James Patterson is one of the best-known and bestselling writers of all time. He is the author of the two top-selling new detective series of the past decade: the Alex Cross novels and the Women's many other bestsellers, including the No. 1 b Diary for Nicholas, Lifeguard, Honeymoon as well as the young adult novels in the Florida.

Praise for James Patterson's novels:

'The man is a master of this genre. We fans will have one wish for him: write even faster' *USA Today*

'Unputdownable. It will sell millions' *The Times*

'Packed with white-knuckled twists' *Daily Mail*

'A novel which makes for sleepless nights' *Daily Express*

'Breakneck pacing and loop-the-loop plotting' *Publishers Weekly*

'A magic hat-trick with the million-dollar-promo thriller... Big warm feelings, usually foreign to thrillers, coax laughter during times of high tension. Reads like a dream' *Kirkus Reviews*

'A fast-paced, electric story that is utterly believable' *Booklist*

'Ticks like a time bomb – full of threat and terror' *Los Angeles Times*

'Absolutely terrific' *Bookseller*

'Patterson's action-packed story keeps the pages flicking by' *The Sunday Times*

'Patterson has a way with plot twists that freshens the material and keeps the adrenaline level high' *Publishing News*

'Cross is one of the best and most likeable characters in the modern thriller genre' *San Francisco Examiner*

'A fine writer with a good ear for dialogue and pacing. His books are always page-turners' *Washington Times*

Also by James Patterson and published by Headline

When the Wind Blows
Cradle and All
Miracle on the 17th Green (*with Peter de Jonge*)
Suzanne's Diary for Nicholas
The Beach House (*with Peter de Jonge*)
The Jester (*with Andrew Gross*)
The Lake House
Sam's Letters for Jennifer
SantaKid
Honeymoon (*with Howard Roughan*)
Lifeguard (*with Andrew Gross*)
Beach Road (*with Peter de Jonge*)
Judge and Jury (*with Andrew Gross*)
Step on a Crack (*with Michael Ledwidge*)
The Quickie (*with Michael Ledwidge*)
You've Been Warned (*with Howard Roughan*)

Alex Cross novels
Cat and Mouse
Pop Goes the Weasel
Roses are Red
Violets are Blue
Four Blind Mice
The Big Bad Wolf
London Bridges
Mary, Mary
Cross
Double Cross

The Women's Murder Club series
1st to Die
2nd Chance (*with Andrew Gross*)
3rd Degree (*with Andrew Gross*)
4th of July (*with Maxine Paetro*)
The 5th Horseman (*with Maxine Paetro*)
The 6th Target (*with Maxine Paetro*)

Maximum Ride series
Maximum Ride: The Angel Experiment
Maximum Ride: School's Out Forever
Maximum Ride: Saving the World and Other Extreme Sports

An Alex Cross Omnibus

CAT AND MOUSE
&
POP GOES
THE WEASEL

headline

CAT AND MOUSE first published in Great Britain in 1997
by HEADLINE BOOK PUBLISHING

POP GOES THE WEASEL first published in Great Britain in 1999
by HEADLINE BOOK PUBLISHING

First published in this omnibus edition in 2008
by HEADLINE PUBLISHING GROUP

1

Cataloguing in Publication Data is available from the British Library

ISBN 978 0 7553 4345 4

Typeset in Times by Palimpsest Book Production Limited,
Grangemouth, Stirlingshire

Printed and bound in Great Britain by
Clays Ltd, St Ives plc

Headline's policy is to use papers that are natural, renewable and recyclable
products and made from wood grown in sustainable forests. The logging and
manufacturing processes are expected to conform to the environmental regulations
of the country of origin.

HEADLINE PUBLISHING GROUP
An Hachette Livre UK Company
338 Euston Road
London NW1 3BH

www.headline.co.uk
www.hachettelivre.co.uk

CAT AND MOUSE

James Patterson

Catch a Spider

Chapter One

Washington, DC.

The Cross house was twenty paces away and the proximity and sight of it made Gary Soneji's skin prickle. It was Victorian-style, white-shingled, and extremely well kept. As Soneji stared across Fifth Street, he slowly bared his teeth in a sneer that could have passed for a smile. This was perfect. He had come here to murder Alex Cross and his family.

His eyes moved slowly from window to window, taking in everything from the crisp, white lace curtains to Cross's old piano on the sunporch to a Batman and Robin kite stuck in the rain gutter of the roof. *Damon's kite*, he thought.

On two occasions he caught sight of Cross's elderly grandmother as she shuffled past one of the downstairs windows. Nana Mama's long, purposeless life would soon be at an end. That made him feel so much better. *Enjoy every moment – stop and smell the roses*, Soneji reminded himself. *Taste the roses, eat Alex Cross's roses – flowers, stems, and thorns.*

He finally moved across Fifth Street, being careful to stay in the shadows. Then he disappeared into the thick yews and forsythia bushes that ran like sentries alongside the front of the house.

He carefully made his way to a whitewashed cellar door, which was to one side of the porch, just off the kitchen. It had a Master padlock, but he had the door open in seconds.

He was inside the Cross house!

He was in the cellar: The cellar was a clue for those who collected them. The cellar was worth a thousand words. A thousand forensic pictures, too.

It was important to everything that would happen in the very near future. The Cross murders!

There were no large windows, but Soneji decided not to take any chances by turning on the lights. He used a Maglite flashlight. Just to look around, to learn a few more things about Cross and his family, to fuel his hatred, if that was possible.

The cellar was cleanly swept, as he had expected it would be. Cross's tools were haphazardly arranged on a pegged Masonite board. A stained Georgetown ballcap was hung on a hook. Soneji put it on his own head. He couldn't resist.

He ran his hands over folded laundry laid out on a long wooden table. He felt close to the doomed family now. He despised them more than ever. He felt around the hammocks of the old woman's bra. He touched the boy's small Jockey underwear. He felt like a total creep, and he loved it.

Soneji picked up a small red reindeer sweater. It would fit Cross's little girl, Jannie. He held it to his face and tried to smell the girl. He anticipated Jannie's murder and only wished that Cross would get to see it, too.

He saw a pair of Everlast gloves and black Pony shoes tied around a hook next to a weathered old punching bag. They belonged to Cross's son, Damon, who must be nine years old now. Gary Soneji thought he would punch out the boy's heart.

Finally, he turned off the flashlight and sat all alone in the dark. Once upon a time, he had been a famous kidnapper and murderer. It was going to happen again. He was coming back with a vengeance that would blow everybody's mind.

He folded his hands in his lap and sighed. He had spun his web perfectly.

Alex Cross would soon be dead, and so would everyone he loved.

Chapter Two

London, England.

The killer who was currently terrorizing Europe was named *Mr Smith*, no first name. It was given to him by the Boston press, and then the police had obligingly picked it up all over the world. He accepted the name, as children accept the name given by their parents, no matter how gross or disturbing or pedestrian the name might be.

Mr Smith – so be it.

Actually, he had a thing about names. He was obsessive about them. The names of his victims were burned into his mind and also into his heart.

First and foremost, there was Isabella Calais. Then came Stephanie Michaela Apt, Ursula Davies, Robert Michael Neel, and so many others.

He could recite the complete names backward and forward, as if they had been memorized for a history quiz or a bizarre round of Trivial Pursuit. That was the ticket – this chase was *trivial pursuit*, wasn't it?

So far, no one seemed to understand, no one got it. Not the fabled FBI. Not the storied Interpol, not Scotland Yard or any of the local police forces in the cities where he had committed murders.

No one understood the secret pattern of the victims, starting with Isabella Calais in Cambridge, Massachusetts, March 22, 1993, and continuing today in London.

The victim of the moment was Derek Cabott. He was a chief inspector – of all the hopelessly inane things to do with your life. He was 'hot' in London, having recently apprehended an IRA killer. His murder would electrify the town, drive everyone mad. Civilized and sophisticated London loved a gory murder as well as the next burg.

This afternoon Mr Smith was operating in the wealthy, fashionable Knightsbridge district. He was there *to study the human race* – at least that was the way the newspapers described it. The press in London and across Europe also called him by another name – *Alien*. The *prevailing* theory was that Smith was an extraterrestrial. *No human could do the things that he did.* Or so they said.

Mr Smith had to bend low to talk into Derek Cabott's ear, to be more intimate with his prey. He played music while he worked – all kinds of music. Today's selection was the overture to *Don Giovanni. Opera buffa* felt right to him.

Opera felt right for this *live* autopsy.

'Ten minutes or so after your death,' Mr Smith said, 'flies will already have picked up the scent of gas accompanying the decomposition of your tissue. Green flies will lay the tiniest eggs within the orifices of your body. Ironically, the language reminds me of Dr Seuss – "green flies and ham." What could that mean? I don't know. It's a curious association, though.'

Derek Cabott had lost a lot of blood, but he wasn't giving up. He was a tall, rugged man with silver-blond hair. A never-say-never sort of chap. The inspector shook his head back and forth until Smith finally removed his gag.

'What is it, Derek?' he asked. 'Speak.'

'I have a wife and two children. Why are you doing this to me? Why me?' he whispered.

'Oh, let's say because you're Derek. Keep it simple and unsentimental. You, Derek, are a piece of the puzzle.'

He tugged the inspector's gag back into place. No more chitchat from Derek.

Mr Smith continued with his observations as he made his next surgical cuts and *Don Giovanni* played on.

'Near the time of death, breathing will become strained, intermittent. It's exactly what you're feeling now, as if each breath could be your last. Cessation will occur within two or three minutes,' whispered Mr Smith, whispered the dreaded *Alien*. 'Your life will end. May I be the first to congratulate you. I sincerely mean that, Derek. Believe it or not, *I envy you*. I wish I were Derek.'

Part One

Train Station Murders

Chapter One

'I am the great Cornholio! Are you challenging me? I am Cornholio!' the kids chorused and giggled. Beavis and Butt-head strike again – in my neighborhood.

I bit my lip and decided to let it go. Why fight it? Why fan the fires of preadolescence?

Damon, Jannie, and I were crowded into the front seat of my old black Porsche. We needed to buy a new car, but none of us wanted to part with the Porsche. We were schooled in tradition, in the classics. We loved the old car, which we had named 'The Sardine Can' and 'Old Paintless.'

Actually, I was preoccupied at twenty to eight in the morning. Not a good way to start the day.

The night before, a thirteen-year-old girl from Ballou High School had been found in the Anacostia River. She had been shot, and then drowned. The gunshot had been to her mouth. What the coroners call a 'hole in one.'

A bizarre statistic was creating havoc with my stomach and central nervous system. *There were now more than a hundred unsolved murders of young, inner-city women committed in just the past three years*. No one had called for a major investigation. No one in power seemed to care about the dead black and Hispanic girls.

As we drove up in front of the Sojourner Truth School, I saw Christine Johnson welcoming kids and their parents as they arrived, reminding everyone that this was a community with good, caring people. She was certainly one of them.

I remembered the very first time we met. It was the previous fall and the circumstances couldn't have been any worse for either of us.

We had been thrown together – *smashed* together someone said to me once – at the homicide scene of a sweet baby girl named Shanelle Green. Christine was the principal of the school that Shanelle attended, and where I was now delivering my own kids. Jannie was new to the Truth School this semester. Damon was a grizzled veteran, a fourth grader.

'What are you mischief makers gawking at?' I turned to the kids, who were looking back and forth from my face to Christine's as if they were watching a championship tennis match.

'We're *gawking* at you, Daddy, and you're *gawking* at Christine!' Jannie said and laughed like the wicked child-witch of the North that she can be sometimes.

'She's Mrs Johnson to you,' I said as I gave Jannie my best squinting evil eye.

Jannie shrugged off my baleful look and frowned at me as only she can. 'I know that, Daddy. She's the *principal* of my school. I know exactly who she is.'

My daughter already understood many of life's important connections and mysteries. I was hoping that maybe someday she would explain them to me.

'Damon, do you have a point of view we should hear?' I asked. 'Anything you'd like to add? Care to share some good-fellowship and wit with us this morning?'

My son shook his head no, but he was smiling, too. He liked Christine Johnson just fine. Everybody did. Even Nana Mama approved, which is unheard of, and actually worried me some. Nana and I never seemed to agree about *anything*, and it's getting worse with age.

The kids were already climbing out of the car, and Jannie gave me a kiss goodbye. Christine waved and walked over.

'What a fine, upstanding father you are,' she said. Her brown eyes twinkled. 'You're going to make some lady in the neighborhood very happy one of these days. Very good with children, reasonably handsome, driving a classy sports car. My, my, my.'

'My, my, back at you,' I said. To top everything off, it was a beautiful morning in early June. Shimmering blue skies, temperature in the low seventies, the air crisp and relatively clean. Christine was wearing a soft beige suit with a blue shirt, and beige flat-heeled shoes. Be still my heart.

A smile slid across my face. There was no way to stop it, to hold it back, and besides I didn't want to. It fit with the fine day I was starting to have.

'I hope you're not teaching my kids that kind of cynicism and irony inside that fancy school of yours.'

'Of course I am, and so are all my teachers. We speak Educanto with the best of them. We're trained in cynicism, and we're all experts in irony. More important, we're excellent skeptics. I have to get inside now, so we don't miss a precious moment of indoctrination time.'

'It's too late for Damon and Jannie. I've already programmed them. A child is fed with milk and praise. They have the sunniest dispositions in the neighborhood, probably in all of Southeast, maybe in the entire city of Washington.'

'Oh we've noticed that, and we accept the challenge. Got to run. Young minds to shape and change.'

'I'll see you tonight?' I said as Christine was about to turn away and head toward the Sojourner Truth School.

'Handsome as sin, driving a nice Porsche, of course you'll see me tonight,' she said. Then she turned away and headed toward the school.

We were about to have our first 'official' date that night. Her husband, George, had died the previous winter, and now Christine felt she was ready to have dinner with me. I hadn't pushed her in any way, but I couldn't wait. Half-a-dozen years after the death of my wife, Maria, I felt as if I were coming out of a deep rut, maybe even a clinical depression. Life was looking as good as it had in a long, long time.

But as Nana Mama has often cautioned, 'Don't mistake the edge of a rut for the horizon.'

Chapter Two

A lex Cross is a dead man. Failure isn't an option.
    Gary Soneji squinted through a telescopic sight he'd removed from a Browning automatic rifle. The scope was a rare beauty. He watched the oh-so-touching affair of the heart. He saw Alex Cross drop off his two brats and then chat with his pretty lady friend in front of the Sojourner Truth School.

Think the unthinkable, he prodded himself.

Soneji ground his front teeth as he scrunched low in the front seat of a black Jeep Cherokee. He watched Damon and Janelle scamper into the schoolyard, where they greeted their playmates with high and low fives. Years before he'd almost become famous for kidnapping two school brats right here in Washington. Those were the days, my friend! Those were the days.

For a while he'd been the dark star of television and newspapers all over the country. Now it was going to happen again. He was sure that it was. After all, it was only fair that he be recognized as the best.

He let the aiming post of the rifle sight gently come to rest on Christine Johnson's forehead. *There, there, isn't that nice.*

She had very expressive brown eyes and a wide smile that seemed genuine from this distance. She was tall, attractive, and had a commanding presence. *The school principal.* A few loose hairs lay curled on her cheek. It was easy to see what Cross saw in her.

What a handsome couple they made, and what a tragedy this was going to be, what a damn shame. Even with all the wear and tear, Cross still looked good, impressive, a little like Muhammad Ali in his prime. His smile was dazzling.

As Christine Johnson walked away and headed towards the red-brick school building, Alex Cross suddenly glanced in the direction of Soneji's Jeep.

The tall detective seemed to be looking right into the driver's side of the windshield. Right into Soneji's eyes.

That was okay. Nothing to worry about, nothing to fear. He knew what he was doing. He wasn't taking any risks. Not here, not yet.

It was all set to start in a couple of minutes, but in his mind it had already happened. It had happened a hundred times. He knew every single move from this point until the end.

Gary Soneji started the Jeep and headed toward Union Station. The scene of the crime-to-be, the scene of his masterpiece theater.

'Think the unthinkable,' he muttered under his breath, 'then *do* the unthinkable.'

Chapter Three

After the last bell had rung and most of the kids were safe and sound in their classrooms, Christine Johnson took a slow walk down the long deserted corridors of the Sojourner Truth School. She did this almost every morning, and considered it one of her special treats to herself. You had to have treats sometimes, and this beat a trip to Starbucks for café latte.

The hallways were empty and pleasantly quiet – and always sparkling clean, as she felt a good school ought to be.

There had been a time when she and a few of her teachers had actually mopped the floors themselves, but now Mr Gomez and a porter named Lonnie Walker did it two nights a week, every week. Once you got good people thinking in the right way, it was amazing how many of them agreed a school should be clean and safe, and were willing to help. Once people believed the right thing could actually happen, it often did.

The corridor walls were covered with lively, colorful artwork by the kids, and everybody loved the hope and energy it produced. Christine glanced at the drawings and posters every morning, and it was always something different, another child's perspective, that caught her eye and delighted her inner person.

This particular morning, she paused to look at a simple yet dazzling crayon drawing of a little girl holding hands with her mommy and daddy in front of a new house. They all had round faces and happy smiles and a nice sense of purpose. She checked out a few illustrated stories: 'Our Community,' 'Nigeria,' 'Whaling.'

But she was out here walking for a different reason today. She was thinking about her husband, George, and how he died, and why. She wished she could bring him back and talk to him now. She wanted to hold George at least one more time. *Oh God, she needed to talk to him.*

She wandered to the far end of the hall to Room 111, which was light yellow and called *Buttercup*. The kids had named the rooms themselves, and the names changed every year in the fall. It was *their* school, after all.

Christine slowly and quietly opened the door a crack. She saw Bobbie Shaw, the second-grade teacher, scrubbing notes on the blackboard. Then she noticed row after row of mostly attentive faces, and among them Jannie Cross.

She found herself smiling as she watched Jannie, who happened to be talking to Ms Shaw. Jannie Cross was so animated and bright, and she had such a sweet perspective on the world. She was a lot like her father. *Smart, sensitive, handsome as sin.*

Christine eventually walked on. Preoccupied, she found herself climbing the concrete stairs to the second floor. Even the walls of the stairwells were decorated with projects and brightly colored artwork, which was part of the reason most of the kids believed that this was 'their school.' Once you understood something was 'yours,' you protected it, felt a part of it. It was a simple enough idea, but one that the government in Washington seemed not to get.

She felt a little silly, but she checked on Damon, too.

Of all the boys and girls at the Truth School, Damon was probably her favorite. He had been even before she met Alex. It wasn't just that Damon was bright, and verbal, and could be very charming – Damon was also a really good person. He showed it time and again with the other kids, with his teachers, and even when his little sister entered the school this past semester. He'd treated her like his best friend in the world – and maybe he already understood that *she was.*

Christine finally headed back to her office, where the usual ten-to-twelve-hour day awaited her. She was thinking about Alex now, and she supposed that was really why she had gone and looked in on his kids.

She was thinking that she wasn't looking forward to their dinner date tonight. She was afraid of tonight, a little panicky, and she thought she knew why.

Chapter Four

At a little before eight in the morning, Gary Soneji strolled into Union Station, as if he owned the place. He felt tremendously good. His step quickened and his spirits seemed to rise to the height of the soaring train-station ceilings.

He knew everything there was to know about the famous train gateway for the capital. He had long admired the neoclassical façade that recalled the famed Baths of Caracalla in ancient Rome. He had studied the station's architecture for hours as a young boy. He had even visited the Great Train Store, which sold exquisite model trains and other railroad-themed souvenirs.

He could hear and feel the trains rattling down below. The marble floors actually shook as powerful Amtrak trains departed and arrived, mostly on schedule, too. The glass doors to the outside world *rumbled*, and he could hear the panes *clink* against their frames.

He loved this place, everything about it. It was truly magical. The key words for today were *train* and *cellar*, and only he understood why.

Information was power, and he had it all.

Gary Soneji thought that he might be dead within the next hour, but the idea, the image, didn't trouble him. Whatever happened was meant to, and besides, he definitely wanted to go out with a bang, not a cowardly whimper. Why the hell not? He had plans for a long and *exciting career after his death*.

Gary Soneji was wearing a lightweight black jumpsuit with a red Nike logo. He carried three bulky bags. He figured that he looked like just another yuppified traveler at the crowded train station. He appeared to be overweight and his hair was gray, for the time being. He was actually five foot ten, but the lifts in his shoes got him up to six-one today. He still had a trace of his former good looks. If somebody had wanted to guess his occupation, they might say *teacher*.

The cheap irony wasn't lost on him. He'd been a teacher once, one of the worst ever. He had been *Mr Soneji – the Spider Man*. He had kidnapped two of his own students.

He had already purchased his ticket for the Metroliner, but he didn't head for his train just yet.

Instead, Gary Soneji crossed the main lobby, hurrying away from the waiting room. He took a stairway next to the Center Café and climbed to the balcony on the second floor, which looked out on the lobby, about twenty feet below.

He gazed down and watched the lonely people streaming across the cavernous lobby. Most of these assholes had no idea how undeservedly lucky they were this particular morning. They would be safely on board their little commuter trains by the time the 'light and sound' show began in just a few minutes.

What a beautiful, beautiful place this is, Soneji thought. How many times he'd dreamed about this scene.

This very scene at Union Station!

Long streaks and spears of morning sunlight shafted down through delicate skylights. They reflected off the walls and the high gilded ceiling. The main hall before him held an information booth, a magnificent electronic train-arrival-and-departure board, the Center Café, Sfuzzi, and America restaurants.

The concourse led to a waiting area that had once been called 'the largest room in the world.' What a grand and historic venue he had chosen for today, his birthday.

Gary Soneji produced a small key from his pocket. He flipped it in the air and caught it. He opened a silver-gray metallic door that led into a room on the balcony.

He thought of it as *his room*. Finally, he had his own room – *upstairs* with everyone else. He closed the door behind him.

'Happy birthday, dear Gary, happy birthday to you.'

Chapter Five

This was going to be incredible, beyond anything he'd attempted so far. He could almost do this next part blindfolded, working from memory. He'd done the drill so many times. In his imagination, in his dreams. He had been looking forward to this day for more than twenty years.

He set up a folding aluminum tripod mount inside the small room, and positioned a Browning BAR on it. The rifle was a dandy, with a milspec scoping device and an electronic trigger he had customized himself.

The marble floors continued to shake as his beloved trains entered and departed the station, huge mythical beasts that came here to feed and rest. There was nowhere he'd rather be than here. He loved this moment so much.

Soneji knew everything about Union Station, and also about mass murders conducted in crowded public places. As a boy, he had obsessed on the so-called 'crimes of the century.' He had imagined himself committing such acts and becoming feared and famous. He planned perfect murders, random ones, and then he began to carry them out. He buried his first victim on a relative's farm when he was fifteen. The body still hadn't been found, not to this day.

He *was* Charles Starkweather; he *was* Bruno Richard Hauptmann; he *was* Charlie Whitman. Except that he was much smarter than any of them; and he wasn't crazy like them.

He had even appropriated a name for himself: Soneji, pronounced *Soh-nee-gee*. The name had seemed scary to him even at thirteen or fourteen. It still did. *Starkweather, Hauptmann, Whitman, Soneji.*

He had been shooting rifles since he was a boy in the deep, dark woods surrounding Princeton, New Jersey. During the past year, he'd done more shooting, more hunting, more practicing than ever before. He was primed and ready for this morning. Hell, he'd been ready for years.

Soneji sat on a metal folding chair and made himself as comfortable as he could. He pulled up a battleship-gray tarp that blended into the background of the train terminal's dark walls. He snuggled under the tarp. He was going to disappear, to be part of the scenery, *to be a sniper in a very public place. In Union Station!*

An old-fashioned-sounding train announcer was singing out the track and time for the next Metroliner to Baltimore, Wilmington, Philadelphia, and New York's Penn Station.

Soneji smiled to himself – *that was his getaway train.*

He had his ticket, and he still planned to be on it. No problem, just book it. He'd be on the Metroliner, or bust. Nobody could stop him now, except maybe Alex Cross, and even that didn't matter anymore. His plan had contingencies for every possibility, even his own death.

Then Soneji was lost in his thoughts. His memories were his cocoon.

He had been nine years old when a student named Charles Whitman opened fire out of a tower at the University of Texas in Austin. Whitman was a former Marine, twenty-five years old. The outrageous, sensational event had galvanized him back then.

He'd collected every single story on the shootings, long pieces from *Time, Life, Newsweek*, the *New York Times*, the *Philadelphia Inquirer, The Times* of London, *Paris Match, Los Angeles Times, Baltimore Sun*. He still had the precious articles. They were at a friend's house, being held for posterity. They were *evidence – of past, present, and future crimes.*

Gary Soneji knew he was a good marksman. Not that he needed to be a crackerjack in this bustling crowd of targets. No shot he'd have to make in the train terminal would be over a hundred yards, and he was accurate at up to five hundred yards.

Now, I step out of my own nightmare and into the real world, he thought as the moment crystallized. A cold, hard shiver ran through his body. It was delicious, tantalizing. He peered through the Browning's telescope at the busy, nervous, milling crowd.

He searched for the first victim. *Life was so much more beautiful and interesting through a target scope.*

Chapter Six

You are there.
He scanned the lobby with its thousands of hurrying commuters and summer vacation travelers. Not one of them had a clue about his or her mortal condition at that very moment. No one ever seemed to believe that something horrible could actually happen *to them.*

Soneji watched a lively brat-pack of students in bright blue blazers and starched white shirts. Preppies, goddamn preppies. They were giggling and running for their train with unnatural delight. He didn't like happy people at all, especially dumb-ass children who thought they had the world by the nuts.

He found that he could distinguish smells from up here: diesel fuel, lilacs and roses from the flower vendors, meat and garlic shrimp from the lobby's restaurants. The odors made him hungry.

The target circle in his customized scope had a black site post rather than the more common bull's-eye. He preferred the post. He watched a montage of shapes and motion and colors swim in and out of death's way. This small circle of the Grim Reaper was his world now, self-contained and mesmerizing.

Soneji let the aiming post come to rest on the broad, wrinkled forehead of a weary-looking businesswoman in her early- to mid-fifties. The woman was thin and nervous, with haggard eyes, pale lips. 'Say good night, Gracie,' he whispered softly. 'Good night, Irene. Good night, Mrs Calabash.'

He almost pulled the trigger, almost started the morning's massacre, then he eased off at the last possible instant.

Not worthy of the first shot, he thought, chastising himself for impatience. *Not nearly special enough. Just a passing fancy. Just another middle-class cow.*

The aiming post settled in and held as if by a magnet on the lower spine of a porter pushing an uneven load of boxes and suitcases. The porter was a tall, good-looking black – *much like Alex Cross*, Soneji thought. His dark skin gleamed like mahogany furniture.

That was the attraction of the target. He liked the image, but who would get the subtle, special message other than himself? No, he had to think of others, too. This was a time to be selfless.

He moved the aiming post again, the circle of death. There was an amazing number of commuters in blue suits and black wing tips. Business sheep.

A father and teenage son floated into the circle, as if they had been put there by the hand of God.

Gary Soneji inhaled. Then he slowly exhaled. It was his shooting ritual, the one he'd practiced for so many years alone in the woods. *He had imagined doing this so many times. Taking out a perfect stranger, for no good reason.*

He gently, very gently, pulled the trigger toward the center of his eye.

His body was completely still, almost lifeless. He could feel the faint pulse in his arm, the pulse in his throat, the approximate speed of his heartbeat.

The shot made a loud cracking noise, and the sound seemed to follow the flight of the bullet down toward the lobby. Smoke spiraled upward, inches in front of the rifle barrel. Quite beautiful to observe.

The teenager's head exploded inside the telescopic circle. Beautiful. The head flew apart before his eyes. The Big Bang in miniature, no?

Then Gary Soneji pulled the trigger a second time. He murdered the father before he had a chance to grieve. He felt absolutely nothing for either of them. Not love, not hate, not pity. He didn't flinch, wince, or even blink.

There was no stopping Gary Soneji now, no turning back.

Chapter Seven

*R*ush *hour! Eight-twenty a.m. Jesus God Almighty, no! A madman was on the loose inside Union Station.*

Sampson and I raced alongside the double lanes of stalled traffic that covered Massachusetts Avenue as far as the eye could see. *When in doubt, gallop.* The maxim of the old Foreign Legion.

Car and truck drivers honked their horns in frustration. Pedestrians were screaming, walking fast, or running away from the train station. Police squad cars were on the scene everywhere.

Up ahead on North Capitol I could see the massive, all-granite Union Station terminal with its many additions and renovations. Everything was somber and gray around the terminal except the grass, which seemed especially green.

Sampson and I flew past the new Thurgood Marshall Justice Building. We heard gunshots coming from the station. They sounded distant, muffled by the thick stone walls.

'It's for goddamn real,' Sampson said as he ran at my side. 'He's here. No doubt about it now.'

I knew he would be. An urgent call had come to my desk less than ten minutes earlier. I had picked up the phone, distracted by another message, a fax from Kyle Craig of the FBI. I was scanning Kyle's fax. He desperately needed help on his huge *Mr Smith* case. He wanted me to meet an agent, Thomas Pierce. I couldn't help Kyle this time. I was thinking of getting the hell out of the murder business, not taking on more cases, especially a serious bummer like *Mr Smith*.

I recognized the voice on the phone. 'It's Gary Soneji, Dr Cross. It really *is* me. I'm calling from Union Station. I'm just passing through DC, and I hoped against hope that you'd like to see me again. Hurry, though. You'd better scoot if you don't want to miss me.'

Then the phone went dead. Soneji had hung up. He loved to be in control.

Now, Sampson and I were sprinting along Massachusetts Avenue. We were moving a whole lot faster than the traffic. I had abandoned my car at the corner of Third Street.

We both wore protective vests over our sport shirts. We were 'scooting,' as Soneji had advised me over the phone.

'What the hell is he doing in there?' Sampson said through tightly gritted teeth. 'That son of a bitch has always been crazy.'

We were less than fifty yards from the terminal's glass and wood front doors. People continued to stream outside.

'He used to shoot guns as a boy,' I told Sampson. 'Used to kill pets in his neighborhood outside Princeton. He'd do sniper-kills from the woods. Nobody ever solved it at the time. He told me about the sniping when I interviewed him at Lorton Prison. Called himself the pet assassin.'

'Sounds like he graduated to people,' Sampson muttered.

We raced up the long driveway, heading toward the front entrance of the ninety-year-old terminal. Sampson and I were moving, burning up shoe leather, and it seemed like an eternity since Soneji's phone call.

There was a pause in the shooting – then it began again. Weird as hell. It definitely sounded like rifle reports coming from inside.

Cars and taxis in the train terminal's driveway were backing out, trying to get away from the scene of gunfire and madness. Commuters and day travelers were still pushing their way out of the building's front doors. I'd never been involved with a sniper situation before.

In the course of my life in Washington, I'd been inside Union Station several hundred times. Nothing like this, though. Nothing even close to this morning.

'He's got himself trapped in there. Purposely trapped! Why the hell would he do that?' Sampson asked as we came up to the front doors.

'Worries me, too,' I said. Why had Gary Soneji called me? Why would he effectively trap himself in Union Station?

Sampson and I slipped into the lobby of Union Station. The shooting from the balcony – from up high somewhere – suddenly started up again. We both went down flat on the floor.

Had Soneji already seen us?

Chapter Eight

I kept my head low as my eyes scanned the huge and portentous train-station lobby. I was desperately looking for Soneji. Could he see me? One of Nana's sayings was stuck in my head: *Death is nature's way of saying 'howdy.'*

Statues of Roman legionnaires stood guard all around the imposing main hall of Union Station. At one time, politically correct Pennsylvania Railroad execs had wanted the warriors fully clothed. The sculptor, Louis Saint-Gaudens, had managed to sneak by every third statue in its accurate historical condition.

I saw three people already down, probably dead, on the lobby floor. My stomach dropped. My heart beat even faster. One of the victims was a teenage boy in cutoff shorts and a Redskins practice jersey. A second victim appeared to be the father. Neither of them was moving.

Hundreds of travelers and terminal employees were trapped inside arcade shops and restaurants. Dozens of frightened people were squashed into a small Godiva Chocolates store and an open café called America.

The firing had stopped again. What was Soneji doing? And where was he? The temporary silence was maddening and spooky. There was supposed to be lots of noise here in the train terminal. Someone scraped a chair against the marble floor and the screeching sound echoed loudly.

I palmed my detective's badge at a uniformed patrolman who had barricaded himself behind an overturned café table. Sweat was pouring down the uniformed cop's face to the rolls of fat at his neck. He was only a few feet inside one of the doorways to the front lobby. He was breathing hard.

'You all right?' I asked as Sampson and I slid down behind the table. He nodded, grunted something, but I didn't believe him. His eyes were open wide with fear. I suspected he'd never been involved with a sniper either.

'Where's he firing from?' I asked the uniform. 'You seen him?'

'Hard to tell. But he's up in there somewhere, that general area.' He pointed to the south balcony that ran above the long line of doorways at the front of Union Station. Nobody was using the doors now. Soneji was in full control.

'Can't see him from down here,' Sampson snorted at my side. 'He might be moving around, changing position. That's how a good sniper would work it.'

'Has he said anything? Made any announcements? Any demands?' I asked the patrolman.

'Nothing. He just started shooting people like he was having target practice. Four vics so far. Sucker can shoot.'

I couldn't see the fourth body. Maybe somebody, a father, mother, or friend, had pulled one of the victims in off the floor. I thought of my own family. Soneji had come to our house once. And he had called me here – invited me to his coming-out party at Union Station.

Suddenly, from up on the balcony above us, a rifle barked! The flat crack of the weapon echoed off the train station's thick walls. This was a shooting gallery with human targets.

A woman screamed inside the America restaurant. I saw her go down hard as if she'd slipped on ice. Then there were lots of moans from inside the café.

The firing stopped again. *What the hell was he doing up there?*

'Let's take him out before he goes off again,' I whispered to Sampson. 'Let's do it.'

Chapter Nine

Our legs pumping in unison, our breath coming in harsh rasps, Sampson and I climbed a dark marble stairway to the overhanging balcony. Uniformed officers and a couple of detectives were crouched in shooting positions up there.

I saw a detective from the train-station detail, which is normally a small-crimes unit. Nothing like this, nothing even close to dealing with a sharpshooting sniper.

'What do you know so far?' I asked. I thought the detective's name was Vincent Mazzeo, but I wasn't sure. He was pushing fifty and this was supposed to be a soft detail for him. I vaguely remembered that Mazzeo was supposed to be a pretty good guy.

'He's inside one of those anterooms. See that door over there? The space he secured has no roof cover. Maybe we can get at him from above. What do you think?'

I glanced up toward the high copper ceiling. I remembered that Union Station was supposed to be the largest covered colonnade in the United States. It sure looked it. Gary Soneji had always liked a big canvas. He had another one now.

The detective took something out of his shirt pocket. 'I got a master key. This gets us into some of the antechambers. Maybe the room he's in.'

I took the key. He wasn't going to use it. He wasn't going to play the hero. He didn't want to meet up with Gary Soneji and his sharpshooter's rifle this morning.

Another burst of gunfire suddenly came from in the anteroom.

I counted. There were six shots – just like the last time.

Like a lot of psychos, Soneji was into codes, magical words, numbers. I wondered about *sixes. Six, six, six?* The number hadn't come up in the past with him.

The shooting abruptly stopped again. Once more it was quiet in the station. My nerves were on edge, badly strained. There were too many people at risk here, too many to protect.

Sampson and I moved ahead. We were less than twenty feet from the ante-room where he was shooting. We pressed against the wall, Glocks out.

'You okay?' I whispered. We had been here before, similar bad situation, but that didn't make it any better.

'This is fun shit, huh, Alex? First thing in the morning, too. Haven't even had my coffee and doughnut.'

'Next time he fires,' I said, 'we go get him. He's been firing six shots each time.'

'I noticed,' Sampson said without looking at me. He patted my leg. We took in big sips of air.

We didn't have to wait long. Soneji began another volley of shots. *Six shots. Why six shots each time?*

He knew we'd be coming for him. Hell, he'd invited me to his shooting spree.

'Here we go,' I said.

We ran across the marble-and-stone corridor. I took out the key to the ante-room, squeezed it between my index finger and thumb.

I turned the key.

Click!

The door wouldn't open! I jiggled the handle. Nothing.

'What the hell?' Sampson said behind me, anger in his voice. 'What's wrong with the door?'

'I just locked it,' I told him. *'Soneji left it open for us.'*

Chapter Ten

Downstairs, a couple and two small children started to run. They rushed toward the glass doors and possible freedom. One of the kids tripped and went down hard on his knee. The mother dragged him forward. It was terrifying to watch, but they made it.

The firing started again!

Sampson and I burst into the anteroom, both of us crouched low, our guns drawn.

I caught a glimpse of a dark gray tarp straight ahead.

A sniper rifle pointed out from the cover and camouflage of the tarp. Soneji was underneath, hidden from view.

Sampson and I fired. Half-a-dozen gunshots thundered in the close quarters. Holes opened in the tarp. The rifle was silent.

I rushed across the small anteroom and ripped away the tarp. I groaned – a deep, gut-wrenching sound.

No one was underneath the tarp. No Gary Soneji!

A Browning automatic rifle, spattered with blood, was strapped on a metal tripod. A timing device was attached to a rod and the trigger. The whole thing was customized. The rifle would fire at a programmed interval. Six shots, then a pause, then six more shots. No Gary Soneji.

I was already moving again. There were metal doors on the north and south walls of the small room. I yanked open the one closest to me. *I expected a trap.*

But the connecting space was empty. There was another gray metal door on the opposing wall. The door was shut. Gary Soneji still loved to play games. His favorite trick: He was the only one with the rules.

I rushed across the second room and opened door number two. Was that the game? A surprise? A booby-prize behind either door one, two, or three?

I found myself peering inside another small space, another empty chamber. No Soneji. Not a sign of him anywhere.

The room had a metal stairway – it looked as if it went to another floor. Or maybe a crawlspace above us.

I climbed the stairs, stopping and starting so he wouldn't get a clear shot from above. My heart was pounding, my legs trembling. I hoped that Sampson was close behind. I needed cover.

At the top of the stairway, a hatchway was open. No Gary Soneji here either. I had been lured deeper and deeper into some kind of trap, into his web.

My stomach was rolling. I felt a sharp pain building up behind my eyes. Soneji was still somewhere in Union Station. He had to be. *He'd said he wanted to see me.*

Chapter Eleven

Soneji sat as calm as a small-town banker, pretending to read the *Washington Post* on the 8:45 a.m. Metroliner to Penn Station in New York. His heart was still palpitating, but none of the excitement showed on his face. He wore a gray suit, white shirt, striped blue tie – he looked just like all the rest of the commuter assholes.

He had just tripped the light fantastic, hadn't he? He had gone where few others ever would have dared. He had just outdone the legendary Charles Whitman, and this was only the beginning of his prime-time exposure. There was a saying he liked a lot. *Victory belongs to the player who makes the next-to-last mistake.*

Soneji drifted in and out of a reverie in which he returned to his beloved woods around Princeton, New Jersey. He could see himself as a boy again. He remembered everything about the dense, uneven, but often spectacularly beautiful terrain. When he was eleven, he had stolen a .22-caliber rifle from one of the surrounding farms. He kept it hidden in a rock quarry near his house. The gun was carefully wrapped in an oilcloth, foil, and burlap bags. The .22-caliber rifle was the only earthly possession that he cared about, the only thing that was truly his.

He remembered how he would scale down a steep, very rocky ravine to a quiet place where the forest floor leveled off, just past a thick tangle of bayberry prickers. There was a clearing in the hollow, and this was the site of his secret, forbidden target practice in those early years. One day he brought a rabbit's head and a calico cat from the nearby Ruocco farm. There wasn't much that a cat liked more than a fresh rabbit's head. Cats were such little ghouls. Cats were like him. To this day, they were magical for him. The way they stalked and hunted was the greatest. That was why he had given one to Dr Cross and his family.

Little Rosie.

After he had placed the severed bunny's head in the center of the clearing, he untied the neck of the burlap and let the kitty free. Even though he had punched a few airholes in the bag, the cat had almost suffocated. 'Sic 'em. Sic the bunny!' he commanded. The cat caught the scent of the fresh kill and took off in a pouncing run. Gary put the .22 rifle on his shoulder and watched. He sighted on the moving target. He caressed the trigger of his deuce-deuce, and then he fired. He was learning how to kill.

You're such an addict! He chastised himself now, back in the present, on the Metroliner train. Little had changed since he'd been the original Bad Boy in the Princeton area. His stepmother – the gruesome and untalented whore of Babylon – used to lock him in the basement regularly back then. She would leave him alone in the dark, sometimes for as long as ten to twelve hours. He learned to love the darkness, to be the darkness. He learned to love the cellar, to make it his favorite place in the world.

Gary beat her at her own game.

He lived in the underworld, his own private hell. He truly believed he was the Prince of Darkness.

Gary Soneji had to keep bringing himself back to the present, back to Union Station and his beautiful plan. The Metro police were searching the trains.

The police were outside right now! Alex Cross was probably among them.

What a great start to things, and this was only the beginning.

Chapter Twelve

He could see the police jackasses roaming the loading platforms at Union Station. They looked scared, lost and confused, and already half-beaten. That was good to know, valuable information. It set a tone for things to come.

He glanced toward a businesswoman sitting across the aisle. She looked frightened, too. Frozen. Stiff. White knuckles showing on her clenched hands. Shoulders thrown back like a military school cadet.

Soneji spoke to her. He was polite and gentle, the way he could be when he wanted to. 'I feel like this whole morning has to be a bad dream. When I was a boy, I used to go – *one, two, three, wake up!* I could bring myself out of a nightmare that way. It's sure not working today.'

The woman across the aisle nodded as if he'd said something profound. He'd made a connection with her. Gary had always been able to do that, reach out and touch somebody if he needed to. He figured he needed to now. It would look better if he was talking to a travel companion when the police came through the train car.

'One, two, three, wake up,' she said in a low voice across the aisle. 'God, I hope we're safe down here. I hope they've caught him by now. Whoever, *whatever* he is.'

'I'm sure they will,' Soneji said. 'Don't they always? Crazy people like that have a way of catching themselves.'

The woman nodded once, but didn't sound too convinced. 'They do, don't they. I'm sure you're right. I hope so. That's my prayer.'

Two DC police detectives were stepping inside the club car. Their faces were screwed tight. Now it would get interesting. He could see more cops approaching through the dining car, which was just one car ahead. There had to be hundreds of cops inside the terminal now. It was showtime. Act Two.

'I'm from Wilmington, Delaware. Wilmington's home.' Soneji kept talking to the woman. 'Otherwise I'd have left the station already. That's if they let us back upstairs.'

'They won't. I tried,' the woman told him. Her eyes were frozen, locked in an odd place. He loved that look. It was hard for Soneji to glance away, to focus on the approaching policemen and the threat they might present.

'We need to see identifications from everyone,' one of the detectives was announcing. He had a deep, no-nonsense voice that got everybody's attention. 'Have IDs with pictures out when we come through. Thank you.'

The two detectives got to his row of seats. This was it, wasn't it? Funny, he didn't feel much of anything. He was ready to take both cops out.

Soneji controlled his breathing and also his heartbeat. *Control, that was the ticket.* He had control over the muscles in his face, and especially his eyes. He'd changed the color of his eyes for today. Changed his hair colour from blond to gray. Changed the shape of his face. He looked soft, bloated, as harmless as your average traveling salesman.

He showed a driver's license and Amex card in the name of Neil Stuart from Wilmington, Delaware. He also had a Visa card and a picture ID for the Sports Club in Wilmington. There was nothing memorable about the way he looked. Just another business sheep.

The detectives were checking his ID when Soneji spotted Alex Cross outside the train car. *Make my day.*

Cross was coming his way, and he was peering in through the windows at passengers. Cross was still looking pretty good. He was six-three and well built. He carried himself like an athlete, and looked younger than forty-one.

Jesus, Jesus, Jesus, what a mindblower. Trip the goddamn light fantastic. I'm right here, Cross. You could almost touch me if you wanted to. Look in at me. Look at me, Cross. I command you to look at me now!

The tremendous anger and fury growing inside him was dangerous, Soneji knew. He could wait until Alex Cross was right on top of him, then pop up and put half-a-dozen shots into his face.

Six head shots. Each of the six would be well deserved for what Cross had done to him. Cross had ruined his life – no, Alex Cross had destroyed him. Cross was the reason all of this was happening now. Cross was to blame for the murders in the train station. It was all Alex Cross's fault.

Cross, Cross, Cross! Was this the end now? Was this the big finale? How could it be?

Cross looked so almighty as he walked, so above-the-fray. He had to give that to Cross, he was two or three inches taller than the other cops, smooth brown skin. *Sugar* – that's what his friend Sampson called him.

Well – he had a surprise for Sugar. Big unexpected surprise. Mindscrewer for the ages surprise.

If you catch me, Dr Cross – you catch yourself. Do you understand that? Don't worry – you will soon enough.

'Thank you, Mr Stuart,' said the detective as he handed Soneji back his credit card and the Delaware driver's license.

Soneji nodded and offered a thin smile to the detective, and then his eyes flicked back to the window.

Alex Cross was right there. *Don't look so humble, Cross. You're not that great.*

He wanted to start shooting now. He was in heat. He experienced something like hot flashes. He could do Alex Cross right now. There was no doubt about it. He hated that face, that walk, everything about the doctor-detective.

Alex Cross slowed his step. Then Cross looked right in at him. He was five feet away.

Gary Soneji slowly moved his eyes up to Cross, then very naturally over to the other detectives, then back to Cross.

Hello, Sugar.

Cross didn't recognize him. How could he? The detective looked right at his face – then he moved on. He kept on walking down the platform, picking up speed.

Cross had his back to him and it was an almost irresistibly inviting target. A detective up ahead was calling to him, motioning for Cross to come. He loved the idea of shooting Cross in the back. A cowardly murder, that was the best. That's what people really hated.

Then Soneji relaxed back into his train seat.

Cross didn't recognize me. I'm that good. I'm the best he's ever faced by far. I'll prove it, too.

Make no mistake about it. I will win.

I am going to murder Alex Cross and his family, and no one can stop it from happening.

Chapter Thirteen

It was past five-thirty in the evening before I even got to *think* about leaving Union Station. I'd been trapped inside all day, talking to witnesses, talking to Ballistics, the medical examiner, making rough sketches of the murder scene in my notepad. Sampson was pacing from about four o'clock on. I could see he was ready to blow out of there, but he was used to my thoroughness.

The FBI had arrived, and I'd gotten a call from Kyle Craig who had stayed down in Quantico working on Mr Smith. There was a mob of news reporters outside the terminal. How could it get any worse? I kept thinking, *the train has left the station*. It was one of those wordplays that gets in your head and won't leave.

I was bleary-eyed and bone-weary by day's end, but also as sad as I remembered being at a homicide scene. Of course this was no ordinary homicide scene. I had put Soneji away, but somehow I felt responsible that he was out again.

Soneji was nothing if not methodical: He had wanted me at Union Station. Why, though? The answer to that question still wasn't apparent to me.

I finally snuck out of the station through the tunnels, to avoid the press and whatnot. I went home and showered and changed into fresh clothes.

That helped me a little. I lay on my bed and shut my eyes for ten minutes. I needed to clear my head of everything that had happened today.

It wasn't working worth a damn. I thought of calling off the night with Christine Johnson. A voice of warning was in my head. *Don't blow it. Don't scare her about The Job. She's the one.* I already sensed that Christine had problems with my work as a homicide detective. I couldn't blame her, especially not today.

Rosie the cat came in to visit. She cuddled against my chest. 'Cats are like Baptists,' I whispered to her. 'You know they raise hell, but you can't ever catch them at it.' Rosie purred agreement and chuckled to herself. We're friends like that.

When I finally came downstairs, I got 'the business' from my kids. Even Rosie joined in the fun, racing around the living room like the family's designated cheerleader.

'You look so nice, Daddy. You look *beautiful.*' Jannie winked and gave me the A-OK sign.

She was being sincere, but she was also getting a large charge out of my 'date' for the night. She obviously delighted in the idea of my getting all dolled up just to see the principal from her school.

Damon was even worse. He saw me coming down the stairs and started giggling. Once he started, he couldn't stop. He mumbled, 'Beautiful.'

'I'll get you for this,' I told him. 'Ten times over, maybe a hundred times. Wait until you bring somebody home to meet your pops. Your day will come.'

'It's worth it,' Damon said, and continued to laugh like the little madman that he can be. His antics got Jannie going so bad that she was finally rolling around on the carpet. Rosie hopped back and forth over the two of them.

I got down on the floor, growled like Jabba the Hut, and started wrestling with the kids. As usual, they were healing me. I looked over at Nana Mama, who was standing in the doorway between the kitchen and dining room. She was strangely quiet, not joining in as she usually does.

'You want some of this, old woman?' I said as I held Damon and lightly rubbed my chin against his head.

'No, no. But you're sure nervous as Rosie tonight,' Nana said and finally started to laugh herself. 'Why, I haven't seen you like this since you were around fourteen and off to see Jeanne Allen, if I remember the name correctly. Jannie's right, though, you do look, let's say, rather dashing.'

I finally let Damon up off the floor. I stood and brushed off my snazzy dinner clothes. 'Well, I just want to thank all of you for being so supportive in my time of need.' I said it with false solemnity and a hurt look on my face.

'You're welcome!' they all chorused. 'Have a good time on your date! You look *beautiful*!'

I headed out to the car, refusing to look back and give them the satisfaction of one final taunting grin or another rousing huzzah. I did feel better, though, strangely revived.

I had promised my family, but also myself, that I was going to have some kind of normal life now. Not just a career, not a series of murder investigations. And yet as I drove away from the house, my last thought was, *Gary Soneji is out there again. What are you going to do about it?*

For starters, I was going to have a terrific, peaceful, exciting dinner with Christine Johnson.

I wasn't going to give Gary Soneji another thought for the rest of the night. I was going to be *dashing*, if not downright *beautiful*.

Chapter Fourteen

K inkead's in Foggy Bottom is one of the best restaurants in Washington or anywhere else I've ever eaten. The food there might even be better than home, though I'd never tell Nana that. I was pulling out the stops tonight, trying to anyway, doing the best I could.

Christine and I had agreed to meet at the bar around seven. I arrived a couple of minutes before seven, and she walked in right behind me. Soul mates. So began the first date.

Hilton Felton was playing his usual seductive-as-hell jazz piano downstairs, as he did six nights a week. On the weekends, he was joined by Ephrain Woolfolk on bass. Bob Kinkead was in and out of the kitchen, garnishing and inspecting every dish. Everything seemed just right. Couldn't be better.

'This is a really terrific place. I've been wanting to come here for years,' Christine said as she looked around approvingly at the cherry-wood bar, the sweeping staircase up to the main restaurant.

I had never seen her like this, all dressed up, and she was even more beautiful than I had thought. She had on a long black slip dress that showed off nicely toned shoulders. A cream-colored shawl fringed in black lace was draped over one arm. She wore a necklace made from an old-fashioned brooch that I liked a lot. She had on black flat-heeled pumps, but she was still nearly six feet tall. She smelled of flowers.

Her velvet-brown eyes were wide and sparkling with the kind of delight I suspected she saw in her children at school, but which was absent on the faces of most adults. Her smile was effortless. She seemed happy to be here.

I wanted to look like anything but a homicide detective, so I had picked out a black shirt given to me by Jannie for my birthday. She called it my 'cool guy shirt.' I also wore black slacks, a snazzy black leather belt, black loafers. I already knew that I looked 'beautiful.'

We were escorted to a cozy little booth in the mezzanine section. I usually try to keep 'physical allure' in its place, but heads turned as Christine and I walked across the dining room.

I'd completely forgotten what it was like to be out with someone and have that happen. I must admit that I sort of liked the feeling. I was remembering what it was like to be with someone you want to be with. I was also remembering what it was like to feel whole, or almost whole, or at least on the way to being whole again.

Our cozy booth overlooked Pennsylvania Avenue and also had a view of Hilton tinkering away at his piano. Kind of perfect.

'So how was your day?' Christine asked after we settled into the booth.

'Uneventful,' I said and shrugged. 'Just another day in the life of the DCPD.'

Christine shrugged right back at me. 'I heard something on the radio about a shooting at Union Station. Weren't you involved just a little bit with Gary Soneji at one point in your illustrious career?'

'Sorry, I'm off-duty now,' I said to her. 'I love your dress, by the way.' *I also love that old brooch that you turned into a necklace. I like that you wore flats just in case I needed to be taller tonight, which I don't.*

'Thirty-one dollars,' she said and smiled shyly, wonderfully. The dress looked like a million on her. I thought so anyway.

I checked her eyes to see if she was all right. It had been more than six months since her husband's death, but that isn't really a lot of time. She seemed fine to me. I suspected she'd tell me if that changed.

We picked out a nice bottle of Merlot. Then we shared Ipswich clams, which were full belly and a little messy, but a good start to dinner at Kinkead's. For a main dish, I had a velvety salmon stew.

Christine made an even better choice. Lobster with buttery cabbage, bean purée and truffle oil.

All the while we ate, the two of us never shut up. Not for a minute. I hadn't felt so free and easy around someone in a long, long time.

'Damon and Jannie say you're the best principal ever. They paid me a dollar each to say that. What's your secret?' I asked Christine at one point. I found that I was fighting off an urge simply to babble when I was around her.

Christine was thoughtful for a moment before she answered. 'Well, I guess the easiest and maybe the truest answer is that it just makes me feel good to teach. The other answer I like goes something like this. If you're right-handed, it's really hard to write with your left hand. Well, most kids are *all left hand* at first. I try to always remember that. That's my secret.'

'Tell me about today at school,' I said, staring into her brown eyes, unable not to.

She was surprised by my question. 'You really want to hear about my day at school? Why?'

'I absolutely do. I don't even know why.' *Except that I love the sound of your voice. Love the way your mind works.*

'Actually, today was a great day,' she said, and her eyes lit up again. 'You sure you want to hear this, Alex? I don't want to bore you with work stuff.'

I nodded. 'I'm sure. I don't ask a whole lot of questions I don't want to hear the answers to.'

'Well then, I'll tell you about my day. Today, all the kids had to pretend they were in their seventies and eighties. The kids had to move a little more slowly than they're used to. They had to deal with infirmities, and being alone, and usually not being the center of attention. We call it "*getting under other people's skin*," and we do it a lot at the Truth School. It's a great program and I had a great day, Alex. Thanks for asking. That's nice.'

Christine asked me about my day again, and I told her as little as possible. I didn't want to disturb her, and I didn't need to relive the day myself. We talked about jazz, and classical music, and Amy Tan's latest novel. She seemed to know about everything, and was surprised I had read *The Hundred Secret Senses*, and even more surprised that I liked it.

She talked about what it was like for her growing up in Southeast, and she told me a big secret of hers: She told me about 'Dumbo-Gumbo.'

'All through grade-school days,' Christine said, 'I was Dumbo-Gumbo. That's what some of the other kids called me. I have big ears, you see. Like Dumbo the flying elephant.'

She pulled back her hair. 'Look.'

'Very pretty,' I said to her.

She laughed. 'Don't blow your credibility. I *do* have big ears. And I do have this *big* smile, lots of teeth and *gums*.'

'So some smart-ass kid came up with Dumbo-Gumbo?'

'My brother, Dwight, did it to me. He also came up with "Gumbo Din." He still hasn't said he's sorry.'

'Well, I'm sorry for him. Your smile is dazzling, and your ears are just right.'

She laughed again. I loved to hear her laugh. I loved everything about her actually. I couldn't have been happier with our first night out.

Chapter Fifteen

The time flew by like nothing at all. We talked about charter schools, a national curriculum, a Gordon Parks exhibit at the Corcoran Gallery of Art, lots of silly stuff, too. I would have guessed it was maybe nine-thirty when I happened to glance at my watch. It was actually ten to twelve.

'It's a school night,' Christine said. 'I have to go, Alex. I really do. My coach will turn into a pumpkin and all that.'

Her car was parked on Nineteenth Street and we walked there together. The streets were silent, empty, glittering under overhead lamps.

I felt as if I'd had a little too much to drink, but I knew I hadn't. I was feeling carefree, remembering what it was like to be that way.

'I'd like to do this again sometime. How about tomorrow night?' I said and started to smile. God, I liked the way this was going.

Suddenly, something was wrong. I saw a look I didn't like – sadness and concern. Christine peered into my eyes.

'I don't think so, Alex. I'm sorry,' she said. 'I'm really sorry. I thought I was ready, but I guess maybe I'm not. There's a saying – scars grow with us.'

I sucked in a breath. I wasn't expecting that. In fact, I don't remember ever having been so wrong about how I was getting along with someone. It was like a sudden punch to the chest.

'Thanks for taking me to just about the nicest restaurant I've ever been to. I'm really, really sorry. It's nothing that you did, Alex.'

Christine continued to look into my eyes. She seemed to be searching for something, and I guess not finding it.

She got into her car without saying another word. She seemed so efficient suddenly, so in control. She started it up and drove away. I stood in the empty street and watched until her car's blazing brake lights disappeared.

It's nothing that you did, Alex. I could hear her words repeating in my head.

Chapter Sixteen

B ad Boy was back in Wilmington, Delaware. He had work to do here. In some ways, this might even be the best part.

Gary Soneji strolled the well-lit streets of Wilmington, seemingly without a care in the world. Why should he worry? He was skillful enough at makeup and disguises to fool the stiffs living here in Wilmington. He'd fooled them in Washington, hadn't he?

He stopped and stared at a huge, red-type-on-white poster near the train station. 'Wilmington – A Place To Be Somebody,' it read. What a terrific, un-intentional joke, he thought.

So was a three-story mural of bloated whales and dolphins that looked as if it had been stolen from some beach town in Southern California. Somebody ought to hire the Wilmington town council to work on *Saturday Night Live.* They were good, real good.

He carried a duffel bag, but didn't draw any attention to himself. The people he saw on his little walk looked as if they had outfitted themselves from the pages of the Sears catalogue, circa 1961. Lots of twill that didn't exactly flatter girth; putrid-colored plaid; comfortable brown shoes on everybody.

He heard the grating mid-Atlantic accent a few times, too. 'I've got to phewn heum' ('I've got to phone home'). A plain and ugly dialect for plain and ugly thoughts.

Jesus, what a place to have lived. How the hell had he survived during those sterile years? Why had he bothered to come back now? Well, he knew the answer to that question. Soneji knew why he'd come back.

Revenge.

Payback time.

He turned off North Street and onto his old street, Central Avenue. He stopped across from a white-painted brick house. He stared at the house for a long time. It was a modest Colonial, two stories. It had belonged to Missy's grandparents originally, which was why she hadn't moved.

Click your heels together, Gary. Jesus, there's no place like home.

He opened his duffel bag and took out his weapon of choice. He was especially proud of this one. He'd been waiting for a long time to use it.

Gary Soneji finally crossed the street. He marched up to the front door as if he owned the place, just as he had four years ago, the last time he'd been here, the day Alex Cross had barged into his life along with his partner, John Sampson.

The door was open – how sweet – his wife and daughter were waiting up for him, eating Poppycock and watching *Friends* on television.

'Hi. Remember me?' Soneji said in a soft voice.

They both started to scream.

His own sweet wife, Missy.

His darling little girl, Roni.

Screaming like strangers, because they knew him so well, and because they had seen his weapon.

Chapter Seventeen

If you ever began to face all the facts, you probably wouldn't get up in the morning. The war room inside police headquarters was filled beyond capacity with ringing telephones, percolating computers, state-of-the-art surveillance equipment. I wasn't fooled by all the activity or the noise. We were still nowhere on the shootings.

First thing, I was asked to give a briefing on Soneji. I was supposed to know him better than anyone else, yet somehow I felt that I didn't know enough, especially now. We had what's called a roundtable. Over the course of an hour, I shorthanded the details of his kidnapping of two children a few years earlier in Georgetown, his eventual capture, the dozens of interviews we'd had at Lorton Prison prior to his escape.

Once everybody on the task force was up to speed, I got back to work myself. I needed to find out who Soneji was, who he really was; and why he had decided to come back now; why he had returned to Washington.

I worked through lunch and never noticed the time. It took that long just to retrieve the mountain of data we had collected on Soneji. Around two in the afternoon, I found myself painfully aware of *pushpins* on the Big Board, where we were collecting 'important' information.

A war room just isn't a war room without pushpin maps and a large bulletin board. At the very top of our board was the name that had been given to the case by the chief of detectives. He had chosen 'Web,' since Soneji had already picked up the nickname 'Spider' in police circles. Actually, I'd coined the nickname. It came out of the complex webs he was always able to spin.

One section of the Big Board was devoted to 'civilian leads.' These were mostly reliable eyewitness accounts from the previous morning at Union Station. Another section was 'police leads,' most of which were the detectives' reports from the train terminal.

Civilian leads are 'untrained eye' reports; police leads are 'trained eye.' The thread in all of the reports so far was that no one had a good description of what Gary Soneji looked like now. Since Soneji had demonstrated unusual skill with disguises in the past, the news wasn't surprising, but it was disturbing to all of us.

Soneji's personal history was displayed on another part of the board. A long, curling computer printout listed every jurisdiction where he had ever been charged with a crime, including several unsolved homicides from his early years in Princeton, New Jersey.

Polaroid pictures depicting the evidence we had so far were also pinned up. Captions had been written in marker on the photos. The captions read: 'known skills, Gary Soneji'; 'hiding locations, Gary Soneji'; 'physical characteristics, Gary Soneji'; 'preferred weapons, Gary Soneji.'

There was a category for 'known associates' on the board, but this was still bare. It was likely to remain that way. To my knowledge, Soneji had always worked alone. *Was that assumption still accurate?* I wondered. Had he changed since our last run-in?

Around six-thirty that night, I got a call from the FBI evidence labs in Quantico, Virginia. Curtis Waddle was a friend of mine, and knew how I felt about Soneji. He had promised he'd pass on information as fast as he got it himself.

'You sitting down, Alex? Or you pacing around with one of those insipid, state-of-the-artless cordless phones in your hand?' he asked.

'I'm pacing, Curtis. But I'm carrying around an old-fashioned phone. It's even black. Alexander Graham Bell himself would approve.'

The lab head laughed and I could picture his broad, freckled face, his frizzy red hair tied with a rubber-band in a ponytail. Curtis loves to talk, and I've found you have to let him go on or he gets hurt and can even get a little spiteful.

'Good man, good man. Listen, Alex, I've got something here, but I don't think you're going to like it. I don't like it. I'm not even sure if we trust what we have.'

I edged in a few words. 'Uh, what do you have, Curtis?'

'The blood on the stock and barrel of the rifle at Union Station? We've got a definite match on it. Though, as I said, I don't know if I trust what we have. Kyle agrees. Guess what? It's not Soneji's blood.'

Curtis was right. I didn't like hearing that at all. I hate surprises in any murder investigation. 'What the hell does that mean? Whose blood is it then, Curtis? You know yet?'

I could hear him sigh, then blow out air in a *whoosh*. 'Alex, it's *yours*. Your blood was on the sniper rifle.'

Part Two

Monster Hunt

Chapter Eighteen

It was rush hour in Penn Station in New York City when Soneji arrived. He was on time, right on schedule, for the next act. *Man, he had lived this exact moment a thousand times over before today.*

Legions of pathetic burnouts were on the way home, where they would drop onto their pillows (no goose down for these hard cases), sleep for what would seem like an instant, and then get back up the following morning and head for the trains again. Jesus – and they said *he* was crazy!

This was absolutely, positively, the best – he'd been dreaming of this moment for more than twenty years. *This very moment!*

He had planned to get to New York between five and five-thirty – and here he was. Heeere's Gary! He'd imagined himself, *saw* himself, coming up out of the deep dark tunnels at Penn Station. He knew he was going to be out-of-his-head furious when he got upstairs, too. Knew it before he began to hear the piped-in circus music, some totally insane John Philip Sousa marching band ditty, with an overlay of tinny-sounding train announcements.

'You may now board through Gate A to Track 8, Bay Head Junction,' a fatherly voice proclaimed to the clueless.

All aboard to Bay Head Junction. All aboard, you pathetic morons, you freaking robots!

He checked out a poor moke porter who wore a dazed, flat look, as if life had left him behind about thirty years ago.

'You just can't keep a bad man down,' Soneji said to the passing redcap. 'You dig? You hear what I'm saying?'

'Fuck off,' the redcap said. Gary Soneji snorted out a laugh. Man, he got such a kick out of the surly downtrodden. They were everywhere, like a league these days.

He stared at the surly redcap. He decided to punish him – to let him live.

Today's not your day to die. Your name stays in the Book of Life. Keep on walking.

He was furious – just as he knew he would be. He was seeing red. The blood rushing through his brain made a deafening, pounding sound. Not nice. Not conducive to sane, rational thought. *The blood? Had the bloodhounds figured it out yet?*

The train station was filled to the gills with shoving, pushing, and grumbling New Yorkers at their worst. These goddamn commuters were unbelievably aggressive and irritating.

Couldn't any of them see that? Well hell, sure they could. And what did they do about it? They got even more aggressive and obnoxious.

None of them came close to approaching his own seething anger, though. Not even close. His hatred was pure. Distilled. He *was* anger. He did the things most of them only fantasized about. Their anger was fuzzy and unfocused, bursting in their bubbleheads. He saw anger clearly, and he acted upon it swiftly.

This was so fine, being inside Penn Station, creating another scene. He was really getting into the spirit now. He was noticing everything in full-blast, touchy-feely 3-D. Dunkin' Donuts, Knot Just Pretzels, Shoetrician Shoe Shine. The omnipresent rumble of the trains down below – it was just as he'd always imagined it.

He knew what would come next – and how it would all end.

Gary Soneji had a six-inch knife pressed against his leg. It was a real collector's item. Had a mother-of-pearl handle and a tight serpentine blade on both sides. 'An ornate knife for an ornate individual,' a greasy salesman had told him once upon a long time ago. 'Wrap it up!' he'd said. Had it ever since. For special occasions like today. Or once to kill an FBI agent named Roger Graham.

He passed Hudson News, with all of its glossy magazine faces staring out at the world, staring at him, trying to work their propaganda. He was still being shoved and elbowed by his fellow commuters. Man, didn't they ever stop?

Wow! He saw a character from his dreams, from way back when he was a kid. There was *the guy*. No doubt about it. He recognized the face, the way the guy held his body, everything about him. *It was the guy in the gray-striped business getup, the one who reminded him of his father.*

'You've been asking for this for a long time!' Soneji growled at Mr Gray Stripes. 'You asked for this.'

He drove the knife blade forward, felt it sink into flesh. It was just as he had imagined it.

The businessman saw the knife plunge near his heart. A frightened, bewildered look crossed his face. Then he fell to the station floor, stone cold dead, his eyes rolled back and his mouth frozen in a silent scream.

Soneji knew what he had to do next. He pivoted, danced to his left, and cut a second victim who looked like a slacker type. The guy wore a 'Naked Lacrosse' T-shirt. The details didn't matter, but some of them stuck in his mind. He cut a black man selling *Street News*. Three for three.

The thing that really mattered was *the blood*. Soneji watched as the precious blood spilled onto the dirty, stained, and mottled concrete floor. It spattered the clothes of commuters, pooled under the bodies. The blood was a clue, a Rorschach test for the police and FBI hunters to analyze. The blood was there for Alex Cross to try and figure out.

Gary Soneji dropped his knife. There was incredible confusion, shrieking everywhere, panic in Penn Station that finally woke the walking dead.

He looked up at the maze of maroon signs, each with neat Helvetic lettering: *Exit 31st St, Parcel Checking, Visitor Information, Eighth Avenue Subway.*

He knew the way out of Penn Station. It was all preordained. He had made this decision a thousand times before.

He scurried back down into the tunnels again. No one tried to stop him. He was the Bad Boy again. Maybe his stepmother had been right about that. His *punishment* would be to ride the New York subways.

Brrrr. Scar-ry!

Chapter Nineteen

Seven that evening. I was caught in the strangest, most powerful epiphany. I felt that I was outside myself, *watching myself.* I was driving by the Sojourner Truth School, on my way home. I saw Christine Johnson's car and stopped.

I got out of my car and waited for her. I felt incredibly vulnerable. A little foolish. I hadn't expected Christine to be at the school this late.

At quarter past seven, she finally wandered out of the school. I couldn't catch my breath from the instant I spotted her. I felt like a schoolboy. Maybe that was all right, maybe it was good. At least I was feeling again.

She looked as fresh and attractive as if she'd just arrived at the school. She had on a yellow-and-blue-flowered dress cinched around her narrow waist. She wore blue sling-back heels and carried a blue bag over one shoulder. The theme song from *Waiting to Exhale* floated into my head. I was waiting, all right.

Christine saw me, and she immediately looked troubled. She kept on walking, as if she were in a hurry to be somewhere else, anywhere else but here.

Her arms were crossed across her chest. *A bad sign*, I thought. The worst possible body language. Protective and fearful. One thing was clear already: Christine Johnson didn't want to see me.

I knew I shouldn't have come, shouldn't have stopped, but I couldn't help myself. I needed to understand what had happened when we left Kinkead's. Just that, nothing more. A simple, honest explanation, even if it hurt.

I sucked in a deep breath and walked up to her. 'Hi,' I said, 'you want to take a walk? It's a nice night.' I almost couldn't speak, and I am never at a loss for words.

'Taking a break in one of your usual twenty-hour workdays?' Christine half-smiled, tried to anyway.

I returned the smile, felt queasy all over. I shook my head. 'I'm off work.'

'I see. Sure, we can walk a little bit, a few minutes. It is a nice night, you're right.'

We turned down F Street and entered Garfield Park, which was especially pretty in the early summer. We walked in silence. Finally, we stopped near a ballfield swarming with little kids. A frenzied baseball game was in progress.

We weren't far from the Eisenhower Freeway and the *whoosh* of rush-hour traffic was steady, almost soothing. Tulip poplars were in bloom, and there was coral honeysuckle. Mothers and fathers were playing with their kids; everybody in a nice mood tonight.

This had been my neighborhood park for almost thirty years, and during the daylight hours it can almost be idyllic. Maria and I used to come here all the time when Damon was a toddler and she was pregnant with Jannie. Much of that is starting to fade away now, which is probably a good thing, but it's also sad.

Christine finally spoke. 'I'm sorry, Alex.' She had been staring at the ground, but now she raised her lovely eyes to mine. 'About the other night. The bad scene at my car. I guess I panicked. To be honest, I'm not even sure what happened.'

'Let's be honest,' I said. 'Why not?'

I could tell this was hard for her, but I needed to know how she felt. I needed more than she'd told me outside the restaurant.

'I want to try and explain,' she said. Her hands were clenched. One of her feet was tapping rapidly. Lots of bad signs.

'Maybe it's all my fault,' I said. 'I'm the one who kept asking you to dinner until—'

Christine reached out and covered my hand with hers. 'Please let me finish,' she said. The half-smile came again. 'Let me try to get this out once and for all. I was going to call you anyway. I was planning to call you tonight. I would have.

'You're nervous now, and so am I. God, am I nervous,' she said quietly. 'I know I've hurt your feelings, and I don't like that. It's the last thing I meant to do. You don't deserve to be hurt.'

Christine was shivering a little. Her voice was shaking, too, as she spoke. 'Alex, my husband died because of the kind of violence you have to live with every day. You accept that world, but I don't think I can. I'm just not that kind of person. I couldn't bear to lose someone else I was close to. Am I making sense to you? I'm feeling a little confused.'

Everything was becoming clearer to me now. Christine's husband had been killed in December. She said that there had been serious problems in the marriage, but she loved him. She had seen him shot to death in their home, seen him die. I had held her then. I was part of the murder case.

I wanted to hold her again, but I knew it was the wrong thing to do. She was still hugging herself tightly. I understood her feelings.

'Please listen to me, Christine. I'm not going to die until probably in my late eighties. I'm too stubborn and ornery to die. That would give us longer together than either of us has been alive so far. Forty-plus years. It's also a long time to avoid each other.'

Christine shook her head a little. She continued to look into my eyes. Finally, a smile peeked through.

'I *do* like the way your crazy mind works. One minute, you're Detective Cross – the next minute you're this very open, very sweet child.' She put her hands up to her face. 'Oh, God, I don't even know what I'm *saying*.'

Everything inside me said to do it, every instinct, every feeling. I slowly, carefully, reached out and took Christine into my arms. She fit so right. I could feel myself melting and I liked it. I even liked that my legs felt shaky and weak.

We kissed for the first time and Christine's mouth was soft and very sweet. Her lips pushed against mine. She didn't pull away, as I'd expected she might. I ran the tips of my fingers along one cheek, then the other.

Her skin was smooth and my fingers tingled at the tips. It was as if I had been without air for a long, long time and suddenly could breathe again. I could breathe. I felt alive.

Christine had shut her eyes, but now she opened them. Our eyes met, and held. 'Just like I imagined it,' she whispered, 'times about four hundred and fifty.'

Then the worst thing imaginable happened – my pager *beeped*.

Chapter Twenty

At six o'clock in New York City, police cruisers and EMS van sirens were wailing everywhere in the always highly congested five-block radius around Penn Station. Detective Manning Goldman parked his dark-blue Ford Taurus in front of the post office building on Eighth Avenue and ran toward the multiple-murder scene.

People stopped walking on the busy avenue to watch Goldman. Heads turned everywhere, trying to find out what was going on, and how this running man might fit in.

Goldman had long, wavy caramel-and-gray hair and a gray goatee. A gold stud glinted from one earlobe. Goldman looked more like an aging rock or jazz musician than a homicide detective.

Goldman's partner was a first-year detective named Carmine Groza. Groza had a strong build and wavy black hair, and reminded people of a young Sylvester Stallone, a comparison he hated. Goldman rarely talked to him. In his opinion, Groza had never uttered a single word worth listening to.

Groza nonetheless followed close behind his fifty-eight-year-old partner, who was currently the oldest Manhattan homicide detective working the streets, possibly the smartest, and definitely the meanest, grumpiest bastard Groza had ever met.

Goldman was known to be somewhere to the right of Pat Buchanan and Rush Limbaugh when it came to politics but, like most rumors, or what he called 'caricature assassinations,' this one was off the mark. On certain issues – the apprehension of criminals, the rights of criminals versus the rights of other citizens, and the death penalty – Goldman was definitely a radical conservative. He knew that anyone with half a brain who worked homicide for a couple of hours would come to exactly the same conclusions that he had. On the other hand, when it came to a woman's right to choose, same-sex marriages, or even Howard Stern, Goldman was as liberal as his thirty-year-old son, who just happened to be a lawyer with the ACLU. Of course, Goldman kept that to himself. The last thing he wanted was to ruin his reputation as an insufferable bastard. If he did that, he might have to talk to up-and-coming young assholes like 'Sly' Groza.

Goldman was still in good shape – better than Groza, with his steady diet of fast foods and high-octane colas and sugary teas. He ran against the tide of people streaming out of Penn Station. The murders, at least the ones he knew about so far, had taken place in and around the main waiting area of the train station.

The killer had chosen the rush hour for a reason, Goldman was thinking as the train-station waiting area came into view. Either that, or the killer just happened to go wacko at a time when the station was jam-packed with victims-to-be.

So what brought the wacko to Penn Station at rush hour? Manning Goldman wondered. He already had one scary theory that he was keeping to himself so far.

'Manning, you think he's still in here someplace?' Groza asked from behind.

Groza's habit of calling everybody by their first names, as if they were camp counselors together, really got under his skin.

Goldman ignored his partner. No, he didn't believe the killer was still in Penn Station. The killer was on the loose in New York. That bothered the hell out of him. It made him sick to his stomach, which wasn't all that hard these days, the past couple of years, actually.

Two pushcart vendors were artfully blocking the way to the crime scene. One cart was called Montego City Slickers Leather, the other From Russia With Love. He wished they would go back to Jamaica and Russia, respectively.

'NYPD. Make way. Move these ashcarts!' Goldman yelled at the vendors.

He pushed his way through the crowd of onlookers, other cops, and train-station personnel who were gathered near the body of a black man with braided hair and tattered clothing. Bloodstained copies of *Street News* were scattered around the body, so Goldman knew the dead man's occupation and his reason for being at the train station.

As he got up close, he saw that the victim was probably in his late twenties. There was an unusual amount of blood. Too much. The body was surrounded by a bright-red pool.

Goldman walked up to a man in a dark-blue suit with a blue-and-red Amtrak pin prominent on his lapel.

'Homicide Detective Goldman,' he said, flashing his shield. 'Tracks ten and eleven.' Goldman pointed at one of the overhead signs. 'What train would have come in on those tracks – just before the killings?'

The Amtrak manager consulted a thick booklet he kept in his breast pocket.

'The last train on ten . . . that would have been the Metroliner from Philly, Wilmington, Baltimore, originating in Washington.'

Goldman nodded. It was exactly what he'd been afraid of when he'd heard that a spree killer had struck at the train station, and that he was able to get away. That fact meant he was clearheaded. The killer had a plan in mind.

Goldman suspected that the Union Station and Penn Station killers might be one and the same – and that now the maniac was here in New York.

'You got any idea yet, Manning?' Groza was yapping again.

Goldman finally spoke to his partner without looking at him. 'Yeah, I was just thinking that they've got earplugs, bunghole plugs, so why not *mouth* plugs.'

Then Manning Goldman went to scare up a public phone. He had to make a call to Washington, DC. He believed that Gary Soneji had come to New York. Maybe he was on some kind of twenty- or thirty-city spree killer tour.

Anything was a possibility these days.

Chapter Twenty-One

I answered my pager and it was disturbing news from the NYPD. There had been another attack at a crowded train station. It kept me at work until well past midnight.

Gary Soneji was probably in New York City. Unless he had already moved on to another city he'd targeted for murder. Boston? Chicago? Philadelphia?

When I got home, the lights were off. I found lemon meringue pie in the refrigerator and finished it off. Nana had a story about Oseola McCarty attached to the fridge door. Oseola had washed clothes for more than fifty years in Hattiesburg, Mississippi. She had saved one hundred and fifty thousand dollars and donated it to the University of Southern Mississippi. President Clinton had invited her to Washington and given her the Presidential Citizen's Medal.

The pie was excellent, but I needed something else, another kind of nourishment. I went to see my shaman.

'You awake, old woman?' I whispered at Nana's bedroom door. She always keeps it ajar in case the kids need to talk or cuddle with her during the night. *Open twenty-four hours, just like 7-Eleven*, she always says. It was like that when I was growing up, too.

'That depends on your intentions,' I heard her voice in the dark. 'Oh, *is that you, Alex*?' she cackled and had a little coughing spell.

'Who else would it be? You tell me that? In the middle of the night at your bedroom door?'

'It could be anyone. Hugger-mugger. Housebreaker in this dangerous neighborhood of ours. Or one of my gentlemen admirers.'

It goes like that between us. Always has, always will.

'You have any particular boyfriends you want to tell me about?'

Nana cackled again. 'No, but I suspect you have a girlfriend you want to talk to me about. Let me get decent. Put on some water for my tea. There's lemon meringue pie in the fridge, at least there *was* pie. You *do* know that I have gentlemen admirers, Alex?'

'I'll put on the tea,' I said. 'The lemon meringue has already gone to pie heaven.'

A few minutes passed before Nana appeared in the kitchen. She was wearing the cutest housedress, blue stripes with big white buttons down the front. She looked as if she were ready to begin her day at half past twelve in the morning.

'I have two words for you, Alex. Marry her.'

I rolled my eyes. 'It's not what you think, old woman. It's not that simple.'

She poured some steaming tea for herself. 'Oh, it is absolutely that simple, granny son. You've got that spring in your step lately, a nice gleam in your eyes. You're *long gone*, mister. You're just the last one to hear about it. Tell me something. This is a serious question.'

I sighed. 'You're still a little high from your sweet dreams. What? Ask your silly question.'

'Well, it's this. If I was to charge you, say, ninety dollars for our sessions, *then* would you be more likely to take my fantastic advice?'

We both laughed at her sly joke, her unique brand of humor.

'Christine doesn't want to see me.'

'Oh, dear,' Nana said.

'Yeah, oh, dear. She can't see herself involved with a homicide detective.'

Nana smiled. 'The more I hear about Christine Johnson, the more I like her. Smart lady. Good head on those pretty shoulders.'

'Are you going to let me talk?' I asked.

Nana frowned and gave me her serious look. 'You always get to say what you want, just not at the exact moment you want to say it. Do you love this woman?'

'From the first time I saw her, I felt something extraordinary. Heart leads head. I know that sounds crazy.'

She shook her head and still managed to sip steaming hot tea. 'Alex, as smart as you are, you sometimes seem to get everything backwards. You don't sound crazy at all. You sound like you're better for the first time since Maria died. Will you look at the evidence that we have here? You have a spring back in your step again. Your eyes are bright and smiling. You're even being nice to me lately. Put it all together – your heart is working again.'

'She's afraid that I could die on the job. Her husband was murdered, remember?'

Nana rose from her chair at the kitchen table. She shuffled around to my side, and she stood very close to me. She was so much smaller than she used to be, and that worried me. I couldn't imagine my life without her in it.

'I love you, Alex,' she said. 'Whatever you do, I'll still love you. *Marry her*. At least live with Christine.' She laughed to herself. 'I can't believe I said that.'

Nana gave me a kiss, and then headed back to bed.

'I *do too* have suitors,' she called from the hall.

'Marry one,' I called back at her.

'I'm not in love, lemon meringue man. You are.'

Chapter Twenty-Two

First thing in the morning, six-thirty-five to be exact, Sampson and I took the Metroliner to New York's Penn Station. It was almost as fast as driving to the airport, parking, finagling with the airlines – and besides, I wanted to do some thinking about *trains*.

A theory that Soneji was the Penn Station slasher had been advanced by the NYPD. I'd have to know more about the killings in New York, but it was the kind of high-profile situation that Soneji had been drawn to in the past.

The train ride was quiet and comfortable, and I had the opportunity to think about Soneji for much of the trip. What I couldn't reconcile was why Soneji was committing crimes that appeared to be acts of desperation. They seemed suicidal to me.

I had interviewed Soneji dozens of times after I had apprehended him a few years ago. That was the Dunne-Goldberg case. I certainly didn't believe he was suicidal then. He was too much of an egomaniac, even a megalomaniac.

Maybe these were copycat crimes. *Whatever* he was doing now didn't track. *What had changed? Was it Soneji who was doing the killings? Was he pulling some kind of trick or stunt? Could this be a clever trap? How in hell had he gotten my blood on the sniper's rifle in Union Station?*

What kind of trap? For what reason? Soneji obsessed on his crimes. Everything had a purpose with him.

So why kill strangers in Union and Penn Stations? Why choose railroad stations?

'Oh ho, smoke's curling out of your forehead, Sugar. You aware of that?' Sampson looked over at me and made an announcement to the nice folks seated around us in the train car.

'Little wisps of white smoke! See? Right *here*. And *here*.'

He leaned in close and started hitting me with his newspaper as if he were trying to put out a small fire.

Sampson usually favors a cool deadpan delivery to slapstick. The change of pace was effective. We both started to laugh. Even the people sitting around us smiled, looking up from their newspapers, coffees, laptop computers.

'Phew. Fire seems to be out,' Sampson said and chuckled deeply. 'Man, your head is *hot* as Hades to the touch. You must have been brainstorming some powerful ideas. Am I right about that?'

'No, I was thinking about Christine,' I told Sampson.

'You lying sack. You *should* have been thinking about Christine Johnson. Then I would have had to beat the fire out someplace else. How you two doing? If I might be so bold as to ask?'

'She's great, she's the best, John. Really something else. She's smart and she's funny. Ho ho, ha ha.'

'And she's almost as good-looking as Whitney Houston, and she's sexy as hell. But none of that answers my question. What's happening with you two? You trying to hide your love on me? My spy, Ms Jannie, told me you had a date the other night. Did you have a big date and not tell me about it?'

'We went to Kinkead's for dinner. Had a good time. Good food, great company. One little minor problem, though: She's afraid I'm going to get myself killed, so she doesn't want to see me anymore. Christine's still mourning her husband.'

Sampson nodded, slid down his shades to check me out sans light filtration. 'That's interesting. Still mourning, huh? Proves she's a good lady. By the by, since you brought up the forbidden topic, something I should tell you, all-star.

You ever get capped in action, your family will mourn you for an indecent length of time. Myself, I would carry the torch of grief up to and through the funeral service. That's it, though. Thought you should know. So, are you two star-crossed lovers going to have another date?'

Sampson liked to talk as if we were girlfriends in a Terry McMillan novel. We could be like that sometimes, which is unusual for men, especially two tough guys like us. He was on a roll now. 'I think you two are so cute together. Everybody does. Whole town is talking. The kids, Nana, your aunties.'

'They are, are they?'

I got up and sat down across the aisle from him. Both seats were empty. I spread out my notes on Gary Soneji and started to read them again.

'Thought you would never get the hint,' Sampson said as he stretched his wide body across both seats.

As always, there was nothing like working a job with him. Christine was wrong about my ever getting hurt. Sampson and I were going to live forever. We wouldn't even need DHEA or melatonin to help.

'We're going to get Gary Soneji's ass in a sling. Christine's going to fall hard for you, like you obviously already fell for her. Everything will be beautiful, Sugar. Way it has to be.'

I don't know why, but I couldn't quite make myself believe that.

'I know you're thinking negative shit already,' Sampson said without even looking over at me, 'but just watch. Nothing but happy endings this time.'

Chapter Twenty-Three

Sampson and I arrived in New York City around nine o'clock in the morning. I vividly remembered an old Stevie Wonder tune about getting off the bus in New York for the first time. The mixture of hopes and fears and expectations most people associate with the city seems a universal reaction.

As we climbed the steep stone steps from the underground tracks in Penn Station, I had an insight about the case. If it was right, it would definitely tie Soneji to both train-station massacres.

'I might have something on Soneji,' I told Sampson as we approached the bright lights gleaming at the top of the stairs. He turned his head toward me but kept on climbing.

'I'm not going to guess, Alex, because my mind doesn't ever go where yours does.' Then he mumbled, 'Thank the Lord and Saviour Jesus for that. Addlehead brother.'

'You trying to keep me amused?' I asked him. I could hear music coming from the main terminal now – it sounded like Vivaldi's *The Four Seasons*.

'Actually, I'm trying not to let the fact that Gary Soneji is on this current mad-ass rampage upset my equilibrium or otherwise depress the hell out of me. Tell me what you're thinking.'

'When Soneji was at Lorton Prison, and I interviewed him, he always talked about how his stepmother kept him in the cellar of their house. He was obsessed about it.'

Sampson's head bobbed. 'Knowing Gary as we do, I can't completely blame the poor woman.'

'She would keep him down there for hours at a time, sometimes a whole day, if his father happened to be away from home. She kept the lights off, but he learned to hide candles. He would read by candlelight about kidnappers, rapists, mass murderers, all the other bad boys.'

'And so, Dr Freud? These mass killers were his boyhood role models?'

'Something like that. Gary told me that when he was in the cellar, he would fantasize about committing murders and other atrocities – *as soon as he was let out*. His idée fixe was that release from the cellar would give him back his freedom and power. He'd sit in the cellar obsessing on what he was going to do as soon as he got out. You happen to notice any cellarlike locations around here? Or maybe at Union Station?'

Sampson showed his teeth, which are large and very white, and can give you the impression that he likes you maybe more than he does. 'The train tunnels represent the cellar of Gary's childhood house, right? When he gets out of the tunnels, all hell breaks loose. He finally takes his revenge on the world.'

'I think that's part of what's going on,' I said. 'But it's never that simple with Gary. It's a start anyway.'

We had reached the main level of Penn Station. This was probably how it had been when Soneji arrived here the night before. More and more I was thinking that the NYPD had it right. Soneji could definitely be the Penn Station killer, too.

I saw a mob of travelers lingering beneath the slipping numbers of the Train Departures board. I could almost see Gary Soneji standing where I was now, taking it all in – *released from the cellar to be Bad Boy again! Still wanting to do famous crimes and succeeding beyond his craziest dreams.*

'Dr Cross, I presume.'

I heard my name as Sampson and I wandered into the brightly lit waiting area of the station. A bearded man with a gold ear stud was smiling at his small joke. He extended his hand.

'I'm Detective Manning Goldman. Good of you to come. Gary Soneji was here yesterday.' He said it with absolute certainty.

Chapter Twenty-Four

S ampson and I shook hands with Goldman and also his partner, a younger detective who appeared to defer to Goldman. Manning Goldman wore a bright-blue sports shirt with three of the buttons undone. He had on a ribbed undershirt that exposed silver and reddish-gold chest hairs sprouting toward his chin. His partner was dressed from head to toe in black. Talk about your odd couples, but I still preferred Oscar and Felix.

Goldman started in on what he knew about the Penn Station stabbings. The New York detective was high-energy, a rapid-fire talker. He used his hands constantly, and appeared confident about his abilities and opinions. The fact that he'd called us in on his case was proof of that. He wasn't threatened by us.

'We know that the killer came up the stairs at track ten here, just like the two of you just did. We've talked to three witnesses who may have seen him on the Metroliner from Washington,' Goldman explained. His swarthy, dark-haired partner never said a word. 'And yet, we don't have a good ID of him – each witness gave a different description – which doesn't make any sense to me. You have any ideas on that one?'

'If it's Soneji, he's good with makeup and disguises. He's devious and clever. He enjoys fooling people, especially the police. Do you know where he got on the train?' I asked.

Goldman consulted a black leather notebook. 'The stops for that particular train were DC, Baltimore, Philadelphia, Wilmington, Princeton Junction, and New York. We assumed he got on in DC.'

I glanced at Sampson, then back at the NYPD detectives. 'Soneji used to live in Wilmington with his wife and little girl. He was originally from the Princeton area.'

'That's information we didn't have,' Goldman said. I couldn't help noticing that he was talking only to me, as if Sampson and Groza weren't even there. It was peculiar, and made it uncomfortable for the rest of us.

'Get me a schedule for yesterday's Metroliner, the one that arrived at five-ten. I want to double-check the stops,' he barked at Groza. The younger detective skulked off to do Goldman's bidding.

'We heard there were three stabbings, three deaths?' Sampson finally spoke.

I knew that he'd been sizing up Goldman. He'd probably come to the conclusion that the detective was a New York asshole of the first order.

'That's what it says on the front pages of all the daily newspapers,' Goldman cracked out of the side of his mouth. It was a nasty remark, delivered curtly.

'The reason I was asking—' Sampson started to say, still keeping his cool.

Goldman cut him off with a rude swipe of the hand. 'Let me show you the sites of the stabbings,' he said as he turned his attention back to me. 'Maybe it will jog something else you know about Soneji.'

'Detective Sampson asked you a question,' I said.

'Yeah, but it was a pointless question. I don't have time for p.c. crap or pointless questions. Like I said, let's move on. Soneji is on the loose in my town.'

'You know much about knives? You cover a lot of stabbings?' Sampson asked. I could tell that he was starting to lose it. He towered over Manning Goldman. Actually, both of us did.

'Yeah, I've covered quite a few stabbings,' Goldman said. 'I also know where you're going. It's extremely unlikely for Soneji to be able to kill three out of three with a knife. Well, the knife he used had a double serpentine blade, extremely sharp. He cut each victim like some surgeon from NYU Medical Center. Oh, yeah, he tipped the knife with potassium cyanide. Kill you in under a minute. I was getting to that.'

Sampson backed off. The mention of poison on the knife was news to us. John knew we needed to hear what Goldman had to say. We couldn't let this get personal here in New York. Not yet anyway.

'Soneji have any history with knives?' Goldman asked. He was talking to me again. 'Poisons?'

I understood that he wanted to pump me, to use me. I didn't have a problem with it. Give and take is as good as it gets on most multijurisdictional cases.

'Knives? He once killed an FBI agent with a knife. Poisons? I don't know. I wouldn't be surprised. He also shot an assortment of handguns and rifles while he was growing up. Soneji likes to kill, Detective Goldman. He's a quick study, so he could have picked it up. Guns and knives, and poisons, too.'

'Believe me, he did pick it up. He was in and out of here in a couple of minutes. Left three dead bodies just like *that*,' Goldman snapped his fingers.

'Was there much blood at the scene?' I asked Goldman. It was the question I'd had on my mind all the way from Washington.

'There was a *helluva* lot of blood. He cut each victim deep. Slashed two of their throats. Why?'

'There could be an angle connected with all the blood.' I told Goldman one of my findings at Union Station. 'The sniper in DC made a mess. I'm pretty sure Soneji did it on purpose. He used hollow-points. He also left traces of my blood on his weapon,' I revealed to Goldman.

He probably even knows I'm here in New York, I thought. *And I'm not completely sure who is tracking whom.*

Chapter Twenty-Five

For the next hour, Goldman, with his partner practically walking up his heels, showed us around Penn Station, particularly the three stabbing sites. The body markings were still on the floor, and the cordoned-off areas were causing more than the usual congestion in the terminal.

After we finished with a survey of the station, the NYPD detectives took us up to the street level, where it was believed Soneji had caught a cab headed uptown.

I studied Goldman, watched him work. He was actually pretty good. The way he walked around was interesting. His nose was poised just a little higher than those of the rest of the general population. His posture made him look haughty, in spite of the odd way he was dressed.

'I would have guessed he'd use the subway to escape,' I offered as we stood out on noisy Eighth Avenue. Above our heads, a sign announced that Kiss was appearing at Madison Square Garden. Shame I'd have to miss it.

Goldman smiled broadly. 'I had the same thought. Witnesses are split on which way he went. I was curious whether you'd have an option. I think Soneji used the subway, too.'

'Trains have a special significance for him. I think trains are part of his ritual. He wanted a set of trains as a kid, but never got it.'

'Ah, *quod erat demonstrandum*,' Goldman said and smirked. 'So now he kills people in train stations. Makes perfect sense to me. Wonder he didn't blow up the whole fucking train.'

Even Sampson laughed at Goldman's delivery on that one.

After we had finished the tour of Penn Station and the surrounding streets, we made a trip downtown to One Police Plaza. By four o'clock I knew what the NYPD had going – at least everything that Manning Goldman was prepared to tell me at this time.

I was almost sure that Gary Soneji was the Penn Station killer. I personally contacted Boston, Philly, and Baltimore and suggested tactfully that they pay attention to the train terminals. I passed on the same advice to Kyle Craig and the FBI.

'We're going to head back to Washington,' I finally told Goldman and Groza. 'Thanks for calling us in on this. This helps a lot.'

'I'll call if there's anything. You do the same, hey?' Manning Goldman put out his hand, and we shook. 'I'm pretty sure we haven't heard the last of Gary Soneji.'

I nodded. I was sure of it, too.

Chapter Twenty-Six

*I*n *his mind*, Gary Soneji lay down beside Charles Joseph Whitman on the roof of the University of Texas tower, circa 1966.

All in his goddamn incredible mind!

He had been up there with Charlie Whitman *many, many times before* – ever since 1966, when the spree killer had become one of his boyhood idols. Over the years, other killers had captured his imagination, but none were like Charlie Whitman. Whitman was an American original, and there weren't many of those left.

Let's see now, Soneji ran down the names of his favorites: James Herberty, who had opened fire without warning inside the McDonald's in San Ysidio, California. He had killed twenty-one, killed them at an even faster clip than they could dish out greasy hamburgers. Soneji had actually copycatted the McDonald's shootings a few years earlier. That was when he'd first met Cross face to face.

Another of his personal favorites was postman Patrick Sherill, who'd blown away fourteen co-workers in Edmond, Oklahoma, and also probably started the postman-as-madman paranoia. More recently, he had admired the handiwork of Martin Bryant at the Port Arthur penal colony in Tasmania. Then there was Thomas Watt Hamilton, who invaded the mind space of virtually everyone on the planet after his shooting spree at a primary school in Dunblane, Scotland.

Gary Soneji desperately wanted to invade everybody's mind space, to become a large, disturbing icon on the world's Internet. He was going to do it, too. He had everything figured out.

Charlie Whitman was still his sentimental favorite, though. Whitman was the original, the 'madman in the tower.' A Bad Boy down there in Texas.

God, how many times had he lain on that same tower, in the blazing August sun, along with Bad Boy Charlie?

All in his incredible mind!

Whitman had been a twenty-five-year-old student of architectural engineering at the University of Texas when he'd gone tapioca pudding. He'd brought an arsenal up onto the observation deck of the limestone tower that soared three hundred feet above the campus, and where he must have felt like God.

Just before he'd gone up in the clock tower, he had murdered his wife and mother. Whitman had made Charlie Starkweather look like a piker and a real chump that afternoon in Texas. The same could be said for Dickie Hickock and Perry Smith, the white-trash punks Truman Capote immortalized in his book *In Cold Blood*. Charles Whitman made those two look like crap, too.

Soneji never forgot the actual passage from the *Time* magazine story on the Texas tower shootings. He knew it word for word: '*Like many mass murderers, Charles Whitman had been an exemplary boy, the kind that neighborhood mothers hold up as a model to their own recalcitrant youngsters. He was a Roman Catholic altar boy, and a newspaper delivery boy.*'

Cool goddamn beans.

Another master of disguise, right. Nobody had known what Charlie was thinking, or what he was ultimately going to pull off.

He had carefully positioned himself under the VI numeral of the tower's clock. Then Charles Whitman opened fire at 11:48 in the morning. Beside him on the six-foot runway that went around the tower were a machete, a Bowie knife, a 6mm Remington bolt-action rifle, a 35mm Remington, a Luger pistol, and a .357 Smith & Wesson revolver.

The local and state police fired thousands of rounds up onto the tower, almost shooting out the entire face of the clock – but it took over an hour and a half to bring an end to Charlie Whitman. The whole world marveled at his audacity, his unique outlook and perspective. The whole goddamn world took notice.

Someone was pounding on the door of Soneji's hotel room! The sound brought him back to the here and now. He suddenly remembered where he was.

He was in New York City, in Room 419 of the Plaza, which he always used to read about as a kid. He had always fantasized about coming by train to New York and staying at the Plaza. *Well, here he was.*

'Who's there?' he called from the bed. He pulled a semiautomatic from under the covers. Aimed it at the peephole in the door.

'Maid service,' an accented Spanish female voice said. 'Would you like your bed turned down?'

'No, I'm comfortable as is,' Soneji said and smiled to himself. *Well actually, señorita, I'm preparing to make the NYPD look like the amateurs that cops usually are. You can forget the bed turndown and keep your chocolate mints, too. It's too late to try and make up to me now.*

On second thoughts – 'Hey! You can bring me some of those chocolate mints. I like those little mints. I need a little sweet treat.'

Gary Soneji sat back against the headboard and continued to smile as the maid unlocked the door and entered. He thought about doing her, boffing the scaggy hotel maid, but he figured that wasn't such a good idea. He wanted to spend one night at the Plaza. He'd been looking forward to it for years. It wasn't worth the risk.

The thing that he loved the most, what made it so perfect, was that nobody had any idea where this was going.

Nobody would guess the end to this one.

Not Alex Cross, not anybody.

Chapter Twenty-Seven

I vowed I would not let Soneji wear me down this time. I wouldn't let Soneji take possession of my soul again.

I managed to get home from New York in time for a late dinner with Nana and the kids. Damon, Jannie, and I cleaned up downstairs and then we set the table in the dining room. Keith Jarrett was playing ever so sweetly in the background. This was nice. This was the way it was supposed to be and there was a message in that for me.

'I'm so impressed, Daddy,' Jannie commented as we circled the table, putting out the 'good' silverware, and also glasses and dinner plates I'd picked out years ago with my wife, Maria. 'You went all the way to New York. You came all the way back again. You're here for dinner. Very good, Daddy.'

She beamed and giggled and patted me on my arm as we worked. I was a good father tonight. Jannie approved. She bought my act completely.

I took a small formal bow. 'Thank you, my darling daughter. Now this trip to New York I was on, about how far would you say that might be?'

'Kilometers or miles?' Damon broke in from the other side of the table, where he was folding napkins like fans, the way they do in fancy restaurants. Damon can be quite the little scene stealer.

'Either measurement would be fine,' I told him.

'Approximately two hundred forty-eight miles, one way,' Jannie answered. 'Howzat?'

I opened my eyes as wide as I could, made a funny face, and let my eyes roll up into my forehead. I can still steal a scene or two myself. 'Now, *I'm* impressed. Very good, Jannie.'

She took a little bow and then did a mock curtsy. 'I asked Nana how far it was this morning,' she confessed. 'Is that okay?'

'That's cool,' Damon offered his thought on his sister's moral code. 'It's called research, Velcro.'

'Yeah, that's cool, Baby,' I said, and we all laughed at her cleverness and sense of fun.

'Round-trip, it's four hundred ninety-six miles,' Damon said.

'You two are . . . smart!' I exclaimed in a loud, playful voice. 'You're both smarty pants, smart alecks, smarties of the highest order!'

'What's going on in there? What am I missing out on?' Nana finally called from the kitchen, which was overflowing with good smells from her cooking. She doesn't like to miss anything. Ever. To my knowledge, she just about never has.

'G. E. College Bowl,' I called out to her.

'You will lose your shirt, Alex, if you play against those two young scholars,' she warned. 'Their hunger for knowledge knows no bounds. Their knowledge is fast becoming encyclopedic.'

'En-cy-clo-pedic!' Jannie grinned.

'Cakewalk!' she said then, and did the lively old dance that had originated back in plantation times. I'd taught it to her one day at the piano. The cakewalk music form was actually a forerunner of modern jazz. It had fused polyrhythms from West Africa with classical melodies and also marches from Europe.

Back in plantation days, whoever did the dance best on a given night won a cake. Thus the phrase 'that takes the cake.'

All of this Jannie knew, and also how to actually do the damn dance in high style, and with a contemporary twist or two. She can also do James Brown's famous Elephant Walk and Michael Jackson's Moonwalk.

After dinner, we did the dishes and then we had our biweekly boxing lesson in the basement. Damon and Jannie are not only smart, they're tough little weasels. Nobody in school picks on those two. 'Brains and a wicked left hook!' Jannie brags to me sometimes. 'Hard combination to beat.'

We finally retired to the living room after the Wednesday-night fights. Rosie the cat was curled up on Jannie's lap. We were watching a little of the Orioles baseball game on television when Soneji slid into my head again.

Of all the killers I had ever gone up against, he was the scariest. Soneji was single-minded, obsessive, but he was also completely whacked-out, and that's the proper medical term I learned years ago at Johns Hopkins. He had a powerful imagination fueled by anger, and he acted on his fantasies.

Months back, Soneji had called to tell me that he'd left a cat at our house, a little present. He knew that we had adopted her, and loved little Rosie very much. He said that every time I saw Rosie the cat, I should think: *Gary's in the house, Gary is right there.*

I had figured that Gary had seen the stray cat at our house, and just made up a nasty story. Gary loved to lie, especially when his lies hurt people. That night, though, with Soneji running out of control again, I had a bad thought about Rosie. It frightened the hell out of me.

Gary is in the house. Gary is right here.

I nearly threw the cat out of the house, but that wasn't an option, so I waited until morning to do what had to be done with Rosie. *Goddamn Soneji. What in hell did he want from me? What did he want from my family?*

What could he have done to Rosie before he left her at our house?

Chapter Twenty-Eight

I felt like a traitor to my kids and also to poor little Rosie. I was feeling subhuman as I drove thirty-six miles to Quantico the next morning. I was betraying the kids' trust and possibly doing a terrible thing, but I didn't see that I had any other choice.

At the start of our trip, I had Rosie trapped in one of those despicable, metal-wire pet carriers. The poor thing cried and meowed and scratched so hard at the cage and at me that I finally had to let her out.

'You be good now,' I gave her a mild warning. Then I said, 'Oh, go ahead and raise hell if you want to.'

Rosie proceeded to lay a huge guilt trip on me, to make me feel miserable. Obviously, she'd learned this lesson well from Damon and Jannie. Of course, she had no idea how angry she ought to be at me. But maybe she did. Cats are intuitive.

I was fearful that the beautiful red-and-brown Abyssinian would have to be destroyed, possibly this morning. I didn't know how I could ever explain it to the kids.

'Don't scratch up the car seats. And don't you dare jump on top of my head!' I warned Rosie, but in a pleasant, conciliatory voice.

She meowed a few times, and then we had a more or less peaceful and pleasant ride to the FBI quarters in Quantico. I had already spoken to Chet Elliott in the Bureau's SAS or Scientific Analysis Section. He was waiting for Rosie and me. I was carrying the cat in one arm, with her cage dangling from the other.

Now things were going to get very hard. To make things worse, Rosie got up on her hind legs and nuzzled my face. I looked into her beautiful green eyes and I could hardly stand it.

Chet was outfitted in protective gear: a white lab coat, white plastic gloves, even gold-tinted goggles. He looked like the king of the geeks. He peered at Rosie, then at me and said, 'Weird science.'

'Now what happens?' I asked Chet. My heart had sunk to the floorboards when I'd spotted him in his protective gear. He was taking this seriously.

'You go over to Admin,' he said. 'Kyle Craig wants to see you. Says it's important. Of course, everything with Kyle is important as hell and can't wait another second. I know he's crazed about Mr Smith. We all are. Smith is the craziest fucker yet, Alex.'

'What happens to Rosie?' I asked.

'First step, some X-rays. Hopefully, little Red here isn't a walking bomb, compliments of our friend Soneji. If she isn't, we'll pursue toxicology. Examine her for the presence of drugs or poison in the tissues and fluids. You run along. Go see Uncle Kyle. Red and I will be just fine. I'll try to do right by her, Alex. We're all cat-people in my family. I'm a cat-person, can't you tell? I understand about these things.'

He nodded his head and then flipped down his swimmer-style goggles. Rosie rubbed up against him, so I figured she knew he was okay. So far, anyway.

It was later that worried me, and almost brought tears to my eyes.

Chapter Twenty-Nine

I went to see what Kyle had on his mind, though I thought I knew what it was. I dreaded the confrontation, the war of the wills that the two of us sometimes get into. Kyle wanted to talk about his Mr Smith case. Smith was a violent killer who had murdered more than a dozen people in America and Europe. Kyle said it was the ugliest, most chilling spree he had ever seen, and Kyle isn't known for hyperbole.

His office was on the top floor of the Academy Building, but he was working out of a crisis room in the basement of Admin. From what he'd told me, Kyle was practically camping out inside the war room, with its huge Big Board, state-of-the-art computers, phones, and a whole lot of FBI personnel, none of whom looked too happy on the morning of my visit.

The Big Board read: MR SMITH 17 – GOOD GUYS 0, in bright-red letters.

'Looks like you're in your glory again. Nowhere to go but up,' I said. Kyle was sitting at a big walnut desk, lost in study of the evidence board, at least he seemed to be.

I already knew about the case – more than I wanted to. 'Smith' had started his string of gory murders in Cambridge, Massachusetts. He had then moved on to Europe, where he was currently blazing a bewildering trail.

Smith's work was so strange and kinky and *unhinged* that it was seriously discussed in the media that he might be an alien, as in a visitor from outer space. At any rate, 'Smith' definitely seemed inhuman. No human could have committed the monstrosities that he had. That was the working theory.

'I thought you'd never get here,' Kyle said when he saw me.

I raised my hands defensively. 'Can't help. Won't do it, Kyle. First, because I'm already overloaded with Soneji. Second, because I'm losing my family on account of my work habits.'

Kyle nodded. 'All right, all right. I hear you. I see the larger picture. I even understand and sympathize, to a degree. But since you're here, with a little time on your hands, I do need to talk to you about Mr Smith. Believe me, Alex, you've never seen anything like this. You've got to be a little curious.'

'I'm not. In fact, I'm going to leave now. Walk right out that door I came in.'

'We've got an unbelievably ugly problem on our hands, Alex, Just let me talk, and you listen. Just *listen*,' Kyle pleaded.

I relented, but just a little. 'I'll listen. That's all. I'm not getting involved with this.'

Kyle made a small, ceremonial bow in my direction. 'Just listen,' Kyle said. 'Listen and keep an open mind, Alex, This is going to blow your mind, I guarantee it. It's blown mine.'

Then Kyle proceeded to tell me about an agent named Thomas Pierce. Pierce was in charge of the Mr Smith case. What *was* intriguing was that Smith had brutally murdered Pierce's fiancée some years back.

'Thomas Pierce is the most thorough investigator and the most brilliant person I've ever met,' Kyle told me. 'At first, we wouldn't let him anywhere near the Smith case, for obvious reasons. He worked it on his own. He made progress where we hadn't. Finally, he made it clear that if he couldn't work on Smith, he'd leave the Bureau. He even threatened to try and solve the case on his own.'

'You put him on the case?' I asked Kyle.

'He's very persuasive. In the end, he made his case to the director. He sold Burns. Pierce is logical, and he's creative. He can analyze a problem like nobody I've ever seen. He's been fanatical on Mr Smith. Works eighteen- and twenty-hour days.'

'But even Pierce can't crack this case,' I said and pointed at the Big Board.

Kyle nodded. 'We're finally getting close, Alex. I desperately need your input. And I want you to meet Thomas Pierce. You have to meet Pierce.'

'I said I'd listen,' I told Kyle. 'But I don't have to meet anyone.'

Nearly four hours later, Kyle finally let me out of his clutches. He *had* blown my mind, all right – about Mr Smith *and* about Thomas Pierce – but I wasn't getting involved. I couldn't.

I finally made my way back to SAS to check on Rosie. Chet Elliott was able to see me right away. He was still wearing his lab coat, gloves, and the gold-tinted goggles. His slow-gaited walk toward me said *bad news*. I didn't want to hear it.

Then he surprised me and grinned. 'We don't see anything wrong with her, Alex. I don't think Soneji did anything to her. He was just mind-humping you. We checked her for volatile compounds – nada. Then for nonvolatile organic compounds that would be unusual in her system – also negative. Forensic serology took some blood. You ought to leave Red with us for a couple of days, but I doubt we'll find anything. You can leave her here, period, if you like. She's a really cool cat.'

'I know.' I nodded and breathed a sigh of relief. 'Can I see her?' I asked Chet.

'Sure can. She's been asking for you all morning. I don't know why, but she seems to like you.'

'She knows I'm a cool cat, too.' I smiled.

He took me back to see Rosie. She was being kept in a small cage, and she looked pissed as hell. I'd brought her here, hadn't I? I might as well have administered the lab tests myself.

'Not my fault,' I explained as best I could. 'Blame that nutcase Gary Soneji, not me. Don't look at me like that.'

She finally let me pick her up and she even nuzzled my cheek. 'You're being a very brave good girl,' I whispered. 'I owe you one, and I always pay my debts.'

She purred and finally licked my cheek with her sandpaper tongue. *Sweet lady, Rosie O'Grady.*

Chapter Thirty

London, England.

M r Smith was dressed like an anonymous street person in a ripped and soiled black anorak. The killer was walking quickly along Lower Regent Street in the direction of Piccadilly Circus.

Going to the Circus, oh boy, oh boy! He was thinking. His cynicism was as thick and heavy as the air in London.

No one seemed to notice him in the late-afternoon crowds. No one paid much attention to the poor in any of the large, 'civilized' capitals. Mr Smith had noticed that, and used it to his advantage.

He hurried along with his duffel bag until he finally reached Piccadilly, where the crowds were even denser.

His attentive eyes took in the usual traffic snarl, which could be expected at the hub of five major streets. He also saw Tower Records, McDonald's, the Trocadero, far too many neon ads. Backpackers and camera-hounds were every-where on the street and sidewalks.

And a single alien creature – himself.

One being who didn't fit in any way with the others.

Mr Smith suddenly felt so alone, incredibly lonely in the middle of all these people in London town.

He set down the long, heavy duffel bag directly under the famous statue in the Circus – *Eros*. Still, no one was paying attention to him.

He left the bag sitting there, and he walked toward Haymarket.

When he was a few blocks away, he called the police, as he always did. The message was simple, clear, to the point. *Their time was up.*

'Inspector Derek Cabott is in Piccadilly Circus. He's in a gray duffel bag. What's left of him. You blew it. Cheers.'

Chapter Thirty-One

S ondra Greenberg of Interpol spotted Thomas Pierce as he walked toward the crime scene at the center of Piccadilly Circus. Pierce stood out in a crowd, even one like this.

Thomas Pierce was tall; his long blond hair was pulled back in a pony-tail; and he usually wore dark glasses. He did not look like your typical FBI agent, and, in fact, Pierce was nothing like any agent Greenberg had ever met or worked with.

'What's all the excitement about?' he asked as he got up close. 'Mr Smith out for his weekly kill. Nothing so unusual.' His habitual sarcasm was at work.

Sondra looked around at the packed crowd at the homicide scene and shook her head. There were press reporters and television news trucks everywhere.

'What's being done by the local geniuses? The police?' said Pierce.

'They're canvassing. *Obviously*, Smith has been here.'

'The bobbies want to know if anyone saw a little green man? Blood drip-ping from his little green teeth?'

'Exactly, Thomas. Have a look?'

Pierce smiled and it was entirely captivating. Definitely not the American FBI's usual style. 'You said that like, *spot of tea? . . . Have a look?*'

Greenberg shook her head of dark curls. She was nearly as tall as Pierce, and pretty in a tough sort of way. She always tried to be nice to Pierce. Actually, it wasn't hard.

'I guess I'm finally becoming jaded,' she said. 'I wonder why.'

They walked toward the crime scene, which was almost directly under the towering, waxed aluminum figure of Eros. One of London's favorite landmarks, Eros was also the symbol for the *Evening Standard*. Although people believed the statue was a representation of erotic love, it had actually been commissioned as a symbol for Christian charity.

Thomas Pierce flashed his ID and walked up to the 'body bag' that Mr Smith had used to transport the remains of Chief Inspector Cabott.

'It's as if he's *living* a Gothic novel,' Sondra Greenberg said. She was kneeling beside Pierce. Actually, they looked like a team, even like a couple.

'Smith called you here, too – to London? Left voice-mail?' Pierce asked her.

Greenberg nodded. 'What do you think of the body? The latest kill? Smith packed the bag with body parts in the most careful and concise way. Like you would if you had to get everything into a suitcase.'

Thomas Pierce frowned. 'Freak, goddamn butcher.'

'Why Piccadilly? A hub of London. Why under Eros?'

'He's leaving clues for us, obvious clues. We just don't understand,' Thomas Pierce said as he continued to shake his head.

'Right you are, Thomas. Because we don't speak Martian.'

Chapter Thirty-Two

*C*rime *marches on and on.*

Sampson and I drove to Wilmington, Delaware, the following morning. We had visited the city made famous by the Duponts during the original manhunt for Gary Soneji a few years before. I had the Porsche floored the entire ride, which took a couple of hours.

I had already received some very good news that morning. We'd solved one of the case's nagging mysteries. I had checked with the blood bank at St Anthony's. A pint of my blood was missing from our family's supply. Someone had taken the trouble to break in and take my blood. *Gary Soneji? Who else? He continued to show me that nothing was safe in my life.*

'Soneji' was actually a pseudonym Gary had used as part of a plan to kidnap two children in Washington. The strange name had stuck in news stories, and that was the name the FBI and media used now. His real name was Gary Murphy. He had lived in Wilmington with his wife, Meredith, who was called Missy. They had one daughter, Roni.

Actually, Soneji was the name Gary had appropriated when he fantasized about his crimes as a young boy locked in the cellar of his house. He claimed to have been sexually abused by a neighbor in Princeton, a grade-school teacher named Martin Soneji. I suspected serious problems with a relative, possibly his paternal grandfather.

We arrived at the house on Central Avenue at a little past ten in the morning. The pretty street was deserted, except for a small boy with Rollerblades. He was trying them out on his front lawn. There should have been local police surveillance here, but, for some reason, there wasn't. At least I didn't see any sign of it yet.

'Man, this perfect little street kills me,' Sampson said. 'I still keep looking for Jimmy Stewart to pop out of one of these houses.'

'Just as long as Soneji doesn't,' I muttered.

The cars parked up and down Central Avenue were almost all American makes, which seemed quaint nowadays: Chevys, Olds, Fords, some Dodge Ram pickup trucks.

Meredith Murphy wasn't answering her phone that morning, which didn't surprise me.

'I feel sorry for Mrs Murphy and especially the little girl,' I told Sampson as we pulled up in front of the house. 'Missy Murphy had no idea who Gary really was.'

Sampson nodded. 'I remember they seemed nice enough. Maybe too nice. Gary fooled them. Ole Gary the Fooler.'

There were lights burning in the house. A white Chevy Lumina was parked in the driveway. The street was as quiet and peaceful as I remembered it from our last visit, when the peacefulness had been short-lived.

We got out of the Porsche and headed toward the front door of the house. I touched the butt of my Glock as we walked. I couldn't help thinking that Soneji could be waiting, setting some kind of trap for Sampson and me.

The neighborhood, the entire town, still reminded me of the 1950s. The house was well kept and looked as if it had recently been painted. That had been part of Gary's careful façade. It was the perfect hiding place: a sweet little house on Central Avenue, with a white picket fence and a stone walkway bisecting the front lawn.

'So what do you figure is going on with Soneji?' Sampson asked as we came up to the front door. 'He's changed some, don't you think? He's not the careful planner I remember. More impulsive.'

It seemed that way. 'Not everything's changed. He's still playing parts, acting. But he's on a rampage like nothing I've seen before. He doesn't seem to care if he's caught. Yet everything he does is planned. He *escapes*.'

'And why is that, Dr Freud?'

'That's what we're here to find out. And that's why we're going to Lorton Prison tomorrow. Something weird is going on, even for Gary Soneji.'

I rang the front doorbell. Sampson and I waited for Missy Murphy on the porch. We didn't fit into the small-town-America neighborhood, but that wasn't so unusual. We didn't exactly fit into our own neighborhood back in DC either. That morning we were both wearing dark clothes and dark glasses, looking like musicians in somebody's blues band.

'Hmm, no answer,' I muttered.

'Lights blazing inside,' Sampson said. 'Somebody must be here. Maybe they just don't want to talk to Men in Black.'

'Ms Murphy,' I called out in a loud voice, in case someone was inside, but not answering the door. 'Ms Murphy, open the door. It's Alex Cross from Washington. We're not leaving without talking to you.'

'Nobody home at the Bates Motel,' Sampson grunted.

He wandered around the side of the house, and I followed close behind. The lawn had been cut recently and the hedges trimmed. Everything looked so neat and clean and so harmless.

I went to the back door, the kitchen, if I remembered. I wondered if he could be hiding inside. Anything was possible with Soneji – the more twisted and unlikely, the better for his ego.

Things about my last visit were flashing back. Nasty memories. It was Roni's birthday party. She was seven. Gary Soneji had been inside the house that time, but he had managed to escape. A regular Houdini. A very smart, very creepy creep.

Soneji could be inside now. Why did I have the unsettling feeling that I was walking into a trap?

I waited on the back porch, not sure what to do next. I rang the bell. Something was definitely wrong about the case, everything about it was wrong. Soneji here in Wilmington? Why here? Why kill people in Union and Penn Stations?

'Alex!' Sampson shouted. 'Alex! Over here! Come quick. Alex, *now*!'

I hurried across the yard with my heart in my throat. Sampson was down on all fours. He was crouched in front of a doghouse that was painted white, and shingled to look like the main residence. What in hell was inside the doghouse?

As I got closer, I could see a thick black cloud of flies.

Then I heard the buzzing.

Chapter Thirty-Three

'Oh, goddamn it, Alex, look at what that madman did. Look at what he did to her!'

I wanted to avert my eyes, but I had to look. I crouched down low beside Sampson. Both of us were batting away horse flies and other unpleasant, crawling insects. White larvae were all over everything – the doghouse, the lawn. I held a handkerchief bunched over my nose and mouth, but it wasn't enough to stifle the putrid smell. My eyes began to water.

'What the hell is wrong with him?' Sampson said. 'Where does he get his insane ideas?'

Propped up inside the doghouse was the body of a golden retriever, or what remained of it. Blood was spattered everywhere on the wooden walls. The dog had been decapitated.

Firmly attached to the dog's neck was the head of Meredith Murphy. Her head was propped perfectly, even though it was too large proportionately for the retriever's body. The effect was beyond grotesque. It reminded me of the old Mr Potato Head toys. Meredith Murphy's open eyes stared out at me.

I had met Meredith Murphy only once, and that had been almost four years before. I wondered what she could have done to enrage Soneji like this. He had never talked much about his wife during our sessions. He had despised her, though. I remembered his nicknames for her: 'Simple Cipher,' 'The Headless Hausfrau,' 'Blonde Cow.'

'What the hell is going on inside that sick, sorry son of a bitch's head? You understand this?' Sampson muttered through his handkerchief-covered mouth.

I thought that I understood psychotic rage states, and I had seen a few of Soneji's, but nothing prepared me for the past few days. The current murders were extreme, and bloody. They were also clustered, happening much too frequently.

I had the grim feeling Soneji couldn't turn off his rage, not even after a new kill. None of the murders satisfied his need anymore.

'Oh, God.' I rose to my feet. 'John, his little girl,' I said. 'His daughter, Roni. What has he done with her?'

The two of us searched the wooded half-lot, including a copse of bent, wind-battered evergreens on the northeast side of the house. No Roni. No other bodies, or grossly severed parts, or other grisly surprises.

We looked for the girl in the two-car garage. Then in the tight, musty crawl-space under the back porch. We checked the trio of metal garbage cans neatly lined alongside the garage. Nothing anywhere. Where was Roni Murphy? Had he taken her with him? Had Soneji kidnapped his daughter?

I headed back toward the house, with Sampson a step or two behind me. I broke the window in the kitchen door, unlocked it, and rushed inside. I feared the worst. Another murdered child?

'Go easy, man. Take it slow in here,' Sampson whispered from behind. He knew how I got when children were involved. He also sensed this could be a trap Soneji had set. It was a perfect place for one.

'Roni!' I called out. 'Roni, are you in here? Roni, can you hear me?'

I remembered her face from the last time I'd been in this house. I could have drawn her picture if I had to.

Gary had told me once that Roni was the only thing that mattered in his life, the only good thing he'd ever done. At the time, I believed him. I was probably projecting my feelings for my own kids. Maybe I was fooled into thinking that Soneji had some kind of conscience and feelings because that was what I wanted to believe.

'Roni! It's the police. You can come out now, honey. Roni Murphy, are you in here? Roni?'

'Roni!' Sampson joined in, his deep voice just as loud as mine, maybe louder.

Sampson and I covered the downstairs, throwing open every door and closet as we went. Calling out her name. Dear God, I was praying now. It was sort of a prayer anyway. *Gary – not your own little girl. You don't have to kill her to show us how bad you are, how angry. We get the message. We understand.*

I ran upstairs, taking the creaking wooden steps two at a time. Sampson was close behind me, a shadow. It usually doesn't show on his face, but he gets as upset as I do. Neither of us is jaded yet.

I could hear it in his voice, in the shallow way he was breathing. 'Roni! Are you up here? Are you hiding somewhere?' he called out.

'Roni! It's the police. You're safe now, Roni! You can come out.'

Someone had ransacked the master bedroom. Someone had invaded this space, desecrated it, broken every piece of furniture, overturned beds and bureaus.

'You remember her, John?' I asked as we checked the rest of the bedrooms.

'I remember her pretty good,' Sampson said in a soft voice. 'Cute little girl.'

'Oh, no – *nooo . . .*'

Suddenly I was running down the hallway, back down the stairs. I raced through the kitchen and pulled open a hollow-core door between the refriger-ator and a four-burner stove.

We both hurried down into the basement, into the *cellar* of the house.

My heart was out of control, *beating, banging, thudding* loudly inside my chest. I didn't want to be here, to see any more of Soneji's handiwork, his nasty surprises.

The cellar of his house.

The symbolic place of all Gary's childhood nightmares.

The cellar.

Blood.

Trains.

The cellar in the Murphy house was small and neat. I looked around. *The trains were gone!* There had been a train set down here the first time we came to the house.

I didn't see any signs of the girl, though. Nothing looked out of place. We threw open work cabinets. Sampson yanked open the washer, then the clothes dryer.

There was an unpainted wooden door to one side of the water heater and a fiberglass laundry sink. There was no sign of blood in the sink, no blood-stained clothes. Was there a way outside? Had the little girl run away when her father came to the house?

The closet! I yanked open the door.

Roni Murphy was bound with rope and gagged with old rags. Her blue eyes were large with fear. She was alive!

She was shaking badly. He didn't kill her, but he had killed her childhood, just as his had been killed. A few years before, he had done the same thing with a girl called Maggie Rose.

'Oh, sweet girl,' I whispered as I untied her and took out the cloth gag her father had stuffed into her mouth. 'Everything is all right now. Everything is okay, Roni. You're okay now.'

What I didn't say was, *Your father loved you enough not to kill you – but he wants to kill everything and everyone else.*

'You're okay, you're okay, baby. Everything is okay,' I lied to the poor little girl. 'Everything is okay now.'

Sure it is.

Chapter Thirty-Four

Once upon a long time ago, Nana Mama had been the one who had taught me to play the piano.

In those days, the old upright sat like a constant invitation to make music in our family room. One afternoon after school, she heard me trying to play a little boogie-woogie. I was eleven years old at the time. I remember it well, as if it were yesterday.

Nana swept in like a soft breeze and sat next to me on the piano bench, just the way I do now with Jannie and Damon.

'I think you're a little ahead of yourself with that cool jazz stuff, Alex. Let me show you something beautiful. Let me show you where you might start your music career.'

She made me practice my Czerny finger exercises every day until I was ready to play and appreciate Mozart, Beethoven, Handel, Haydn – all from Nana Mama. She taught me to play from age eleven until I was eighteen, when I left for school at Georgetown and then Johns Hopkins. By that time, I was ready to play that cool jazz stuff, and to know what I was playing, and even know why I liked what I liked.

When I came home from Delaware, very late, I found Nana on the porch and she was playing the piano. I hadn't heard her play like that in many years.

She didn't hear me come in, so I stood in the doorway and watched her for several minutes. She was playing Mozart and she still had a feeling for the music that she loved. She'd once told me how sad it was that no one knew where Mozart was buried.

When she finished, I whispered, 'Bravo, Bravo. That's just beautiful.'

Nana turned to me. 'Silly old woman,' she said and wiped away a tear I hadn't been able to see from where I was standing.

'Not silly at all,' I said. I sat down and held her in my arms on the piano bench. 'Old yes, really old and cranky, but never silly.'

'I was just thinking,' she said, 'about that third movement in Mozart's Piano Concerto No. 21, and then I had a memory of how I used to be able to play it, a long, long time ago.' She sighed. 'So I had myself a nice cry. Felt real good, too.'

'Sorry to intrude,' I said as I continued to hold her close.

'I love you, Alex,' my grandmother whispered. 'Can you still play "Clair de Lune"? Play Debussy for me.'

And so with Nana Mama close beside me, I played.

Chapter Thirty-Five

The groan-and-grunt work continued the following morning.

First thing, Kyle faxed me several stories about his agent, Thomas Pierce. The stories came from cities where Mr Smith had committed murders: Atlanta, St Louis, Seattle, San Francisco, London, Hamburg, Frankfurt, Rome. Pierce had helped to capture a murderer in Fort Lauderdale in the spring, unrelated to Smith.

Other headlines: *For Thomas Pierce, The Crime Scene Is in the Mind; Murder Expert Here in St Louis; Thomas Pierce – Getting into Killers' Heads; Not All Pattern Killers Are Brilliant – But Agent Thomas Pierce Is; Murders of the Mind, the Most Chilling Murders of All.*

If I didn't know better, I'd have thought Kyle was trying to make me jealous of Pierce. I wasn't jealous. I didn't have the time for it right now.

A little before noon, I drove out to Lorton Prison, one of my least favorite places in the charted universe.

Everything moves slowly inside a high-security federal prison. It is like being held underwater, like being drowned by unseen human hands. It happens over days, over years, sometimes over decades.

At an administrative max facility, prisoners are kept in their cells twenty-two to twenty-three hours a day. The boredom is incomprehensible to anyone who hasn't served time. *It is not imaginable.* Gary Soneji told me that, created the drowning metaphor when I interviewed him years back at Lorton.

He also thanked me for giving him the experience of being in prison, and he said that one day he would reciprocate if he possibly could. More and more, I had the sense that my time had come, and I had to guess what the excruciating payback might be.

It was not imaginable.

I could almost feel myself drowning as I paced inside a small administrative room near the warden's office on the fifth floor at Lorton.

I was waiting for a double-murderer named Jamal Autry. Autry claimed to have important information about Soneji. He was known inside Lorton as the Real Deal. He was a predator, a three-hundred-pound pimp who had murdered two teenage prostitutes in Baltimore.

The Real Deal was brought to me in restraints. He was escorted into the small, tidy office by two armed guards with billy clubs.

'You Alex Cross? Gah-damn. Now ain't that somethin',' Jamal Autry said with a middle-South twang.

He smiled crookedly when he spoke. The lower half of his face sagged like the mouth and jaw of a bottom feeder. He had strange, uneven piggy eyes that were hard to look at. He continued to smile as if he were about to be paroled today, or had just won the inmates' lottery.

I told the two guards that I wanted to talk to Autry alone. Even though he was in restraints, they departed reluctantly. I wasn't afraid of this big load, though. I wasn't a helpless teenage girl he could beat up on.

'Sorry, I missed the joke,' I finally said to Autry. 'Don't quite know why it is that you're smiling.'

'Awhh, don't worry 'bout it, man. You get the joke okay. Eventually,' he said with his slow drawl. 'You'll get the joke, Dr Cross. See, *it's on you.*'

I shrugged. 'You asked to see me, Autry. You want something out of this and so do I. I'm not here for your jokes or your private amusement. You want to go back to your cell, just turn the hell around.'

Jamal Autry continued to smile, but he sat down on one of two chairs left for us. 'We boff want something,' he said. He began to make serious eye contact with me. He had the don't-mess-with-me look now. His smile evaporated.

'Tell me what you've got to trade. We'll see where it goes,' I said. 'Best I can do for you.'

'Soneji said you a hard-ass. Smart for a cop. We'll see what we see,' he drawled.

I ignored the bullshit that flowed so easily from his over-large mouth. I couldn't help thinking about the two sixteen-year-old girls he'd murdered. I imagined him smiling at them, too. Giving them the look. 'The two of you talked sometimes? Soneji was a friend of yours?' I asked him.

Autry shook his head. The look stayed fixed. His piggy eyes never left mine. 'Naw, man. Only talked when he needed somethin'. Soneji rather sit in his cell, stare out into far space, like Mars or someplace. Soneji got no friends in here. Not me, not anybody else.'

Autry leaned forward in his chair. He had something to tell me. Obviously, he thought it was worth a lot. He lowered his voice as if there were someone in the room besides the two of us.

Someone like Gary Soneji, I couldn't help thinking.

Chapter Thirty-Six

'Lookit, Soneji didn't have no friends in here. He didn't need nobody. Man had a guest in his attic. Know what I mean? Only talked to me when he wanted something.'

'What kind of things did you do for Soneji?' I asked.

'Soneji had simple needs. Cigars, fuck-books, mustard for his Froot-Loops. He paid to keep certain individuals away. Soneji always had money.'

I thought about that. Who gave Gary Soneji money while he was in Lorton? It wouldn't have come from his wife – at least I didn't think so. His grandfather was still alive in New Jersey. Maybe the money had come from his grandfather. He had only one friend that I knew of, but that had been way back when he was a teenager.

Jamal Autry continued his bigmouthed spiel. 'Check it out, man. Protection Gary bought from me was good – the best. Best anybody could do in here.'

'I'm not sure I follow you,' I said. 'Spell it out for me, Jamal. I want all the details.'

'You can protect *some* of the people *some* of the time. That's all it is. There was another prisoner here, name of Shareef Thomas. Real crazy nigger, originally from New York City. Ran with two other crazy niggers – Goofy and Coco Loco. Shareef's out now, but when he inside, Shareef did whatever the hell he wanted. Only way you control Shareef, you cap him. *Twice*, just to make sure.'

Autry was getting interesting. He definitely had something to trade. 'What was Gary Soneji's connection with Shareef?' I asked.

'Soneji tried to cap Shareef. Paid the money. But Shareef was smart. Shareef was lucky, too.'

'Why did Soneji want to kill Shareef Thomas?'

Autry stared at me with his cold eyes. 'We have a deal, right? I get privileges for this?'

'You have my full attention, Jamal. I'm here, I'm listening to you. Tell me what happened between Shareef Thomas and Soneji.'

'Soneji wanted to kill Shareef 'cause Shareef was fuckin' him. Not just one time either. He wanted Gary to know he was *the man*. He was the one man even crazier than Soneji in here.'

I shook my head and leaned forward to listen. He had my attention, but something wasn't tracking for me. 'Gary was separated from the prison population. Maximum security. How the hell did Thomas get to him?'

'Gah-damn, I told you, things get done in here. Things always get done. Don't be fooled what you hear on the outside, man. That's the way it is, way it's always been.'

I stared into Autry's eyes. 'So you took Soneji's money for protection, and Shareef Thomas got to him anyway? There's more, isn't there?'

I sensed that Autry was relishing his own punch line, or maybe he just liked having the power over me.

'There's more, yeah. Shareef gave Gary Soneji the Fever. Soneji has the bug, man. He's dying. Your old friend Gary Soneji is dying. He got *the message from God*.'

The news hit me like a sucker punch. I didn't let it show, didn't give away any advantage, but Jamal Autry had just made some sense of everything Soneji had done so far. He had also shaken me to the quick. *Soneji has the Fever. He has AIDS. Gary Soneji is dying. He has nothing to lose anymore.*

Was Autry telling the truth or not? Big question, important question.

I shook my head. 'I don't believe you, Autry. Why the hell should I?' I said.

He looked offended, which was part of his act. 'Believe what you want. But you *ought* to believe. Gary got the message to me in here. Gary *contacted* me this week, two days ago. Gary let me know he has the Fever.'

We had come full circle. Autry knew that he had me from the minute he walked into the room. Now I got to hear the punch line of his joke – the one he'd promised at the start. First, though, I had to be his straight man for a little while longer.

'Why? Why would he tell you he's dying?' I played my part.

'Soneji said you'd come here asking questions. He knew you were coming. He knows you, man – better than you know him. Soneji wanted me to give you the message personally. He gave me the message, just for you. *He said to tell you that.*'

Jamal Autry smiled his crooked smile again. 'What do you say now, Dr Cross? You get what you come here for?'

I had what I needed all right. Gary Soneji was dying. He wanted me to follow him into hell. He was on a rampage with nothing to lose, nothing to fear from anyone.

Chapter Thirty-Seven

When I got home from Lorton Prison I called Christine Johnson. I needed to see her. I needed to get away from the case. I held my breath as I asked her to dinner at Georgia Brown's on McPherson Square. She surprised me – she said yes.

Still on pins and needles, but kind of liking the feeling, I showed up at her place with a single red rose. Christine smiled beautifully, took the rose and put it in water as if it were an expensive arrangement.

She was wearing a gray calf-length skirt and a matching soft gray V-necked blouse. She looked stunning again. We talked about our respective days on the drive to the restaurant. I liked her day a lot better than mine.

We were hungry, and started with hot buttermilk biscuits slathered with peach butter. The day was definitely improving. Christine ordered Carolina shrimp and grits. I got the Carolina Perlau – red rice, thick chunks of duck, shrimp, and sausage.

'No one has given me a rose in a long time,' she told me. 'I love that you thought to do that.'

'You're being too nice to me tonight,' I said as we started to eat.

She tilted her head to one side and looked at me from an odd angle. She did that now and again. 'Why do you say that I'm being too nice?'

'Well, you can tell I'm not exactly the best company tonight. It's what you're afraid of, isn't it? That I can't turn off my job.'

She took a sip of wine. Shook her head. Finally she smiled, and the smile was so down-to-earth. 'You're *so* honest. But you have a good sense of humor about it. Actually, I hadn't noticed that you weren't operating at one hundred and ten percent.'

'I've been distant and into myself all night,' I said. 'The kids say I get twilight zoned.'

She laughed and rolled her eyes. 'Stop it, stop it. You are the least into-yourself man I think I've ever met. I'm having a very nice time here. I was planning on a bowl of Corn Pops for my dinner at home.'

'Corn Pops and milk are good. Curl up in bed with a movie or book. Nothing wrong with that.'

'That was my plan. I finally gave in and started *The Horse Whisperer*. I'm glad you called and spoiled it for me, took me out of my own twilight zone.'

'You must really think I'm crazy,' Christine said and smiled a little later during dinner. 'Lawdy, Miss Clawdy, I believe I *am* crazy.'

I laughed. 'For going out with me? Absolutely crazy.'

'No, for telling you I didn't think we should see each other, and now late dinner at Georgia Brown's. Forsaking my Corn Pops and *Horse Whisperer*.'

I looked into her eyes, and I wanted to stay right there for a very long time, at least until Georgia Brown's asked us to leave. 'What happened? What changed?' I asked.

'I stopped being afraid,' she said. 'Well, almost stopped. But I'm getting there.'

'Yeah, maybe we both are. I was afraid, too.'

'That's nice to hear. I'm glad you told me. I couldn't imagine that you get afraid.'

I drove Christine home from Georgia Brown's around midnight. As we rode on the John Hansen Highway, all I could think about was touching her hair, stroking the side of her cheek, maybe a few other things. Yes, definitely a few other things.

I walked Christine to her front door and I could hardly breathe. Again. My hand was lightly on her elbow. She had her house key clasped in her hand.

I could smell her perfume. She told me it was called Gardenia Passion, and I liked it a lot. Our shoes softly scraped the cement.

Suddenly, Christine turned and put her arms around me. The movement was graceful, but she took me by surprise.

'I have to find something out,' she said.

Christine kissed me, just as we had a few days before. We kissed sweetly at first, then harder. Her lips were soft and moist against mine, then firmer, more urgent. I could feel her breasts press against me; then her stomach, her strong legs.

She opened her eyes, looked at me, and she smiled. I loved that natural smile – loved it. *That smile – no other one.*

She gently pulled herself away from me. I felt the separation and I didn't want her to go. I sensed, I knew, I should leave it at that.

Christine opened her front door and slowly backed inside. I didn't want her to go in just yet. I wanted to know what she was thinking, all her thoughts.

'The first kiss wasn't an accident,' she whispered.

'No, it wasn't an accident,' I said.

Chapter Thirty-Eight

*G*ary Soneji was in the cellar again.
  Whose dank, dark cellar was it, though?
That was the $64,000 question.

He didn't know what time it was, but it had to be very early in the morning. The house upstairs was as quiet as death. He liked that image, the rub of it inside his mind.

He loved it in the dark. He went back to being a small boy. He could still feel it, as if it had happened only yesterday. His stepmother's name was Fiona Morrison, and she was pretty, and everybody believed she was a good person, a good friend and neighbor, a good mother. It was all a lie! She had locked him away like a hateful animal – *no*, worse than an animal! He remembered shivering in the cellar, and peeing in his pants in the beginning, and sitting in his own urine as it turned from warm to icy cold. He remembered the feeling that he wasn't like the rest of his family. He wasn't like anybody else. There was nothing about him that anybody could love. There was nothing good about him. He had no inner core.

He sat in the dark cellar now and wondered if he was where he thought he was.

Which reality was he living in?

Which fantasy?

Which horror story?

He reached around on the floor in the dark. *Hmmm.* He wasn't in the cellar in the old Princeton house. He could tell he wasn't. Here the cold cement floor was smooth. And the smell was different. Dusty and musty. Where was he?

He turned on his flashlight. Ahhh!

No one was going to believe this one! No one would guess whose house this was, whose cellar he was hiding in now.

Soneji pushed himself up off the floor. He felt slightly nauseated and achy, but he ignored the feeling. The pain was incidental. He was ready to go upstairs now.

No one would believe what he was going to do next. How outrageous.

He was several steps ahead of everybody else.

He was way ahead.

As always.

Chapter Thirty-Nine

Soneji entered the living room and saw the correct time on the Sony television's digital clock. It showed 3:24 in the morning. Another witching hour.

Once he reached the upstairs part of the house, he decided to crawl on his hands and knees.

The plan was good. Damn it, he *wasn't* worthless and useless. He hadn't deserved to be locked in the cellar. Tears welled in his eyes and they felt hot and all too familiar. His stepmother always called him a crybaby, a little pansy, a fairy. She never stopped calling him names, until he fried her mouth open in a scream.

The tears burned his cheeks as they ran down under his shirt collar. He was dying, and he didn't deserve to die. He didn't deserve any of this. So now someone had to pay.

He was silent and careful as he threaded his way through the house, slithering on his belly like a snake. The floorboards underneath him didn't even creak as he moved forward. The darkness felt charged with electricity and infinite possibilities.

He thought about how frightened people were of intruders inside their houses and apartments. They ought to be afraid, too. There were monsters preying just outside their locked doors, often watching their windows at night. There were Peeping Garys in every town, small and large. And there were thousands more, twisted perverts, just waiting to come inside and feast. The people in their so-called safe houses were monster-fodder.

He noticed that the upstairs part of the house had green walls. *Green walls. What luck!* Soneji had read somewhere that hospital operating walls were often painted green. If the walls were white, doctors and nurses sometimes saw ghost images of the ongoing operation, the blood and gore. It was called the 'ghosting effect,' and green walls masked the blood.

No more intruding thoughts, no matter how relevant, Soneji told himself. No more interruptions. Be perfectly calm, be careful. The next few minutes were the dangerous ones.

This particular house was dangerous – which was why the game was so much fun, such a mind trip.

The bedroom door was slightly ajar. Soneji slowly, patiently, inched it open.

He heard a man softly snoring. He saw another digital clock on a bedside table. *Three-twenty-three*. He had *lost* time.

He rose to his full height. He was finally out of the cellar, and he felt an incredible surge of anger now. He felt rage, and it was justified.

Gary Soneji angrily sprang forward at the figure in bed. He clasped a metal pipe tightly in both his hands. He raised it like an ax. He swung the pipe down as hard as he could.

'Detective Goldman, so nice to meet you,' he whispered.

Chapter Forty

T he Job was always there, waiting for me to catch up, demanding everything I could give it, and then demanding some more.

The next morning I found myself hurrying back to New York. The FBI had provided me with a helicopter. Kyle Craig was a good friend, but he was also working his tricks on me. I knew it, and he knew I did. Kyle was hoping that I would eventually get involved in the Mr Smith case, that I would meet agent Thomas Pierce. I knew that I wouldn't. Not for now anyway, maybe not ever. I had to meet Gary Soneji again first.

I arrived before 8:30 a.m. at the busy New York City heliport in the East Twenties. Some people call it 'the New York Hellport.' The Bureau's black Belljet floated in low over the congested FDR Drive and the East River. The plane dropped down as if it owned the city, but that was just FBI arrogance. No one could own New York – except maybe Gary Soneji.

Detective Carmine Groza was there to meet me and we got into his unmarked Mercury Marquis. We sped up the FDR Drive to the exit for the Major Deegan. As we crossed over into the Bronx, I remembered a funny line from the poet Ogden Nash: 'The Bronx, no thonx.' I needed some more funny lines in my life.

I still had the irritating noise of the helicopter's rotor blades roaring inside my head. It made me think of the nasty *buzzing* in the doghouse in Wilmington. Everything was happening too fast again. Gary Soneji had us off balance, the way he liked it, the way he always worked his nastiness.

Soneji got in your face, applied intense pressure, and then waited for you to make a crucial mistake. I was trying not to make one right now, not to end up like Manning Goldman.

The latest homicide scene was up in Riverdale. Detective Groza talked nervously as he drove the Deegan. His chattering reminded me of an old line I try to live by – *never miss a good chance to shut up.*

Logically, the Riverdale area should be part of Manhattan, he said, but it was actually part of the Bronx. To confuse matters further, Riverdale was the site of Manhattan College, a small private school having no affiliation with either Manhattan or the Bronx. New York's mayor, Rudy Giuliani, had attended Manhattan, Groza said.

I listened to the detective's idle chitchat until I felt he had talked himself out. He seemed a different man from the one I'd met earlier in the week at Penn Station when he was partnered with Manning Goldman.

'Are you okay?' I finally asked him. I had never lost a partner, but I had come close with Sampson. He had been stabbed in the back. That happened in North Carolina, of all places. My niece, Naomi, had been kidnapped. I have counseled detectives who have lost partners, and it's never an easy thing.

'I didn't really like Manning Goldman,' Groza admitted, 'but I respected things he did as a detective. No one should die the way he did.'

'No, no one should die like that,' I agreed. *No one was safe.* Not the wealthy, certainly not the poor, and not even the police. It was a continuing refrain in my life, the scariest truth of our age.

We finally turned off the crowded Deegan Expressway and got onto an even busier, much noisier Broadway. Detective Groza was clearly shook up that morning. I didn't show it, but so was I.

Gary Soneji was showing us how easy it was for him to get into a cop's home.

Chapter Forty-One

M anning Goldman's house was located in an upscale part of Riverdale known as Fieldstone. The area was surprisingly attractive – for the Bronx. Police cruisers and a flock of television vans and trucks were parked on the narrow and pretty residential streets. A FOX-TV helicopter hovered over the trees, peeking through the branches and leaves.

The Goldman house was more modest than the Tudors around it. Still, it seemed a nice place to live. Not a typical cop's neighborhood, but Manning Goldman hadn't been a typical cop.

'Goldman's father was a big doctor in Mamaroneck,' Groza continued to chatter. 'When he passed away, Manning came into some money. He was the black sheep in his family, the rebel – a cop. Both of his brothers are dentists in Florida.'

I didn't like the look and feel of the crime scene, and I was still two blocks away. There were too many blue-and-whites and official-looking city cars. Too much help, too much interference.

'The mayor was up here early. He's a pisser. He's all right, though,' Groza said. 'A cop gets killed in New York, it's a huge thing. Big news, lots of media.'

'Especially when a detective gets killed right in his own home,' I said.

Groza finally parked on the tree-lined street, about a block from the Goldman house. Birds chattered away, oblivious to death.

As I walked toward the crime scene, I enjoyed one aspect of the day, at least, the anonymity I felt in New York. In Washington, many reporters know who I am. If I'm at a homicide scene, it's usually a particularly nasty one, a big case, a violent crime.

Detective Carmine Groza and I were ignored as we walked through the crowd of looky-loos up to the Goldman house. Groza introduced me around inside and I was allowed to see the bedroom where Manning Goldman had been brutally murdered. The NYPD cops all seemed to know who I was and why I was there. I heard Soneji's name muttered a couple of times. Bad news travels fast.

The detective's body had already been removed from the house, and I didn't like arriving at the murder scene so late. Several NYPD techies were working the room. *Goldman's blood was everywhere*. It was splattered on the bed, the walls, the beige-carpeted floor, the desk and bookcases, and even on a gold menorah. I already knew why Soneji was so interested in spilling blood now – his blood was deadly.

I could feel Gary Soneji here in Goldman's room, *I could see him*, and it stunned me that I could imagine his presence so strongly, physically and emotionally. I remembered a time when Soneji had entered my home in the night with a knife. *Why would he come here?* I wondered. *Was he warning me, playing with my head?*

'He definitely wanted to make a high-profile statement,' I muttered, more to myself than to Carmine Groza. 'He knew that Goldman was running the case in New York. He's showing us that he's in complete control.'

There was something else, though. There had to be more to this than I was seeing so far. I paced around the bedroom. I noticed that the computer on the desk was turned on.

I spoke to one of the techies, a thin man with a small, grim mouth. Perfect for homicide scenes. 'The computer was on when they found Detective Goldman?' I asked.

'Yeah. The Mac was on. It's been dusted.'

I glanced at Groza. 'We know he's looking for Shareef Thomas, and that Thomas was originally from New York. He's supposed to be back here now. Maybe he made Goldman pull up Thomas's file before he killed him.'

For once Detective Groza didn't answer. He was quiet and unresponsive. I wasn't completely certain myself. Still, I trusted my instincts, especially when it came to Soneji. I was following in his bloody footsteps and I didn't think I was too far behind.

Chapter Forty-Two

The surprisingly hospitable New York police had gotten me a room for the night at the Marriott Hotel on Forty-second Street. They were already checking on Shareef Thomas for me. What could be done was being taken care of, but Soneji was on the loose for another night on the town.

Shareef Thomas had lived in DC, but he was originally from Brooklyn. I was fairly certain Soneji had followed him here. Hadn't he told me as much through Jamal Autry at Lorton Prison? He had a score to settle with Thomas, and Soneji settled his old scores. I ought to know.

At eight-thirty I finally left Police Plaza, and I was physically whipped. I was driven uptown in a squad car. I'd packed a duffel bag, so I was set for a couple of days, if it came to that. I hoped that it wouldn't. I like New York City under the right circumstances, but this was hardly Fifth Avenue Christmas shopping in December, or a Yankee World Series game in the fall.

Around nine, I called home and got our automatic answering machine – Jannie. She said, 'Is this ET? You calling *home*?' She's cute like that. She must have known the phone call would be from me. I always call, no matter what.

'How are you, my sweet one? Light of my life?' Just the sound of her voice made me miss her, miss being home with my family.

'Sampson came by. He was checking on us. We were supposed to do boxing tonight. Remember, Daddy?' Jannie played her part with a heavy hand, but it worked. 'Bip, bip, bam. Bam, bam, bip,' she said, creating a vivid picture out of sound.

'Did you and Damon practice anyway?' I asked. I was imagining her face as we talked. Damon's face. Nana's too. The kitchen where Jannie was talking. I missed having supper with my family.

'We sure did. I knocked his block right off. I put out his lights for the night. But it's not the same without you. Nobody to show off for.'

'You just have to show off for yourself,' I told her.

'I know, Daddy. That's what I did. I showed off for myself, and myself said good show.'

I laughed out loud into the phone receiver. 'I'm sorry about missing the boxing lesson with you two pit bulls. Sorry, sorry, sorry,' I said in a bluesy, sing-song voice. 'Sorry, sorry, sorry, sorry.'

'That's what you *always* say,' Jannie whispered, and I could hear the crackle of hurt in her voice. 'Someday, it's not going to work anymore. Mark my words. Remember where you heard it first. Remember, remember, remember.'

I took her counsel to heart in the lonely New York City hotel room as I ate a room-service burger and looked out over Times Square. I remembered an old joke among shrinks: '*Schizophrenia beats eating alone.*' I thought about my kids, and about Christine Johnson, and then about Soneji and Manning Goldman, murdered in his own house. I tried to read a few pages of *Angela's Ashes*, which I'd packed in my bag. I couldn't handle the beautifully described Limerick ghetto that night.

I called Christine when I thought I had my head screwed on straight. We talked for almost an hour. Easy, effortless talk. Something was changing between us. I asked her if she wanted to spend some time together that weekend, maybe in New York if I still had to be here. It took some nerve for me to ask. I wondered if she could hear it in my voice.

Christine surprised me again. She wanted to come to New York. She laughed and said she could do some early Christmas shopping in July, but I had to *promise* to make time for her.

I promised.

I must have slept some finally, because I woke in a strange bed, in a stranger town, wrapped in my bedsheets as if I were trapped in a straitjacket.

I had a strange, discomforting thought. Gary Soneji is tracking *me*. It's not the other way round.

Chapter Forty-Three

*H**e was the Angel of Death.* He had known that since he was eleven or twelve years old. He had killed someone back then, just to see if he could do it. The police had never found the body. Not to this day. Only he knew where all the bodies were buried, and he wasn't telling.

Suddenly, Gary Soneji drifted back to reality, to the present moment in New York City.

Christ, I'm snickering and laughing to myself inside this bar on the East Side. I might have even been talking to myself.

The bartender at Dowd & McGoey's had already spotted him, talking to himself, nearly in a trance. The sneaky, red-haired Irish prick was pretending to polish beer glasses, but all the time he was watching out of the corner of his eye. *When Irish eyes are spying.*

Soneji immediately beckoned the barman over with a wave and a shy smile. 'Don't worry, I'm cutting myself off. Starting to get a little out of control here. What do I owe you, Michael?' The name was emblazoned on the barman's shirt tag.

The phoney, apologetic act seemed to work okay, so he settled his bill and left. He walked south for several blocks on First Avenue, then west on East Fiftieth Street.

He saw a crowded spot called Tatou. It looked promising. He remembered his mission: He needed a place to stay the night in New York, someplace safe. The Plaza hadn't really been such a good idea.

Tatou was filled to the rafters with a lively crowd come to talk, rubberneck, eat and drink. The first floor was a supper club; the second floor was set up for dancing. *What was the scene here about?* he wondered. He needed to understand. Attitude was the answer he came up with. Stylish businessmen and professional women in their thirties and forties came to Tatou, probably straight from work in midtown. It was a Thursday night. Most of them were trying to set up something interesting for the weekend.

Soneji ordered a white wine and he began to eye the men and women lined up along the bar. They looked so perfectly in tune with the times, so desperately cool. *Pick me, choose me, somebody please notice me*, they seemed to plead.

He chatted up a pair of lady lawyers who, unfortunately, were joined at the hip. They reminded him of the strange girls in the French movie *La Cérémonie*. He learned that Theresa and Jessie had been roommates for the past eleven years. Jesus! They were both thirty-six. Their clocks were ticking very loudly. They worked out religiously at the Vertical Club on Sixty-first Street. Summered in Bridgehampton, a mile from the water. They were all wrong for him and, apparently, for everyone else at the bar.

Soneji moved on. He was starting to feel a little pressure. The police knew he was using disguises. Only not what he might look like on a given day. Yesterday, he was a dark-haired Spanish-looking man in his mid-forties. Today, he was blond, bearded, and fit right in at Tatou. Tomorrow, who knew? He could make a dumb mistake, though. He could be picked up and everything would end.

He met an advertising art director, a creative director in a large ad factory on Lexington Avenue. Jean Summerhill was originally from Atlanta, she told him. She was small and very slim, with blond hair, lots of it. She wore a single trendy braid down one side, and he could tell she was full of herself. In an odd way, she reminded him of his Meredith, his Missy. Jean Summerhill had her own place, a condo. She lived alone, in the seventies.

She was too pretty to be in here alone, looking for company in all the wrong places, but Soneji understood why once they'd talked: Jean Summerhill was too smart, too strong and individualistic for most men. She scared men off without meaning to, or even knowing that she had.

She didn't scare him, though. They talked easily, the way strangers sometimes do at a bar. Nothing to lose, nothing to risk. She was very down-to-earth. A woman with a need to be seen as 'nice'; unlucky in love, though. He told her that and, since it was what she wanted to hear, Jean Summerhill seemed to believe him.

'You're easy to talk to,' she said over their third or fourth drink. 'You're very calm. Centered, right?'

'Yeah, I am a little boring,' Soneji said. He knew he was anything but that. 'Maybe that's why my wife left me. Missy fell for a rich man, her boss on Wall Street. We both cried the night that she told me. Now she lives in a big apartment over on Beekman Place. Real fancy digs.' He smiled. 'We're still friends. I just saw Missy recently.'

Jean looked into his eyes. There was something sad about the look. 'You know what I like about you,' she said,' it's that you're not afraid of me.'

Gary Soneji smiled. 'No, I guess I'm not.'

'And I'm not afraid of you either,' Jean Summerhill whispered.

'That's the way it should be,' Soneji said. 'Just don't lose your head over me. Promise?'

'I'll do my best.'

The two of them left Tatou and went to her condo together.

Chapter Forty-Four

I stood all alone on Forty-second Street in Manhattan, anxiously waiting for Carmine Groza to show. The homicide detective finally picked me up at the front entrance of the Marriott. I jumped into his car and we headed to Brooklyn. Something good had finally happened on the case, something promising.

Shareef Thomas had been spotted at a crackhouse in the Bedford-Stuyvesant section of Brooklyn. Did Gary Soneji know where Thomas was, too? How much, if anything, had he learned from Manning Goldman's computer files?

At seven on Saturday morning, traffic in the city was a joy to behold. We raced west to east across Manhattan in less than ten minutes. We crossed the East River on the Brooklyn Bridge. The sun was just coming up over a group of tall apartment buildings. It was a blinding yellow fireball that gave me an instant headache.

We arrived in Bed-Stuy a little before seven-thirty. I'd heard of the Brooklyn neighborhood, and its tough reputation. It was mostly deserted at that time of the morning. Racist cops in DC have a nasty way of describing this kind of inner-city area. They call them 'self-cleaning ovens.' You just close the door and let it clean itself. Let it burn. Nana Mama has another word for America's mostly neglectful social programs for the inner cities: genocide.

The local bodega had a handpainted sign scrawled in red letters on yellow: FIRST STREET DELI AND TOBACCO, OPEN 24 HOURS. The store was closed. So much for the sign.

Parked in front of the deserted deli was a maroon-and-tan van. The vehicle had silver tinted windows and a 'moonlight over Miami' scene painted on the side panels. A lone female addict slogged along in a knock-kneed swaying walk. She was the only person on the street when we arrived.

The building that Shareef Thomas was in turned out to be two-storied, with faded gray shingles and some broken windows. It looked as if it had been condemned a long time ago. Thomas was still inside the crackhouse. Groza and I settled in to wait. We were hoping Gary Soneji might show up.

I slid down into a corner of the front seat. In the distance, I could see a peeling billboard high above a red-brick building: COP SHOT $10,000 REWARD. Not a good omen, but a fair warning.

The neighborhood began to wake up and show its character around nine or so. A couple of elderly women in blousy white dresses walked hand in hand toward the Pentecostal church up the street. They made me think of Nana and her buddies back in DC. Made me miss being home for the weekend, too.

A girl of six or seven was playing jump rope down the street. I noticed she was using salvaged electrical wire. She moved in a kind of listless trance.

It made me sad to watch the little sweetheart play, I wondered what would become of her? What chance did she have to make it out of here? I thought of Jannie and Damon and how they were probably 'disappointed' in me for being away on Saturday morning. *Saturday is our day off, Daddy. We only have Saturdays and Sundays to be together.*

Time passed slowly. It almost always does on surveillance. I had a thought about the neighborhood – *tragedy can be addictive, too.* A couple of suspicious-looking guys in sleeveless T-shirts and cutoff shorts pulled up in an unmarked black truck around ten-thirty. They set up shop, selling watermelons, corn on the cob, tomatoes, and collard greens on the street. The melons were piled high in the scummy gutter.

It was almost eleven o'clock now and I was worried. Our information might be wrong. Paranoia was starting to run a little wild in my head. Maybe Gary Soneji had already visited the crackhouse. He was good at disguises. He might even be in there now.

I opened the car door and got out. The heat rushed at me and I felt as if I were stepping into a blast oven. Still, it was good to be out of the car, the cramped quarters.

'What are you doing?' Groza asked. He seemed prepared to sit in the car all day, playing everything by the book, waiting for Soneji to show.

'Trust me,' I said.

Chapter Forty-Five

I took off my white shirt and tied it loosely around my waist. I narrowed my eyes, let them go in and out of focus.

Groza called out: 'Alex.' I ignored him and I began to shuffle toward the dilapidated crackhouse. I figured I looked the street-junkie part okay. It wasn't too hard. God knows I'd seen it played enough times in my own neighborhood. My older brother was a junkie before he died.

The crackhouse was being operated out of an abandoned building on a dead-end corner. It was pretty much standard operating procedure in all big cities I have visited: DC, Baltimore, Philly, Miami, New York. Makes you wonder.

As I opened the graffiti-painted front door, I saw that the place was definitely bottom of the barrel, even for crackhouses. This was end-of-the-line time. Shareef Thomas had the Virus, too.

Debris was scattered everywhere across the grimy, stained floor. Empty soda cans and beer bottles. Fast-food wrappers from Wendy's and Roy's and Kentucky Fried. Crack vials. Hanger wires used to clean out crack pipes. Hot time, summer in the city.

I figured that a down-and-out dump like this would be run by a single 'clerk.' You pay the guy two or three dollars for a space on the floor. You can also buy syringes, pipes, papers, butane lighters, and maybe even a soda pop or cerveza.

'Fuck-it' and 'AIDS' and 'Junkies of the World' were scrawled across the walls. There was also a thick, smoky fog that seemed allergic to the sunlight. The stink was fetid, worse than walking around in a city dump.

It was incredibly quiet, strangely serene, though. I noticed everything at a glance, but no Shareef Thomas. No Gary Soneji either. At least I didn't see him yet.

A Latino-looking man with a shoulder holster over a soiled 'Bacardi' T-shirt was in charge of the early-morning shift. He was barely awake, but still managed to look in control of the place. He had an ageless face and a thick mustache.

It looked as if Shareef Thomas had definitely fallen down a few notches. If he was here, he was hanging with the low end of the low. Was Shareef dying? Or just hiding? Did he know Soneji might be looking for him?

'What do you want, chief?' the Latino man asked in a low grumble. His eyes were thin slits.

'Little peace and quiet,' I said. I kept it respectful. As if this were church, which it was for some people.

I handed him two crumpled bills and he turned away with the money. 'In there,' he said.

I looked past him into the main room, and I felt as if a hand were clutching my heart and squeezing it tight.

About ten or twelve men and a couple of women were sitting or sprawled on the floor and on a few soiled, incredibly thin mattresses. The pipeheads were mostly staring into space, doing nothing, and doing it well. It was as if they were slowly fading or evaporating into the smoke and dust.

No one noticed me, which was okay, which was good. Nobody much cared who came or left this hellhole. I still hadn't spotted Shareef. Or Soneji.

It was as dark as a moonless night in the main room of the crackhouse. No lights except for an occasional match being struck. The sound of the match-head strike, then a long, extended hiss.

I was looking for Thomas, but I was also carefully playing my part. Just another strung-out junkie pipehead. Looking for a spot to smoke, to nod out in peace, not here to bother anyone.

I spotted Shareef Thomas on one of the mattresses, near the rear of the dark, dingy room. I recognized him from pictures I'd studied at Lorton. *I forced my eyes away from him.*

My heart started to pump like crazy. Could Soneji be here, too? Sometimes he seemed like a phantom or ghost to me. I wondered if there was a door back out. I had to find a place to sit down before Thomas became suspicious of me.

I made it to a wall and started to slide down to the floor. I watched Shareef Thomas out of the corner of my eye. Then all kinds of unexpected madness and chaos broke out inside the crackhouse.

The front door was thrown open and Groza and two uniforms burst in. So much for trust. 'Muhfucker,' a man near me woke up and moaned in the smoky shadows.

'Police! Don't move!' Carmine Groza yelled. 'Nobody move. Everybody stay cool!' He sounded like a street cop anyway.

My eyes stayed glued to Shareef Thomas. He was already getting up off the mattress, where he'd been content as a cat just a few seconds ago. Maybe he wasn't stoned at all. Maybe he *was* hiding.

I grabbed for the Glock under my rolled-up shirt, tucked at the small of my back. I brought it around in front of me. I hoped against hope I wouldn't have to use it in these close quarters.

Thomas raised a shotgun that must have been hidden alongside his mattress. The other pipeheads seemed unable to move and get out of the way. Every red-rimmed eye in the room was opened wide with fear.

Thomas's Street Sweeper exploded! Groza and the uniformed cops hit the floor, all three of them. I couldn't tell if anyone had been hit up front.

The Latino at the door yelled, 'Cut this shit out! Cut the shit!' He was down low on the floor himself, screaming without raising his head into the line of fire.

'Thomas!' I yelled at the top of my voice.

Shareef Thomas was moving with surprising speed and alertness. Quick, sure reflexes, even under the influence. He turned the shotgun on me. His dark eyes glared.

There is nothing to compare with the sight of a shotgun pointed right at you. I had no choice now. I squeezed the trigger of the Glock.

Shareef Thomas took a thunderbolt in his right shoulder. He spun hard left, but he didn't go down. He pivoted smoothly. He'd been here before. So had I.

I fired a second time, hit him in the throat or lower jaw. Thomas flew back and crashed into the paper-thin walls. The whole building shook. His eyeballs flipped back and his mouth sagged open wide. He was gone before he hit the crackhouse floor.

I had killed our only connection to Gary Soneji.

Chapter Forty-Six

I heard Carmine Groza shouting into his radio. The words chilled me. 'Officer down at 412 Macon. *Officer down!*'

I had never been on the scene when another officer was killed. As I got to the front of the crackhouse, though, I was certain one of the uniforms was going to die. Why had Groza come in here like that? Why had he brought in patrolmen with him? Well, it didn't matter much now.

The uniformed man lay on his back on the littered floor near the front door. His eyes were already glazed and I thought he was in shock. Blood was trickling from the corner of his mouth.

The shotgun had done its horrifying work, just as it would have done me. Blood was splashed on the walls and across the scarred wooden floor. A scorched pattern of bullet holes was tattooed in the wall above the patrolman's body. There was nothing any of us could do for him.

I stood near Groza, still holding my Glock. I was clenching and unclenching my teeth. I was trying not to be angry with Groza for overreacting and causing this to happen. I had to get myself under control before I spoke.

The uniformed cop to my left was muttering 'Christ, Christ,' over and over again. I could see how traumatized he was. The uniformed man kept wiping his hand across his forehead and over his eyes, as if to wipe out the bloody scene.

EMS arrived in a matter of minutes. We watched while two medics tried desperately to save the patrolman's life. He was young and looked to be only in his mid-twenties. His reddish hair was in a short brush-cut. The front of his dark-blue shirt was soaked with blood.

In the rear of the crackhouse another medic was trying to save Shareef Thomas, but I already knew that Thomas was gone.

I finally spoke to Groza, low and serious. '*We* know that Thomas is dead, but there's no reason Soneji has to know. This could be how we get to him. If Soneji *thought* Thomas was alive at a New York hospital.'

Groza nodded. 'Let me talk to somebody downtown. Maybe we could take Thomas to a hospital. Maybe we could get the word to the press. It's worth a shot.'

Detective Groza didn't sound very good and he didn't look too good. I was sure I didn't either. I could still see the ominous billboard in the distance: COP SHOT $10,000 REWARD.

Chapter Forty-Seven

No one in the police manhunt would ever guess the beginning, the middle, but especially the end. None of them could imagine where this was heading, where it had been going from the first moment inside Union Station.

Gary Soneji had all the information, all the power. He was getting famous again. He was somebody. He was on the news at ten-minute intervals.

It didn't much matter that they were showing pictures of him. Nobody knew what he looked like today, or yesterday, or tomorrow. They couldn't go around and arrest everyone in New York, could they?

He left the late Jean Summerhill's apartment around noon. The pretty lady had definitely lost her head over him. Just like Missy in Wilmington. He used her key and locked up tight. He walked west on Seventy-third Street until he got to Fifth, then he turned south. The train was back on the track again.

He bought a cup of black coffee in a cardboard container with Greek gods all over the sides. The coffee was absolute New York City swill, but he slowly sipped it anyway. He wanted to go on another rampage right here on Fifth Avenue. He really wanted to go for it. He imagined a massacre, and he could already see the *live* news stories on CBS, ABC, CNN, FOX.

Speaking of news stories, Alex Cross had been on TV that morning. Cross and the NYPD had nabbed Shareef Thomas. Well hooray for them. It proved they could follow instructions at least.

As he passed chic, well-dressed New Yorkers, Soneji couldn't help thinking how smart he was, how much brighter than any of these uptight assholes. If any of these snooty bastards could get inside his head, just for a minute, then they'd know.

No one could, though, no one had ever been able to. No one could guess. *Not the beginning, the middle, or the end.*

He was getting very angry now, almost uncontrollably so. He could feel the rage surging as he walked the overcrowded streets. He almost couldn't see straight. Bile rose in his throat.

He flung his coffee, almost a full cup of the steamy liquid, at a passing businessman. He laughed right in the shocked, outraged face. He howled at the sight of coffee dripping from the New Yorker's aquiline nose, his squarish chin. Dark coffee stained the expensive shirt and tie.

Gary Soneji could do anything he wanted to, and most often, he did. Just you watch.

Chapter Forty-Eight

At seven that night, I was back in Penn Station. It wasn't the usual commuter crowd, so it wasn't too bad on Saturdays. The murders that had taken place at Union Station in Washington, and here, were spinning around in my mind. The dark train tunnels were the 'cellar' to Soneji, symbols of his tortured boyhood. I had figured out that much of the delusionary puzzle. When Soneji came up and out of the cellar, he exploded at the world in a murderous rage . . .

I saw Christine coming up the stairs from the train tunnels.

I began to smile in spite of the locale. I smiled, and shifted my weight from foot to foot, almost dancing. I felt light-headed and excited, filled with hope and desire that I hadn't felt in a long time. She had really come.

Christine was carrying a small black bag with 'Sojourner Truth School' printed on it. She was traveling light. She looked beautiful, proud, more desirable than ever, if that was possible. She was wearing a white short-sleeved dress with a jewel neckline and her usual flats in black patent leather. I noticed people looking at her. They always did.

We kissed in a corner of the train station, keeping our privacy as best we could. Our bodies pressed together and I could feel her warmth, her bones, her flesh. I heard the bag she was carrying drop at her feet.

Her brown eyes looked into mine and they were wide and questioning at first, but then became very soft and light. 'I was a little afraid you wouldn't be here,' she said. 'I had visions of you off on some police emergency, and me standing here alone in the middle of Penn Station.'

'There's no way I would let that happen,' I said to her. 'I'm so glad you're here.'

We kissed again, pressing even harder together. I didn't want to stop kissing

Christine, holding her tightly. I wanted to take her where we could be alone. My body nearly convulsed. It was that bad, that good.

'I tried,' she said and grinned, 'but I couldn't stay away from you. New York scares me a little, but here I am.'

'We're going to have a great time. You'll see.'

'You promise? Will it be unforgettable?' she teased me.

'Unforgettable. I promise,' I said.

I held her tightly in my arms. I couldn't let her go.

Chapter Forty-Nine

The beginning of 'unforgettable' felt like this, looked like this, sounded like this.

The Rainbow Room at eight-thirty on a Saturday night. Christine and I waltzed off the glitzy elevator, arm in arm. We were immediately swept into another era, another lifestyle, maybe another life. A fancy silver-on-black placard near the elevator door read: 'The Rainbow Room, Step into an MGM Musical.' Hundreds of minispotlights kicked off from the dazzling chrome and crystal. It was over the top, and just about perfect.

'I'm not sure if I'm dressed right for an MGM musical, but I don't particularly care. What a wonderful idea,' Christine said as we made our way past overdone, outrageous-looking ushers and usherettes. We were directed to a desk that looked down onto the deco ballroom but also had panoramic views of New York. The room was jam-packed on a Saturday night; every table and the dance floor was filled.

Christine was dressed in a simple black sheath. She wore the same necklace, made from an old-fashioned brooch, that she wore at Kinkead's. It had belonged to her grandmother. Because I'm six-three, she wasn't afraid to wear dressier shoes with high heels, rather than her comfortable flats. I had never realized it before, but I liked being with a woman who was nearly as tall as I am.

I had dressed up, too. I'd chosen a charcoal-gray, summer-weight suit, crisp white shirt, blue silk tie. For tonight anyway, I was definitely not a police detective from DC. I didn't look like Dr Alex Cross from Southeast. Maybe more like Denzel Washington playing the part of Jay Gatsby. I liked the feeling, for a night on the town anyway. Maybe even for a whole weekend.

We were escorted to a table in front of a large window that overlooked the glittering East Side of Manhattan. A five-piece Latin band was onstage, and they were cooking pretty good. The slowly revolving dance floor was still full. People were having a fine time, lots of people dancing the night away.

'It's funny, beautiful, and ridiculous, and I think it's as special as anywhere I've been,' Christine said once we were seated. 'That's about all the superlatives you're going to hear from me tonight.'

'You haven't even seen me dance,' I said.

'I already know that you can dance,' Christine laughed and told me. 'Women always know which men can dance, and which men can't.'

We ordered drinks, straight Scotch for me, Harvey's Bristol Cream for Christine. We picked out a bottle of Sauvignon Blanc, and then spent a few delicious minutes just taking in the spectacle of the Rainbow Room.

The Latin combo was replaced by a 'big band combo,' which played swing and even took a swipe at the blues. A whole lot of people still knew how to jitterbug and waltz and even tango, and some of them were pretty good.

'You ever been here before?' I asked Christine as the waiter came with our drinks.

'Only while I was watching *The Prince of Tides* alone in my bedroom at home,' she said and smiled again. 'How about you? Come here often, sailor?'

'Just the one time I was chasing down this split-personality ax-murderer in New York. He went right out that picture window over there. Third from the left.'

Christine laughed. 'I wouldn't be surprised if it was true, Alex. I wouldn't be a bit surprised.'

The band started to play 'Moonglow,' which is a pretty song, and we had to get up and dance. Gravity just pulled us. At that moment, I couldn't think of too many things in the world I wanted to do more than hold Christine in my arms. Actually, I couldn't think of anything at all.

At some point in time, Christine and I had agreed to take a risk and see what would happen. We'd both lost people we loved. We knew what it meant to be hurt, and yet here we were, ready to go out on the dance floor of life again. I think I'd wanted to slow-dance with Christine from the very first time I saw her at the Sojourner Truth School.

Now, I tucked her in close and my left arm encircled her waist. My right hand clasped hers. I felt her soft intake of breath. I could tell she was a little nervous, too.

I started to hum softly. I might have been floating a little, too. My lips touched hers and my eyes closed. I could feel the silk of her dress under my fingers. And yes, I could dance pretty well, but so could she.

'Look at me,' she whispered, and I opened my eyes. She was right. It was much better that way.

'What's going on here? What *is* this? I don't think I've ever felt like this, Alex.'

'Neither have I. But I could get used to it. I know that I like it.'

I lightly brushed her cheek with my fingers. The music was working and Christine seemed to flow with me. Graceful, moonlit choreography. All my body parts were moving. I was finding it hard to breathe.

Christine and I were in harmony together. We both could dance well enough, but together it was something special. I moved slowly and smoothly with her. The palm of her hand felt magnetized to mine. I spun her slowly, a playful half-turn underneath my arm.

We came back together and our lips were inches apart. I could feel the warmth of her body right through my clothes. Our lips met again, for just an instant, and the music stopped. Another song began.

'Now *that* is a hard act to follow,' she said as we sashayed back to our table after the slow-dance. 'I knew you could dance. Never a doubt in my mind. But I didn't know you could *dance*.'

'You haven't seen anything. Wait until they play a samba,' I told her. I was still holding her hand, couldn't let go. Didn't want to.

'I *think* I can samba,' she said.

We danced a lot, we held hands constantly, and I think we even ate dinner. We definitely danced some more, and I could not let go of Christine's hand. She couldn't let go of mine. We talked nonstop, and later, I couldn't remember most of what had been said. I think that happens high above New York City in the Rainbow Room.

The first time I looked at my watch all night it was nearly one o'clock and I couldn't believe it. That same mysterious time-loss thing had happened a couple of times when I'd been with Christine. I paid our bill, our *big* bill, and I noticed that the Rainbow Room was nearly empty. Where had everybody gone?

'Can you keep a secret?' Christine whispered as we were going down to the lobby in the walnut-paneled elevator. We were alone in the car with its soft yellow light. I was holding her in my arms.

'I keep lots of secrets,' I said.

'Well, here it is,' Christine said as we reached the bottom floor with just the lightest *bump*. She held me inside after the door had opened. She wasn't going to let me out of the softly lit elevator until she finished saying what she had to say.

'I really like that you got me my own room at the Astor,' she said. 'But Alex, I don't think I'll be needing it. Is that okay?'

We stood very still in the elevator and began to kiss again. The doors shut, and the elevator slowly climbed back up to the roof. So we kissed going up, and we kissed on the way back down to the lobby, and it wasn't nearly a long-enough round-trip.

'You know what, though?' she finally said as we reached the ground floor of Rockefeller Center a second time.

'What, though?' I asked her.

'That's what's *supposed* to happen when you go to the Rainbow Room.'

Chapter Fifty

I t *was* unforgettable. Just like the magical Nat King Cole song, and the more recent version with Natalie Cole.

We were standing at the door to my hotel room, and I was completely lost in the moment. I had let go of Christine's hand to open the door – and I was *lost*. I fumbled the key slightly and missed the lock. She gently placed her hand on mine and we glided the key into the lock, turned the tumblers together.

An eternity of seconds passed, at least it seemed that way. I knew that I would never forget any of this. I wouldn't let skepticism or cynicism diminish it either.

I knew what was happening to me. I was feeling the dizzying effect of a return to intimacy. I hadn't realized how much I'd missed it. I had let myself be numb, let myself live numb for the past few years. It's easy enough to do, so easy that you don't even realize your life has become a deep rut.

The hotel door slowly opened, and I had the thought that the two of us were giving up something of our past now. Christine turned to me at the threshold. I heard the faint swish of her silk dress.

Her beautiful face tilted toward mine. I reached for her and balanced her chin with my fingertips. I felt as if I hadn't been able to breathe properly all night, not from the moment she'd arrived at Penn Station.

'Musician's hands. Piano player fingers,' she said. 'I love the way you touch me. I always knew I would. I'm not afraid anymore, Alex.'

'I'm glad. Neither am I.'

The heavy wooden door of the hotel room seemed to close all by itself.

It didn't really matter where we were right now, I was thinking. The twinkling lights outside, or maybe a boat gliding by on the river, gave the impression that the floor was gently moving, much as the dance floor at the Rainbow Room had moved under our feet.

I had switched hotels for the weekend, moving to the Astor on Manhattan's

East Side. I'd wanted someplace special. The room was on the twelfth floor, facing out on the river.

We were drawn to the picture window, attracted by the strobing lights of the New York skyline to the southeast. We watched the silent, strangely beautiful movement of traffic passing the United Nations, moving toward the Brooklyn Bridge.

I remembered taking the bridge earlier today on our way to a crackhouse in Brooklyn. It seemed so long ago. I saw the face of Shareef Thomas, then the dead policeman's, then Soneji's, but I shut down those images immediately. I wasn't a police detective here. Christine's lips were on my skin, lightly bussing my throat.

'Where did you go just now? You went away, didn't you?' she whispered. 'You were in a dark place.'

'Just for a few seconds.' I confessed the truth, my flaw. 'A flashback from work. It's gone.' I was holding her hand again.

She kissed me lightly on the cheek, a paper-thin kiss, then very lightly on the lips. 'You can't lie, can you, Alex? Not even tiny white lies.'

'I try not to. I don't like lies. If I lie to you, then who am I?' I said and smiled. 'What's the point?'

'I love that about you,' she whispered. 'Lots of other things, too. I find something else every time I'm with you.'

I nuzzled the top of her head, then I kissed Christine's forehead, her cheek, her lips, and finally the sweet hollow of her throat. She was trembling a little. So was I. Thank God that neither of us was afraid, right. I could feel the pulse tripping under her skin.

'You're so beautiful,' I whispered. 'Do you know that?'

'I'm way too tall, too thin. *You're* the beautiful one. You are, you know. Everybody says so.'

Everything felt electric and so right. It seemed a miracle that we had found each other, and now we were here together. I was so glad, felt so lucky, that she had decided to take a chance with me, that I had taken a chance, too.

'Look in the mirror there. See how beautiful you are,' she said. 'You have the sweetest face. You *are* trouble though, aren't you, Alex?'

'I won't give you too much trouble tonight,' I said.

I wanted to undress her, to do everything for and to Christine. A funny word, strange word was in my head, *rapture*. She slid her hand over the front of my pants and felt how hard I was.

'Hmmm,' she whispered and smiled.

I began to unzip her dress. I couldn't remember wanting to be with someone like this, not for a long time anyway. I ran my hand over her face, memorizing every part, every feature. Christine's skin was so soft and silky underneath my fingers.

We started to dance again, right there in the hotel room. There wasn't any music, but we had our own. My hand pressed just below her waist, folding her in close to me.

Moonlit choreography again. We slowly rocked back and forth, back and forth, a sensuous cha-cha-cha next to the broad picture window. I held her buttocks in the palms of my hands. She wiggled into a position she liked. I liked it, too. A whole lot.

'You dance real good, Alex. I just knew you would.'

Christine reached down and tugged at my belt until the prong came free. She unzipped me, lightly fondled me. I loved her touch, anywhere, everywhere. Her lips were on my skin again. Everything about her was erotic, irresistible, unforgettable.

We both knew to do this slowly, no need to hurry anything tonight. Rushing would spoil this, and it mustn't be spoiled in any way.

I held the thought that we'd both been here before, but never like this. We were in this very special place for the first time. This would only happen one time.

My kisses slowly swept over her shoulders and I could feel her breasts rising and falling against me. I felt the flatness of her stomach, and her legs pressing. I cupped Christine's breasts in my hands. Suddenly I wanted everything, all of her at once.

I sank to my knees. I ran my hands up and down her soft legs, along her waist.

I rose to my feet. I unzipped her black sheath the rest of the way and it trailed down her long arms to the floor. It made a shimmering black puddle surrounding her ankles, her slender feet.

Finally, when there were no more clothes and we looked at each other, Christine watched my eyes and I watched hers. Her eyes shamelessly traveled down my chest, past my waist. I was still highly aroused. I wanted to be inside her so much.

She took a half-step back. I couldn't breathe. I could hardly bear this. But I didn't want it to stop. I was feeling again, remembering how to feel, remembering how good it could be.

She pulled her hair to one side, behind one ear. Such a simple, graceful movement.

'Do that again,' I smiled.

She laughed and repeated the movement with her hair. 'Anything that you want.

'Stay there,' she whispered. 'Don't move, Alex. Don't come closer – we might both catch fire. I mean it.'

'This could take the rest of the weekend,' I said and started to laugh.

'I hope it does.'

I heard the tiniest *click*.

Was that the door to our room?
Had I closed it?
Was someone out there?
Jesus, no.

Chapter Fifty-One

S uddenly nervous and paranoid, I peered back at the door to the hotel room. It was closed and locked tight. Nobody there, nothing to worry about. Christine and I were safe here. Nothing bad was going to happen to either of us tonight.

Still, the moment of fear and doubt had raised the hairs on my neck. Soneji has a habit of doing that to me. *Damn it, what did he want from me?*

'What's wrong, Alex? You just left me again.' Christine touched me, brought me back. Her fingers were like feathers on the side of my cheek. 'Just be here with me, Alex.'

'I'm here. I just thought I heard something.'

'I know you did. No one is there. You locked the door behind us. We're fine. It's okay, it's okay.'

I pulled Christine close against my body again and she felt electric and incredibly warm. I drew her down onto the bed and rolled over her, holding my weight on the palms of my hands. I dipped and kissed her sweet face again, then each of her breasts; I pulled at the nipples with my lips, licked them with my tongue. I kissed between her legs, down her long legs, her slender ankles, her toes. *Just be here with me, Alex.*

She arched herself toward me and she gasped, but she was smiling radiantly. She was moving her body against me and we had already found a nice rhythm. We were both breathing faster and faster.

'Please, do it now,' she whispered, her teeth biting into my shoulder near the clavicle. 'Please now, *right now*. I want you inside.' She rubbed my sides with the palms of her hands. She rubbed me like kindling sticks.

A fire ignited. I could feel it spreading through my body. I entered her for the first time. I slid inside slowly, but I went as deep as I could go. My heart was pounding, my legs felt weak. My stomach was taut and I was so hard it hurt.

I was all the way inside Christine. I knew I'd wanted to be here for a long time. I had the thought that I was made for this, for being in this bed with this woman.

Gracefully and athletically, she rolled on top of me and sat up proud and tall. We began to rock slowly like that. I felt our bodies surge and peak, surge and peak, surge.

I heard my own voice crying yes, yes, yes. Then I realized it was both our voices.

Then Christine said something so magical. She whispered, '*You're the one.*'

Part Three

The Cellar of Cellars

Chapter Fifty-Two

Paris, France.

Dr Abel Sante was thirty-five years old, with longish black hair, boyish good looks, and a beautiful girlfriend named Regina Becker, who was a painter, and a very good one, he thought. He had just left Regina's apartment, and was winding his way home on the back streets of the sixth arrondissement at around midnight.

The narrow streets were quiet and empty and he loved this time of day for collecting his thoughts, or sometimes for not thinking at all. Abel Sante was musing on the death of a young woman earlier today, a patient of his, twenty-six years old. She had a loving husband and two beautiful daughters. He had a perspective about death that he thought was a good one: Why should leaving the world, and rejoining the cosmos, be any scarier than entering the world, which wasn't very scary at all?

Dr Sante didn't know where the man, a street person in a soiled gray jacket and torn, baggy jeans, had come from. Suddenly the man was at his side, nearly attached to his elbow.

'Beautiful,' the man said.

'I'm sorry, excuse me?' Abel Sante said, startled, coming out of his inner thoughts in a hurry.

'It's a beautiful night and our city is so perfect for a late walk.'

'Yes, well it's been nice meeting you,' Sante said to the street person. He'd noticed that the man's French was slightly accented. Perhaps he was English, or even American.

'You shouldn't have left her apartment. Should have stayed the night. A gentleman always stays the night – unless of course he's asked to leave.'

Dr Abel Sante's back and neck stiffened. He took his hands from his trouser pockets. Suddenly he was afraid, very much so.

He shoved the street person away with his left elbow.

'What are you talking about? Why don't you just get out of here?'

'I'm talking about you and Regina. Regina Becker, the painter. Her work's not bad, but not good enough, I'm afraid.'

'Get the hell away from me.'

Abel Sante quickened his pace. He was only a block from his home. The other man, the street person, kept up with him easily. He was larger, more athletic than Sante had noticed at first.

'You should have given her babies. That's my opinion.'

'Get away. Go!'

Suddenly, Sante had both fists raised and clasped tightly. This was insane! He was ready to fight, if he had to. He hadn't fought in twenty years, but he was strong and in good shape.

The street person swung out and knocked him down. He did it easily, as if it were nothing at all.

Dr Sante's pulse was racing rapidly. He couldn't see very well out of his left eye, where he'd been struck.

'*Are you a complete maniac? Are you out of your mind?*' he screamed at the man, who suddenly looked powerful and impressive, even in the soiled clothes.

'Yes, of course,' the man answered. 'Of course I'm out of my mind. *I'm Mr Smith* – and you're next.'

Chapter Fifty-Three

Gary Soneji hurried like a truly horrifying city rat through the low dark tunnels that wind like intestines beneath New York's Bellevue Hospital. The fetid odor of dried blood and disinfectants made him feel sick. He didn't like the reminders of sickness and death surrounding him.

No matter, though, he was properly revved for today. He was wired, flying high. *He was Death. And Death was not taking a holiday in New York.*

He had outfitted himself for his big morning: crisply pressed white pants, white lab coat, white sneakers; a laminated hospital photo ID around his neck on a beaded silver chain.

He was here on morning rounds. Bellevue. *This was his idea of rounds anyway!*

There was no way to stop any of this: his train from hell, his destiny, his last hurrah. No one could stop it because no one would ever figure out where the last train was headed. Only he knew that, only Soneji himself could call it off.

He wondered how much of the puzzle Cross had already pieced together. Cross wasn't in his class as a thinker, but the psychologist and detective wasn't without crude instincts in certain specialized areas. Maybe he was underestimating Dr Cross, as he had once before. Could he be caught now? Perhaps, but it really didn't matter. The game would continue to its end without him. That was the beauty of it, the evil of what he had done.

Gary Soneji stepped into a stainless-steel elevator in the basement of the well-known Manhattan hospital. A pair of porters shared the narrow car with him, and Soneji had a moment of paranoia. They might be New York cops working undercover.

The NYPD actually had an office on the main floor of the hospital. It was there under 'normal' circumstances. *Bellevue. Jesus, what a sensational madhouse this was. A hospital with a police station inside.*

He eyed the porters with a casual and disinterested city-cool look. *They can't be policemen*, he thought. *Nobody could look that dumb.* They were what they looked like – slow-moving, slow-thinking hospital morons.

One of them was pushing around a stainless-steel cart with *two* bum wheels. It was a wonder that any patient ever made it out of a New York City hospital alive. Hospitals here were run with about the same personnel standards as a McDonald's restaurant, probably less.

He knew one patient who wasn't going to leave Bellevue alive. The news reports said that Shareef Thomas was being kept here by the police. Well, Thomas was going to suffer before he left this so-called 'vale of tears.' Shareef was about to undergo a world of suffering.

Gary Soneji stepped out of the elevator onto the first floor. He sighed with relief. The two porters went about their business. They weren't cops. No, they were dumber and dumbest.

Canes, wheelchairs, and metal walkers were everywhere. The hospital artifacts reminded him of his own mortality. The halls on the first floor were painted off-white, the doors and radiators were a shade of pink like old gum. Up ahead was a strange coffee shop, dimly lit like a subway passageway. *If you ate in that place*, he thought to himself, *they ought to lock you up in Bellevue!*

As he walked from the elevator, Soneji caught his own reflection in a stainless-steel pillar. *The master of a thousand faces*, he couldn't help thinking. It was true. His own stepmother wouldn't recognize him now, and if she did, she would scream her bloody lungs out. She'd know he'd come all the way to hell to get her.

He walked down the corridor, singing very softly in a reggae lilt, 'I shot the Shareef, but I did not shoot the dep-u-tee.'

No one paid him any mind. Gary Soneji fit right in at Bellevue.

Chapter Fifty-Four

S oneji had a perfect memory, so he would recall everything about this morning. He would be able to play it back for himself with incredible detail. This was true for all of his murders. He scanned the narrow, high-ceilinged hallways as if he had a surveillance camera mounted where his head was. His powers of concentration gave him a huge advantage. He was almost supernaturally aware of everything going on around him.

A security guard was riffing with young black males outside the coffee shop. They were all mental defectives for sure, the toy cops especially.

No threat there.

Silly baseball caps were bobbing everywhere. New Jork Janquis. San Francisco Jints. San Jose Sharks. None of the ball-cap wearers looked as if they could play ball worth spit. Or harm, or stop him.

The Hospital Police Office was up ahead. The lights were out, though. Nobody home right now. So where were the hospital patrol cops? Were they waiting for him someplace? Why didn't he see any of them? Was that the first sign of trouble?

At the inpatient elevator, a sign read: ID REQUIRED. Soneji had his ready. For today's masquerade, he was Francis Michael Nicolo, RN.

A framed poster was on the wall: Patients' Rights and Responsibilities. Signs stared out from behind fuzzy Plexiglas everywhere he looked. It was worse than a New York highway: Radiology, Urology, Hematology. *I'm sick, too*, Soneji wanted to yell out to the powers that be. *I'm as sick as anybody in here. I'm dying. Nobody cares. Nobody has ever cared.*

He took the central elevator to four. No problems so far, no hassles. No police. He got off at his stop, pumped to see Shareef Thomas again, to see the look of shock and fear on his face.

The hallway on four had a hollowed-out basement feel to it. Nothing seemed to absorb sound. The whole building felt as if it were made entirely of concrete.

Soneji peered down the corridor to where he knew Shareef was being kept. His room was at the far end of the building. Isolated for safety, right? So this was the high-and-mighty NYPD in action. What a joke. Everything was a joke, if you thought about it long and hard enough.

Soneji lowered his head and started to walk toward Shareef Thomas's hospital room.

He had bribed a hospital security guard who brought the meals up to four and was aware of the tight security. He was as dead now as Robert Fishenauer, the supervisor who had helped Soneji escape from prison.

Chapter Fifty-Five

Carmine Groza and I were inside the private hospital room waiting for Soneji, hoping that he would show. We had been here for hours. How would I know what Soneji looked like now? That was a problem, but we would take them one at a time.

We never heard a noise at the door. Suddenly it was swinging open. Soneji exploded into the room, expecting to find Shareef Thomas. He stared at Groza and me.

His hair was dyed silver gray and combed straight back. He looked like a man in his fifties or early sixties – but the height was about right. His light-blue eyes widened as he looked at me. It was the eyes that I recognized first.

He smiled the same disdainful and dismissive smirk I'd seen so many times, sometimes in my nightmares. He thought he was so damn superior to the rest of us. He *knew* it.

Soneji said only two words: 'Even better.'

'New York police! Freeze,' Groza barked a warning in an authoritative tone.

Soneji continued to smirk as if this surprise reception pleased him no end, as if he'd planned it himself. His confidence, his arrogance, were incredible to behold.

He's wearing a bulletproof vest – my mind registered a bulge around his upper body. *He's protected. He's ready for whatever we do.*

There was something clasped tightly in his left hand. I couldn't tell what. He'd entered the room with the arm half-raised.

He flipped a small green bottle in his hand toward Groza and me. Just the *flip* of his hand. The bottle clinked as it hit the wooden floor. It bounced a second time. Suddenly I understood . . . but too late, seconds too late.

'Bomb!' I yelled at Groza. 'Hit the floor! Get down!'

Groza and I dove away from the bed and the caroming green bottle. We managed to put up sitting chairs as shields. The flash inside the room was incredibly bright, a splintered shock of white light with an afterglow of the brightest yellow. Then everything around us seemed to catch fire.

For a second or two, I was blinded. Then I felt as if I were burning up. My trousers and shoes were engulfed in flames. I covered my face, mouth, and eyes with my hands. 'Jesus, God,' Groza screamed.

I could hear a sizzle, like bacon on a grill. I prayed it wasn't me that was cooking. Then I was choking and gurgling and so was Groza. Flames burst and danced across my shirt, and through it all I could hear Soneji. He was laughing at us.

'Welcome to hell, Cross,' he said. 'Burn, baby, burn.'

Chapter Fifty-Six

G roza and I stripped the bed of blankets and sheets and beat out our burning trousers. We were lucky, at least I hoped we were. We smothered the flames. The ones on our legs and shoes.

'He wanted to burn Thomas alive,' I told Groza. 'He's got *another* firebomb. I saw another green bottle, at least one.'

We hobbled as best we could down the hospital corridor, chasing after Soneji. Two other detectives were already down outside, wounded. Soneji *was* a phantom.

We followed him down several twisting flights of back stairs. The sound of the footrace echoed loudly on the stairway. My eyes were watering, but I could see okay.

Groza alerted and clued in other detectives on his two-way. 'Suspect has a firebomb! Soneji has a bomb. Probably a knife also. Use extreme care.'

'What the hell does he want?' the detective yelled at me as we kept moving. 'What the hell's he going to do now?'

'I think he wants to die,' I gasped. 'And he wants to be even more famous. Go out with a bang. That's his way. Maybe right here at Bellevue.'

Attention was what Gary Soneji had always craved. From his boyhood years, he'd been obsessed with stories of 'crimes of the century.' I was sure that Soneji wanted to die now, but he had to do it with a huge noise. He wanted to control his own death.

I was wheezing and out of breath when we finally got to the lobby floor. Smoke had seared my throat, but otherwise I was doing okay. My brain was fuzzy and unclear about what to do next.

I saw a blur of hectic movement ahead, maybe thirty yards across the front lobby.

I pushed through the nervous crowd trying to exit the building. Word had spread about the fire upstairs. The flow of people in and out of Bellevue was always as steady as at a subway turnstile, and that was *before* a bomb went off inside.

I made it onto the stoop in front of the hospital. It was raining hard, gray and awful outside. I looked everywhere for Soneji.

A cluster of hospital staff and visitors were under the front awning, smoking cigarettes. They seemed unaware of the emergency situation, or maybe these workers were just used to them. The brick path leading away from the building was crowded with more pedestrians coming and going in the downpour. The umbrellas were blocking my vision.

Where the hell had Gary Soneji gone? Where could he have disappeared to? I had the sinking feeling that I'd lost him again. I couldn't stand any more of this.

Out on First Avenue, food vendors under colorful umbrellas stained with dirt were peddling gyros, hot dogs, and New York-style pretzels.

No Soneji anywhere.

I kept searching, frantically looking up and down the busy, noisy street. I couldn't let him get away. I would never get another chance as good as this. There was an opening in the crowd. I could see for maybe half a block.

There he was!

Soneji was moving with a small clique of pedestrians headed north on the sidewalk. I started to go after him. Groza was still with me. We both had our guns out. We couldn't risk a shot in the crowds, though. Lots of mothers and children and elderly people, patients coming and going from the hospital.

Soneji peered to the left, the right, and then behind. He saw us coming. I was sure he'd seen me.

He was improvising his escape, a way out of the extreme and dangerous mess. The sequence of recent events showed deterioration in his thinking. He was losing his sharpness and clarity. *That's why he's ready to die now. He's tired of dying slowly. He's losing his mind. He can't bear it.*

A Con Ed crew had blocked off half the intersection. Hard hats bobbed in the rain. Traffic was trying to maneuver around the road-work, nonstop honkers everywhere.

I saw Soneji make a sudden break from the crowd. What the hell? He was running toward First Avenue, racing down the slippery street. He was weaving, running in a full sprint.

I watched as Gary Soneji spun quickly to his right. *Do us all a favor. Go down!* He ran along the side of a white and blue city bus that had stopped for passengers.

He was still slipping, sliding. He almost fell. Then he was inside the goddamn bus.

The bus was standing-room only. I could see Soneji frantically waving his arms, screaming orders at the other passengers. *Jesus God, he's got a bomb on that city bus.*

Chapter Fifty-Seven

Detective Groza staggered up beside me. His face was smudged with soot and his flowing black hair was singed. He signaled wildly for a car, waving both arms. A police sedan pulled up beside us and we jumped inside.

'You all right?' I asked him.

'I guess so. I'm here. Let's go get him.'

We followed the bus up First Avenue, weaving in and out of traffic, siren full blast. We almost hit a cab, missed by inches, if that.

'You sure he's got another bomb?'

I nodded. 'At least one. Remember the Mad Bomber in New York? Soneji probably does. The Mad Bomber was famous.'

Everything was crazy and surreal. The rain was coming down harder, making loud bangs on the sedan's roof.

'He has hostages,' Groza spoke into the two-way on the dash. 'He's on a city bus heading up First Avenue. He appears to have a bomb. The bus is an M-15. All cars stay on the bus. Do not intercept at this point. He has a goddamn bomb on the M-15 bus.'

I counted half-a-dozen blue-and-whites already in pursuit. The city bus was stopping for red lights, but it was no longer picking up passengers. People standing in the rain, bypassed at stops, waved their arms angrily at the M-15. None of them understood how lucky they were that the bus doors didn't open for them.

'Try to get close,' I told the driver. 'I want to talk to him. Want to see if he'll talk anyway. It's worth a try.'

The police sedan accelerated, then weaved on the wet streets. We were getting closer, inching alongside the white and blue bus. A poster advertised the musical *The Phantom of the Opera* in bold type. *A real live phantom was on board the bus.* Gary Soneji was back in the spotlight that he loved. He was playing New York now.

I had the side window of the car rolled down. Rain and wind attacked my face, but I could see Soneji inside the bus. *Jesus, he was still improvising* – he had somebody's child, a bundle of pink-and-blue cradled in his arm. He was screaming orders, his free arm swinging in angry circles.

I leaned as far as I could outside the car. 'Gary!' I yelled. 'What do you want?' I called out again, fighting the traffic noise, the loud roar of the bus. *'Gary! It's Alex Cross!'*

Passengers inside the bus were looking out at me. They were terrified, beyond terror, actually.

At Forty-second Street and First, the bus made a sudden, sweeping left turn! I looked at Groza. 'This the regular route?'

'No way,' he said. 'He's making his own route up as he goes.'

'What's on Forty-second Street? What's up ahead? Where the hell could he be going?'

Groza threw up his hands in desperation. 'Times Square is across town, home of the skells, the city's worst derelicts and losers. Theater district's there, too. Port Authority Bus Terminal. We're coming up on Grand Central Station.'

'Then he's going to Grand Central,' I told Groza. 'I'm sure of it. This is the way he wants it. In a train station!' Another cellar, a glorious one that went on for city blocks. *The cellar of cellars.*

Gary Soneji was already out of the bus and running on Forty-second Street. He was headed toward Grand Central Station, headed toward home. He was still carrying the baby in one arm, swinging it loosely, showing us how little he cared about the child's life.

Goddamn him to hell. He was on the homestretch, and only he knew what that meant.

Chapter Fifty-Eight

I made my way down the crowded stone-and-mortar passageway from Forty-second Street. It emptied into an even busier Grand Central Station. Thousands of already harried commuters were arriving for work in the midtown area. They had no idea how truly bad their day was about to become.

Grand Central is the New York end for the New York Central, the New York, New Haven, and Hartford trains and a few others. And for three IRT subway lines. Lexington Avenue, Times Square–Grand Central Shuttle, and Queens.

The terminal covers three blocks between Forty-second and Forty-fifth Streets. Forty-one tracks are on the upper level and twenty-six on the lower, which narrows to a single four-track line to Ninety-sixth Street.

The lower level is a huge labyrinth, one of the largest anywhere in the world. Gary's cellar.

I continued to push against the densely packed rush-hour crowd. I made it through a waiting room, then emerged into the cavernous and spectacular main concourse. Construction work was in progress everywhere. Giant cloth posters for Pan Am Airlines and American Express and Nike sneakers hung down over the walls. The gates to dozens of tracks were visible from where I stood.

Detective Groza caught up with me in the concourse. We were both running on adrenaline. 'He's still got the baby,' he huffed. 'Somebody spotted him running down to the next level.'

Leading a merry chase, right? Gary Soneji was heading to the cellar. That wouldn't be good for the thousands of people crowding inside the building. He had a bomb, and maybe more than one.

I led Groza down more steep stairs, under a lit sign that said OYSTER BAR ON THIS LEVEL. The entire station was still under massive construction and renovation, which only added to the confusion. We pushed past crowded bakeries and delis. Plenty to eat here while you waited for your train, or possibly to be blown up.

Detective Groza and I reached the next level. We entered a spacious arcade, surrounded by more railway-track doorways. Signs pointed the way to the subways, to the Times Square Shuttle.

Groza had a two-way cupped near his ear. He was getting up-to-the-second reports from around the station. 'He's down in the tunnels. We're close,' he told me.

Groza and I raced down another steep deck of stone steps. We ran side by side. It was unbearably hot down below and we were sweating. The building was vibrating. The gray stone walls and the floor shook beneath our feet. We were in hell now, the only question was, which circle?

I finally saw Gary Soneji up ahead. Then he disappeared again. He still had the baby, or maybe it was just the pink-and-blue blanket puffed in his arms.

He was back in sight. Then he *stopped* suddenly. Soneji turned and stared down the tunnel. He wasn't afraid of anything anymore. I could see it in his eyes.

'Dr Cross,' he yelled. 'You follow directions beautifully.'

Chapter Fifty-Nine

Soneji's dark secret still worked, still held true for him: Whatever would make people intensely angry, whatever would make them inconsolably sad, whatever would hurt them – *that's what he did.*

Soneji watched Alex Cross approaching. *Tall and arrogant black bastard. Are you ready to die, too, Cross?*

Right when your life seems so promising. Your young children growing up. And your beautiful new lover.

Because that's what's going to happen. You're going to die for what you did to me. You can't stop it from happening.

Alex Cross kept walking toward him, parading across the concrete train platform. He didn't look afraid. Cross definitely walked the talk. That was his strength, but it was also his folly.

Soneji felt as if he were floating in space right now. He felt so free, as if nothing could hurt him anywhere. He could be exactly who he wanted to be, act as he wished. He'd spent his life trying to get here.

Alex Cross was getting closer and closer. He called out a question across the train platform. It was always a question with Cross.

'What do you want, Gary? What the hell do you want from us?'

'Shut your hole! What do you think I want?' Soneji shouted back. 'You! I finally caught *you.*'

Chapter Sixty

I heard what Soneji said, but it didn't matter anymore. The thing between us was going down now. I kept coming toward him. One way or the other, this was the end.

I walked down a flight of three or four stone steps. I couldn't take my eyes off Soneji. I couldn't. I refused to give up now.

Smoke from the hospital fire was in my lungs. The air in the train tunnel didn't help. I began to cough.

Could this be the end of Soneji? I almost couldn't believe it. What the hell did he mean *he finally caught me*?

'Don't anybody move. Stop! Not another step!' Soneji yelled. He had a gun. The baby. 'I'll tell you who moves, and who doesn't. That includes you, Cross. So *just stop walking.*'

I stopped. No one else moved. It was incredibly quiet on the train platform, deep in the bowels of Grand Central. There were probably twenty people close enough to Soneji to be injured by a bomb.

He held the baby from the bus up high, and that had everybody's attention. Detectives and uniformed police stood paralyzed in the wide doorways around the train tunnel. We were all helpless, powerless to do anything to stop Soneji. We had to listen to him.

He began to turn in a small, tight, frenzied circle. His body twirled around and around. A strange whirling dervish. He was clutching the infant in one arm, holding the tiny baby like a doll. I had no idea what had become of the child's mother.

Soneji almost seemed in a trance. He looked crazy now – maybe he was. 'The good Dr Cross is here,' he yelled down the platform. 'How much do you know? How much do you *think* you know? Let *me* ask the questions for a change.'

'I don't know enough, Gary,' I said, keeping my answer as low-key as possible. Not playing to the crowd, *his* crowd. 'I guess you still like an audience.'

'Why yes, I do, Dr Cross. I love an appreciative crowd. What's the point of a great performance with no one to see it? I crave the look in all of your eyes, your fear, your hatred.' He continued to turn, to spin as if he were playing a theater-in-the-round. 'You'd all like to kill me. You're all killers, too!' he screeched.

Soneji did another slow spin around, his gun pointed out, the baby cradled in his left arm. The infant wasn't crying, and that worried me sick. The bomb could be in a pocket of his trousers. It was somewhere. I hoped it wasn't in the baby's blanket.

'You're back there in the cellar? Aren't you?' I said. At one time I had believed Gary Soneji was schizophrenic. Then I was certain he wasn't. Right now, I wasn't sure of anything.

He gestured with his free arm at the underground caverns. He continued to walk slowly toward the rear of the platform. We couldn't stop him. 'As a kid, this is where I always dreamed I would escape to. Take a big, fast train to Grand Central Station in New York City. Get away clean and free. *Escape* from everything.'

'You've done it. You finally won. Isn't that why you led us here? To catch you?' I said.

'I'm *not* done. Not even close. I'm not finished with you yet, Cross,' he sneered.

There was his threat again. It made my stomach drop to hear him talk like that. 'What about me?' I called. 'You keep making threats. I don't see any action.'

Soneji stopped moving. He stopped backing toward the rear of the platform. Everyone was watching him now, probably thinking none of this was real. I wasn't even sure if I did.

'This doesn't end here, Cross. *I'm coming for you*, even from the grave if I have to. There's no way you can stop this. You remember that! Don't you forget now! I'm sure you won't.'

Then Soneji did something I would never understand. His left arm shot up. He threw the baby high in the air. The people watching gasped as the child tumbled forward.

They sighed audibly as a man fifteen feet down the platform caught the baby perfectly.

Then, the infant started to cry.

'Gary, no!' I shouted at Soneji. He was running again.

'Are you ready to die, Dr Cross?' he screamed back at me. *'Are you ready?'*

Chapter Sixty-One

Soneji disappeared through a silver, metallic door at the rear of the platform. He was quick, and he had surprise on his side. Gunshots rang out – Groza fired – but I didn't think Soneji had been hit.

'There's more tunnels back there, lots of train tracks down here,' Groza told me. 'We're walking into a dark, dirty maze.'

'Yeah, well let's go anyway,' I said. 'Gary loves it down here. We'll make the best of it.'

I noticed a maintenance worker and grabbed his flashlight. I pulled out my Glock. Seventeen shots. Groza had a .357 Magnum. Six more rounds. How many shots would it take to kill Soneji? Would he ever die?

'He's wearing a goddamn vest,' Groza said.

'Yeah, I saw that.' I clicked the safety off the Glock. 'He's a Boy Scout – *always prepared*.'

I opened the door through which Soneji had disappeared, and it was suddenly as dark as a tomb. I leveled the barrel of the Glock in front of me and continued forward. This was the cellar, all right, his private hell on a very large scale.

Are you ready to die, Dr Cross?

There's no way you can stop it from happening.

I bobbed and weaved as best I could and the light from the flashlight shook all over the walls. I could see dim light, dusty lamps up ahead, so I turned off the flash. My lungs hurt. I couldn't breathe very well, but maybe some of the physical distress was claustrophobia and terror.

I didn't like it in his cellar. This is how Gary must have felt when he was just a boy. Was he telling us that? Letting us experience it?

'Jesus,' Groza muttered at my back. I figured that he felt what I felt, disoriented and afraid. The wind howled from somewhere inside the tunnel. We couldn't see much of anything up ahead.

You had to use your imagination in the dark, I was thinking as I proceeded forward. Soneji had learned how to do that as a boy. There were voices behind us now, but they were distant. The ghostly voices echoed off the walls. Nobody was hurrying to catch up with Soneji in the dark, dingy tunnel.

The brakes of a train screeched on the other side of the blackened stone walls. The subway was down here, just parallel to us. There was a stench of garbage and waste that kept getting worse the farther we walked.

I knew that street people lived in some of these tunnels. The NYPD had a Homeless Unit to deal with them.

'Anything there?' Groza muttered, fear and uncertainty in his voice. 'You see anything?'

'Nothing,' I whispered. I didn't want to make any more noise than we had to. I sucked in another harsh breath. I heard a train whistle on the other side of the stone walls.

There was dim light in parts of the tunnel. A scrim of garbage lay underfoot, discarded fast-food wrappers, torn and grossly soiled clothing. I had already seen a couple of oversized rats scurrying alongside my feet, out food shopping in the Big Apple.

Then I heard a scream right on top of me. My neck and back stiffened. It was Groza! He went down. I had no idea what had hit him. He didn't make another sound, didn't move on the tunnel floor.

I whirled around. Couldn't see anyone at first. The darkness seemed to swirl.

I caught a flash of Soneji's face. One eye and half his mouth in dark profile. He hit me before I could get the Glock up. Soneji screamed – a brutal, primal yell. No recognizable words.

He hit me with tremendous power. A punch to the left temple. I remembered how incredibly strong he was, and how crazy he had become. My ears rang, and my head was spinning. My legs were wobbly. He'd almost taken me out with the first punch. Maybe he could have. But he wanted to punish me, wanted his revenge, his payback.

He screamed again – this time inches from my face.

Hurt him back, I told myself. *Hurt him now, or you won't get another chance.*

Soneji's strength was as brutal as it had been the last time we met, especially fighting in close like this. He had me wrapped in his arms and I could smell his breath. He tried to crush me with his arms. White lights flickered and danced before my eyes. I was nearly out on my feet.

He screamed again. I butted with my head. It took him by surprise. His grip loosened, and I broke away for a second.

I threw the hardest punch of my life and heard the crunch of his jaw. Soneji didn't go down! What did it take to hurt him?

He came at me again, and I struck his left cheek. I felt bone crush under my fist. He screamed, then moaned, but he didn't fall, didn't stop coming after me.

'You can't hurt me,' he gasped, growled. 'You're going to die. You can't stop it from happening. You can't stop this now.'

Gary Soneji came at me again. I finally got the Glock out and raised it. *Hurt him, hurt him, kill him right now.*

I fired! And although it happened fast, it seemed like slow-motion to me. I thought I could *feel* the gunshot travel through Soneji's body. The shot bulldozed through his lower jaw. It must have blown his tongue away, his teeth.

What remained of Soneji reached out to me, tried to hold on, to claw at my face and throat. I pushed him away. *Hurt him, hurt him, kill him.*

He staggered several steps down the darkened tunnel. I don't know where he got the strength. I was too tired to chase him, but I knew I didn't have to.

He fell toward the stone floor. He dropped like a deadweight. As he hit the ground, the bomb in his pocket ignited. Gary Soneji exploded in flames. The tunnel behind him was illuminated for at least a hundred feet.

Soneji screamed for a few seconds, then he burned in silence – a human torch in his cellar. He had gone straight to hell.

It was finally over.

Chapter Sixty-Two

The Japanese have a saying – after victory, tighten your helmet cord. I tried to keep that in mind.

I was back in Washington early on Tuesday, and I spent the whole day at home with Nana and the kids and with Rosie the cat. The morning started when the kids prepared what they called a 'bubba-bath' for me. It got better from there. Not only didn't I tighten my helmet cord, I took the damn thing off.

I tried not to be upset by Soneji's horrible death, or his threat against me.

I'd lived with worse from him in the past. Much worse. Soneji was dead and gone from all of our lives. I had seen him blown to hell with my own eyes. I'd helped blow him there.

Still, I could hear his voice, his warning, his threat at different times during my day at home.

You're going to die. You can't stop it from happening.

I'm coming for you, from the grave if I have to.

Kyle Craig called from Quantico to congratulate me and ask how I was doing. Kyle still had an ulterior motive. He tried to suck me into his Mr Smith case, but I told him no. Definitely no way. I didn't have the heart for Mr Smith right now. He wanted me to meet his superagent Thomas Pierce. He asked if I'd read his faxes on Pierce. *No.*

That night I went to Christine's house, and I knew I had made the right decision about Mr Smith and the FBI's continuing problems with the case. I didn't spend the night because of the kids, but I could have. I wanted to. 'You promised you'd be around until we were both at least in our eighties. This is a pretty good start,' she said when I was leaving for the night.

On Wednesday, I had to go to the office to start closing down the Soneji case. I wasn't thrilled that I had killed him, but I was glad it was over. Everything but the blasted paperwork.

I got home from work around six. I was in the mood for another 'bubba-bath,' maybe some boxing lessons, a night with Christine.

I walked in the front door of my house – and all hell broke loose.

Chapter Sixty-Three

Nana and the kids were standing before me in the living room. Sampson, several detective friends, neighbors, my aunties, a few uncles, and all of their kids were with them. Jannie and Damon started the group yell on cue, 'Surprise, Daddy! Surprise party!' Then everybody else in kingdom come joined in. 'Surprise, Alex, surprise!'

'Who's Alex? Who's Daddy?' I played dumb at the door. 'What the hell is going on here?'

Toward the back of the room I could see Christine, at least her smiling face. I waved at her, even as I was being hugged and pounded on the back and shoulders by all my best friends in the world.

I thought Damon was acting a little too respectful, so I swooped him up in my arms (this was probably the last year I would be able to do it) and we hollered assorted sports and war cries, which seemed to fit the party scene.

It's not usually a very charitable idea to celebrate the death of another human being but, in this case, I thought a party was a terrific idea. It was an appropriate and fitting way to end what had been a sad and scary time for all of us. Somebody had hung a droopy, badly hand-painted banner over the doorway between the living room and dining area. The banner read: *Congratulations, Alex! Better luck next lifetime, Gary S!*

Sampson led me into the backyard, where even more friends were waiting in ambush. Sampson had on baggy black shorts, a pair of combat boots, and his shades. He wore a beat-up Homicide cap and had a silver loop in one ear. He was definitely ready to party, and so was I.

Detectives from all around DC had come to offer their hearty congratulations, but also to eat my food and drink my liquor.

Succulent kabobs and racks of baby-back ribs were arranged beside home-made breads, rolls, and an impressive array of hot-sauce bottles. It made my eyes water just to look at the feast. Aluminum tubs overflowed with beer and ale and soda pop on ice. There was fresh corn on the cob, colorful fruit salads, and summer pastas by the bowlful.

Sampson grabbed my arm tight, and hollered so I could hear him over the noise of joyful voices and also Toni Braxton wailing her heart out on the CD player. 'You party on, Sugar. Say hello to all your other guests, all your peeps. I plan to be here until closing time.'

'I'll catch you later,' I told him. 'Nice boots, nice shorts, nice legs.'

'Thank you, thank you, thank you. You got that son of a bitch, Alex! You did the right thing. May his evil, hair-bag ass burn and rot in hell. I'm just sorry I wasn't there with you.'

Christine had taken a quiet spot in the corner of the yard under our shade tree. She was talking with my favorite aunt, Tia, and my sister-in-law, Cilla. It was like her to put herself last on the greeting line.

I kissed Tia and Cilla, and then reached out and gave Christine a hug. I held her and didn't want to let go. 'Thank you for coming here for all this madness,' I said. 'You're the best surprise of all.'

She kissed me, and then we pulled apart. I think we were overly conscious that Damon and Jannie had never seen us together. Not like this anyway.

'Oh shit,' I muttered. 'Look there.'

The two little devil-demons *were* watching us. Damon winked outrageously, and Jannie made an okay sign with her busy and quick little fingers.

'They're way, way ahead of us,' Christine said and laughed. 'Figures, Alex. We should have known.'

'Why don't you two head on up to bed?' I kidded the kids.

'It's only six o'clock, Daddy!' Jannie yelped, but she was grinning and laughing and so was everybody else.

It was a wild, let-loose party and everybody quickly got into the spirit. The monkey of Gary Soneji was finally off my back. I spotted Nana talking to some of my police friends.

I heard what she was saying as I passed. It was pure Nana Mama. 'There is *no* history that I know of that has led from slavery to freedom, but there is sure a history from the slingshot to the Uzi,' she said to her audience of homicide detectives. My friends were grinning and nodding their heads as if they understood what she was saying, where she was coming from. I did. For better or for worse, Nana Mama had taught me how to think.

On the lighter side there was dancing to everything, from Marsalis to hip-hop. Nana even danced some. Sampson ran the barbecue in the backyard, featuring hot-and-spicy sausages, barbecued chicken, and more ribs than you would need for a Redskins tailgate party.

I was called upon to play a few tunes, so I banged out ''S Wonderful,' and then a jazzy version of 'Ja – da, ja – da, ja – da, jing, jing, jing.'

'Here's a stupid little melody,' Jannie hammed it up at my side, 'but it's so *soothing* and *appealing* to me.'

I grabbed some slow-dances with Christine as the sun set and the night progressed. The fit of our bodies was still magical and right. Just as I remembered it from the Rainbow Room. She seemed amazingly comfortable with my family and friends. I could tell that they *approved* of her big time.

I sang along with a Seal tune as we danced in the moonlight. 'No, we're never going to survive – Unless – We get a little cra-azy.'

'Seal would be sooo proud,' she whispered in my ear.

'Mmm. Sure he would.'

'You are such a good, smooth dancer,' she said against my cheek.

'For a gumshoe and a flatfoot,' I said. 'I only dance with you, though.'

She laughed, and then punched my side. 'Don't you lie! I *saw* you dancing with John Sampson.'

'Yes, but it didn't mean anything. It was only for the cheap sex.'

Christine laughed and I could feel a small quiver in her stomach. It reminded me of how much life she had in her. It reminded me that she wanted kids, and that she ought to have them. I remembered everything about our night at the Rainbow Room, and afterward at the Astor. I felt as if I had known her forever. *She's the one, Alex.*

'I have summer school in the morning,' Christine finally told me. It was already past midnight. 'I brought my car. I'm okay. I've been drinking kiddie cocktails mostly. You enjoy your party, Alex.'

'You sure?'

Her voice was firm. 'Absolutely. I'm fine. I'm cool. And I'm outta here.'

We kissed for a long time, and when we had to come up for air, we both laughed. I walked her out to her car. 'Let me drive you home at least,' I protested as I stood with my arms around her. 'I want to. I insist.'

'No, then my car would still be here. *Please* enjoy your party. Be with your friends. You can see me tomorrow, if you like. I'd like that. I won't take no for an answer.'

We kissed again, and then Christine got in her car and drove away to Mitchellville.

I missed her already.

Chapter Sixty-Four

I could still feel Christine's body against me, smell her new Donna Karan perfume, hear the special music of her voice. Sometimes you just get lucky in life. Sometimes the universe takes care of you pretty good. I wandered back to the party taking place in my house.

Several of my detective friends were still hanging out, including Sampson. There was a joke going around about Soneji having 'angel lust.' 'Angel lust' was what they called cadavers at the morgue with an erection. The party was going *there*.

Sampson and I drank way too much beer, and then some B&B on the back-porch steps – after everyone else was long gone.

'Now *that* was a hell of a party,' Two-John said. 'The all-singing, all-dancing model.'

'It was pretty damn good. Of course, we are still *standing*. Sitting up anyway. I feel real good, but I'm going to feel pretty bad.'

Sampson was grinning and his shades were placed slightly crooked on his face. His huge elbows rested on his knees. You could strike a match on his arms or legs, probably even on his head.

'I'm proud of you, man. We all are. You definitely got the twenty-thousand-pound gorilla off your back. I haven't seen you smiling so much in a long, long while. More I see of Ms Christine Johnson, the more I like her, and I liked her to begin with.'

We were on the porch steps, looking over Nana's garden of wildflowers, her roses that bloomed so abundantly, and garden-lilies, looking over the remains of the party, all that food and booze.

It was late. It was already tomorrow. The wildflower garden had been there since we were little kids. The smell of bone meal and fresh dirt seemed particularly ageless and reassuring that night.

'You remember the first summer we met?' I asked John. 'You called me watermelon-ass, which burned me, because it was complete bullshit. I had a tight butt, even then.'

'We tangled good in Nana's garden, right in the brierpatch over yonder. I couldn't believe you would tangle with me. Nobody else would do that, still don't. Even back then you didn't know your limitations.'

I smiled at Sampson. He finally had taken off his shades. It always surprises me how sensitive and warm his eyes are. 'You call me watermelon-ass, we'll tangle again.'

Sampson continued to nod and grin. Come to think of it, I hadn't seen him smiling so much in a long while. Life was good tonight. The best it had been in a while.

'You really like Ms Christine. I think you've found yourself another special person. I'm sure of it. You're down for the count, champ.'

'You jealous?' I asked him.

'Yeah, of course I am. Damn straight. Christine is all that and a bag of chips. But I would just fuck it up if I ever found somebody sweet and nice like that. You're easy to be with, Sugar. Always have been, even when you had your little watermelon-ass. Tough when you have to be, but you can show your feelings, too. Whatever it is, Christine likes you a lot. Almost as much as you like her.'

Sampson pushed himself up off the sagging back-porch step, which I needed to replace soon.

'God willing, I'm going to walk on home. Actually, I'm going to Cee Walker's house. The beautiful diva left the party a little early, but she was kind enough to give me a key. I'll be back, pick up my car in the morning. Best not to drive when you can hardly walk.'

'Best not to,' I agreed. 'Thanks for the party.'

Sampson waved goodbye, saluted, and then he went round the corner of the house, which he bumped on the way out.

I was alone on the back-porch steps, staring out over Nana's moonlit garden, smiling like the fool I can be sometimes, but maybe not often enough.

I heard Sampson call out. Then his deep laugh came from the front of the house.

'Good night, watermelon-ass.'

Chapter Sixty-Five

I came fully awake, and I wondered what I was afraid of, what the hell was happening here. My first conscious fear was that *I was having a heart attack in my own bed.*

I was spacey and woozy, still flying high from the party. My heart was beating loudly, thundering in my chest.

I thought that I had heard a deep, low, pounding noise from somewhere inside the house. The noise was *close*. It sounded as if a heavy weight, maybe a club, had been striking something down the hallway.

My eyes weren't adjusted to the darkness yet. I listened for another noise.

I was frightened. I couldn't remember where I left my Glock last night. What could possibly make that heavy *pounding* sound inside the house?

I listened with all the concentration I could command.

The refrigerator purred down in the kitchen.

A distant truck changed gears on the mean streets.

Still, something about that sound, the pounding noise, bothered me a lot. *Had there even been a sound?* I wondered. *Was it just the first warnings of a powerful headache coming on?*

Before I realized what was happening, a shadowy figure rose from the other side of the bed.

Soneji! He's kept his promise. He's here in the house!

'Aaagghhgghh!' the attacker screamed and swung at me with a large club of some sort.

I tried to roll, but my body and mind weren't cooperating. I'd had too much to drink, too much party, too much fun.

I felt a powerful blow to my shoulder. My whole body went numb. I tried to scream, but suddenly I had no voice. I couldn't scream. I could barely move.

The club descended swiftly again – this time it struck my lower back.

Someone was trying to beat me to death. Jesus, God. I thought of the loud pounding sounds. *Had he gone to Nana's room first? Damon and Jannie's? What was happening in our house?*

I reached for him and managed to grab his arm. I yanked hard and he shrieked again, a high-pitched sound, but definitely a man's voice.

Soneji? How could it be? I'd seen him die in the tunnels of Grand Central Station.

What was happening to me? Who was in my bedroom? Who was upstairs in our house?

'Jannie? Damon? . . .' I finally mumbled, tried to call to them. *'Nana? Nana?'*

I began scratching at his chest, his arms, felt something sticky, probably drawing blood. Then my left wrist went numb. I was fighting with only one arm now, and barely able to do that.

'Who are you? What are you doing? *Damon! Damon!*' I called out again. Much louder this time.

He broke loose and I fell out of the bed, face first. The floor came at me hard, *struck*, and my face went numb.

My whole body was on fire. I began to throw up on the carpet.

The bat, the sledgehammer, the crowbar – whatever in hell it was – came down again and seemed to split me in two. I was burning up with pain.

I could feel and smell blood everywhere around me on the floor. My blood?

'I told you there was no way to stop me!' he screamed. 'I told you.'

I looked up and saw his gun, thought I recognized the face looming above me. *Gary Soneji? Could it possibly be Soneji? How could that possibly be? It couldn't!*

He began shooting. I understood that I was dying, and I didn't want to die. I wanted to run, to see my kids one more time. Just one more look at them.

I knew I couldn't stop the attack. Knew there was nothing I could do to stop this horror from happening.

I thought of Nana and Jannie, Damon, Christine. My heart ached for them. *Then I let God do His will.*

Part Four

Thomas Pierce

Chapter Sixty-Six

M atthew Lewis happily drove the graveyard shift on the city bus line that traveled along East Capitol Street in DC. He was absently whistling a Marvin Gaye song, 'What's Goin' On,' as he piloted his bus through the night.

He had driven the same route for nineteen years and was mostly glad to have the work. He also enjoyed the solitude. Lewis had always been a fairly deep thinker, according to his friends and Alva, his wife of twenty years. He was a history buff, and interested in government, sometimes a little sociology, too. He had developed the interests in his native Jamaica and had kept up with them.

For the past few months, he had been listening to self-improvement tapes from an outfit called the Teaching Company, in Virginia. As he rode along East Capitol at five in the morning, he was really getting into an excellent lecture called 'The Good King – the American Presidency Since the Depression.' Sometimes he'd knock off two or three lectures in a single night, or maybe he'd listen to a particularly good tape a couple of times in a night.

He saw the sudden movement out of the corner of his eye. He swerved the steering wheel. The brakes screeched. His bus skidded hard right and wound up diagonally across East Capitol.

The bus emitted a loud hiss. There wasn't any traffic coming, thank goodness, just a string of green lights as far as he could see.

Matthew Lewis threw open the bus doors and climbed out. He hoped he'd missed whoever, or whatever, had run into the street.

He wasn't sure, though, and he was afraid of what he might find. Except for the drone of his tape inside the bus, it was quiet. This was so weird and as bad as can be, he thought to himself.

Then he saw an elderly black woman lying in the street. She was wearing a long blue-striped bathrobe. Her robe was open and he could see her red nightgown. Her feet were bare. His heart bucked dangerously.

He ran across the street to help her, and thought he was going to be sick. In his headlights he saw that her nightgown wasn't red. It was bright-red blood, all over her. The sight was gruesome and awful. It wasn't the worst thing he'd encountered in his years on the night route, but it was right up there.

The woman's eyes were open and she was still conscious. She reached out a frail, thin arm toward him. *Must be domestic violence*, he thought. *Or maybe a robbery at her home.*

'Please help us,' Nana Mama whispered. 'Please help us.'

Chapter Sixty-Seven

Fifth Street was blocked off and completely barricaded to traffic. John Sampson abandoned his black Nissan and ran the rest of the way to Alex's house. Police cruiser and ambulance sirens were wailing everywhere on the familiar street that he almost thought of as his own.

Sampson ran as he never had before, in the grip of the coldest fear of his life. His feet pounded heavily on the sidewalk stones. His heart felt heavy, ready to break. He couldn't catch a breath, and he was certain he would throw up if he didn't stop running this second. The hangover from the night before had dulled his senses, but not nearly enough.

Metro police personnel were still arriving at the confused, noisy, throbbing scene. Sampson pushed his way past the neighborhood looky-loos. His contempt for them had never been more obvious or more intense. People were crying everywhere Sampson looked – people he knew, neighbors and friends of Alex. He heard Alex's name being spoken in whispers.

As he reached the familiar wooden picket fence that surrounded the Cross property, he heard something that turned his stomach inside out. He had to steady himself against the whitewashed fence.

'They're all dead inside. The whole Cross family gone,' a pock-faced woman in the crowd was shooting off her mouth. She looked like a character from the TV show *Cops*, had the same crude lack of sensitivity.

He spun round toward the source of the words, toward the hurt. Sampson gave the woman a glazed look and pushed forward into the yard, past collapsible sawhorses and yellow crime-scene tape.

He took the front porch steps in two long, athletic strides, and nearly collided with EMS medics hurrying a litter out of the living room.

Sampson stopped cold on the Crosses' front porch. He couldn't believe any of this. Little Jannie was on the litter and she looked so small. He bent over, and then collapsed hard on his knees. The porch shook beneath his weight.

A low moan escaped his mouth. He was no longer strong, no longer brave. His heart was breaking and he choked back a sob.

When she saw him, Jannie started to cry. 'Uncle John, Uncle John.' She said his name in the tiniest, saddest, hurt voice.

Jannie isn't dead, Jannie is alive, Sampson thought, and the words almost tumbled out of his mouth. He wanted to shout the truth to the looky-loos. *Stop your damn rumors and lies!* He wanted to know everything, all at once, but that just wasn't possible.

Sampson leaned in close to Jannie, his goddaughter, whom he loved as if she were his own child. Her nightgown was smeared with blood. The coppery smell of blood was strong and he was almost sick again.

More blood ribboned through Jannie's tight, carefully braided hair. She was so proud of her braids, her beautiful hair. *Oh, dear God. How could this happen? How could it be? He remembered her singing 'Ja – da, ja – da,' just the night before.*

'You're okay, baby,' Sampson whispered, the words catching like barbed wire in his throat. 'I'm going to be back here with you in a minute. You're okay, Jannie. I need to run upstairs. I'll be right back, baby. Be right back. Promise you.'

'What about Damon? What about my daddy?' Jannie whimpered as she softly cried.

Her eyes were wide with fear, with a terror that made Sampson's heart break all over again. She was just a little girl. How could anyone do this?

'Everybody's okay, baby. They're okay,' Sampson whispered again. His tongue was thick, his mouth as dry as sandpaper. He could barely get out the words. *Everybody's okay, baby.* He prayed that was true.

The EMS medics did their best to wave Sampson away, and they carried Jannie down to a waiting ambulance. More ambulances were still arriving in front, and more police cruisers as well.

He pushed his way into the house, which was crowded with police – both street officers and detectives. When the first alarm came, half of the precinct must have rushed over to the Cross house. He had never seen so many cops in one place.

He was late as usual – the *late* John Sampson, Alex liked to call him. He'd slept at a woman's house, Cee Walker's, and couldn't be reached right away. His beeper was off, taking a night off after Alex's party – after the big celebration.

Someone knew Alex would have his guard down, Sampson thought, being a homicide detective already. *Who knew? Who did this terrible thing?*

What in the name of God happened here?

Chapter Sixty-Eight

Sampson bolted up the narrow, twisting stairs to the second floor of the house. He wanted to shout above the blaring noise, the buzz of the incipient police investigation, to yell Alex's name, to see him appear out of one of the bedrooms.

He had had way too much to drink the night before and he was reeling, feeling shaky, rubbery all over. He rushed into Damon's room and let out a deep moan. The boy was being transferred from his bed to a litter. Damon looked so much like his father, so much like Alex when he was Damon's age.

He looked worse than Jannie. The side of his face was beaten raw. One of Damon's eyes was closed, swollen to twice its size. Deep purple and scarlet bruises were around the eye. There were contusions and lacerations.

Gary Soneji was dead – he'd gone down in Grand Central Station. He couldn't have done this horrible thing at Alex's house.

And yet, he had promised that he would!

Nothing made sense to Sampson yet. He wished he were dreaming this nightmare, but knew he wasn't.

A detective named Rakeem Powell grabbed him by the shoulder, grabbed him hard and shook him. 'Damon's all right, John. Somebody came in here, beat the living hell out of the kids. Looks like he just used fists. Hard punches. Didn't mean to kill them, though, or maybe the cowardly fuck couldn't finish the job. Who the hell knows at this point. Damon's all right. *John?* Are you all right?'

Sampson pushed Rakeem away, threw him off impatiently. 'What about Alex? Nana?'

'Nana was beaten bad. Bus driver found her on the street, took her to St Tony's. She's conscious, but she's an old woman. Skin rips when they're old. Alex got shot in his bedroom, John. They're up there with him.'

'Who's in there?' Sampson groaned. He was close to tears, and he never cried. He couldn't help himself now, couldn't hide his feelings.

'Christ, who isn't?' Rakeem said and shook his head. 'EMS, us, FBI. Kyle Craig is here.'

Sampson broke away from Rakeem Powell and lunged toward the bedroom. *Everybody wasn't dead inside the house – but Alex had been shot. Somebody came here to get him! Who could it have been?*

Sampson tried to go into Alex's bedroom, but he was held back by men he didn't know – probably FBI from the look of them.

Kyle Craig was in the room. He knew that much. The FBI was here already. 'Tell Kyle I'm here,' he told the men at the door. 'Tell Kyle Craig it's Sampson.'

One of the FBI agents ducked inside. Kyle came out immediately, pushed his way into the hall to Sampson.

'Kyle, what the hell?' Sampson tried to talk. '*Kyle*, what happened?'

'He's been shot twice. Shot and beaten,' Kyle said. 'I need to talk to you, John. Listen to me, just *listen* to me, will you?'

Chapter Sixty-Nine

S ampson tried to hold back his fears, his true feelings, tried to control the chaos in his mind. Detectives and police personnel were clustered at the bedroom door in the narrow hallway. A couple of them were crying. Others were trying not to.

None of this could be happening!

Sampson turned away from the bedroom. He was afraid he was going to lose it, something he never did. Kyle hadn't stopped talking, but he couldn't really follow what Kyle was saying. He couldn't concentrate on the FBI man's words.

He inhaled deeply, trying to fight off the reverberations of shock. It *was* shock, wasn't it? Then hot tears started to stream down his cheeks. He didn't care if Kyle saw. The pain in his heart cut so deep, cut right to the bone. His nerve endings were already rubbed raw. Never anything like this before.

'Listen to me, John,' Kyle said, but Sampson wasn't listening.

Sampson's body slumped heavily against the wall. He asked Kyle how he'd gotten here so fast. Kyle had an answer, always an answer for everything. Still – nothing was really making sense to Sampson, not a word of it.

He was looking at something over the FBI man's shoulder. Sampson couldn't believe it. Through the window, he could see an FBI helicopter. It was landing in the vacant lot just across Fifth Street. Things were getting stranger and stranger.

A figure lurched out of the helicopter, crouched under the rotor blades, then started toward the Cross house. It almost seemed as if he were levitating above the blowing grass in the yard.

The man was tall and slender, with dark sunglasses, the kind with small round lenses. His long blond hair was bound in a ponytail. He didn't look like FBI.

There was definitely something different about him, something radical for the Bureau. He almost looked angry as he pushed the looky-loos away. He also looked as if he were in charge, at least in charge of himself.

Now . . . what was this? Sampson thought. *What's going on here?*

'Who the hell is that?' he asked Kyle Craig. 'Who is that, Kyle? Who is that goddamn ponytailed asshole?'

Chapter Seventy

My name is Thomas Pierce, but the press usually call me 'Doc.' I was once a medical student at Harvard. I graduated, but never worked a day in a hospital, never practiced medicine. Now I'm part of the Behavioral Science Unit of the FBI. I'm thirty-three years old. Truthfully, the only place I might look like a 'Doc' is in an episode of the TV show *ER*.

I was rushed from the training compound at Quantico to Washington early that morning. I had been ordered to investigate the attack on Dr Alex Cross and members of his immediate family. To be candid, I didn't want to be involved in the case for a number of reasons. Most important, I was already part of a difficult investigation, one that had drained nearly all of my energy – the Mr Smith case.

Instinctively, I knew that some people would be angry with me because of the shooting of Alex Cross and my being at the crime scene so quickly. I knew with absolute certainty I would be seen as opportunistic, when that couldn't be farther from the truth.

There was nothing I could do about it now. The Bureau wanted me there. So I put it out of my mind. I tried to anyway. I was performing my job, the same as Dr Cross would have done for me under comparably unfortunate circumstances.

I was certain of one thing, though, from the moment I arrived. I knew I looked as shocked and outraged as anyone else standing sentinel in the crowd gathered at the house on Fifth Street. I probably looked angry to some of them. I *was* angry. My mind was full of chaos, fear of the unknown, fear of failure, too. I was close to the state of mind described as 'toast.' Too many days, weeks, months in a row with Mr Smith. Now this new bit of blasphemy.

I had listened to Alex Cross speak once at a profiler seminar at the University of Chicago. He had made an impression. I hoped that he would live, but the reports were all bad. Nothing I'd heard so far left room for hope.

I figured that was why they'd brought me in on the case right away. The vicious attack on Cross would mean major headlines, and put intense pressure on both the Washington police and the Bureau. I was there on Fifth Street for the simplest of reasons – to relieve the pressure.

I felt an unpleasant aura, residue from the recent violence, as I approached the tidy, white-shingled Cross house. Some policemen I passed were red-eyed and a few seemed almost to be in shock. It was all very strange and disquieting.

I wondered if Alex Cross had died since I had left Quantico. I already had a sixth sense for the terrible and unexpected violence that had taken place inside the modest, peaceful-looking house. I wished that none of the others were at the crime scene, so I could absorb everything without all these distractions.

That was what I had been brought here to do. Observe the scene of unbelievable mayhem. Get a gut feeling for what might have happened in the early hours of the morning. Figure everything out quickly and efficiently.

Out of the corner of my eye, I saw Kyle Craig coming out of the house. He was in a hurry, as he always is. I sighed. *Now it begins, now it begins.*

Kyle crossed Fifth Street in a quick jog. He came up to me and we shook hands. I was glad to see him. Kyle is smart and very organized, and also supportive of those he works with. He's famous for getting things done.

'They just moved Alex,' he said. 'He's hanging on.'

'What's the prognosis? Tell me, Kyle.' I needed to know everything. I was there to collect facts. This was the start of it.

Kyle averted his eyes. 'Not good. They say he won't live. They're sure he won't live.'

Chapter Seventy-One

The press corps intercepted Kyle and me as we headed toward the Cross house. There were already a couple dozen reporters and cameramen at the scene. The vultures effectively blocked our way, wouldn't let us pass. They knew who Kyle was and possibly they knew about me, too.

'Why is the FBI already involved?' one of them shouted above the street noise and general commotion. Two news helicopters fluttered overhead. They loved this sort of disaster. 'We hear this is connected to the Soneji case. Is that true?'

'Let me talk to them,' Kyle whispered close to my ear.

I shook my head. 'They'll want to talk to me about it anyway. They'll find out who I am. Let's get the silly shit over with.'

Kyle frowned, but then he nodded slowly. I tried to control my impatience as I walked toward the horde of reporters.

I waved my hands over my head and that quieted some of them. The media are extremely visual, I've learned the hard way, even the print journalists, the so-called wordsmiths. They all watch far too many movies. Visual signals work best with them.

'I'll answer your questions,' I volunteered and served up a thin smile, 'as best I can anyway.'

'First question, who are you?' a man with a scraggly red beard and Salvation Army store taste in clothes hollered from the front of the pack. He looked like the reclusive novelist Thomas Harris, and maybe he was.

'That's an easy one,' I answered, 'I'm Thomas Pierce. I'm with BSU.'

That quieted the reporters for a moment. Those who didn't recognize my face knew the name. The fact that I'd been brought in on the Cross case was news in itself. Camera flashes exploded in front of me, but I was used to them by now.

'Is Alex Cross still alive?' someone called out. I had expected that to be the *first* question, but there's no way to predict with the press corps.

'Dr Cross is alive. As you can see, I just got here, so I don't know much. So far, we have no suspects, no theories, no leads, nothing particularly interesting to talk about,' I said.

'What about the Mr Smith case?' a woman reporter shouted at me. She was a dark-haired anchor-person type, perky as a chipmunk. 'Are you putting Mr Smith on hold now? How can you work two big cases? What's up, Doc?' the reporter said and smiled. She was obviously smarter and wittier than she looked.

I winced, rolled my eyes, and smiled back at her. 'No suspects, no theories, no leads, nothing interesting to talk about,' I repeated. 'I have to go inside. The interview's over. Thanks for your concern. I know it's genuine in this god-awful case. I admire Alex Cross, too.'

'Did you say admire or admired?' another reporter shouted at me from the back.

'Why did they bring you in on this, Mr Pierce? Is Mr Smith involved?'

I couldn't help arching my eyebrows at the question. I felt an unpleasant itch in my brain. 'I'm here because I get lucky sometimes, all right? Maybe I'll get lucky again. I have to go into the trenches now. I promise that I'll tell you if and when we have anything. I sincerely doubt that Mr Smith attacked Alex Cross last night. And I said *admire*, present tense.'

I pulled Kyle Craig out of there with me, holding on to his arm for support as much as anything. He grinned as soon as we had our backs to the horde.

'That was pretty goddamn good,' he said. 'I think you managed to confuse the hell out of them, even beyond the usual blank stares.'

'Mad dogs of the fourth estate,' I shrugged. 'Smears of blood on their lips and cheeks. They couldn't care less about Cross or his family. Not one question about the kids. Edison said, "We don't know a millionth of one percent about *anything!*" The press doesn't get that. They want everything in black-and-white. They mistake simplicity and simple-mindedness for the truth.'

'Make nice with the DC police,' Kyle cajoled, or maybe he was giving me a friendly warning. 'This is an emotional time for them. That's Detective John Sampson on the porch. He's a friend of Alex. Alex's closest friend in fact.'

'Great,' I muttered. 'Just who I don't want to see right now.'

I glanced at Detective Sampson. He looked like a bad storm about to happen. *I didn't want to be here. Didn't want or need any of this.*

Kyle patted my shoulder. 'We need you on this one. Soneji promised this would happen,' he suddenly told me. 'He *predicted* it.'

I stared at Kyle Craig. He'd delivered his stunning thunderbolt of news in his usual deadpan, understated way, sort of like Sam Shepard on Quaalude.

'Say again? What was that last bit?'

'Gary Soneji warned Alex that he'd get him, even if he died. Soneji said he couldn't be stopped. It looks like he made good on his promise. I want you to tell me how. Tell me how Soneji did it. *That's* why you're here, Thomas.'

Chapter Seventy-Two

My nerves were already on edge. My awareness was heightened to a level I found almost painful. I couldn't believe I was here in Washington, involved in this case. *Tell me how Gary Soneji did this?* Tell me how it could have happened. That's all I had to do.

The press had one thing right. It's fair to say that I am the FBI's current hotshot profiler. I should be used to graphic, violent crime scenes, but I'm not. It stirs up too much white noise, too many memories of Isabella. *Of Isabella and myself. Of another time and place, another life.*

I have a sixth sense, which is nothing paranormal, nothing like that at all. It's just that I can process raw information and data better than most people, better than most policemen anyway. I feel things very powerfully, and sometimes my 'felt' hunches have been useful not only to the FBI but also to Interpol and Scotland Yard.

My methods differ radically from the Federal Bureau's famed investigative process, however. In spite of what they say, the Bureau's Behavioral Science Unit believes in formalistic investigation with much less room for surprising hunches. I subscribe to a belief in the widest possible array of hunches and instincts, followed by the most exacting science.

The FBI and I are polar opposites, yet to their credit they continue to use me. Until I screw up badly, which I could do at any moment. Like right now.

I had been working hard at Quantico, reporting in on the gruesome and complex 'Mr Smith' investigation, when the news arrived about the attack on Cross. Actually, I had been in Quantico for less than a day, having just returned from England where 'Smith' was blazing his killer trail and I was in lukewarm pursuit.

Now I was in Washington, at the center of a raging storm over the Cross family attack. I looked at my watch, a TAG Heuer 6000 given to me by Isabella, the only material possession I really care about. It was a few minutes past eight when I entered the Cross frontyard. I noted the time. Something about it bothered me, but I wasn't sure what it was yet.

I stopped beside a battered and rusting EMS truck. The roof lights were flashing, the rear doors thrown open. I looked inside and saw a boy – it had to be Damon Cross.

The boy had been badly beaten. His face and arms were bloody, but he was alert and talking in a soft voice to the medics, who tried to be gentle and comforting.

'Why wouldn't he have killed the children? Why just thrash out at them?' Kyle said. We had the same mind-set on that question.

'His heart wasn't in it.' I said the first thing that came into my head, the first *feeling* I had. 'He was compelled to make a symbolic gesture toward the Cross children, but no more than that.'

I turned to look at Kyle. 'I don't know, Kyle. Maybe he was frightened. Or in a hurry. Maybe he was afraid of waking Cross.' All of those thoughts invaded my mind, almost in an instant. *I felt as if I had briefly met the attacker.*

I looked up at the old house, the Cross house. 'Okay, let's go to the bedroom, if you don't mind. I want to see it before the techies do their number in there. I need to see Alex Cross's room. I don't know, but I think something is seriously fucked-up here. This certainly wasn't done by Gary Soneji *or* his ghost.'

'How do you know that?' Kyle grabbed my arm and made eye contact. 'How can you know for sure?'

'Soneji would have killed the two kids and the grandmother.'

Chapter Seventy-Three

Alex Cross's blood was spattered everywhere in the corner bedroom. I could see where a bullet had exited through the window directly behind Cross's bed. The glass fracture was clean and the radial lines even: The shooter had fired from a standing position, directly across the bed. I made my first notes, and also a quick sketch of the small, unadorned bedroom.

There was other 'evidence.' A shoe print had been discovered near the cellar. The Metro police were working on a 'walking picture' of the assailant. A white male had been spotted around midnight in the mostly black neighborhood. For a moment, I was almost glad I'd been rushed up here from Virginia. There was so much raw data to take in and process, almost too much. The mussed bed, where Cross had apparently slept on top of a hand-sewn quilt. Photos of his children on the walls.

Alex Cross had been moved to St Anthony's Hospital, but his bedroom was intact, just the way the mysterious assailant had left it.

Had he left the room like this on purpose? Was this his first message to us? Of course it was.

I looked at the papers still out on Cross's small work desk. They were notes on Gary Soneji. They had been left undisturbed by the assailant. Was that important?

Someone had taped a short poem to the wall over the desk. *Wealth covers sins – the poor/Are naked as a pin.*

Cross had been reading a book called *Push*, a novel. A piece of lined yellow paper was stuck inside, so I read it: *Write the talented author about her wonderful book!*

The time I spent in the room passed like a snap of the fingers, almost a mind fugue. I drank several cups of coffee. I remembered a line from the offbeat TV show *Twin Peaks*, 'Damn fine cup of coffee, and hot!'

I had been inside Cross's bedroom for almost an hour and a half, lost in forensic detail, hooked on the case in spite of myself. It was a nasty and disturbing puzzle, but a very intriguing one. Everything about the case was intense, and highly unusual.

I heard footsteps thumping outside in the hallway and looked up, my concentration interrupted. The bedroom door suddenly swung open and thudded against the wall.

Kyle Craig popped his head inside. He looked concerned. His face was white as chalk. Something had happened. 'I have to go right now. Alex has gone into cardiac arrest!'

Chapter Seventy-Four

'I'll go with you,' I said to Kyle. I could tell that Kyle badly needed company. I wanted to see Alex Cross before he died, if that was what it had come to, and it sounded like it, felt like it to me.

On the ride over to St Anthony's I gently questioned Kyle about the extent of Dr Cross's injuries and the tenor of concern at the hospital. I also made a guess about the cause of the cardiac arrest.

'It sounds like it's due to blood loss. There's a lot of blood in the bedroom. It's all over the sheets, the floor, the walls. Soneji was obsessed with blood, right? I heard that at Quantico before I left this morning.'

Kyle was quiet for a moment in the car, and then he asked the question I expected. I'm sometimes a step or two ahead in conversations.

'Do you ever miss it, not being a doctor anymore?'

I shook my head, frowned a little. 'I really don't. Something delicate and essential broke inside me when Isabella died. It will never be repaired, Kyle, at least I don't think so. I couldn't be a doctor now. I find it hard to believe in healing anymore.'

'I'm sorry,' he whispered solemnly.

'And I'm sorry about your friend. I'm sorry about Alex Cross,' I said to him.

In the spring of 1993, I had just graduated from Harvard Medical School. My life seemed to be spiraling upward at dizzying speed, when the woman I loved more than life itself was murdered in our apartment in Cambridge. Isabella Calais was my lover, and she was my best friend. She was one of the first victims of 'Mr Smith.'

After the murder, I never showed up at Massachusetts General, where I'd been accepted as an intern. I didn't even contact them. I knew I would never practice medicine. In an odd way, my life had ended with Isabella's, at least that was how I saw it.

Eighteen months after the murder, I was accepted into the FBI's Behavioral Science Unit, what some wags call the 'b.s. group.' It was what I wanted to do, what I needed to do. Once I had proved myself in the BSU, I asked to be put on the Mr Smith case. My superiors fought the move at first, but finally they gave in.

'Maybe you'll change your mind one day,' Kyle said. I had a feeling that he personally believed I would. Kyle likes to believe that everyone thinks as he does: With perfectly clear logic and a minimum of emotional baggage.

'I don't think so,' I told him, without sounding argumentative, or even too firm on the point. 'Who knows, though?'

'Maybe after you finally catch Smith.' He persisted with his point.

'Yes, maybe then,' I said.

'You don't think Smith—' he started to say, but then backed off from the absurd notion that Mr Smith could be involved with the attack here in Washington.

'No,' I said, 'I do not. Smith couldn't have made this attack. They would all be dead and mutilated if he had.'

Chapter Seventy-Five

At St Anthony's Hospital, I left Kyle and roamed about playing 'Doc.' It didn't feel too bad to be working in a hospital, contemplating what it might have been like. I tried to find out as much as I could about Alex Cross's condition, and his chances of surviving his wounds.

The staff nurses and doctors were surprised that I understood so much about trauma and gunshot wounds, but no one pressed me as to how or why. They were too busy trying to save Alex Cross's life. He had done pro bono work at the hospital for years and no one there could bear to let him die. Even the porters liked and respected Cross, calling him a 'regular brother.'

I learned that the cardiac arrest had been caused by the loss of blood, as I had guessed. According to the doctor in charge, Alex Cross had gone into massive arrest minutes after he arrived at the ER. His blood pressure had dipped dangerously low: 60 over 0.

The staff's prognosis was that he could probably die during the surgery necessary to repair his massive internal injuries, but that he would definitely die without the surgery. The more I heard, the more I was certain they were right. An old saying of my mother's ran through my head, 'May his body rise to heaven, before the devil finds out he's dead.'

Kyle caught up with me in the busy and chaotic hallway on the fourth floor at St Anthony's. A lot of people working there knew Cross personally. They were all visibly upset and helpless to do anything about it. The hospital scene was raw and emotional, and I couldn't help being swept up in the tragedy, even more so than I had been at the Cross house.

Kyle was still pale, his brow furrowed and punctuated by blisters of sweat. His eyes had a distant look as he gazed down the hospital corridor. 'What did you find out? I know you've been poking around,' he said. He rightly suspected that I would have already conducted my own mini investigation. He knew my style, even my motto: Assume nothing, question everything.

'He's in surgery now. He's not expected to make it.' I gave him the bad news. Unsentimental, the way I knew he wanted it. 'That's what the doctors believe. But what the hell do doctors know?' I added.

'Is that what you think?' Kyle asked.

The pupils of his eyes were the tiniest, darkest points. He was taking this as badly as I'd seen him react to anything since I'd known him. He was being very emotional for Kyle. I understood how close he and Cross had been.

I sighed and shut my eyes. I wondered if I should tell him what I really thought. Finally, I opened them. I said, 'It might be better if he doesn't make it, Kyle.'

Chapter Seventy-Six

'C'mon with me,' he said, pulling me along. 'I want you to meet someone. C'mon.'

I followed Kyle down one floor to a room on three. The patient in the room was an elderly black woman.

Her head was swathed in Webril, a stretchy woven bandage. The head bandage resembled a turban. A few wisps of gray hair hung loose from the dressing. Telfa bandages covered the abrasions on her face.

There were two IV lines, 'cut downs,' one for blood and one for fluids and antibiotics. She was hooked to a cardiac monitor.

She looked up at us as if we were intruders, but then she recognized Kyle.

'How is Alex? Tell me the truth,' she said in a hoarse, nearly whispering voice that still managed to be firm. 'No one here will tell me the truth. Will you, Kyle?'

'He's in surgery now, Nana. We won't know anything until he comes out,' Kyle said, 'and maybe not even then.'

The elderly woman's eyes narrowed. She shook her head sadly.

'I asked you for the truth. I deserve at least that much. *Now, how is Alex?* Kyle, is Alex still alive?'

Kyle sighed loudly. It was a weary sound, and a sad one. He and Alex Cross had been working together for years.

'Alex's condition is extremely grave,' I said, as gently as I could. 'That means—'

'I know what grave means,' she said. 'I taught school for forty-seven years. English, history, Boolean algebra.'

'I'm sorry,' I said, 'I didn't mean to sound condescending.' I paused for a second or two, then continued to answer her question.

'The internal injuries involve a kind of "ripping," probably with a high degree of contamination to the wounds. The most serious wound is to his abdomen. The shot passed through the liver and apparently nicked the common hepatic artery. That's what I was told. The bullet lodged in the rear of the stomach, where it's now pressing onto the spinal column.'

She winced, but she was listening intently, waiting for me to finish. I was thinking that if Alex Cross was anything near as strong as this woman, as willful, then he must be something special as a detective.

I went on.

'Because of the nick to the artery there was considerable blood loss. The contents of the stomach itself and the small bowel can be sources of E. coli infection. There's a danger of inflammation of the abdominal cavity – peritonitis, and possibly pancreatitis, all of which can be fatal. The gunshot wound is the *injury*, the infection is the *complication*. The second shot went through his left wrist, but missed the radial artery and exited, without shattering bone. That's what we know so far. That's the truth.'

I stopped at that point. My eyes never left those of the elderly woman, and hers never left mine.

'Thank you,' she said in a resigned whisper. 'I appreciate that you didn't condescend to me. Are you a doctor here at the hospital? You speak as if you were.'

I shook my head. 'No, I'm not. I'm with the FBI. I studied to be a doctor.'

Her eyes widened and seemed even more alert than when we had come in. I sensed that she had tremendous reserves of strength. 'Alex is a doctor *and* a detective.'

'I'm a detective, too,' I said.

'I'm Nana Mama. I'm Alex's grandmother. What's your name?'

'Thomas,' I told her. 'My name is Thomas Pierce.'

'Well, thank you for speaking the truth.'

Chapter Seventy-Seven

Paris, France.

The police would never admit it, but *Mr Smith had control of Paris now. He had taken the city by storm and only he knew why.* The news of his fearsome presence spread along boulevard Saint-Michel, and then rue de Vaugirard. This sort of thing wasn't supposed to happen in the *'très luxe'* sixth arrondissement.

The seductively chic shops along boulevard Saint-Michel lured tourists and Parisians alike. The Panthéon and beautiful Jardin du Luxembourg were nearby. Lurid murders weren't supposed to happen here.

Clerks from the expensive shops were the first to leave their posts and hurriedly walk or run toward No. 11 rue de Vaugirard. They wanted to *see* Smith, or at least his handiwork. They wanted to see the so-called alien with their own eyes.

Shoppers and even owners left the fashionable clothing shops and cafés. If they didn't walk up rue de Vaugirard, they at least looked down to where several police black-and-whites and also an army bus were parked. High above the eerie scene, pigeons fluttered and squawked. They seemed to want to see the famous criminal as well.

Across Saint-Michel stood the Sorbonne, with its foreboding chapel, its huge clock, its open cobblestone terrace. A second bus filled with soldiers was parked in the plaza. Students tentatively wandered up rue Champollion to have a look-see. The tiny street had been named after Jean-François Champollion, the French Egyptologist who had discovered the key to Egyptian hieroglyphics while deciphering the Rosetta stone.

A police inspector named René Girard shook his head as he pulled onto rue Champollion and saw the crowd. Girard understood the common man's sick fascination with 'Mr Smith.' It was the fear of the unknown, especially fear of sudden, horrible death, that drew people's interest to these bizarre murders. Mr Smith had gained a reputation because his actions were so completely incomprehensible. He actually did seem to be an 'alien.' Few people could conceive of another human acting as Smith routinely did.

The inspector let his eyes wander. He took in the electronic sign hanging at the Lycée St Louis corner. Today it advertised 'Tour de France Femina' and also something called 'Formation d'artistes.' More madness, he thought. He coughed out a cynical laugh.

He noticed a sidewalk artist contemplating his sidewalk chalk masterpiece. The man was oblivious to the police emergency. The same could be said of a homeless woman blithely washing her breakfast dishes in the public fountain.

Good for both of them. They passed Girard's test for sanity in the modern age.

As he climbed the gray-stone stairway leading to a blue-painted door, he was tempted to turn toward the crowd of onlookers massed on rue de Vaugirard, and to scream, 'Go back to your little chores and your even smaller lives. Go see an art movie at Cinéma Champollion. This has nothing whatsoever to do with you. Smith takes only interesting and deserving specimens – so you people have absolutely nothing to worry about.'

That morning, one of the finest young surgeons at L'École Pratique de Médecine had been reported missing. If Mr Smith's pattern held, within a couple of days the surgeon would be found dead and mutilated. That was the way it had been with all the other victims. It was the only strand that represented anything like a repeating pattern. *Death by mutilation.*

Girard nodded and said hello to two flics and another low-ranking inspector inside the surgeon's expensively furnished apartment. The place was magnificent, filled with antique furniture, expensive art, with a view of the Sorbonne.

Well, the golden boy of L'École Pratique de Médecine had finally gotten a bad break. Yes, things had suddenly gotten very bleak for Dr Abel Sante.

'Nothing, no sign of a struggle?' Girard asked the closest flic as he entered the apartment.

'Not a trace, just like the others. The poor rich bastard is gone, though. He's disappeared, and Mr Smith has him.'

'He's probably in Smith's space capsule,' the other flic said, a youngish man with longish red hair and trendy sunglasses.

Girard turned brusquely. '*You!* Get the hell out of here! Go out on the street with the rest of the madmen and the goddamned pigeons! I would hope Mr Smith might take *you* for his *space capsule* but, unfortunately, I suspect his standards are too high.'

Having said his piece and banished the offending police officer, the inspector went to examine the handiwork of Mr Smith. He had a *procès-verbal* to write up. He had to make some sense out of the madness somehow. All of France, all of Europe, waited to hear the latest news.

Chapter Seventy-Eight

F BI headquarters in Washington is located on Pennsylvania Avenue between Ninth and Tenth Streets. I spent from four until almost seven in a BOGSAAT with a half-dozen special agents, including Kyle Craig. BOGSAAT is a *bunch of guys sitting around a table*. We vigorously discussed the Cross attack inside a Strategic Ops Center conference room.

At seven that night, we learned that Alex Cross had made it through the first round of surgery. A cheer went up around the table. I told Kyle that I wanted to go back to St Anthony's Hospital.

'I need to see Alex Cross,' I told him. 'I really do need to see him, even if he can't talk. No matter what condition he's in.'

Twenty minutes later, I was in an elevator headed to the sixth floor of St Anthony's. It was quieter there than the rest of the building. The high floor was a little spooky, especially under the circumstances.

I entered a private recovery room near the center of the semidarkened floor. I was too late. Someone was already in there with Cross.

Detective John Sampson was standing vigil by the bed of his friend. Sampson was tall and powerful, at least six foot six, but he looked incredibly weary, as if he were ready to fall over from exhaustion and the long day's stress.

Sampson finally looked at me, nodded slightly, then turned his attention back to Dr Cross. His eyes were a strange mixture of anger and sadness. I sensed that he knew what was going to happen here.

Alex Cross was hooked up to so many machines it was a visceral shock to see him. I knew that he was in his early forties. He looked younger than his age. That was the only good news.

I studied the charts at the base of the bed. He had suffered severe–moderate blood loss secondary to the tearing of the radial artery. He had a collapsed lung, numerous contusions, hematomas, and lacerations. The left wrist had been injured. There was blood poisoning, and the morbidity of the injuries put him on the 'could be about to check out' list.

Alex Cross was conscious, and I stared into his brown eyes for a long time. What secrets were hidden there? What did he know? Had he actually seen the face of his assailant? *Who did this to you? Not Soneji. Who dared to go into your bedroom?*

He couldn't talk and I could see nothing in his eyes. No awareness that I was there with Detective Sampson. He didn't seem to recognize Sampson either. Sad.

Dr Cross was getting excellent care at St Anthony's. The hospital bed had a Stryker frame attached to it. The injured wrist was encased in an Elastoplast cast and the arm was anchored to a trapeze bar. He was receiving oxygen through a clear tube that ran into an outlet in the wall. A fancy monitor called a Slavescope was providing pulse, temp, blood pressure, and EKG readings.

'Why don't you leave him alone?' Sampson finally spoke after a few minutes. 'Why don't you leave both of us? You can't help here. Please, go.'

I nodded, but continued to look into the eyes of Alex Cross for a few more seconds. Unfortunately, he had nothing to tell me.

I finally left Cross and Sampson alone. I wondered if I would ever see Alex Cross again. I doubted that I would. I didn't believe in miracles anymore.

Chapter Seventy-Nine

That night, I couldn't get Mr Smith out of my head, as usual, and now Alex Cross and his family were residing there as well. I kept revisiting different scenes from the hospital, and from the Cross house. Who had entered the house? Who had Gary Soneji gotten to? That had to be it.

The crisscrossing flashbacks were maddening and running out of control. I didn't like the feeling, and I didn't know if I could conduct an investigation, still less two, under these stressful, almost claustrophobic, conditions.

It had been twenty-four hours from hell. I had flown to the United States from London. I'd landed at National Airport, in DC, and gone to Quantico, Virginia. Then I had been rushed back to Washington where I worked until ten in the evening on the Cross puzzle.

To make things worse, if they could get any worse, I found I couldn't sleep when I finally got to my room at the Washington Hilton & Towers. My mind was in a chaotic state that steadfastly refused sleep.

I didn't like the working hypothesis on Cross that I had heard from the FBI investigators at headquarters that night. They were stuck in their usual rut: They were like slow students who scan classroom ceilings for answers. Actually, most police investigators reminded me of Einstein's incisive definition of insanity. I had first heard it at Harvard: *'Endlessly repeating the same process, hoping for a different result.'*

I kept flashing back to the upstairs bedroom where Alex Cross had been brutally attacked. I was looking for something – but what was it? I could see his blood spattered on the walls, on the curtains, the sheets, the throw rug. *What was I missing? Something?*

I couldn't sleep, goddamnit.

I tried work as a sedative. It was my usual antidote. I had already begun extensive notes and sketches on the scene of the attack. I got up and wrote some more. My PowerBook was beside me, always at the ready. My stomach wouldn't stop rolling and my head throbbed in a maddening way.

I typed: *Could Gary Soneji possibly still be alive? Don't rule anything out yet, not even the most absurd possibility.*

Exhume Soneji's body if necessary.

Read Cross's book – Along Came a Spider.

Visit Lorton Prison, where Soneji was held.

I pushed aside my computer after an hour's work. It was nearly two in the morning. My head felt stuffed, as if I had a terrible, nagging cold. I still couldn't sleep. I was thirty-three years old; I was already beginning to feel like an old man.

I kept seeing the bloody bedroom at the Cross house. No one can imagine what it's like to live with such imagery day and night. I saw Alex Cross – the way he looked at St Anthony's Hospital. Then I was remembering victims of Mr Smith, his 'studies,' as he called them.

The terrifying scenes play on and on and on in my head. Always leading to the same place, the same conclusion.

I can see another bedroom. It is the apartment Isabella and I shared in Cambridge, Massachusetts.

With total clarity, I remembered running down the narrow hallway that terrible night. I remember my heart pushing into my throat, feeling larger than a clenched fist. I remember every pounding step that I took, everything I saw along the way.

I finally saw Isabella, and I thought it must be a dream, a terrible nightmare.

Isabella was in our bed, and I knew that she was dead. No one could have survived the butchery I witnessed there. No one did survive – neither of us.

Isabella had been savagely murdered at twenty-three, in the prime of her life, before she could be a mother, a wife, the anthropologist she'd dreamed of becoming. I couldn't help myself, couldn't stop. I bent and held what was left of Isabella, *what was left.*

How can I ever forget any of it? How can I turn that sight off in my mind?

The simple answer is, I cannot.

Chapter Eighty

I was on the hunt again, the loneliest road on this earth. Truthfully, there wasn't much else that had sustained me during the past four years, not since Isabella's death.

The moment I awoke in the morning, I called St Anthony's Hospital. Alex Cross was alive, but in a coma. His condition was listed as extremely critical. I wondered if John Sampson had remained at his bedside. I suspected he had.

By nine in the morning, I was back at the Cross house. I needed to study the scene in much greater depth, to gather every fact, every splinter and fragment. I tried to organize everything I knew, or thought I knew at this early stage of the investigation. I was reminded of a maxim that was frequently used at Quantico: All truths are half-truths and possibly not even that.

A fiendish 'ghoul' had supposedly struck back from the grave and attacked a well-known policeman and his family in their home. The ghoul had warned Dr Cross that he would come. There was no way to stop it from happening. It was the ultimate in cruel and effective revenge.

For some reason, though, the assailant had failed to execute. None of the family members, or even Alex Cross, had been killed. That was the perplexing and most baffling part of the puzzle for me. That was the key!

I arrived at the cellar in the Cross house just before eleven in the morning. I had asked the Metro police and FBI technicians not to mess around down there until I was finished with my survey of the other floors. My data gathering, my science, was a methodical step-by-step process.

The attacker had hidden himself (herself?) in the basement while a party had been in progress upstairs and in the backyard. There was a partial footprint near the entryway to the cellar. It was a size nine. It wasn't much to go on, not unless the perpetrator had wanted us to find the print.

One thing struck me right away. *Gary Soneji had been locked in a cellar as a child. He'd been excluded from family activities in the rest of the house. He'd been physically abused in the cellar. Just like the one in the Cross house.*

The attacker had definitely hidden in the cellar. That couldn't be a coincidence.

Had he known about Gary Soneji's explicit warning to Cross? That possibility was disturbing as hell. I didn't want to settle on any theories or premature conclusions yet. I just needed to collect as much raw data and information as I could.

Possibly because I'd been to medical school, I approached cases as a clinical scientist would.

Collect all the data first. Always the data.

It was quiet in the cellar, and I could focus and concentrate all of my attention on my surroundings. I tried to imagine the attacker lurking here during the party, and then afterward, as the house grew quiet, until Alex Cross finally went to bed.

The attacker was a coward.

He wasn't in a rage state. He was methodical.

It was not a crime of passion.

The intruder had struck out at each of the children first, but not fatally. He had beaten Alex Cross's grandmother, but had spared her. *Why?* Only Alex Cross was meant to die and so far even that hadn't happened.

Had the attacker failed? Where was the intruder now?

Was he still in Washington? Checking out the Cross house right now? Or at St Anthony's Hospital, where the Metro police were guarding Alex Cross.

As I passed an ancient coal stove, I noticed the metal door was slightly ajar. I poked it open with my handkerchief and peered inside. I couldn't see very well and took out a penlight. There were inches of ash that were light gray in color. Someone had burned a flammable substance recently, possibly newspapers or magazines.

Why start a fire in the middle of summer? I wondered.

A small hand shovel was on a worktable near the stove. I used the shovel to sift through the ashes.

I carefully scraped along the stove's bottom.

I heard a *clink*. A metal-against-metal noise.

I scooped out a shovelful of ash. Something came with the ash. It was hard, heavier. My expectations weren't high. I was still just collecting data, anything and everything, even the contents of an old stove. I emptied the ashes onto the worktable in a pile, then smoothed it out.

I saw what the small shovel had struck. I flipped over the new evidence with the tip of the shovel. *Yes*, I said to myself. I finally had something, the first bit of evidence.

It was Alex Cross's detective shield, and it was burned and charred.

Someone wanted us to find the shield.

The intruder wants to play! I thought. *This is cat and mouse.*

Chapter Eighty-One

Île-de-France.

D r Abel Sante was normally a calm and collected man. He was widely
known in the medical community to be erudite, but surprisingly down-to-
earth. He was a nice man, too, a gentle physician.

Now he desperately tried to put his mind somewhere other than where his body
was. Just about anywhere else in the universe would do just fine.

He had already spent several hours remembering minute details from his
pleasant, almost idyllic, boyhood in Rennes; then his university years at the
Sorbonne and L'École Pratique de Médecine; he had replayed tennis and golf
sporting events; he had relived his seven-year love affair with Regina Becker
– dear, sweet Regina.

He needed to be somewhere else, to exist anywhere else but where he actually was. He needed to exist in the past, or even the future, but not in the
present. He was reminded of *The English Patient* – both the book and the movie.
He was Count Almasy now, wasn't he? Only his torture was even worse than
Almasy's horribly burned flesh. He was in the grasp of Mr Smith.

He thought about Regina constantly now, and he realized that he loved her
fiercely, and what a fool he'd been not to marry her years ago. What an arrogant bastard, and what a huge fool!

How dearly he wanted to live now, and to see Regina again. Life seemed
so damned precious to him at this moment, in this terrible place, under these
monstrous conditions.

No, this wasn't a good way to be thinking. It brought him down – it brought
him back to reality, to the present. *No, no no! Go somewhere else in your mind.
Anywhere but here.*

The present line of thought brought him to this tiny compartment, this infini-
tesimal x on the globe where he was now a prisoner, and where no one could
possibly find him. Not the flics, not Interpol, not the entire French Army, or
the English, or the Americans, or the Israelis!

Dr Sante could easily imagine the furor and outrage, the panic continuing
in Paris and throughout France. NOTED PHYSICIAN AND TEACHER ABDUCTED! The

headline in *Le Monde* would read something like that. Or, NEW MR SMITH HORROR IN PARIS.

He was the horror! He was certain that tens of thousands of police, as well as the army, were searching for him now. Of course, every hour he was missing, his chances for survival grew dimmer. He knew that from reading past articles about Mr Smith's unearthly abductions, and what had happened to the victims.

Why me? God Almighty, he couldn't stand this infernal monologue anymore.

He couldn't stand this nearly-upside-down position, this terribly cramped space, for one more second.

He just couldn't bear it. Not one more second!

Not one more second!

Not one more second!

He couldn't breathe!

He was going to die in here.

Right here, in a goddamn dumbwaiter. Stuck between floors, in a godforsaken house in Île-de-France somewhere on the outskirts of Paris.

Mr Smith had put him in the dumbwaiter, stuffed him inside like a bundle of dirty laundry, and then left him there – for God only knew how long. It seemed like hours, at least several hours, but Abel Sante really wasn't sure anymore.

The excruciating pain came and went, but mostly it rushed through his body in powerful waves. His neck, his shoulders, and his chest ached so badly, beyond belief, beyond his tolerance for pain. The feeling was as if he'd been slowly crushed into a squarish heap. If he hadn't been claustrophobic before, he was now.

But that wasn't the worst part of this. No, it wasn't the worst. The most terrifying thing was that he knew what all of France wanted to know, what the whole world wanted to know.

He knew certain things about Mr Smith's identity. He knew precisely how he talked. He believed that Mr Smith might be a philosopher, perhaps a university professor or student.

He had even *seen* Mr Smith.

He had looked out from the dumbwaiter – upside down, no less – and stared into Smith's hard, cold eyes, seen his nose, his lips.

Mr Smith saw that.

Now there was no hope for him.

'Damn you, Smith. Damn you to hell. I know your shitty secret. I know everything now. You *are* a fucking alien! *You aren't human.*'

Chapter Eighty-Two

'Y̲ou really think we're going to track down this son of a bitch? You think this guy is dumb?'

John Sampson asked me point-blank, challenging me. He was dressed all in black, and he wore Ray-Ban sunglasses. He looked as if he were already in mourning. The two of us were flying an FBI Belljet helicopter from Washington to Princeton, New Jersey. We were supposed to work together for a while.

'You think Gary Soneji did this somehow? Think he's Houdini? You think maybe he's still alive?' Sampson went on. 'What the hell do you think?'

'I don't know yet,' I sighed. 'I'm still collecting data. It's the only way I know how to work. No, I don't *think* Soneji did it. He's always worked alone before this. Always.'

I knew that Gary Soneji had grown up in New Jersey, then gone on to become one of the most savage murderers of the times. It didn't seem as if his run were over yet. Soneji was part of the ongoing mystery.

Alex Cross's notes on Soneji were extensive. I was finding useful and interesting insights all through the notes, and I was less than a third of the way through. I had already decided that Cross was a sharp police detective but an even better psychologist. His hypotheses and hunches weren't merely clever and imaginative; they were often right. There's an important difference in that, which many people fail to see, especially people in medium-high places.

I looked up from my reading.

'I've had some luck with difficult killers before. All except the one I really want to catch,' I told Sampson.

He nodded, but his eyes stayed locked onto mine. 'This Mr Smith something of a cult hero now? Over in Europe, especially, the Continent, London, Paris, Frankfurt.'

I wasn't surprised that Sampson was aware of the ongoing case. The tabloids had made Mr Smith their latest icon. The stories were certainly compelling reading. They played up the angle that Smith might be an alien. Even newspapers like the *New York Times* and *The Times* of London had run stories stating that police authorities believed Smith might be an extraterrestrial being who had come here to study humans. To *grok*, as it were.

'Smith has become the evil ET. Something for *X-Files* fans to contemplate between TV episodes. Who knows, perhaps Mr Smith *is* a visitor from outer space, at least from some other parallel world. He doesn't have anything in common with human beings, I can vouch for that. I've visited the murder scenes.'

Sampson nodded. 'Gary Soneji didn't have much in common with the human race,' he said in his deep, strangely quiet voice. 'Soneji was from another planet, too. He's an ALF, alien life-form.'

'I'm not sure he fits the same psychological profile as Smith.'

'Why is that?' he asked. His eyes narrowed. 'You think your mass killer is smarter than our mass killer?'

'I'm not saying that. Gary Soneji was very bright, but he made mistakes. So far, Mr Smith hasn't made any.'

'And that's why you're going to solve this hinky mystery? Because Gary Soneji makes mistakes?'

'I'm not making predictions,' I told Sampson. 'I know better than that. So do you.'

'Did Gary Soneji make a mistake at Alex's house?' he suddenly asked, his dark eyes penetrating.

I sighed out loud. 'I think someone did.'

The helicopter was settling down to land outside Princeton. A thin line of cars silently streamed past the airfield on a state highway. People watched us from the cars. It could safely be assumed that everything had started here. The house where Gary Soneji had been raised was less than six miles away. This was the monster's original lair.

'You're sure Soneji's not still alive?' John Sampson asked one more time. 'Are you absolutely sure about that?'

'No,' I finally said. 'I'm not sure of anything yet.'

Chapter Eighty-Three

A ssume nothing, question everything.

As we set down in the small private airfield, I could feel the hair on the back of my neck standing on end. *What was wrong here? What was I feeling about the Cross case?*

Beyond the thin ribbons of landing strip were acre upon acre of pine forests and hills. The beauty of the countryside, the incredible shades of green, reminded me of something Cézanne had once said: 'When color is at its richest, form is at its fullest.' I never looked at the world in quite the same way after hearing that.

Gary Soneji was brought up near here, I thought to myself. *Was it possible that he could still be alive? No, I didn't believe that. But could there be connections?*

We were met in New Jersey by two field agents who brought a blue Lincoln sedan for our use. Sampson and I proceeded first to Rocky Hill where Soneji grew up, and then over to Lambertville to see his grandfather. I knew that Sampson and Alex Cross had been to Princeton less than a week ago. Still, I had questions of my own, theories that needed field-testing.

I also wanted to see the entire area where Gary Soneji had grown up, where his madness had been inflicted and nurtured. Mostly I wanted to talk with someone neither Cross nor Sampson had spent much time investigating, a brand-new suspect.

Assume nothing, question everything . . . and everyone.

Seventy-five-year-old Walter Murphy, Gary's grandfather, was waiting for us on a long, whitewashed porch. He didn't ask us inside his house.

The porch had a nice view out from the farmhouse. I saw multiflora rose everywhere, an impenetrable bramble. The nearby barn was also over-run by sumac and poison ivy. I guessed that the grandfather was letting this happen.

I could feel Gary Soneji at his grandfather's farm, I felt him everywhere.

According to Walter Murphy, he'd had no inkling that Gary was capable of murder. Not at any time. Not a clue.

'Some days I think I've gotten used to what's happened, but then suddenly it's fresh and incomprehensible to me all over again,' he told us as the mid-day breeze ruffled his longish white hair.

'Did you stay close to Gary as he got older?' I asked cautiously. I was studying his build, which was large. His arms were thick and looked as if they could still do physical damage.

'I remember long talks with Gary from the time he was a boy right up until it was alleged he'd kidnapped those two children in Washington.' *Alleged*.

'And you were taken by surprise?' I said. 'You had no idea?'

Walter Murphy looked directly at me – for the first time. I knew that he resented my tone, the irony in it. How angry could I make him? How much of a temper did the old man have?

I leaned in and listened more closely. I watched every gesture, every tic. *Collected the data.*

'Gary always wanted to fit in, just like everybody else does,' he said abruptly. 'He trusted me because he knew I accepted him for what he was.'

'What was it about Gary that needed to be accepted?'

The old man shifted his eyes to the peaceful-looking pine woods surrounding the farm. *I could feel Soneji in those woods. It was as if he were watching us.*

'He could be hostile at times, I'll admit. His tongue was sharp, double-barbed. Gary had an air of superiority that ruffled some tail feathers.'

I kept at Walter Murphy, didn't give him space to breathe. 'But not when he was around you?' I asked. 'He didn't ruffle your feathers?'

The old man's clear blue eyes returned from their trip into the woods. 'No, we were always close. I know we were, even if the expensive shrinks say it wasn't possible for Gary to feel love, to feel anything for anybody. I was never the target for any of his temper explosions.'

That was a fascinating revelation, but I sensed it was a lie. I glanced at Sampson. He was looking at me in a new way.

'These explosions at other people, were they ever premeditated?' I asked.

'Well, you know damn well he burned down his father and stepmother's house. They were in it. So were his stepbrother and stepsister. He was supposed to be away at school. He was an honor student at the Peddie School in Highstown. He was making friends there.'

'Did you ever meet any of the friends from Peddie?' The quickening tempo of my questions made Walter Murphy uneasy. Did he have his grandson's temper?

A spark flared in the old man's eyes. Unmistakable anger was there now. Maybe the real Walter Murphy was appearing.

'No, he never brought his friends from school around here. I suppose you're suggesting that he didn't have friends, that he just wanted to seem more normal than he was. Is that your two-bit analysis? Are you a forensic psychologist, by the way? Is that your game?'

'Trains?' I said.

I wanted to see where Walter Murphy would go with it. This was important, a test, a moment of truth and reckoning.

C'mon, old man. Trains?

He looked off into the woods again, still serene and beautiful. 'Mmm. I'd forgotten, hadn't thought of the trains in a while. Fiona's son, her real son, had an expensive set of Lionel trains. Gary wasn't allowed to even be in the same room with them. When he was ten or eleven, the train set disappeared. The whole damn set, gone.'

'What happened to the train set?'

Walter Murphy almost smiled. 'They all knew Gary had taken it. Destroyed it, or maybe buried it somewhere. They spent an entire summer questioning him as to the train set's whereabouts, but he never told them squat. They grounded him for the summer and he still never told.'

'It was his secret, his power over them.' I offered a little more 'two-bit analysis.'

I was beginning to feel certain disturbing things about Gary and his grandfather. I was starting to know Soneji and maybe, in the process, getting closer to whoever had attacked the Cross house in Washington. Quantico was researching possible copycat theories. I liked the partner angle – except for the fact that Soneji had never had one before.

Who had crept into Cross's house? And how?

'I was reading some of Dr Cross's detective logs on the way here,' I told the grandfather. 'Gary had a recurring nightmare. It took place here on your farm. Are you aware of it? Gary's nightmare at your farm?'

Walter Murphy shook his head. He was blinking his eyes, twitching. He knew something.

'I'd like your permission to do something here,' I finally said. 'I'll need two shovels. Picks, if you have them.'

'And if I say no?' he raised his voice suddenly. It was the first time he'd been openly uncooperative.

And then it struck me. The old man is acting, too. That's why he understood so much about Gary. He looks off into the trees to set his mind and gain control for the next few lines he has to deliver. *The grandfather is an actor! Just not as good as Gary.*

'Then we'll get a search warrant,' I told him. 'Make no mistake. We will do the search anyway.'

Chapter Eighty-Four

'What the hell is this all about?' Sampson asked as we trudged from the ramshackle barn to a gray fieldstone fireplace that stood in an open clearing. 'You think this is how we catch the Bug-Eyed Monster? Beating up on this old man?'

Both of us carried old metal shovels, and I had a rusted pickax also.

'I told you – *data*. I'm a scientist by training. Trust me for about half an hour. The old man is tougher than he looks.'

The stone fireplace had been built for family cookouts a long time ago, but apparently had not been used in recent years. Sumac and other vines were creeping over the fireplace, as if to make it disappear.

Just beyond the fireplace was a rotting, wooden-plank picnic table with splintered benches on either side. Pines, oaks, and sugar maples were everywhere.

'Gary had a recurring dream. That's what brought me here. This is where the dream takes place. Near the fireplace and the picnic table at Grandpa Walter's farm. It's quite horrible. The dream comes up several times in the notes Alex made on Soneji when he was inside Lorton Prison.'

'Where Gary should have been *cooked*, until he was crispy on the outside, slightly pink toward the center,' Sampson said.

I laughed at his dark humor. It was the first light moment I'd had in a long time and it felt good to share it with someone.

I picked out a spot midway between the old fireplace and a towering oak tree that canted toward the farmhouse. I drove the pickax into the ground, drove it hard and deep. *Gary Soneji. His aura, his profound evil. His paternal grand-daddy. More data.*

'In his bizarre dreams,' I told Sampson, 'Gary committed a gruesome murder when he was a young boy. He *may* have buried the victim out here. He wasn't sure himself. He felt he couldn't separate dreams from reality sometimes. Let's spend a little time searching for Soneji's ancient burial ground. Maybe we're about to enter Gary's earliest nightmare.'

'Maybe I don't want to enter Gary Soneji's earliest nightmare,' Sampson said, laughing again. The tension between us was definitely breaking some. This was better.

I lifted the pickax high and swung down with great force. I repeated the action again and again, until I found a smooth, comfortable, working rhythm.

Sampson looked surprised as he watched me handle the pick. 'You've done this kind of fieldwork before, boy,' he said, and began to dig at my side.

'Yes, I lived on a farm in El Toro, California. My father, his father, and my grandfather's father were all small-town doctors. But they continued to live on our family horse farm. I was supposed to go back there to set up practice, but then I never finished my medical training.'

The two of us were hard at work now. Good, honest work: looking for old bodies, searching for ghosts from Gary Soneji's past. Trying to goad Grandfather Murphy.

We took off our shirts, and soon both of us were covered with sweat and dust.

'This was like a *gentleman's* farm? Back in California? The one you lived on as a boy?'

I snorted out a laugh as I pictured the *gentleman's* farm. 'It was a very small farm. We had to struggle to keep it going. My family didn't believe a doctor should get rich taking care of other people. "You shouldn't take a profit from other people's misery," my father said. He still believes that.'

'Huh. So your whole family's weird?'

'That's a reasonably accurate portrait.'

Chapter Eighty-Five

As I continued to dig in Walter Murphy's yard, I thought back to our farm in Southern California. I could still vividly see the large red barn and two small corrals.

When I lived there we owned six horses. Two were breeding stallions, Fadl and Rithsar. Every morning I took rake, pitchfork, and wheelbarrow, and I cleared the stalls; and then made my trip to the manure pile. I put down lime and straw, washed out and refilled the water buckets, made minor repairs. Every single morning of my youth. So yes, I knew how to handle a shovel and pickax.

It took Sampson and me half an hour before we had a shallow ditch stretching toward the ancient oak tree in the Murphy yard. The sprawling tree had been mentioned several times in Gary's recounting of his dreams.

I had almost expected Walter Murphy to call the police on us, but it didn't happen. I half-expected Soneji to suddenly appear. That didn't happen either.

'Too bad old Gary didn't just leave us a map.' Sampson grunted and groaned under the hot, beating sun.

'He was very specific about his dream. I think he wanted Alex to come out here. Alex, or somebody else.'

'Somebody else did. The two of us. Ho shit, there's something down here. Something under my feet,' Sampson said.

I moved around toward his spot in the trench. The two of us continued to dig, picking up the pace. We worked side by side, sweating profusely. *Data*, I reminded myself. *It's all just data on the way to an answer. The beginning of a solution.*

And then I recognized the fragments we had uncovered in the shallow grave, in Gary's hiding place near the fireplace.

'Jesus Christ, I don't believe it. Oh God, Jesus!' Sampson said.

'Animal bones. Looks like the skull and upper thigh bone of a medium-sized dog,' I said to Sampson.

'Lots of bones!' he added.

We continued to dig even faster. Our breathing was harsh and labored. We had been digging in the summer heat for nearly an hour. It was in the nineties, sticky-hot, and claustrophobic. We were in a hole up to our waists.

'Shit! Here we go again. You recognize this from any of your med-school anatomy classes?' Sampson asked.

We were looking down at fragments from a human skeleton. 'It's the scapula and mandible. It could be a young boy or girl,' I told him.

'So this is the handiwork of young Gary? This Gary's first kill? Another kid?'

'I don't know for sure. Let's not forget about Grandpa Walter. Let's keep looking. If it is Gary, maybe he left a sign. These would be his earliest souvenirs. They would have been precious to him.'

We kept on digging and, minutes later, we found another cache. Only the sound of our labored breathing broke the silence.

There were more bones, possibly from a large animal, possibly a deer, but probably human.

And there was something else, a definite sign from young Gary. It had been wrapped in tinfoil, which I now carefully removed.

It was a Lionel locomotive, undoubtedly the one he had stolen from his step-brother.

The toy train that launched a hundred deaths.

Chapter Eighty-Six

Christine Johnson knew she had to go to the Sojourner Truth School, but once she got there, she wasn't sure she was ready for work yet. She was nervous, distracted, and not herself. Maybe school would help to get her mind off Alex, though.

She stopped at Laura Dixon's first-grade class on her morning walk. Laura was one of her best friends in the world, and her classes were stimulating and fun. Besides, first graders were so damn cute to be around. 'Laura's babies,' she called them. Or, 'Laura's cuddly kittens and perky puppies.'

'Oh, *look* who it is, look who's come to visit. Aren't we the luckiest first-grade class in the whole world!' the teacher cried when she spotted Christine at the door.

Laura was just a smidgen over five foot tall, but she was still a very *big* girl, large at the hips and breasts. Christine couldn't keep from smiling at her friend's greeting. Trouble was, she was also incredibly close to tears. She realized she *wasn't* ready for school.

'Good morning, Ms Johnson!' the first graders chorused like a practiced glee club. God, they were wonderful! So bright and enthusiastic, sweet and good.

'Good morning back at you,' Christine beamed. There, she felt a little better.

A big letter *B* was scrawled on the blackboard, as well as Laura's sketches of a *B*umblebee *B*uzzing around *B*atman and a *B*ig *B*lue *B*oat.

'Don't let me interrupt progress,' she said. 'I'm just here for a little refresher course. *B* is for *B*eautiful *B*eginnings, *B*abies.'

The class laughed, and she felt *connected* with them, thank God. It was at times like this when she dearly wished she had kids of her own. She loved the first graders, loved kids, and, at thirty-two, it was definitely time.

Then, out of nowhere, an image flashed from the terrible scene a few days earlier. Alex being moved from his house on Fifth Street to one of the ambulances! She had been called to the scene by neighbors, friends of hers. Alex was conscious. He said, 'Christine, you look so beautiful. Always.' And then they took him away from her.

The image from that morning and his final words made her shiver to remember. The Chinese had a saying that had been in her mind for a while, troubling her: *Society prepares the crime; the criminal only commits it.*

'Are you all right?' Laura Dixon was at her side, had seen Christine falter at the door.

'Excuse us, ladies and gentlemen,' she said to her class. 'Ms Johnson and I have to chat for a minute right outside the door. You may chat as well. Quietly. Like the ladies and gentlemen that you are, I trust.'

Then Laura took Christine's arm and walked her out into the deserted hallway.

'Do I look *that* bad?' Christine asked. 'Does it show all over my face, Laura?'

Laura hugged her tightly and the heat from her friend's ample body felt good. Laura *was* good.

'Don't you try to be so *goddamn* strong, don't try to be so brave,' Laura said. 'Have you heard anything more, sweetheart? Tell Laura. Talk to me.'

Christine mumbled into Laura's hair. It felt so good to hold her, to hold on to someone. 'Still listed as critical. Still no visitors. Unless you happen to be high up in the Metro police or the FBI.'

'Christine, Christine,' Laura whispered softly. 'What am I going to do with you?'

'What, Laura? I'm okay now. I really am.'

'You are so strong, girl. You are about the best person I have ever met. I love you dearly. That's all I'll say for right now.'

'That's enough. Thank you,' Christine said. She felt a little better, not quite so hollowed-out and empty, but the feeling didn't last very long.

She started to walk back to her office.

As she turned down the east corridor, she spotted the FBI's Kyle Craig waiting for her near her office. She hurried down the hallway toward him. *This is not good*, she told herself. *Oh dear God, no. Why is Kyle here? What does he have to tell me?*

'Kyle, what is it?' Her voice trembled and nearly went out of control.

'I have to talk to you,' he said, taking her hand. 'Please, just listen. Come inside your office, Christine.'

Chapter Eighty-Seven

That night, back in my room at the Marriott in Princeton, I couldn't sleep again. It was two cases running concurrently in my mind. I skimmed several chapters from a rather pedestrian book about trains, just to gather *data*.

I was starting to familiarize myself with the vocabulary of trains: vestibules, step boxes, roomettes, annunciators, the deadman control. I knew that trains were a key part to the mystery I had been asked to solve.

What part had Gary Soneji played in the attack at Alex Cross's house?

Who was his partner?

I went to work at my PowerBook, which I'd set up on the hotel-room desk. As I would later relate to Kyle Craig, I no sooner sat down than the specially designed alarm in the computer started to *beep*. A fax was waiting for me.

I knew instantly what it was – Smith was calling. He had been contacting me for over a year, on a regular basis. Who was tracking whom? I sometimes asked myself.

The message was classic Smith. I read it, line by line.

Paris – Wednesday.

In Foucault's Discipline and Punish, *the philosopher suggests that in the modern age we are moving from individual punishment to a paradigm of generalized punishment. I, for one, believe that this is an unfortunate happenstance. Do you see where I might be going with this line of thinking, and what my ultimate mission might be?*

I'm missing you over here on the Continent, missing you terribly. Alex Cross isn't worth your valuable time and energy.

I've taken one here in Paris in your honor – a doctor! A doctor, a surgeon, just like you wanted to be once upon a time.

Always,

Mr Smith.

Chapter Eighty-Eight

This was the way the killer communicated with me for more than a year. Fax or e-mail messages arrived on the PowerBook at any time of day or night. I would then transmit them to the FBI. Mr Smith was so contemporary, a creature of the nineties.

I relayed the fax to the Behavioral Science Unit at Quantico. Several of the profilers were still working. I could visualize the scene of consternation and frustration. My trip to France was approved.

Kyle Craig telephoned my room at the Marriott a few minutes after the fax had been relayed to Quantico. Mr Smith was giving me another window of opportunity to catch him, usually only a day or so, but sometimes only hours. Smith was challenging me to save the kidnapped doctor in Paris.

And yes, I did believe Mr Smith was far superior to Gary Soneji. Both his mind and his methodology outstripped Soneji's more primitive approach.

I was carrying my travel bag and computer when I saw John Sampson. He was outside in the parking lot of the hotel. It was a little past midnight. I wondered what he'd been up to in Princeton that night.

'What the hell is this, Pierce? Where do you think you're going?' he said in a loud, angry voice. He towered over me in the parking lot. His shadow stretched out thirty or forty feet from the lights of the building.

'Smith contacted me about thirty minutes ago. He does this just before he makes a kill. He gives me a location and challenges me to stop the murder.'

Sampson's nostrils flared. He was shaking his head from side to side. There was only one case in his mind.

'So you're just dropping what we're working on here? You weren't even going to tell me, were you? Just leave Princeton in the dead of night.' His eyes were cold and unfriendly. I had lost his trust.

'John, I left a message explaining everything to you. It's at the front desk. I already spoke to Kyle. I'll surely be back in a few days. Smith never takes long. He knows it's too dangerous. I need time to think about this case anyway.'

Sampson frowned and he continued to shake his head. 'You said it was important to visit Lorton Prison. You said Lorton is the one place where Soneji could have gotten somebody to do his dirty work. His partner probably came from Lorton.'

'I still plan to visit Lorton Prison. Right now, I have to try and prevent a murder. Smith abducted a doctor in Paris. He's dedicating the kill to me.'

John Sampson wasn't impressed with anything I'd said.

'Trust me a little,' I said, but he turned and walked away.

I didn't get a chance to tell him the other thing, the part that bothered me the most. I hadn't told Kyle Craig either.

Isabella had come from Paris. Paris was her home. I hadn't been there since her murder.

Mr Smith knew that.

Chapter Eighty-Nine

It was a beautiful spot, and Mr Smith wanted to spoil it, to ruin it forever inside his mind. The small stone house with its earth-grouted walls and white-shuttered windows and country-lace curtains was peaceful and idyllic. The garden was surrounded by twig fencing. Under a lone apple tree sat a long wooden table, where friends, family, and neighbors might gather to eat and talk.

Smith carefully spread out pages from *Paris-Monde* across the linoleum floor of the spacious farmhouse kitchen. Patti Smith – not a relation – was screeching from his CD player. She sang 'Summer Cannibals,' and the blatant irony wasn't lost on him.

The newspaper front page screamed as well – *Mr Smith Takes Surgeon Captive in Paris!*

And so he had, so he had.

The *idée fixe* that had captured the public's fancy and fear was that Mr Smith might be an alien visitor roaming and ravaging the earth for dark, unknown, perhaps *unknowable* reasons. He didn't share any traits with humans, the lurid news stories reasoned. He was described as 'not of the earth,' 'incapable of any human emotion.'

His name – Mr Smith – came from 'Valentine Michael Smith,' a visitor from Mars in Robert Heinlein's science-fiction novel, *Stranger in a Strange Land*. The book had always been a cult favorite. *Stranger* was the single book in Charles Manson's backpack when he was captured in California.

He studied the French surgeon lying nearly unconscious on the kitchen floor. One FBI report stated that 'Mr Smith seems to appreciate beauty. He has a human artist's eye for composition. Observe the studied way in which he arranges the corpses.'

A human artist's eye for beauty and composition. Yes, that was true enough.

He had loved beauty once, lived for it, actually. The artful arrangements were one of the clues he left for his . . . *his followers.*

Patti Smith finished her song, and the Doors immediately came on. 'People Are Strange.' The moldy oldie was wonderful mood music as well.

Smith let his gaze wander around the country kitchen. One entire wall was a stone fireplace. Another wall was white tile, with antique shelves that held copper pots, white café au lait bowls, antique jam jars, or *confitures fines*, as they were called here. He knew that, knew just about everything about everything. There was an antique black cast-iron stove with brass knobs. And a large white porcelain sink. Adjacent to the sink, just above a butcher-block work-table, hung an impressive array of kitchen knives. The knives were beautiful, absolutely perfect in every way.

He was avoiding looking at the victim, wasn't he?

He knew that he was. He always did.

Finally, he lowered his eyes and looked into the victim's.

So this was Abel Sante.

This was lucky number nineteen.

Chapter Ninety

The victim was a very successful thirty-five-year-old surgeon. He was good-looking in a Gallic sort of way, in excellent shape even without very much meat left on his bones. He seemed a nice person, an 'honorable' man, a 'good' doctor.

What was human? What exactly was human-ness? Mr Smith wondered. That was the fundamental question he still had, after physical exams like this, in nearly a dozen countries around the world.

What was human? What, exactly, did the word mean?

Could he finally find an answer here in this French country kitchen? The philosopher Heidegger believed the *self is revealed* by what we truly care about. Was Heidegger onto something? What was it that Mr Smith truly cared about? That was a fair question to ask.

The French surgeon's hands were tightly tied behind his back. The ankles were bound to the hands; the knees were bent back toward the head. The remaining length of rope was attached to the neck in a noose.

Abel Sante had already realized that any struggling, any thrashing about, created intense strangulation pressure. As the legs eventually tired, they would become numb and painful. The urge to straighten them would be overpowering. If he did this, it would induce self-strangulation.

Mr Smith was ready. He was on a schedule. The autopsy would start at the top of the body, then work its way down. The correct order: neck, spine, chest. Then abdomen, pelvic organs, genitalia. The head and brain would be examined last, in order to allow the blood to drain as much as possible – *for maximum viewing*.

Dr Sante screamed, but no one could hear him out here. It was an ungodly sound and almost made Smith scream, too.

He entered the chest via a classic 'Y' incision. The first cut went across the chest from shoulder to shoulder, continued over the breasts, then traveled from the tip of the sternum. He cut down the entire length of the abdomen to the pubic area.

The brutal murder of an innocent surgeon named Abel Sante.

Absolutely inhuman, he thought to himself.

Abel Sante – he was the key to everything, and none of the police masterminds could figure it out. None of them were worth shit as detectives, as investigators, as anything. It was so simple, if only they would use their minds.

Abel Sante.

Abel Sante.

Abel Sante.

The autopsy finished, Mr Smith lay down on the kitchen floor with what was left of poor Dr Sante. He did this with every victim. Mr Smith hugged the bleeding corpse against his own body. He whispered and sighed, whispered and sighed. It was always like this.

And then, Smith sobbed loudly. 'I'm so sorry. I'm so sorry. Please forgive me. Somebody forgive me,' he moaned in the deserted farmhouse.

Abel Sante.

Abel Sante.

Abel Sante.

Didn't anyone get it?

Chapter Ninety-One

On the American Airlines flight to Europe, I noticed that mine was the only overhead lamp glaring as the flight droned over the Atlantic.

Occasionally, one of the stewardesses stopped to offer coffee or liquor. But for the most part, I just stared into the blackness of the night.

There had never been a mass killer to match Mr Smith's unique approach to violence, not from a scientific vantage point anyway. That was one thing the Behavioral Science Unit at Quantico and I agreed on. Even the contrarians at Interpol, the international clearing house for police information, agreed with us.

In point of fact, the community of forensic psychologists is, or at least had been, in relative agreement about the different repeat – or pattern-murderer types; and also the chief characteristics of their disorders. I found myself reviewing the data as I flew.

Schizoid personality disorder types, as they are currently called, tend to be introverted and indifferent to social relationships. This freak is a classic loner. He tends to have no close friends or close relationships, except possibly family. He exhibits an inability to show affection in acceptable ways. He usually chooses solitary activities for his free time. He has little or no interest in sex.

Narcissists are different. They exhibit little or no concern for anyone but themselves, though they sometimes pretend to care about others. True narcissists can't empathize. They have an inflated sense of self, can become highly unstable if criticized, and feel they are entitled to special treatment. They are preoccupied with grandiose feelings of success, power, beauty, and love.

Avoidant personality disorder types usually won't get involved with other people unless they're completely sure of acceptance. These types avoid jobs and situations involving social contact. They are usually quiet and embarrass easily. They're considered 'sneaky dangerous.'

Sadistic personality disorder types are the ultimate in badness, as destructive individuals go. They habitually use violence and cruelty to establish control. They enjoy inflicting physical and psychological pain. They like to tell lies, simply for the purpose of inflicting pain. They are obsessed with involving violence, torture, and especially the death of others.

As I said, all of this ran through my mind as I sat in my airplane seat high over the Atlantic. What interested me mostly, though, was the conclusion I'd reached about Mr Smith, and which I had recently shared with Kyle Craig at Quantico.

At different times during the long and complex investigation, Mr Smith *had fit all four of these classic murderer types.* He would seem to fit one personality disorder type almost perfectly – then change into another – back and forth at whim. He might even be a fifth type of psychopathic killer, a whole new breed of disorder type.

Perhaps the tabloids were right about Mr Smith, and he *was* an alien. He wasn't like any other human. I knew that. *He had murdered Isabella.*

This was really why I couldn't sleep on the flight to Paris. It was why I could never sleep anymore.

Chapter Ninety-Two

W ho could ever begin to forget the cold-blooded murder of a loved one? I couldn't. Nothing has diminished its vividness or unreality in four years. It goes like this, exactly the way I told it to the Cambridge police.

It is around two in the morning, and I use my key to open the front door of our two-bedroom apartment on Inman Street in Cambridge. Suddenly, I stop. I have the sense that something is wrong in the apartment.

Details inside are particularly memorable. I will never forget any of it. A poster in our foyer: *Language is more than speech.* Isabella is a closet linguist, a lover of words and word games. So am I. It's an important connection between us.

A favorite Noguchi rice-paper lamp of Isabella's.

Her treasured paperbacks from home, most of them Folio. White uniform spines with black lettering, so perfect and neat.

I'd had a few glasses of wine at Jillian's with some other medical students, recent graduates like myself. We were letting off steam after too many days and nights and weeks and years in the Harvard pressure cooker. We were comparing notes about the hospitals each of us would be working at in the fall. We were promising to stay in touch, knowing that we probably wouldn't.

The group included three of my best friends through medical school. Maria Jane Ruocco, who would be working at Children's Hospital in Boston; Chris Sharp, who was soon off to Beth Israel; Michael Fescoe, who had landed a prize internship at NYU. I had been fortunate, too. I was headed to Massachusetts General, one of the best teaching hospitals in the world. My future was assured.

I was high from the wine, but not close to being drunk, when I got home. I was in a good mood, unusually carefree. Odd, guilty detail – I was horny for Isabella. *Free.* I remember singing 'With or Without You' on the way back in my car, a ten-year-old Volvo befitting my economic status as a med student.

I vividly remember standing in the foyer, seconds after I flicked on the hall lights. Isabella's Coach purse is on the floor. The contents are scattered about in a three- or four-foot radius. Very, very strange.

Loose change, her favorite Georg Jensen earrings, lipstick, assorted makeup containers, compact, cinnamon gum – all there on the floor.

Why didn't Isabella pick up her purse? Is she pissed at me for going out with my med-school chums?

That wouldn't be like Isabella. She is an open woman, liberal-minded to a fault.

I start back through the narrow, winding apartment, looking for her everywhere. The apartment is laid out railroad-style, small rooms on a tight track leading to a single window that looks onto Inman Street.

Some of our secondhand scuba equipment is sitting in the hall. We had been planning a trip to California. Two air tanks, weight belts, wet suits, two sets of rubber fins clutter the hallway.

I grab a speargun – just in case. *In case of what?* I have no idea. How could I?

I become more and more frantic, and then afraid. 'Isabella!' I call at the top of my voice. '*Isabella?* Where are you?'

Then I stop, everything in the world seems to stop. I let go of the speargun, let it fall, crash and clatter against the bare hardwood floor.

What I see in our bedroom will never leave me. I can still *see, smell*, even *taste*, every obscene detail. Maybe this is when my sixth sense is born, the strange feeling that is so much a part of my life now.

'Oh God! Oh Jesus, no!' I scream loud enough for the couple who live above us to hear. *This isn't Isabella*, I remember thinking. Those words of total disbelief. I may have actually spoken them aloud. *Not Isabella. It couldn't be Isabella. Not like this.*

And yet – I recognize the flowing auburn hair that I so love to stroke, to brush; the pouting lips that can make me smile, make me laugh out loud, or sometimes duck for cover; a fan-shaped, mother-of-pearl barrette Isabella wears when she wants to look particularly coquettish.

Everything in my life has changed in a heartbeat, or lack of one. I check for signs of breathing, a sign of life. I can feel no pulse in the femoral or carotid arteries. Not a beat. Nothing at all. *Not Isabella. This can't be happening.*

Cyanosis, a bluish coloration of the lips, nail beds, and skin is already taking place. Blood is pooled on the underside of her body. The bowels and bladder have relaxed, but these bodily secretions are nothing to me. They are nothing under the circumstances.

Isabella's beautiful skin looks waxy, almost translucent, as if it isn't her after all. Her pale-green eyes have already lost their liquid and are flattening out. They can no longer see me, can they? I realize they will never look at me again.

The Cambridge police arrive at the apartment somehow. They are everywhere all at once, looking as shocked as I know I look. My neighbors from the building are there, trying to comfort me, trying to calm me, trying not to be sick themselves.

Isabella is gone. We never even got to say goodbye. Isabella is dead, and I can't bring myself to believe it. An old James Taylor lyric, one of our favorites, weaved through my head: '*But I always thought that I'd see you, one more time again.*' The song was 'Fire and Rain.' It was our song. It still is.

A terrible fiend was loose in Cambridge. He had struck less than a dozen blocks from Harvard University. He would soon receive a name: *Mr Smith*, a literary allusion that could have happened only in a university town like Cambridge.

The worst thing, what I would never forget or forgive – the final thing – *Mr Smith had cut out Isabella's heart.*

My reverie ended. My plane was landing at Charles de Gaulle Airport. I was in Paris.

So was Smith.

Chapter Ninety-Three

I checked into the Hôtel de la Seine. Up in my room, I called St Anthony's Hospital in Washington. Alex Cross was still in a grave condition. I purposely avoided meeting with the French police or the crisis team. The local police are never any help anyway. I preferred to work alone, and did so for half a day.

Meanwhile, Mr Smith contacted the Sûreté. He always did it this way; a call to the local police, a personal affront to everyone involved in chasing him. Bad news, always terrible news. *All of you have failed to catch me. You've failed, Pierce.*

He had revealed where the body of Dr Abel Sante could be found. He taunted us, called us pathetic losers and incompetents. He always mocked us after a kill.

The French police, as well as members of Interpol, were gathered in large numbers at the entrance to the Parc de Montsouris. It was ten after one in the morning when I arrived there.

Because of the possibility of crowds of onlookers and the press, the CRS, a special force of the Paris police, had been called in to secure the scene.

I spotted an inspector from Interpol whom I knew and waved in her direction. Sondra Greenberg was nearly as obsessed about catching Mr Smith as I was. She was stubborn, excellent at her job. She had as good a chance as anyone of catching Mr Smith.

Sondra looked particularly tense and uneasy as she walked toward me. 'I don't think we need all these people, all this *help*,' I said smiling thinly. 'It shouldn't be too damn hard to find the body, Sandy. He told us where to look.'

'I agree with you,' she said, 'but you know the French. This was the way they decided it should be done. *Le grand* search party for *le grand* alien space criminal.' A cynical smile twisted along the side of her mouth.' Good to see you, Thomas. Shall we begin our little hunt? How is your French, by the way?'

'Il n'y a rien à voir, Madame, rentrez chez vous!'

Sandy laughed out of the side of her mouth. Some of the French policemen were looking at us as if we were both crazy. 'I will *like hell* go home. Fine, though. *You* can tell the flics what we'd like them to do. And then they'll do the exact opposite, I'm quite sure.'

'Of course they will. They're French.'

Sondra was a tall brunette, willowy on top but with heavy legs, almost as if two body types had been fused. She was British, witty and bright, yet tolerant, even of Americans. She was devoutly Jewish and militantly gay. I enjoyed working with her, even at times like this.

I walked into the Parc de Montsouris with Sandy Greenberg, arm in arm. Once more into the fray.

'Why do you think he sends us *both* messages? Why does he want us both here?' she mused as we tramped across damp lawns that glistened under street-lamps.

'We're the stars in his weird galaxy. That's my theory anyway. We're also authority figures. Perhaps he likes to taunt authority. He might even have a modicum of respect for us.'

'I sincerely doubt that,' Sandy said.

'Then perhaps he likes showing us up, making himself feel superior. How about that theory?'

'I rather like it, actually. He could be watching us right now. I know he's an egomaniac of the highest order. *Hello there, Mr Smith from planet Mars. Are you watching? Enjoying the hell out of this?* God, I hate that creepy bastard!'

I peered around at the dark elm trees. There was plenty of cover here if someone wanted to observe us.

'Perhaps he's here. He might be able to change shapes, you know. He could be that *balayeur des rues*, or that gendarme, or even that *fille de trottoir* in disguise,' I said.

We began to search at quarter past one. At two in the morning, we still hadn't located the body of Dr Abel Sante. It was strange and worrisome to everyone in the search party. It was obvious to me that Smith wanted to make it hard for us to locate the body. He had never done that before. He usually discarded bodies the way people throw away gum wrappers. *What was Smith up to?*

The Paris newspapers had evidently gotten a tip that we were searching the small park. They wanted a hearty serving of blood and guts for their breakfast editions. TV helicopters hovered like vultures overhead. Police barricades had been set up out on the street. We had everything except a victim.

The crowd of onlookers already numbered in the hundreds – and it was two o'clock in the morning. Sandy peered out at them. 'Mr Smith's sodding fan club,' she sneered. 'What a time! What a civilization! Cicero said that, you know.'

My beeper went off at half past two. The noise startled Sandy and me. Then hers went off. *Dueling beepers. What a world, indeed.*

I had received a fax or a voice-mail or an e-mail. I was certain it was Smith. I looked at Sandy.

'What the hell is he pulling this time?' she said. She looked frightened. 'Or maybe it's a *she* – what is *she* pulling?'

We removed our laptops from our shoulder bags.

Sandy was already checking her machine for messages. I got to mine first.

Pierce, the fax read, *welcome back to the real work, to the real chase. I lied to you. That was your punishment for unfaithfulness. I wanted to embarrass you, whatever that means. I wanted to remind you that you can't trust me, or anyone else – not even your friend, Ms Greenberg. Besides, I really don't like the French. I've thoroughly enjoyed torturing them here tonight.*

Poor Dr Abel Sante is at the Buttes-Chaumont Park. He's up near the temple. I swear it. I promise you.

Trust me. Ha, ha! Isn't that the quaint sound you humans make when you laugh? I can't quite make the sound myself. You see, I've never actually laughed.

Always,

Mr Smith.

Sandy Greenberg was shaking her head, muttering curses in the night air. She had gotten the message, too.

'Buttes-Chaumont Park,' she repeated the location. Then she added, 'He says that I shouldn't trust you. *Ha, ha!* Isn't that the quaint sound we humans make when we laugh?'

Chapter Ninety-Four

The huge, unwieldy search team swept across Paris to the north-east, heading toward the Buttes-Chaumont Park. The syncopated wail of police sirens was a disturbing, fearsome noise. Mr Smith still had Paris in an uproar in the early-morning hours.

'He's in control now,' I said to Sandy Greenberg as we sped along dark Parisian streets in a blue Citroën I had rented. The car tires made a ripping sound on the smooth road surface. The noise fit with everything else that was happening. 'Smith is in his glory, however ephemeral it may turn out to be. This is his time, his moment,' I rattled on.

The English investigator frowned. 'Thomas, you continue to ascribe human emotions to Smith. When are you going to get it through your skull that we're looking for a *little green man*?'

'I'm an empirical investigator. I'll believe it only when I *see* a little green man with blood dripping from his little green mouth.'

Neither of us had ever given a millisecond's credence to the 'alien' theories, but space-visitor jokes were definitely a part of the dark humor of this manhunt. It helped to keep us going, knowing that we would soon be at a particularly monstrous and disturbing murder scene.

It was nearly three in the morning when we arrived at the Buttes-Chaumont. What difference did the late hour make to me? I never slept anymore.

The park was deserted, but brightly lit with streetlamps and police and army searchlights. A low, bluish-gray fog had settled in, but there was still enough visibility for our search. The Buttes-Chaumont is an enormous area, not unlike Central Park in New York. Back in the mid-1800s, a man-made lake was dug there and fed by the St Martin's Canal. A mountain of rocks was then constructed, and it is full of caves and waterfalls now. The foliage is dense almost anywhere you choose to roam, or perhaps to hide a body.

It took only a few minutes before a police radio message came for us. Dr Sante had been located not far from where we had entered the park. Mr Smith was finished playing with us. For now.

Sandy and I got out of the patrol car at the gardener's house near the temple and we began to climb the steep stone steps. The flics and French soldiers around us weren't just tired and shell-shocked, they looked afraid. The body-recovery scene would stay with all of them for the rest of their lives. I had read John Webster's *The White Devil* while I was an undergrad at Harvard. Webster's weird seventeenth-century creation was filled with devils, demons, and werewolves – *all of them human*. I believed Mr Smith was a human demon. The worst kind.

We pushed our way forward through thick bushes and brush. I could hear the low, pitiful whine of search dogs nearby. Then I saw four high-strung, shivering animals leading the way.

Predictably, the new crime scene was a unique one. It was quite beautiful, with an expansive view of Montmartre and Saint-Denis. During the day, people came here to stroll, climb, walk pets, live life as it should be lived. The park closed at 11:00 p.m. for safety reasons.

'Up ahead,' Sandy whispered. 'There's something.'

I could see soldiers and police loitering in small groups. Mr Smith had definitely been here. A dozen or more 'packets,' each wrapped in newspaper, were carefully laid out on a sloping patch of grass.

'Are we sure this is it?' one of the inspectors asked me in French. His name was Girard. 'What the hell is this? Is he making a joke?'

'It is not a joke, I can promise you that. Unwrap one of the bundles. Any one will do,' I instructed the French policeman. He just looked at me as if I were mad.

'As they say in America,' Girard said in French, 'this is your show.'

'Do you speak English?' I spit out the words.

'Yes, I do,' he answered brusquely.

'Good. Go fuck yourself,' I said.

I walked over to the eerie pile of 'packages,' or perhaps 'gifts' was the better word. There were a variety of shapes, each packet meticulously wrapped in newspaper. Mr Smith the artiste. A large round packet looked as if it might be a head.

'French butcher shop. That's his motif for tonight. It's all just meat to him,' I muttered to Sandy Greenberg. 'He's mocking the French police.'

I carefully unwrapped the newspaper with plastic gloves. 'Christ Jesus, Sandy.'

It wasn't quite a head – *only half a head*.

Dr Abel Sante's head had been cleanly separated from the rest of the body, like an expensive cut of meat. It was sliced in half. The face was washed, the skin carefully pulled away. Only half of Sante's mouth screamed at us – a single eye reflected a moment of ultimate terror.

'You're right. It *is* just meat to him,' Sandy said. 'How can you stand being right about him all the time?'

'I can't,' I whispered. 'I can't stand it at all.'

Chapter Ninety-Five

Outside Washington, an FBI sedan stopped to pick up Christine Johnson at her apartment. She was ready and waiting, standing vigil just inside the front door. She was hugging herself, always hugging herself lately, always on the edge of fear. She'd had two glasses of red wine and had to force herself to stop at two.

As she hurried to the car she kept glancing around to see if a reporter was staking out her apartment. They were like hounds on a fresh trail. Persistent, sometimes unbelievably insensitive and rude.

A black agent whom she knew, a smart, nice man named Charles Dampier, hopped out and held the car's back door open for her. 'Good evening, Ms Johnson,' he said as politely as one of her students at school. She thought that he had a little crush on her. She was used to men acting like that, but tried to be kind.

'Thank you,' she said as she got into the gray-leather backseat. 'Good evening, guys,' she said to Charles and the driver, a man named Joseph Denjeau.

During the ride, no one spoke. The agents had obviously been instructed not to make small talk unless she initiated it. *Strange, cold world they live in*, Christine thought to herself. *And now I guess I live there, too. I don't think I like it at all.*

She had taken a bath before the agents arrived. She sat in the tub with her red wine and reviewed her life. She understood the good, bad, and ugly about herself pretty well. She knew she had always been a little afraid to jump off the deep end in the past, but she'd wanted to, and she'd gotten oh-so-close. There was definitely a streak of wildness inside her, *good* wildness, too. She had actually left George for six months during the early years of their marriage. She'd flown to San Francisco and studied photography at Berkeley, lived in a tiny apartment in the hills. She had loved the solitude for a while, the time for thinking, the simple act of recording the beauty of life with her camera every day.

She had come back to George, taught, and eventually got the job at the Sojourner Truth School. Maybe it was being around the children, but she absolutely loved it at the school. God, she loved kids, and she was good with them, too. She wanted children of her own so badly.

Her mind was all over the place tonight. Probably the late hour, and the second glass of Merlot. The dark Ford sedan cruised along deserted streets at midnight. It was the usual route, almost always the same trail from Mitchellville to DC She wondered if that was wise, but figured they knew how to do their jobs.

Occasionally Christine glanced around, to see if they were being followed. She felt a little silly doing it. Couldn't help it, though.

She was part of a case that was important to the press now. And dangerous, too. They had absolutely no respect for her privacy or feelings. Reporters would show up at the school and try to question other teachers. They called her at home so frequently that she finally changed her number to an unlisted one.

She heard the *whoop* of nearby police or ambulance sirens and the unpleasant sound brought her out of her reverie. She sighed. She was almost there now.

She shut her eyes and took deep, slow breaths. She dropped her head down near her chest. She was tired and thought she needed a good cry.

'Are you all right, Ms Johnson?' agent Dampier inquired. *He's got eyes in the back of his head. He's been watching me*, Christine thought. *He's watching everything that happens, but I guess that's good.*

'I'm fine.' She opened her eyes and offered a smile. 'Just a little tired is all. Too many early mornings and late nights.'

Agent Dampier hesitated, then he said, 'I'm sorry it has to be this way.'

'Thank you,' she whispered. 'You make it a lot easier for me with your kindness. And *you're* a real good driver,' she kidded agent Denjeau, who mostly kept quiet, but laughed now.

The FBI sedan hurtled down a steep concrete ramp and entered the building from the rear. This was a delivery entrance, she knew by now. She noticed that she was hugging herself again. Everything about the nightly trip seemed so unreal to her.

Both agents escorted her upstairs, right to the door, at which point they stepped back and she entered alone.

She gently closed the door and leaned against it. Her heart was pounding – it was always this way.

'Hello, Christine,' Alex said, and she went and held him so tight, *so tight*, and everything was suddenly so much better. Everything made sense again.

Chapter Ninety-Six

My first morning back in Washington, I decided to visit the Cross house on Fifth Street again. I needed to look over Cross's notes on Gary Soneji one more time. I had a deepening sense that Alex Cross knew his assailant, had met the person at some time before the vicious attack.

As I drove to the house through the crowded DC streets I went over the physical evidence again. The first really significant clue was that the bedroom where Cross was attacked had been tightly controlled. There was little or no evidence of chaos, of someone being out of his mind. There was ample evidence that the assailant was in what is called a cold rage.

The other significant factor was the evidence of 'overkill' in the bedroom. Cross had been struck half-a-dozen times before he was shot. That would seem to conflict with the tight control at the crime scene, but I didn't think so: Whoever came to the house had a deep hatred for Cross.

Once inside the house, the attacker operated as Soneji would have. The assailant had hidden in the cellar. Then he copycatted an earlier attack Soneji had made at the house. No weapons had been found, so the attacker was definitely clearheaded. No souvenirs had been taken from Cross's room.

Alex Cross's detective shield had been left behind. The attacker wanted it found. What did that tell me – that the killer was proud of what he had accomplished?

Finally, I kept returning to the single most striking and meaningful clue so far. It had jumped at me from the first moment I arrived on Fifth Street and began to collect data.

The attacker had left Alex Cross and his family alive. Even if Cross died, the assailant had departed from the house with the knowledge that Cross was still breathing.

Why would the intruder do that? He could have killed Cross. Or was it always part of a plan to leave Cross alive? If so, why?

Solve that mystery, answer that question – case solved.

Chapter Ninety-Seven

The house was quiet, and it had a sad and empty feeling, as houses do when a big, important piece of the family is missing.

I could see Nana Mama working feverishly in her kitchen. The smell of baking bread, roast chicken, and baked sweet potatoes flowed through the house, and it was soothing and reassuring. She was lost in her cooking, and I didn't want to disturb her.

'Is she okay?' I asked Sampson. He had agreed to meet me at the house, though I could tell he was still angry about my leaving the case for a few days.

He shrugged his shoulders. 'She won't accept that Alex isn't coming back, if that's what you mean,' he said. 'If he dies, I don't know what will happen to her.'

Sampson and I climbed the stairs in silence. We were in the hallway when the Cross children appeared out of a side bedroom.

I hadn't formally met Damon and Jannie, but I had heard about them. Both children were beautiful, though still showing bruises from the attack. They had inherited Alex's good looks. They had bright eyes and their intelligence showed.

'This is Mr Pierce,' Sampson said, 'he's a friend of ours. He's one of the good guys.'

'I'm working with Sampson,' I told them. 'Trying to help him.'

'Is he, Uncle John?' the little girl asked. The boy just stared at me – not angry, but wary of strangers. I could see his father in Damon's wide brown eyes.

'Yes, he is working with me, and he's very good at it,' Sampson said. He surprised me with the compliment.

Jannie stepped up close to me. She was the most beautiful little girl, even with the lacerations and a bruise the size of a baseball on her cheek and neck. Her mother must have been a beautiful woman.

She reached out and shook my hand. 'Well, you can't be as good as my daddy, but you can use my daddy's bedroom,' she said, 'but only until he comes back home.'

I thanked Jannie, and nodded respectfully at Damon. Then I spent the next hour and a half going over Cross's extensive notes and files on Gary Soneji. *I was looking for Soneji's partner*. The files dated back over four years. I was convinced that whoever attacked Alex Cross didn't do it randomly. There had to be a powerful connection with Soneji, *who claimed to always work alone*. It was a knotty problem and the profilers at Quantico weren't making headway with it either.

When I finally trudged back downstairs, Sampson and Nana were both in the kitchen. The uncluttered and practical-looking room was cozy and warm. It brought back memories of Isabella, who had loved to cook and was good at it, too, memories of our home and life together.

Nana looked up at me, her eyes as incisive as I remembered. 'I remember you,' she said. 'You were the one who told me the truth. Are you close to anything yet? Will you solve this terrible thing?' she asked.

'No, I haven't solved it, Nana,' I told her the truth again. 'But I think Alex might have. Gary Soneji might have had a partner all along.'

Chapter Ninety-Eight

A recurring thought was playing constantly inside my head: *Who can you trust? Who can you really believe? I used to have somebody – Isabella.*

John Sampson and I boarded an FBI Belljet Ranger around eleven the following morning. We had packed for a couple of days' stay.

'So who is this partner of Soneji's? When do I get to meet him?' Sampson asked during the flight.

'You already have,' I told him.

We arrived in Princeton before noon and went to see a man named Simon Conklin. Sampson and Cross had questioned him before. Alex Cross had written several pages of notes on Conklin during the investigation of the sensational kidnapping of two young children a few years back: Maggie Rose Dunne and Michael 'Shrimpie' Goldberg. The FBI had never really followed up on the exten-sive reports at the time. They wanted the high-profile kidnapping case closed.

I'd read the notes through a couple of times now. Simon Conklin and Gary had grown up on the same country road, a few miles outside the town of Princeton. The two friends thought of themselves as 'superior' to other kids, and even to most adults. Gary had called himself and Conklin the 'great ones.' They were reminiscent of Leopold and Loeb, two highly intelligent teens who had committed a famous thrill killing in Chicago one year.

As boys, Simon Conklin and Gary had decided that life was nothing more than a cock-and-bull 'story' conveniently cooked up by the people in charge. Either you followed the 'story' written by the society you lived in, or you set out to write your own.

Cross double-underscored in the notes that *Gary had been in the bottom fifth of his class at Princeton High School, before he transferred to the Peddie School. Simon Conklin had been number one, and gone on to Princeton University.*

A few minutes past noon, Sampson and I stepped out into the dirt and gravel parking lot of a dreary little strip mall between Princeton and Trenton, New Jersey. It was hot and humid and everything looked bleached out by the sun.

'Princeton education sure worked out well for Conklin,' Sampson said with sarcasm in his voice. 'I'm really impressed.'

For the past two years, Simon Conklin had managed an adult bookstore in the dilapidated strip mall. The store was located in a single-story, red-brick building. The front door was painted black and so were the padlocks. The sign read ADULT.

'What's your feeling about Simon Conklin? Do you remember much about him?' I asked as we walked toward the front door. I suspected there was a back way out, but I didn't think he would run on us.

'Oh, Simon Says is definitely a world-class freakazoid. He was high on my Unabomber list at one time. Has an alibi for the night Alex was attacked.'

'He would,' I muttered. 'Of course he would. He's a clever boy. Don't ever forget that.'

We walked inside the seedy, grungy store and flashed our badges. Conklin stepped out from behind a raised counter. He was tall and gangly and painfully thin. His milky-brown eyes were distant, as if he were someplace else. He was instantly unlikable.

He had on faded black jeans and a studded black leather vest, no shirt under the vest. If I hadn't known a few Harvard flameouts myself, I wouldn't have imagined he had graduated from Princeton and ended up like this. All around him were pleasure kits, masturbators, dildos, pumps, restraints. Simon Conklin seemed right in his element.

'I'm starting to enjoy these unexpected visits from you assholes. I didn't at first, but now I'm getting into them,' he said. 'I remember you, Detective Sampson. But *you're* new to the traveling team. You must be Alex Cross's unworthy replacement.'

'Not really,' I said. 'Just haven't felt like coming around to this shithole until now.'

Conklin snorted, a phlegmy sound that wasn't quite a laugh. 'You haven't felt like it. That means you have feelings that you occasionally act on. How quaint. Then you *must* be with the FBI's Criminal Investigative Analysis Program. Am I right?'

I looked away from him and checked out the rest of the store.

'Hi,' I said to a man perusing a rack with Spanish Fly Powder, Sta-Hard, and the like. 'Find anything you like today? Are you from the Princeton area? I'm Thomas Pierce with the FBI.'

The man mumbled something unintelligible into his chin and then he scurried out, letting a blast of sunlight inside.

'Ouch. That's not nice,' Conklin said. He snorted again, not quite a laugh.

'I'm not very nice sometimes,' I said to him.

Conklin responded with a jaw-cracking yawn. 'When Alex Cross got shot, I was with a friend all night. Your very thorough cohorts already spoke to my squeeze, Dana. We were at a party in Hopewell till around midnight. Lots and lots of witnesses.'

I nodded, looked as bored as he did. 'On another, more promising subject, tell me what happened to Gary's trains? The ones he stole from his stepbrother?'

Conklin wasn't smiling anymore. 'Look, actually I'm getting a little tired of the bullshit. The repetition bores me and I'm not into ancient history. Gary and I were friends until we were around twelve years old. After that, we never spent time together. He had his friends, and so did I. *The end.* Now get the hell out of here.'

I shook my head. 'No, no, Gary never had any other friends. He only had time for the "great ones." He believed you were one of them. He told that to Alex Cross. I think you were Gary's friend until he died. That's why you hated Dr Cross. You had a reason to attack his house. You had a motive, Conklin, and you're the *only* one who did.'

Conklin snorted out of his nose and the side of his mouth again. 'And if you can prove that, then I go directly to jail. I do not pass Go. But you can't prove it. *Dana. Hopewell. Several witnesses.* Bye-bye, assholes.'

I walked out the front door of the adult bookstore. I stood in the blazing heat of the parking lot and waited for Sampson to catch up with me.

'What the hell is going on? Why did you just walk out like that?' he asked.

'Maybe Conklin is the leader,' I said. 'Maybe Soneji was *the follower.*'

Chapter Ninety-Nine

Sooner or later almost every police investigation becomes a game of cat and mouse. The difficult, long-running ones always do. First you have to decide, though: *Who is the cat? Who is the mouse?*

For the next few days, Sampson and I kept Simon Conklin under surveillance. We let him know we were there, waiting and watching, always just around the next corner, and the corner after that. I wanted to see if we could pressure Conklin into a telling action, or even a mistake.

Conklin's reply was an occasional jaunty salute with his middle finger. That was fine. We were registering on his radar. He knew we were there, always there, watching. I could tell we were unnerving him, and I was just beginning to play the game.

John Sampson had to return to Washington after a few days. I had expected that. The DC police department couldn't let him work the case indefinitely. Besides, Alex Cross and his family needed Sampson in Washington.

I was alone in Princeton, the way I liked it, actually.

Simon Conklin left his house on Tuesday night. After some maneuvering of my own, I followed in my Ford Escort. I let him see me early on. Then I dropped back in the heavy traffic out near the malls, and I let him go free.

I drove straight back to his house and parked off the main road, which is hidden from sight by thick scrub pines and brambles. I walked through the dense woods as quickly as I could. I knew I might not have a lot of time.

No flashlight, no lights of any kind. I knew where I was going now. I was pumped up and ready. I had figured it all out. I understood the game now, and my part in it. My sixth sense was active.

The house was brick and wood and it had a quirky hexagonal window in the front. Loose, chipped, aqua-colored shutters occasionally banged against the house. It was more than a mile from the closest neighbor. No one would see me break in through the kitchen door.

I was aware that Simon Conklin might circle back behind me – if he was as bright as he thought he was. I wasn't worried about that. I had a working theory about Conklin and his visit to Cross's house. I needed to test it out.

I suddenly thought about Mr Smith as I was picking the lock. *Smith was obsessed with studying people, with breaking and entering into their lives.*

The inside of the house was absolutely unbearable: Simon Conklin's place smelled like Salvation Army furniture laced with BO and immersed in a McDonald's deep fryer. No, it was actually worse than that. I held a handker-chief over my nose and mouth as I began to search the filthy lair. I was afraid that I might find a body in here. Anything was possible.

Every room and every object was coated with dust and grime. The best that could be said of Simon Conklin was that he was an avid reader. Volumes were spread open in every room, half-a-dozen on his bed alone.

He seemed to favor sociology, philosophy, and psychology: Marx, Jung, Bruno Bettelheim, Malraux, Jean Baudrillard. Three unpainted floor-to-ceiling bookcases were crammed with books piled horizontally. My initial impression of the place was that it had already been ransacked by someone.

All of this fit with what had really happened at Alex Cross's house.

Over Conklin's rumpled, unmade bed was a framed Vargas girl, signed by the model, with a lipstick kiss next to the butt.

A rifle was stashed under the bed. It was a Browning BAR – the same model Gary Soneji had used in Washington. A smile slowly broke across my face.

Simon Conklin knew the rifle was circumstantial evidence, that it proved nothing about his guilt or innocence. *He wanted it found. He wanted Cross's badge found. He liked to play games. Of course he did.*

I climbed down creaking wooden stairs to the basement. I kept the house lights off and used only my penlight.

There were no windows in the cellar. There was dust and cobwebs, and a loudly dripping sink. Curled photographic prints were clipped to strings dangling from the ceiling.

My heart was beating in double time. I examined the dangling pictures. They were photos of Simon Conklin himself, different pics of the auteur cavorting in the buff. They appeared to have been taken inside the house.

I shined the light haphazardly around the basement, glancing everywhere. The floor was dirt and there were large rocks on which the old house was built. Ancient medical equipment was stored: a walker, an aluminum-framed potty, an oxygen tank with hoses and gauges still attached, a glucose monitor.

My eyes trailed over to the far side, the southern wall of the house. *Gary Soneji's train set!*

I was in the house of Gary's best friend, his only friend in the world, the man who had attacked Alex Cross and his family in Washington. I was certain of it. I was certain I had solved the case.

I was better than Alex Cross.

There, I've said it.

The truth begins.

Who is the cat? Who is the mouse?

Part Five

Cat and Mouse

Chapter One Hundred

A dozen of the best FBI agents available stood in an informal grouping on the airfield in Quantico, Virginia. Directly behind them, two jet-black helicopters were waiting for takeoff. The agents couldn't have looked more solemn or attentive, but also puzzled.

As I stood before them, my legs were shaking and my knees were hitting together. I had never been more nervous, more unsure of myself. I had also never been more focused on a murder case.

'For those of you who don't know me,' I said, pausing not for effect, but because of nerves, 'I'm Alex Cross.'

I tried to let them see that physically I was fine. I wore loose-fitting khaki trousers and a long-sleeved navy-blue cotton knit shirt open at the collar. I was doing my best to disguise a mess of bruises and lacerations.

A lot of troubling mysteries had to unfold now. Mysteries about the savage, cowardly attack at my house in Washington – and who had done it; dizzying mysteries about the mass-murderer Mr Smith; and about Thomas Pierce of the FBI.

I could see by their faces that some of the agents remained confused. They clearly looked as if they'd been blind-sided by my appearance.

I couldn't blame them, but I also knew that what had happened was necessary. It seemed like the only way to catch a terrifying and diabolical killer. That was the plan, and the plan was all-consuming.

'As you can all see, rumors of my imminent demise have been greatly exaggerated. I'm just fine, actually,' I said and cracked a smile. That seemed to break the ice a little with the agents.

'The official statements out of St Anthony's Hospital – "not expected to live," "very grave condition," "highly unusual for someone in Dr Cross's condition to pull through" – were overstatements, and sometimes outright lies. The releases were manufactured for Thomas Pierce's benefit. The releases were a hoax. If you want to blame someone, blame Kyle Craig,' I said.

'Yes, definitely blame me,' Kyle said. He was standing at my side, along with John Sampson and Sondra Greenberg from Interpol. 'Alex didn't want to go this way. Actually, he didn't want any involvement at all, if my memory serves me.'

'That's right, but now I am involved. I'm in this up to my eyebrows. Soon you will be, too. Kyle and I are going to tell you everything.'

I took a breath, then I continued. My nervousness was mostly gone.

'Four years ago, a recent Harvard Medical School grad named Thomas Pierce discovered his girlfriend murdered in their apartment in Cambridge. That was the police finding at the time. It was later corroborated by the Bureau. Let me tell you about the actual murder. Now let me tell you what Kyle and I believe really happened. This is how it went down that night in Cambridge.'

Chapter One Hundred and One

Thomas Pierce had spent the early part of the night out drinking with friends at a bar called Jillian's in Cambridge. The friends were recent med-school graduates and they'd been drinking hard since about two in the afternoon.

Pierce had invited Isabella to the bar, but she'd turned him down and told him to have fun, let off some steam. He deserved it. That night, as he had been doing for the past six months, a doctor named Martin Straw came over to the apartment Isabella and Pierce shared. Straw and Isabella were having an affair. He had promised he would leave his wife and children for her.

Isabella was asleep when Pierce got to the apartment on Inman Street. He knew that Dr Martin Straw had been there earlier. He had seen Straw and Isabella together at other times. He'd followed them on several occasions around Cambridge and also on day trips out into the countryside.

As he opened the front door of his apartment, he could feel, in every inch of his body, that Martin Straw had been there. Straw's scent was unmistakable, and Thomas Pierce wanted to scream. He had never cheated on Isabella, never even come close.

She was fast asleep in their bed. He stood over her for several moments and she never stirred. He had always loved the way she slept, loved watching her like this. He had always mistaken her sleeping pose for innocence.

He could tell that Isabella had been drinking wine. He smelled the sweet odor from where he stood.

She had on perfume that night. For Martin Straw.

It was Jean Patou's Joy – very expensive. He had bought it for her the previous Christmas.

Thomas Pierce began to cry, to sob into his hands.

Isabella's long auburn hair was loose and strands and bunches flowed free on the pillows. For Martin Straw.

Martin Straw always lay on the left side of the bed. He had a deviated septum that he should have tended to, but doctors put off operations, too. He couldn't breathe very well out of the right nostril.

Thomas Pierce knew this. He had *studied* Straw, tried to understand him, his so-called humanity.

Pierce knew he had to act now, knew that he couldn't take too much time.

He fell on Isabella with all his weight, his force, his power. His tools were ready. She struggled, but he held her down. He clutched her long swanlike throat with his strong hands. He wedged his feet under the mattress for leverage.

The struggle exposed her bare breasts and he was reminded of how 'sexy' and 'absolutely beautiful' Isabella was; how they were 'perfect together'; 'Cambridge's very own Romeo and Juliet.' What bullshit it was. A sorry myth. The perception of people who couldn't see straight. She didn't really love him, but how he had loved her. Isabella made him *feel* for the one and only time in his life.

Thomas Pierce looked down at her. Isabella's eyes were like sand-blasted mirrors. Her small, beautiful mouth fell open to one side. Her skin still felt satin-soft to his touch.

She was helpless now, but she could see what was happening. Isabella was aware of her crimes and the punishment to come.

'I don't know what I'm doing,' he finally said. 'It's as if I'm outside myself, watching. And yet . . . I can't tell you how alive I feel right now.'

Every newspaper, the news magazines, TV, and radio reported what happened in gruesome detail, but nothing like what really happened, what it was like in the bedroom, staring into Isabella's eyes as he murdered her.

He cut out Isabella's heart.

He held her heart in his hands, still pumping, still alive, and watched it die.

Then he impaled her heart on a spear from the scuba equipment.

He *'pierced'* her heart. That was the clue he left. The very first clue.

He had the feeling, the sixth sense, that he actually watched Isabella's spirit leave her body. Then he thought he felt his own soul depart. He believed that he died that night, too.

Smith was born from death that night in Cambridge.

Thomas Pierce was Mr Smith.

Chapter One Hundred and Two

'Thomas Pierce *is* Mr Smith,' I said to the agents gathered at Quantico. 'If any of you still doubt that, even a little bit, please don't. It could be dangerous to you and everyone else on this team. Pierce is Smith, and he's murdered nineteen people so far. He will murder again.'

I had been speaking for several moments, but now I stopped. There was a question from the group. Actually, there were several questions. I couldn't blame them – I was full of questions myself.

'Can I backtrack for just a second here? Your family *was* attacked?' a young crew-cut agent asked. 'You *did* sustain injuries?'

'There *was* an attack at my house. For reasons that we don't understand yet, the intruder stopped short of murder. My family is all right. Believe me, I want to understand about the attack, and the intruder, more than anyone does. I want that bastard, whoever he is.'

I held up my cast for all of them to see. 'I took a bullet in my wrist. A second entered my abdomen, but passed through. The hepatic artery was not nicked, as was reported. I was definitely banged-up, but my EKG never showed "a pattern of decreased activity." That was for Pierce's benefit. Kyle? You want to fill in some more of the holes you helped create?'

This was Kyle Craig's master plan, and he spoke to the agents.

'Alex is right about Pierce. He is a cold-blooded killer and what we hope to do tonight is dangerous. It's unusual, but this situation warrants it. For the past several weeks, Interpol and the Bureau have been trying to set a foolproof trap for the elusive Mr Smith, who we believe to be Thomas Pierce,' Kyle repeated. 'We haven't been able to catch him at anything conclusive, and we don't want to do something that might spook him, make him run.'

'He's one scary, spooky son of a bitch, I'll tell you that much,' John Sampson said from his place alongside me. I could tell he was holding back, keeping his anger inside. 'And the bastard is *very careful*. I never caught him in anything close to a slipup while I was working with him. Pierce played his part perfectly.'

'So did you, John,' Kyle offered a compliment. 'Detective Sampson has been in on the ruse, too,' he explained.

A few hours earlier, Sampson had been with Pierce in New Jersey. He knew him better than I did, though not as well as Kyle or Sondra Greenberg of Interpol, who had originally profiled Pierce, and was with us now at Quantico.

'How is he acting, Sondra?' Kyle asked Greenberg. 'What have you noticed?'

The Interpol inspector was a tall, impressive-looking woman. She'd been working the case for nearly two years in Europe. 'Thomas Pierce is an arrogant bastard. Believe me, he's laughing at all of us. He's one hundred percent sure of himself. He's also high-strung. He never stops looking over his shoulder. Sometimes, I don't think he's human either. I do believe he's going to blow soon. The pressure we've applied is working.'

'That's becoming more evident,' Kyle picked up the thread. 'Pierce was very cool in the beginning. He had everyone fooled. He was as professional as any agent we've ever had. Early on, no one in the Cambridge police believed he had murdered Isabella Calais. He never made a mistake. His grief over her death was astonishing.'

'He's for real, ladies and gents.' Sampson spoke up again. 'He's smart as hell. Pretty good investigator, too. His instincts are sharp and he's disciplined. He did his homework, and he went right to Simon Conklin. I think he's competing with Alex.'

'So do I,' Kyle nodded at Sampson. 'He's very complex. We probably don't know the half of it yet. That's what scares me.'

Kyle had come to me about Mr Smith before the Soneji shooting spree had started. We had talked again when I'd taken Rosie to Quantico for tests. I worked with him on an unofficial basis. I helped with the profile on Thomas Pierce, along with Sondra Greenberg. When I was shot at my house, Kyle rushed to Washington out of concern. But the attack was nowhere near as bad as everyone thought, or as we led them to believe.

It was Kyle who decided to take a big chance. So far, Pierce was running free. Maybe if he brought him in on the case, on *my* case? It would be a way to watch him, to put pressure on Pierce. Kyle believed that Pierce wouldn't be able to resist. Big ego, tremendous confidence. Kyle was right.

'Pierce is going to blow,' Sondra Greenberg said again. 'I'm telling you. I don't know everything that's going on in his head, but he's close to the limit.'

I agreed with Greenberg. 'I'll tell you what could happen next. The two personas are starting to fuse. Mr Smith and Thomas Pierce could merge soon. Actually, it's the Thomas Pierce part of his personality that seems to be diminishing. I think he just might have *Mr Smith take out Simon Conklin*.'

Sampson leaned into me and whispered. 'I think it's time that you met Mr Pierce *and* Mr Smith.'

Chapter One Hundred and Three

This was it. The end. It had to be.

Everything we could think of was tightly in place by seven o'clock that night in Princeton. Thomas Pierce had proved to be elusive in the past, almost illusory. He kept mysteriously slipping in and out of his role as 'Mr Smith.' But he was clearly about to blow.

How he accomplished his black magic, no one knew. There were never any witnesses. No one was left alive.

Kyle Craig's fear was that we would never catch Pierce in the act, never be able to hold him for more than forty-eight hours. Kyle was convinced that Pierce was smarter than Gary Soneji, cleverer than any of us.

Kyle had objected to Thomas Pierce's assignment to the Mr Smith case, but he'd been overruled. He had watched Pierce, listened to him, and became more and more convinced that Pierce was involved – at least with the death of Isabella Calais.

Pierce never seemed to make a mistake, though. He covered all of his tracks. Then a break came. Pierce was seen in Frankfurt, Germany, on the same day a victim disappeared there. Pierce was supposed to be in Rome.

It was enough for Kyle to approve a search of Pierce's apartment in Cambridge. Nothing was found. Kyle brought in computer experts. They *suspected* that Pierce might be sending himself messages, supposedly from Smith, but there was no proof. Then Pierce was seen in Paris on the day Dr Abel Sante disappeared. His logs stated that he was in London all day. It was circumstantial, but Kyle knew he had his killer.

So did I.

Now we needed concrete proof.

Nearly fifty FBI agents were in the Princeton area, which seemed like the last place in the world where a shocking crime ought to occur, or a notorious murder spree end.

Sampson and I waited in the front seat of a dark sedan parked on an anonymous looking street. We weren't part of the main surveillance team, but we stayed close. We were never more than a mile, or at most two, from Pierce. Sampson was restless and irritable through the early night. It had gotten excruciatingly personal between him and Pierce.

I had a very personal reason to be in Princeton myself. I wanted a crack at Simon Conklin. Unfortunately, Pierce was between me and Conklin for now.

We were a few blocks from the Marriott in town where Pierce was staying.

'Quite a plan,' Sampson mumbled as we sat and waited.

The FBI tried just about everything else. Kyle thinks this will work. He feels Pierce couldn't resist solving the attack at my house. It's the ultimate competition for him. Who knows?'

Sampson's eyes narrowed. I knew the look – sharp, comprehending. 'Yeah, and you had no part in any of the hinky shit, right?'

'Maybe I did offer a suggestion about why the setup might be attractive to Thomas Pierce, to his huge ego. Or why he might be cocky enough to get caught.'

Sampson rolled his eyes back into his forehead, the way he'd been doing since we were about ten years old. 'Yeah, maybe you did. By the way, he's an even bigger pain in the ass than you are to work with. Anal as shit, to coin a phrase.'

We waited on the side street in Princeton as night blanketed the university town. It was déjà vu all over again. John Sampson and Alex Cross on a stakeout duty.

'You still love me,' Sampson said and grinned. He doesn't get giddy too often, but when he does – watch out. 'You do love me, Sugar?'

I put my hand high on his thigh. 'Sure do, big fellow.'

He punched me in the shoulder – *hard*. My arm went numb. My fingers tingled. The man can *hit*.

'I want to put the hurt on Thomas Pierce! I'm going to put the hurt on Pierce!' Sampson yelled out in the car.

'Put the hurt on Thomas Pierce,' I yelled with him. 'And Mr Smith, too!'

'Put the hurt on Mr Smith and Mr Pierce,' we sang in unison, doing our imitation of the *Bad Boy* movie.

Yeah!

We were back. Same as it ever was.

Chapter One Hundred and Four

Thomas Pierce felt that he was invincible, that he couldn't be stopped.

He waited in the dark, trancelike, without moving. He was thinking about Isabella, seeing her beautiful face, seeing her smile, hearing her voice. He stayed like that until the living-room light was switched on and he saw Simon Conklin.

'Intruder in the house,' Pierce whispered. 'Sound familiar? Ring any bells for you, Conklin?'

He held a .357 Magnum pointed directly at Conklin's forehead. He could blow him right out the front door and down the porch stairs.

'What the—?' Conklin was blinky-eyed in the bright light. Then his dark eyes grew beady and hard. 'This is unlawful entry!' Conklin screamed. 'You have no right to be here in my house. Get the hell out!'

Pierce couldn't hold back a smile. He definitely *got* the humor in life, but sometimes he didn't take enough pleasure in it. He got up out of the chair, holding the gun perfectly still in front of him.

There wasn't much space to move in the living room, which was filled with tall stacks of newspapers, books, clippings, and magazines. Everything was categorized by date and subject. He was pretty sure that not-so-Simple Simon had an obsessive-compulsive disorder.

'Downstairs. We're going to your basement,' he said. 'Down to *the cellar.*'

The light was already on downstairs. Thomas Pierce had gotten everything ready. An old cot was set up in the center of the crowded basement room. He had cleared away stacks of survivalist and sci-fi books to make room for the cot.

He wasn't sure, but he thought Conklin's obsession had to do with the end of the human race. He hoarded books, journals, and newspaper stories that supported his pathological idea. The cover of a science journal was taped to the cellar wall. It read: 'Sex Changes in Fish – A Look at Simultaneous and Sequential Hermaphrodites.'

'What the hell?' Simon Conklin yelled when he saw what Pierce had done.

'That's what they all say,' Thomas Pierce said and shoved him. Conklin stumbled down a couple of stairs.

'You think I'm afraid of you?' Conklin whirled and snarled. 'I'm not afraid of you.'

Pierce nodded his head once and cocked an eyebrow. 'I hear you, and I'm going to straighten that out right now.'

He shoved Conklin hard again and watched him tumble down the rest of the stairs. Pierce walked slowly down toward the heap. 'You *starting* to get afraid of me now?' he asked.

He whacked Conklin with the side of the Magnum and watched as blood spit from Simon Conklin's head. 'You starting to get afraid now?'

He bent down and put his mouth close to Conklin's hairy ear.

'You don't understand very much about pain. I know that about you,' he whispered. 'You don't have much in the way of guts either. You were the one in the Cross house, but you *couldn't* kill Alex Cross, could you? You *couldn't* kill his family. You punked out at his house. You blew it. That's what I *already know.*'

Thomas Pierce was enjoying the confrontation, the satisfaction of it. He was curious about what made Simon Conklin tick. He wanted to 'study' Conklin, to understand his humanity. To know Simon Conklin was to know something about himself.

He stayed in Conklin's face. 'First, I want you to *tell* me that you're the one who snuck into Alex Cross's house. *You did it!* Now just tell me you did it. What you say here will *not* be held against you, and will *not* be used in a court of law. It's just between us.'

Simon Conklin looked at him as if he were a complete madman. *How perceptive.*

'You're crazy. You can't do this. This won't matter in court,' Conklin squealed.

Pierce's eyes widened in disbelief. He looked at Conklin as if *he* were the madman. 'Didn't I just say precisely that? Weren't you listening? Am I talking to myself here? No, it won't matter in *their* court. This is *my* court. So far, you're losing your case, Simple Simon. You're smart, though. I'm confident you can do a much better job over the next few hours.'

Simon Conklin gasped. A shiny, stainless-steel scalpel was pointed at his chest.

Chapter One Hundred and Five

'*Look at me!* Would you focus on what I'm saying, Simon. I'm not another gray suit from the FBI . . . I have important questions to ask. I want you to answer them truthfully. You *were* the one at Cross's house! You attacked Cross. Let's proceed from there.'

With a swift move of his left arm, Pierce pulled Conklin roughly up off the cellar floor. His physical strength was a shock to Conklin.

Pierce put his scalpel down and hog-tied Conklin to the cot with rope.

Pierce leaned in close to Simon Conklin once he was tied down and help-less. 'Here's a news flash – I don't like your superior attitude. Believe me, *you aren't superior*. Somehow, and this amazes me, I don't think I've made myself clear yet. You're a *specimen*, Simon. Let me show you something creepy.'

'Don't!' Conklin screeched. He was helpless as Pierce made a sudden inci-sion in the upper chest. He couldn't believe what was happening. Simon Conklin screamed.

'Can you concentrate better now, Simon? See what's on the table here? It's your tape recorder. I just want you to confess. Tell me what happened inside Dr Cross's house. I want to hear everything.'

'Leave me alone,' Conklin whispered weakly.

'No! That's not going to happen. You will never be alone again. All right, forget the scalpel and the tape recorder. I want you to focus on *this*. Ordinary can of Coca-Cola. *Your Coke*, Simon.'

He shook the bright-red can, shook it up good, and popped it open. Then he pulled Conklin's head back. Grabbed a handful of long, greasy hair. Pierce pushed the harmless-looking can under Conklin's nostrils.

The soda exploded upward, fizz, bubbles, sugary-brown water. It shot up Conklin's nose and toward the brain. It was an army interrogator's trick. Excruciatingly painful, and it always worked.

Simon Conklin choked horribly. He couldn't stop coughing, gagging.

'I hope you appreciate the kind of resourcefulness I'm showing. I can work with any household object. Are you ready to confess? Or would you like some more Coke?'

Simon Conklin's eyes were wider than they had ever been before. 'I'll *say* whatever you want! Just please stop.'

Thomas Pierce shook his head back and forth. 'I just want the truth. I want the facts. I want to know I solved the case that Alex Cross couldn't.'

He turned on the tape recorder and held it under Conklin's bearded chin. 'Tell me what happened.'

'I was the one who attacked Cross and his family. Yes, yes, it was me,' Simon Conklin said in a choked voice that made each word sound even more emotional. 'Gary made me. He said if I didn't, somebody would come for me. They'd torture and kill me. Somebody he knew from Lorton Prison. That's the truth, I swear it is. Gary was the leader, not me!'

Thomas Pierce was suddenly almost tender, his voice soft and soothing. 'I figured that, Simon. I'm not stupid. So Gary made you do it. Now, when you got to the Cross house, you couldn't kill him, could you? You'd fantasized about it, but then you couldn't do it.'

Simon Conklin nodded. He was exhausted and frightened. He wondered if Gary had sent this madman and thought that maybe he had.

Pierce motioned with the Coke can for him to keep going. He took a hit of the Coke as he listened. 'Go on, Simon. Tell me all about you and Gary.'

Conklin was crying, bawling like a child, but he was talking. 'We got beat up a lot when we were kids. We were inseparable. I was there when Gary burned down his own house. His stepmother was inside with her two kids. So was his father. I watched over the two kids he kidnapped in DC. I was the one at Cross's house. You were right! It might as well have been Gary. He planned everything.'

Pierce finally took away the tape recorder and shut it off. 'That's much better, Simon. I do believe you.'

What Simon Conklin had just said seemed like a good break point – somewhere to end. The investigation was over. He'd proved he was better than Alex Cross.

'I'm going to tell you something. Something amazing, Simon. You'll appreciate this, I think.'

He raised the scalpel and Simon Conklin tried to squirm away. He knew what was coming.

'Gary Soneji was a pussycat compared to me,' Thomas Pierce said. *'I'm Mr Smith.'*

Chapter One Hundred and Six

S ampson and I rushed through Princeton, breaking just about every speed limit. The agents trailing Thomas Pierce had temporarily lost him. The elusive Pierce, or was it Mr Smith – was on the loose. They thought they had him again, at Simon Conklin's. Everything was chaos.

Moments after we arrived, Kyle gave the signal to move in on the house. Sampson and I were supposed to be *Jafos* at the scene – *just a fucking observer*. Sondra Greenberg was there. She was a *Jafo*, too.

A half-dozen FBI agents, Sampson, myself, and Sondra hurried through the yard. We split up. Some went in the front and others through the back of the ramshackle house. We were moving quickly and efficiently, handguns and rifles out. Everybody wore windbreakers with 'FBI' printed large on the back.

'I think he's here,' I told Sampson. 'I think we're about to meet Mr Smith!'

The living room was darker and gloomier than I remembered from an earlier visit. We didn't see anyone yet, neither Pierce nor Simon Conklin nor Mr Smith. The house looked as if it had been ransacked and it smelled terrible.

Kyle gave a hand signal and we fanned out, hurrying through the house. Everything was tense and unsettling.

'See no evil, hear no evil,' Sampson muttered at my side, 'but it's here all the same.'

I wanted Pierce to go down, but I wanted to get Simon Conklin even more. I figured it was Conklin who had come into my house and attacked my family. I needed five minutes alone with Conklin. Therapy time – for me. Maybe we could talk about Gary Soneji, about the 'great ones,' as they called themselves.

An agent called out – *'The basement! Down here! Hurry!'*

I was out of breath and hurting already. My right side burned like hell. I followed the others down the narrow, twisting stairs. 'Awhh Jesus,' I heard Kyle say from his position up ahead.

I saw Simon Conklin lying spread-eagled across an old striped-blue mattress on the floor. The man who had attacked me and my family had been mutilated.

Thanks to countless anatomy classes at Johns Hopkins, I was better prepared than the others for the gruesome murder scene. Simon Conklin's chest, stomach, and pelvic area had been cut open, as if a crackerjack medical examiner had just performed an on-the-scene autopsy.

'He's been gutted,' an FBI agent muttered, and turned away from the body. 'Why in the name of God?'

Simon Conklin had no face. A bold incision had been made at the top of his skull. The cut went through the scalp and clear down to the bone. Then the scalp had been pulled down over the front of the face.

Conklin's long black hair hung from his scalp to where the chin should have been. It looked like a beard. I suspected that this meant something to Pierce. *What did obliterating a face mean to him, if anything?*

There was an unpainted wooden door in the cellar, another way out, but none of the agents stationed outside had seen him leave. Several agents were trying to chase down Pierce. I stayed inside with the mutilated corpse. I couldn't have run down Nana Mama right then. For the first time in my life, I understood what it would be like to be physically old.

'He did this in just a couple of minutes?' Kyle Craig asked. 'Alex, could he work this fast?'

'If he's as crazy as I think he is, yeah, he could have. Don't forget he did this in med school, not to mention his other victims. He has to be incredibly strong, Kyle. He didn't have morgue tools, no electric saws. He used a knife, and his hands.'

I was standing close to the mattress, staring down at what remained of Simon Conklin. I thought of the cowardly attack on me, on my family. I'd wanted him caught, but not like this. Nobody deserved this. Only in Dante were such fierce punishments imposed on the damned.

I leaned in closer and peered at the remains of Simon Conklin. *Why was Thomas Pierce so angry at Conklin? Why had he punished Conklin like this?*

The basement of the house was eerily quiet. Sondra Greenberg looked pale, and was leaning against a cellar wall. I would have thought she'd be used to the murder scenes, but maybe that wasn't possible for anybody.

I had to clear my throat before I could speak again. 'He cut away the front quadrant of the skull,' I said. 'He performed a frontal craniotomy. It looks like Thomas Pierce is practicing medicine again.'

Chapter One Hundred and Seven

I had known Kyle Craig for ten years, and been his friend for nearly that long. I had never seen him so troubled and disconsolate about a case before, no matter how difficult or gruesome. The Thomas Pierce investigation had ruined his career, or at least he thought so, and maybe he was right.

'How the hell does he keep slipping away?' I said. We were still in Princeton the next morning, having breakfast at PJ's Pancake House. The food was excellent, but I just wasn't hungry.

'That's the worst part of it – he knows everything we would do. He anticipates our actions and procedures. He was one of us.'

'Maybe he *is* an alien,' I said to Kyle, who nodded wearily.

Kyle ate the remainder of his soft, runny eggs in silence. His face was bent low over his plate. He wasn't aware how comically depressed he looked.

'Those eggs must be real good.' I finally broke the silence with something other than the scraping sound of Kyle's fork on the plate.

He looked up at me with his usual deadpan look. 'I really messed this up, Alex. I should have taken Pierce in when I had the chance. We talked about it down in Quantico.'

'You would have had to let him go, release him in a few hours. Then what would you do? You couldn't keep Pierce under surveillance forever.'

'Director Burns wanted to sanction Pierce, take him out, but I strongly disagreed. I thought I could get him. I told Burns I would.'

I shook my head. I couldn't believe what I'd just heard. 'The Director of the FBI approved a sanction on Pierce? Jesus.'

Kyle ran his tongue back and forth over his teeth. 'Yes, and not just Burns. This went all the way to the attorney general's office. God knows where else. I had them convinced Pierce was Mr Smith. Somehow the idea of an FBI field agent who's also a multiple killer didn't sit very well with them. We'll never catch him now. There's no real pattern, Alex, at least nothing to follow. No way to trace him. He's laughing at us.'

'Yeah, he probably is,' I agreed. 'He's definitely competitive on some level. He likes to feel superior. There's a whole lot more to this, though.'

I had been thinking about the possibility of some kind of abstract or artistic pattern since I'd first heard about the complicated case. I was well aware of the theory that each of the murders was different, and worse, seemed arbitrary. That would make Pierce almost impossible to catch. The more I thought about the series of murders, though, and especially about Thomas Pierce's history, the more I suspected that there had to be a pattern, a mission behind all of this. The FBI had simply missed it. Now I was missing it, too.

'What do you want to do, Alex?' Kyle finally asked. 'I understand if you're not going to work this one, if you're not up to it.'

I thought about my family back home, about Christine Johnson and the things we'd talked over, but I didn't see how I could step away from this awful case right now. I was also somewhat afraid of retribution from Pierce. There was no way to predict how he might react now.

'I'll stay with you for a few days. I'll be around, Kyle. No promises beyond that. Shit, I *hate* that I said that. Damn it!' I pounded the table and the plates and flatware jumped.

For the first time that morning, Kyle offered up half a smile, 'So, what's your plan? Tell me what you're going to do.'

I shook my head back and forth. I still couldn't believe I was doing this. 'My plan is as follows. I'm going home to Washington, and that's non-negotiable. Tomorrow or the next day, I'll fly up to Boston. I want to see Pierce's apartment. He wanted to see my house, didn't he? Then, we'll see, Kyle. Please keep your evidence-gatherers on a leash before I get to his apartment. *Look, photograph*, but don't move anything around. Mr Smith is a very orderly man. I want to see how Pierce's place looks, how he arranged it for us.'

Kyle was back to the deadpan look, superserious, which I actually prefer. 'We're not going to get him, Alex. He's been given a warning. He'll be more careful from now on. Maybe he'll disappear like some killers do, just vanish off the face of the earth.'

'That would be nice,' I said, 'but I don't think it's going to happen. There *is* a pattern, Kyle. We just haven't found it.'

Chapter One Hundred and Eight

As they say in the wild, Wild West, you have to get right back on the horse that threw you. I spent two days back in Washington, but it seemed more like a couple of hours. Everybody was mad at me for getting into the hunt. Nana, the kids, Christine. So be it.

I took the first flight into Boston and was at Thomas Pierce's apartment in Cambridge by nine in the morning. Reluctantly, the dragonslayer was back in play.

Kyle Craig's original plan to catch Pierce was one of the most audacious ever to come out of the usually conservative Federal Bureau, but it probably had to be. The question now – had Thomas Pierce been able to get out of the Princeton area somehow? Or was he still down there?

Had he circled back to Boston? Fled to Europe? Nobody knew for sure. It was also possible that we might not hear from Pierce, or from Mr Smith, for a long time.

There was a pattern. We just had to find it.

Pierce and Isabella Calais had lived together for three years in the second-floor apartment of a town house in Cambridge. The front door of the place opened onto the kitchen. Then came a long railroad-style hallway. The apartment was a revelation. *There were memories and reminders of Isabella Calais everywhere.*

It was strange and overwhelming, as if she still lived here and might suddenly appear from one of the rooms.

There were photographs of her in every single room. I counted more than twenty pictures of Isabella on my first pass, a quick sight-seeing tour of the apartment.

How could Pierce bear to have this woman's face everywhere, looking at him, staring silently, accusing him of the most unspeakable murder?

In the pictures, Isabella Calais has the most beautiful auburn hair, worn long and perfectly shaped. She has a lovely face and the sweetest, natural smile. It was easy to see how he could have loved her. But her brown eyes had a far-off look in some of the pictures, as if she weren't quite there.

Everything about their apartment made my head spin, my insides, too. Was Pierce trying to tell us, or maybe tell himself, that he felt absolutely nothing – no guilt, no sadness, no love in his heart?

As I thought about it, I was overwhelmed with sadness myself. I could imagine the torture that must be his life every day – never to experience real love or deep feelings. In his crazed mind did Pierce think that by dissecting each of his victims he would find the answer to himself?

Maybe the opposite was true.

Was it possible that Pierce needed to feel her presence, to *feel* everything with the greatest intensity imaginable? Had Thomas Pierce loved Isabella Calais more than he'd thought he was capable of loving anyone? Had Pierce felt redeemed by their love? When he'd learned of her affair with a doctor named Martin Straw, had it driven him to madness and the most unspeakable of acts: The murder of the only person he had ever loved?

Why were her pictures still looming everywhere in the apartment? Why had Thomas Pierce been torturing himself with this constant reminder?

Isabella Calais was watching me as I moved through every room in the apartment. What was she trying to say?

'Who is he, Isabella?' I whispered. 'What is he up to?'

Chapter One Hundred and Nine

I began a more detailed search of the apartment. I paid careful attention not just to Isabella's things, but to Pierce's, too. Since both had been students, I wasn't surprised by the academic texts and papers lying about.

I found a curious test-tube rack of corked vials of sand. Each vial was labeled with the name of a different beach: Laguna, Montauk, Normandy, Parma, Virgin Gorda, Oahu. I thought about the curious notion that Pierce had bottled something so vast, infinite, and random to give it order and substance.

So what was his organizing principle for Mr Smith's murders? What would explain them?

There were GT Zaskar mountain bikes stored inside the apartment and two GT Machete helmets. Isabella and Thomas biked together through New Hampshire and across into Vermont. More and more, I was sure that he had loved her deeply. Then his love had turned to a hatred so intense few of us could imagine it.

I recalled that the first Cambridge police reports had convincingly described Pierce's grief at the murder scene as 'impossible to fake.' One of the detectives had written, 'He is shocked, surprised, utterly heartbroken. Thomas Pierce not considered a suspect at this time.'

What else, what else? There had to be a clue here. There had to be a pattern.

A framed quote was hung in the hallway. *Without God, We Are Condemned To Be Free.* Was it Sartre? I thought so. I wondered whose thinking it really represented. Did Pierce take it seriously himself or was he making a joke? *Condemned* was a word that interested me. Was Thomas Pierce a condemned man?

In the master bedroom there was a bookcase with a well-preserved, three-volume set of H. L. Mencken's *The American Language*. It rested on the top shelf. Obviously, this was a prized possession. Maybe it had been a gift? I remembered that Pierce had been a dual major as an undergraduate: biology and philosophy. Philosophy texts were everywhere in the apartment. I read the spines: Jacques Derrida, Foucault, Jean Baudrillard, Heidegger, Habermas, Sartre.

There were several dictionaries as well: French, German, English, Italian, and Spanish. A compact, two-volume set of the *Oxford English Dictionary* had type so small it came with a magnifying glass.

There was a framed diagram of the human voice mechanism directly over Pierce's work desk. And a quote: '*Language is more than speech.*' Several books by the linguist and activist Noam Chomsky were on his desk. What I remembered about Chomsky was that he had suggested a complex biological component of language acquisition. He had a view of the mind as a set of mental organs. I *think* that was Chomsky.

I wondered what, if anything, Noam Chomsky or the diagram of the human voice mechanism had to do with Smith, or the death of Isabella Calais.

I was lost in my thoughts, when I was startled by a loud *buzzing* noise. It came from the kitchen at the other end of the hall.

I thought I was alone in the apartment, and the buzzing spooked me. I took my Glock from its shoulder holster and started down the long narrow hallway. Then I began to run.

I entered the kitchen with my gun in position and then understood what the buzzing was. I had brought along a PowerBook that Pierce had left in his hotel room in Princeton. *Left on purpose? Left as another clue?* A special alarm on the laptop personal computer was the source of the noise.

Had he sent a message to us? A fax or voice-mail? Or perhaps someone was sending a message to Pierce? Who would be sending him messages?

I checked voice-mail first.

It was Pierce.

His voice was strong and steady and almost soothing. It was the voice of someone in control of himself and the situation. It was eerie under the circumstances, to be hearing it alone in his apartment.

Dr Cross – at least I suspect it's you I've reached. This is the kind of message I used to receive when I was tracking Smith.

Of course, I was using the messages for misdirection, sending them myself. I wanted to mislead the police, the FBI. Who knows, maybe I still do.

At any rate, here's your very first message – Anthony Bruno, Brielle, New Jersey.

Why don't you come to the seashore and join me for a swim? Have you arrived at any conclusions about Isabella yet? She is important to all of this. You're right to be in Cambridge.

Smith/Pierce

Chapter One Hundred and Ten

The FBI provided me with a helicopter out of Logan International Airport to fly me to Brielle, New Jersey. I was on board the Disorient Express and there was no getting off.

I spent the flight obsessing about Pierce, his apartment, Isabella Calais, *their* apartment, his studies in biology and modern philosophy, Noam Chomsky. I wouldn't have thought it possible, wouldn't have dreamed it possible, but Pierce was already eclipsing Gary Soneji and Simon Conklin. I despised everything about Pierce. Seeing the pictures of Isabella Calais had done it for me.

Alien? I wrote on the foolscap pad lying across my lap. *He identifies with descriptor.*

Alienated? Alienated from what? Idyllic upbringing in California. Doesn't fit any of the psychopathic profiles we used before. He's an original. He secretly enjoys that, doesn't he?

No discernible pattern to murders that links with a psychological motive. Murders seem haphazard and arbitrary! He revels in his own originality.

Dr Sante, Simon Conklin, now Anthony Bruno. Why them? Does Conklin count? Seems impossible to predict Thomas Pierce's next move. His next kill.

Why go south toward the New Jersey Shore?

It had occurred to me that he was originally from a shore town. Pierce had grown up near Laguna Beach in Southern California. Was he going home, in a manner of speaking? Was the New Jersey Shore as close to home as he could get – as close as he dared go?

I now had a reasonable amount of information about his background in California before he came east. He had lived on a working farm not far from the famous Irvine Ranch properties. Three generations of doctors in the family. Good, hardworking people. His siblings were all doing well, and not one of them would ever dream that Thomas was capable of any of this mayhem and murder.

FBI says Mr Smith is disorganized, chaotic, unpredictable, I scribbled in my pad.

What if they're wrong? Pierce is responsible for much of their data about Smith. Pierce created Mr Smith, then did the profile on him.

I kept revisiting his and Isabella's apartment in my mind. The place was so very neat and organized. The home had a definite *organizing principle*. It revolved around

Isabella – her pictures, clothes, even her perfume bottles had been left in place. The smell of L'Air du Temps and Je Reviens permeated their bedroom to this day.

Thomas Pierce had loved her. *Pierce had loved.* Pierce had felt passion and emotion. That was another thing the FBI was wrong about. He'd killed because he thought he was losing her, and he couldn't bear it. Was Isabella the only person who had ever loved Pierce?

Another small piece of the puzzle suddenly fell into place. I was so struck by it that I said it aloud in the helicopter. *'Her heart on a spear!'*

He had 'pierced' her heart! Jesus Christ! He had confessed to the very first murder! He had confessed!

He'd left a clue, but the police missed it. What else were we missing? What was he up to now? What did 'Mr Smith' represent inside his mind? Was everything representational for him? Symbolic? Artistic? Was he creating a kind of language for us to follow? Or was it even simpler? He had 'pierced' her heart. Pierce wanted to be caught. Caught and punished.

Crime and punishment.

Why couldn't we catch him?

I landed in New Jersey around five at night. Kyle Craig was waiting for me. Kyle was sitting on the hood of a dark-blue town car. He was drinking Samuel Adams beer out of a bottle.

'You find Anthony Bruno yet?' I called out as I walked toward him. 'You find the body?'

Chapter One Hundred and Eleven

*M*r *Smith goes to the seashore.* Sounded like an unimaginative children's story.

There was enough moonlight for Thomas Pierce to make his way along the long stretch of glowing white sand at Point Pleasant Beach. He was carrying a corpse, what was left of it. He had Anthony Bruno loaded on his back and shoulders.

He walked just south of popular Jenkinson's Pier and the much newer Seaquarium. The boarded-up arcades of the amusement park were tightly packed along the beach shoulder. The small, grayish buildings looked forlorn and mute in their shuttered state.

As usual, music ran through his head – first Elvis Costello's 'Clubland,' then

Beethoven's Piano Sonata No. 21, then 'Mother Mother' by Tracy Bonham. The savage beast inside him wasn't calmed, not even close, but at least he could feel a beat.

It was quarter to four in the morning and even the surf-casting fishermen weren't out yet. He'd seen only one police patrol car so far. The police in the tiny beach town were a joke anyway.

Mr Smith against the Keystone Cops.

This whole funky seashore area reminded him of Laguna Beach, at least the *tourista* parts of Laguna. He could still picture the surf shops that dotted the Pacific Coast Highway back home – the Southern California artifacts: Flogo sandals, Stussy T's, neoprene gloves and wet suits, beach boots, the unmistakable smell of board wax.

He was physically strong – had a working man's build. He carried Anthony Bruno over one shoulder without much effort. He had cut out all the vital parts, so there wasn't much of Anthony anymore. Anthony was a shell. No heart, liver, intestines, lungs, or brain.

Thomas Pierce thought about the FBI's continuing search. The Bureau's fabled 'manhunts' were overrated – a holdover from the glory days of John Dillinger and Bonnie and Clyde. He knew this to be so after years of observing the Bureau chase Mr Smith. They would never have caught Smith, not in a hundred years.

The FBI was looking for him in all the wrong places. They would surely have 'numbers,' meaning excessive force, their trademark maneuver. They would be all over the airports, probably expecting him to head back to Europe. And what about the wild cards in the search, people like Alex Cross? Cross had made his bones, no doubt about that. Maybe Cross was more than he seemed to be. Pierce had never believed Kyle when Kyle told him that Cross might not survive the attack on his house. He knew it was a ploy. At any rate, he relished the thought of Dr Cross being in on this, too. He liked the competition.

The dead weight on his back and shoulder was starting to get heavy. It was almost morning, close to daybreak. It wouldn't do to be found lugging a disemboweled corpse across Point Pleasant Beach.

He carried Anthony Bruno another fifty yards to a glistening white lifeguard's chair. He climbed the creaking rungs of the chair, and propped the body in the seat.

The remains of the corpse were naked and exposed for the world to see. Quite a sight. *Anthony was a clue.* If anybody on the search team had half a brain and was using it properly.

'I'm not an alien. Do any of you follow that?' Pierce shouted above the ocean's steady roar.

'I'm human. I'm perfectly normal. I'm just like you.'

Chapter One Hundred and Twelve

It was all a mind game, wasn't it – Pierce against the rest of us. While I had been at his apartment in Boston, a team of FBI agents went out to Southern California to meet with Thomas Pierce's family. The mother and father still lived on the same farm, between Laguna and El Toro, where Thomas Pierce had grown up.

Henry Pierce practiced medicine, mostly among the indigent farmworkers in the area. His lifestyle was modest and the reputation of the family impeccable. Pierce had an older brother and sister, doctors in Northern California, who were also well regarded and worked with the poor.

Not a person the profilers spoke to could imagine Thomas a murderer. He'd always been a good son and brother, a gifted student who seemed to have close friends and no enemies.

Thomas Pierce fit no brief for a pattern killer that I was familiar with. He was an original.

'*Impeccable*' was a word that jumped out of the FBI profiler reports. Maybe Pierce didn't want to be impeccable.

I re-reviewed the news articles and clippings about Pierce from the time of Isabella Calais's gruesome murder. I was keeping track of the more perplexing notions on three-by-five index cards. The packet was growing rapidly.

Laguna Beach – commercial shore town. Parts similar to Point Pleasant and Bay Head. Had Pierce killed in Laguna in the past? Had the disease now spread to the Northeast?

Pierce's father was a doctor. Pierce didn't 'make it' to Dr Pierce, but as a med student he had performed autopsies.

Looking for his humanity when he kills? Studying humans because he fears he has no human qualities himself?

He had a dual major as an undergrad: biology and philosophy. Fan of the linguist Noam Chomsky. Or is it Chomsky's political writings that turn Pierce on? Plays word and math games on his PowerBook.

What were we all missing so far?

What was I missing?

Why was Thomas Pierce killing all of these people?

He was 'impeccable,' wasn't he?

Chapter One Hundred and Thirteen

Pierce stole a forest-green BMW convertible in the expensive, quaint, quite lovely shore town of Bay Head, New Jersey. On the corner of East Avenue and Harris Street, a prime location, he hot-wired and grabbed the vehicle as slickly as a pickpocket working the boardwalks down at Point Pleasant Beach. He was so good at this, overqualified for the scut work.

He drove west through Brick Town at moderate speeds, to the Garden State Parkway. He played music all the way – Talking Heads, Alanis Morissette, Melissa Etheridge, Blind Faith. Music helped him to *feel something*. It always had, from the time he'd been a boy. An hour and a quarter later he entered Atlantic City.

He sighed with pleasure. He loved it instantly – the shameless tawdriness, the grubbiness, the tattered sinfulness, the soullessness of the place. He felt as if he were 'home,' and he wondered if the FBI geniuses had linked the Jersey Shore to Laguna Beach yet?

Entering Atlantic City, he had half-expected to see a beautifully maintained expanse of lawn sloping down to the ocean. Surfers with peroxided, gnarly hair; volleyball played around the clock.

But no, no, this was New Jersey. Southern California, his real home, was thousands of miles away. He mustn't get confused now.

He checked into Bally's Park Place. Up in his room, he started to make phone calls. He wanted to 'order in.' He stood at a picture window and watched the ghostly waves of the Atlantic punish the beach again and again. Far down the beach he could see Trump Plaza. The audacious and ridiculous penthouse apartments were perched on the main building, like a space shuttle ready to take off.

Yes, ladies and gentlemen, of course there was a pattern. Why couldn't anyone figure it out? Why did he always have to be misunderstood?

At two in the morning, Thomas Pierce sent the trackers another voice-mail message: *Inez in Atlantic City*.

Chapter One Hundred and Fourteen

G *oddamn him!* Half a day after we recovered the body of Anthony Bruno, we got the next message from Pierce. He had taken another one already.

We were on the move immediately. Two dozen of us rushed to Atlantic City and prayed he was still there, that someone named Inez hadn't already been butchered and 'studied' by Mr Smith and discarded like the evening trash.

Giant billboards screamed all along the Atlantic City Expressway. Caesar's Atlantic City, Harrah's, Merv Griffin's Resorts Casino Hotel, Trump's Castle, Trump Taj Mahal. Call 1-800-GAMBLER, Now *that* was funny.

Inez, Atlantic City, I kept hearing inside my head. *Sounds like Isabella.*

We set up shop in the FBI field office, which was only a few blocks from the old Steel Pier and the so-called 'Great Wooden Way.' There were usually only four agents in the small office. Their expertise was organized crime and gambling, and they weren't considered movers and shakers inside the Bureau. They weren't prepared for a savage, unpredictable killer who had once been a very good agent.

Someone had bought a stack of newspapers and they were piled high on the conference table. The New York, Philly, and Jersey headline writers were having a field day with this one.

ALIEN KILLER VISITS JERSEY SHORE . . . FBI KILLER-DILLER IN ATLANTIC CITY . . . MR SMITH MANHUNT: Hundreds of Federal agents flock to New Jersey Shore . . . MONSTER ON THE LOOSE IN NEW JERSEY!

Sampson came up to the beach from Washington. He wanted Pierce as badly as any of us. He, Kyle, and I worked together, brainstorming over what Pierce-Mr Smith might do next. Sondra Greenberg from Interpol worked with us, too. She was seriously jet lagged, and had deep circles under her eyes, but she knew Pierce and had been at most of the European murder sites.

'He's not a goddamn split personality?' Sampson asked. 'Smith and Pierce?'

I shook my head. 'He seems to be in control of his faculties at all times. He created "Smith" to serve some other purpose.'

'I agree with Alex,' Sondra Greenberg said from across the table, 'but *what* is the sodding purpose?'

'Whatever it was, it worked,' Kyle joined in. 'He had us chasing Mr Smith halfway around the world. We're still chasing. No one has ever jerked around the Bureau like this.'

'Not even the great Herbert Hoover?' Sondra said and winked.

'Well,' Kyle softened, 'as a pure psychopath, Hoover was in a class by himself.'

I was up and pacing again. My side was hurting, but I didn't want anyone to know about it. They would try to send me home, make me miss the fun. I let myself ramble – sometimes it works.

'He's trying to tell us something. He's communicating in some strange way. *Inez*? The name reminds us of Isabella. He's obsessed with Isabella. You should see the apartment in Cambridge. Is Inez a substitute for Isabella? Is Atlantic City a substitute for Laguna Beach? Has he brought Isabella home? Why bring Isabella home?'

It went on and on like that: wild hunches, free association, insecurity, fear, unbearable frustration. As far as I could tell nothing worthwhile was said all day and late into the night, but who could really tell.

Pierce didn't try to make further contact. There were no more voice messages. That surprised us a little. Kyle was afraid he'd moved on, and that he would keep moving until he drove us completely insane. Six of us stayed in the field office throughout the night and into the early morning. We slept in our clothes, on chairs, tables, and the floor.

I paced inside the office, and occasionally outside on the glittery, fog-laden boardwalk. As a last desperate resort, I bought a bag of Fralinger's salt water taffy and tried to get sick to my stomach.

What kind of logic system is he using? Mr Smith is his creation, his Mr Hyde. What is Smith's mission? Why is he here? I wondered, occasionally talking to myself as I strolled the mostly deserted boardwalk.

Inez is Isabella?

It couldn't be that simple. Pierce wouldn't make it simple for us.

Inez is not Isabella. There was only one Isabella. So why does Pierce keep killing again and again?

I found myself at the corner of Park Place and Boardwalk, and that finally brought a smile. *Monopoly. Another kind of game? Is that it?*

I wandered back to the FBI field office and got some sleep. But not nearly enough. A few hours at most.

Pierce was here.

So was Mr Smith.

Chapter One Hundred and Fifteen

*A flat, still sandy, still meadowy region . . . a superb range of ocean beach –
miles and miles of it. The bright sun, the sparkling waves, the foam, the
view – a sail here and there in the distance.* Walt Whitman had written that
about Atlantic City a hundred years before. His words were inscribed on the
wall of a pizza-and-hotdog stand now. Whitman would have been stricken to
see his words on such a backdrop.

I went by myself for another stroll on the Atlantic City boardwalk around
ten o'clock. It was Saturday, and so hot and sunny that the eroding beach was
already dotted with swimmers and sunbathers.

We still hadn't found Inez. We didn't have a single clue. We didn't even
know who she was.

I had the uncomfortable feeling that Thomas Pierce was watching us, or that
I might suddenly come upon him in the dense, sweltering crowds. I had my
pager just in case he tried to contact us at the field office.

There was nothing else to be done right now. Pierce-Mr Smith was in control
of the situation and our lives. A madman was in control of the planet. It seemed
like it anyway.

I stopped near Steeplechase Pier and the Resorts Casino Hotel. People were
playing under a hot sun in the high, rolling surf. They seemed to be enjoying
themselves and didn't appear to have a care in the world. How nice for them.

This was the way it should be, and it reminded me of Jannie and Damon,
my own family, and of Christine. She desperately wanted me to leave this job
and I couldn't blame her. I didn't know if I could walk away from police work,
though. I wondered why that was so. *Physician, heal thyself.* Maybe I would
someday soon.

As I continued my walk along the boardwalk, I tried to convince myself that
everything that could be done to catch Pierce was being done. I passed a
Fralinger's, and a James Candy store. And the old Peanut Shoppe, where a
costumed Mr Peanut was stumbling about in the mid-ninety-degree heat.

I had to smile as I saw the Ripley's Believe It Or Not Museum up ahead,
where you could see a lock of George Washington's hair, and a roulette table
made of jelly beans. No, *I could not believe it.* I didn't think anyone on the
crisis team could, but here we were.

I was jolted out of my thoughts by the beeper vibrating against my leg. I ran to a nearby phone and called in.

Pierce had left another message. Kyle and Sampson were already out on the boardwalk. Pierce was near the Steel Pier. He claimed that Inez was with him! *He said we could still save them!*

Pierce specifically said *them*.

I shouldn't have been running around like this. My side began to throb and hurt like hell. I'd never been out of shape like this, not in my life, and I didn't like the feeling. I hadn't felt so vulnerable and relatively helpless before.

Finally, I realized: *I'm actually afraid of Pierce, and of Mr Smith.*

By the time I got near the Steel Pier, my clothes were dripping wet and I was breathing hard. I pulled off my sport shirt and waded out into the crowd bare-chested. I pushed my way past old-style jitneys and newer step vans, past tandem bikes and joggers.

I was taped and bandaged and I must have looked like an escapee from a local ER. Even so, it was hard to stand out on a beach like the one at Atlantic City. An ice-cream man hauling a box on his shoulder cried out, 'Hitch your tongue to a sleigh ride! Get your Fudgie Wudgies here!'

Was Thomas Pierce watching us and laughing? He could be the ice-cream man, or anyone else in this frenetic mob scene.

I cupped my hands over my eyes and looked up and down the beach. I spotted policemen and FBI agents wading into the crowd. There must have been at least fifty thousand sunbathers on the beach. I could faintly hear electronic bells from the slot machines in one of the nearby hotels.

Inez. Atlantic City. Jesus!

A madman on the loose near the famous Steel Pier.

I looked for Sampson or Kyle, but I didn't see either of them. I searched for Pierce, and for Inez, and for Mr Smith.

I heard a loud voice, and it stopped me in my tracks. *'This is the FBI.'*

Chapter One Hundred and Sixteen

The voice boomed over a loudspeaker. Probably from one of the hotels, or maybe a police hookup. 'This is the FBI,' Kyle Craig announced. 'Some of our agents are on the beach now. Cooperate with them and also with the

Atlantic City police. Do whatever they ask. There's no reason for undue concern. Please cooperate with police officers.'

The huge crowd became strangely quiet. Everyone was staring around, looking for the FBI. No, there was no reason for *undue concern* – not unless we actually found Pierce. Not unless we discovered Mr Smith operating on somebody in the middle of this beach crowd.

I made my way toward the famous amusement pier, where as a young boy I had actually seen the famous diving horse. People were standing out in the low surf, just looking in toward shore. It reminded me of the movie *Jaws*.

Thomas Pierce was in control here.

A black Belljet helicopter hovered less than seventy yards from shore. A second helicopter came into view from the northeast. It swept in close to the first, then fluttered away in the direction of the Taj Mahal Hotel complex. I could make out sharpshooters positioned in the helicopters.

So could Pierce, and so could the people on the beach. I knew there were FBI marksmen in the nearby hotels. Pierce would know that. Pierce was FBI. He knew everything we did. That was his edge and he was using it against us. He was winning.

There was a disturbance up closer to the pier. People were pushing forward to see, while others were moving away as fast as they could. I moved forward.

The beach crowd's noise level was building again. En Vogue played from somebody's blaster. The smell of cotton candy and beer and hotdogs was thick in the air. I began to run toward the Steel Pier, remembering the diving horse and Lucy the Elephant from Margate, better times a long time ago.

I saw Sampson and Kyle up ahead.

They were bending over something. *Oh God. Oh God, no. Inez, Atlantic City!* My pulse raced out of control.

This was not good.

A dark-haired teenage girl was sobbing against an older man's chest. Others gawked at the dead body, which had been clumsily wrapped in beach blankets. I couldn't imagine how it had gotten here – but there it was.

Inez, Atlantic City. It had to be her.

The murdered woman had long bleach-blond hair and looked to be in her early twenties. It was hard to tell now. Her skin was purplish and waxy. The eyes had flattened because of a loss of fluid. Her lips and nail beds were pale. He had operated on Inez: The ribs and cartilage had been cut away, exposing her lungs, esophagus, trachea, and heart.

Inez sounds like Isabella.

Pierce knew that.

He hadn't taken out Inez's heart.

The ovaries and fallopian tubes were neatly laid out beside the body. The tubes looked like a set of earrings and a necklace.

Suddenly, sunbathers were pointing to something out over the ocean.

I turned and I looked up, shading my eyes with one hand.

A prop plane was lazily making its way down the shoreline from the north. It was the kind of plane you rented for commercial messages. Most of the messages on forty-foot banners hyped the hotels, local bars, area restaurants and casinos.

A banner waved behind a sputtering plane that was getting closer and closer. I couldn't believe what I was reading. It was another message.

Mr Smith is gone for now! Wave goodbye.

Chapter One Hundred and Seventeen

E arly the next morning, I headed home to Washington. I needed to see the kids, needed to sleep in my own bed, to be far, far away from Thomas Pierce and his monstrous creation – *Mr Smith*.

Inez had turned out to be an escort from a local service. Pierce had called her to his room at Bally's Park Place. I was starting to believe that Pierce could *find intimacy only with his victims now*, but what else was driving him to commit these horrifying murders? Why Inez? Why the Jersey Shore?

I had to escape for a couple of days, or even a few hours, if that was all I could get. At least we hadn't already gotten another name, another location to rush off to.

I called Christine from Atlantic City and asked her if she wanted to have dinner with my family that night. She said yes, she'd like that a lot. She said she'd 'be there with bells on.' That sounded unbelievably good to me. The best medicine I could imagine for what ailed me.

I kept the sound of her voice in my head all the way home to Washington. She would be there with bells on.

Damon, Jannie, and I spent a hectic morning getting ready for the party. We shopped for groceries at Citronella, and then at the Giant. *Veni, vidi, Visa.*

I had *almost* put Pierce-Smith out of my mind, but I still had my Glock in an ankle holster to go grocery shopping.

At the Giant, Damon scouted on ahead to find some RC Cola and tortilla chips. Jannie and I had a chance to talk the talk. I knew she was dying to *bzzz-bzzz-bzzz*. I can always tell. She has a fine, overactive imagination, and I couldn't wait to hear what was on her little mind.

Jannie was in charge of pushing the shopping cart, and the metal handle of the cart was just above her eye level. She stared at the immense array of cereals in our aisle, looking for the best deals. Nana Mama had taught her the fine art of grocery shopping, and she can do most of the math in her head.

'Talk to me,' I said. 'My time is your time. Daddy's home.'

'For today.' She sent a hummer right past my ear, brushed me right back from home plate with a high, hard one.

'It's not easy being green,' I said. It was an old favorite line between us, compliments of Kermit the Frog. She shrugged it off today. No sale. No easy deals.

'You and Damon mad at me?' I asked in my most soothing tones. 'Tell me the truth, girlfriend.'

She softened a little. 'Oh, it's not so much that, Daddy. You're doing the best you can,' she said, and finally looked my way. 'You're trying, right? It's just hard when you go away from home. I get lonely for you. It's not the same when you're away.'

I shook my head, smiled, and wondered where she got much of her thinking from. Nana Mama swore that Jannie has a mind of her own.

'You okay with our dinner plans?' I asked, treading carefully.

'Oh *ab*-solutely,' she suddenly beamed. 'That's not a problem at all. I *love* dinner parties.'

'Damon? Is he okay with Christine coming over tonight?' I asked my confidante.

'He's a little scared 'cause she's the principal of our school. But he's cool, too. You know Damon. He's the man.'

I nodded. 'He *is* cool. So dinner's not a problem? You're not even a little scared?'

Jannie shook her head. 'Nope. Not because of that. Dinners can't scare me. Dinner is dinner.'

Man, she was smart, and so subtle for her age. It was like talking to a very wise adult. She was already a poet, and a philosopher, too. She was going to be competition for Maya Angelou and Toni Morrison one day. I loved that about her.

'Do you have to keep going after him? After this bum Mr Smith?' Jannie finally asked me. 'I guess you do.' She answered her own question.

I echoed her earlier line. 'I'm doing the best I can.'

Jannie stood up on her tippy-toes. I bent low to her, but not as far as I used to. She kissed me on the cheek, a nice *smacker*, as she calls the kisses.

'You're the bee's knees,' she said. It was one of Nana's favorite things to say and she'd adopted it.

'Boo!' Damon peeked around the soda-pop aisle at the two of us. His head was framed against a red, white, and blue sea of Pepsi bottles and cans. I pulled Damon close, and I kissed him on the cheek, too. I kissed the top of his head, held him in a way I would have liked my father to have held me a long time ago. We made a little spectacle of ourselves in the grocery-store aisle. Nice spectacle.

God, I loved the two of them, and what a continued dilemma it presented. The Glock on my ankle weighed a ton and felt as hot as a poker from a fire. I wanted to take it off and never put the weapon on again.

I knew I wouldn't, though. Thomas Pierce was still out there somewhere, and Mr Smith, and all the rest of them. For some reason I felt it was my responsibility to make them all go away, to make things a little safer for everyone.

'Earth to Daddy,' Jannie said. She had a small frown on her face. 'See? You went away again. You were with Mr Smith, weren't you?'

Chapter One Hundred and Eighteen

C hristine can save you. If anyone can, if it's possible for you to be salvaged at this point in your life.

I got to her place around six-thirty that night. I'd told her I would pick her up out in Mitchellville. My side was hurting again, and I definitely felt like damaged goods, but I wouldn't have missed this for anything.

She came to the front door in a bright-tangerine sundress and heeled espadrilles. She looked slightly beyond great. She wore a bar pin with tiny silver bells. She *did* have bells on.

'Bells.' I smiled.

'You bet. You thought I was kidding.'

I took her in my arms right there on the red-brick front stoop, with blooming red and white impatiens and climbing roses all around us. I hugged Christine tightly against my chest and we started to kiss.

I was lost in her sweet, soft mouth, in her arms. My hands flew up to her face, lightly tracing her cheekbones, her nose, her eyelids.

The shock of intimacy was rare and overwhelming. So good, so fine, and missing for such a long time.

I opened my eyes and saw that she was looking at me. She had the most expressive eyes I'd ever seen. 'I love the way you hold me, Alex,' she whispered, but her eyes said much more. 'I love your touch.'

We backed into the house, kissing again.

'Do we have time?' She laughed.

'Shhh. Only a crazy person wouldn't. We're not crazy.'

'Of course we are.'

The bright-tangerine sundress fell away to the floor. I liked the feel of shantung, but Christine's bare skin felt even better. She was wearing Shalimar and I liked that, too. I had the feeling that I had been here before with her, maybe in a dream. It was as if I had been imagining this moment for a long time and now it was here.

She helped me with her white-lace demibra. We slid down the matching panties, two pairs of hands working together. Then we were naked, except for the fine rope necklace with a fire opal around her neck. I remembered a poem, something magical about the nakedness of lovers, but with just a touch of jewelry to set it off. Baudelaire? I bit gently into her shoulder. She bit back.

I was so hard it hurt, but the pain was exquisite, the pain had its own raw power. I loved this woman completely, and I was also turned on by her, every inch of her being.

'You know,' I whispered, 'you're driving me a little crazy.'

'Oh. Just a little?'

I let my lips trail down along her breasts, her stomach. She was lightly scented with perfume. I kissed between her legs and she began to gently call my name, then not so gently. I entered Christine as we stood against the cream living-room wall, as we seemed to push our bodies *into* the wall.

'I love you,' I whispered.

'I love you, Alex.'

She was strong and gentle and graceful, all at the same time. We danced, but not in the metaphorical sense. We really *danced*.

I loved the sound of her voice, the softest cry, the song she sang when she was with me like this.

Then I was singing, too. I had found my voice again, for the first time in many years. I don't know how long we were like that. Time wasn't part of this. Something in it was eternal, and something was so very real and right now in the present.

Christine and I were soaking wet. Even the wall behind me was slippery and wet. The wild ride at the beginning, the rocking and rolling, had transformed itself into a slower rhythm that was even stronger. I knew that no life was right without this kind of passion.

I was barely moving inside her. She tightened around me and I thought I could feel the edges of her. I surged deeper and Christine seemed to swell around me. We began to move into each other, trying to get closer. We shuddered, and got closer still.

Christine climaxed, and then the two of us came together. We danced and we sang. I felt myself melting into Christine and we were both whispering *yes, yes, yes, yes, yes, yes*. No one could touch us here, not Thomas Pierce, no one.

'Hey, did I tell you I loved you?'

'Yes, but tell me again.'

Chapter One Hundred and Nineteen

K ids are so damn much smarter than we usually give them credit for. Kids know just about everything, and they often know it before we do.

'You two are *late*! You have a flat tire – or were you just smooching?' Jannie wanted to know as we came in the front door. She can say some outrageous things and get away with them. She knows it, and pushes the envelope every chance she gets.

'We were smooching,' I said. 'Satisfied?'

'Yes I am,' Jannie smiled. 'Actually, you're not even late. You're right on time. Perfect timing.'

Dinner with Nana and the children wasn't an anticlimax. It was such a sweet, funny time. It was what being home is all about. We all pitched in and set the table, served the food, then ate with reckless abandon. The meal was swordfish steaks, scalloped potatoes, summer peas, buttermilk biscuits. Everything was served piping hot, expertly prepared by Nana, Jannie, and Damon. Dessert was Nana's world-famous lemon meringue pie. She made it specially for Christine.

I believe the simple yet complex word that I'm searching for is *joy*.

It was so obvious around the dinner table. I could see it in the bright and lively eyes of Nana and Damon and Jannie. I had already seen it in Christine's eyes. I watched her at dinner and I had the thought that she could have been somebody famous in Washington, anything she wanted to be. She chose to be a teacher, and I loved that about her.

We repeated stories that had been in the family for years, and are always repeated at such occasions. Nana was lively and funny all through the night. She gave us her best advice on aging: 'If you can't recall it, forget it.'

Later on, I played the piano and sang rhythm-and-blues songs. My wrist gave me trouble but I was doing OK. Jannie showed off and did the cakewalk to a jazzy version of 'Blueberry Hill.' Even Nana did a minute of jitterbugging, protesting, 'I really can't dance, I never could dance,' as she did just beautifully.

One moment, one picture, sticks out in my mind, and I'm sure it will be there until the day I die. It was just after we'd finished dinner and were cleaning up the kitchen.

I was washing dishes in the sink, and as I reached to get another platter I stopped in midturn, frozen in the moment.

Jannie was in Christine's arms, and the two of them looked just beautiful together. I had no idea how she had gotten there, but they were both laughing and it was so natural and real. As I never had before, I knew and understood that Jannie and Damon were missing so much without a mother.

Joy – that's the word. So easy to say, so hard to find in life sometimes.

In the morning, I had to go back to work.

I was still the dragonslayer.

Chapter One Hundred and Twenty

I shut myself away to think, to quietly obsess about Thomas Pierce and Mr Smith.

I made suggestions to Kyle Craig about moves that Pierce might make, and precautions he should think about taking. Agents were dispatched to watch Pierce's apartment in Cambridge. Agents camped out at his parents' house outside Laguna Beach, and even at the gravesite of Isabella Calais.

Pierce had been passionately in love with Isabella Calais! She had been the only one for him! Isabella and Thomas Pierce! That was the key – Pierce's obsessive love for her.

He's suffering from unbearable guilt, I wrote in my notepad.

If my hypothesis is right, then what clues are missing?

Back at Quantico, a team of FBI profilers was trying to solve the problem on paper. They had all worked closely with Pierce in the BSU. Absolutely nothing in Pierce's background was consistent with the psychopathic killers they had dealt with before. Pierce had never been abused, either physically or sexually. There was no violence of any kind in his background. At least not as far as anyone knew. There was no warning, no hint of madness, no sign until he blew sky-high. *He was an original. There had never been a monster anything like him. There were no precedents.*

I wrote: *Thomas Pierce was deeply in love. You are in love, too.*

What would it mean to murder the only person in the world who you loved?

Chapter One Hundred and Twenty-One

I couldn't manage any sympathy, or even a modicum of clinical empathy, for Pierce. I despised him, and his cruel, cold-blooded murders, more than I had any of the other killers I had taken down – even Soneji. Kyle Craig and Sampson felt the same, and so did most of the Federal Bureau, especially the good folks in Behavioral Science. We were the ones in a rage state now. We were obsessed with stopping Pierce. Was he using that to beat our brains in?

The following day, I worked at home again. I locked myself away with my computer, several books, and my crime-scene notepads. The only time I took off was to walk Damon and Jannie to school, and then have a quick breakfast with Nana.

My mouth was full of poached egg and toast when she leaned across the kitchen table and launched one of her famous sneak attacks on me.

'Am I correct in saying that you don't want to discuss your murder case with me?' she asked.

'I'd rather talk about the weather or just about anything else. Your garden looks beautiful. Your hair looks nice.'

'We all like Christine very much, Alex. She's knocked our socks off. In case you wanted to know but forgot to ask. She's the best thing that's happened to you since Maria. So, what are you going to do about it? What are your plans?'

I rolled my eyes back, but I had to smile at Nana's dawn offensive. 'First, I'm going to finish this delicious breakfast you fixed. Then I have some dicey work to do upstairs. How's that?'

'You mustn't lose her, Alex. Don't do that,' Nana advised and warned at the same time. 'You won't listen to a decrepit old woman, though. What do I know about anything? I just cook and clean around here.'

'And talk,' I said with my mouth full. 'Don't forget talk, old woman.'

'Not just talk, sonny boy. Pretty sound psychological analysis, necessary cheerleading at times, and expert guidance counseling.'

'I have a game plan,' I said, and left it at that.

'You better have a winning game plan.' Nana got the last word in. 'Alex, if you lose her, you will never get over it.'

The walk with the kids and even talking with Nana revitalized me. I felt clear and alert as I worked at my old rolltop for the rest of the morning.

I had started to cover the bedroom walls with notes and theories, and the beginnings of *even more theories* about Thomas Pierce. The pushpin parade had taken control. From the looks of the room, it seemed as if I knew what I was doing, but contrary to popular opinion, looks are almost always deceiving. I had hundreds of clues, and yet I didn't have a clue.

I remembered something Mr Smith had written in one of his messages to Pierce, which Pierce had then passed on to the FBI. *The god within us is the one that gives the laws and can change the laws. And God is within us.*

The words had seemed familiar to me, and I finally tracked down the source. The quote was from Joseph Campbell, the American mythologist and folklorist who had taught at Harvard when Pierce was a student there.

I was trying different perspectives to the puzzle. Two entry points in particular interested me.

First, Pierce was curious about language. He had studied linguistics at Harvard. He admired Noam Chomsky. What about language and words, then?

Second, Pierce was extremely organized. He had created the false impression that Mr Smith was disorganized. He had purposely misled the FBI and Interpol.

Pierce was leaving clues from the start. Some of them were obvious.

He wants to be caught. So why doesn't he stop himself?

Murder. Punishment. Was Thomas Pierce punishing himself, or was he punishing everybody else? Right now, he was certainly punishing the hell out of me. Maybe I deserved it.

Around three o'clock, I took a stroll and picked up Damon and Jannie at the Sojourner Truth School. Not that they needed someone to walk them home. I just missed the hell out of them. I needed to see them, couldn't keep myself away.

Besides, my head ached and I wanted to get out of the house, away from all of my thoughts.

I saw Christine in the schoolyard. She was surrounded by little children. I remembered that she wanted to have kids herself. She looked so happy, and I could see that the kids loved to be around her. Who in their right mind wouldn't? She made it look so natural to be turning jump rope in a navy business suit.

She smiled when she saw me approaching across the schoolyard full of kids. The smile warmed the cockles of my heart, and all my other cockles as well.

'Look who's taking a break for air,' she said, 'three potato, four.'

'When I was in high school,' I told her as she continued to turn her end of a Day-Glo pink jump rope, 'I had a girlfriend over at John Carroll. This was in my sophomore and junior years.'

'Mmm, hmmm. Nice Catholic girl? White blouse, plaid skirt, saddle shoes?'

'She was very nice. Actually, she's a botanist now. See, nice? I used to walk all the way over to South Carolina Avenue just on the off chance I might see Jeanne for a couple of minutes after she finished school. I was seriously smitten.'

'Must have been the saddle shoes. Are you trying to tell me that you're smitten again?' Christine laughed. The kids couldn't quite hear us, but they were laughing anyway.

'I am way beyond smitten. I am smote.'

'Well that's good,' she said and continued to turn the pink rope and smile at her kids, 'because so am I. And when this case is over, Alex—'

'Anything you want, just say the word.'

Her eyes brightened even more than was usual. 'A weekend away from everything. Maybe at a country inn, but anywhere remote will do just fine.'

I wanted to hold Christine so much. I wanted to kiss her right there, but that wasn't going to happen in the crowded schoolyard.

'It's a date,' I said. 'It's a promise.'

'I'll hold you to it. *Smote*, that's good. We can try that on our weekend away.'

Chapter One Hundred and Twenty-Two

B ack home, I worked on the Pierce case until supper time. I ate a quick meal of hamburgers and summer squash with Nana and the kids. I took some more heavy heat for being an incurable and unrepentant workaholic. Nana cut me a slice of pie, and I retreated to my room again. Well fed, but deeply unsatisfied.

I couldn't help it – I was worried. Thomas Pierce might already have grabbed another victim. He could be performing an 'autopsy' tonight. He could send us a message at any time.

I reread the notes I had plastered on the bedroom wall. I felt as if the answer were on the tip of my tongue and it was driving me crazy. People's lives hung in the balance.

He had 'pierced' the heart of Isabella Calais.

His apartment in Cambridge was an obsessive shrine to her memory.

He had returned 'home' when he went to Point Pleasant Beach. The opportunity to catch him was there – if we were smart enough, if we were as good as he was.

What were we missing, the FBI and me?

I played more word games with the assortment of clues.

He always 'pierces' his victims. I wondered if he was impotent or had become impotent, unable to have a sexual relationship with Isabella.

Mr Smith operates like a doctor – which Pierce nearly was – which his father and his siblings are. He had failed as a doctor.

I went to bed early, around eleven, but I couldn't sleep. I guess I'd just wanted to try and turn the case off. I finally called Christine and we talked for about an hour. As we talked and I listened to the music of her voice, I couldn't help thinking about Pierce and Isabella Calais.

Pierce had loved her. Obsessive love. What would happen if I lost Christine now? What happened to Pierce after the murder? Had he gone mad?

After I got off the phone, I went back at the case again. For a while, I thought his pattern might have something to do with Homer's *Odyssey*. He was heading home after a series of tragedies and misfortunes? *No, that wasn't it.*

What the hell was the key to his code? If he wanted to drive all of us mad, it was working.

I began to play with the names of the victims, starting with Isabella and ending with Inez. *I* goes full circle to *I*? Full circle? Circles? I looked at the clock on the desk – it was almost one-thirty in the morning, but I kept at it.

I wrote – *I*.

I. Was that something? It could be a start. The personal pronoun *I*? I tried a few combinations with the letters of the names.

I – S – U . . . R
C – A – D . . .
I – A – D . . .

I stopped after the next three letters: IMU. I stared at the page. I remembered 'pierced,' the obviousness of it. The simplest wordplay.

Isabella, Michaela, Ursula. Those were the names of the first three victims – in order. *Jesus Christ!*

I looked at the names of all the victims – in order of the murders. I looked at the first, last, and middle names. I began mixing and matching the names. My heart was pounding. There was something here. Pierce had left us another clue, a series of clues, actually.

It was right there in front of us all the time. No one got it, because Smith's crimes appeared to be without any pattern. But Pierce had started that theory himself.

I continued to write, using either the first or last or middle names of the victims. It started IMU. Then *R*, for Robert. *D* for Dwyer. Was there a subpattern for selecting the name? It could be an arithmetic sequence.

There was a pattern to Pierce Smith, after all. His mission began that very first night in Cambridge, Massachusetts. He *was* insane, but I had caught on to his pattern. It started with his love of wordplay.

Thomas Pierce wanted to be caught! But then something changed. He had become ambivalent about his capture. Why?

I looked at what I had assembled. 'Son of a bitch,' I muttered. 'Isn't this something. He has a ritual.'

I – Isabella Calais.
M – Stephanie Michaela Apt.
U – Ursula Davies.

R – Robert Michael Neel.
D – Brigid Dwyer.
E – Mary Ellen Klauk.
R – Robin Anne Schwartz.
E – Clark Daniel Ebel.
D – David Hale.
I – Isadore Morris.
S – Theresa Anne Secrest.
A – Elizabeth Allison Gragnano.
B – Barbara Maddalena.
E – Edwin Mueller.
L – Laurie Garnier.
L – Lewis Lavine.
A – Andrew Klauk.
C – Inspector Derek Cabott.
A – Dr Abel Sante.
L – Simon Lewis Conklin.
A – Anthony Bruno.
I – Inez Marquez.
S – ?

It read: I MURDERED ISABELLA CALAIS.

He had made it so easy for us. He was taunting us from the very beginning. Pierce wanted to be stopped, wanted to be caught. So why the hell hadn't he stopped himself? Why had the string of brutal murders gone on and on?

I MURDERED ISABELLA CALAIS.

The murders were a confession, and maybe Pierce was almost finished. Then what would happen? And who was *S*?

Was it Smith himself? Did S stand for Smith?

Would he symbolically murder Smith? Then Mr Smith would disappear forever?

I called Kyle Craig and then Sampson, and I told them what I had found. It was past two in the morning, and neither of them was overjoyed to hear my voice or the news. They didn't know what to do with the word jumble and neither did I.

'I'm not sure what it gives us,' Kyle said, 'what it proves, Alex.'

'I'm not either. Not yet. It does tell us he's going to kill someone with an *S* in his name.'

'George Steinbrenner,' Kyle mumbled. 'Strom Thurmond. Sting.'

'Go back to sleep,' I said.

My head was doing loops. Sleep wasn't an option for me. I half-expected to get another message from Pierce, maybe even that night. He was mocking us. He had been from the beginning.

I wanted to get a message to him. Maybe I ought to communicate with Pierce through the newspapers or TV? We needed to get off the defensive and attack instead.

I lay in the darkness of my bedroom. *Could S be Mr Smith?* I wondered. My head was throbbing. I was past being exhausted. I finally drifted off toward sleep. I was falling off the edge – when I grabbed hold.

I bolted up in bed. I was wide-awake now.

'*S* isn't Smith.'

I knew who *S* was.

Chapter One Hundred and Twenty-Three

Thomas Pierce was in Concord, Massachusetts.

Mr Smith was here, too.

I was finally inside his head.

Sampson and I were ready on a cozy, picturesque side street near the house of Dr Martin Straw, the man who had been Isabella's lover. Martin Straw was S in the puzzle.

The FBI had a trap set for Pierce at the house. They didn't bring huge numbers of agents this time. They were afraid of tipping off Pierce. Kyle Craig was gun-shy and he had every reason to be. Or maybe there was something else going on?

We waited for the better part of the morning and early afternoon. Concord was a self-contained, somewhat constrained town that seemed to be aging grace-fully. The Thoreau and Alcott homes were here somewhere nearby. Every other house seemed to have a historical-looking plaque with a date on it.

We waited for Pierce. And then waited some more. The dreaded *stakeout in Podunk* dragged on and on. Maybe I was wrong about S.

A voice finally came over the radio in our car. It was Kyle. 'We've spotted Pierce. He's here. But something's wrong, Alex. He's headed back toward Route Two,' Kyle said. 'He's not going to Dr Straw's. He saw something he didn't like.'

Sampson looked over at me. 'I told you he was careful. Good instincts. He *is* a goddamn Martian, Alex.'

'He spotted something,' I said. 'He's as good as Kyle always said. He knows how the Bureau works, and he saw something.'

Kyle and his team had wanted to let Pierce enter the Straw house before they took him down. Dr Straw, his wife, and children had been moved from the place. We needed solid evidence against Pierce, as much as we could get. We could lose the case if we got Thomas Pierce to court without it. We definitely could lose.

A message crackled over the shortwave. 'He's headed toward Route Two. Something spooked him. He's on the run!'

'He has a shortwave! He's intercepting us!' I grabbed the mike and warned Kyle. 'No more talk on the radio. Pierce is listening. That's how he spotted us.'

I started the engine and gunned the sedan away from the curb. I pushed the speed up to sixty on heavily populated Lowell Road. We were actually closer to Route 2 than the others. We still might be able to cut Pierce off.

A shiny, silver BMW passed us, coming from the opposite direction on the road. The driver sat on her horn as we sped by. I couldn't blame her. Sixty was a dangerous speed on the narrow village street. Everything was going crazy again, caroming out of control at the whim of a madman.

'There he is!' Sampson yelled.

Pierce's car was heading into Concord Center, the most congested area of town. He was moving way too fast.

We sped past Colonial-style houses, then upscale shops, and finally approached Monument Square. I caught glimpses of the Town House, Concord Inn, the Masons' Hall – then a sign for Route 62 – another for Route 2.

Our sedan whisked by car after car on the village streets. Brakes screeched around us. Other cars honked, justifiably angry and afraid of the car chase in progress.

Sampson was holding his breath and so was I. There's a joke about black men being pulled over illegally in suburban areas. The *DWB* violation. Driving while black. We were up to seventy inside the city limits.

We made it in one piece out of the town center – Walden Street – Main – then back onto Lowell Road approaching the highway.

I whipped around onto Route 2 and nearly spun out of control. My wrist was still weak. The pedal was down to the floor. This was our best chance to get Thomas Pierce, maybe our last chance. Up ahead, Pierce knew this was it, too.

I was doing close to ninety now on Route 2, passing cars as if they were standing still. Pierce's Thunderbird must have been pushing eighty-five. He'd spotted us early in the chase.

'We're catching this squirrely bastard now!' Sampson hollered at me. 'Pierce goes down!'

We hit a deep pothole and the car momentarily left the road. We landed with a jarring *thud*. The wound in my side screamed. My head hurt. Sampson kept hollering in my ear about Pierce going down.

I could see his dark Thunderbird bobbing and weaving up ahead. Just a couple of car lengths separated us.

He's a planner, I warned myself. *He knew this might happen.*

I finally caught up to Pierce and pulled alongside him. Both cars were doing close to ninety. Pierce took a quick glance over at us.

I felt strangely exhilarated. Adrenaline powered through my body. *Maybe we had him.* For a second or two, I was as totally insane as Pierce.

Pierce saluted with his right hand. 'Dr Cross,' he called through the open window, 'we finally meet!'

Chapter One Hundred and Twenty-Four

'*I know about the FBI sanction!*' Pierce yelled over the whistle and roar of the wind. He looked cool and collected, oblivious to reality. 'Go ahead, Cross. I want you to do it. Take me out, Cross!'

'There's no sanction order!' I yelled back. 'Pull your car over! No one's going to shoot you.'

Pierce grinned – his best killer smile. His blond hair was tied in a tight pony-tail. He had on a black turtleneck. He looked successful – a local lawyer, shop owner, doctor. 'Doc.'

'Why do you think the FBI brought such a small unit,' he yelled. 'Terminate with prejudice. Ask your friend Kyle Craig. That's why they wanted me *inside* Straw's house!'

Was I talking to Thomas Pierce?

Or was this Mr Smith?

Was there a difference anymore?

He threw his head back and roared with laughter. It was one of the oddest, craziest things I've ever seen. The look on his face, the body language, his calmness. He was daring us to shoot him at ninety miles an hour on Route 2 outside Concord, Massachusetts. He wanted to crash and burn.

We hit a stretch of highway with thick fir woods on either side. Two of the FBI cars caught up. They were pinned on Pierce's tail, pushing, taunting him. Had the Bureau come here planning to kill Pierce?

If they were going to take him, this was a good place – a secluded pocket away from most commuter traffic and houses.

This was the place to terminate Thomas Pierce.

Now was the time.

'You know what we have to do,' Sampson said to me.

He's killed more than twenty people that we know of, I was thinking, trying to rationalize. *He'll never give up.*

'Pull over,' I yelled at Pierce again.

'I murdered Isabella Calais,' he screamed at me. His face was crimson. 'I can't stop myself. I don't want to stop. I like it! I found out I like it, Cross!'

'Pull the hell over,' Sampson's voice boomed. He had his Glock up and aimed at Pierce. 'You butcher! You piece of shit!'

'I murdered Isabella Calais and I can't stop the killing. You hear what I'm saying, Cross? I murdered Isabella Calais, and I can't stop the killing.'

I understood the chilling message. I'd gotten it the first time.

He was adding more letters to his list of victims. Pierce was creating a new, longer code: I murdered Isabella Calais, and I can't stop the killing. If he got away, he'd kill again and again. Maybe Thomas Pierce *wasn't* human, after all. He'd already intimated that he was his own god.

Pierce had an automatic out. He fired at us.

I yanked the steering wheel hard to the left with my right arm, trying desperately to get us out of the line of fire. Our car leaned hard on its left front and rear wheels. Everything was blurred and out of focus. I gripped the wheel. I thought we were going over.

Pierce's Thunderbird shot off Route 2, rocketing down a side road. I don't know how he made the turnoff at the speed he was traveling. Maybe he didn't care whether he made it or not.

I managed to set our sedan back down on all four wheels. The FBI cars following Pierce shot past the turn. None of us could stop. Next, came a ragged ballet of skidding stops and U-turns, the screech and whine of tires and brakes. We'd lost sight of Pierce. He was behind us.

We raced back to the turnoff, then down a twisting, chevroned country road. We found the Thunderbird abandoned about two miles from Route 2.

My heart was thudding hard inside my chest. *Pierce wasn't in the car. Pierce wasn't here.*

The woods on both sides of the road were thick and offered lots of cover. Sampson and I climbed out of our car.

We hurried back into the dense thicket of fir trees, Glocks out. It was almost impossible to get through the underbrush. There was no sign of Thomas Pierce anywhere.

Pierce was gone.

Chapter One Hundred and Twenty-Five

Thomas Pierce had vanished into thin air again. I was almost convinced he might actually live in a parallel world. Maybe he was an alien.

Sampson and I were headed to Logan International Airport. We were going home to Washington. Rush-hour traffic in Boston wasn't cooperating with the plan.

We were still half a mile from the Callahan Tunnel, gridlocked in a line that was barely moving. Grunting and groaning cars and trucks surrounded us. Boston was rubbing our faces in our failure.

'Metaphor for our cause. The whole goddamn manhunt for Pierce,' Sampson said about the traffic jumble, the mess. A good thing about Sampson – he gets either stoic or funny when things go really badly. He refuses to wallow in shit. He swims right out of it.

'I'm getting an idea,' I told him, giving him some warning.

'I knew you were flying around somewhere in your private universe. Knew you weren't really here, sitting in this car with me, listening to what I'm saying.'

'We'd just be stuck here in the tunnel traffic if we stayed put.'

Sampson nodded. 'Uh-huh. We're in Boston. Don't want to have to come back tomorrow, follow up on one of your hunches then. Best to do it now. Chase those wild geese while the chasing is good. I don't like you driving.'

I pulled out of the tight lane of stalled traffic. 'There's just one wild goose that I can think to chase.'

'You going to tell me where we're headed? I need to put my vest back on?'

'Depends on what you think of my hunches.'

I followed forest-green signs toward Storrow Drive, heading out of Boston the way we came. Traffic was heavy in that direction, too. There were too many people everywhere you went these days, too much crowding, and too much chaos, too much stress on everybody.

'Better put your vest back on,' I told Sampson.

He didn't argue with me. Sampson reached into the backseat and fished around for our vests.

I wiggled into my own vest as I drove. 'I think Thomas Pierce wants this to end. I think he's ready now. I saw it in his eyes.'

'So, he had his chance back there in Concord. *"Pull off the road. Pull over, Pierce!"* You remember any of that? Sound familiar, Alex?'

I glanced at Sampson. 'He needs to be in control. *S* was for Straw, but *S* is also for *Smith*. It's important to him that he finish this.'

Out of the corner of my eye I could see Sampson staring. 'And? So? What the hell is that supposed to mean?'

'He wants to end on *S*. It's magical for him. It's the way he has it figured, the way it has to be. It's his mind game, and he plays it obsessively. He can't stop playing. He told us that. He's still playing.'

Sampson was clearly having trouble with this. We had just missed capturing Pierce an hour ago. Would he put himself at risk again? 'You think he's that crazy?'

'I think he's that crazy, John. I'm sure of it.'

Chapter One Hundred and Twenty-Six

Half-a-dozen police squad cars were gathered on Inman Street in Cambridge. The blue-and-white cruisers were outside the apartment where Thomas Pierce and Isabella Calais had once lived, where Isabella had been murdered four years before.

EMS ambulances were parked near the graystone front stoop. Sirens bleated and wailed. If we hadn't turned around at the Callahan Tunnel we would have missed it.

Sampson and I showed our detective shields and kept on moving forward in a hurry. Nobody stopped us. Nobody could have.

Pierce was upstairs.

So was Mr Smith.

The game had come full circle.

'Somebody called in a homicide in progress,' one of the Cambridge uniforms told us on the way up the stone front stairs. 'I hear they got the guy cornered upstairs. Wackadoo of the first order.'

'We know all about him,' Sampson said.

The elevator was stuck so Sampson and I took the stairs to the second floor.

'You think Pierce called all this heat on himself?' Sampson asked as we hurried up the stairs. I was beyond being out of breath, beyond pain, beyond shock or surprise.

This is how he wants it to end.

I didn't know what to make of Thomas Pierce. He had numbed me, and all the rest of us. I was drifting beyond thought, at least logical ideas. There had never been a killer like Pierce. Not even close. He was the most *alienated* human being I'd ever met. Not alien, *alienated*.

'You still with me, Alex?' I felt Sampson's hand gripping my shoulder.

'Sorry,' I said. 'At first, I thought Pierce couldn't feel anything, that he was just another psychopath. Cold rage, arbitrary murders.'

'And now?'

I was inside Pierce's head.

'Now I'm wondering whether Pierce maybe feels *everything*. I think that's what drove him mad. This one can *feel*.'

The Cambridge police were gathered everywhere in the small, twisty hallway. The local cops looked shell-shocked and wild-eyed. A photograph of Isabella stared out from the foyer. She looked beautiful, almost regal, and so very sad.

'Welcome to the wild, wacky world of Thomas Pierce,' Sampson said.

A Cambridge detective explained the situation to us. He had silver-blond hair, an ageless hatchet face. He spoke in a low, confidential tone, almost a whisper. 'Pierce is in the bedroom at the far end of the hall. Barricaded himself in there.'

'The master bedroom, his and Isabella's room,' I said.

The detective nodded. 'Right, the master bedroom. I worked the original murder. I hate the prick. I saw what he did to her.'

'What's he doing in the bedroom?' I asked.

The detective shook his head. 'We think he's going to kill himself. He doesn't care to explain himself to us peons. He's got a gun. The powers-that-be are trying to decide whether to go in.'

'He hurt anybody?' Sampson spoke up.

The Cambridge detective shook his head. 'No, not that we know of. Not yet.'

Sampson's eyes narrowed. 'Then maybe we shouldn't interfere.'

We walked down the narrow hallway to where several more detectives were talking among themselves. A couple of them were arguing and pointing toward the bedroom.

This is how he wants it. He's still in control.

'I'm Alex Cross,' I told the detective-lieutenant on the scene. He knew who I was. 'What has he said so far?'

The lieutenant was sweating. He was a bruiser, and a good thirty pounds over his fighting weight. 'Told us that he killed Isabella Calais, confessed. I think we knew that already. Said he was going to kill himself.' He rubbed his chin with his left hand. 'We're trying to decide if we care. The FBI is on the way.'

I pulled away from the lieutenant.

'Pierce,' I called down the hallway. The talking going on outside the bedroom suddenly stopped. 'Pierce! It's Alex Cross,' I called again. 'I want to come in, Pierce!'

I felt a chill. It was too quiet. Not a sound. Then I heard Pierce from the bedroom. He sounded tired and weak. Maybe it was an act. Who knew what he would pull next?

'Come in if you want. Just you, Cross.'

'Let him go,' Sampson whispered from behind. 'Alex, let it go for once.'

I turned to him. 'I wish I could.'

I pushed through the group of policemen at the end of the hallway. I remembered the poster that hung there: *Without God, We Are Condemned To Be Free.* Was that what this was about?

I took out my gun and slowly inched open the bedroom door. I wasn't prepared for what I saw.

Thomas Pierce was sprawled on the bed he had once shared with Isabella Calais.

He held a gleaming, razor-sharp scalpel in his hand.

Chapter One Hundred and Twenty-Seven

*T*homas Pierce's chest was cut wide open. He had ripped himself apart as he would a corpse at an autopsy. He was still alive, but barely. It was incredible that he was conscious and alert.

Pierce spoke to me. I don't know how, but he did. 'You've never seen Mr Smith's handiwork before?'

I shook my head in disbelief. I had never seen anything like this, not in all my years in Violent Crimes or Homicide. Flaps of skin hung over Pierce's rib cage, exposing translucent muscle and tendons. I was afraid, repulsed, shocked – all at the same time.

Thomas Pierce was Mr Smith's victim. His last?

'Don't come any closer. Just stay there,' he said. It was a command.

'Who am I talking to? Thomas Pierce, or Mr Smith?'

Pierce shrugged. 'Don't play shrink games with me. I'm smarter than you are.'

I nodded. Why argue with him – with Pierce, or was it Mr Smith?

'I murdered Isabella Calais,' he said slowly. His eyes became hooded. He almost looked in a trance. 'I murdered Isabella Calais.'

He pressed the scalpel to his chest, ready to stab himself again, to *pierce*. I wanted to turn away, but I couldn't.

This man wants to cut into his own heart, I thought to myself. *Everything has come full circle to this. Is Mr Smith S? Of course he is.*

'You never got rid of any of Isabella's things,' I said. 'You kept her pictures up.'

Pierce nodded. 'Yes, Dr Cross. I was mourning her, wasn't I?'

'That's what I thought at first. It's what the people at the Behavioral Science Unit at Quantico believed. But then I finally got it.'

'What did you get? Tell me all about myself,' Pierce mocked. He was lucid. His mind still worked quickly.

'The other murders – you didn't want to kill any of them, did you?'

Thomas Pierce glared. He focused on me with a sheer act of will. His arrogance reminded me of Soneji. 'So why did I?'

'You were punishing yourself. Each murder was a re-enactment of Isabella's death. You repeated the ritual over and over. You suffered her death each time you killed.'

Thomas Pierce moaned. 'Ohhh, ohhh, I murdered her here. In this bed! . . . Can you imagine? Of course you can't. No one can.'

He raised the scalpel above his body.

'Pierce, don't!'

I had to do something. I rushed him. I threw myself at him, and the scalpel jammed into my right palm. I screamed in pain as Pierce pulled it out.

I grabbed at the folded yellow-and-white-flowered comforter and pressed it against Pierce's chest. He was fighting me, flopping around like a man having a seizure.

'Alex, no. Alex, look out!' I heard Sampson call out from behind me. I could see him out of the corner of my eye. He was moving fast toward the bed. 'Alex, the scalpel!' he yelled.

Pierce was still struggling beneath me. He screamed obscenities. His strength was amazing. I didn't know where the scalpel was, or if he still had it.

'Let Smith kill Pierce!' he screeched.

'No,' I yelled back. 'I want you alive.'

Then the unthinkable – again.

Sampson fired from point-blank range. The explosion was deafening in the small bedroom. Thomas Pierce's body convulsed on the bed. Both his legs kicked high in the air. He screeched like a badly wounded animal. He sounded inhuman – like an *alien*.

Sampson fired a second time. A strange guttural sound came from Pierce's throat. His eyes rolled way back in his head. The whites showed. The scalpel dropped from his hand.

I shook my head. 'No, John. No more. Pierce is dead. Mr Smith is dead, too. May he rest in hell.'

Chapter One Hundred and Twenty-Eight

I was drained of all feeling, slightly wounded and bandaged, but at least I got home safe and sound and in time to say good night to the kids. Damon and Jannie now had their own rooms. They both wanted it that way. Nana had given Jannie her room on the second floor. Nana had moved down to the smaller bedroom near the kitchen, which suited her fine.

I was so glad to be there, to be home again.

'Somebody's been decorating in here,' I said as I peeked into Jannie's new digs. It surprised her that I was home from the wars. Her face lit up like a jack-o'-lantern on Halloween.

'I did it myself.' Jannie pumped up her arms and 'made muscles' for me. 'Nana helped me hang the new curtains, though. We made them on the sewing machine. You like?'

'You're the hostess with the mostest. I guess I missed all the fun,' I told her.

'You sure did,' Jannie said and laughed. 'C'mere you,' she teased.

I went over to my little girl, and she gave me one of the sweetest hugs in the long and sometimes illustrious history of fathers and daughters.

Then I went to Damon's room, and because it had been both Damon and Jannie's room for so long, I was taken aback, shook up with the change.

Damon had chosen a sporting decor with monster and comedy movie accents. Manly, yet sensitive. I liked what he'd done to his room. It was pure Damon.

'You've got to help me with *my* room,' I told him.

'We missed our boxing lesson tonight,' he said, not in the tone of a major complaint, just setting the record straight.

'You want to go downstairs now?' I raised my fists. 'I'll go a round or two with you, Buster Douglas.'

Damon laughed out loud. 'You think you can take me? I don't *think so.*'

We settled for wrestling on his bed, but I had to agree to a double boxing lesson in the basement the following night. Actually, I couldn't wait. Damon was growing up too fast. So was Jannie. I couldn't have been happier with either of them.

And Christine. I could call her now, see her tomorrow. There was a saying I liked: *Heart leads head.* With Christine, I felt whole again. I felt connected to the eternal river and all that good stuff. I had missed that feeling for too many years.

I was a lucky man.

I had made it home again.

Epilogue

By the Sea, By the Sea

Chapter One Hundred and Twenty-Nine

D amon, Jannie, Nana, Christine, and I arrived at Bermuda International Airport on Sunday, the twenty-fifth of August.

I remember a scene from the airport perfectly – Christine and Jannie were standing on the passport line, holding hands and singing 'Ja – da, ja – da.' It was a mind-photo to have and to hold.

We were blessed with good weather, the very best imaginable. It was sunny and blue skied every day. The days belonged to the kids. We went swimming and snorkeling at Elbow and Horseshoe Bay, and raced mopeds along the Middle Road.

The nights belonged to Christine and me, and we hit the good spots, and hit them hard – the Terrace Bar at the Palm Reef, the Gazebo Lounge at the Princess, the Clay House Inn. I loved being with her more than ever. I felt whole again. I kept remembering the first time I had seen her in the school-yard at Sojourner Truth. *She's the one, Alex. She's the one.*

One morning, I found her walking in the garden with flowers strewn in her hair. 'There's an old saying,' she told me. 'If you have only two pennies, buy a loaf of bread with one, and a lily with the other.'

The kids and I went back to Horseshoe Bay that afternoon. They couldn't get enough of the deep blue sea. Christine took a moped trip into Hamilton to pick up mementos for a few of the teachers at Sojourner Truth. Around five, Damon, Jannie, and I finally returned to the Belmont Hotel, which sat like a sentinel on lush green hills framed by china-blue skies. All around were pastel-colored cottages with white roofs. Nana was sitting out on the porch talking to her new best friends. Paradise regained, I thought.

As I stared out at the perfect blue sky, I regretted that Christine wasn't there to share it. I missed her in that short a time. I hugged the kids and we were all smiling at the obvious.

'You miss her,' Jannie whispered. 'That's good, Daddy. That's very nice.'

When Christine still hadn't returned by six, I struggled between waiting for her at the hotel or driving into Hamilton myself. Maybe she'd had an accident. *Those damn mopeds*, I thought, having found them fun and safe just the day before.

I spotted a tall, slender woman entering through the front gates of the

Belmont. I sighed in relief, but as I hurried down the front stairs, I saw that it wasn't Christine.

Christine still hadn't returned, or called the hotel, by six-thirty. Or by seven. *I called the police.*

Chapter One Hundred and Thirty

Inspector Patrick Busby arrived at seven-thirty. He told me that visitors often lost track of the time and themselves in Bermuda. There were also occasional moped accidents. He promised me that Christine would show up with a mild 'road rash,' or a slightly turned ankle.

I wouldn't have any of it. The inspector and I rode together between the hotel and Hamilton, and then we toured the streets of the capital city. I was silent as I stared out of the car, hoping to get a glimpse of Christine shopping on some side street.

When she still hadn't turned up by nine, Inspector Busby reluctantly agreed that Christine might be missing. He wanted to know if we'd had any kind of argument or disagreement.

'I'm a homicide detective in Washington, DC,' I finally told him. I'd been holding it back because I didn't want this to get territorial. 'I've been involved with high-profile cases involving mass murderers.'

'I see,' Busby said. He was a small, neat black man with a pencil mustache. He looked more like a fussy schoolteacher than a cop. 'Are there any other surprises I should know about, detective?'

'No, that's it. But you see why I'm worried.'

'Yes, I see the reason for your concern. I will put out a missing-persons report.'

I sighed heavily, then went up and talked to the kids and Nana. I tried my best not to alarm them, but Damon and Jannie started to cry. And then Nana Mama did, too.

We had learned nothing more about Christine's whereabouts by midnight. Inspector Busby finally left the hotel at quarter past twelve. He was kind enough to give me his home number and asked me to call right away if I heard from Christine.

At three, I was still up and pacing my hotel room. I had just gotten off the phone with Quantico. The FBI was cross-checking my homicide cases to see if anyone had connections with Bermuda, or anywhere in the Caribbean. They probably wouldn't get back to me until later in the morning.

I stood before tall dormer windows and stared out at black shapes against the moonlit sky and remembered how Christine felt in my arms. I felt incredibly helpless and alone.

I hugged myself tightly. The pain was like a solid column that went from my chest all the way up into my head. I could see her face, her beautiful smile. I remembered dancing with her at the Rainbow Room.

Was Christine out there somewhere on the island? She had to be. I prayed that she was safe. I refused to have any other thought.

The telephone in the room rang, a short burst, at a little past four in the morning. My heart was in my throat.

I rushed across the room and grabbed the phone before the second ring. My hand was trembling.

The strange, muffled voice scared me: 'You have an e-mail.' I couldn't think straight. I couldn't think at all. Then I recognized what it was.

I had brought my laptop personal computer, but left it in the closet.

Who knew that I had my computer here? Who knew a small detail like that about me? Who had been watching me? Watching us?

I couldn't breathe. I couldn't stand it. Finally, I yanked open the closet door. I grabbed the computer, hooked it up, and logged on. I scrolled down the e-mail to the last message.

It was short and very concise.

'She's safe for now. We have her.'

It was worse than anything I could imagine. Each word was branded into my brain, repeating over and over.

She's safe for now.

We have her.

POP GOES THE WEASEL

James Patterson

This is for Suzie and Jack, and the millions of Alex Cross readers who so frequently ask – *can't you write faster?*

Pop Goes the Weasel

Chapter One

Geoffrey Shafer, dashingly outfitted in a single-breasted blue blazer, white shirt, striped tie and narrow gray trousers from H. Huntsman & Son, walked out of his town house at seven thirty in the morning and climbed into a black Jaguar XJ12.

He backed the Jag slowly out of the driveway, then stepped on the accelerator. The sleek sports car rocketed up to fifty before it reached the stop sign at Connecticut Avenue, in the posh Kalorama section of Washington, DC.

When Shafer reached the busy intersection, he didn't stop. He floored the accelerator, picking up more speed.

He was doing sixty-five and ached to crash the Jag into the stately field-stone wall bordering the avenue. He aimed the Jag closer to the wall. He could see the head-on collision, visualize it, feel it all over.

At the last possible second, he tried to avoid the deadly crash. He spun the wheel hard to the left. The sports car fishtailed all the way across the avenue, tires screeching and burning, the smell of rubber thick in the air.

The Jag skidded to a stop, headed the wrong way on the street, the windshield issuing its glossy black stare at a barrage of early oncoming traffic.

Shafer stepped on the accelerator again, and headed forward *against* the oncoming traffic. Every car and truck began to honk loud, sustained blasts.

Shafer didn't even try to catch his breath or bearings. He sped along the avenue, gaining speed. He zoomed across Rock Creek Bridge, made a left, then another left into Rock Creek Parkway.

A tiny scream of pain escaped from his lips. It was involuntary, coming swiftly and unexpectedly. A moment of fear, weakness.

He floored the pedal again and the engine roared. He was doing seventy, then pressing to eighty. He zigged and zagged around slower-moving sedans, sport-utility vehicles, a soot-covered A&P delivery truck.

Only a few honked now. Other drivers on the parkway were terrified, scared out of their minds.

He exited the Rock Creek Parkway at fifty miles an hour, then he gunned it again.

P Street was even more crowded at that hour than the parkway had been. Washington was just waking up and setting off to work. He could still *see* that inviting stone wall on Connecticut. He shouldn't have stopped. He began searching for another rock-solid object, looking for something to hit very hard.

He was doing eighty miles an hour as he approached Dupont Circle. He shot forward like a ground rocket. Two lines of traffic were backed up at a red light. No way out of this one, he thought. Nowhere to go left or right.

He didn't want to rear-end a dozen cars! That was no way to end this – end his life – by smashing into a commonplace Chevy Caprice, a Honda Accord, a delivery truck.

He swerved violently to the left and veered into the lanes of traffic coming east, coming right at him. He could see the panicked, disbelieving faces behind the dusty, grime-smeared windshields. The horns started to blast, a high-pitched symphony of fear.

He ran the next light and just barely squeezed between an oncoming Jeep and a concrete-mixer truck.

He sped down M Street, then onto Pennsylvania Avenue, and headed toward Washington Circle. The George Washington University Medical Center was up ahead – a perfect ending?

The Metro patrolcar appeared out of nowhere, its siren-bullhorn screaming in protest, its rotating beacon glittering, signaling for him to pull over. Shafer slowed down and pulled to the curb.

The cop hurried to Shafer's car, his hand on his holster. He looked frightened and unsure.

'Get out of the car, sir,' the cop said in a commanding voice. 'Get out of the car right now.'

Shafer suddenly felt calm and relaxed. There was no tension left in his body. 'All right. All right. I'm getting out. No problem.'

'You know how fast you were going?' the cop asked in an agitated voice, his face flushed a bright red. Shafer noticed that his hand was still on his gun.

Shafer pursed his lips, thought about his answer. 'Well – I'd say about thirty, Officer,' he finally said. 'Maybe a little over the speed limit.'

Then he took out an ID card and handed it over. 'But you can't do anything about it. I'm with the British Embassy. I have *diplomatic immunity*.'

Chapter Two

That night, as he was driving home from work, Geoffrey Shafer started to feel that he was losing control again. He was beginning to frighten himself. His whole life had begun to revolve around a fantasy game he played called The Four Horsemen. In the game, he was the player called Death. The game was everything to him, the only part of his life with meaning.

He sped across town from the British Embassy, all the way to the Petworth district of Northwest. He knew he shouldn't be there, a white man in a spiffy Jaguar. He couldn't help himself, though, any more than he could that morning.

He stopped the car just before he got to Petworth. Shafer took out his laptop and typed a message to the other players, the Horsemen.

FRIENDS,
DEATH IS ON THE LOOSE IN WASHINGTON.
THE GAME IS ON.

He started the Jag again and rode a few more blocks to Petworth. The usual outrageously provocative hookers were already parading up and down Varnum and Webster Streets. A song called 'Nice and Slow' was playing from a vibrating blue BMW. Ronnie McCall's sweet voice blended into the early evening.

The girls waved to him and showed their large, flat, pert, or flabby breasts. Several wore colorful bustiers with matching hot pants and shiny silver or red platform shoes with pointy heels.

He slowed to a stop beside a small black girl who looked to be around sixteen, and had an unusually pretty face and long slender legs, for such a petite body. She wore too much makeup for his taste. Still, she was hard to resist, so why should he?

'Nice car. Jaguar. I like it a lot,' she cooed, smiled, made a sexy little *o* with her lipsticked mouth. 'You're cute, too, mistah.'

He smiled back at her. 'Jump in, then. Let's go for a test ride. See if it's true love or just infatuation.' He glanced around the street quickly. None of the other girls were working this corner.

'I'm a hundred for full service, sweetie,' she said as she wiggled her tight little butt inside the Jag. Her perfume smelled like eau de bubble gum and she seemed to have bathed in it.

'As I said, get into the car. A hundred dollars is petty cash for me.'

He knew he shouldn't be picking her up in the Jaguar, but he took her for a joy ride anyway. He couldn't help himself now.

He brought the girl to a small wooded park in a part of Washington called Shaw. He parked in a thicket of fir trees that hid the car from sight. He looked at the prostitute and she was even smaller and younger than he had thought.

'How old are you?' he asked.

'How old you want me to be?' she said and smiled. 'Sweetheart, I need the money first. You know how it works.'

'Yes. But do you?' he asked.

He reached into his pocket, and pulled out a switchblade knife. He had it at her throat in an instant.

'Don't hurt me,' she whispered. 'Just be cool.'

'Get out of the car. Slowly. Don't you dare scream. *You* be cool.'

Shafer got out with her, staying close, the knife still pressed to the hollow of her throat.

'This is a fantasy game,' he explained. 'It's all just a game, darling. I play with three other men – in England, Jamaica, and Thailand. Their names are Famine, War, and Conqueror. My name is Death. You're a very lucky girl – I'm the best player of all.'

As if to prove it, he stabbed her for the first time.

Book One

The Jane Doe Murders

Chapter One

Things were going pretty well that day. I was driving a bright-orange school bus through Southeast on a blistering-hot morning in late July and I was whistling a little Al Green as I drove. I was in the process of picking up sixteen boys from their houses and also two foster homes. Door-to-door bus service. Hard to beat.

Just one week earlier I had returned from Boston and the Mr Smith murder case. Mr Smith and a deranged killer named Gary Soneji had both been involved in that one. I needed a rest and I'd taken the morning off to do something I'd been looking forward to for a change.

My partner, John Sampson, and a twelve year old named Errol Mignault sat behind me on the bus. John was wearing Wayfarer shades, black jeans, a black T-shirt that read: ALLIANCE OF CONCERNED MEN. SEND DONATIONS TODAY. He is six-nine, a very solid two hundred fifty pounds. We've been friends since we were ten, when I first moved to DC.

He, Errol, and I were talking about the boxer Sugar Ray Robinson, almost shouting over the bus's blustery, occasionally misfiring engine. Sampson had his huge arm lightly draped over Errol's shoulders. Proper physical contact is encouraged when dealing with these boys.

Finally, we picked up the last little guy on our list, an eight-year-old who lived in Benning Terrace, a tough project known to some of us as Simple City.

As we left the project, an ugly smear of graffiti told visitors everything they needed to know about the neighborhood. It read: YOU ARE NOW LEAVING THE WAR ZONE, AND YOU LIVED TO TELL ABOUT IT.

We were taking the boys out to Lorton Prison in Virginia. They would be visiting their fathers for the afternoon. They were all young, between eight and thirteen. The Alliance transports forty to fifty kids each week to see their fathers and mothers in different prisons. The goal is a lofty one: To bring the crime rate in Washington down by a third.

I'd been out to the prison more times than I cared to remember. I knew the warden at Lorton pretty well. A few years back I'd spent a lifetime there, interviewing Gary Soneji.

Warden Marion Campbell had set up a large room on level one, where the boys met with their fathers. It was a powerful scene, even more emotional than

I'd expected. The Alliance spends time training the fathers who want to participate in the program. There are four steps: how to show love; accept fault and
responsibility; attain parent and child harmonies; new beginnings.

Ironically the boys were all trying to look and act tougher than they actually were. I heard one boy say, 'You weren't in my life before, why should I
listen to you now?' But the fathers were trying to show a softer side.

Sampson and I hadn't made the run to Lorton before. It was our first time,
but I was already sure I'd do it again. There was so much raw emotion and
hope in the room, so much potential for something good and decent. Even if
some of it would never be realized, it showed that an effort was being made,
and something positive could come from it.

What struck me most was the bond that still existed between some of the fathers
and their young sons. I thought about my own boy, Damon, and how lucky we
were. The thing about most of the prisoners in Lorton was that they knew what
they had done was wrong; they just didn't know how to stop doing it.

For most of the hour and a half, I just walked around and listened. I was
occasionally needed as a psychologist, and I did the best I could on short notice.
At one little group, I heard a father say, 'Please tell your mother I love her and
I miss her like crazy.' Then both the prisoner and his son broke into tears and
hugged one another fiercely.

Sampson came up to me after we'd been in the prison for an hour or so. He
was grinning broadly. His smile, when it comes, is a killer. 'Man, I love this.
Do-gooder shit is the best.'

'Yeah, I'm hooked myself. I'll drive the big orange bus again.'

'Think it'll help? Fathers and sons meeting like this?' he asked me.

I looked around the room. 'I think today, right now, this is a success for
these men and their sons. That's good enough.'

Sampson nodded. 'The old one-day-at-a-time approach. Works for me, too.
I am *flying*, Alex.'

So was I, so was I. I'm a sucker for this kind of stuff.

As I drove the young boys home that afternoon. I could see by their faces
that they'd had positive experiences with their fathers. The boys weren't nearly
as noisy and rambunctious on the way back to DC. They weren't trying to be
so tough. They were just acting like kids.

Almost every one of the boys thanked Sampson and me as they got off the
big orange bus. It wasn't necessary. It sure was a lot better than chasing after
homicidal maniacs.

The last boy we dropped off was the eight year old from Benning Terrace.
He hugged both John and me and then he started to cry. 'I miss my dad,' he
said, before running home.

Chapter Two

That night, Sampson and I were on duty in Southeast. We're senior homicide detectives and I'm also liaison between the FBI and the DC police. We got a call at about half past midnight telling us to go to the area of Washington called Shaw. There'd been a bad homicide.

A lone Metro squad car was at the murder scene, and the neighborhood psychos had turned out in pretty fair numbers.

It looked like a bizarre block party in the middle of hell. Fires were blazing nearby, throwing off sparks in two trash barrels, which made no sense, given the sweltering heat of the night.

The victim was a young woman, probably between fourteen and her late teens, according to the radio report.

She wasn't hard to find. Her nude, mutilated body had been discarded in a clump of briar bushes in a small park, less than ten yards off a paved pathway.

As Sampson and I approached the body, a boy shouted at us from the other side of the crime tape. 'Yo, yo, she's just some street whore!'

I stopped and looked at him. He reminded me of the boys we'd just transported to Lorton Prison. 'Dime-a-dozen bitch. Not worth your time, or mine, *dee-fectives,*' he went on with his disturbing rap.

I finally walked up to the young wisecracker. 'How do you know that? You seen her around?'

The boy backed off. But then he grinned, showing off a gold star on one of his front teeth. 'She ain't got no clothes on an' she layin' on her back. Somebody stick her good. Sure sound like a whore to me.'

Sampson eyed the youth, who looked to be around fourteen, but might have been even younger. 'You know who she is?'

'Hell, *no!*' The boy pretended to be insulted. 'Don't know no whores, man.'

The boy finally swaggered off, looking back at us once or twice, shaking his head. Sampson and I walked on and joined two uniformed cops standing by the body. They were obviously waiting for reinforcements. Apparently, we were it.

'You call Emergency Services?' I asked the uniforms.

'Thirty-five minutes ago, and counting,' said the older-looking of the two. He was probably in his late twenties, sporting an attempted mustache and trying to look like he was experienced at scenes like this one.

'That figures.' I shook my head. 'You find any ID anywhere around here?'

'No ID. We looked around in the bushes. Nothing but the body,' said the younger one. 'And the body's seen better days.' He was perspiring badly and looked a little sick.

I put on latex gloves and bent down over the corpse. She did appear to be in her mid to late teens. The girl's throat had been slit from ear to ear. Her face was badly slashed. So were the soles of her feet, which seemed odd. She'd been stabbed a dozen or more times in her chest and stomach. I pushed open her legs.

I saw something, and it made me sick. A metal handle was barely visible between her legs. I was almost sure it was a knife and that it had been driven all the way into her vagina.

Sampson crouched and looked at me. 'What are you thinking, Alex? Another one?'

I shook my head, shrugged my shoulders. 'Maybe, but she's an addict, John. Tracks on her arms and legs. Probably behind her knees, under her arms. Our boy doesn't usually go after addicts. He practices safe sex. The murder's brutal, though. That fits the style. You see the knife?'

Sampson nodded. He didn't miss much. 'Clothes,' he said, 'where the hell did they go? We need to find the clothes.'

'Somebody in the neighborhood probably stripped them off her already,' said the young uniform. There was a lot of disturbance around the body. Several footprints in the dirt. 'That's how it goes around here. Nobody seems to care.'

'We're here,' I said to him. 'We care. We're here for all the Jane Does.'

Chapter Three

Geoffrey Shafer was so happy he almost couldn't hide it from his family. He had to keep from laughing out loud as he kissed his wife, Lucy, on the cheek. He caught a whiff of her Chanel No. 5 perfume, then tasted the brittle dryness of her lips as he kissed her again.

They were standing around like statues in the elegant galley hall of the large Georgian house in Kalorama. The children had been summoned to say goodbye to him.

His wife, the former Lucy Rhys-Cousins, was ash blonde, her sparkling green eyes even brighter than the Bulgari and Spark jewelry that she always wore. Slender, still a beauty of sorts at thirty-seven, Lucy had been at Newnham College, Cambridge, for two years before they were married. She still read useless poetry and literary novels, but spent most of her free time at equally pointless lunches, shopping with her expatriate girlfriends, going to polo matches, or sailing. Occasionally, Shafer sailed with her. He'd been a very good sailor once upon a time.

Lucy had been considered a prize catch, and he supposed that she still would be, for some men. Well, they could have her skinny, bony body and all the passionless sex they could stomach.

Shafer hoisted up four-year-old twins Tricia and Erica, one in each arm. Two mirror images of their mother. He'd have sold the twins for the price of a postage stamp. He hugged the girls and laughed like the good papa he always pretended to be.

Finally, he formally shook twelve-year-old Robert's hand. The debate being waged in the house was over whether Robert should be sent back to England to boarding school, perhaps to Winchester, where his grandfather had gone. Shafer gave his son a crisp military salute. Once upon a time, Colonel Geoffrey Shafer had been a soldier. Only Robert seemed to remember that part of his life now.

'I'm only going away to London for a few days, and this is *work*, not a holiday. I'm not planning to spend my nights at the Athenaeum or anything like that,' he told his family. He was smiling jovially, the way they expected him to be.

'Try to have some fun while you're away, Dad. Have some laughs. God knows, you deserve it,' Robert said, talking in the lower-octave man-to-man's voice that he seemed to be adopting lately.

'Bye, Daddy! Bye, Daddy,' the twins chorused shrilly, making Shafer want to throw them against the walls.

'Bye, Erica-san. Bye, Tricia-san.'

'Remember, Orc's Nest,' Robert said with sudden urgency. '*Dragon* and *The Duelist*.' Orc's Nest was a store for role-playing books and gaming equipment. It was in Earlham Street, just off Cambridge Circus in London. *Dragon* and *The Duelist* were currently the two hot-shit British magazines on role-playing games.

Unfortunately for Robert, Shafer wasn't actually going to London. He had a much better plan for the weekend. He was going to play his own fantasy game right here in Washington.

Chapter Four

He sped due east, rather than toward Washington's Dulles airport, feeling as if a tremendously burdensome weight had been lifted. God, he hated his perfect English family, and even more, their claustrophobic life here in America.

Shafer's own family back in England had been 'perfect' as well. He had two older brothers and they were both excellent students, model youths. His father had been a military attaché and the family had traveled around the globe until he was twelve, when they returned to England and settled in Guildford, about half an hour outside London. Once there, Shafer began to expand on the schoolboy mischief he'd practiced since he was eight. The center of Guildford contained several historic buildings and he set out to gleefully deface all of them. He began with the Abbot's Hospital where his grandmother was dying. He painted obscenities on the walls. Then he moved onto Guildford Castle, the Guildhall, the Royal Grammar School, and the Cathedral. He scrawled more obscene words, and also large penises in bright colors. He had no idea why he took such joy in ruining beautiful things, but he did. He loved it – and he especially loved not getting caught.

Shafer was eventually sent to school at Rugby, where the pranks continued. Then he attended St John's College, Cambridge, where he concentrated on philosophy, Japanese, and shagging as many good-looking women as he possibly could. All his friends were mystified when he went into the army at twenty-one. His language skills were excellent and he was posted to Asia, which was where the mischief rose to a new level and he began to play *the game of games*.

He stopped at a 7-Eleven in Washington Heights for coffee – three coffees, actually. Black, with four sugars in each. He drank most of one of the cups on his way to the counter.

The Indian cashier gave him a cheeky, suspicious look, and he laughed in the bearded wanker's face.

'Do you really think I'd steal a bloody seventy-five-cent cup of coffee? You pathetic jerkoff. You pitiful Paki.'

He threw his money on the counter and left before he killed the clerk with his bare hands, which he could do easily enough.

From the 7-Eleven he drove into the Northeast part of Washington, a middle-class section called Eckington. He began to recognize the streets when he was west of Gallaudet University. Most of the structures were two-storied apartments, with vinyl siding, either red brick, or a hideous Easter-egg blue that always made him wince.

He stopped in front of one of the red-brick garden apartments on Uhland Terrace, near Second Street. This one had an attached garage. A previous tenant had adorned the brick façade with two white concrete cats.

'Hello, pussies,' Shafer said. He felt relieved to be here. He was 'cycling up' – that is, getting high, manic. He loved this feeling, couldn't get enough of it. It was time to play the game.

Chapter Five

A rusted and taped-up purple-and-blue taxi was parked inside the two-car garage. Shafer had been using it for about four months. The taxi gave him anonymity, made him almost invisible anywhere he chose to go in DC. He called it his 'nightmare machine.'

He wedged the Jaguar beside the taxi cab, then he jogged upstairs. Once inside the apartment, he switched on the air-conditioning. He drank another sugar-laced coffee.

Then he took his pills, like a good boy. Thorazine and Librium. Benadryl, Xanax, Vicodin. He'd been using the drugs in various combinations for years. It was mostly a trial and error process, but he'd learned his lessons well. *Feeling better, Geoffrey? Yes, much better, thank you.*

He tried to read today's *Washington Post*, then an old copy of *Private Eye*, and finally a catalog from DeMask, a rubber and leather fetish wholesaler in Amsterdam, the world's largest. He did two hundred pushups, then a few hundred situps, impatiently waiting for darkness to fall over Washington.

At quarter to ten, Shafer began to get ready for a big night on the town. He went into the small, barren bathroom which smelled of cheap cleaner. He stood before the mirror.

He liked what he saw. Very much so. Thick and wavy blond hair that he would never lose. A charismatic, electric smile. Startling blue eyes that had a cinematic quality. Excellent physical shape for a man of forty-four.

He went to work, starting with brown contact lenses. He'd done this so many times, he could almost do it blindfolded. It was a part of his tradecraft. He applied blackface to his face, neck, hands, wrists; thick padding to make his neck seem broader than it was; a dark watch cap to cover every last strand of hair.

He stared hard at himself – and saw a rather convincing-looking black man, especially if the light wasn't too strong. Not bad, not bad at all. It was a good disguise for a night on the town, especially if the town was Washington.

So let the games begin. The Four Horsemen.

At ten twenty-five, he went down to the garage again. He carefully circled around the Jaguar and walked to the purple-and-blue taxi cab. He had already begun to lose himself in delicious fantasy.

Shafer reached into his pants pocket and pulled out three unusual-looking dice. They were twenty-sided, the kind used in most fantasy games, or RPGs. They had numerals on them rather than dots.

He held the dice in his left hand, rolling them over and over.

There were explicit rules to The Four Horsemen; everything was supposed to depend on the dice roll. The idea was to come up with an outrageous fantasy, a mind-blower. The four players around the world were competing. There had never been a game like this – nothing even came close.

Shafer had already prepared an adventure for himself, but there were alternatives for every event. Much depended on the dice.

That was the main point – anything could happen.

He got into the taxi, started it up. Good Lord, was he ready for this!

Chapter Six

He had a gorgeous plan mapped out. He would pick up only those few passengers – 'fares' – who caught his eye, fired up his imagination to the limit. He wasn't in a hurry. He had all night; he had all weekend. He was on a busman's holiday.

His route had been laid out beforehand. First, he drove to the fashionable Adams-Morgan neighborhood. He watched the busy sidewalks, which seemed one long syncopated rhythm of movement. Bar-grazers slouching toward hipness. It seemed that every other restaurant in Adams-Morgan called itself a café. Driving slowly and checking the glittery sights, he passed Café Picasso, Café Lautrec, La Fourchette Café, Bukom Café, Café Dalbol, Montego Café, Sheba Café.

Around eleven thirty, on Columbia Road, he slowed the taxi cab. His heart began to thump. Something very good was shaping up ahead.

A handsome-looking couple was leaving the popular Chief Ike's Mambo

Room. A man and a woman, Hispanic, probably in their late twenties. Sensual beyond belief.

He rolled the dice across the front seat: six, five, four – a total of fifteen. A high count.

Danger! That made sense. A couple was always tricky and risky.

Shafer waited for them to cross the pavement, moving away from the restaurant canopy. *They came right toward him.* How accommodating. He touched the handle of the magnum that he kept under the front seat. He was ready for anything.

As they started to climb into the taxi, he changed his mind. He could do that!

Shafer saw that neither of them was as attractive as he'd thought. The man's cheeks and forehead were slightly mottled; the pomade in his black hair was too thick and greasy. The woman was a few pounds heavier than he liked, plumper than she'd looked from a distance in the flattering streetlights.

'Off duty,' he said, and sped away. Both of them gave him the finger.

Shafer laughed out loud. 'You're in luck tonight! Fools! Luckiest night of your lives and you don't even know it.'

The incomparable thrill of the fantasy had completely taken hold of him. He'd had total power over the couple. He had control of life and death.

'Death *be* proud,' he whispered.

He stopped for more coffee at a Starbucks on Rhode Island Avenue. Nothing like it. He purchased three black coffees and heaped six sugars in each.

An hour later, he was in Southeast. He hadn't stopped for another fare. The streets were crowded to the max with pedestrians. There weren't enough taxis, not even gypsies in this part of Washington.

He regretted having let the Hispanic couple get away. He'd begun to romanticize them in his mind, to visualize them as they'd looked in the streetlight. Remembrance of things past, right? He thought of Proust's monumental opening line: '*For a long time I used to go to bed early.*' And so had Shafer – until he discovered the game of games.

Then he saw her – a perfect brown goddess standing right there before him, as if someone had just given him a wonderful present. She was walking by herself, about a block from E Street, moving fast, purposefully. He was instantly high again.

He loved the way she moved, the swivel of her long legs, the exactness of her carriage.

As he came up behind her, she began looking around, checking the street. Looking for a taxi? Could it be? Did she want him?

She had on a light cream suit, a purple silk shirt, high heels. She looked too classy and adult to be going to a club. She appeared to be in control of herself.

He quickly rolled the twenty-sided dice again and held his breath. Counted the numerals. His heart leaped. This was what the Horsemen was all about.

She was waving her hand at him, signaling. '*Taxi!*' she called. 'Taxi! Are you free?'

He guided the taxi over to the curb and she took three quick, delicate steps toward him. She was wearing shimmery, silken high heels that were just delightful. She was much prettier up close. She was a nine and a half out of ten.

Then he saw that she was carrying flowers, and wondered why. Something special tonight? Well, that was certainly true. The flowers were for her own funeral.

'Oh, thank you so much for stopping.' She spoke breathlessly as she settled into the taxi. He could tell that she was letting herself relax and feel safe. Her voice was soothing, sweet, down-to-earth, and real.

'At your service.' Shafer turned and smiled at her. 'By the way, I'm Death. You're my fantasy for this weekend.'

Chapter Seven

Monday mornings I usually work the soup kitchen at St Anthony's in Southeast, where I've been a volunteer for the past half-dozen years. I do the seven-to-nine shift, three days a week.

That morning I felt restless and uneasy. I was still getting over the Mr Smith case, which had taken me all over the East Coast and to Europe. Maybe I needed a real vacation, a holiday far away from Washington.

I watched the usual lineup of men, women, and children who have no money for food. It was about five deep and went up Twelfth Street to the second corner. It seemed such a pity, so unfair that so many folks still go hungry in Washington, or are fed only once a day.

I had started helping out at the kitchen years before on account of my wife, Maria. She was doing casework as a social worker at St Anthony's when we first met. Maria was the uncrowned princess of St Anthony's; everybody loved her, and she loved me. She was shot, murdered, in a drive-by incident, not far from the soup kitchen. We'd been married four years and had two small children. The case has never been solved, and that still tortures me. Maybe that's what drives me to solve every case that I can, no matter how bad the odds.

At St Anthony's soup kitchen, I help make sure nobody gets too riled up, or causes undue trouble during meals. I'm six-three, around two hundred and five pounds, and built for peacekeeping, if and when it's necessary. I can usually ward off trouble with a few quiet words and non-threatening gestures. Most of these people are here to eat though, not fight or cause trouble.

I also dish out peanut butter and jelly to anyone who wants seconds, or even thirds of the stuff. Jimmy Moore, the Irish-American who runs the soup kitchen with much love and just the right amount of discipline, has always believed in the healing power of PB and J. Some of the regulars at the kitchen call me 'Peanut Butter Man.' They've been doing it for years.

'You don't look so good today,' said a short, ample woman who's been coming to the kitchen for the past year or two. I know her name is Laura, that she was born in Detroit, and has two grown sons. She used to work as a housekeeper on M Street in Georgetown, but the family felt she'd gotten too old for the job, and let her go with a couple weeks' severance and warm words of appreciation.

'You deserve better. You deserve *me*,' Laura said, and laughed mischievously. 'What do you say?'

'Laura, you're too kind with your compliments,' I said, dishing up her usual dish. 'Anyway, you've met Christine. You know I'm already spoken for.'

Laura giggled, and hugged herself with both arms. She had a fine, healthy laugh, even under the circumstances. 'A young girl has to dream, you know. Nice to see you, as always.'

'Same to you, Laura. As always, nice to see you. Enjoy the meal.'

'Oh, I do. You can *see* I do.'

As I said my cheery hellos and dished out heaped portions of peanut butter, I allowed myself to think about Christine. Laura was probably right, maybe I didn't look so good today; I probably hadn't looked too terrific for a few days.

I still remembered a night about two weeks back. I had just finished the multiple-homicide case in Boston. Christine and I stood on the porch in front of her house out in Mitchellville. I was trying to live my life differently, but it's hard to change. I had a saying I really liked: *Heart leads head.*

I could smell the flowers in the night air, roses and impatiens growing in profusion. I could also smell Gardenia Passion, a favorite perfume that Christine was wearing that night.

She and I had known each other for a year and a half. We'd met during a murder investigation that had ended with the death of her husband. Eventually, we began to go out. I was thinking that it had all been leading to this moment on the porch. At least it had been in my mind.

I had never seen Christine when she didn't look good to me, and make me feel light-headed. She's tall, almost five-ten, and that's nice. She has a smile that could probably light up half the country. That night, she was wearing tight faded jeans and a white T-shirt knotted around her waist. Her feet were bare and her nails were dabbed with red. Her beautiful brown eyes were shining.

I reached out and took her into my arms and suddenly everything seemed right with the world. I forgot all about the terrible case I'd just finished; I forgot about a particularly vicious killer known as Mr Smith.

I cupped her sweet, kind face gently in my hands. I like to think that nothing scares me anymore, and many things don't, but I guess the more good things you have in your life, the easier it is to experience fear. Christine felt so precious to me – so maybe I was scared.

Heart leads head.

It isn't the way most men act, but I was learning.

'I love you more than I've ever loved anything in my life, Christine. You help me see and feel things in new ways. I love your smile, your way with people – especially kids – your kindness. I love to hold you like this. I love you more than I can say if I stood here and talked for the rest of the night. I love you so much. Will you marry me, Christine?'

She didn't answer right away. I felt her pull back, just a little, and my heart caught. I looked into her eyes, and what I saw was pain and uncertainty. It nearly broke my heart.

'Oh, Alex, Alex,' she whispered, and looked as if she might cry. 'I can't give you an answer. You just came back from Boston. You were on another horrible, horrible murder case. I can't take that. Your life was in danger again. That terrible madman was in your house. He threatened your family. You can't deny any of that.'

I couldn't. It had been a terrifying experience, and I had nearly died. 'I won't deny anything you said. But I do love you. I can't deny that either. I'll quit the police force if that's what it takes.'

'No.' A softness came into her eyes. She shook her head back and forth. 'That would be all wrong. For both of us.'

We held each other on the porch and I knew we were in trouble. I didn't know how to resolve it. I had no idea. Maybe if I left the force, became a full-time therapist again, led a more normal life for Christine and the kids. But could I do that? Could I really quit?

'Ask me again,' she whispered. 'Ask me again, sometime.'

Chapter Eight

Christine and I had dated since that night, and it had been the way it always is between us. It just felt right, easy, comfortable, and romantic. Still, I wondered if our problem could be fixed. Could she be happy with a homicide detective? Could I stop being one? I didn't know.

I was brought out of my reverie about Christine by the high-pitched, stuttering wail of a siren out on Twelfth Street, just turning off E. I winced when I saw Sampson's black Nissan pull up in front of St Anthony's.

He turned off the siren on his rooftop, but then beeped the car horn, sat on it. I knew he was here for me, probably to take me somewhere that I didn't want to go. The horn continued to blare.

'It's your friend John Sampson,' Jimmy Moore called out. 'You hear him, Alex?'

'I know who it is,' I called back to Jimmy. 'I'm hoping that he goes away.'

'Sure doesn't sound like it.'

I finally walked outside, crossing through the soup-kitchen line and receiving a few jokey jeers. People I had known for a long time accused me of working half a day, or said that if I didn't like the job, could they have it?

'What's up?' I called to Sampson, before I got all the way out to his black sportscar.

Sampson's side window came sliding down. I leaned inside the car. 'You forget? It's my day off,' I reminded him.

'It's Nina Childs,' Sampson said in a low, soft voice he used only when he was angry or very serious. He tried to deaden his facial muscles, to look tough, not emotional, but it wasn't working real well. 'Nina's dead, Alex.'

I shivered involuntarily. I opened the car door and got in. I didn't even go back to the kitchen to tell Jimmy Moore I was leaving. Sampson jerked the car away from the curbside fast. The siren came on again, but now I almost welcomed the mournful wail. It numbed me.

'What do you know so far?' I asked as we rushed along the intensely bleak streets of Southeast, then crossed the slate-gray Anacostia River.

'She was dumped in a row house, Eighteenth and Garnesville. Jerome Thurman is out there with her. Says she's probably been there since the weekend. Some needlepusher found the body. No clothes or ID, Alex,' Sampson said.

I looked over at him. 'So how did they know it was Nina?'

'Uniform guy on the scene recognized her. Knew her from the hospital. Everybody knew Nina.'

I shut my eyes, but I saw Nina Childs' face and I opened them again. She had been the eleven-to-seven charge nurse in the ER unit at St Anthony's Hospital, where once I ran like a tornado with a dying little boy in my arms. Sampson and I had worked with Nina more times than I could remember. Sampson had also dated Nina for over a year, but then they broke it off. She married a neighborhood man who worked for the city. They had two kids, two little babies, and Nina had seemed so happy the last time I saw her.

I couldn't believe she was lying dead in a tenement on the wrong side of the Anacostia. She had been abandoned, like one of the Jane Does.

Chapter Nine

Nina Childs' body had been found in a battered row house in one of the city's most impoverished, destroyed, and dismaying neighborhoods. There was only one patrol car on the scene, and a single rusted and dented EMS van. Homicides in Southeast don't attract much attention. A dog was barking somewhere and it was the only sound on the desolate street.

Sampson and I had to walk past an open-air drug mart on the corner of Eighteenth Street. Mostly young males, but a few children and two women were gathered there defiantly. The drug marts are everywhere in this part of Southeast. The neighborhood youth activity is the crack trade.

'Daily body pick-up, Officers?' said one of the young men, who was wearing black trousers with black suspenders, no shirt, socks, or shoes. He had a prison-yard physique and tattoos everywhere.

'Come to take out the trash?' An older man cackled from behind an unruly patch of salt-and-pepper beard. 'Take that muhfuckin' barkin' – all-night dog while you here. Make yourselves useful,' he added.

Sampson and I ignored them and continued walking across Eighteenth, then into the boarded-up three-storied row house straight ahead. A black-and-white boxer leaned out of a third-floor window, like a lifetime resident, and wouldn't stop barking. Otherwise the building appeared deserted.

The front door had been jimmied a hundred times, so it just swung open for us. The building smelled of fire, garbage, water damage. There was a gaping hole in the ceiling from a burst steam pipe. It was so wrong for Nina to have ended up in this sad, abominable place.

For over a year I had been unofficially investigating unsolved murders in Southeast, many of them Jane Does. My count was well over a hundred, but no one else in the department was willing to agree to the number, or anything close to it. Several of the murdered women were drug abusers or prostitutes. But not Nina.

We carefully descended a circular stairwell that had a shaky, well-worn wooden railing that neither of us would touch. I could see flashlights shining up ahead and I already had my Maglite turned on.

Nina was deep in the basement of the abandoned building. At least somebody had bothered to tape off the perimeter, frozen the crime scene.

I saw Nina's body – and I had to look away.

It wasn't just that she was dead, it was how she'd been killed. I tried to put my mind and eyes somewhere else until I regained some composure.

Jerome Thurman was there with the EMS team. So was a single patrol officer, probably the one who had identified Nina. No ME was present. It wasn't unusual for a medical examiner not to show up for homicides in Southeast.

There were dead flowers on the floor near the body. I focused on the flowers, still not able to look at Nina again. They didn't fit with the other Jane Does, but the killer didn't have a strict pattern. That was one of the problems I was having. It might mean that his fantasy was still evolving – and that he hadn't finished making up his gruesome story yet.

I noted shreds of foil and cellophane wrappers lying everywhere on the floor. Rats are attracted to shiny things and often bring them back to their nests. Thick cobwebs weaved from one end of the basement to the other.

I had to look at Nina again. I needed to look closely.

'I'm Detective Alex Cross. Let me take a look at her, please,' I finally said to the EMS team, a man and a woman in their twenties. 'I'll just be a couple of minutes, then I'll get out of your way.'

'The other detectives already released the body,' the male EMS worker said. He was rail-thin, with long dirty-blond hair. He didn't bother to look up at me. 'Let us finish our job and get the hell out of this cesspool. Whole area is highly infectious, smells like shit.'

'Just back away,' Sampson barked. 'Get up, before I pull your skinny ass up.'

The EMS techie cursed, but he stood and backed away from Nina's body. I moved in close, tried to concentrate and be professional, tried to remember specific details I had gathered about the previous Jane Does in Southeast. I was looking for some connection. I wondered if a single predator could possibly be killing so many people. If that were true, then this would be one of the most savage killing sprees ever.

I took a deep breath and then I knelt over Nina. The rats had been at her, I could see. The killer had done much worse damage.

It looked to me as if Nina had been beaten to death, with punches, and possibly kicks. She might have been struck a hundred times or more. I had rarely seen anyone given this much punishment. Why did it have to happen? She was only thirty-one years old, mother of two, kind, talented, dedicated to her work at St Anthony's.

There was a sudden noise, like a rifleshot, in the building. It reverberated right through the basement walls. The EMS workers jumped.

The rest of us laughed nervously. I knew exactly what the sound was.

'Just rattraps,' I said to the EMS team. 'Get used to it.'

Chapter Ten

I was at the homicide scene for a little over two hours, much longer than I wanted to be there, and I hated every second. I couldn't fix a set pattern for the Jane Doe killings, and Nina Childs' murder didn't help. Why had he struck her so many times and so savagely? What were the flowers doing there? Could this be the work of the same killer?

The way I usually operate at a crime scene, the homicide investigation takes on an almost aerial view. Everything emanates from the body.

Sampson and I walked the entire crime scene – from the basement to each floor and on up to the roof. Then we walked the neighborhood. Nobody had seen anything unusual, which didn't surprise either of us.

Now came the really bad part. Sampson and I drove from the woeful tenement to Nina's apartment in the Brookland section of Washington, east of Catholic University. I knew I was being sucked in again, but there was nothing I could do about it.

It was a sweltering-hot day and the sun hammered Washington without mercy. We were both silent and withdrawn during the ride. What we had to do was the worst thing about our job, telling a family about the death of a loved one. I didn't know how I could do it this time.

Nina lived in a well-kept brown-brick building on Monroe Street. Miniature yellow roses were blooming out front in bright-green window-boxes. It didn't look as if anything bad should happen to someone who lived here. Everything about the place was so bright and hopeful, just as Nina had been.

I was becoming more and more disturbed and upset about the brutal and obscene murder, and the fact that it probably wouldn't get a decent investigation from the department, at least not officially. Nana Mama would chalk it up to her conspiracy theories about the white overlords and their 'criminal disinterest' in the people of Southeast. She had often told me that she felt morally superior to white people, that she would never, ever treat them the way they treated the black people of Washington.

'Nina's sister, Marie, takes care of the kids,' Sampson said as we rode down Monroe. 'She's a nice girl. Had a drug problem one time, beat it. Nina helped her. The whole family is close-knit. A lot like yours. This is going to be real bad, Alex.'

I turned to him. Not surprisingly, he was taking Nina's death even harder than I was. It's unusual for him to show his emotions though. 'I can do it, John. You stay here in the car. I'll go up and talk to the family.'

Sampson shook his head and sighed loudly. 'Doesn't work that way, sugar.'

He snugged the Nissan up to the curb and we both climbed out. He didn't stop me from coming along to the apartment, so I knew he wanted me there with him. He was right. This was going to be bad.

The Childs' apartment took up the first and second floors. The front door was slightly ornate, aluminum. Nina's husband was already at the door. He had on the proletariat uniform of the DC Housing Authority where he worked: mud-stained work boots, blue trousers, a shirt marked DCHA. One of the babies snuggled in his arms, a beautiful girl who looked at me and smiled and cooed.

'Could we come inside for a moment?' Sampson asked.

'It's Nina,' the husband said, and started to break down right there in the doorway.

'I'm sorry, William.' I spoke softly. 'You're right. She's dead. She's been killed. She was found this morning.'

William Childs started to sob loudly. He was a powerful-looking working man, but that didn't matter. He held his bewildered little girl to his chest and tried to control the crying, but he couldn't.

'Oh God, no. Oh, Nina, Nina baby. How could somebody kill her? How could anybody do that? Oh, Nina, Nina, Nina.'

A young, pretty woman came up behind him. She had to be Nina's sister, Marie. She took the baby from her sister's husband, and the little girl began to scream, as if she knew what had happened. I had seen so many families, so many good people, who had lost loved ones on these merciless streets. I knew it would never completely stop, but I felt it ought to get better, and it never did.

The sister motioned for us to come inside, and I noticed a hall table on which were two pocketbooks, as if Nina were still about. The apartment was comfortable and neat, with light bamboo and white-cushioned furniture. The whirr of a window air-conditioner was constant. A Llardo porcelain figure of a nurse was on an end table.

I was still sorting through details about the homicide scene, trying to connect the murder to the other Jane Does. We learned that Nina had attended a health-care charity dinner on Saturday night. William had been working overtime. The family called the police late Saturday night. Two detectives had shown up, but no one had been able to find Nina until now.

Then I was holding the baby, while Nina's sister took the chill off a bottle of formula. It was such a sad and poignant moment, knowing this poor little girl would never see her mother again, never know how truly special her mother had been. It reminded me of my own kids and their mother, and of Christine, who was afraid I would die during some murder investigation like this one.

The older little girl came up to me while I was holding her baby sister. She was two or three at the most. 'I got a new hairstyle,' she said proudly and did a half-turn to show me.

'You did? It's beautiful. Who did those braids for you?'

'My mommy,' said the girl.

It was an hour later that Sampson and I finally left the house. We drove away in silence and despair, the same way we'd come. After a couple of blocks, Sampson pulled over in front of a ramshackle neighborhood bodega covered with beer and soda posters.

He gave a deep sigh, put his hands to his face, and then John cried. I'd never, ever seen him like this before, not in all the years we'd been friends, not even when we were just boys. I reached out and laid a hand on his shoulder, and he didn't move away. Then he told me something he hadn't shared before.

'I loved her, Alex, but I let her get away. I never told her how I felt. We have to get this sonofabitch.'

Chapter Eleven

I sensed I was at the start of another homicide mess. I didn't want it, but I couldn't stop the horror. I had to try to do something about the Jane Does. I couldn't just stand by and do nothing.

Although I was assigned to the Seventh District as a senior detective, my job as liaison with the FBI gave me some extra status and also freedom to occasionally work without too much supervision or interference. My mind was running free and I'd already made some associations with Nina's murder and at least some of the unsolved killings. First, there had been no identification on the victims at the crime scenes. Second, the bodies had frequently been dumped in buildings where they might not be found quickly. Third, not a single witness had seen anyone who might be a suspect or the killer. The most we ever got was that there had been traffic, or people out on the streets, where one of the bodies had been found. That told me that the killer knew how to blend in, and that he possibly was a black man.

Around six that night, I finally headed home. This was supposed to be a day off. I had things to do there, and I was trying to balance the demands of the job and home life as best I could. I put on a happy face and headed inside the house.

Damon, Jannie, and Nana were singing 'Sit Down You're Rockin' de Boat' in the kitchen. The show tune was music to my ears and other essential parts of my anatomy. The kids looked happy as could be. There is a lot to be said for the innocence of childhood.

I heard Nana say. 'How about "I Can Tell The World"?' Then the three of them launched into one of the most beautiful spirituals I know. Damon's voice seemed particularly strong to me. I hadn't really noticed that before.

'I feel like I just walked into a story by Louisa May Alcott,' I said, laughing for the first time that long day.

'I take that as a *high* compliment,' Nana said. She was somewhere between her late seventies and early eighties now, but not telling, and also not showing her age.

'Who's Louise Maise Alcott?' Jannie said, and made a lemon-sucking face. She is a healthy little skeptic, though almost never a cynic. In that way, she takes after both her father and grandmother.

'Look it up tonight, little one. Fifty cents in your pocket for the correct answer,' I told her.

'You're on.' Jannie grinned. 'You can pay me right now if you like.'

'Me too?' Damon asked.

'Of course. You can look up Jane Austen,' I said to him. 'Now what's with the heavenly harmonizing? I like it very much, by the way. I just want to know what the special occasion is.'

'We're just singing while we prepare dinner,' Nana said, and stuck up her nose and twinkled her eyes. 'You play jazz and the blues on the piano, don't you? We harmonize like angels sometimes. No special reason necessary. Good for the soul, and the soul food, I suppose. Can't hurt.'

'Well, don't stop singing on my account,' I said, but they had already stopped. Too bad. Something was going on, I'd figured out that much. A musical mystery to be solved in my own house.

'We still on for boxing after dinner?' I asked cautiously. I was feeling a little vulnerable because I didn't want them to turn me down for the boxing lesson that has become a ritual.

'Of course,' Damon said, and frowned like I must be out of my mind to even ask such a question.

'Of course. Pshaw. Why wouldn't we be?' Jannie said, and brushed off my silly question with a wave of her hand. 'How's Ms Johnson?' she asked then. 'You two talk today?'

'I still want to know what the singing was all about?' I answered Jannie with a question of my own.

'You have valuable information. Well, so do I. Tit for tat,' she said. 'How do you like that?'

A little later, I decided to call Christine at home. Lately, it had seemed more like the way it had been between us before I got involved with the Mr Smith case. We talked for a while, and then I asked her to go out on Friday.

'Of course. I'd like that, Alex. What should I wear?' she asked.

I hesitated. 'Well, I always like what you choose – but wear something special.'

She didn't ask why.

Chapter Twelve

After one of Nana's roast chicken dinners with baked sweet potatoes and homemade bread, I took the kids downstairs for their weekly boxing lesson. Following the Tuesday night fight with the kids, I glanced at my watch and saw that it was already a little past nine.

The doorbell rang a moment later. I set down a terrific book called *The Color of Water* and pushed myself up from my chair in the family room.

'I'll get it. It's probably for me,' I called out.

'Maybe it's Christine. You never know,' Jannie teased, then darted away into the kitchen. Both of the kids adored Christine, in spite of the fact that she was the principal at their school.

I knew exactly who was out on the porch. I had been expecting four homicide detectives from the First District – Jerome Thurman, Rakeem Powell, Shawn Moore and Sampson.

Three of the detectives were standing out on the porch. Rosie the cat and I let them inside. Sampson arrived about five minutes later, and we all gathered in the backyard. What we were doing at the house wasn't illegal, but it wouldn't make us a lot of friends in high places in the police department.

We sat on lawn chairs and I set out beer and low-fat pretzels that two-hundred-seventy-pound Jerome scoffed at. 'Beer and low-fat pretzels. Give me a *break*, Alex. You lost your mind? Hey, you having an affair with my wife? You must have got this bad idea from Claudette.'

'I bought these especially for you, big man. I'm trying to give your heart a break,' I told him, and the others guffawed loudly. We all pick on Jerome.

The five of us had been getting together informally for a couple of weeks. We were beginning to work on The Jane Does, as we called them. Homicide had no official investigation going on; it wasn't trying to link the murders to a serial killer. I'd tried to start one and been turned down by Chief Pittman. He claimed that I hadn't discovered a pattern linking any of the murders, and besides that, he didn't have any extra detectives for duty in Southeast.

'I suppose you've all heard about Nina Childs by now?' Sampson asked the other detectives. All of them had known Nina, and of course Jerome had been at the murder scene with us.

'The good die young.' Rakeem Powell frowned severely and shook his head.

Rakeem is smart and tough and could go all the way in the department. 'Least they do in Southeast.' His eyes went cold and hard.

I told them what I knew, especially that Nina had been found with no ID. I mentioned everything else I had noticed at the tenement crime scene. I also took the occasion to talk some more about the rash of unsolved murders in Southeast. I went over the devastating stats I had compiled, mostly in my free time.

'Statistic like that in Georgetown or the Capitol district, people in this city be enraged. Going ballistic. Be *Washington Post* headlines every day. The president himself be involved. Money no object. National tragedy!' Jerome Thurman railed on and waved his arms around like signal flags.

'Well, we are here to do something about it, 'I said in a calmer voice. 'Money *is* no object with us. Neither is time. Let me tell you what I feel about this killer,' I continued. 'I think I know a few things about him.'

'How'd you come up with the profile?' Shawn Moore asked. 'How can you stand thinking about these kinky bastards as much as you do?'

I shrugged. 'It's what I do best. I've analyzed all the Jane Does,' I said. 'It took me weeks working on my own. Just me and the kinky bastard.'

'Plus, he studies rodent droppings,' said Sampson. 'I saw him bagging the little turds. That's his real secret.'

I grinned, and told them what I had so far. 'I think one male is responsible for at least some of the killings. I don't think he's a brilliant killer, like Gary Soneji or Mr Smith, but he's clever enough not to be caught. He's organized, reasonably careful. I don't think we'll find he has any prior record. He probably has a decent job. Maybe even a family. My FBI friends at Quantico agree with that.

'He's almost definitely caught up in an escalating fantasy cycle. I think he's into his fantasies big time. Maybe he's in the process of becoming someone or something new. He might be forming a new personality for himself. He isn't finished with the killing, not by any means.

'I'll make some educated guesses. He hates his old self, though the people closest to him probably don't realize it. He might be ready to abandon his family, job, any friends he has. At one time he probably had very strong feelings and beliefs about something – law and order, religion, the government – but not anymore. He kills in different ways – there's no set formula. He knows a lot about killing people. He's used different kinds of weapons. He may have traveled overseas. Or maybe he spent time in Asia. I think it's very possible he's a black man. He's killed several times in Southeast – no one's noticed him.'

'Fuck me,' Jerome Thurman said to that. 'Any *good* news, Alex?'

'One thing, and this is a long shot. But it feels right to me. I think he might be suicidal. It fits the profile I'm working on. He's living dangerously, taking a lot of chances. He might just blow himself up.'

'Pop goes the weasel,' Sampson said.

That was how we came to name the killer – the Weasel.

Chapter Thirteen

Geoffrey Shafer looked forward to playing The Four Horsemen every Thursday night, from nine until about one in the morning.

The fantasy game was everything to him. There were three other master players around the world. The players were the Rider on the White Horse, Conqueror; the Rider on the Red Horse, War; the Rider on the Black Horse, Famine; and himself – the Rider on the Pale Horse, Death.

Lucy and the children knew they were forbidden to disturb him for any reason, once he locked himself into the library on the second floor. On one wall was his collection of ceremonial daggers, nearly all of them purchased in Hong Kong and Bangkok. Also on the wall was the oar from the year his college crew were Head of the River. Shafer nearly always won the games he played.

He had been using the Internet to communicate with the other players for years, long before the rest of the world caught on. Conqueror played from the town of Dorking in Surrey, outside London; Famine traveled back and forth between Bangkok, Sydney, Melbourne, and Manila; War usually played out of Jamaica, where he had a large estate by the sea. They had been playing Horsemen for seven years.

Rather than becoming repetitive, the fantasy game had expanded itself. It had grown every year, becoming something new and even more challenging. The object was to create the most delicious and unusual fantasy or adventure. Violence was almost always part of the game, but not necessarily murder. Shafer was the first to claim that his stories weren't fantasies at all, that he lived them in the real world. Now the others would do so as well from time to time. Whether or not they really lived their fantasies, Shafer couldn't tell. The object was to create the evening's most startling fantasy, to get a rise out of the other players.

At nine o'clock his time, Shafer was on his laptop. So were the others. It was rare that one of them missed a session, but if they did, they left lengthy messages and sometimes drawings or even photographs of supposed lovers or victims. Films were occasionally used and the other players had to decide whether or not the scenes were stage-acted or *cinéma vérité*.

Shafer couldn't imagine missing a chapter of the game himself. Death was by far the most interesting character, the most powerful and original. He had missed important social and embassy affairs just to be available for Thursday nights. He had played when he had pneumonia, and once when he'd had a painful double-hernia operation the day before.

The Four Horsemen was unique in so many ways, but most important, because there was no single gamemaster to outline and control the action of the game. Each of the players had complete autonomy to write and visualize his own story, as long as he played by the roll of the dice, and remained inside the parameters of the character.

In effect, in Horsemen, there were four gamemasters. There was no other fantasy game like it. It was as gruesome and shocking as the participants' imaginations and their skills at presentation.

Conqueror, Famine, and War had all signed on.

Shafer began to type.

DEATH HAS TRIUMPHED AGAIN IN WASHINGTON. LET ME TELL YOU THE DETAILS, THEN I'LL LISTEN TO THE GLORIOUS STORIES, THE IMAGINATIVE POWER OF CONQUEROR, FAMINE, AND WAR. I LIVE FOR THIS, AS I KNOW ALL OF YOU DO AS WELL.

THIS WEEKEND, I DROVE MY FANTASTIC TAXI, 'THE NIGHT-MARE MACHINE,' ONCE AGAIN . . . LISTEN TO THIS. I CAME UPON SEVERAL CHOICE AND DELECTABLE VICTIMS, BUT I REJECTED THEM AS UNWORTHY. THEN I FOUND MY QUEEN AND SHE REMINDED ME OF OUR DAYS IN BANGKOK AND MANILA. WHO COULD EVER FORGET THE BLOOD LUST OF THE BOXING ARENA? I HELD A MOCK KICK-BOXING MATCH. GENTLEMEN, I BEAT HER WITH MY HANDS AND FEET. I AM SENDING PICTURES.

Chapter Fourteen

Something was up, and I didn't think that I'd like it very much. I arrived at the Seventh District Police Station just before seven thirty the following morning. I'd been summoned by the powers-that-be to the station, and it was a tough deal. I'd worked until two in the morning trying to get a lead on Nina Childs' murder.

I had a feeling that the day was starting out wrong. I was tense and more uptight than I usually let myself become. I didn't like this early-morning command appearance one bit.

I shook my head, frowned, tried to roll the kinks out of my neck. Finally, I gritted my teeth tightly before opening the mahogany-wood door. Chief of Detectives George Pittman was lying in wait in his office, which consisted of three connecting offices, including a conference room.

The Jefe, as he's called by his many 'admirers,' had on a boxy gray business suit, overstarched white shirt, a silver necktie. His gray-and-white-streaked hair was slicked back. He looked like a banker, and in some ways he was. As he never tires of saying, he is working with a fixed budget, and is always mindful of manpower costs, overtime costs, caseload costs. Apparently, he is an efficient manager, which is why the police commissioner overlooks the fact that he's a bully, bigot, racist and careerist.

Up on his wall were three large, important-looking pushpin maps. The first showed two consecutive months of rapes, homicides, and assaults in Washington. The second map did the same for residential and commercial burglaries. The third map showed auto thefts. The maps and the *Post* say that crime is down in DC, but not where I live.

'Do you know why you're here, why I wanted to see you?' Pittman asked point-blank. No socializing or small talk from the Jefe, no niceties. 'Of course you do, Dr Cross. You're a psychologist. You're supposed to know how the human mind works. I keep forgetting that.'

Be cool, be careful, I told myself. I did the thing Chief Pittman least expected – I smiled, and said softly, 'No, I really don't know. I got a call from your assistant. So I'm here.'

Pittman smiled back, as if I'd made a pretty good joke. Then he suddenly raised his voice, and his face and neck turned a bright red; his nostrils flared, exposing the bristly hairs within.

One of his hands was clenched into a tight fist, while the other was stretched open. His fingers were as rigid as the pencils sticking up from the leather cup on his desk.

'You're not fooling anybody, Cross, least of all me. I'm fully fucking aware that you're investigating homicides in Southeast that you aren't assigned to, the so-called Jane Does. You're doing this against my explicit orders. Some of those cases have been closed for over a year. *I won't have it*, I won't tolerate your insubordination, your condescending attitude. I know what you're trying to pull. Embarrass the department, specifically embarrass me, curry fucking favor with the mayor, make yourself some kind of folk hero in Southeast in the process.'

I hated Pittman's tone and what he was saying, but I had learned one trick a long time ago, and it was probably the most important thing to know about politics inside any organization. It's so simple, but it's the key to every petty kingdom, every fiefdom. Knowledge truly is power; it's everything, and if you don't have any, pretend you do.

So I told Chief Pittman nothing. I didn't contradict him; I didn't admit to a thing. I did nothing. Me and Mahatma Gandhi.

I let him think that maybe I was investigating old cases in Southeast – but I didn't admit to it. I also let him think that maybe I had some powerful connections with Mayor Monroe, and God only knows who else in the City on the Hill. I let him think that maybe I was after his job, or that I might have, God forbid, even loftier aspirations.

'I'm working the homicides assigned to me. Check with the captain. I'm doing my best to close as many cases as I can.'

Pittman nodded curtly – *one* nod. His face was still heart-attack red. 'All right, I want you to close *this* case, and I want you to close it fast. A tourist was robbed and gunned down on M Street last night,' he said. 'A well-respected German doctor from Munich. It's front fucking page in today's *Post*. Not to mention the *International Herald Tribune*, and every newspaper in Germany of course. I want you on *that* murder case and I want it solved pronto.'

'This doctor, he's a white man?' I asked, keeping my expression neutral.

'I told you, he's German.'

'I already have a number of open cases in Southeast,' I said to Pittman. 'A nurse was murdered over the weekend.'

He didn't want to hear it. He shook his head – *one* shake. 'And now you have an important case in Georgetown. Solve it, Cross. You're to work on nothing else. That's a direct order . . . from *the Jefe*.'

Chapter Fifteen

As soon as Cross walked out of Chief Pittman's inner office, a senior homicide detective named Patsy Hampton slipped in through a side door that led to the attached conference room. Detective Hampton had been instructed by Pittman to listen in on everything, to evaluate the situation from a street cop's perspective, to advise and counsel.

Hampton didn't like the job, but those were her orders from Pittman. She didn't like Pittman either. He was wound so tight that if you stuck coal up his ass, in a couple of weeks you'd have a diamond. He was mean, petty, and he was vengeful.

'You see what I'm dealing with here? Cross knows how to push all my buttons. In the beginning he would lose his temper. Now he just ignores what I say.'

'I heard everything,' Hampton said. 'He's slick all right.' She was going to agree with Chief Pittman, no matter what he said.

Patsy Hampton was an attractive woman with sandy-blond hair cut short, and the most piercing blue eyes this side of Stockholm. She was thirty-one years old, and on a very fast track in the department. At twenty-six, she'd been the youngest homicide detective in Washington. She had much loftier goals in mind.

'You're selling yourself short, though. You got to him. I know you did.' She told Pittman what he wanted to hear. 'He just internalizes it pretty well.'

'You're sure he's meeting with those other detectives? 'Pittman asked her.

'They've met three times that I know of, always at Cross's house on Fifth Street. I suspect there have been other times. I heard about it through a friend of Detective Thurman.'

'But they don't meet while any of them are on duty?'

'No, not to my knowledge. They're careful. They meet on their own time.'

Pittman scowled and shook his head. 'That's too goddamn bad. It makes it harder to prove anything really damaging.'

'From what I've heard, they believe the department is holding back resources that could clear a number of unsolved homicides in Southeast and parts of Northeast. Most of the murders involve black and Hispanic women.'

Pittman tensed his jaw and looked away from Hampton. 'The numbers that Cross uses are complete bullshit,' he said angrily. 'They're dogshit. It's all political with him. How much financial resource can we put against the murders of drug addicts and prostitutes in Southeast? It's criminals murdering other criminals. You know how it goes in those black neighborhoods.'

Hampton nodded again, still agreeing when she saw the chance. She was afraid she'd lost him, said the wrong thing by speaking the truth. 'They think that at least some of the victims are innocent women from their neighborhoods. That ER nurse who was killed over the weekend. She was a friend of Cross and Detective John Sampson. Cross thinks a killer could be loose in Southeast, preying on women.'

'A serial killer in the ghetto? Give me a break. We've never had one there. They're rare in any inner city. Why now? Why here? Because Cross wants to find one, that's why.'

'Cross and the others would counter that by saying we've never seriously tried to catch this squirrel.'

Pittman's small eyes suddenly burned into her skull. 'Do you agree with that horseshit, Detective?'

'No, sir. I don't necessarily agree or disagree. I know for a fact that the department doesn't have enough resources anywhere in the city, with the possible exception of Capitol Hill. Now, *that's* political, and it's an outrage.'

Pittman smiled at her answer. The chief knew she was playing him a little, but he liked her anyway. He liked just being in a room with Patsy Hampton. She was such a doll, such a cutie. 'What do you know about Cross, Patsy?'

She sensed that the chief had vented enough. Now he wanted their talk to be more informal. She was certain that he liked her, had a crush on her, but he was too uptight to ever act on his desires, thank God.

'I know Cross has been on the force for just over eight years. He's currently the liaison between the department and the FBI, works with the Violent Criminal Apprehension Program. He's a profiler with a good reputation, from what I hear. Has a PhD in psych from Johns Hopkins. Private practice for three years before he came to us. Widower, two kids, plays the blues on the piano at his house. That enough background? What more do you want to know? I've done my homework. You know me,' Hampton said, and finally smiled.

Pittman was smiling now, too. He had small teeth with spaces between them, and always made her think of Eastern European refugees, or maybe Russian gangsters.

Detective Hampton smiled, though. She knew he liked it when she played along with him – as long as he thought she respected him.

'Any other worthwhile observations at this point?' he asked.

You're such a softy, flabby dick, Patsy Hampton wanted to say, but she just shook her head. 'He has some charm. He's well-connected in political circles. I can see why you're concerned about him.'

'You think Cross is charming?'

'I told you, he's slick. He *is*. People say he looks like the young Muhammad Ali. I think he likes to play the part sometimes. Float like a butterfly, sting like a bee.' She laughed again – and so did he.

'We're going to nail Cross,' Pittman said. 'We'll send him flying back to private practice. Wait and see. You're going to help get it done. You get things done, right, Detective Hampton? You see the bigger picture. That's what I like about you.'

She smiled again. 'That's what I like about me, too.'

Chapter Sixteen

The British Embassy is a plain, federal-style building located at 3100 Massachusetts Avenue. It sits next to the vice-president's house – the Observatory – and also the ambassador's residence, a stately Georgian building with tall, flowing white columns. The Chancery is the actual office building; the embassy is where the ambassador lives.

Geoffrey Shafer sat behind his small mahogany desk at the embassy and stared out onto Massachusetts Avenue. The embassy staff currently counted 415 people, soon to be cut to 414; he was thinking to himself. The staff included defense experts, foreign-policy specialists, trade, public affairs, clerks and secretaries.

Although the US and Britain have an agreement not to spy on each other,

Geoffrey Shafer was nonetheless a spy. He was one of eleven men and women from the Security Service, formerly known as MI6, who worked at the embassy in Washington. These eleven ran agents attached to the consulates-general in Atlanta, Boston, Chicago, Houston, Los Angeles, New York, and San Francisco.

He was feeling restless as hell today, getting up from his desk frequently, pacing back and forth across the carpet that covered the creaking parquet floors. He made phone calls he didn't need to make, tried to get some work done, thought about how much he despised his job and the everyday details of life.

He was supposed to be working on a truly silly communiqué about the government's absurd ongoing commitment to human rights. The Foreign Secretary had rather bombastically proclaimed that Britain would support international condemnation of regimes that violated human rights; support international bodies involved in the cause; denounce human rights abuses, *blah, blah, blah, ad nauseam.*

He glanced through a few of the computer games he enjoyed when he was uptight like this – Riven, MechCommander, Unreal, TOCA, Ultimate Soccer Manager. None of them appealed to him right now; nothing did.

He was starting to crash, and he knew the feeling. *I'm going down and there is only one certain way to stop it: play The Four Horsemen.*

To make matters worse, it was raining and woefully gray-skied outside. The city of Washington, and also the surrounding countryside, looked forlorn and depressing. Christ, he was in a bad mood, even for him.

He continued to stare east across Massachusetts Avenue, looking into the trees bordering a park dedicated to the pacifist bullshit artist Kahlil Gibran. He tried to day-dream, mostly about fucking various attractive women currently working at the embassy.

He had called his psychiatrist, Boo Cassady, at her home office, but she was about to start a session and couldn't talk for long. They agreed to meet after work. A nasty quickie at her place, before he went home to face Lucy and the sniveling brood.

He didn't dare play Horsemen again tonight. It was too soon since the nurse. But God Almighty – he *wanted* to play. He wished he could take somebody out in some very imaginative way, right there inside the embassy.

He did have one excellent thing to do today – saving it until now, three in the afternoon. He had used the dice already, played a bit of Horsemen, just to help him make a personnel decision.

He had called Sarah Middleton just before lunch and told her they needed to have a chat and could she stop by his office, say at three?

Sarah was obviously tense on the phone and told him she could do it earlier, anytime, at his convenience. 'Not busy then, nothing much to do today?' Shafer asked. Three o'clock would be fine, she answered hastily.

His secretary, the bestial Betty formerly from Belgravia, buzzed him promptly at three. At least he'd finally got through to her about punctuality.

Shafer let her buzz him several times, then picked up the phone abruptly, as if she'd interrupted him at something vital to security.

'What is it, Ms Thomas? I'm extremely busy with this communiqué for the Secretary.'

'I'm sorry to interrupt, Mr Shafer, but Ms Middleton is here. You have a three o'clock appointment with her, I understand.'

'*Hmmm.* Do I? Yes, you're right. Can you ask Sarah to wait? I'll need a few more minutes. I'll buzz when I'm ready to see her.'

Shafer smiled contentedly and picked up a copy of *The Red Coat*, the embassy employee newsletter. He knew Betty hated it when he used Ms Middleton's Christian name. Sarah.

He fantasized about Sarah for the next few moments. He'd wanted to have a go at Mzzz Middleton from their first interview, but he was too careful for that. God, he hated the bitch. This was going to be such fun.

He watched the rain hammer down on the traffic crossing Massachusetts Avenue for another ten minutes. Finally Shafer snatched up the phone. He couldn't wait a minute longer. 'I'll see her now. Send Sarah in.'

He fingered his twenty-sided dice. This could be fun, actually. *Terror at the office.*

Chapter Seventeen

The lovely Sarah Middleton entered his office and managed a cordial look, almost a smile. He felt like a boa constrictor eyeing a mouse.

She had naturally curly red hair, a moderately pretty face, a superior figure. Today she wore a very short suit, red V-necked silk blouse, black stockings. It was obvious to Shafer that she was out to catch a husband in Washington.

Shafer's pulse was beating hard. He was aroused by her, always had been. He thought about taking her, and very much liked that phrase. She didn't look as nervous and unsure of herself as she had recently, so that probably meant she was really scared and trying not to show it. He tried his best to think like Sarah. That made it more fun, though he found it a real challenge to be as squirrely and insecure as she would surely be.

'We certainly needed the rain,' Sarah said, and then cringed before the sentence was even finished.

'Sarah, please sit down,' he said. He was trying to keep a straight business face. 'Personally, I loathe the rain. It's one of the many reasons I've never been stationed in London.'

He sighed theatrically behind the rigid tent he'd made with his fingers. He wondered if Sarah noticed the length of his fingers and wondered how large he was elsewhere. He would bet anything that she did. It was how people's minds worked, though women like Sarah would never admit it.

She cleared her throat, then put her hands on her knees. The knuckles of her fingers were white. Christ, he was enjoying her obvious discomfort. She looked ready to jump out of her skin. How about out of her tight little skirt and blouse?

He began to stretch the fingers on his right hand, playing his part as dominator to the hilt. 'Sarah, I think I have some bad news, quite unfortunate really, but can't be avoided.'

She sat nervously forward in her chair. She really was nicely built up top. He was getting hard now. 'What is it, Mr Shafer? What do you mean? You *think* you have bad news? You do or you don't?'

'We have to let you go. *I* have to let you go. Budget cuts, I'm afraid,' he said. 'I know you must find this immensely unfair, and unexpected as well. Particularly when you moved halfway across the world from Australia to take this job, and you've been living in Washington for less than six months. Suddenly, the ax falls.'

He could tell she was actually fighting back tears. Her lips were trembling. Obviously she hadn't expected this. She had no idea. She was a reasonably smart and controlled woman, but she couldn't help herself now.

Excellent. He had succeeded in breaking her down. He wished he had a video camera this minute to record the look on her face and play it back countless times in private.

He saw the very instant that she lost it, and treasured it. He watched her eyes moisten, saw the large tears roll over her cheeks, streaking her working-girl makeup.

He felt the power and it was as good as he'd hoped it would be. A small, insignificant game certainly, but a delicious one. He loved being able to instill such shock and pain.

'Poor Sarah. Poor, poor dear,' he murmured.

Then Shafer did the cruelest, most unforgivable thing. Also the most outrageous and dangerous. He got up from his desk and came around to comfort her. He stood behind her, pressing himself against her shoulders. He knew it was the last thing she wanted, to be touched by him, to feel that he was aroused.

She stiffened, and pulled away from him as if he were on fire. 'Bastard,' she said, between clenched teeth, 'you are a consummate prick!'

Sarah left his office, shaking and in tears, running in that stumbling way women often do in heels. Shafer loved it. The sadistic pleasure, not only of hurting someone, but destroying this innocent woman. He memorized the stunning image for all time. He would play it back, over and over.

Yes, he was a prick. Consummate indeed.

Chapter Eighteen

Rosie the cat was perched on the window sill, watching me dress for my date with Christine. I envied the simplicity of her life: *Love to eat those mousies, mousies what I love to eat.*

I finally headed downstairs. I was taking the night off from work and I was more nervous, distracted and fidgety than I had been in a long time. Nana and the kids knew something was up, but they didn't know what, and it was driving my three favorite busybodies crazy.

'Daddy, tell me what's going on, *please*?' Jannie clasped her hands in prayer and begged.

'I told you no, and no is no. Not even if you get down on your bony little knees,' I said, and smiled. 'I have a date tonight. It's just a date. That's all you need to know, young lady.'

'Is it with Christine?' Jannie asked. 'At least you can tell me *that* much.'

'*That's* for me to know,' I said as I knotted my tie in the mirror beside the stairs. 'And you *not* to find out, my over-inquisitive girlfriend.'

'You're wearing your fancy blue-striped suit, your fancy dancing shoes, that fancy tie you like. You're *so* fancy.'

'Do I look good?' I turned and asked my personal clothier. 'For my date?'

'You look beautiful, Daddy.' My girl beamed and I knew I could believe her. Her eyes were shiny little mirrors that always told the truth. 'You know you do. You know you're handsome as sin.'

'That's my girl,' I said, and laughed again. *Handsome as sin.* She got that one from Nana no doubt.

Damon mimicked his sister. '*You look beautiful, Daddy*. What a little brown-noser. What do you want from Daddy, Jannie?'

'Do I look good?' I turned to Damon.

He rolled his eyes. 'You look all right. How come you're all duded up? You can tell me. Man to man. What's the big deal?'

'Answer the poor children!' Nana finally said.

I looked her way, and offered up a wide grin. 'Don't use the "poor children" to try to get your gossip quotient for the day. Well, I'm off,' I announced. 'I'll be home before sunrise. Moo-ha-ha-ha.' I did my favorite monster imitation and all three of them rolled their eyes.

It was a minute or so before eight, and as I stepped onto the porch, a black Lincoln town car pulled up in front of the house. It was right on time, and I didn't want to be late.

'A limousine?' Jannie gasped, and nearly swooned on the front porch. 'You're going out in a *limousine*?'

'Alex Cross!' Nana said. 'What *is* going on?'

I practically danced down the steps. I got into the waiting car, shut the door, told the driver to go. I waved out the back window and stuck out my tongue as the car smoothly pulled away from our house.

Chapter Nineteen

My last image was of the three of them, Jannie, Damon, and Nana, all mugging and sticking out their tongues at me. We do have some fabulously good times together, I was thinking as the car headed over to Prince Georges County, where I had once confronted a homicidal twelve year old during the halcyon days of the Jack and Jill killers, and where Christine Johnson lived.

I had my mantra all set for tonight – *heart leads head*. I needed to believe that was so.

'A private car? A limousine?' Christine exclaimed when I picked her up at her house in Mitchellville.

She looked as stunningly beautiful as I've ever seen her, and that's saying a lot. She wore a long sleeveless black shift, black satin pumps with straps, and had a floral brocade jacket over her arm. The heels made her a little over six feet tall. God, how I loved this woman, everything about her.

We walked to the car and got inside.

'You haven't told me where we're going tonight, Alex. Just that it's fancy. Someplace special.'

'Ah, but I've told our driver,' I said. I tapped the partition window and the town car moved off into the summer night. Alex the mysterious.

I held Christine's hands as we drove along on the John Hanson Highway, back toward Washington. Her face tilted toward mine and I kissed her in the cozy darkness. I loved the sweetness of her mouth, her lips, the softness and smoothness of her skin. She was wearing a new perfume that I didn't recognize, and I liked that, too. I kissed the hollow of her throat, then her cheeks, her eyes, her hair. I would have been happy to do just this for the rest of the night.

'It is unbelievably romantic,' she finally said. 'It *is* special. You are something else . . . *sugar*.'

We cuddled and hugged all the way into Washington. We talked, but I don't remember the subject. I could feel her breasts rising and falling against me. I was surprised when we arrived at the intersection of Massachusetts and Wisconsin avenues. We were getting close to the surprise.

Christine hadn't asked any more questions. Not until the car eased up in front of Washington National Cathedral, and the driver got out and held the door open for us.

'The National Cathedral?' she said. 'We're going in here?'

I nodded and stared up at the stunning Gothic masterpiece that I'd admired since I was a boy. The Cathedral crowns over fifty acres of lawns and woods and is Washington's highest point, even higher than the Washington Monument. If I remembered correctly, it was the second largest church in the United States, and possibly the prettiest.

I led the way, and Christine followed me inside. She held my hand lightly. We entered the northwest corner of the nave, which extends nearly a tenth of a mile to a massive altar.

Everything felt special and very beautiful, spiritual, just right. We walked up to a pew under the amazing Space Window at mid-nave. Everywhere I looked there were priceless stained-glass windows, over two hundred in all.

The light inside was exquisite; I felt blessed. There was a kaleidoscope of changing colors on the walls: reds, warm yellows, cool blues.

'Beautiful, isn't it?' I whispered. 'Timeless, sublime, all that good Gothic stuff Henry Adams used to write about.'

'Oh, Alex, I think it's the prettiest spot in Washington. The Space Window, the Children's Chapel. I've always loved it here. I told you that, didn't I?' she asked.

'You might have mentioned it once,' I said. 'Or maybe I just knew it.'

We continued walking until we entered the Children's Chapel. It is small, beautiful, and wonderfully intimate. We stood under a stained-glass window that tells the story of Samuel and David as children.

I turned and looked at Christine and my heart was beating so loud I was sure she could hear it. Her eyes were sparkling like jewels in the flickering candlelight. The black dress shimmered and seemed to flow over her body.

I knelt on one knee and looked up at her.

'I've loved you since the first time I saw you at the Sojourner Truth School,' I whispered, so that only she could hear me. 'Except that when I saw you the first time, I had no way of knowing how incredibly special you are on the inside. How wise, how good. I didn't know that I could feel the way I do – whole and complete – whenever I'm with you. I would do anything for you. Or just to be with you for one more moment.'

I stopped for the briefest pause and took a breath. She held my eyes, didn't pull away.

'I love you so much and I always will. Will you marry me, Christine?'

She continued to look into my eyes, and I saw such warmth and love, but also humility, which is always a part of who Christine is. It was almost as if she couldn't imagine my loving her.

'Yes, I will. Oh, Alex, I shouldn't have waited until tonight. But this is so perfect, so special, I'm almost glad I did. Yes, I will be your wife.'

I took an antique engagement ring out and I gently slid it onto Christine's finger. The ring had been my mother's and I'd kept it since she died when I was nine. The exact history of the ring was unclear, except that it went back at least four generations in the Cross family and was my one and only heirloom.

We kissed in the glorious Children's Chapel of the National Cathedral and it was the best moment of my life, never to be forgotten, never to be diminished in any way.

Yes, I will be your wife.

Chapter Twenty

Ten days had passed without another fantasy murder, but now a powerful mood swing had taken hold of Geoffrey Shafer and he let himself go with the flow.

He was flying high as a kite; hyper, manic, bipolar, whatever the doctors wanted to call his condition. He'd already taken Ativan, Librium, Valium, and Depakote, but the drugs only seemed to fuel his jets.

That night at around six he pulled the black Jaguar out of the lot on the north side of the embassy, passing by the larger-than-life Winston Churchill statue, with its stubby right hand raised in a V for victory, its left hand holding his trademark cigar.

Eric Clapton played guitar loudly on the car's CD. He turned up the volume higher, slapping his hands hard on the steering wheel, feeling the rhythm, the beat, the primal urge.

Shafer turned onto Massachusetts Avenue and then stopped at a Starbucks. He hurried in and fixed up three coffees his way. Black as his heart, with six sugars. *Mmm, hmmm.* As usual, he had nearly finished the first before he got to the cash register.

Once he was inside the cockpit of his Jag again, he sipped a second cup at a more leisurely pace. He downed some Benadryl and Nascan. Couldn't hurt, might help. He took out the twenty-sided game dice. He had to play tonight.

Anything twelve or higher would dispatch him directly to Boo Cassady's place for a kinky quickie before he went home to the dreaded family. A seven to eleven was total disaster – straight home to Lucy and the kids. Three, four, five, or six meant he could go to the hideaway, for an unscheduled night of high adventure.

'Come three, four, five. Come baby, come! I need this tonight. Need a fix! I need it!'

He shook the dice for what must have been thirty seconds. He made the suspense last, drew it out. Finally, he released the dice onto the gray leather car seat. He watched the roll closely.

Jesus, he'd thrown a four! Defied the odds! His brain was on fire. He could play tonight. The dice had spoken; fate had spoken.

He excitedly punched a number on his cell phone. '*Lucy,*' he said, and he was smiling already.

'Glad I caught you at home, darling . . . Yes, you guessed it, first try. We're completely swamped here again. Can you believe it? I certainly can't. They think they own me, and I suppose they're half-right. It's the drug-trafficking rubbish again. I'll be home when I can. Don't wait up, though. Love to the kids. Kisses to everybody. Me too, darling. I love you too. You're the best, the most understanding wife alive.'

Very well played, Shafer thought as he breathed a sigh of relief. Excellent performance, considering the drugs he'd taken. Shafer disconnected from his wife, whose family money, unfortunately, paid for the town house, holidays away, even the Jag, and her fashionable Range Rover, of course.

He punched another number on the cell phone.

'Dr Cassady.' He heard her voice almost immediately. She *knew* it was him. He usually called from the car on his way over to see her. They liked to get each other hot and bothered on the phone. Telephone sex as foreplay.

'They've done it to me again.' Shafer whined miserably into the phone, but he was smiling again, loving his flair for the overdramatic.

A short silence, then, 'You mean they did it to us, don't you? There's *no way* you can get away? It's only a bloody job, and one that you detest, Geoff.'

'You know I would if I possibly could. I do hate it here, loathe every moment. And it's even worse at home, Boo. Jesus, you of all people know that.'

He imagined the tight little frown and Boo pursing her lips. 'You sound high, Geoffrey. Are you, dear? Take your pills today?'

'Don't be horrible. Of course I've taken my medications. I *am* rushed. I *am* high. On the ceiling, as a matter of fact. I'm calling between blasted staff meetings. Oh hell, I miss you, Boo. I want to be inside you, deep inside. I want to do your pussy, your ass, your throat. I'm thinking about it right now. Christ, I'm as hard as a rock here in my government issue office. Have to beat it down with a stick. *Cane* it. That's how we British handle such things.'

She laughed and he almost changed his mind about standing her up. 'Go back to work. I'll be at home – if you finish early,' she said. 'I could use a little finishing myself.'

'I love you, Boo. You're so kind to me.'

'I am, and I could probably get into a little caning, too.'

He hung up, and drove to the hideaway in Eckington. He parked the Jag next to the purple-and-blue taxi in the garage. He bounded upstairs to change for the game. God, he loved this, his secret life, his nights away from everything and everyone he loathed.

He was taking too many chances now, but he didn't care.

Chapter Twenty-One

S hafer was totally pumped up for a night on the town. The Four Horsemen was on. Anything could happen tonight. Yet he found that he was introspective and pensive. He could flip from manic to depressive in the blink of an eye.

He watched himself as if he were an observer in a dream. He had been a British intelligence agent, but now that the Cold War was ended, there was little use for his talents. It was only the influence of Lucy's father that had kept him in his job. Duncan Cousins had been a general in the army, and now was chairman of a packaged-goods conglomerate specializing in the sale of detergents, soaps, and drug-store perfume. He liked to call Shafer 'the Colonel,' rubbing in his 'rise to mediocrity.' The General also loved to talk about the glowing successes of Shafer's two brothers, both of whom had made millions in business.

Shafer shifted his thoughts back to the present. He was doing that a lot lately, fading in and out like a radio with a bad connection. He took a settling breath, then pulled the taxi out of the garage. Moments later, he turned onto Rhode Island Avenue. It was beginning to rain again, a light mist that made the passing traffic lights blurry and impressionistic.

Shafer drifted over to the curb and stopped for a tall, slender black man. He looked like a drug dealer, something Shafer had no use for. Maybe he would just shoot the bastard then dump the body. That felt good enough for tonight's action. A sleazebag dope dealer whom nobody would miss.

'Airport,' the man announced haughtily as he climbed inside the taxi. The inconsiderate bastard shook off rainwater onto the seat. Then he shut the creaking car door behind him, and was on his cell phone immediately.

Shafer wasn't going to the airport and neither was his first passenger of the night. He listened in on the phone call. The man's voice was affected, surprisingly cultured.

'I think I'll just make the nine o'clock, Leonard. It's Delta *on* the hour, right? I picked up a cab, thank the Lord Jesus. Most of them won't stop anywhere near where my poor mom lives in Northeast. Then along comes this purple-and-blue absolute wreck of a gypsy cab, and merciful God, it stops for me.'

Christ, he'd been identified. Shafer silently cursed his bad luck. That was the way of the game, though, incredible highs and vicious lows. He would have to take this asshole all the way out to National Airport. If he disappeared, it would be connected to a purple-and-blue cab, an 'absolute wreck of a gypsy cab.'

Shafer stepped on the accelerator and sped out toward National. The airport was backed up, even at nine in the evening. He cursed under his breath. The rain was heavy and it was punctuated by rolling thunder and spits of lightning.

He tried to control his building anger, his darkening mood. It took nearly forty minutes to get to the bloody terminal and drop off the passenger. By that time he'd settled back into another fantasy, had another huge mood swing. He was cycling *up* again.

Maybe he should have gone to see Dr Cassady, after all. He needed more pills, especially Lithium. This was like a carnival ride tonight – up and down, up and down. He wanted to push things as far as he could. He also felt crazed. He was definitely losing control.

Anything could happen when he got like this. That was the thing. He pulled into the queue of taxis waiting to get a fare back to DC.

As he moved closer to the front of the line, there was more thunder. Lightning crackled high above the airport. He could see the prospective victims huddled under a dripping canopy. Flights were undoubtedly being postponed and canceled. He savored the cheap-seat melodrama, the suspense. The victim *du jour* could be anyone, from a corporate executive to a harried secretary, or maybe even a whole family back from a trip to Disney World.

But not once did he look at the queue of potential victims as he inched closer and closer. He was almost there. Just two more taxis in front of him. He could see the queue out of the corner of his eye. Finally, he had to snatch a quick peek.

It was a tall male.

He peeked again, couldn't help himself.

A white male, a businessman, stepped off the curb and was climbing inside the taxi. He was cursing to himself, pissed off about the rain.

Shafer looked the man over. He was American – late thirties – full of himself. Investment analyst, maybe, or a banker – something like that.

'We can *go* – whenever you're in the mood,' the man snapped at him.

'Sorry, sir,' Shafer said, and smiled obsequiously into the rearview mirror.

He dropped the dice on the front seat: *six!* His heart began to hammer.

Six meant *immediate action.* But he was still inside National Airport. There was a heavy lineup of traffic and cops, bright lights glittering everywhere. It was too dangerous, even for him.

The dice had spoken. He had no choice. The game was *on* right now.

A sea of red rear-lights glowed at him. Cars were everywhere. How could he do this here? Shafer began to perspire heavily.

But he had to do it. That was the point of the game. He had to do it now. Had to murder this asshole right here at the airport.

He swerved into the nearest parking area. This was not good. He speeded down a narrow lane. Another bolt of lightning flashed overhead; it seemed to underscore the madness and chaos of the moment.

'Where the *hell* are you going?' the businessman shouted at him. He slammed his palm into the back of the seat. 'This isn't the way out, you ass!'

Shafer glared at the business creep in his rearview mirror. He hated him for calling him an ass. The bastard also reminded him of his brothers.

'I'm not going anywhere,' he yelled back. 'But you're going straight to hell!'

The businessman blustered. 'What did you say to me? What did you just say?'

Shafer fired his Smith & Wesson 9mm and hoped no one would hear it above the thunder and honking horns.

He was soaking wet with perspiration, and he was afraid his black face would run and smear. He was expecting to be stopped now. Waiting for policemen to surround the taxi. Bright red blood was splattered all over the backseat and window. The businessman was slumped in the corner as if he were asleep. Shafer couldn't see where the bloody bullet had exited the taxi.

He made it out of National before he went completely mad. He drove carefully to Benning Heights in Southeast. He couldn't risk being stopped for speeding. But he was out of his head, not sure he was doing the right thing.

He stopped on a side street, checked out the body, stripped it. He decided to dump the corpse out in the open. He was trying his best not to be predictable.

Then he sped away from the crime scene and headed home.

He'd left no identification on the victim. Nothing but the body.

Just a little surprise – a *John* Doe.

Chapter Twenty-Two

I got home from Christine's house at two thirty in the morning, feeling exhilarated, the happiest I'd been in years. I thought about waking Nana and the kids to tell them the news. I wanted to see the surprised looks on their faces. I wished that I had brought Christine home with me, so we could celebrate together.

The phone rang moments after I stepped inside the house. *Oh no*, I thought, *not tonight. Nothing good comes from phone calls at two-thirty a.m.*

I picked up in the living room and heard Sampson's voice on the line. 'Sugar?' he whispered.

'Leave me alone,' I said. 'Try again in the morning. I'm closed for the night.'

'No you're not, Alex. Not tonight. Get over to Alabama Avenue, about three blocks east of Dupont Park. A man was found there naked and dead – in the gutter. The guy is white and there's no ID on him.'

First thing in the morning, I would tell Nana and the kids about Christine and me. I had to go. The murder scene was a ten-minute ride across the Anacostia River. Sampson was waiting for me on a street corner. So was the John Doe.

And a lively, mean-spirited crowd. A naked white body dumped in this neighborhood had prompted lots of curiosity, almost like seeing a deer walking down Alabama Avenue.

'Casper the Friendly Ghost been *offed*.' A heckler contributed his twenty-five cents as Sampson and I stooped down under the yellow plastic crime-scene tape. In the background were rows of dilapidated brick buildings that almost seemed to scream out the names of the lost, the forgotten, the never-had-a-chance.

Stagnant water often pools on the street corners here since the storm drains are hardly ever inspected. I knelt over the twisted, naked body that was partly immersed in the cesspool. There would be no tire marks left at the watery scene. I wondered if the killer had thought of that.

I was making mental notes. No need to write them down – I'd remember everything. The man had manicured fingernails and toenails. No calluses showed on either his hands or feet. He had no bruises or distinct disfiguring marks, other than the cruel gunshot wound that had blown away the left side of his face.

The body was deeply suntanned, except where he'd worn swim trunks. A thin, pale ring ran around his left index finger, where he'd probably worn a wedding band, which was missing.

And there was no ID – just like the Jane Does.

Death was clearly the result of the single, devastating gunshot to the head. Alabama Avenue was the primary scene – where the body was found; but I suspected a secondary homicide scene – where the victim was actually murdered.

'What do you think?' Sampson crouched down close beside me. His knees cracked loudly. 'Sonofabitch killer is pissed off about something.'

'Really bizarre that he wound up here in Benning Heights. I don't know if he's connected to the Jane Does. But if he is, the killer wanted us to find this one in a hurry. Bodies around here usually get dumped in Fort Dupont Park. He's getting stranger and stranger. And you're right, he's very angry with the world.'

My mind was rapidly filling with crime-scene notes, plus the usual stream of homicide detective questions. Why leave the body in a street gutter? Why not in an abandoned building? Why in Benning Heights? Was the killer black? That still made the most sense to me, but a very low percentage of pattern killers are black.

The sergeant from the Crime Scene Unit came strolling up to Sampson and me. 'What do you want from us, Detective?'

I looked back at the naked white body. 'Videotape it, photograph it, sketch it,' I told him.

'And take some of the trash in the gutter and sidewalk?'

'Take everything. Even if it's soaking wet.'

The sergeant frowned. 'Everything? All this wet trash? Why?'

Alabama Avenue is hilly, and I could see the Capitol Building brightly illuminated in the distance. It looked like a faraway celestial body, maybe heaven. It got me thinking about the *haves* in Washington, and the *have-nots*.

'Just take everything. It's how I work,' I said.

Chapter Twenty-Three

Detective Patsy Hampton arrived at the chilling homicide scene around 2:15. The Jefe's assistant had called her apartment about an unusual murder in Benning Heights that might relate to the Jane Does. This one was different in some ways, but there were too many similarities for her to ignore.

She watched Alex Cross work the crime scene. She was impressed that he'd come out at this early hour. She was curious about him, had been for a long time. Hampton knew Cross by reputation, and had followed a couple of his cases. She had even worked a few weeks on the tragic kidnapping of Maggie Rose Dunne and Michael Goldberg.

So far, she had mixed feelings about Cross. He was personable enough, and more than good-looking. He was a tall, strongly-put-together man. She felt that he received undeserved special treatment because he was a forensic psychologist. She'd done her homework on Cross.

Hampton understood that she had been assigned to show Cross up, to win, to knock him down a peg. She knew it would be a tough competition, but she also knew that she was the one to do it; she never failed at anything.

She'd already done her own examination of the crime scene. She had stayed on at the scene only because Cross and Sampson had unexpectedly shown up.

She continued to study Cross – watched him walk the homicide scene several times. He was physically imposing, and so was his partner, who had to be at least six-nine. Cross was six-three and weighed maybe two hundred. He appeared younger than his age, which was forty-one. He seemed to be respected by the assisting patrolmen, even by the EMS personnel. He shook a few hands, patted shoulders, occasionally shared a smile with someone working the crime scene.

Hampton figured that was part of his act though. Everybody had one these days, especially in Washington. Cross's was obviously his charisma and charm.

Hell, she had an act herself. Hers was to appear nonthreatening and 'feminine', then perform contrary to the expectations of the males on the force. She usually caught them off-guard. As she'd risen in the department, the men learned that she could be tough. Surprise, surprise. She worked longer hours than anyone else; she was a hell of a lot tougher than the men; and she never socialized with other cops.

But she'd made one big mistake. She broke into a homicide suspect's car without a warrant, and was caught by another detective, a jealous older male. That was how Pittman got his hooks into her, and now he wouldn't let go.

At around a quarter to three, she walked to her forest-green Explorer, noting that it needed a wash. She already had a few ideas about the dead man in the street. There was no doubt in her mind that she would beat Cross.

Book Two

Death Rides a Pale Horse

Chapter Twenty-Four

George Bayer was Famine among The Four Horsemen. He'd been playing the fantasy game for seven years, and he loved it. At least he had until recently, when Geoffrey Shafer started to go out of control.

Famine was physically unimpressive at around five-eight, a hundred ninety pounds. He was paunchy, balding, wore wire-rim glasses, but he also knew that his appearance was deceiving, and he'd made a living off of those who underestimated him. People like Geoffrey Shafer.

He had reread a forty-page dossier on Shafer during his long plane ride from Asia to Washington. The dossier told him everything about Shafer, and also about the character he played, Death. At Dulles Airport Bayer rented a dark-blue Ford sedan, under a false name. He was still detached and introspective during his thirty-minute drive into the city.

But he was also anxious: He was nervous for all of the Horsemen, especially for himself. He was the one who had to confront Shafer, and he was worried that Shafer might be going mad, that he might blow up in all of their faces.

George Bayer had been an M man, MI6, and he'd known Shafer in the service. He was in Washington to check out Shafer firsthand. It was suspected by the other players that Geoffrey might have gone over the edge, that he was no longer playing by the rules and was a grave danger to them all. Since Bayer had once been stationed in Washington, and knew the town, he was the one to go there.

Bayer didn't want to be seen at the British Embassy on Massachusetts Avenue, but he had spoken to a few friends who he knew would keep silent about having been contacted. The news about Shafer was as bad as he'd suspected. He was seeing women outside his marriage, and he wasn't being discreet. There was a psychologist, who was a sex therapist, and he had been observed going over to her place several times a week, often during working hours. It was rumored that he was drinking heavily and possibly taking drugs. Bayer suspected the latter. He and Shafer had been friends, and done their share of drugs while posted in the Philippines and Thailand. Of course they were younger and more foolish then; at least that was true of Bayer.

The DC police had recently put in a complaint to the embassy about a reckless-driving incident. Shafer might have been high at the time. His current assignments at the embassy were minimal, and he would have been dismissed, or at least sent back to England, if it wasn't for his wife's father, General Duncan Cousins. What a terrible mess Shafer had made of his life.

But that's not the worst of it, is it, Geoffrey? George Bayer was thinking as he drove into the Northeast section of Washington known as Eckington Place. *There's more, isn't there, dear boy? It's much worse than the embassy thinks. It's probably the biggest scandal in the long history of the Secret Service, and you're right at the heart of it. But of course, so am I.*

Bayer locked the doors of his car as he pulled up to a traffic light. The area looked highly suspicious to him, like so much of Washington these days. What a sad, totally insane country America had become. What a perfect refuge for Shafer.

Famine took in the sights on the mean streets as he continued through the decidedly lower-class neighborhood. There was nothing to compare with this in London. Row upon row of two-storied red-brick garden apartments, many of them in dreadful disrepair. Not so much urban decay as urban apathy.

He saw Shafer's lair up ahead and pulled over to the curb. He knew the exact location of the hideaway from the elaborate fantasy tales Shafer had told the other players. He knew the address. Now he needed to know one more thing: Were the murders that Geoffrey claimed he'd committed fantasies, or were they real? Was he actually a cold-blooded killer operating here in Washington?

Bayer walked to the garage door. It took him only a moment to pick the lock and let himself in.

He had heard so much about the 'nightmare machine,' the purple-and-blue taxi that Shafer used for the murders. He was looking at it. The taxi was as real as he was. Now he knew the truth. George Bayer shook his head. Shafer had killed all of those people. This was no longer a game.

Chapter Twenty-Five

Bayer trudged upstairs to the hideaway apartment. His arms and legs felt heavy and he had a slight pain in his chest. His vision was tunneled. He pulled down the dusty blinds and began to look around.

Shafer had boastfully described the garage and taxi several times during the game. He had flaunted the existence of the hideaway and sworn to the other players that it was real and not some fantasy in a role-playing game. Geoffrey had openly dared them to see it for themselves, and that was why Bayer was in Washington.

Well, Geoffrey, the hideaway is real, he agreed. *You are a stone-cold killer. You weren't bluffing, were you?*

At ten o'clock that night Bayer took Shafer's taxi out. The keys were there, almost as a dare. Was it? He figured he had a right to experience exactly what Shafer had. According to Geoffrey, half the fun of the game was foreplay, checking out the possibilities, seeing the whole game board before you made a move.

From ten o'clock until half past eleven Bayer explored the streets of DC, but he didn't pick up a fare. He kept his off-duty sign on. *What a game,* Bayer kept thinking as he drove. *Is this how Geoffrey does it? Is this how he feels when he's prowling the city?*

He was pulled out of his day-dream by an old tramp with a crushed hat, who had wheeled a cart filled with cans and other recyclables right in front of him. He didn't seem to care whether he was run over or not, but Bayer braked hard. That made him think of Shafer. The line between life and death had faded to nothing for him, hadn't it?

Bayer cautiously moved on. He drove past a church. The service was over and a crowd of people were leaving.

He stopped the cab for an attractive black woman in a blue dress and matching high heels. He needed to see what this must be like for Shafer, for Death. He couldn't resist.

'Thank you so much,' the woman said as she slid into the rear of his taxi. She seemed so proper and respectable. He checked her furtively in the mirror. She didn't have much to offer up top. Pretty enough face, though. Long brown legs encased in sheer stockings. He tried to imagine what Shafer might do now, but he couldn't.

Shafer had boasted he was killing people in the poorer sections of Washington, since nobody cared about them anyway. Bayer suspected that he was telling the truth. He knew things about Shafer from when they were in Thailand and the Philippines. He knew Shafer's deepest, darkest secrets.

Bayer drove the attractive and well-spoken black woman to her apartment, and was amused when she gave him a sixty-cent tip for the four dollar ride. Fifteen percent to the penny. He took the money and thanked her graciously.

'An English cab driver,' she said. 'That's unusual. Have a nice evening.'

He continued to drive until past two in the morning. He drank in the sights; played the dizzying game. And then he had to stop again. Two young girls were hailing for a taxi on the corner. The area was called Shaw, and Howard University was very close according to several signs.

The girls were slender, delectable in stacked heels and shiny clothes that glowed in the dark. One of them wore a microskirt, and he could see the tops of black or navy thigh-highs as he stopped to pick them up. *They must be hookers – Shafer's favorite prey,* Bayer thought to himself.

The second prostitute was even prettier and sexier than the first. She wore white stacked sandals, side-striped white athletic pants, a teeny tank top in blue camouflage.

'Where are we going?' Bayer asked as they scampered over to the taxi.

The girl in the miniskirt did the talking. '*We're* going to Princeton Place. That's Petworth, darlin'. Then *you're* going away,' she said. She tossed her head back and issued a taunting laugh. Bayer snickered to himself. He was beginning to get into this now.

The girls climbed in, and Bayer couldn't resist checking them out in the mirror. The foxy one in the microskirt caught him looking. He felt like a schoolboy, found it intoxicating, didn't avert his eyes from hers.

She casually flipped him the finger. He didn't stop looking. Couldn't. *So this was how it felt to Shafer. This was the game of games.*

He couldn't take his eyes off the girls. His heart was pounding. Microskirt wore a tightly fitted ribbed tank top. Her long fingernails were airbrushed in kiwi and mango colors. She had a pager on her belt. Probably a gun in her handbag.

The other girl smiled shyly in his direction. She seemed more innocent. Was she? A necklace that read: BABY GIRL dangled between her young breasts.

If they were going to Petworth, they had to be hooking. They were certainly young and foxy; sixteen, seventeen years old. Bayer could see himself having sex with the girls, and the image was beginning to overpower his imagination. He knew he ought to be careful. This could get completely out of hand. He was playing Shafer's game, wasn't he? And he liked it very much.

'I have a proposition for you,' he said to microskirt.

'All right, darlin',' she said. 'Be one hundred for the half. Plus our ride to Petworth. That's my proposition for you.'

Chapter Twenty-Six

S hafer liked to know when any of the other players traveled, especially if they came to Washington. He had gone through a lot of trouble to hack his way into their computers to keep track of them. Famine had recently bought plane tickets and now he was here in DC. Why?

It wasn't hard to follow George Bayer, once he got to town. Shafer was still reasonably good at it. He'd had plenty of practice at tracking and surveillance, during his years in the Service.

He was disappointed that Famine had decided to 'intersect' with his fantasy. Intersection happened occasionally in the game, but it was rare. Both players were supposed to agree beforehand. Famine was clearly breaking the rules. What did he know, or think he knew?

Then Bayer genuinely surprised him. Not only did he visit Shafer's hideaway but he actually took the taxi for a ride. What the hell was he doing?

At a little past two in the morning, Shafer watched the gypsy cab pick up the two young girls in Shaw. Was Bayer copycatting? Was he setting some kind of trap for Shafer? Or was it something else altogether?

Bayer took the girls to S Street, which wasn't far from the pick-up point. He followed the girls up the darkened stairs of an aging brownstone and then they all disappeared inside.

He had a blue anorak thrown over his right arm and Shafer suspected a pistol was under the coat. Christ! He'd taken two of them. He could have been seen by anyone on the street. The cab could have been spotted.

Shafer parked on the street. He waited and watched. He didn't like being in this part of Shaw, especially without his disguise, and driving the Jaguar. There were some old crumbling brownstones, and a couple of boarded-up, graffiti-covered shacks on the street. No one was outside.

He saw a light blink on the top floor, and figured that was where Bayer had taken the two girls. Probably their flat.

He watched the brownstone from two until close to four. He couldn't take his eyes away. While he waited he imagined dozens of scenarios that might have brought Famine here. He wondered if the others were in Washington, too. Or was Famine acting alone? Was he playing The Four Horsemen right now?

Shafer waited and waited for Bayer to come out of the brownstone. But he didn't come down, and Shafer grew more impatient and worried and angry. He fidgeted. His breathing became labored. He had lurid, paranoid fantasies about what Bayer might have done up there. Had he killed the two girls? Taken their identification? Was this a trap? He thought so. What else could it be?

Still no George Bayer.

Shafer couldn't stand it any longer. He climbed out of the Jaguar. He stood on the street and stared up at the windows of the flat. He wondered if he, too, were being watched. He sensed a trap, wondered if he should flee.

Christ, where the hell was Bayer? What game was Famine playing? Was there a back way out of the building? If so, why had he left the taxi as evidence? Evidence! Damn him!

But then he saw Bayer finally leave the building. He quickly crossed S Street, got into the cab, and drove away.

Shafer decided to go upstairs. He jogged over to the building and found the wooden front door unlocked. He hurried up the steep, winding stairs. He had a flashlight in one hand, turned it on. His semiautomatic was in the other.

Shafer made his way to the fourth floor. He immediately knew which of the two flats was the right one. A poster for Mary J. Blige's *What's the 411* album was on the splintered and scarred door to his right. The girls lived here.

He turned the handle and carefully pushed the door open. He pointed his gun inside, ready.

One of the young girls came out of the bathroom wearing a fluffy black towel on her head, nothing else. She was a hot number with pert little titties. Christ, Famine must have paid for it. What a fool! What a wanker!

'Who the hell are you? What are you doing in here?' the girl shouted angrily.

'I'm Death,' he grinned, and announced, 'I'm here for you and your pretty friend.'

Chapter Twenty-Seven

I had gotten home from the John Doe murder scene at a little past three in the morning. I went to bed, but set my alarm for six thirty. I managed to get myself up before the kids went off to school.

'Somebody was out very, very, very late last night.' Jannie started her teasing before I had made it all the way downstairs and into the kitchen. I continued down and found her and Damon in the breakfast nook with Nana.

'Somebody sure *looks* like they had a late night,' Nana said from her customary cat-bird seat.

'Somebody's cruising for a bruising,' I said to quiet them. 'Now, there's something important I need to tell you before you head out to school.'

'Watch our manners. Always pay attention in class, even if the teacher's boring. Lead with our left if it ever comes to a fight in the school yard,' Jannie offered with a wink.

I rolled my eyes. 'What I was going to say,' I said, 'is that you should be especially nice to Ms Johnson today. You see, last night, Christine said that she'd marry me. I guess that means she's marrying all of us.'

At that point, everything became hugging and loud celebrating in the kitchen. The kids got chocolate milk and bacon grease all over me. I'd never seen Nana happier. And I felt exactly the same. Probably even better than they did.

I eventually made it to work that morning. I had made some progress on the John Doe homicide, and early on Tuesday morning I learned that the man whose body had been dumped on Alabama Avenue was a thirty-four-year-old research analyst named Franklin Odenkirk. He worked at the Library of Congress for the Congressional Research Service.

We didn't release the news to the press, but I did inform Chief Pittman's office as soon as I knew. Pittman would find out anyway.

Once I had a name for the victim, information came quickly and, as it usually is, it was sad. Odenkirk was married and had three small children. He had taken a late flight back from New York that evening, where he'd given a talk at the Rockefeller Institute. The plane landed on time and he deboarded at National around ten. What happened to him after that was a mystery.

For the remainder of Thursday and Friday, I was busy with the murder case. I visited the Library of Congress, and went to the newest structure, the James Madison Building, on Independence Avenue. I talked to nearly a dozen of Frank Odenkirk's coworkers.

They were courteous and cooperative and I was told repeatedly that Odenkirk, while haughty at times, was generally well-liked. He wasn't known to use drugs or drink to excess; wasn't known to gamble either. He was faithful to his wife. He hadn't been involved in a serious argument at the office for as long as he'd been there.

He was with the Education and Public Welfare Division and spent long days in the spectacular Main Reading Room. There was no apparent motive for his murder, which was what I feared. The killing roughly paralleled the Jane Does so far, but of course the chief of detectives didn't want to hear it. There was no Jane Doe killer, according to him. Why? Because he didn't want to shift dozens of detectives to Southeast and begin an extensive investigation on the basis of my instincts and gut feelings. I had heard Pittman joke that Southeast wasn't part of *his city*.

Before I left the Madison Building I was compelled to stop and see the Main Reading Room once again. It was newly renovated and I hadn't been there since the work had been done.

I sat at a reader's table and stared up at the amazing dome high over my head. Around the room were stained-glass representations of the seals of forty-eight states; also bronze statues of figures, including Michelangelo, Plato, Shakespeare, Edward Gibbon, and Homer. I could imagine poor Frank Odenkirk doing his work here, and it bothered me. Why had he been killed? Had it been the Weasel?

The death was a terrible shock to everyone who had worked with him, and a couple of Odenkirk's coworkers broke down while talking to me about his murder.

I wasn't looking forward to interviewing Mrs Odenkirk, but I drove out 295 and 210 to Forest Heights late on Friday afternoon. Chris Odenkirk was home with her mother, and also her husband's parents, who had flown in from Briarcliff Manor in Westchester County, New York. They told me the same story as the people at the Library of Congress. No one in the family knew of anyone who might want to harm Frank. He was a loving father, a supportive husband, a thoughtful son and son-in-law.

At the Odenkirk home, I learned that the deceased had been wearing a green seersucker suit when he left home, his business meeting in New York had run over, and he was nearly two hours late getting to LaGuardia Airport.

He generally took a cab home from the airport in Washington because so many flights arrived late.

Even before I went to the house in Forest Heights I had two detectives sent out to the airport. They showed around pictures of Odenkirk, interviewed airline personnel, shopworkers, porters, taxi dispatchers, and cabdrivers.

Around six I went over to the medical examiner's office to hear the results of the autopsy. All the photos and sketches from the crime scene were laid out. The autopsy had run about two and a half hours. Every cavity of Frank Odenkirk's body had been swabbed and scraped and his brain had been removed.

I talked to the medical examiner while she finished up with Odenkirk at about six thirty. Her name was Angelina Torres, and I'd known her for years. We had both started in our jobs at about the same time. Angelina was a tick under five feet and probably weighed around ninety pounds soaking wet.

'Long day, Alex?' she asked. 'You look used and abused.'

'Long one for you too, Angelina. You look good though. Short, but good.'

She nodded, grinned, then stretched her small, slight arms up over her head. She let out a low groan that approximated the way I felt, too.

'Any surprises for me?' I asked, after allowing her to stretch in peace and moan her little heart out.

I hadn't expected anything, but she had some news. 'One surprise,' Angelina said. 'He was sodomized after he died. Someone had sex with him, Alex. Our killer seems to swing both ways.'

Chapter Twenty-Eight

On the drive home that evening, I needed a break from the murder case. I thought about Christine, and that was much better, easier on the frontal lobe. I even switched off my beeper. I didn't want any distractions for ten or fifteen minutes.

Even though she hadn't talked about it recently, she still felt my job was too dangerous. The trouble was, she was absolutely right. I sometimes worried about leaving Damon and Jannie alone in the world, and now Christine as well. As I drove along the familiar streets of Southeast near Fifth, I considered whether I could actually leave police work. I'd been thinking about going into private practice and working as a psychologist, but I hadn't done anything to make it happen. It probably meant that I didn't really want to do it.

Nana was sitting on the front porch when I arrived home at around seven thirty. She looked peeved, an expression of hers that I know all too well. She can still make me feel like I'm nine or ten years old and she's the one with all the answers.

'Where are the kids?' I called out as soon as I opened the car door and climbed out. A fractured Batman and Robin kite was still up in a tree in the yard and I was annoyed at myself for not getting it down a couple of weeks ago.

'I shackled them to the sink and they're doing the dishes,' Nana said.

'Sorry about missing dinner,' I told her.

'Tell that to your children,' Nana said, frowning up a storm. She's about as subtle as a hurricane. 'You better tell them right now. Your friend Sampson called a little earlier. So did your compatriot Jerome Thurman. There's been more murders, Alex. I used the *plural* noun, just in case you didn't notice. Sampson is waiting for you at the so-called crime scene. Two bodies over in Shaw near Howard University, of all places. Two more young black girls are dead. It won't stop, will it? It never stops in Southeast.'

No, it never does.

Chapter Twenty-Nine

The homicide scene was an old crumbling brownstone in a bad section of S Street in Shaw. A lot of college kids and also young professionals live in the up-and-down, mostly middle-class neighborhood. Lately, prostitution has become a problem there. According to Sampson, the two dead girls were both prostitutes who occasionally worked in the neighborhood but mostly over in Petworth.

A single squad car and an EMS truck were parked at the homicide scene. A uniformed patrolman was posted on the front stoop, and he seemed intent on keeping intruders out. He was young, baby-faced, with smooth butterscotch skin. I didn't know him, so I flashed my detective's shield.

'Detective Cross.' He grunted. I sensed that he'd heard of me.

'What do we have so far?' I asked, before I went inside and trudged up four steep flights. 'What do you hear, Officer?'

'Two girls dead upstairs. Both pros, apparently. One of them lived in the building. Murders were called in anonymously. Maybe a neighbor, maybe the pimp. They're sixteen, seventeen, maybe younger. Too bad. They didn't deserve this.'

I nodded, took a deep breath, and then quickly climbed up steep, winding, creaking stairs to the fourth floor. Prostitutes make for difficult police investigations, and I wondered if the Weasel knew that. On average, a hooker out of Petworth might turn a dozen or more tricks a night, and that's a lot of forensic evidence, just on her body.

The door to apartment 4A was wide open and I could see inside. It was an efficiency – one large room, kitchenette, bath. A fluffy white area rug lay between two daybeds. A lava lamp was undulating green blobs next to several dildos.

Sampson was crouched on the far side of one daybed. He looked like an NBA power forward searching the floor for a missing contact lens.

I walked into a small, untidy room that smelled of incense, peach blossom fragrance, greasy food. A bright red and yellow McDonald's container of fries was open on the couch.

Dirty clothes covered the chairs: bike shorts, short-shorts, Karl Kani urban clothes. At least a dozen bottles of nail polish, remover, files, and cotton balls lay on the floor. There was a heavy, cloying smell of fruity perfume.

I went around the bed to look at the victims. Two very young women, both naked from the waist down. The Weasel had been here – I could feel it.

The girls were lying one on top of the other, looking like lovers. They looked as if they were having sex on the floor.

One girl wore a blue tank top, the other had on black lingerie. They both had on 'slides,' stacked bath sandals that are popular nowadays. Most of the Jane Does had been left naked, but unlike many of the others, we would be able to identify these two fairly easily.

'No actual ID on either girl,' Sampson said, without looking up from his work.

'One of them rents the apartment, though,' I told him.

He nodded. 'Probably pays cash. She's in a cash business.'

Sampson was wearing latex rubber gloves and he was bent down close to the two women.

'The killer wore gloves,' Sampson said, still without looking up at me. 'Don't seem to be fingerprints anywhere. That's what the techie says. First look-through. They both were shot, Alex. Single shot to the forehead.'

I was still looking around the room, collecting information, letting the details of the murder scene flow over me. I noticed an array of hair products: Soft Sheen, Care Free Curl, styling gel, several wigs. On top of one of the wigs was a green army garrison cap with stripes. It's commonly called a 'cunt cap' among military personnel because it's effective for picking up women, especially in the South. There was also a pager.

The girls were young and pretty. They had skinny little legs, small, bony feet, silver toe rings that looked like they came from the same shop. Their discarded clothes amounted to insignificant little bundles on the bloodied hardwood floor.

In one corner of the small room, there were vestiges of brief childhoods: a lotto game, a stuffed blue bear that was threadbare and looked about as old as the girls, a Barbie doll, a ouija board.

'Take a good look, Alex. It gets weirder and weirder. Our Weasel is starting to freak out.'

I sighed and bent down to see what Sampson had discovered. The smaller, and perhaps the younger of the two girls was lying on top. The girl underneath was on her back. Her glazed brown eyes stared straight up at a broken light fixture in the ceiling, as if she had seen something terrible up there.

The girl on top had been positioned with her face, actually her mouth, tilted down into the other girl's crotch.

'Killer played real cute games with them after they were dead,' Sampson said. 'Move the one on top a little. Lift her head, Alex. You see it?'

I saw it. A completely new MO for the Jane Does, at least the ones I knew about. The phrase 'stuck on each other' ran through my mind. I wondered if that was the killer's 'message.' The girl on top was connected to the one underneath – by her tongue.

Sampson sighed and said, 'I think her tongue is stapled inside the other girl. I'm pretty sure that's it, Alex. The Weasel stapled them together.'

I looked at the two girls and shook my head. 'I don't think so. A staple, even a surgical one, would come apart on the tongue's surface . . . Crazy glue would work.'

Chapter Thirty

The killer was working faster so I had to do the same. The two dead girls didn't remain Jane Does for very long. I had their names before the ten o'clock news that night. I continued to ignore the explicit orders of the chief of detectives and to investigate what I felt like.

Early the next morning, Sampson and I met at Stamford, the high school that Tori Glover and Marion Cardinal had attended. The murdered girls were seventeen and fourteen years old.

The memory of the homicide scene had left me with a queasy, sick feeling that wouldn't go away. I kept thinking, *Christine is right. Get out of this, do something else. It's time.*

The principal at Stamford was a small, frail-looking red-haired woman named Robin Schwartz. Her resource officer, Nathan Kemp, had gotten together some students who knew the victims. He had set aside a couple of classrooms for Sampson, Jerome Thurman, and me to use for interviews. Jerome would work in one room, Sampson and me in the other.

Summer school was still in session and Stamford was busy as a mall on a Saturday. We passed the cafeteria on the way there and it was packed at ten thirty. No empty seats anywhere. The room reeked of French fries, the same greasy smell that was in the girls' apartment.

A few kids were making noise, but they were mostly well behaved. The music of Wu/Tang and Jodeci leaked from earphones. The school seemed to be well-run and orderly. Between classes a few boys and girls embraced tenderly, with loosely locked pinkies and the gentlest brushes of cheeks.

'These were not bad girls,' Nathan Kemp told us as we walked. 'I think you'll hear that from other students. Tori dropped out last semester, but her home life was the main reason. Marion was an honor student at Stamford. I'm telling you, guys, these were not bad girls.'

Sampson, Thurman, and I spent the rest of the afternoon with the kids. We learned that Tori and Marion were popular all right. They were loyal to their friends, funny, usually fun to be around. Marion was described as 'blazing,' which meant she was great. Tori was 'buggin' sometimes,' which meant she could be a little crazy. Most of the kids hadn't known that the girls were tricking in Petworth, but Tori Glover was said to always have money.

One particular interview would stick in my mind for a while. Evita Cardinal was a senior at Stamford, and also a cousin of Marion's. She wore white athletic pants and a purple stretchy top. A pair of black-rimmed, yellow-tinted sunglasses were propped on top of her head.

She started to cry her eyes out as soon as she sat down across the desk from me.

'I'm real sorry about Marion,' I said, and I was. 'We just want to catch whoever did this terrible thing. Detective Sampson and I both live nearby in Southeast. My kids go to the Sojourner Truth School.'

The girl looked at me. Her eyes were red-rimmed and wary. 'You won't catch nobody,' she finally said. It was the prevailing attitude in the neighborhood, and it happened to be mostly true. Sampson and I weren't even supposed to be here. I had told my secretary I was out working the murder of Frank Odenkirk. A few other detectives were covering for us.

'How long have Tori and Marion been working in Petworth? Do you know any other girls from school who work over there?'

Evita shook her head. '*Tori* was the one working the street in Petworth. Not Marion. My cousin was a good person. They both were. Marion was my little doggie,' Evita said, and the tears came flowing again.

'Marion *was* there with Tori.' I told her what I knew to be the truth. 'We talked to people who saw her on Princeton Place that night.'

The cousin glared at me. 'You don't know what you're talkin' about, Mister Detective. You're *wrong*. You ain't got the straight.'

'I'm listening to you, Evita. That's why I'm here.'

'Marion wasn't there to sell her body or like that. She was just afraid for Tori. She went to *protect* Tori. She never did nothin' bad for money, and I know that for a fact.'

The girl started to sob again. 'My cousin was a good person, my best girl-friend. She was tryin' to just protect Tori and she got herself killed for it. The police won't do nothin'. You never come back here again after today. Never happen. You don't care about us. We're nothin' to nobody,' Evita Cardinal said, and that seemed to say it all.

Chapter Thirty-One

*W*e're *nothin' to nobody*. It was a horrifying and absolutely true statement, and it was at the deepest roots of the Jane Doe investigation, the search for the Weasel. It pretty well summed up George Pittman's cynical philosophy about the inner city. It was also the reason I was feeling tired and numb to the bone by six thirty that night. I believed that the Jane Doe murders were escalating.

On the other hand, I hadn't seen nearly enough of my own kids for the last few days, so I decided I'd better head home. On the way, I thought about Christine and calmed down immediately. Since the time I was a young boy, I've been having a recurring day-dream. I'm standing alone on a cold, barren planet. It's scary, but more than anything, it's lonely and unsettling. Then a woman comes up to me. We begin to hold hands, to embrace, and then every-thing is all right. That woman was Christine, and I had no idea how she had gotten out of my dreams and into the real world.

Nana, Damon, and Jannie were just leaving the house when I pulled up into the driveway. What was this? I wondered.

Wherever they were going, everybody was dolled up and looking especially nice. Nana and Jannie wore their best dresses and Damon had on a blue suit, white shirt and tie. Damon almost never wears what he calls his 'monkey' or 'funeral' suit.

'Where's everybody going?' I said as I climbed out of the old Porsche. 'What's going on? You all aren't moving out on me?'

'It's nothing.' Damon said, strangely evasive, eyes darting all over the front yard.

'Damon's in the Washington Boys' Choir at school!' Jannie proudly blurted out. 'He didn't want you to know until he made it for sure. Well, he made it. Damon's a *chorister* now.'

Her brother swatted her on the arm. Not hard, but enough to show he wasn't pleased with Jannie for telling his secret.

'Hey!' Jannie said, and put up her dukes like the little semipro boxer that she is becoming under my watchful eye.

'Hey, hey!' I said, and moved in like a big time referee, like that guy Mills Lane, who does the big pro fights. 'No prizefighting outside the ring. You know the rules of the fight game. Now what's this about a choir?'

'Damon tried out for the Boys' Choir and he was selected,' Nana said, and beamed gloriously as she looked over at Damon. 'He did it all by himself.'

'You sing, too?' I said, and beamed at him as well. 'My, my, my.'

'He could be in Boyz II Men, Daddy. Boyz II Boyz, maybe. He's smoo-ooth and silky. His voice is pure.'

'Is that so, Sister Soul?' I said to my baby girl.

'Zatso.' Jannie continued to prattle as she patted Damon on the back. I could tell she was incredibly proud of him. She was his biggest fan, even if he didn't realize it yet. Some day he would.

Damon finally couldn't hold back a big smile, then he shrugged it off. 'No big thing. I sing all right.'

'*Thousands* of other boys tried out,' Jannie said. 'It *is* a big thing, biggest in your small life, brother.'

'Hundreds,' Damon corrected her. 'Only hundreds of kids tried out. I guess I just got lucky.'

'*Hundreds* of *thousands!*' Jannie gushed, and scooted away before he swatted her like the little gnat she can be sometimes. 'And you were *born* lucky.'

'Can I come to the practice?' I asked. 'I'll be good. I'll be quiet. I won't embarrass anybody too much.'

'If you can spare the time.' Nana threw a neat jab. She sure doesn't need any boxing lessons from me. 'Your busy work schedule and all. If you can spare the time, come along with us.'

'Sure, Dad,' said Damon, finally.

So I came along.

Chapter Thirty-Two

I happily walked the six short blocks to the Sojourner Truth School with Nana and the kids. I wasn't dressed up. They were in their finery, but it didn't matter. There was suddenly a bounce in my step. I took Nana's arm, and she smiled as I tucked her hand into the crook of my arm.

'Now that's better. Seems like old times,' I exclaimed.

'You're such a shameless charmer sometimes,' Nana said and laughed out loud. 'Ever since you were a little boy like Damon. You certainly can be one when you want to.'

'You helped make me what I am, old woman,' I confided to her.

'Proud of it, too. And I'm *so* proud of Damon.'

We arrived at the Sojourner Truth School and went directly to the small auditorium in back. I wondered if Christine might be there, but she wasn't anywhere to be seen. Then I wondered if she already knew Damon had made the Boys' Choir, if he had told her first. I kind of liked the thought that he might have told her. I wanted them to be close. I knew that Damon and Jannie needed a mother, not just a father and great-grandmother.

'We're not too good yet,' Damon informed me, before he left to join the other boys. His face clearly showed the fear and anxiety of possibly being embarrassed. 'This is just our second practice. Mr Dayne says we're horrid as a tubful of castor oil. He's tough as nails, Dad. He makes you stand for an hour straight without moving.'

'Mr Dayne's tougher than you, Daddy, tougher than Ms Johnson,' Jannie said, and grinned wickedly. 'Tough as *nails*.'

I had heard that Nathaniel Dayne was a demanding maestro, the Great Dayne, but that his choirs were among the finest in the country and most of the boys seemed to profit immensely from the dedicated training and discipline. He was already organizing the boys up on the stage. He was a very broad man of below-average height. I guessed he carried about two hundred fifty pounds on his five-foot-seven-inch frame. He wore a black suit with a black shirt buttoned at the collar, no tie. He started the boys off with a few playful verses of 'Three Blind Mice' that didn't sound half-bad.

'I'm really happy for Damon. He looks so proud up there,' I whispered to Nana and Jannie. 'He is a handsome devil, too.'

'Mr Dayne is starting a girls' choir in the fall,' Jannie loud-whispered in my ear. 'You watch. I mean, you *listen*. I'll make it.'

'Go for it, girl,' Nana said, and gave Jannie a hug. She is very good at encouraging others.

Dayne suddenly called out loudly, 'Ugh. I hear a *swoop*. I don't want any swoops here, gentlemen. I want clean diction and pure pitch. I want silver and silk. I do not want *swoops*.'

Out of the corner of my eye, I suddenly saw Christine in the hallway. She was watching Dayne and the boys, but then she looked my way. Her face was principal-serious for just a moment. Then she smiled and winked.

I walked over to see her. Be still my heart.

'That's my boy,' I said with mock proudness as I came up to her. She was dressed in a soft gray pantsuit with a coral-pink blouse. God, I loved seeing her now, being with her, hanging out, doing nothing, the works.

Christine smiled. Actually, she laughed a little at me. 'He does everything so damn well.' She didn't hold back, no matter what. 'I was hoping you might be here, Alex,' she whispered. 'I was just this very minute missing you like crazy. You know that feeling?'

'Yes, that feeling and I are well acquainted.'

We held hands as the choir practiced Bach's 'Jesu, Joy of Man's Desiring.' Everything felt so right, and it was hard to get used to.

'Sometimes . . . I still have this dream about George being shot and dying,' she said as we were standing there. Christine's husband had been murdered in her home, and she had seen him die. It was one of the big reasons she was hesitant about being with me: the fear that I might die in the line of duty; also the fear that I could bring terror and violence into the house.

'I remember everything about the afternoon I heard Maria was shot. It eases with time, but it never goes away.'

Christine knew that. She had figured out the answers to most of her questions, but she liked to talk things through. We were both that way.

'And yet I continue to work here in Southeast. I come to the inner city every day. I could choose a nice school in Maryland or Virginia.'

I nodded. 'Yes, Christine, you do choose to work here.'

'And so do you.'

'And so do I.'

She held my hand a little tighter. 'I guess we were made for each other,' she said. 'Why fight it?'

Chapter Thirty-Three

E arly the next morning I was back in the write-up room at the Seventh District Station working the John Doe homicide. I was the first one in there.

Apparently, no one had noticed Frank Odenkirk as he was leaving the airport. His clothing still hadn't been recovered. The ME reported that he had definitely been sodomized after he'd been killed. As I had suspected, there was no semen. The killer had used a condom. Just as with the Jane Does.

The police commissioner was involved in the Odenkirk case, and was putting added pressure on the department. It was making everyone angry and a little crazy. Chief Pittman was riding his detectives hard, and the only case he seemed interested in was the Odenkirk killing, especially since a suspect in the German tourist murder had been arrested.

At around eleven that morning, Rakeem Powell stopped by my desk. He bent low and whispered, 'Might have something interesting, Alex. Downstairs in the jail, if you've got a minute. Could be a first break on those two murdered girls in Shaw.'

The jail was down a set of steep concrete stairs, just past a tight warren of small interrogation rooms, a holding room and a booking room. All over the ceiling and walls, prisoners had scratched their street names or used black ink from fingerprinting to write the names. This was incredibly dumb of them, since it gave us their street names for our files.

It's purposely kept dark down in the jail. Each cell is six by five feet, with a metal bed and a combination water fountain/toilet. Sneakers had been tossed in the hallways outside several of the cells. It's what experienced prisoners do who don't want to take the laces out of their sneakers. Laces aren't allowed in the jail for safety reasons.

A small-time drug runner and petty thief named Alfred 'Sneak' Streek was seated like the Fresh Prince of DC in one of the holding cells. The street punk looked up at me as I entered his cell. A slicky-sick smirk crossed his face.

Sneak was sporting wraparound sunglasses, dusty dreadlocks, a bright-green and yellow crocheted hat. His white T-shirt had a drawing of Haile Selassie's face and read: HEAD HUNTER. RASTAFARIAN.

'You from the DA's office? I *don't think so*. No dealee, no talkee, my man,' he said to me. 'So get lost.'

Rakeem ignored him as he talked to me. 'Sneak claims to have some useful information about the Glover and Cardinal homicides. He would like us to extend him some courtesy in return for what he claims to know. He's jammed up on a charge that he may have broken into an apartment in Shaw. He was caught coming out of a bedroom window with a Sony TV in his arms. Imagine that. Not very Sneaky of him.'

'I didn't rob no ticky-tacky apartment. I don't even *watch* TV, my man. And I don't see no assistant district attorney present with the *au-tho-rity* to make a deal.'

'Take off your sunglasses,' I said to him.

He ignored me, so I took them off for him. As one well-known street saying goes, 'His eyes were like tombstones.' I could tell at a glance that Sneak wasn't just running drugs anymore; he was using.

I stood across from Sneak in the jail cell and stared him down. He was probably in his early twenties, angry, cynical, lost in space and time. 'If you didn't rob the apartment, then why would you be interested in seeing a lawyer from the district attorney's office? That doesn't make too much sense to me, Alfred. Now here's what I'll do for you and it's a one-time offer, so listen carefully. If I walk out of here, I *don't* come back.'

Sneak half-listened to what I was saying.

'If you give us information that directly helps solve the murders of those two young girls, *then* we will help you on the robbery charges. I'll go to the mat myself. If you don't give up the information then I'm going to leave you in here with Detective Powell and Detective Thurman. You won't get this generous, one-time offer again. That's another promise, and as these detectives know, I always keep my word.'

Sneak still didn't say anything. A glaze was coming over his eyes. He tried to stare *me* down, but I'm usually better at it than the average TV booster.

I finally shrugged a look at Rakeem Powell and Jerome Thurman. 'Okay, fine. Gentlemen, we need to know what he knows about those murdered girls in Shaw. He gets nothing from us when you're finished with him. It's possible that he's involved with the homicides himself. He could even be our killer, and we need to solve this thing fast. You treat him that way until we know differently.'

I started to get up, when suddenly Sneak spoke.

'Back Door Man. He hang at Downing Park. He, Back Door, maybe see who done those girls. That's how he say it at the park. Say he saw the killer. So how you gonna help me?'

I walked out of the cell. 'I told you the deal, Alfred. We solve the case, your information helps, I'll help you.'

Chapter Thirty-Four

Maybe we were close to something. Two Metro cruisers and two unmarked sedans pulled up to the fenced-in entrance of tiny Downing playground in Shaw. Rakeem Powell and Sampson went with me to visit with Joe 'Back Door' Booker, a well-known neighborhood menace.

I knew Back Door by sight and spotted him right away. He was short, no more than five-seven, goateed, and so good with a basketball that he sometimes played in work boots, just to show off. He had on dusty orange construction boots today. Also a faded black nylon jacket and black nylon pants that accordioned at the ankles.

A full-court basketball game was in progress, a fast, high-level game, somewhere between college and pro in terms of athletic ability. The court couldn't have been more basic – black macadam, faded white lines, metal backboards and rims with chain nets.

Players from two or three other teams sat around waiting their turn to play winners. Nylon shorts and pants and the Nike *swoosh* were everywhere. The court was surrounded by four walls of heavy wire fencing and was known as the 'cage.' Everybody looked up as we arrived, Booker included.

'We got next!' Sampson called out.

The players on and off the court exchanged looks and a couple of them grinned at Sampson's one-liner. They knew who we were. The steady *thump, thump, thump* on the game ball hadn't stopped.

Back Door was on the court. It wasn't unusual for his team to hold winners for an entire afternoon. He had been in and out of reformatories and prisons since he was fourteen, but he could play ball. He was taunting another player who was on the court in gray suit pants, high-tops, a bare chest. 'You suck,' said Back Door. 'Take those church pants off. I play you in baseball, tennis, bowling, *any* game – you suck. Stop suckin'.'

Rakeem Powell blew the silver referee's whistle he always carries. Rakeem works as a soccer ref in his spare time. The whistle is unorthodox, but it gets attention in noisy places. The game stopped.

The three of us walked up to Booker, who was standing near the foul circle at one basket. Sampson and I towered over him. But so did most of the players.

It didn't matter, he was still the best ballplayer out there. He could probably beat Sampson and me if we played him two on one.

'Awhh, leave the brother alone. He didn't do nothin',' one of the other, taller men complained in a deep voice. He had prison-style tattoos all over his back and arms. 'He was here playin' ball, man.'

'Door been here *all day*,' said somebody else. 'Door been here for days. Hasn't lost *a game* in days!'

Several of the young men laughed at the playground humor. Sampson turned to the biggest man on the court. 'Shut the hell up. Stop dribbling that rock, too. Two young sisters been murdered. That's why we're here. This is no game with us.'

The dribbler shut up and picked up the game ball. The yard became strangely quiet. We could hear a jump rope striking the sidewalk in a fast rhythm. Three little girls playing just outside the cage were saying, '*Little Miss Pinky dressed in blue, died last night at half past two.*' It was a jump-rope rhyme, sadly true around here.

I put my arm around Booker's shoulder and walked him away from his friends.

Sampson continued to do the talking. 'Booker, this is going to be so fast and easy you and your friends will be laughing your asses off about it before we're back in our cars.'

'Yeah, uh-huh,' said Joseph Booker, trying to be cool in the extreme heat of Sampson's and my glare.

'I'm serious as a heart attack, little man. You saw something that can help us with the murder of Tori Glover and Marion Cardinal. Simple as that. You talk and we walk right back out of here.'

Booker glared up at Sampson as if he were staring down the sun. 'I didn't see shit. Like Luki say, I been here for days. I never lose to these sorry chumps.'

I held up my hand, palm out, inches from his squashed moonpie face.

'I'm on a stopwatch here, Booker, so please don't interrupt my flow. I promise you, two minutes and we're out of here. Now here's what's in it for you. One, we go away and you gentlemen finish your game. Two, Detectives Powell and Sampson will owe you one. Three, a hundred dollars now for your time and trouble.

'The clock is ticking,' I said. '*Tick, tick, tick*. Easy money.'

He finally nodded and held out his hand.

'I seen those two girls get picked up. Around two, three in the mornin' on E Street. I *didn't* see no driver, nobody's face or nothin'. Too dark, man. But he was driving a cab. Look like purple-and-blue gypsy. Somethin' like that. Girls get into the back of the cab, drive off.'

'Is that it?' I asked him. 'I don't want to have to come back here later. Break up your game again.'

Booker considered what I'd said, then spoke again. 'Cab driver a white man. Seen his arm stickin' out the side window. Aint' no white boys drivin' the night shift in Shaw, least none I seen.'

I nodded, waited a bit, then I smiled at the other players. 'Gentlemen, as you were. Play ball.'

Thump, thump, thump.

Swish.

Booker could really play ball.

Chapter Thirty-Five

The new pieces of information gave us something to run with. We'd done an incredible amount of thankless street work and something had finally paid off. We had the color of the gypsy cab that had picked up the girls around the time of the murders. The fact that the driver was white was the best lead we had so far.

Sampson and I drove to my house, rather than back to the station. It would be easier to work on the new leads from Fifth Street. It took me about five minutes to come up with more information from a contact at the Taxi Commission. No fleets operating in DC currently had purple-and-blue cabs. That probably meant the car was an illegal gypsy, as Booker had said. I learned that a company called Vanity Cabs had once used purple-and-blue cars, but Vanity had been out of business since '95. The Taxi Commission rep said that half a dozen or so of the old cars might still be on the street. Originally, the fleet had been fifteen cars, which wasn't that many, even if all of them were still around, which was highly doubtful.

Sampson called all the cab companies that regularly did business in Southeast, especially around Shaw. According to their records, there were only three white drivers who had been working that night.

We were working in the kitchen. Sampson was on the phone and I was using the computer. Nana had fixed fresh coffee and also set out fruit and half a pecan pie.

Rakeem Powell called the house at around 4:15. I picked up. 'Alex, Pittman's watchdog is sniffing around here something fierce. Fred Cook wants to know what you and Sampson are working on this afternoon. Jerome told him the Odenkirk murder.'

I nodded and said, 'If the murders in Southeast are connected in any way, that's the truth.'

'One more thing,' Rakeem said, before he let me go. 'I checked with Motor Vehicles. Might be something good for us. A purple gypsy got a summons for running a stop sign around one in the morning over in Eckington, near the university, Second Street. Maybe that's where our boy lives.'

I clapped my hands and congratulated Rakeem. Our long hours working the Jane Doe cases were finally beginning to pay off.

Maybe we were about to catch the Weasel.

Chapter Thirty-Six

He had been much more careful lately. The visit to Washington by George Bayer, Famine, had been a warning, a shot over his head, and Shafer had taken it seriously. The other players could be as dangerous as he was. It was they who had taught him how to kill, not the other way round. Famine, Conqueror, and War were not to be underestimated, especially if he wanted to win the game.

The day after Famine's visit, the others had informed him that Bayer had come to Washington, that he was being watched. He supposed that was his *second* warning. His activity had frightened them and now they were retaliating. It was all part of the game.

After work that night, he headed to the hideaway in Eckington. He spotted what looked like a half-dozen or so policemen canvassing the street.

He immediately suspected the other Horsemen. They had turned him in, after all. Or were they playing a mind game with him? What were the cops doing here?

He parked the Jaguar several blocks away, then headed toward the hideaway and garage on foot. He had to check this out. He had on a pin-striped suit, city shirt, and tie. He knew he looked respectable enough. He carried a leather brief-case, and definitely looked like a businessman coming home late.

Two African-American policemen were doing door-to-door questioning on Uhland Terrace. This wasn't good – the police were less than five blocks from the hideaway.

Why were they here? His brain was reeling, adrenaline rushing through his nervous system like a flash flood. Maybe this had nothing to do with him, but he couldn't be too careful. He definitely suspected the other players, especially George Bayer. *But why?* Was this the way they planned to end the game, by bringing him down?

When the two policemen up ahead disappeared down a side street of Uhland, Shafer decided to stop at one of the brownstones where they'd been asking questions. It was a small risk, but he needed to know what was happening.

A couple of old men were seated on the stoop. An ancient radio played an Orioles baseball game.

'They ask you about some kind of trouble in the neighborhood?' Shafer asked the men in as casual a tone as he could manage. 'They stopped me up the block.'

One of the men just stared at him, terminally pissed off, but the other one nodded and spoke up. 'Sure did, mister. Lookin' for a cab, purple-and-blue gypsy. Connected to some killings, they say. Though I don't recall seeing any purple ones lately. Used to be a cab company called Vanity. You remember, Earl? They had the purple people-eaters.'

'That was some years ago,' the other man said, nodding. 'They went belly up.'

'I guess they were Metro police. Never showed me any ID, though,' Shafer said, and shrugged. He was being careful to speak with an American accent, which he was good at imitating.

'Detectives Cross and Sampson.' The more talkative of the two men volunteered their names. 'Detective Cross showed me his badge. It was the real deal.'

'Oh, I'm sure it was,' Shafer said, and saluted the two old men. 'Good to see the police in the neighborhood, actually.'

'You got that right.'

'Have a nice night.'

'Yeah, you too.'

Shafer circled back to his car, and drove to the embassy. He went straight to his office, where he felt safe and protected. He calmed himself, then turned on his computer and did a thorough search on DC detectives named Cross and Sampson. He found more than he hoped for, especially on Detective Cross.

He thought about how the new developments might change the game. Then he sent out a message to the Horsemen. He told them about Cross and Sampson – that the detectives had decided to 'play the game.' So, naturally, he had plans for them too.

Chapter Thirty-Seven

Zachary Scott Taylor was a thorough, analytical, and very hard-nosed reporter on the *Washington Post*. I respected the hell out of him. His relentless cynicism and skepticism were a little too much for me to take on a daily basis; otherwise we might have been even closer friends. But we had a good relationship and I trusted him more than I did most journalists.

I met him that night at the Irish Times, on F Street, near Union Station. The restaurant-bar is in an anachronistic stand-alone brick building surrounded by modern office structures. Zachary called it 'a dumpy little toilet of a bar, a perfect place for us to meet.'

In the time-honored tradition of Washington, I have occasionally been one of his trusted sources, and I was about to tell the reporter something important. I hoped he would agree, and that he could convince his editors at the *Post* about the story.

'How're Master Damon and Ms Jannie?' Zachary asked as he sat across from me in a darkened corner under an old photo of a stern-looking man in a black top hat. Zachary is tall, gaunt and thin; he remembered the man in the old photo a little bit. Zachary always talks too fast – with the words running into one another – *How'reMasterDamonandMsJannie?* There was just a hint of Virginia softening his accent.

The waitress eventually came over to our table. He ordered black coffee and I had the same.

'Two coffees?' she asked, to make sure she'd heard us right.

'Two of your very *finest* coffees,' Zachary said.

'This isn't Starbucks, y'know,' she said.

I smiled at the waitress's brio, then at what Zachary had said – his first words to me. I'd probably mentioned my kids' names to him once, but he had an encyclopedic memory for all kinds of disparate information.

'You should go get yourself a couple of kids, Zachary,' I told him, smiling broadly.

He glanced up at an ancient whirring ceiling fan that looked as if it might suddenly spin out of the ceiling. It seemed a nice metaphor for modern life in America, an aging infrastructure threatening to spin out of control.

'Don't have a wife yet, Alex. Still looking for the right woman,' said Zachary.

'Well, okay then, get yourself a wife first, then get a couple of kids. Might take the edge off your neuroses.'

The waitress placed steaming cups of black coffee in front of us. 'Will that be *all*?' she said. She shook her head, then left us.

'Maybe I don't want the edge taken off my rather stunning neurotic behavior. Maybe I believe that's what makes me such a damn fine reporter, and that without it my work would be pedestrian shit, and then I'd be nothing in the eyes of Don Graham and company.'

I sipped the day or two old coffee. 'Except that if you had a couple of kids, you could never be nothing.'

Zachary squinted one eye shut and smacked the left side of his lips. He was a very animated thinker.

'Except if the kids didn't love, or even like me very much.'

'And you don't consider yourself lovable? But actually you are, Zachary. Trust me. You're just fine. Your kids would adore the hell out of you and you would adore them. You'd have a mutual adoration society.'

He finally laughed and clapped his hands loudly. We usually laugh a good bit when we're together.

'So will you marry me and have my children?' He grinned at me over the top of his steaming cup. 'This is a pick-up joint, after all. Singles from the Bureau of Labor Statistics and the Government Printing Office come here, hoping to bed a staffer from Kennedy's or Glenn's.'

'Actually, it's the best offer I've had all day. Who called this meeting anyway? Why are we here at this dive, drinking really bad coffee?'

Taylor slurped his. 'Coffee's fairly strong, isn't it? That's something to be thankful for. What's up, Alex?'

'You interested in another Pulitzer?' I asked him.

He pretended to think it over, but his eyes lit up. 'Well, I might be. You see, I need to balance the look of my mantelpiece. One of my dates told me that. Never did see the young woman again. She worked for Gingrich, as a matter of fact.'

For the next forty-five minutes or so, I told Zachary exactly what I thought was up. I told him about one hundred and fourteen unsolved murders in Southeast and parts of Northeast DC. I detailed the contrasting investigation of the cases of Frank Odenkirk and the German tourist in Georgetown, and the black teenagers Tori Glover and Marion Cardinal. I filled him in on the chief of detectives, his proclivities and his biases, at least my perception of them. I even admitted that I disliked Pittman intensely, and Zachary knows I'm not that way about too many folks who don't murder for a living.

He shook his head back and forth, back and forth, while I talked, and didn't stop when I was finished. 'Not that I doubt any of what you're saying, but do you have any documentation?' he asked.

'You're such a stickler for details,' I said. 'Reporters are such wusses when you come right down to it.'

I reached down under my seat and lifted up two thick manila folders. His eyes brightened.

'This should help with the story. Copies of sixty-seven of the unsolved homicide reports. Also a copy of the Glover and Cardinal investigation. Note the number of detectives assigned to each. Check the case hours logged. You'll see a huge discrepancy. That's all I could get my hands on – but the other reports exist.'

'Why would this be happening, this malicious neglect?' he asked me.

I nodded at the wisdom of his question. 'I'll give you the most cynical reason,' I said. 'Some Metro cops like to refer to Southeast as "self-cleaning ovens." That sound like the beginnings of malicious neglect to you? Some victims in Southeast are called NHIs – that's No Humans Involved. The latter is a phrase used by Chief Pittman.'

Zachary quickly leafed through the reports. Then he shook my hand. 'I'm going home to my lonely abode, made bearable only by my single Pulitzer. I have all these fascinating police files on NHIs to read, then hopefully a chilling news exposé to write. We'll see. As always, it's been a party, Alex. My best to

Damon, Jannie, Nana Mama. I'd like to meet them one day. Put some faces with the names.'

'Come to the next Washington Boys' Choir performance,' I said. 'All our faces will be there. Damon is a *chorister*.'

Chapter Thirty-Eight

I worked that night until eight thirty, and then I drove to Kinkead's in Foggy Bottom to meet up with Christine. Kinkead's is one of our favorite restaurants and also an excellent place to listen to jazz, and snuggle up to each other.

I sat at the bar and enjoyed the sounds of Hilton Felton and Ephrain Woolfolk until Christine arrived, coming from an event at school. She was right on time, though. She is punctual. Very considerate. Perfect in almost every way, at least in my eyes. *Yes, I will be your wife.*

'You hungry? Want to go to a table?' I asked, after we had hugged as if we'd been separated for many years and thousands of miles.

'Let's just sit here at the bar for a few minutes. You mind?' she asked. Her breath smelled lightly of spearmint. Her face was so soft and smooth that I *had* to lightly cup it in both my hands.

'Nothing I'd rather do in the whole wide world,' I said.

Christine ordered a Harvey's Bristol Cream and I had a mug of beer, and we talked as the music flowed over, around, and right through our bodies. It had been a long day, and I needed this.

'I've been waiting for this all day long. I couldn't wait. Am I being too corny and romantic again?' I said, and grinned.

'Not for me. Never too corny, never too romantic. That won't happen, Alex.' Christine smiled. I loved to see her like this. Her eyes twinkled and danced. I sometimes get lost in her eyes, fall into the deep pools, all that good stuff that people yearn for but few seem to get nowadays, which is sad.

She stared back and my fingers lightly caressed her cheek. Then I held her under her chin. 'Stardust' was playing. It's one of my favorite songs, even under ordinary circumstances. I wondered if Hilton and Ephrain were playing the tune for us, and when I looked at him, Hilton gave me a sly wink.

We moved closer together and danced in place. I could feel her heart beating; feel it right up against my chest. We must have stayed like that for ten or fifteen minutes. No one at the bar seemed to notice; no one bothered us – offered to refill our drinks, or escort us to our table. I guess they understood.

'I really like Kinkead's,' Christine whispered. 'But you know what? I'd rather be home with you tonight. Some place a little more private. I'll make you eggs, whatever you'd like. Is that all right? Do you mind?'

'No, I don't mind at all. That's a perfect idea. Let's go.'

I paid our bar bill, made my regrets about the dinner reservation. Then we went to Christine's.

'We'll start with dessert,' she said and smiled wickedly. I liked that about her too.

Chapter Thirty-Nine

I had been waiting a long time to be in love again, but this was worth it and then some. I grabbed hold of Christine as soon as we were inside her house. My hands began to trace her waist, her hips; they played over her breasts, her shoulders, then touched the delicate bones of her face. We liked to do this slowly, no need to rush. I kissed her lips, then gently scratched her back and shoulders. I pulled her closer, closer.

'You have the gentlest touch,' she whispered against my cheek. 'I could do this all night. Be just like this. You want some wine? Anything? I'll give you anything I have.'

'I love you,' I told her, still lightly scratching her lower back. 'We *will* do this forever. I have no doubt of it.'

'I love you so much,' she whispered, then I heard her breath softly catch. 'So please, try to be careful, Alex. At work.'

'Okay, I will. But not tonight,' I said.

Christine smiled. 'Not tonight. Tonight you can live dangerously. We both will. You *are* handsome, and debonair for a policeman.'

'Or even for an international jewel thief.'

I swept her up and carried her down the hallway to the bedroom. 'Mmm. Strong, too,' she said. She flicked on a hall lamp as we passed. It was just enough light to see where we were going.

'How about a trip somewhere?' I said. 'I need to get away.'

'That sounds good. Yes – before school starts. Anywhere. Take me away from all this.'

Her room smelled of fresh flowers. There were pink and red roses on the nightstand. She has a passion for flowers and gardening.

'You planned this all along, didn't you?' I said. 'You *did*. This is entrapment. You sly girl.'

'I was thinking about it all day,' she confessed and sighed contentedly. 'I thought about being with you all day, in my office, in the hallways, the schoolyard, and then in my car on the way to the restaurant. I've been having erotic day-dreams about you all day.'

'I hope I can live up to them.'

'You will. No doubt about it.'

I took off her black silk blouse in one sweeping motion. I put my mouth to a breast, pulling at it through her demi bra. She was wearing a brushed leather skirt and I didn't take it off, just slowly pushed it up. I knelt and kissed her ankles, the tops of her feet, then slowly came up her long legs. She massaged my neck, my back and shoulders.

'You *are* dangerous tonight,' she said. 'That's a good thing.'

'Sexual healing.'

'Mmm, please. Heal me all over, Doctor.'

She bit down hard into my shoulder, then even harder into the side of my neck. We were both breathing fast. She moved against me then opened her legs for me. I moved inside her. She felt incredibly warm. The bedsprings began to sing and the headboard rocked into the wall.

She pushed her hair to one side, behind an ear. I love the way she does that.

'You feel so good. Oh, Alex, don't stop, don't stop, don't stop,' she whispered.

I did as I was told and I loved every moment, every movement we made together, and I even wondered for a second if we had made a baby.

Chapter Forty

Much later that night we rustled up some eggs with Vidalia onions and cheddar and mozzarella cheeses, opened a nice bottle of Pinot Noir. Then I started a fire, in August, with the air-conditioner turned up high.

We sat in front of the fire, laughed and talked, and planned a quick trip away from Washington. We settled on Bermuda, and Christine asked if we could bring Nana and the kids. I felt as if my life were changing fast, going to a new good place. If only I could get lucky and catch the Weasel somehow. That could be the perfect ending to my career with the Metro police.

I went home to Fifth Street late, got in just before three. I didn't want Damon and Jannie to wake in the morning and not find me there. I was up by eight o'clock the next morning, bounding downstairs to the delectable smells of fresh coffee and Nana's world-famous sticky buns.

The terrible twosome were just about ready to dash off to the Sojourner Truth School where they were taking advanced classes in the morning. They looked like a pair of shiny angels. I didn't get to feel this good very often, so I was going all the way with it.

'How was your date last night, Daddy?' Jannie said, making her biggest goo-goo eyes at me.

'Who said I had a date?' I made room for her on my knee. She ate a bite of the humongous sweet bun Nana had set on my plate.

'Let's just say a little birdie told me,' she chirped.

'Uh-huh. Little birdie makes good sticky buns,' I said. 'My date was pretty good. How was yours? You had a date, right? Didn't sit home alone, did you?'

'Your date was *pretty* good? You came home with the milkman.' Jannie laughed out loud. Damon was giggling, too. She can get us all going when she wants to; she's been that way since she was a baby.

'Jannie Cross,' Nana said, but she let it go. There was no use trying to make Jannie act like a typical seven year old at this point. She was too bright, too outspoken, too full of life and fun. Besides, we have a philosophy as a family: He or she who laughs, lasts.

'How come you two don't live together first?' Jannie asked. 'That's what they all do in the movies and on TV.'

I found myself grinning and starting to frown at the same time. 'Don't get me going on the silly stuff they do on TV and in the movies, little girl. They always get it wrong. Christine and I are going to get married soon, and *then* we'll all live together.'

'You *sure* you asked her?' they all exclaimed.

'I did.'

'And she said yes?'

'Why do you all look so surprised? Of course she said yes. Who could resist being a part of this family?'

'Hooray!' Jannie whooped loudly. I could tell she meant it from the bottom of her little heart.

'Hooray!' echoed Nana. 'Thank God. Oh, thank God.'

'I agree,' Damon piped in. 'It's time that we had a more normal life around here.'

Everybody was congratulating me for several minutes until Jannie finally said: 'I have to go to *school* now, *Pa-pa*. I wouldn't want to disappoint Ms Johnson by being late, now would I? Here's your morning newspaper.'

Jannie handed me the *Washington Post* and my heart jumped a little in my chest. This was a good day indeed. I saw Zachary Taylor's story in the bottom right of the front page. It wasn't the banner headline it deserved to be, but he'd gotten the story on page one.

Potential scandal over unsolved murders in Southeast DC. Possible racial bias seen in police activity.

'Potential scandal indeed,' Nana said, and squeegeed her lower face. 'Genocide always is, isn't it?'

Chapter Forty-One

I entered the station house around eight and Chief Pittman's assistant-lackey came scurrying up to me. Old Fred Cook had been a bad detective once, and now was an equally bad and devious administrator, but Fred was as smooth a buttkisser as could be found in the department or anywhere else in Washington.

'The chief of detectives wants to see you in his office, post-haste. It's important,' Fred told me. 'Better move it.'

I nodded at him and tried to keep my good mood intact. 'Of course it is, he's the chief of detectives. You have any helpful hints for me, Fred? You happen to know what this is about, what I should expect?'

'It's a big deal,' said Cook, unhelpful and happy about it. 'That's about all I can tell you, Alex.'

He walked away, leaving me hanging. I could feel the bile rising in my throat. My good mood had already deserted me.

I walked down the creaking hardwood floors of the hallway to the Jefe's office. I had no idea what to expect; but I sure wasn't prepared for what I found.

I immediately thought about what Damon had said that morning: *It's time that we had a more normal life around here.*

Sampson was seated inside the chief's office. Rakeem Powell and Jerome Thurman were both in there, too.

'Come in, Dr Cross.' Chief Pittman beckoned with an outstretched hand. 'Please come in. We've been waiting for you to arrive.'

'What is this?' I said, pulling up a chair next to Sampson's, whispering in his ear.

'Don't know yet, but it's not too good,' he said. 'The Jefe hasn't said one word to us. Looks like the canary who ate the cat, though.'

Pittman came around in front of his desk and leaned his ample buttocks back against it. He seemed particularly full of himself, and shit, this morning. His mousy gray hair was plastered back and looked like a helmet on his bullet head.

'I can tell you what you want to know, Detective Cross,' he said. 'In fact, I didn't want to tell these other detectives until you got here. As of this morning, Detectives Sampson, Thurman, and Powell have been suspended from active duty. They have been working on cases outside the auspices of this department. Evidence is still being gathered about the full extent of these activities; and also, if any other detectives were involved.'

I started to speak up, but Sampson grabbed my arm – hard. 'Be cool, Alex.'

Pittman looked at the three of them. 'Detectives Sampson, Thurman, Powell, you can go. Your union representative has been informed of the situation. You have questions, or issues with my decision, inform your representative.'

Sampson's mouth was set hard. He didn't say a word to the Jefe, though. He got up and left the office. Thurman and Powell trailed close behind him. Neither of them spoke to Pittman either. The three of them were hardworking, dedicated detectives, and I couldn't stand to watch this happen.

I wondered why the Jefe had spared me so far. I also wondered why Shawn Moore wasn't there. The cynical answer was that Pittman wanted to set us against one another, to make us believe that Shawn had spoken against us.

Pittman reached across his desk and picked up a folded copy of the *Washington Post*. 'You happen to see this article today? Bottom right?'

He pushed the newspaper toward me. I had to catch the paper to keep it from falling to the floor.

'Scandal over unsolved murders in Southeast,' I said. 'Yes, I did. I read it at home.'

'I'll bet you did. Mr Taylor, of the *Post*, quotes unidentified sources in the police department. You have anything to do with the article?' Pittman asked and stared hard at me.

'Why would I talk to the *Washington Post*?' I asked a question in answer to his. 'I told you about the problem in Southeast. I think a repeat killer may be working there. Why go any farther with it than that? Suspending those detectives sure won't help solve the problem. Especially if this sicko is approaching rage, which I believe he is.'

'I don't buy this serial-killer story. I don't see any pattern that's consistent. No one else does but you.' Pittman shook his head and frowned. He was hot, angry, trying to control himself.

He reached out his hand toward me again. His fingers were like uncooked sausages. He lowered his voice almost to a whisper. 'I'd like to fuck you over good, and I will. But for now, it wouldn't be expedient to pull you off the Odenkirk homicide. It wouldn't *look* good, and I suspect it would end up in the *Post*, too.

I look forward to your daily reports on the so-called John Doe case. You know, it is time you got some of those unsolved murders off the books. You'll report directly to me on this. I'm going to be all over you, Cross. Any questions?'

I quickly left Chief Pittman's office. Before I hit him.

Chapter Forty-Two

S ampson, Thurman, and Rakeem Powell had already left the building by the time I got out of the Jefe's office. I felt as if I could easily go postal. I nearly walked back inside Pittman's office and wiped up the floor with him.

I went to my desk and thought about what to do next, tried to calm myself down before I did anything rash and stupid. I thought about my responsibilities to the people in Southeast and that helped me. Still, I almost went back after Pittman.

I called Christine and let out some steam. Then, spur of the moment, I asked if she could get away for our long weekend, possibly starting on Thursday night. Christine said that she could go. I went and filled out a vacation form and left it on Fred Cook's desk. It was the last thing he and Pittman would expect from me. But I'd already decided the best thing would be to get away from here, cool down, then decide on a plan to move forward.

As I headed out of the building, another detective stopped me. 'They're over at Hart's bar,' he said. 'Sampson said to tell you they reserved a seat for you.'

Hart's is a very seedy, very popular gin mill on Second Street. It isn't a cops' bar, which is why some of us like it. It was eleven in the morning and the bar room was already crowded, lively, even friendly.

'Here he is!' Jerome Thurman saluted me with a half-full beer mug as I walked inside. Half-a-dozen other detectives and friends were there, too. The word had gotten around fast about the suspensions.

There was a whole lot of laughter and shouting going on. 'It's a bachelor's party!' Sampson said, and grinned. 'Got you, sugar. With a little help from Nana. You should see the look on your face!'

For the next hour and a half, friends kept arriving at Hart's. By noon the bar was full, and then the regular customers started arriving for their lunch-hour nips. The owner, Mike Hart, was in his glory. I hadn't really thought about a bachelor's party, but now that I was in the middle of one, I was glad it happened. A lot of men still guard their emotions and feelings, but not so much at a bachelor's party, at least not at a good one thrown by the people closest to you.

This was a good one. The suspensions that were handed down earlier that morning were mostly forgotten for a few hours. I was congratulated and hugged more times than I could count, and even kissed once or twice. Everybody was calling me 'sugar,' following Sampson's lead. The 'love' word was used, and overused. I was roasted and toasted in sentimental speeches that seemed hilarious at the time. Just about everybody had too much to drink.

By four in the afternoon, Sampson and I were steadying each other, making our way into the blinding daylight on Second Street. Mike Hart himself had called us a cab.

For a brief, clear moment, I was reminded of the purple-and-blue gypsy cab we were looking for – but then the thought evaporated into the nearly white sunlight.

'Sugar,' Sampson whispered against my skull as we were climbing into our cab. 'I love you more than life itself. It's true. I love your kids, love your Nana, love your wife-to-be, the lovely Christine. Take us home,' he said to the driver. 'Alex is getting married.'

'And he's the best man,' I said to the driver, who smiled.

'Yes, I am,' said Sampson, 'the very best.'

Chapter Forty-Three

On Thursday night, Shafer played The Four Horsemen again. He was locked inside his study, but through the early part of the night he could hear the sounds of his family throughout the house. He felt intensely isolated; he was nervous, jittery, and angry for no apparent reason.

While he waited to log on with the other players, he found himself thinking back to the wild car ride through Washington. He relived a particular feeling over and over: The imagined moment of sudden impact with an unmovable object. He saw it as blinding light, and physical objects, and *himself*, shattering like glass and then becoming part of the universe again. Even the pain he would feel would be part of the reassembling of matter into other fascinating forms and shapes.

I am suicidal, he finally thought. *It's just a matter of time. I really am Death.*

When it was exactly nine o'clock, he began to type in a message on his computer. The Horsemen were online, waiting for his response to the visit and warning by George Bayer. He didn't want to disappoint them. What they had done had made him more enthusiastic about playing the game. He wrote:

STRANGELY, DEATH WASN'T SURPRISED WHEN FAMINE APPEARED IN WASHINGTON. OF COURSE HE HAD EVERY RIGHT TO COME. JUST AS DEATH COULD GO TO DORKING, OR SINGAPORE, OR MANILA, OR KINGSTON, AND PERHAPS DEATH WILL PAY ONE OF YOU A VISIT SOON.

THAT'S THE BEAUTY OF THE GAME WE PLAY – ANYTHING CAN HAPPEN.

ULTIMATELY, THE ISSUE IS TRUST, ISN'T IT? DO I TRUST THAT YOU WILL ALLOW ME TO CONTINUE TO PLAY THE FANTASY GAME AS I WISH? AFTER ALL, THAT IS WHAT MAKES THE GAME DISTINCTIVE AND ALLURING, THE FREEDOM WE EXPERIENCE.

THAT *IS* THE GAME NOW, ISN'T IT? WE HAVE EVOLVED INTO SOMETHING NEW. WE HAVE RAISED THE TABLE STAKES. SO LET'S HAVE SOME REAL EXCITEMENT, FELLOW HORSEMEN. I HAVE A FEW IDEAS TO TRY OUT ON YOU. EVERYTHING IS IN THE SPIRIT OF THE GAME. NO UNNECESSARY RISKS WILL BE TAKEN.

LET'S PLAY THE GAME AS IF OUR LIVES DEPENDED ON IT.

PERHAPS MINE ALREADY DOES?

AS I TOLD YOU – WE HAVE TWO NEW PLAYERS. THEY ARE WASHINGTON DETECTIVES NAMED ALEX CROSS AND JOHN SAMPSON. WORTHY OPPONENTS. I'M WATCHING THEM, BUT I CAN'T HELP WONDERING WHETHER SOON THEY'LL BE WATCHING ME.

LET ME TELL YOU ABOUT A FANTASY SCENARIO THAT I'VE CREATED TO WELCOME THEM TO OUR GAME. I'M SENDING PICTURES NOW – DETECTIVES CROSS AND SAMPSON.

Chapter Forty-Four

It took us a day to get organized for our trip, but everybody seemed to enjoy the spontaneity, and also the special treat that we would all be together on a vacation for the first time. And so, Damon, Jannie, Nana, Christine, and I left DC in the afternoon and arrived in high spirits at Bermuda International Airport late on Thursday evening, the twenty-fifth of August.

I definitely wanted to be out of Washington for a few days. The Mr Smith murder chase had been followed too quickly by the Jane Doe investigation. I needed a rest. I had a friend who was part owner of a hotel in Bermuda, and it wasn't a particularly long airplane ride. It was perfect for us.

One scene from the airport will always stick in my mind – Christine singing 'Ja-da, ja-da' with Jannie stuck at her side. I couldn't help thinking that they looked like mother and daughter and that touched me deeply. They were so affectionate and playful, so natural. It was a mind-photo for me to have and to hold. One of those moments that I knew I'd never forget, even as I watched the two of them dancing and singing as if they'd known each other forever.

We were blessed with extraordinarily good weather for our holiday. It was sunny and blue-skied every day, morning until nightfall, when the sky turned a magical combination of reds, oranges, and purples. The days belonged to all of us, but especially the kids. We went swimming and snorkeling at Elbow Beach and Horseshoe Bay, and then raced mopeds along the picturesque Middle and Harbor Roads.

The nights belonged to Christine and me, and we made the most of them. We hit all the best spots: the Terrace Bar at the Palm Reef, the Gazebo Lounge at the Princess, the Clay House Inn, Once Upon a Table in Hamilton, Horizons in Paget. I loved being with her and that thought kept drifting through my mind. I felt that what we shared had been strengthened because I had backed off and given her time and space. And I felt whole again. I kept remembering the very first time I had seen her in the schoolyard at Sojourner Truth. *She's the one, Alex.* That thought still played in my head too.

We sat at the Terrace Bar overlooking the city and harbor of Hamilton. It was dotted with small islands, white sails, ferries back and forth to Warwick and Paget. We held hands and I couldn't stop staring into her eyes, didn't want to.

'Big thoughts?' she finally said.

'I've been thinking a lot about going into private practice again,' I told her. 'I think it might be the best thing to do.'

She stared into my eyes. 'I don't want you to do it for me, Alex. Please don't make me the cause of your leaving your job with the police. I know you love it. Most days you do.'

'The job has been tearing at me lately. Pittman isn't just a difficult boss, I think he's a bad guy. What happened to Sampson and the others is just bullshit. They were working unsolved cases on their own time. I'm tempted to give the story to Zach Taylor at the *Post*. People would riot if they knew the truth. Which is why I *won't* give it to the *Post*.'

She listened and tried to help but she didn't push, and I appreciated that. 'It does sound like a terrible, complicated, nasty mess, Alex. I'd like to punch out Pittman, too. He's choosing politics over protecting people. I'm sure you'll know what to do when the time is right.'

The next morning, I found her walking in the garden, with tropical flowers strewn in her hair. She looked radiant, even more than usual, and I fell in love all over again.

'There's an old saying I've been hearing since I was a little girl,' she told me as I joined her. 'If you have only two pennies, buy a loaf of bread with one, and a lily with the other.'

I kissed her hair, in between the flowers. I kissed her sweet lips, her cheeks, the hollow in her throat.

The kids and I went back to Horseshoe Bay beach early that afternoon. They couldn't get enough of the deep blue sea, swimming, snorkeling, building sand castles, and of course it was almost time to start school again so everything about our vacation was extra special and intense.

Christine took a moped trip into Hamilton to pick up mementos for a few of the teachers at Sojourner Truth. We all waved until she was out of sight on Middle Road. Then back into the water!

Around five o'clock, Damon, Jannie, and I finally returned to the Belmont Hotel, which sat like a sentinel on lush green hills framed by china-blue skies. All around, everywhere we looked, were pastel-colored cottages with white roofs. Nana was sitting out on the porch, talking to a couple of her new best friends. Paradise regained, I thought, and felt something deep and sacred coming back to life inside me.

As I stared out at the cloudless blue sky, I regretted that Christine wasn't there to share it. I actually missed her in just that short a time. I hugged Jannie and Damon and we were all smiling at the obvious. We loved being here together and we were so damn fortunate to have one another.

'You miss her,' Jannie whispered. It was a statement, not a question. 'That's good, Daddy. That's the way it should be, right.'

When Christine still hadn't returned by six o'clock, I struggled between conflicting thoughts of waiting for her at the hotel or driving into Hamilton myself. Maybe she'd had an accident. *Those damn mopeds*, I thought, having found them fun and perfectly safe just the afternoon before.

I finally spotted a tall, slender woman entering through the front gates of the Belmont, walking against a background of hibiscus and oleander. I sighed in relief, but as I started down the front stairs, I saw that it wasn't Christine.

Christine still hadn't returned, or called the hotel, by six thirty. Or by seven o'clock.

I finally called the police.

Chapter Forty-Five

Inspector Patrick Busby from the Hamilton PD arrived at the Belmont Hotel around seven thirty. He was a small, balding man and from a distance he looked to be in his late fifties or sixties. As he approached the front porch, I could tell he was no more than forty, around the same age as me.

He listened to my story, then said that visitors often lost track of time and themselves in Bermuda. There were also occasional moped accidents on the Middle Road. He promised me that Christine would show up soon with a mild 'road rash,' or a 'slightly turned ankle.'

I wouldn't have any of it. She was always punctual, or at the very least, she would have called.

I knew that somehow she'd call if she had a minor accident. So the inspector and I rode together between the hotel and Hamilton, and then we toured the streets of the capital city, particularly Front and Reid Streets. I was silent and solemn-faced as I stared out of the car, hoping to get a glimpse of Christine shopping on some side street, forgetful of the hour. But we didn't see her anywhere, and she still hadn't called the hotel.

When she hadn't turned up by nine, Inspector Busby reluctantly agreed that Christine might be missing. He asked a lot of questions that showed me he was a decent cop. He wanted to know if we'd had any kind of argument or disagreement.

'I'm a homicide detective in Washington, DC,' I finally told him. I'd been holding it back because I didn't want this to get territorial. 'I've been involved with high-profile cases involving mass murders in the past. I've known some very bad men. There might be a connection. I hope not, but that could be.'

'I see,' Busby said. He was such a precise, neat man, with his thin pencil mustache. He looked more like a fussy schoolteacher than a cop, more like a psychologist than I did. 'Are there any other surprises I should know about, Detective Cross?' he asked.

'No, that's it. But you see why I'm worried, and why I called you. I'm working on a series of nasty murders in Washington right now.'

'Yes, I see a reason for your concern now. I will put out a missing persons report forthwith.'

I sighed heavily, then went upstairs and talked to the kids and Nana. I tried my best not to alarm them, but Damon and Jannie started to cry. And then Nana did, too.

We had learned nothing more about Christine or her whereabouts by midnight. Inspector Busby finally left the hotel at quarter past twelve. He was kind actually, and considerate enough to give me his home number; he asked me to call right away if I heard from Christine. Then he said my family and I would be in his prayers.

At three, I was still up and pacing my hotel room on the third floor, and doing some praying myself. I had just gotten off the phone with Quantico. The FBI was cross-checking all of my homicide cases to see if anyone I'd investigated had connections with Bermuda. They were concentrating on the current series of unsolved murders in Southeast. I'd faxed them my profile on the Weasel.

I didn't have any logical reason to suspect the killer might be here in Bermuda, and yet I feared that he might be. It was just the kind of feeling that the Jefe had been rejecting about the murders in Southeast.

I understood that the Bureau probably wouldn't get back to me until later in the morning. I was tempted to call friends at Interpol, but I held off . . . And then I called Interpol too.

The hotel room was filled with mahogany Queen Anne furniture and wicker, and had dusty-pink carpets. It felt empty, and lonely. I stood like a ghost before tall, water-stained dormer windows and stared out at shifting black shapes against the moonlit sky and remembered how Christine felt in my arms. I felt incredibly helpless and alone without her. I also couldn't believe this had happened.

I hugged myself tightly and became aware of an incredible pain all around my heart. The tightening pain was like a solid column that went from my chest all the way up into my head. I could see her face, her beautiful smile. I remembered dancing with her one night at the Rainbow Room in New York, and dinners at Kinkead's in Washington, and one special night at her place when we'd laughed and thought maybe we'd made a baby. Was Christine out there somewhere on the island? She had to be. I prayed again that she was safe. She had to be safe. I refused to have any other thought for more than a couple of seconds.

The telephone in the room rang, a short burst, at a little past four in the morning.

My heart was stuck in my throat. My skin crawled, felt as if it were shrinking and no longer fit my body. I rushed across the room and grabbed the phone before the second ring. My hand was trembling.

The strange, muffled voice scared me: 'You have e-mail.'

I couldn't think straight. I couldn't think at all.

I'd brought my laptop with me on vacation.

Who knew that I had my computer here? Who knew a small detail like that about me? Who had been watching me? Watching us?

I yanked open the closet door. I grabbed the computer, hooked it up, and logged on. I scrolled down the e-mail to the last message.

It was short and very concise.

SHE'S SAFE FOR NOW. WE HAVE HER.

The curt, cold message was worse than anything I could imagine. Each word was branded into my brain, repeating over and over.

She's safe for now.

We have her.

Book Three

Elegy

Chapter Forty-Six

S ampson arrived at the Belmont Hotel the day after Christine disappeared. I hurried down to the small front lobby to meet him. He threw his large arms around me, clasping me tightly, but gently, as if he were holding a child in his arms.

'You okay? You holding up?' he asked.

'Not even close,' I told him. 'I spent half a day checking the e-mail address I got last night. It came from curtain@mindspring.com. The address was falsified. Nothing is going right.'

'We'll get Christine back. We'll find her.' He muttered what he knew I wanted to hear, but I was sure that he truly believed it in his heart. Sampson is the most positive human being I've ever met. He won't be denied.

'Thanks for coming. It means a lot to all of us. I can't think straight about anything. I'm really rattled, John. I can't even begin to imagine who could have done this. Maybe the Weasel. I don't know.'

'If you *could* think straight now,' John said, 'I'd be more worried about you than usual. That's why I'm here.'

'I kind of knew you'd come.'

'Of course you did. I'm Sampson. Occam's razor and all that deep philosophical shit at work here.'

There were a half-dozen guests in the hotel lobby and all of them looked our way. The hotel staff knew about Christine's disappearance, and I'm sure that the guests at the Belmont knew as well, as did just about everybody else on the small, chatty island.

'The story's on the front page of the local newspaper,' Sampson said. 'People were reading copies at the airport.'

I told him, 'Bermuda is small, mostly peaceful and orderly. The disappearance of a tourist, or any kind of violent crime, is unusual here. I don't know how the paper got the story so quickly. The leak must have come out of the police station.'

'Local police won't help us. Probably get in the way,' Sampson muttered as we walked over to the hotel registration desk. He signed in, then we trudged upstairs to show Nana and the kids that Uncle John was here.

Chapter Forty-Seven

The following morning, the two of us met for hours with the police in Hamilton. They were professionals, but a kidnapping was a rarity for them. They let us set up in their station house on Front Street. I still couldn't concentrate or focus the way I needed to.

Bermuda is a twenty-one-square-mile island. While the British colony is small, we soon discovered that there are more than twelve hundred roads. Sampson and I split up and covered as much of the island as we possibly could. For the next two days we went from six in the morning until ten or eleven at night, without a break. I didn't want to stop, not even to sleep.

We didn't do any better than the locals, though. No one had seen anything. We'd reached a dead end. Christine had disappeared without a trace.

We were bone tired. After we finished at the station house on the third night, Sampson and I went for a late swim at Elbow Beach, just down the road from the hotel.

I had learned to swim at the municipal pool in DC. Nana had insisted that I learn. She was fifty-four at the time, and stubborn. She made up her mind to learn and took lessons from the Red Cross with us. The majority of people in Southeast didn't know how to swim back then, and she felt it was symbolic of the limiting inner-city experience.

So one summer, we all tackled swimming with Nana at the municipal pool. We went for lessons three mornings a week, and usually practiced an extra hour after that. Nana herself was soon able to swim fifty or more laps. She had stamina, same as now. I rarely get into the water without flashing back to those fine summer days of my youth, when I became a reasonably good swimmer.

Now, Sampson and I floated on the calm surface, out about a hundred yards or so from shore. The sky above was the deepest shade of evening blue, sparkling with countless stars. I could see the curving white line of the beach as it stretched several miles in either direction. Palm and casuarina trees shimmied in the sea breeze.

I felt devastated, totally overwhelmed as I floated on the sea. I kept seeing Christine with my eyes open or closed. I couldn't believe she was gone. I teared up as I thought about what had happened, the unfairness of life sometimes.

'You want to talk about the investigation? My thoughts so far? Little things

I learned today? Or give it a rest for the night?' Sampson asked me as we floated peacefully on our backs. 'Talk? Or quiet time?'

'Talk, I guess. I can't think about anything else except Christine. I can't think straight. Say whatever you're thinking. Something bothering you in particular?'

'Little thing, but maybe it's important.'

I didn't say anything. I just let him go on.

'What puzzles me is the first newspaper stories.' Sampson paused and then continued. 'Busby says he didn't talk to anybody the first night. Not a single person, he claims. You didn't either. Story was in the morning edition, though.'

'It's a small island, John. I told you that and you've seen it yourself.'

But Sampson kept at it, and I began to think that maybe there was something in it.

'Listen, Alex, only you, Patrick Busby, and whoever took Christine knew. *He* called it in to the paper. The kidnapper did it himself. I talked to the girl at the paper who got the call. She wouldn't say anything yesterday, but she finally told me late today. She thought it was just a concerned citizen calling. I think somebody's playing with your head, Alex. Somebody's running a nasty game on you.'

We have her.

A game? What kind of nasty game? Who were the players? Was one of them the Weasel? Was it possible that he was still here in Bermuda?

Chapter Forty-Eight

I couldn't sleep back at the hotel. I still couldn't concentrate or focus and it was incredibly frustrating. It was as if I were losing my mind.

A *game*? No, this wasn't a game. This was shock and horror. This was a living nightmare beyond anything I had ever experienced. Who could have done this to Christine? Why? Who was the Weasel?

Every time I closed my eyes, tried to sleep, I could see Christine's face, see her waving goodbye that final time on the Middle Road, see her walking through the hotel gardens with flowers in her hair.

I could hear Christine's voice all through the night – and then it was morning again. My guilt over what had happened to her had doubled, tripled.

Sampson and I continued to canvass Middle Road, Harbour Road, South Road. Every person we spoke to in the police and military believed that Christine didn't simply disappear on the island. Sampson and I heard the same song and dance every day for a week. No one – shopkeepers, taxi or bus drivers – had seen her in Hamilton or St George, so it was possible that she'd never arrived in either town that afternoon.

No one, not one witness remembered seeing her moped on the Middle or Harbour Roads, so maybe she never even got that far.

Most disturbing of all was that there hadn't been any further communication to me about her since the e-mail on the night she'd disappeared. The e-mail address was fake. Whoever had contacted me was a skillful hacker able to conceal their identity. The words I'd seen that night were always on my mind.

She's safe for now.

We have her.

Who was 'we'? And why wasn't there any further contact? What did they want from me? Did they know that they were driving me insane? Was that what they wanted to do? Did the 'Weasel' represent more killers than one? Suddenly that made a lot of sense to me.

Sampson returned to Washington on Sunday, and he took Nana and the kids with him. They didn't want to leave without me, but it was time for them to go. I couldn't make myself leave Bermuda yet. It would have felt as if I were abandoning Christine.

On Sunday night, Patrick Busby showed up at the Belmont Hotel around nine. He asked me to ride with him out past Southampton, about a six-mile drive that he said would take us twenty minutes or more. Bermudians measure distance in a straight line, but all the roads run in wiggles and half-circles, so it always takes longer to travel than you would think.

'What is it, Patrick? What's out in Southampton?' I asked as we rode along Middle Road. My heart was in my throat. He was scaring me with his silence.

'We haven't found Ms Johnson. However, a man may have witnessed the abduction. I want you to hear his story. You decide for yourself. You're the big city detective, not me. You can ask whatever questions you like. Off the record, of course.'

The man's name was Perri Graham, and he was staying in a room at the Port Royal Golf Club. We met him at his tiny apartment in the staff quarters. He was tall and painfully thin, with a longish goatee. He clearly wasn't happy to see Inspector Busby or me on his doorstep.

Busby had already told me that Graham was originally from London, and now worked as a porter and maintenance man at the semiprivate golf club. He had also lived in New York City and Miami, and had a criminal record for selling crack in New York.

'I already told him everything I saw.' Perri Graham spoke defensively as soon as he opened the front door of his room and saw the two of us standing there. 'Go away. Let me be. Why would I hold back anything or—'

I cut him off. 'My name is Alex Cross. I'm a homicide detective from

Washington. The woman you saw was my fiancée, Mr Graham. May we come in and talk? This will only take a few minutes.'

He shook his head back and forth in frustration.

'I'll tell you what I know. *Again*,' he finally said, relenting. 'Yeah, come in. Only because you called me Mr Graham.'

'That's all I want. I'm not here to bother you about anything else.'

Busby and I walked inside the room, which was little more than an alcove. The tile floors and all the furniture were strewn with wrinkled clothes, mostly underwear.

'A woman I know lives in Hamilton,' he said in a weary voice. 'I went to visit her this Tuesday past. We drank too much wine. Stayed the evening, you know how it is. I got up somehow. Had to be at the club by noon, but I knew I'd be late and get docked some of my pay. Don't have a car or nothing, so I hitched a ride from Hamilton, out South Shore Road. Walked along near Paget, I suppose. Damn hot afternoon, I remember. I went down to the water, cool off if I could.

'I came back up over a knobbly hill, and I witnessed an accident on the roadway. It was maybe a quarter of a mile down the big hill there. You know it?'

I nodded and held my breath as I listened to him. I remembered the stifling heat of that afternoon, everything about it. I could still see Christine driving off on a shiny blue moped, waving and smiling. The memory of her smile, which had always brought me such joy, now put a tight knot in my stomach.

'I saw a white van hit a woman riding a blue moped. I can't be sure, but it almost looked like the van hit her on purpose. Driver, he jumped out of the van right away and helped her up. She didn't look like she was hurt badly. Then he helped her inside the van. Put the moped inside, too. Then he drove off. I thought he was taking her to the hospital. Thought nothing else of it.'

'You sure she wasn't badly hurt?' I asked.

'Not sure. But she got right up. She was able to stand all right.'

There was a catch in my voice when I spoke again. 'And you didn't tell anybody about the accident, not even when you saw the news stories?'

The man shook his head. 'Didn't see no stories. Don't bother with the local news much. Just small time shit and worthless gossip. But then my girl, she keep talking about it. I didn't want to go to the police, but she made me do it, made me talk to this inspector here.'

'You know what kind of van it was?' I asked.

'White van. I think it was maybe a rented one. Clean and new.'

'License plate?'

Graham shook his head. 'Don't have no idea.'

'What did the man in the van look like?' I asked him. 'Any little thing you remember is helpful, Mr Graham. You've already helped a lot.'

He shrugged, but I could tell that he was trying to think back to that afternoon. 'Nothing special about him. Not as tall as you, but tall. Look like anybody else. Just a black man, like any other.'

Chapter Forty-Nine

In a small apartment in a suburb of Washington called Mount Rainier, Detective Patsy Hampton lay in bed, restlessly flipping through the pages of the *Post*. She couldn't sleep, but there was nothing unusual about that. She often had trouble sleeping, ever since she'd been a little girl in Harrisburg, Pennsylvania. Her mother said she must have a guilty conscience about something.

She watched a rerun episode of *ER*, then fetched herself a Stonyfield yogurt with blueberries and logged onto America Online. She had e-mail from her father, now relocated in Delray Beach, Florida; and also from an old college roommate from the University of Richmond, whom she had never been that close to anyway.

The roommate had just heard from a mutual friend that Patsy was a hotshot police detective in Washington, and what an exciting life she must lead. The roommate wrote that she had four children and lived in a suburb of Charlotte, North Carolina, but that she was bored with everything in her life. Patsy Hampton would have given anything to have just one child.

She wandered back to the kitchen and got a cold bottle of Evian mineral water. She was aware that her life had become ridiculous lately. She spent too much time on her job, but also too much time by herself in the apartment, especially weekends. It wasn't that she couldn't get dates – she was just turned off by men in general lately.

She still fantasized about finding someone compatible, having children. But increasingly, she thought about the depressing and maddening cycle of trying to meet someone interesting. She usually ended up with guys who were hopelessly boring *or* thirty-something jackasses who still acted like teenagers, though without the charm of youth. *Hopeless, hopeless, hopeless*, she thought as she sent off a cheery lie to her dad in Florida.

The phone rang and she glanced at her wristwatch – it was twenty past twelve. She snatched up the receiver. 'Hampton speaking.'

'It's Chuck, Patsy. Really sorry to call so late. Is it okay? You awake?'

'Sure, no problem, Chucky Cheese. I'm up with the other vampires, yourself included, I guess.'

It was kind of late but she was glad to hear from Chuck Hufstedler, who was a computer geek at the FBI in Washington. The two of them helped each other out sometimes, and she'd recently talked to him about the unsolved murders in Washington, especially the Jane Does. Chuck told her that he was also in contact with Alex Cross, but Cross had trouble of his own right now. His fiancée had been kidnapped, and Patsy Hampton wondered if it had anything to do with the murders in Southeast.

'I'm wide awake, Chuck. What's up? What's on your big mind?'

He started with a disclaimer, which said volumes about Chuck's incredibly low self-esteem. 'Maybe nothing, but maybe something a little interesting on those killings in Southeast, and particularly the two young girls in Shaw. This really comes out of left field, though.'

The FBI computer expert had her attention. 'That's where this killer lives, Chuck, *deep* left field. Tell me what you have. I'm wide awake and listening. Talk to me, Chucky Cheese.'

Chuck hemmed and hawed. He was always like that, which was too bad because he was basically a real nice guy. 'You know anything about RPGs, Patsy?' he asked.

'I know that it stands for role-playing games and, let's see, there's a popular one called Dragon and Dungeons, Dungeons and Dragons – whatever the order.'

'It's Dungeons and Dragons, or Advanced Dungeons and Dragons. Confession time, kiddo. I occasionally play an RPG myself – it's called Millennium's End. I play a couple of hours a day usually. More on weekends.'

'New to me. Go on, Chuck.' God, she thought, cyberspace confessions in the middle of the night.

'Very popular game, even with so-called adults. The characters in Millennium's End work for Black Eagle Security. It's a private organization of troubleshooters who hire out for investigative services around the world. The characters are all good guys, crusaders for good.'

'Uh-huh, Chuck. Say six Hail Marys, now make an Act of Contrition, then get to the damn point. It *is* around twelve thirty, pal.'

'Right, I am heartily sorry, and deeply embarrassed, too. Anyway, there's a chatroom online that I visited. It's called the Gamesters' Chatroom and it's on AOL. As I speak, there's a fascinating discussion going on about a new kind of game. It's more an *anti*-game, though. All the role-playing games I know are about *good* characters trying to conquer chaos and evil. The game under discussion has a couple of evil characters *trying to overcome good*. Specifically, Patsy, one of the characters is attacking and murdering women in the Southeast part of DC. Lots of lurid detail on the murders. These aren't the actual players – but they know about the game. The game itself is probably protected. Thought you should know. It's called The Four Horsemen.'

Patsy Hampton was definitely wide awake now. 'I'm on it. Thanks, Chuck. Let's keep this between the two of us for the moment, okay?'

'Yeah. Okay.'

It took her a couple of minutes to log onto AOL, then get into the Gamesters' Chatroom. She didn't participate, just read what the others had to say. This was interesting. She wondered if she had just stumbled onto her first big break in the Jane Doe case.

The others in the room were named Viper, Landlocked, J-Boy, and Lancelot. They chattered on and on about the hottest fantasy games and cutting-edge magazines, which nearly succeeded in putting her to sleep. The Four Horsemen came up twice, but only in passing as a point of reference. Lancelot was the one who mentioned it. Chuck was right, these probably weren't the actual players, but they knew about the game somehow.

The fantasy nerds were starting to wear really thin with her by quarter past one. Finally, out of frustration, she typed out a message for the little shitheels. She called herself Sappho.

I CAME IN LATE, BUT HORSEMEN SOUNDS LIKE A NEAT KIND OF REVOLUTIONARY GAME TO ME, LANCELOT. PRETTY AUDACIOUS STUFF, NO?

Lancelot shot back:

NOT REALLY, *SAPPO*. THERE'S A LOT OF IT GOING AROUND LATELY. ANTI-HEROES, SICKOS. ESPECIALLY IN VAMPIRE GAME CIRCLES.

Hampton typed:

HAVEN'T I READ ABOUT MURDERS LIKE THESE IN THE NEWS-PAPERS? BY THE WAY, IT'S SAPPHO, LIKE THE POET.

Lancelot replied:

YEAH, BUT LOTS OF RPGS USE CURRENT EVENTS. NO BIGGIE, REALLY. *SAPPO*.

Hampton grinned. He was an obnoxious little nerd, but she had him – for the moment anyway. And she needed him. How much did he know about The Four Horsemen? Could he be a player? She tried to peek at Lancelot's profile, but he had restricted access to it.

YOU'RE FUNNY. ARE YOU A PLAYER, LAUGHALOT, OR JUST AN ART CRITIC?

I DON'T LIKE THE BASIC CONCEPT OF HORSEMEN. ANYWAY, IT'S A PRIVATE GAME. *STRICTLY* PRIVATE. ENCRYPTED.

YOU KNOW ANY OF THE PLAYERS? I MIGHT LIKE TO TRY IT
OUT MYSELF?

There was no response to the question. Patsy thought maybe she'd pushed too
hard, too fast. Damn! She should have known better. Damn, damn! Come back,
Lancelot. Earth to Lancelot.

I REALLY WOULD LIKE TO PLAY THE FOUR HORSEMEN. BUT
I'M COOL ABOUT IT. NO BIGGIE. LANCELOT?

Patsy Hampton waited, and then Lancelot left the chatroom. Lancelot was gone.
And so was her connection to somebody playing a so-called fantasy game about
committing gruesome murders in Washington – murders that had really
happened.

Chapter Fifty

I returned to Washington during the first week of September and I had never
felt stranger in my own skin. I'd gone to Bermuda with my family and
Christine, and now I was coming home without her. Whoever had taken Christine
had contacted me only once. I missed her nearly every moment of every day,
and I felt so far away from where she might still be.

It was an unusually cool and windy day when I got back to the city. It almost
seemed as if summer had suddenly changed to the middle of fall. I felt as if I
had been away much longer than I had. I had been in a fog of unreality in
Bermuda, and I felt nearly the same once I was back in DC again. I'd never
felt this badly before, never so lost, so unhinged, battered.

I wondered if Christine and I were part of a madman's elaborate fantasy,
what profilers call an escalating fantasy. If so, who was this madman and where
was he now? Was it the Weasel? Did I know him from some time in my past?
The heartless, spineless bastard had communicated *we have her*. And that was
it. No further word. Now only silence, which was deafening.

I took a taxi from the airport and I thought of Frank Odenkirk, who had
innocently taken a cab one night in August and wound up murdered on Alabama
Avenue near Dupont Park. I hadn't thought about the Odenkirk case during the
past three weeks. I rarely had a thought about the Jane Doe murders while in

Bermuda, but I was guiltily reminded of them now. Others had suffered painful losses because of the killer.

I wondered if any progress had been made, and who in the department was running the case, at least the Odenkirk part of it. On the other hand, I didn't feel that I could work on any of the other unsolved murders right now. I felt my place was still in Bermuda, and strange as it sounds, I nearly headed back as soon as I landed.

Then I could see our house up ahead on Fifth Street. Something strange was happening – there was a crowd.

Chapter Fifty-One

L ots of people were standing on the porch and they were also clustered in front of the house when the cab arrived. Cars were parked and double-parked all along the street.

I recognized Aunt Tia. My sister-in-law Cilla and Nana were on the porch with the kids. Sampson was there with a girlfriend named Millie, a lawyer from the Justice Department.

Some of them waved as I pulled up, so I knew everything was all right. This wasn't more trouble. But what was it?

I saw my niece, Naomi, and her husband, Seth Taylor, who had come all the way from Durham, North Carolina. Jerome Thurman, Rakeem Powell, and Shawn Moore were standing on the front lawn.

'Hey, Alex, good to see you.' Jerome's deep voice boomed out at me as I passed near him on my way to the porch. I finally set down my travel bag and started shaking hands, giving out hugs, receiving back pats and kisses from all sides.

'We're all here for you,' Naomi said. She came over to me and hugged me tightly. 'We love you so much. But we'll go away if you don't want us here now.'

'No, no. I'm glad you're here, Scootchie,' I said, and kissed my niece on both cheeks. A while back, she'd been abducted in Durham, North Carolina. I had been there for her and so had Sampson. 'It's good that you and Seth are here. It's good to see everybody. You can't imagine how good it is.'

I hugged relatives and friends, my grandmother, my two beautiful kids, and I realized again how lucky I was to have so many good people in my life. Two teachers from the Sojourner Truth School had also come to the house. They were friends of Christine, and they started to cry when they came up to me.

They wanted to know if any progress had been made and if there was anything they could do.

I told them that we had a witness to the abduction, and that we were more hopeful than ever. The teachers were buoyed by the news, which wasn't nearly as good as I made it sound. Nothing more had come of the one eyewitness account to the abduction. No one else had seen the white van that took away Christine.

Jannie finally cornered me in the backyard around nine o'clock. I had just spent half an hour with Damon in the basement, talking man to man, shadow-boxing a little bit.

Damon had told me that he was having trouble remembering Christine's face, exactly what she looked like. I told him that it happened with people and that it was all right. We finally shared a long hug.

Jannie had patiently waited to talk with me.

'My turn?' she asked.

'Absolutely, sweetheart.'

Jannie then took my hand and pulled me forward into the house. She quietly led me upstairs, not to her room, but to mine.

'If you get lonely in here tonight, you can come to my room. I *mean* it,' she said as she gently shut the door on the two of us. She is so wise and has such a good perspective on so many things. Both she and Damon are such good kids. Nana says they have 'sound character,' and it is building nicely. So far, so good.

'Thank you, sweetie. I will come to your room if it gets bad in here. You're very thoughtful and nice.'

'I am, Daddy. You helped me be this way, and I'm glad of it. Now I have a real serious question for you, Daddy. It's hard, but I have to ask anyway.'

'You go ahead,' I told her, feeling uncomfortable under her serious little gaze. I wasn't completely focused, and I didn't know if I could handle one of Jannie's hard questions. 'I'm listening, sweetheart,' I said. 'Fire away.'

She had let go of my hand, but she took it up again, held my big hand tightly in both her small ones.

'Daddy, is Christine dead?' she asked me. 'You can tell me if she is. Please tell the truth, though. I want to know.'

I almost lost it, sitting on the edge of the bed with Jannie. I'm sure she had no idea how much her question hurt, or how hard it was to answer.

I was hanging over the edge of a dark abyss, just about gone, but I pulled myself together and took a deep breath. Then I tried to answer my little girl's honest question as best I could.

'I don't know yet,' I told her. 'That's the truth. We're still hoping to find her, sweetie. We found one witness so far.'

'But she might be dead, Daddy?'

'Let me tell you the best thing I know about dying,' I said to Jannie. 'The very best thing that I know. Just about the only thing, in fact.'

'You go away, and then you're with Jesus forever,' Jannie said. The way she spoke, though, I wasn't sure if she really believed what she was saying. It sounded like one of Nana's 'gospel truths,' or maybe she'd heard it in church.

'Yes, that can be a great comfort to know, baby. But I was thinking of something else. Maybe it's the same thing, but a different way to look at it.'

Her intense little eyes held mine, wouldn't let go. 'You can tell me, Daddy. Please. I want to hear it. I'm very interested in this.'

'It's not a bad thing, but it helps me whenever somebody dies. Think about this. We come into life so easily – from somewhere, from the universe, from God. Why should it be any harder when we leave life? We come – from a good place. We leave – and go to a good place. Does that make any sense to you, Jannie?'

She nodded and continued to stare deeply into my eyes. 'I understand,' she whispered. 'It's like it's in balance.'

She paused a second, thinking it over, then she spoke. 'But Daddy, Christine isn't dead. I just know it. She *isn't* dead. She hasn't gone to that good place yet. So don't you lose hope.'

Chapter Fifty-Two

The character and traits of Death were so much like his own, Shafer was thinking as he sped south along I-95. Death wasn't brilliant, but he was always thorough, and he always won in the end.

As the black Jag raced past the exits for various small towns, Shafer wondered if he wanted to be caught now, if he needed to be unmasked, finally to show his true face to everyone. Boo Cassady believed that he was hiding, even from her, but more importantly, from himself. Maybe she was right. Maybe he did want Lucy and the kids to see who he really was. And the police. But especially the uptight and sanctimonious staff at the embassy.

I am Death – it's who I am. I am a multiple killer – it's who I am. I am not Geoffrey Shafer anymore, maybe I never was. But if I was, it was a long, long time ago.

Shafer had always had a natural mean streak, a vengeful, nasty way. He remembered it from his early years traveling with his family through Europe, then Asia, and finally back to England. His father had been in the military and was always a real tough guy around the house. He struck Shafer and his two brothers often, but not nearly as often as he hit their mother, who died of a fall when Shafer was twelve.

Shafer was large as a boy, and he was one 'tough hombre', a real bully. Other boys feared him, even his brothers, Charles and George, who believed that Geoff was capable of anything. He was.

Nothing in his early days prepared him for being the man who finally emerged once he joined MI6. It was there that he learned he was capable of killing another human being – and Shafer found that he loved it. He had discovered his calling, his true passion in life. He was the ultimate tough guy; Shafer was Death.

He continued traveling south on the interstate highway. Because it was late, traffic was light, mostly high-speeding trucks headed toward Florida, he supposed.

He mentally composed a message to the other fantasy game players.

DEATH GOES TO FREDERICKSBURG, MARYLAND, TONIGHT. A GOOD-LOOKING THIRTY-SEVEN-YEAR-OLD WOMAN LIVES THERE WITH HER MIRROR-IMAGE FIFTEEN-YEAR-OLD DAUGHTER. THE WOMAN IS DIVORCED, A SMALL-TOWN LAWYER, A PROSECUTOR. THE DAUGHTER IS AN HONOR STUDENT AND A FOOTBALL CHEERLEADER. THE TWO WOMEN WILL BE SLEEPING. DEATH HAS COME TO MARYLAND, BECAUSE WASHINGTON IS TOO DANGEROUS NOW. (YES, I TOOK YOUR WARNING TO HEART.) THE DC POLICE ARE SEARCHING FOR THE JANE DOE MURDERER. A WELL-THOUGHT-OF DETECTIVE NAMED PATSY HAMPTON IS ON THE CASE, AND DETECTIVE CROSS HAS RETURNED FROM BERMUDA. IT WILL BE INTERESTING TO SEE IF HIS CHARACTER HAS CHANGED IN ANY WAY. CHARACTER IS EVERYTHING, DON'T YOU AGREE?

I CAN SEE THE CAHILL HOUSE UP AHEAD. I CAN PICTURE BOTH OF THE LOVELY CAHILL WOMEN. THEY LIVE IN A FOUR-BEDROOM RANCH HOUSE. THE SUBURBAN STREET IS VIRTUALLY SILENT AT 1:00 A.M. NO ONE COULD POSSIBLY CONNECT THESE TWO MURDERS TO THE JANE DOES. I WISH YOU COULD BE HERE WITH ME. I WISH YOU COULD FEEL EXACTLY AS I DO.

Chapter Fifty-Three

S hafer parked his Jag on the shadowy street and felt strangely alone and afraid. He was actually scaring himself. The things he thought and did. No one had a twisted mind like his – no one thought like this. No one ever had such outlandish fantasies and ideas, and then acted them out.

The other players had complicated and very sick fantasy lives of course, but they paled in comparison to his. Famine claimed authorship of a series of psycho-sexual murders in Thailand and the Philippines. War liked to think of himself as the uncrowned head of the group – he claimed to influence the adventures of the others. Conqueror was confined to a wheelchair and made up stories about using his infirmity to lure his prey close enough for the kill.

Shafer doubted that any of them actually had the guts to play the game out in the real world.

But perhaps they would surprise him. Maybe each of the others was living out a homicidal fantasy. Wouldn't that be something?

The Cahill women thought they were so perfectly safe inside the ranch house, less than fifty yards away. He could see a green wooden fence surrounding a stone terrace and lap swimming pool in the back. The house had sliding doors to the pool area. So many possibilities for him to consider.

He might enter the house and murder both of them execution-style. Then he would drive directly back to Washington.

The local police and FBI would be totally baffled. The story might even make network TV. Two women shot and murdered while they slept, a mother and daughter whom everybody in their small town admired. No motive for the horrific crime, no suspects.

He was hard now, and it was difficult to walk. That was comical to Shafer, his absurd hard-on waddle. His mouth formed a smile.

A dog was barking, two or three houses down the street – a small, wimpy dog, from the sound of it. Then a larger dog joined in. They sensed danger, didn't they? They knew he was here.

Shafer knelt beside a maple tree at the edge of the backyard. He stood in shadows while the moon cast a soft white light across the yard.

He slid the twenty-sided dice out of his pocket, then let them fall on the tufts of lawn. *Here we go. Playing by the rules. Let's see what the night has to offer*. He counted the numerals on the special dice. They appeared fuzzy in the dark.

Shafer couldn't believe what he saw. He wanted to howl like the crazed and bewildered neighborhood dogs.

The dice count was seven.

Death had to leave! This instant! There could be no murders tonight!

No! He wouldn't do it! To hell with the dice. He wouldn't leave. He couldn't. He was losing all impulse control, wasn't he? Well, so be it. Alea jacta est, he remembered from his schoolboy Latin class. Julius Caesar before he crossed the Rubicon – *the die is cast*.

This was a monumental night. For the first time, he was breaking the rules. He was changing the game forever.

He needed to kill someone and the urge was everything to him.

He hurried to the house before he changed his mind. He was nervous. Adrenaline punched through his system. He used his glass cutter at first, but then just smashed in a small window with a gloved hand.

Once inside he moved quickly down the darkened hallway. He was sweating – so unlike him. He entered Deirdre's bedroom. She was asleep, despite the breaking of the glass. Her bare arms were thrown up over her head, the surrender position.

'Lovely,' he whispered.

She was wearing white bikini panties and a matching bra. Her long legs were spread delicately, expectantly. In her dreams, she must have known he was coming. Shafer believed that dreams told you the truth, and you had better listen.

He was still hard and was so glad he'd chosen to disobey the rules.

'Who the hell are you?' he heard, suddenly. The voice came from behind. Shafer whirled around.

It was Lindsay, the daughter. She wore nothing but coral-pink underwear, a brassière and briefs. He calmly raised his gun until it pointed between her eyes.

'Shhh. You don't want to know, Lindsay,' he said, in the calmest voice, not bothering to disguise his English accent. 'But I'll tell you anyway.'

He fired the gun.

Chapter Fifty-Four

For the second time in my life I understood what it felt like to be a victim of a terrible crime rather than the detective investigating it. I was disconnected and out of it. I needed to be doing something positive on a case, or get back to volunteer work at St Anthony's, anything to take my mind off what had happened.

I had to be busy, but I knew I'd lost my ability to concentrate, something that had come so naturally to me. I came across a pair of shocking murders in Maryland that bothered me for some unspecified reason. I didn't follow up on them. I should have.

I wasn't myself; I was lost. I still spent endless hours thinking about Christine, remembering everything about our time together, seeing her face wherever I went.

Sampson tried to push me. He *did* push me. He and I made the rounds of the streets of Southeast. We put the word out that we were looking for a purple-and-blue cab, possibly a gypsy. We canvassed door-to-door in the Shaw neighborhood where Tori Glover and Marion Cardinal had been found. Often we were still going at ten or eleven at night.

I didn't care. I couldn't sleep anyway.

Sampson cared. He was my friend.

'You're supposed to be working the Odenkirk case, right? I'm not supposed to be working at all. The Jefe would be livid. I kind of like that,' Sampson said as we trudged along S Street late one evening. Sampson had lived in this neighborhood for years. He knew all the local hangarounds.

'Jamal, you know anything I should know?' he called out to a goateed youth sitting in shadows on a graystone stoop.

'Don't know nothin'. Just relaxin' my mind. Catchin' a cool night breeze. How 'bout yourself?'

Sampson turned back to me. 'Damn crackrunners working these streets everywhere you look nowadays. Real good place to commit a murder and never get caught. You talk to the police in Bermuda lately?'

I nodded and my eyes stared at a fixed point up ahead. 'Patrick Busby said the story of Christine's disappearance is off the front pages. I don't know if that's good or bad. It's probably bad.'

Sampson agreed. 'Takes the pressure off them. You going back down there?'

'Not right away. But yeah, I have to go back. I have to find out what happened.'

He looked me in the eye. 'Are you here with me right now? Are you *here*, sugar?'

'Yeah, I'm here. Most of the time. I'm functioning okay.' I pointed up at a nearby red brick building. 'That place would have a view of the front entryway into the girl's building. Any of those windows. Let's get back to work.'

Sampson nodded. 'I'm here as long as you want to be.'

There was something about pounding the streets that appealed to me that night. We talked to everyone in the building that we could find at home, about half the apartments. Nobody had seen a purple-and-blue cab on the street; nobody had seen Tori or Marion either. Or so they said.

'You see any connections anywhere?' I asked as we came down the steep stairs of a fourth-floor walk-up. 'What do you see? What the hell am I missing?'

'Not a thing, Alex. Nothing to miss. Weasel didn't leave a clue. Never does.'

We got back down to the entrance, and met up with an elderly man carrying three clear plastic bags of groceries from the Stop & Shop.

'We're homicide detectives,' I said to him. 'Two young girls were murdered across the street.'

The man nodded. 'Tori and Marion. I know 'em. You want to know 'bout that fella watchin' the buildin'? He was sittin' there most the night. Inside a slick fancy black car,' he said. 'Mercedes, I think. You think maybe he's the killer?'

Chapter Fifty-Five

'I been away awhile, y'see. Visitin' wit' my two old bat sisters in North Carolina for a week of good memories, home-cooked food,' the elderly man said as we climbed to the fourth floor. 'That was why I was missed during the earlier time through here by your detectives.'

This was old-school police work, I was thinking as I climbed stairs – the kind too many detectives try to avoid. The man's name was DeWitt Luke and he was retired from Bell Atlantic, the huge phone company that services most of the Northeast. He was the fifty-third interview I'd had so far in Shaw.

'Saw him sittin' there around one in the mornin'. Didn't think much of it at first. Probably waitin' for somebody. Seemed to be mindin' his own business. He was still there at two, though. Sittin' in his car. Seemed kinda strange to me.' He paused for a long moment as if trying to remember.

'Then what happened?' I prompted the man.

'Fell asleep. But I got up to pee around three thirty. He was *still* in that shiny black car. So I watched him closer this time. He was watchin' the other side of the street. Like some kind of damn spy or somethin'. Couldn't tell what he was lookin' at, but he was studyin' somethin' real hard over there. I thought he might be the police. 'Cept his car was too nice.'

'You got that right,' Sampson said, and barked out a laugh. 'No Mercedes in my garage.'

'I pulled up a card-table chair behind the darkened window in my apartment. Made sure there were no lights on, so he couldn't see me. By now he'd caught my attention some. Remember the old movie *Rear Window*? I tried to figure out why he might be down there sittin', waitin'. Jealous lover, jealous husband, maybe some kinda night stalker. But he wasn't botherin' anybody so far as I could see.'

I spoke again. 'You never got a better look than that? Man sitting in the car?'

'Around the time I got up to pee, he got out of the car. Opened the door, but the inside light didn't come on. That struck me strange, it bein' such a nice car and all. Fueled my mind even more. I squinted my eyes, get a better look.' Another long pause.

'And?'

'He was tall, a blond gentleman. White fella. We don't get too many of them around here at night, or even in the daytime, for that matter.'

Chapter Fifty-Six

Detective Patsy Hampton's investigation of the Jane Doe murders was starting to show forward movement and positive results. She thought she might have something good in the works. She had confidence in her ability to solve the murders. She knew from experience that she was smarter than everybody else.

It helped to have Chief Pittman and all the department's resources on her side. She had spent the past day and a half with Chuck Hufstedler at the FBI building. She knew she was using Chuck a little, but he didn't seem to mind. He was lonely, and she *did* like his company. She and Chuck were still sitting around at three thirty in the afternoon when Lancelot entered the Gamesters' Chatroom again. *Laughalot*, she remembered.

'He couldn't resist, could he?' Hampton said to Hufstedler. 'Gotcha, you fantasy freak.'

Hufstedler looked at her, his thick black eyebrows arched. 'Three thirty in the afternoon, Patsy. What does that say? Tell you what it says to me. *Maybe* he's playing from work. But I bet our Lancelot is a school kid.'

'Or he's somebody who likes to play with school kids.' She offered a thought that upset her even as she uttered the words.

This time, she didn't try to make contact with Lancelot. She and Chuck just listened in on a stultifying discussion of several role-playing games. In the meantime, he was trying to trace Lancelot.

'He's pretty good at this, a real hacker. He's built a lot of security into his system. Hopefully, we'll get to him anyway.'

'I have confidence in you, Cheeseman.'

Lancelot stayed in the chatroom past four thirty. By then it was all over. Chuck had his name and address: Michael Ormson, Hutchins Place in Foxhall.

At a few minutes before five, two dark-blue vans pulled up in front of the Ormson house on the Georgetown Reservoir. Five agents in blue FBI wind-breakers and Detective Patsy Hampton surrounded the large Tudor-style house with an acre or two of front and back lawn and majestic views.

Senior FBI Agent Brigid Dwyer and Hampton proceeded to the front door and found it unlocked. With weapons drawn they quietly entered the house and discovered Lancelot in the den.

He looked to be around thirteen years old. A baby geek. He was sitting at a computer in his shorts and black socks.

'Hey, what the heck is going on? Hey! What are you doing in my house? I didn't do anything wrong? Who are you guys?' Michael Ormson asked in a high-pitched, peeved, but quivering voice.

He was skinny. His face was covered with acne. His back and shoulders had a rash that looked like eczema. Chuck Hufstedler had been right on target. Lancelot was a teenage geek playing with his fancy computer after school. He wasn't the Weasel, though. This boy *couldn't* be the Weasel.

'Are you Michael Ormson?' Patsy Hampton asked the boy. She had lowered her weapon but hadn't holstered it.

The young boy dropped his head and looked ready to weep. 'Oh God, oh God,' he moaned. 'Yes, I'm Michael Ormson. Who are you guys? Are you going to tell my parents?'

Chapter Fifty-Seven

M ichael's father and mother were immediately contacted at their jobs at
Georgetown University Hospital and the US Naval Observatory, respectively. The Ormsons were currently separated, but they both made it to Foxhall
in less than ten minutes, even with rush-hour traffic starting to build. The other
two Ormson children, Laura and Anne Marie, had come home from high school.

Patsy Hampton convinced the parents to let her talk to their son at the house.
She told the Ormsons that they could be present, and could interrupt, and even
stop the interview at any time they wished. Otherwise, she and Agent Dwyer
would have to take Michael to FBI headquarters for the interview.

The Ormsons, Mark and Cindy, agreed to let Michael talk. They were clearly
frightened, especially of the FBI personnel, but they seemed to trust Detective
Hampton. Most people did, she knew. She was pretty, sincere, and had a
disarming smile that she used when she needed to.

'I'm interested in the game called The Four Horsemen,' Hampton said to
the boy. 'That's the only reason I'm here, Michael. I need your help.'

The teenager dropped his chin to his chest again, and shook his head back
and forth. Hampton watched the nervous boy, and decided to take a chance
with him. She had a hunch that she wanted to play.

'Michael, whatever you think you've done wrong, it's nothing to us. It's *nothing*.
We don't care what you've done on your computer. This isn't about you or your
family *or* your hacking. There have been some terrible murders in Washington,
and there might be a connection to this game called The Four Horsemen. Please
help us, Michael. You're the only one who can. You're the only one.'

Mark Ormson, who was a radiologist at Georgetown University Hospital,
leaned forward on the black leather couch in the den. He looked more frightened now than when he'd gotten home. 'I'm beginning to think I better get a
lawyer,' he said.

Patsy Hampton shook her head and smiled kindly at both parents. 'This is
not about your son, Mr and Mrs Ormson. He's not in any trouble with us, I
assure you.'

She turned back to the teenager. '*Michael*, what do you know about The
Four Horsemen? We know you're not one of the players. We know it's a very
private game.'

The boy finally looked up. She could tell that he liked her, and maybe trusted her some. 'Hardly anything, ma'am. I don't know too much.'

Hampton nodded. 'This is very important to us, Michael. Someone is killing people in the Southeast part of Washington – *for real*, Michael. This is not a fantasy game. I think you can help us. You can save others from getting murdered.'

Michael dropped his head again. He had hardly looked at his mother and father since they arrived. 'I'm good with computers. You probably already figured that out.'

Detective Hampton kept nodding, giving the boy positive reinforcement. 'We know you are, Michael. We had trouble tracing you here. You're *very* good with computers. My friend Chuck Hufstedler at the FBI was really impressed. When all this is over, you can see where he works. You'll like him, and you'll love his equipment.'

Michael finally smiled, showing off large protruding teeth with braces. 'Back at the beginning of summer, probably late in June, this guy came into the Gamesters' Chatroom – where you found me.'

Patsy Hampton tried to hold eye contact with the boy. She needed him badly; she had a feeling that this was a big break, the biggest so far.

Michael continued to speak softly. 'He sort of, like, he took over the conversation. Actually, he was pretty much a control freak about it. He kept putting down Highlander, D&D, Millennium, all the hot games that are out now. Wouldn't let anybody else get a word in. Almost seemed like he was high on something.

'He kept hinting about this completely different game he played called The Four Horsemen. It was like he didn't want to tell us about it, but then he would give out bits and pieces anyway, but not much. He wouldn't shut up.

'He said the characters in D&D, Dune, Condottiere were predictable and boring – which I must admit, they are sometimes. Then he said some of the characters in his game were *chaotic evil* instead of *lawful good*. He said they weren't fake heroes like in most RPGs; his characters were more like people in real life. They were basically selfish, didn't really care about others, didn't follow society's rules. He said Horsemen was the ultimate fantasy game. That was all he would tell us about The Four Horsemen, but it was enough. I mean, you could see it was a game for total psychos.'

'What was his call name?' Agent Dwyer asked Michael.

'Call name, or his real name?' Michael asked, and offered up a sly, superior smile.

Agent Dwyer and Hampton looked at each other. *Call name, or real name?* They turned back to Michael.

'I traced him, just like you tracked me. I got through his encryptions. I know his name, and I know where he lives. Even where he works. It's Shafer – Geoffrey Shafer. He works at the British Embassy on Massachusetts Avenue. He's some kind of information analyst there, according to the embassy's web site. He's forty-four years old.'

Michael Ormson looked sheepishly around the room. He finally made eye contact with his parents, who looked relieved. Then he looked back at Hampton. 'Is any of that stuff helpful to you? Did I help?'

'Yes, you did, Laughalot.'

Chapter Fifty-Eight

Geoffrey Shafer had vowed he would not get high on pharmaceuticals tonight. He'd also decided he was going to keep his fantasies under control, under wraps. He understood precisely what the psycho-babbling profilers on the murder cases would be thinking: His fantasy life was escalating and he was approaching a rage state. And the profilers would be exactly right – which was why he was playing it cool for a while.

He was a skillful cook, skilled at a lot of things, actually. He sometimes put together elaborate meals for his family, and even large dinner parties with friends. When he cooked, he liked to have the family with him in the kitchen; he loved an audience, even them.

'Tonight, we'll be eating classic Thai,' he announced to Lucy and the children as they watched him work. He was feeling a little hyper, and reminded himself not to let things get out of hand at home. Maybe he ought to take some Valium before he began to cook. All he'd taken was a little Xanax.

'What sets Thai food apart from other Southeast Asian cuisines are the explicit rules for proportions of ingredients, especially seasonings,' he said as he prepared a centerpiece of carved vegetables.

'Thai is a distinctive cuisine, blending Chinese, Indonesian, Indian, Portuguese, Malaysian. Bet you didn't know that, Tricia and Erica.'

The little girls laughed – confused – so much like their mother.

He put jasmine blossoms in Lucy's hair. Then a blossom each for the twins. He tried the same with Robert but his son pulled away, laughing.

'Nothing too hot tonight, darling,' Lucy said. 'The children.'

'The children, of course, dear. Speaking of hot, the real heat comes from capsaicin, which is stored in the ribs of these chili peppers. Capsaicin is an irritant and burns whatever it touches, even skin, so it's wise to wear gloves. I'm not wearing gloves, of course, because I'm not wise. Also I'm a little crazy.' He laughed. Everyone did. But Lucy looked worried.

Shafer served the dinner himself, without any help, and he announced each dish, both in Thai and English. '*Plaa meuk yaang*, or roast squid. Delicious.' '*Mieng kum*, leaf rolls with "treasurers." Yummy.' '*Plaa yaang kaeng phet*, grilled snapper with red curry sauce. Delectable. A *little* hot, though. Hmmm.'

He watched them tentatively sample each course, and as they tasted the snapper, tears began to run down their faces. Erica began to choke.

'Daddy, it's too hot!' Robert gulped, and complained.

Shafer smiled and nodded blithely. He loved this, the flowing tears, his perfect family in pain. He savored each exquisite moment of their suffering. He'd managed to turn the dinner into a tantalizing game, after all.

At quarter to nine he kissed Lucy and started off on his 'constitutional,' as he called his nightly disappearing act. He went out to the Jag and drove a few blocks to Phelps Place, which was a quiet street without many lights.

He took liberal doses of Thorazine *and* Librium, then injected himself with Toradol. He took another Xanax.

Then he went to his doctor's.

Chapter Fifty-Nine

Shafer didn't like the arrogant, asshole doormen at Boo Cassady's building and they didn't like him, he decided.

Who needed their approval anyway? They were shiftless, lazy incompetents, incapable of doing much more than holding open doors and offering up ingratiating smiles to fat-cat tenants.

'I'm here to see Dr Cassady,' Shafer announced to the familiar black wanker with *Mal* jauntily pinned on his lapel. It was probably there so that he wouldn't forget his own name.

'Right,' said Mal.

'Isn't that – right, *sir*?'

'Right, sir. I'll ring up Dr Cassady. Wait right here, sir.'

He could hear Boo through the doorman's staticky phone receiver. She had no doubt left explicit instructions that he be let up immediately. She certainly knew he was coming – they'd talked during the car ride from his house.

'You can go up now, sir,' the doorman finally said.

'I'm fucking her brains out, Mal,' Shafer said. He waltzed to the elevators with a grin. 'You watch that door now. Don't let anyone take it.'

Boo was in the hallway to meet him when the elevator cruised to a stop on ten. She was wearing at least five thousand dollars' worth of clothes from Escada. She had a great body, but she looked like a bullfighter or a marching band leader in the gaudy outfit. No wonder her first two husbands had divorced her. The second husband had been a therapist and treating MD. Still, she was a good, steady mistress who gave much better than she got. More importantly, she was able to get him Thorazine, Librium, Ativan, Xanax. Most of the drugs were samples from drug company representatives. Her husband had left them behind when they'd split. The amount of 'samples' left by the drug reps amazed Shafer, but she assured him it was common. She had other friends who were doctors and she hinted to Shafer that they helped her out for an occasional fuck. She could get all the drugs he needed.

Shafer wanted to take her right there in the hall and knew Boo would like the spontaneity and the passion that was so clearly missing from her life. Not tonight, though. He had more basic needs: the drugs.

'You don't look too happy to see me, Geoff,' she complained. She took his face in her manicured hands. Christ, her long, varnished red nails scared him. 'What happened, darling? Something's happened. Tell Boo what it is.'

Shafer took her in his arms and held her tightly against his chest. She had large soft breasts, great legs, too. He stroked her frosted-blond hair and nuzzled her with his chin. He loved the power he had over her – his goddamned shrink.

'I don't want to talk about it just yet. I'm here with you. I feel much better already.'

'What happened, darling? What's wrong? You have to share these things with me.'

So he made up a story on the spot, acted it out. Nothing to it. 'Lucy claims she knows about us. God, she was paranoid *before* I started to see you. Lucy always threatens to ruin my life. She says she'll leave me. Sue for what fucking little I have. Her father will have me fired, then blackball me with the government *and* the private sector, which he's perfectly capable of doing. The worst thing is she's poisoning the children, turning them against me. They use the same belittling phrases that she does: "colossal failure," "under-achiever," "get a real job, Daddy." Some days I wonder whether it isn't true.'

Boo kissed him lightly on the forehead. 'No, no, darling. You're well thought of at the embassy. I know you're a loving dad. You just have a bitchy, mean-spirited, spoiled-rotten wife who gets you down on yourself. Don't let her do it.'

He knew what she wanted to hear next, so he told her. 'Well, I won't have a bitchy wife for much longer. I swear to God I won't, Boo. I love you dearly, and I'm going to leave Lucy soon.'

He looked at her heavily made-up face and watched as tears formed and ruined her look. 'I love you, Geoff,' she whispered, and Shafer smiled as if he were pleased to hear it.

God, he was so good at this.

Lies.

Fantasies.

Role-playing games.

He unbuttoned the front of her mauve silk blouse, fondled her, then carried her inside to the sofa.

'This is my idea of therapy,' he whispered hotly in Boo's ear. 'This is all the therapy I need.'

Chapter Sixty

I had been up since before five that morning. Finally, I called Inspector Patrick Busby in Bermuda. I wanted to call every day, sometimes more than once, but I stopped myself.

It would only make things worse, strain my relations with the local police, and signal that I didn't trust them to handle the investigation properly.

'Patrick, it's Alex Cross calling from Washington. Did I catch you at a good time? Can you talk for a moment now?' I asked. I always tried to sound as upbeat as possible.

I wasn't, of course. I had been pacing the house, and already had breakfast with Nana. Then I'd waited impatiently until eight thirty to call Busby at the station house in Hamilton. He was an efficient man, and I knew he was there every morning by eight.

I could picture the thin, wiry policeman as we talked on the phone. I could see the tidy cubicle office where he worked. And superimposed over everything, I could still see Christine on her moped waving goodbye to me on that perfectly sunny afternoon.

'I have a few things for you from my contact at Interpol,' I said. I told him about an abduction of a woman in Jamaica earlier in the summer, and another in Barbados; both were similar, though not identical, to Christine's disappearance. I didn't think they were connected really, but I wanted to give him something, anything.

Patrick Busby was a thoughtful and patient man; he remained silent until I had finished talking before asking his usual quota of logical questions. I had observed that he was flawed as an interrogator because he was so polite. But at least he hadn't given up.

'I assume that neither abduction was ever solved, Alex. How about the women who were taken? Were they found?'

'No, neither woman was seen again. Not a sign of them. They're still missing.'

He sighed into the phone receiver. 'I hope your news is helpful in some way, Alex. I'll certainly call the other islands and check into it further. Anything else from Interpol or the FBI?'

I wanted to keep him on the line, the lifeline, as I now thought of it. 'A few far-flung possibilities in the Far East, Bangkok, the Philippines, Malaysia. Women abducted and murdered – all Jane Does. To be honest, nothing too promising at this point.'

I imagined him pursing his thin lips and nodding thoughtfully. 'I understand, Alex. Please keep giving me whatever you get from your sources. It's difficult for us to get help outside this small island. My calls for assistance frequently aren't returned. I sincerely wish that I had some good news for you on my end, but I'm afraid I don't.

'Other than Perri Graham, no one saw the man with the van. No one seems to have seen Christine Johnson in Hamilton or St George either. It's truly a baffling mystery. I don't believe that she ever got to Hamilton. It's frustrating for us, too. My prayers are with you and your wonderful family and, of course, John Sampson.'

I thanked Patrick Busby and hung up the phone. Slowly I went upstairs and dressed for work.

I still had nothing really substantial on the murder of Frank Odenkirk, and the Jefe was contacting me daily on e-mail. I certainly knew how the Odenkirk family felt. The media heat about the homicide had died down, though, as it often does. Unfortunately, so had the *Post* stories about the unsolved murders in Southeast.

While I was taking a hot shower, I thought about DeWitt Luke and the mysterious 'watcher' on S Street. What was the man in the Mercedes doing out there so long? Did he have some connection to the murders of Tori Glover and Marion Cardinal? None of this was making complete sense to me. That was the truly maddening thing about the Jane Doe murders and the Weasel. He wasn't like other repeat killers. He wasn't a criminal genius like Gary Soneji, but he was effective. *He got the job done, didn't he?*

I needed to think more about why someone had been lurking outside Tori Glover's apartment. Was he a private detective? A stalker? Or was he actually the murderer? One possibility hit me. Maybe the man in the car was an accomplice of the killer. Two of them working together. I'd seen that before in North Carolina.

I turned up the water, made it hotter. I thought it would help me to concentrate better. Steam out the cobwebs in my brain. Bring me back from the dead.

Nana finally banged on the pipes from downstairs in the kitchen. 'Get down here and go to work, Alex. You're using all my hot water up,' she yelled above the noise of the shower.

'Last time I looked, my name was on the water and gas bills,' I shouted back.

'It's still my hot water. Always was, always will be,' Nana replied.

Chapter Sixty-One

E very day, every night, I was out on the streets of Southeast, working harder than ever, but with nothing much to show for it. I continued to search for the mysterious purple-and-blue cab, and for the late-model black Mercedes DeWitt Luke had seen on S Street.

Sometimes I felt as if I were sleepwalking, but I kept at it, sleepwalking as fast as I could. Everything about the investigation seemed a longshot at best. I received tips and leads every day that had to be followed up; none of them went anywhere, though.

I got home at a little past seven that night but, tired as I was, I still let the kids drag me downstairs for their boxing lesson. Damon was showing me a lot of hand speed, and also some pretty good footwork and power for his age. He always had good spirit, and I was confident that he wouldn't abuse his burgeoning boxing skills at school.

Jannie was more a student of boxing, though she seemed to recognize the value of being able to defend herself. She was quick at mastering techniques, seeing connections, even if her heart wasn't completely into the sport. She preferred to torture her brother and me with her taunts and wit.

'Alex, telephone,' Nana called down from the top of the cellar stairs. I looked at my watch, saw it was twenty to eight.

'Practice your footwork,' I told the kids. Then I trudged up the steep stone stairs. 'Who is it?'

'Wouldn't say who it was,' Nana said as I got up to the kitchen. She was making shrimp and corn fritters and the room was also filled with the glorious smells of honey-baked apples and gingerbread. It was a late dinner for us – Nana had waited until I got home.

I picked up the phone on the kitchen counter. 'Alex Cross.'

'I know who you are, Detective Cross.'

A chill went right through me, and my hands shook.

'There's a pay phone outside the Budget Drugs on Fourth Street. *She's safe for now. We have her*. But hurry. Hurry! Maybe she's on the pay phone right now. I'm serious. *Hurry!*'

Chapter Sixty-Two

I exploded out the back kitchen door without saying a word to Nana or the kids. I didn't have time to explain where I was going, or why. Besides, I didn't really know exactly what was happening. Had I just spoken to the Weasel?

I'm serious. Hurry! Maybe she's on the pay phone right now!

I sprinted across Fifth Street, then down a side alley and over to Fourth. I dashed another four blocks south toward the Anacostia River. People on the streets watched me running. I was like a tornado suddenly roaring through Southeast.

I could see the metal frame of a pay phone from more than a block away as I approached Budget Drugs. A young girl was leaning against the graffiti-covered wall of the drugstore, talking on the phone.

I pulled out my detective's shield as I raced the final block toward her.

The phone gets a lot of use. Some people don't have phones in their homes in the neighborhood.

'Police. I'm a homicide detective. *Get off the phone!*' I told the girl, who looked nineteen or so. She stared at me as if she couldn't care less that a DC policeman was trying to commandeer the phone.

'I'm *using* this phone, mister. Don't care who you are. You can wait your turn like everybody else.' She turned away from me. 'Probably just calling your honey.'

I yanked the receiver away from her, disconnected her call.

'The fuck you think you are!' the girl shouted at me, her face screwed in anger. 'I was talking. The fuck you thinking.'

'I'm thinking you better get out of my face. This is a life-and-death situation. Get away from this phone. *Now! Get out of here!*' I could see she had no intention of leaving. 'There's been a kidnapping!' I was yelling like a madman.

She finally backed away. She was afraid that I was really crazy, and maybe I was.

I stood there with my hand on the phone receiver, trembling, waiting for the call to come in. I was winded. Sweat covered my body.

I stared up and down Fourth Street.

Nothing obvious or suspicious. I didn't see a purple-and-blue cab parked anywhere. No one watching me. Somebody definitely knew who I was. They had contacted me at the Belmont Hotel; they had called me at home.

I could still hear the words echoing loudly inside my head.

She's safe for now.
We have her.

Those were the words sent to me six weeks before in Bermuda. I hadn't heard anything from the sender until now.

My heart was pounding, sounding as if it were amplified in my ears. Adrenaline was rushing like powerful rivers through my bloodstream. I couldn't stand this. The caller had stressed that I *hurry*.

A young man approached the pay phone. He stared at my hand on the receiver. 'Wuzup, man? I need to use the phone. The phone? You hear me?'

'Police business.' I gave him a hard stare. 'Take a walk, please. Go!'

'Don't look like no police business to me,' he mumbled.

The man moved away, looking over his shoulder as he retreated down Fourth, frowning, but not stopping to argue with me.

The caller liked to be completely in control, I was thinking as I stood there helpless in front of the busy drugstore. He'd made me wait this long since the Bermuda call, possibly to demonstrate his power. Now he was doing it again. What did he really want, though? Why had he taken Christine? *We* have her, he'd said, and repeated the very same words when he called my house. Was there really a *we*? What kind of group did he represent? What did they want?

I stood at the pay phone for ten minutes, fifteen, twenty. I felt as if I were going mad, but I would stay there all night if I had to. I began to wonder if this was the right phone, but I knew it was. He had been crystal clear, calm, in control.

For the first time in weeks I allowed myself to truly hope that Christine might be alive. I imagined her face, deep brown eyes that showed so much love, and warmth. Maybe, just maybe, I would be allowed to talk to her.

I let my anger build toward the unknown caller. But then I cut it off, shut down my emotions, and waited with a cool head.

People came and went, in and out of the drugstore. A few wanted to use the phone. They took one look at me, then moved on, looked for another phone.

At five minutes to nine, the phone rang. I lifted the receiver instantly.

'This is Alex Cross,' I said.

'Yes, I know who you are. That's already been established. Here's what you should do. *Back all the way off. Just back away. Before you lose everything you care about.* It can happen so easily. In a snap. You're smart enough to understand that, aren't you?'

Then the caller hung up. The line was dead.

I banged the phone with the receiver. I cursed loudly. The manager from the drugstore had come outside and was staring at me.

'I'm going to call the police,' he said. 'That's a public phone.' I didn't bother to tell him I was the police.

Chapter Sixty-Three

Was it the Weasel who had called? Was I dealing with one killer, or more than one?

If only I had some idea who the caller was and who he meant by *we*. The message scared me just as much as the first one had, maybe even more; but it also gave me hope about Christine still being alive.

With hope came a jolting surge of pain. If only they would put Christine on the phone. I needed to hear her voice.

What did they want? *Back all the way off*. Back off from what?

The Odenkirk murder case? The Jane Does? Perhaps even Christine's disappearance? Was Interpol or the FBI getting close to something that had scared them? We weren't close to anything that could solve any of the cases, and I knew timing was critical.

Early Wednesday morning, Sampson and I drove to Eckington. A woman over there knew where a purple-and-blue cab was garaged. We'd followed up a dozen or so leads like this already, but it didn't matter. Every lead had to be investigated, every single one.

'Cab owner's name is Arthur Marshall,' I told Sampson as we walked from my car toward a red-brick garden apartment that had seen better days. Trouble is, Arthur Marshall seems to be a false identity. Landlady has him working at a Target store. According to Target, he doesn't. Never worked at any Target store. Hasn't been seen around for a while, according to the landlady.'

'Maybe we spooked him,' Sampson said.

'I hope not, but you may be right.'

I glanced around at the lower-middle-class neighborhood as we walked. Overhead, the sky was a bright-blue canvas, nearly empty of clouds. The street was packed with one- and two-story homes. Bright orange fliers were sticking out from the mailboxes. Every window was a possible lookout for the Weasel. *Back away*, he had warned. I couldn't. Not after what he'd done. I knew that I was taking a risk though.

He probably spotted us canvassing the streets. If he was responsible for the Jane Doe murders, he had been working undetected for a long while. He was skillful, good at killing, at not getting caught.

The landlady told us what she knew about Arthur Marshall, which wasn't much more than the information she needed to rent him a one-bedroom apartment and the attached garage. She gave us a set of keys for the place and said we could go look for ourselves.

The second house was similar to the landlady's except that it was painted Easter-egg blue. Sampson and I entered the garage first.

The purple-and-blue cab was there.

Arthur Marshall had told the landlady that he owned the cab and operated it as a part-time job. That was a possibility, but it seemed unlikely. The Weasel was close. I could feel it now. Had he known we would find the cab? Probably. Now what? What came next? What was his plan? His fantasy?

'I'm going to have to figure out how to get some techies in here,' I told Sampson. 'There has to be something in the cab, or maybe upstairs in the apartment. Hair, fibers, prints.'

'Hopefully no damn body parts,' Sampson said, and grimaced. It was typical cop humor, and so automatic that I didn't give it a second thought. 'Body parts are always popping up in these cases, Alex. I don't want to see it. I like feet attached to ankles, heads attached to necks, even if all the parts happen to be dead.'

Sampson searched around the front seat of the cab, with latex-gloved hands. 'Papers in here. Candy and gum wrappers, too. Why not call in a favor from Kyle Craig? Get the FBI boys over here.'

'Actually, I talked to Kyle last night,' I said. 'The Bureau's been involved for some time. He'll help out if we say the word.'

Sampson tossed me a pair of gloves and I examined the cab's backseat. I saw what could be bloodstains in the fabric of the seat cushion. The stains would be easy enough to check out.

John and I finally climbed upstairs into the apartment above the garage. It was dusty, grimy, without much furniture. Eerie and unpleasant on the eyes. It didn't look as if anyone lived there, but if someone did, they were really weird. The landlady had said as much.

The kitchen was mostly empty. An expensive juicer was the only personal indulgence. Not a low-end model – *expensive*. I took out my handkerchief and opened the refrigerator. There was nothing in it but bottled water and some aging fruit. The fruit was rotting and I hated to think of what else we might find here in the apartment.

'Health nut,' Sampson offered.

'Nut anyway,' I said. 'There's a sense of animal fear in here. He gets very tense, excited, when he comes to this place.'

'Yeah,' Sampson said, 'I know the feeling.'

We entered the bedroom, which had a small cot, a couple of stuffed chairs, nothing else. The sense of fear was here, too.

I opened the closet door and what I saw stopped me dead. There was a pair of khaki pants, a blue chambray shirt, a blue blazer – and something else.

'John, come here,' I called. 'John!'

'Oh, shit. Do I have to? Not more bodies.'

'Just come here. It's him. This is the Weasel's place. I'm sure of it. It's worse than a body.'

I opened the closet door wider and let Sampson see what I'd found there.

'Shit,' he groaned. *'Goddamn* it, Alex.'

Someone had put up pictures. Half-a-dozen black-and-white photographs were taped to the wall of the closet. It wasn't a killer's shrine. It was meant to be found.

There were pictures of Nana, Damon, Jannie, me, and Christine. Christine almost seemed to be smiling at the camera, that incredible smile of hers, those big welcoming eyes.

The pictures had been taken in Bermuda. Whoever had rented this apartment had taken them. Finally, I had something to link Christine's abduction to the murders in Washington. I knew who had taken her.

Back off.

Before you lose everything.

I sensed fear again. It was my own.

Chapter Sixty-Four

Patsy Hampton had decided that she wasn't ready to confide in Chief George Pittman just yet. She didn't want the Jefe interfering or crowding her. Also, she flat out didn't trust or like the bastard.

She still hadn't made up her mind what to do about Alex Cross. Cross was a complication. The more she checked him out, the better he looked. He seemed to be a very good, dedicated detective and she felt bad about keeping Chuck Hufstedler's information away from him. Chuck had been Cross's source first, but she'd used the techie's crush on her to gain an advantage. She didn't like herself for doing that.

She drove her Jeep to the British Embassy late that afternoon. She had Geoffrey Shafer under limited surveillance – hers. She could get more teams, but that would mean going to Pittman now, and she didn't want anyone to know what she had. She didn't want to be crowded.

She had done preliminary homework on Shafer. He was in the Security Service, which meant he was British Intelligence, operating outside England. Most likely he was a spy working out of the embassy on Massachusetts Avenue. His reputation was okay, good, actually. His current assignment supposedly had to do with the British Government's human-rights program, which meant the assignment was bullshit. He lived in Kalorama, and that was a high-rent district he shouldn't be able to afford on his salary. So, who the hell was this Shafer chap?

Hampton sat parked in her vehicle outside the embassy on California Street. She smoked a Marlboro Light and started to think things through. She really ought to talk to Cross about where he was with his investigation. Did he know anything that could help? Maybe he was onto Shafer? It was almost criminal for her not to contact Cross and share what she'd gotten from Chucky Cheese.

Pittman's dislike for Cross was well-known; he considered him competition. She didn't know Cross that well, but he got too many headlines. Still, she wished she knew what Cross had in his files, and especially if Geoffrey Shafer might have appeared on Cross's radar.

There was too much fricking noise on the fricking street near the British Embassy. Workers were doing construction on the Turkish Chancery across California Street. Hampton already had a headache – her life was one big headache – and she wished they would stop pounding and hammering and battering and sawing. For some reason or other, there was a crowd of people swarming all over the National Mosque today.

At a few minutes past five Shafer got into his Jaguar in a parking lot outside the glass-walled Rotunda.

She'd seen him twice before and he was in very good shape. Attractive, too, though not a physical type she herself responded to. Shafer sure didn't hang around long after the workday ended. Hampton figured he either had some place to go or he really hated his day job. Possibly both.

She stayed a safe distance behind the black Jag, following it along crowded Massachusetts Avenue. Shafer didn't seem to be heading home, and he wasn't going to Southeast either.

Where are we going tonight? she wondered as she tailed him. *And what does it have to do with the Four Horsemen? What game are you really playing? What are your fantasies?*

Are you a bad man, a murderer, Geoffrey? You don't look like it, Blondie. Such a nice spiffy car for a scumbag killer.

Chapter Sixty-Five

A fter work, Geoffrey Shafer joined the clogged artery of rush-hour traffic inching along Massachusetts. Turning out of the embassy he had spotted the black Jeep behind him.

The tail was still there as he drove down Massachusetts Avenue.

Who was in the Jeep? One of the other players? DC police? Detective Alex Cross? They had found the garage in Eckington. Now they'd found him. It had to be the bloody police.

He watched the black Jeep as it trailed four cars behind him. There was only one person inside and it looked like a woman. Could it possibly be Lucy? Had she discovered the truth about him? God, had she finally figured out who and what he was?

He picked up his mobile phone and made a call home. Lucy picked up after a couple of rings.

'Darling, I'm coming home, after all. There's a bit of a lull at the office. We can order in or something – unless you and the children already have plans.'

She blathered on in the usual maddening way. She and the twins had been going to see a movie, *Antz*, but they'd rather stay at home with him. They could order from Pizza Hut. It would be fun for a change.

'Yes, what fun,' Shafer said, and cringed at the thought. Pizza Hut served indigestible cardboard drenched with very bad tomato soup. He hung up, then took a couple of Vicodin and a Xanax. He thought he could feel cracks slowly opening up in his skull.

He made a dangerous U-turn on Massachusetts Avenue and headed toward home. He passed the Jeep going in the opposite direction and was tempted to wave. A woman driver. Now, who was she?

The pizza got to the house at around seven and Shafer opened an expensive bottle of Cabernet Sauvignon. He washed down another Xanax with the wine in the downstairs bathroom. Felt a little confused, fuzzy around the edges. That was all right, he supposed.

Jesus Christ, he couldn't stand being with his family, though; he felt as if he were going to crawl out of his skin. Ever since he'd been a boy in England he'd had a repetitive fantasy that he was actually a reptile and could shed his own skin. He'd had the dream long before he'd read any Kafka; he *still* had the disturbing dream.

He rolled three dice in his hand as he sipped his wine, played the game at the dinner table. If the number seventeen came up, he would murder them all tonight. He swore he would do it. First the twins, then Robert, and finally Lucy.

She kept prattling on and on about her day. He smiled blithely as she told him about her shopping trip to Bloomingdale's and Bath & Body Works and Bruno Cipriani at the mall. He considered the supreme irony of taking truckloads of antidepressants, and being more depressed. Jesus, he was cycling down again. How low could he go?

'Come, seventeen,' he finally said aloud.

'What, darling?' Lucy suddenly asked. 'Did you just say something?'

'He's already playing tonight's game,' said Robert, and snickered. 'Right, Daddy? It's your fantasy game. Am I right?'

'Right, son,' Shafer replied, thinking, *Christ, I am mad!*

He let the dice gently fall on the dining table, though. He would kill them – if their number came up. The dice rolled over and over, finally banking off the greasy pizza box.

'Daddy and his games,' Lucy said, and laughed. Erica and Tricia laughed. Robert laughed.

Six, five, one, he counted. *Damn, damn.*

'Are the two of us going to play tonight?' Robert asked.

Shafer forced a smile. 'Not tonight, Rob Boy. I'd like to, but I can't. I have to go out again.'

Chapter Sixty-Six

This was getting very interesting. Patsy Hampton watched Shafer leave the large and expensive house in Kalorama around eight thirty. He was off on another of his nightly jaunts. The guy was a regular vampire.

She knew that Cross and his friends called the killer the Weasel, and it certainly fit Shafer. There was something uncomfortable about him, something bent.

She followed the black Jag, but he didn't head toward Southeast, which disappointed her. He drove to a trendy supermarket, Sutton on the Run, which was just off Dupont Circle. Hampton knew the pricey store and called it Why Pay Less.

He parked the sports car illegally, then jogged inside. *Diplomatic immunity.* That pissed her the hell off. What a weasel he was, real Euro-trash.

While he was in the market, Hampton made a command decision. She was pretty sure she was going to talk to Alex Cross. She had thought a lot about it, the pros and cons. Now she figured that she might be endangering lives in Southeast by not sharing at least some of what she knew. If someone died, she wouldn't be able to bear it. Besides, Cross would have gotten the information if she hadn't interceded with Chuck Hufstedler.

Shafer shuffled back out of Sutton on the Run and glanced around crowded Dupont Circle. He had a small bag of overpriced groceries clutched in one arm. Groceries for whom, though? He didn't look in the direction of her Jeep, which was just peeking around the corner.

She followed the black Jag at a safe distance in the light traffic. He got on Connecticut Avenue. She didn't think he'd spotted her, though he was an MI6 man, so she needed to be careful.

Shafer wasn't far from Embassy Row. He wouldn't be going back to work now, would he? Why the groceries if he was headed to the embassy?

The Jaguar eventually turned into the underground garage of a prewar building in Woodley Park. THE FARRAGUT was engraved on a brass sign in front.

Patsy Hampton waited a few minutes, then she pulled into the garage behind the attendant in a small kiosk and identified herself.

'The Jag that came in before me, ever see it here before?' she asked.

The man nodded. He was around her age and she could tell he wanted to impress her if he could. 'Sure. I don't know him to talk to, though. Comes here to visit a lady on ten. Dr Elizabeth Cassady. She's a shrink. I assume he's a patient. He's got a funny look in his eyes,' the attendant said, 'but so do most people.'

'How about me?' Hampton asked.

'Nah. Well, maybe a little,' the attendant said, and grinned.

Shafer stayed upstairs with Dr Cassady for nearly two hours. Then he came down and went straight back to the house in Kalorama.

Patsy Hampton followed him, then watched the house for another half-hour. She thought that Shafer was probably in for the night. She drove to a nearby diner but didn't go inside right away. She picked up her mobile phone before she had too many second thoughts. She knew Cross's street, and got the phone number through information. Was it too late to call? Screw it, she was going through with this.

She was surprised when the phone was picked up on the first ring. She heard a pleasant male voice. Nice. Strong.

'Hello. Alex Cross.'

She almost hung up on him. Interesting that he'd intimidated her for a moment. 'This is Detective Patsy Hampton. I've been doing some work on the Jane Does. I've been following a man who is a suspect. I think we should talk.'

'Where are you, Patsy?' Cross said, without hesitation. 'I'll come to you. Just tell me where.'

'I'm at the City Limits diner on Connecticut Avenue.'

'I'm on my way,' said Cross.

Chapter Sixty-Seven

I wasn't totally surprised that Pittman had assigned someone to the Jane Does. Especially after Zach Taylor's article in the *Washington Post*. I was interested in any leads Detective Hampton might have turned up.

I had seen Patsy Hampton around and she obviously knew who I was. She was supposed to be on a fast track; she was a smart and effective senior homicide detective, though from what I'd heard, she was also a lone wolf. She didn't have any friends in the department, as far as I knew.

She was much prettier than I remembered. She was in very trim, athletic shape, probably early thirties, short blond hair, piercing blue eyes that cut through the diner haze.

She'd put on bright-red lipstick for our meeting, or maybe she wore it all the time. I wondered what was on her mind and what her motives were. I didn't think I could trust her.

'You or me first?' Detective Hampton asked, after we'd ordered coffee. We were seated at a table in the City Limits diner, near a window looking out on Connecticut Avenue.

'I'm afraid I don't know what this is about,' I told her.

She sipped her coffee and gave me a look over the cup's rim. She was a strong-willed, confident person. Her eyes told me that much.

'You really didn't know someone else was working the Jane Does?'

I shook my head. 'Pittman said that the cases were closed. I took him at his word. He suspended some good detectives for working the cases after hours.'

'There's a lot of seriously nasty crap going on in the department. So what's new though,' she said as she set down her cup. She gave a deep sigh. 'I thought I could deal with it by myself. Now I'm not so sure.'

'Pittman assigned you to the Jane Does? Personally?'

She nodded, then her blue eyes narrowed. 'He assigned me to the Glover and Cardinal murders, and any others I wanted to look into. Gave me free rein.'

'And you say you have something?'

'Maybe. I've got a possible suspect. He's involved in a role-playing game that features victims being murdered, mostly in Southeast. It's all after-the-fact stuff, so he could have read the news stories and then fantasized about them. He works at the British Embassy.'

This was a new piece of information, and it surprised me. 'How far have you gone with this?'

'Not to Pittman, if that's what you mean. I've done a little discreet checking on the suspect. Trouble is, he seems to be a solid citizen. Very good at his job – supposedly. At least that's the official word from the embassy. Nice family in Kalorama. I've been watching Shafer a little, hoping I'd get lucky. His first name is Geoffrey.'

I knew she was supposed to be a little bit of a loose cannon, and that she didn't suffer fools gladly. 'You're out here alone tonight?' I asked her.

Hampton shrugged. 'That's how I usually operate. Partners slow me down. Chief Pittman knows how I like to work. He gave me the green light. All green, all day long.'

I knew that she was waiting for me to give her something – if I had anything. I decided to play along. 'We found a cab that the killer apparently used in Southeast. He kept it in a garage in Eckington.'

'Anybody see the suspect in the neighborhood?' She asked the right first question.

'The landlady saw him. I'd like to show her pictures of your guy. Or you want to do it yourself?'

Her face was impassive. 'I'll do it. First thing in the morning. Anything revealing in the apartment?'

I decided to be straight with her. She'd initiated the meeting, after all. 'Photographs of me and my family covered a wall in a closet. They were taken of us in Bermuda. While we were on vacation. He was there watching us all the time.'

Hampton nodded gently. 'I heard your fiancée disappeared in Bermuda. Word gets around.'

'There were photographs of Christine too,' I said.

Her blue eyes softened. I got a quick look behind her tough façade. 'I'm really sorry about your loss.'

'I haven't given up yet,' I told her. 'Listen, I don't want any credit for solving these cases, just let me help. He called me at home last night. Somebody did. Told me to back off. I assume that he meant this investigation, but I'm not supposed to be on it. If Pittman hears about us—'

Detective Hampton interrupted me. 'Let me think about everything you've said. You know that Pittman will totally crucify me if he finds out. You have no idea. Trouble is, I don't trust him.' Hampton's gaze was intense and direct. 'Don't mention any of this to your buddies, or Sampson. You never know. Just let me sleep on it. I'll try to do the right thing. I'm not such a hardass really. Just a little weird, you know.'

'Aren't we all,' I said, and smiled. Hampton was a tough detective, but I felt okay about her. I took something out of my pocket. A beeper.

'Keep this. If you get in trouble or get another lead, you can beep me anytime. If you find something out, please let me know. I'll do the same. If Shafer's the one, I want to talk to him before we bring him in. This is personal for me. You can't imagine how personal.'

Hampton continued to make eye contact, studying me. She reminded me of someone I'd known a while back, another complicated woman cop named Jezzie Flanagan. 'I'll think about it. I'll let you know.'

'All right. Thanks for calling me in on this.'

She stood. 'You're not in on it yet. Like I said, I'll let you know.' Then she touched my hand. 'I really am sorry about your friend.'

Chapter Sixty-Eight

We both knew I was in, though. We'd made some kind of a deal in the City Limits diner. I just hoped I wasn't being set up by Hampton and Pittman or God knows who else.

During the next two days we talked four times. I still wasn't sure that I could trust her, but I didn't have a choice. I had to keep moving forward. She had already visited the landlady who'd rented out the apartment and garage in Eckington. The landlady hadn't recognized the pictures of Shafer. Possibly he'd worn some kind of disguise when he met with her.

If Patsy Hampton was setting me up, she was one of the best liars I'd met, and I've known some good ones. During one of the calls, she confessed that Chuck Hufstedler had been her source, and that she'd gotten him to keep the information from me. I shrugged it off. I didn't have the time or energy to be angry at either of them.

In the meantime, I spent a lot of time at home. I didn't believe the killer would come after my family, not when he already had Christine, but I couldn't tell that for sure. When I wasn't there, I made sure Sampson or somebody else was checking on the house.

On the third night after I met her, Patsy Hampton and I had a breakthrough of sorts. She actually invited me to join her on the stakeout at Shafer's town house in Kalorama Heights.

He had arrived home from work before six and remained there until past nine.

He had a nice-looking ex-pat family, three children, a wife, a nanny. He lived very well. Nothing about his life or surroundings suggested he might be a killer.

'He seems to go out every night around this time,' Hampton told me as we watched him walk to a shiny black Jag parked in a graveled driveway on the side of the house.

'Creature of habit,' I said. A *weasel*.

'Creature anyway,' she said. We both smiled. The ice was breaking up a little between us. She admitted that she had checked me out thoroughly. She'd decided that Chief Pittman was the bad guy in all of this, not me.

The Jaguar pulled out of the drive and we followed Shafer to a night spot in Georgetown. He didn't seem to be aware of us. The problem was that we had to catch him doing something; we had no concrete evidence that he was our killer.

Shafer sat by himself at the bar and we watched him from the street. Did he perch by the window on purpose? I wondered. Did he know we were watching? Was he playing with us?

I had a bad feeling that he was. This was all some kind of bizarre game to him. He left the bar around a quarter to twelve and returned home just past midnight.

'Bastard.' Patsy grimaced, and shook her head. Her blond hair was soft and had a nice bounce to it. She definitely reminded me of Jezzie Flanagan, a Secret Service agent I'd worked with on the kidnapping of two children in Georgetown.

'He's in for the night?' I asked. 'What was that all about? He leaves the house to watch the Orioles baseball game at a bar in Georgetown?'

'That's how it's been the last few nights. I think he knows we're out here.'

'He's an intelligence officer. He knows surveillance. We also know he likes to play fantasy games. At any rate, he's home for the night, so I'm going home too, Patsy. I don't like leaving my family alone too long.'

'Good night, Alex. Thanks for the help. We'll get him. And maybe we'll find your friend soon.'

'I hope so.'

On the drive home, I thought a little about Detective Patsy Hampton. She struck me as a lonely person, and I wondered why. She was thoughtful and interesting once you got past her tough façade. I wondered if anyone could really get through the façade though.

There was a light on in our kitchen when I rolled into the driveway. I strolled around to the back door and saw Damon and Nana, in their bathrobes at the stove. Everything seemed all right.

'Am I breaking up a pajama party?' I asked as I eased in through the back door.

'Damon has an upset stomach. I heard him in the kitchen so I came out to get in his way.'

'I'm all right. I just couldn't sleep. I saw you were still out,' he said. 'It's after midnight.'

He looked worried, and also a little sad. Damon had really liked Christine and he told me a couple of times that he was looking forward to having a mom again. He'd already begun to think of her that way. He and Jannie missed Christine a whole lot. Twice, they'd had important women taken away from them.

'I was working a little late. That's all. It's a very complicated case, Damon, but I think I'm making progress,' I said. I went to the cabinet and took out two tea bags.

'I'll make you tea,' Nana offered.

'I can do it,' I said, but she reached for the bags and I let her take them away from me. It doesn't pay to argue with Nana, especially not in her kitchen.

'You want some tea and milk, big guy?' I asked Damon.

'All right,' he said. He pronounced it *ah-yite*, as they do in the playgrounds, and probably even at the Sojourner Truth School.

'You sound like that poor excuse of an NBA point guard Alan Iverson,' Nana said to him. She didn't much like street slang, never had. She had started off as an English teacher and never lost her love of books and language. She loved Toni Morrison, Alice Walker, Maya Angelou, and also Oprah Winfrey for bringing their books to a wider audience.

'He's the fastest guard in the league, *Grandma Moses*. Shows what you know about basketball,' said Damon. 'You probably think Magic Johnson is still playing in the league. And *Wilt Chamberlain*.'

'I like Marbury with the Timberwolves, and Stoudamire with Portland, formerly with Toronto,' Nana said, and gave a little triumphant smile. '*Ah-yite?*'

Damon laughed. Nana probably knew more about NBA point guards than either of us. She could always get you if she wanted to.

We sat at the kitchen table and drank tea with milk and too much sugar, and we were mostly quiet, but it was kind of nice. I love family, always have. Everything that I am flows from that. Finally, Damon got up from the table. He went to the sink and rinsed out his cup.

'I can probably sleep now,' he reported to us. 'Give it a try anyway.'

He came back to the table and gave Nana and me a kiss before he went back upstairs to bed. 'You miss her, don't you?' he whispered against my cheek.

'Of course I miss Christine,' I said to Damon. 'All the time. Every waking minute.' I didn't make mention of the fact that I was out late because I was observing the sonofabitch who may have abducted her. Nor did I say anything about the other detective on surveillance, Patsy Hampton.

When Damon left, Nana put her hand in mine and we sat like that for a few minutes before I went up to bed.

'I miss her, too,' Nana finally said. 'I'm praying for you both, Alex.'

Chapter Sixty-Nine

The next evening, at around six, I took off early from work and went to Damon's choir practice at the Sojourner Truth School. I'd put together a good-sized file on Geoffrey Shafer, but I didn't have anything that concretely linked him to any of the murders. Neither did Patsy Hampton. Maybe he was just a fantasy-game player. Or maybe the Weasel was just being more careful since his taxi had been found.

It tore me up to go to the Truth School, but I had to go. I realized how hard it must be for Damon and Jannie to go there every day. The school brought back too many memories of Christine. It was as if I was suffocating, all the breath being squeezed out of my lungs. At the same time, I was in a cold sweat that coated the back of my neck and forehead.

A little while after the practice began, Jannie quietly reached over and took my hand. I heard her sigh softly. We were all doing a lot more touching and emoting since Bermuda, and I don't think we have ever been closer as a family.

She and I held hands through most of the choir practice, which included the Welsh folk song 'All Through the Night'; Bach's 'My heart ever faithful, sing praises'; and a very special arrangement of the spiritual 'O Fix Me.'

I kept imagining that Christine would suddenly appear at the school, and once or twice I actually turned back toward the archway that led to her office. Of course she wasn't there, which filled me with inconsolable sadness and the deepest emptiness. I finally cleared my mind of all thought, just shut down, and let my whole self be the music, the glorious sound of the boys' voices.

After we got home from the choir practice, Patsy Hampton checked in with me from her surveillance post. It was a little past eight. Nana and the kids were putting out cold chicken, slices of pears and apples, Cheddar cheese, a salad of endive and bibb lettuce.

Shafer was still home and, of all things, a children's birthday party was going on there, Patsy reported. 'Lots of smiling kids from the neighborhood, plus a rent-a-clown called Silly Billy. Maybe we're on the wrong track here, Alex.'

'I don't think so. I think our instincts are right about him.'

I told her I would come over at around nine to keep her company; that was the time when Shafer usually left the house.

Just past eight thirty the phone in the kitchen rang again as we were digging into the cold, well-spiced, delicious chicken. Nana frowned as I picked up the phone.

I recognized the voice.

'I told you to back off, didn't I? Now you have to pay some consequences for disobeying. It's your fault! There's a pay phone at the old Monkey House at the National Zoo. The zoo closes at eight, but you can get in through the gardening-staff gate. Maybe Christine Johnson is there at the zoo waiting for you. You better get over there quick and find out. Run, Cross, run. Hurry! *We have her.*'

The caller hung up and I charged upstairs for my Glock. I called Patsy Hampton and told her I'd gotten another call, presumably from the Weasel. I'd be at the National Zoo.

'Shafer's still at his kid's birthday party,' she told me. 'Of course, he could have called from the house. I can see Silly Billy's truck from where I'm parked.'

'Keep in contact with me, Patsy. Phones and beepers. Beeper for *emergencies* only. Be careful with him.'

'Okay. I'm fine here, Alex. Silly Billy doesn't pose too much of a threat. Nothing will happen at his house. Go to the zoo, Alex. *You* be careful.'

Chapter Seventy

I was at the National Zoo by ten to nine. I was thinking that the zoo was actually pretty close to Dr Cassady's apartment at the Farragut. Was it a coincidence that I was so close to Shafer's shrink? I didn't believe in coincidences anymore.

I called Patsy Hampton before I left the car, but she didn't pick up this time. I didn't beep her – this wasn't an emergency, or not so far.

I knew the zoo from lots of visits with Damon and Jannie, but even better from when I was a boy and Nana used to bring me, and sometimes Sampson, who was nearly six foot by the time he was eleven. The main entrance to the zoo was at the corner of Connecticut and Hawthorne Avenues, but the old Monkey House was nearly a mile diagonally across the grounds from there.

No one seemed to be around, but the gardening-staff gate was unlatched – as the caller said it would be. He knew the zoo, too. More games, I kept thinking. He definitely loved to play.

As I hurried into the park, a steep horizon of trees and hills blocked out the lights from the surrounding city. There was only an occasional foot lamp for light, and it was eerie and frightening to be in there alone. Of course, I was sure I wasn't alone.

The Monkey House was farther inside the gates than I had remembered. I finally located it in the dark. It looked like an old Victorian railway station. Across a cobblestoned circle there was a more modern structure that I knew was the Reptile House.

A sign over the twin doors of the old Monkey House read: WARNING: QUARANTINE – DO NOT ENTER! More eeriness. I tried the tall twin doors, but they were securely locked.

On the wall beside the doors I saw a faded blue-and-white sign – the international pictograph indicating there was a phone inside. *Was that the phone he wanted me to use?*

I shook the doors, which were old and wooden and rattled loudly. Inside, I could hear monkeys starting to scream and act out. First the smaller primates: spider monkeys, chimpanzees, gibbons. Then the deeper grunt of a gorilla.

I caught sight of a dim red glow across the cobblestoned circle. Another pay phone was over there.

I hurried across the square. Checked my watch. It was two minutes past nine. *He kept me waiting the last time.*

I thought about his game-playing. Was this all a role-playing game to him? How did he win? Lose?

I worried that I wasn't at the right phone. I didn't see any others, but there was always the one locked inside the old Monkey House.

Was that the phone he wanted me to use? I felt frantic and hyper. So many dangerous emotions were building up inside me.

I heard a long, sustained '*aaaaahhhh*,' like the sound of a football crowd at the opening kickoff. It startled me until I realized it was the apes in the Monkey House.

Was something wrong in there? *An intruder?* Something or someone near the phone?

I waited another five minutes, and then it dragged on to ten minutes. It was driving me crazy. I almost couldn't bear it any longer, and I thought about beeping Patsy.

Then my beeper went off, and I jumped!

It was Patsy. It had to be an emergency.

I stared at the silent pay phone; I waited a half-minute or so. Then I snatched it up.

I called the beeper number and left the number of the pay phone. *I waited some more.*

Patsy didn't call me back.

Neither did the mystery caller.

I was in a sweat.

I had to make a decision now. I was caught in a very bad place. My head was starting to reel.

Suddenly the phone rang. I grabbed at it, almost dropped the receiver. My heart was pounding like a bass drum.

'We have her.'

'*Where?*' I yelled into the receiver.

'She's at the Farragut, of course.'

The Weasel hung up. He never said she was safe.

Chapter Seventy-One

I couldn't imagine why Christine would be at the Farragut in Washington, but he'd said she was there. Why would he do that if she wasn't? What was he doing to me? To her?

I ran toward where I thought Cathedral Avenue was located. But it was very dark in the zoo, almost pitch-black. My vision was tunneling, maybe because I was close to being in shock. I couldn't think straight.

My mind in a haze, I tripped over a dark slab of rock, went down on one knee. I cut my hands, tore my pants. Then I was up again, running through thick high bushes that grabbed and ripped at my face and arms.

Animals all around the zoo howled, moaned, bellowed insanely. They sensed something was wrong. I could make out the sounds of grizzlies and elephant seals. I realized that I had to be approaching Arctic Circle, but I couldn't remember where it was in relation to the rest of the zoo or the city streets.

Up ahead was a high Gibraltar-like rock. I clambered up the rock to try and get my bearings.

Down below I saw a cluster of cages, shuttered gift stores and snack bars, two large veldts. I knew where I was now. I hurriedly climbed back down the rock and started to run again. Christine was at the Farragut. Would I finally find her? Could it actually be happening?

I passed African Alley, then the Cheetah Conservation Station. I came to a vast field and what looked like large haystacks scattered everywhere. I realized that they were bison. I was somewhere near the Great Plains Way.

The beeper in my pocket went off again.

Patsy! An emergency! Where was she? Why hadn't she called back at the pay-phone number I'd given her?

I was soaked in sweat and almost hyperventilating. Thank God I could finally see Cathedral Avenue, then Woodley Road up ahead.

I was a long way from where I'd parked my car, but I was close to the Farragut apartment building.

I ran another hundred yards in the dark, then climbed the stone wall separating the zoo from the city streets. There was blood smeared on my hands, and I didn't know where it had come from. The knee I'd scraped? Scratches from swinging branches? I could hear the loud wail of sirens in the near distance. Was it coming from the Farragut?

I headed there in a sprint. It was a little past ten o'clock. Over an hour and a half had already gone by since the call to my house.

The beeper was buzzing inside my shirt pocket.

Chapter Seventy-Two

Something bad had happened at the Farragut. The burping screams of approaching sirens were getting louder as I raced down Woodley. I was reeling, feeling dizzy. I couldn't focus my mind. I realized that, for one of the few times in recent years, I was close to panic.

Neither the police nor the EMS had arrived at the apartment building yet. I was going to be the first on the scene.

Two doormen and several tenants in bathrobes were clustered in front of the underground garage entrance. It couldn't be Christine. It just couldn't be. I raced across a quadrant of lawn toward them. Was the Weasel here at the Farragut?

They saw me coming and looked as frightened as I felt inside. I must have been quite a sight. I remembered that I'd fallen once or twice inside the zoo. I probably looked like a madman, maybe even like a killer. There was blood on my hands and who knew where else.

I reached for my wallet, shook it open to expose my detective's shield.

'Police. What's happened here?' I shouted. 'I'm a police detective. My name is Alex Cross.'

'Somebody has been murdered, Detective.' One of the doormen finally spoke. 'This way. Please.'

I followed the doorman down the steeply sloped concrete driveway leading into the garage.

'It's a woman,' he said. 'I'm pretty sure she's gone. I called nine-one-one.'

'Oh God,' I gasped out loud. My stomach clutched. Patsy Hampton's Jeep was tucked back in a corner space. The door of the Jeep was open and light spilled outside.

I felt terrible fear, pain, and shock as I hurried around the door. Patsy Hampton was sprawled across the front seat. I could tell she was probably dead.

We have her. That was what the message meant. Jesus God, no. They had murdered Patsy Hampton. They had told me to back off. For God's sake, no.

Her bare legs were twisted and pinned under the steering wheel. Her upper body was crumpled over, at almost a right angle. Her head was thrown back and lay partly off the seat, on the passenger's side. Her blond hair was matted with blood. Her vacant blue eyes stared up at me.

Patsy was wearing a white knit sport shirt. There were deep lacerations around her throat. Bright-red blood was still oozing from the wound. She was naked below the waist. I didn't see any clothes anywhere.

I suspected she'd been strangled with some kind of wire, and that she'd only been dead for a few minutes. A rope or garotte had been used in some of the Jane Doe murders. The Weasel liked to use his hands, to work close to his victims, possibly to watch and feel their pain, maybe even while he was sexually assaulting them.

I saw what looked like paint chips around the deep, ugly neck wounds. Paint chips?

Something else seemed very strange to me. The Jeep's radio had been partly dislodged, but left behind. I didn't understand why the radio had been tampered with, but it didn't seem important right now.

I leaned back out of the Jeep. 'Is anyone else hurt? Have you checked?'

The doorman shook his head. 'No. I don't think so. I'll go look.'

Sirens finally screeched inside the garage. I saw red and blue lights flashing and whirling against the ceiling and walls. Some of the tenants had made it into the garage as well. Why did they have to come and gape at this terrible crime?

A very bad thought flashed in my head. I climbed out of the Jeep, grabbing Patsy's keys out of the ignition. I hurried around to the back. I pushed the release and the rear door came open. My heart was thundering again. I didn't want to look inside, but when I did, there was nothing. *Jesus, Jesus, Jesus. We have her! Was Christine here too? Where?*

I looked around the garage. Up near the entrance I spotted Geoffrey Shafer's sports car, the black Jaguar. He was there at the Farragut. Patsy must have followed him.

I ran across the garage to the Jag. I felt the hood, then the exhaust pipe. Both were still warm. The car hadn't been in the garage very long. The doors were locked. I couldn't break in. I was all too aware of the search and seizure constraints.

I stared inside the Jaguar. In the backseat, I could see dress shirts on wire hangers. The hangers were white and I thought of the chips in Detective Hampton's wounds. Had he strangled her with a hanger? Was Shafer the Weasel? Was he still in the building? What about Christine? Was she here, too?

I said a few words to the patrolmen who'd just arrived, the first on the scene after me. Then I took them with me.

The helpful doorman told me which floor Shafer's therapist's apartment was on. The number was 10D, the penthouse. Like all buildings in DC, the Farragut was restricted to a height no more than the Capitol dome.

I took the elevator with the two uniformed cops, both in their twenties, both scared shitless I'd bet. I was close to rage. I knew I had to be careful; I had to act professionally, to control my emotions somehow. If there was an arrest, there would be questions to answer, such as what I was doing here in the first place. Pittman would be on my case in a second.

I talked to the policemen on the way up, more to calm myself than anything else.

'You okay, Detective?' one of them asked me.

'I'm fine. I'm all right. The killer might still be in the building. The victim was a detective, one of our own. She was on surveillance here. The suspect has a relationship with a woman upstairs.'

The faces of both young cops tightened. It was bad enough to have seen the murdered woman in her car, but to learn that she was a policewoman, a detective on surveillance, made it worse. Now they were about to confront a cop killer.

We hurried out of the elevator to apartment 10D. I led the way and pressed the bell. I saw what appeared to be drops of blood on the hallway carpet near the door. I noticed the blood on my hands, saw the two cops staring at them.

No answer from inside the apartment, so I pounded my fist on the door. Was everyone okay in there? 'Police, open up! DC police!'

I could hear a woman shouting inside. I had my Glock out, the safety off. I was angry enough to kill Shafer. I didn't know if I could hold myself back.

The uniformed patrolmen took their pistols out of their holsters, too. After just a few seconds I was ready to kick down the door, search and seizure constraints or not. I kept seeing Patsy Hampton's face, her dead, vacant eyes, the savage wounds in her crushed throat.

Finally, the door to the apartment slowly opened.

A blonde woman was standing there. Dr Cassady, I assumed. She wore an expensive-looking light-blue suit with lots of gold buttons, but she was barefoot. She looked frightened and angry.

'What do you want?' she demanded. 'What the hell is going on here? Do you know what you've done? You've interrupted a therapy session.'

Chapter Seventy-Three

Geoffrey Shafer stepped into the doorway and stood a few feet behind the irate therapist. He was tall and imposing and very blond. *He was the Weasel, wasn't he?*

'What the hell's the problem here? Who are you, sir, and what do you want?' he asked, in a clipped English accent.

'There's been a murder,' I said. 'I'm Detective Cross.' I showed them my badge. I kept looking past Shafer and Dr Cassady, trying to spot something that would give me probable cause to come inside the apartment. There were lots of plants on the sills, hanging in windows – philodendron, azalea, English ivy. Dhurrie rugs in light pastels, over-stuffed furniture.

'No. There's certainly no murderer here,' the therapist said. 'Leave this instant.'

'You should do as the lady says,' Shafer said.

Shafer didn't look like a murderer. He was dressed in a navy suit, a white shirt, moiré tie, a pocket square. Impeccable taste. Completely unruffled and unafraid.

Then I glanced to look at his shoes. I almost couldn't believe it. The gods had finally smiled at me.

I pulled out my Glock and pointed it at Shafer. At the Weasel. I went up to him and bent on one knee. My whole body was trembling. I examined the right leg of his trousers.

'What the *hell* are you doing?' he asked, pulling away from me. 'This is completely absurd.'

'I'm with the British Embassy,' Shafer then stated. 'I'll repeat, I'm with the British Embassy. You have no right to be here.'

'Officers,' I called to the two patrolmen who were still outside the door. I tried to act calm, but I wasn't. 'Come here and look. You see this?'

Both patrolmen moved closer to Shafer. They entered the living room.

'*Stay out of this apartment!*' The therapist raised her voice close to a scream.

'Remove your trousers,' I said to Shafer. 'You're under arrest.'

Shafer lifted his leg and gave a look. He saw a dark stain, Patsy Hampton's blood, smudged on the cuff of his trousers. Fear shot through his eyes and he finally lost his cool.

'You put that blood there! You did it,' he yelled at me. He pulled out an identification badge. 'I am an official at the British Embassy. I don't have to put up with this outrage. I have diplomatic immunity. I will not take off my trousers for you. Call the embassy immediately! *I demand diplomatic immunity.*'

'Get out of here now!' Dr Cassady yelled loudly. Then she pushed one of the patrolmen.

It was just what Shafer needed. He broke free, and ran back through the living room. He rushed into the first room down the hallway, slammed the door, and locked it.

The Weasel was trying to get away. It couldn't happen. I couldn't let it. I got to the door seconds behind him. 'Come out of there, Shafer! You're under arrest for the murder of Detective Patsy Hampton.'

Dr Cassady came screaming down the hall after me.

I heard the toilet flush in the bathroom. No, no, no! I reared back powerfully, and kicked in the door.

Shafer was pulling off his trousers, standing on one leg. I tackled him hard, knocked him over, then held him face down against the tile floor. He screamed curses at me, flailed his arms, bucked his lower body. I pushed his face harder into the floor.

The therapist tried to pull me off Shafer. She was scratching my face, pounding my back with her fists. It took both policemen to restrain her.

'You can't do this to me!' Shafer was yelling at the top of his voice, twisting and turning beneath me, a powerful stallion of a man.

'This is illegal. I have diplomatic immunity!'

I turned to one of the officers.

'Cuff him.'

Chapter Seventy-Four

It was a long and very sad night at the Farragut, and I didn't leave until past three. I had never lost a partner before, although I had once come close with Sampson, in North Carolina. I realized that I'd already come to think of Patsy Hampton as a partner, and a friend. At least we had the Weasel in custody.

I slept in the next morning, allowing myself the small luxury of not setting the alarm. Still, I was wide awake by seven. I'd been dreaming about Patsy Hampton, and also about Christine; different, vivid scenes with each of them, the kind of frenetic dreams where you wake up feeling as tired as when you went to bed. I said a prayer for both of them before I finally rolled out of bed. We had the Weasel. Now I had to get the truth out of him.

I slipped on a somewhat worn white satin robe. Muhammad Ali had worn it in his training camp in Manila before the Joe Frazier fight. Sampson gave it to me for my fortieth birthday. He appreciated that while most people would use the robe as some kind of sacred exhibit in their house, I routinely wear it to breakfast.

I love the old robe, which is unusual for me since I'm not particularly into mementos and souvenirs. Maybe part of it is that I'm supposed to resemble Ali physically, or so people tell me. I might be a little better looking, but he was definitely the better man.

When I got down to the kitchen, Nana and the kids were sitting at the table watching the small portable TV she keeps there, but doesn't use very often. She prefers to read or chitchat and, of course, cook.

'Ali.' Jannie looked up at me and grinned, but then her eyes went back to the TV. 'You should watch this, Daddy.'

Nana muttered into her cup of tea, 'Your British murderer is all over the news this morning. TV and the newspaper, too. "Diplomatic Immunity May Bar Prosecution of British Embassy Suspect," "Spy Linked to Detective Slay." They already interviewed people in Union Station and on Pennsylvania Avenue. Everybody's mad as a hatter about this diplomatic immunity disgrace, as they call it. It's just terrible.'

'I'm mad. It's not right,' Damon said. 'Not if he did it. Did he, Dad? Did he do it?'

I nodded. 'He did it.' I poured milk into my coffee. I wasn't quite ready to deal with Geoffrey Shafer, or the kids, or especially the terrible, senseless murder the night before. 'Anything else on the news?'

'The Wizards kicked butt,' Damon said with a straight face. 'Rod Strickland had a double-double.'

'*Shhhh.*' Nana gave us both a mighty look of irritation. 'CNN carried stories *from London*. The media there is already comparing this to that unfortunate nanny case in Massachusetts. They say that Geoffrey Shafer is a decorated war hero and that he claims, with good reasons, he was framed by the police. I assume that means you, Alex.'

'Yes, it does. Let's watch CNN for a few minutes,' I said. Nobody objected, so I switched the channel. A hard knot was forming in my stomach. I didn't like what I was seeing and hearing on TV.

Almost immediately, a reporter came on the screen from London. He introduced himself, and then proceeded to give a pompous thirty-second summary of the previous evening's events.

The reporter looked gravely into the camera. 'And now, in a dramatic development, we have learned that the Washington Police Department is investigating a bizarre twist. According to the American press, the senior detective who arrested Geoffrey Shafer might himself be a suspect in the murder case.'

I shook my head and frowned. 'I'm innocent,' I said, to Nana and the kids. They knew that of course.

'Until proven guilty,' said Jannie, with a little wink.

Chapter Seventy-Five

There was a loud hubbub out in front of the house and Jannie ran to the living-room window to look. She hurried back to the kitchen with wide eyes, loud-whispering: 'It's TV cameras and the newspapers outside. CNN, NBC, lots of them, like that other time with Gary Soneji. Remember?'

'Of course we remember,' said Damon. 'Nobody's retarded in this house except you.'

'Oh good Lord, Alex,' Nana said, 'don't they know decent people are eating breakfast?' She shook her head, rolled her eyes. 'The vultures are here again. Maybe I should throw some meat scraps out the front door.'

'*You* go talk to them, Jannie,' I said, and looked back at the TV. I don't know why I was feeling so cynical, but I was. My remark quieted her down for a half-second, but then she figured it was a joke. She pointed a finger at herself. 'Gotcha!'

I knew they wouldn't go away, so I finally took my mug of coffee and headed toward the front door. I walked out into a beautiful fall morning, temperature probably in the low sixties.

Leaves rustled merrily in the elm and maple trees, dappled sunshine fell on the heads of the TV crew and print journalists gathered at the edges of our front lawn.

The vultures.

'Don't be absurd and ridiculous around here,' I said, and then calmly sipped my coffee as I stared at the noisy press mob. 'Of course I didn't kill Detective Patsy Hampton, or frame anyone for her murder.'

Then I turned on my heels and walked back inside without answering a single question from any of them.

Nana and the kids were right behind the big wooden door, listening. 'That was pretty good,' Nana said, and her eyes sparkled and beamed.

I went upstairs and got dressed for work. 'Go to school. *Now!*' I called back to Jannie and Damon. 'Get straight As. Play nicely with your friends. Pay no attention to the craziness everywhere around you.'

'Yes, Daddy!'

Chapter Seventy-Six

On account of his request for diplomatic immunity, we weren't allowed to question Geoffrey Shafer about Detective Hampton's murder, or anything else. I was incredibly frustrated. We had the Weasel, and we couldn't go near him.

Investigators were lying in wait for me that morning at the station house, and I knew it was going to be a long and excruciating day. I was interviewed by Internal Affairs, then the city's chief counsel, and finally Mike Kersee from the district attorney's office.

Pay no attention to the craziness everywhere around you, I reminded myself over and over, but my own good advice wasn't working too well.

Around three o'clock, the district attorney himself showed up. Ron Coleman is a tall, slender, athletic-looking man; we had worked together many times when he was coming up in the DA's office. I had always found him to be conscientious, well-informed, and directionally committed to rationality and sanity. He'd never seemed very political, so it was a shock to almost everyone when Mayor Monroe appointed him the DA. Monroe loves to shock people though.

Coleman made an announcement. 'Mr Shafer already has an attorney, and he is one of the bright stars of our galaxy. He has retained none other than Jules Halpern. Halpern's probably the one who planted the story that you're a suspect, which you aren't, as far as I know.'

I stared at Coleman. I couldn't believe what I'd just heard. 'As far as you know? What does that mean, Ron?'

The DA shrugged. 'We're probably going to go with Cathy Fitzgibbon on our side. I think she's our best litigator. We'll back her up with Lynda Cole and maybe Daniel Weston, who are also top-notch. That's my take on it as of this morning.'

I knew all three of the prosecutors and they had good reputations, particularly Fitzgibbon. They were on the young side, but tireless, smart, dedicated, a lot like Coleman himself.

'You sound like you're preparing for a war, Ron.'

He nodded. 'As I said, Jules Halpern is Shafer's defense attorney. He rarely loses. In fact, I don't know if he's ever lost a big case like this one. He turns down all the losers, Alex.'

I looked directly into Coleman's dark eyes. 'We have Patsy Hampton's blood on the killer's clothes. We have blood in the bathroom drain, and I'll bet we'll have Shafer's fingerprints somewhere in Hampton's car before the end of the day. We may have the wire hanger he used to strangle her. Ron?'

'Yes, Alex. I know what you're going to say. I know your question. It's the same one that I have.'

'Shafer *has* diplomatic immunity. So why bring in Jules Halpern?'

'That's a very good goddamn question we both came up with. I suspect Halpern's been hired to get us to drop the charges completely.'

'We have substantial evidence. He was *washing Patsy Hampton's blood* off himself in the bathroom. There's residue in the sink.'

Coleman nodded and shrank back into his easy chair. 'I don't understand why Jules Halpern is involved. I'm sure we'll know before too long, though.'

'I'm *afraid* we'll know soon,' I said.

I decided to leave the station by the back way that night, just in case there was press lying in wait out front on Alabama Avenue. As I stepped outside, a small, balding man in a light-green suit popped out from behind the adjacent stone wall.

'That's a good way to get yourself shot,' I told him. I was only half-kidding.

'Occupational hazard,' he lisped. 'Don't shoot the messenger, Detective.'

He smiled thinly as he handed me a white letter-sized envelope. 'Alex Cross, you've hereby been served with a Summons and Complaint. Have a nice night, Detective,' he said in his sibilant whine. Then he walked away as surreptitiously as he'd appeared.

I opened the envelope and quickly scanned the letter. I groaned. Now I knew why Jules Halpern had been retained, and what we were up against.

I had been named in a civil suit for 'false arrest' and 'defamation of the character of Colonel Geoffrey Shafer.' The suit was for fifty million dollars.

Chapter Seventy-Seven

The next morning I was summoned to the District of Columbia Law Department offices downtown. This was not good, I decided. The city's chief counsel, James Dowd, and Mike Kersee from the DA's office were already ensconced in red leather club chairs.

So was Chief of Detectives Pittman, and he was putting on quite a show from his front-row seat. 'You mean to tell me that because Shafer has diplomatic immunity he can avoid criminal prosecution in criminal court? But he can traipse right into our *civil* court and get protection against false arrest and defamation?'

Kersee nodded and made clucking noises with his tongue and teeth. 'Yes, sirree-bob, that's it, exactly. Our ambassadors and their staffs enjoy the same kind of immunity in England and everywhere else around the world. No amount of political pressure will get the Brits to waive immunity. Shafer is a war hero from the Falklands. Supposedly, he's pretty well-respected inside the Security Service, although lately he seems to have been in some trouble.'

'What kind of trouble?' I asked.

'*They won't tell us.*'

Pittman was still badgering the lawyers. 'What about that clown from the Baltic Embassy? The one who wiped out the sidewalk café? *He* went to trial.'

Mike Kersee shrugged. 'He was just a low-level staffer from a low-level country that we could threaten. We can't do that with England.'

'Why the hell not?' Pittman frowned and thumped his hand hard against the arm of his chair. 'England isn't worth shit anymore.'

The phone on Dowd's desk rang, and he raised his hand for quiet. 'That's probably Jules Halpern. He said he'd call at ten and he's an efficient bastard. If it is, I'll put him on the speaker box. This should be as interesting as a rectal exam with a cactus.'

Dowd picked up and exchanged pleasantries with the defense attorney for about thirty seconds. Then Halpern cut him off. 'I believe we have matters of substance to discuss. My schedule is rather tight today. I'm sure you're hard pressed as well, Mr Dowd.'

'Yes, let's get down to business,' Dowd said, raising his thick, curly black eyebrows. 'As you know, the police have a qualified privilege to arrest anyone if they have probable cause. You simply don't have a civil case, Counselor—'

Halpern interrupted Dowd before he had finished speaking. '*Not* if that person identifies himself from the outset as having diplomatic immunity, which my client did. Colonel Shafer stood in the doorway of his *therapist's* apartment waving his British Secret Service shield like a stop sign, saying that he had immunity.'

Dowd sighed loudly into the phone. 'There was blood on his trousers, Counselor. He's a murderer, Counselor, *and* a cop killer. I don't think I need to say anymore on the subject. With respect to the alleged defamation, the police also have a qualified privilege to talk to the press when a crime has been committed.'

'And I suppose that the chief of detectives' statement in front of reporters, and several hundred million others around the world, isn't slander *per se*?'

'That's correct, it isn't. There's a qualified privilege with respect to public figures such as your client.'

'My client is not a *public* figure, Mr Dowd. He is a very private individual. He is an intelligence agent. His very livelihood, if not his life, depends on his being able to work undercover.'

The chief counsel was already exasperated, possibly because Halpern's responses were so calm, and yet always delivered rapid-fire. 'All right, Mr Halpern. So why are you calling us?'

Halpern paused long enough to make Dowd curious. Then he began again. 'My client has authorized me to make a very unusual offer. I have strongly advised him against it, but he maintains his right to do so.'

Dowd looked startled. I could tell that he hadn't been expecting any kind of deal offer. Neither had I. What was this about?

'Go ahead, Mr Halpern,' said Dowd. His eyes were wide and alert as they roamed around the room looking at us. 'I'm listening.'

'I'll bet you are, and all your esteemed colleagues as well.'

I leaned forward to hear every word.

Jules Halpern continued with the real reason for his call. 'My client wants all possibility of a civil case being brought against him waived.'

I rolled my eyes. Halpern wanted to make certain that no one could sue his client in civil court after the criminal court case was concluded. He had no doubt seen how O.J. Simpson had been set free in one court, then bankrupted in the other.

'Impossible!' said Dowd. 'There's no way in hell that will ever happen. No way.'

'Listen to me. There is a way, or I wouldn't have broached the subject. If this is done, and if he and I can be convinced of a speedy route for a criminal trial, my client will *waive diplomatic immunity*. Yes, you heard me correctly. Geoffrey Shafer wants to prove his innocence in a court of law. He insists on it, in fact.'

Dowd was shaking his head in disbelief. So was Mike Kersee. His eyes were glazed with astonishment as he glanced across the room at me.

None of us could believe what we had just heard from the defense attorney.

Geoffrey Shafer wanted to go to trial.

Book Four

Trial and Errors

Chapter Seventy-Eight

C onqueror had watched her work Kensington High Street for nearly six weeks. She became his obsession, his fantasy woman, his 'game piece.' He knew everything there was to know about her. He felt, he knew, that he was starting to act like Shafer. They all were, weren't they?

The girl's name was Noreen Anne and a long time ago, *three years* to be exact, she had traveled to London from Cork, in Ireland, with lovely dreams of being a fashion model on the world stage.

She was seventeen then, nearly five foot ten, slender, blonde, and with a face that all the boys and even older men back home told her was destined for magazine covers, or maybe even the cinema.

So what was she doing here on Kensington High Street at half past one in the morning? She wondered about it as she forced a coquettish smile and occasionally waved a hand at the leering men in slowly passing cars that made the rounds of the High Street, DeVere Gardens, Exhibition Road.

They thought she was pretty all right, just not pretty enough for British or American magazine covers, and not good enough, not classy enough to marry, or be someone's girlfriend.

Well, at least she had a plan, and she thought it was a good one. Noreen Anne had saved nearly two thousand quid since she'd begun to walk the streets. She thought she needed another three thousand or so, and then she would head back to Ireland. She'd start a small beauty shop, because she did know the secrets of beauty, and also a lot about the dreams women have.

So, in the meantime, here I am in front of Kensington Palace Hotel, she thought. *Freezing my fine butt off.*

'Excuse me, miss,' she heard, and turned with a start. She hadn't heard anyone come up on her.

'I couldn't help noticing you standing here. You're an extraordinary beauty. But of course you know that, don't you?'

Noreen Anne felt relief the moment she saw who it was. This one wouldn't hurt her, couldn't if he tried. She could hurt him if it came to that.

He was old, in his late sixties or seventies; he was obscenely fat; and he was seated in a wheelchair.

And so she went off with Conqueror.

It was all part of the game.

Chapter Seventy-Nine

The Americans had promised a speedy route to trial and the fools had actually delivered.

Five months had passed since the murder of Detective Patsy Hampton. Alex Cross had been shuttling back and forth to Bermuda, but still had no idea where Christine had disappeared to. Shafer had been out of jail, but on a very short leash. He hadn't played the game once since Hampton's murder. The game of games had been on hold and it was driving him mad.

Now Shafer sat in his black Jag in the parking lot directly under the courthouse, feeling hopeful. He was eager to stand trial on the count of Aggravated, Premeditated Murder in the First Degree. The rules of play had been established, and he appreciated that.

The suppression hearing from weeks before was still a vivid memory for him. He relished every minute of it – the preliminary hearing was held before jury selection, to determine what evidence would be allowed at the trial. It was held in the spacious chambers of Judge Michael Fescoe. The judge set the rules, so in a way he was the gamemaster. How fabulously droll, how delicious.

Shafer's lawyer, Jules Halpern, argued that Shafer was in a therapy session at Dr Cassady's home office; and he therefore had every right to privacy. 'That privacy was violated. First, Dr Cassady refused to let Detective Cross and the other officers come inside. Second, Colonel Shafer showed his identification to the detective. It proved that he was with the British Embassy and had diplomatic immunity. Cross barged into the therapist's office anyway. Consequently, any evidence obtained, if indeed any evidence was obtained, is the result of unlawful search.'

Judge Fescoe took the rest of the day to consider, then made his decision the next morning. 'As I listened to both sides, it seemed to me that the issues were straightforward and not all that unusual in a murder case. Mr Shafer does, indeed, have diplomatic immunity. However, it is my opinion that Detective Cross acted in a reasonable and lawful manner when he went to Dr Cassady's apartment. He suspected a grave crime had been committed. Dr Cassady opened the door, allowing Detective Cross plain view of Mr Shafer's attire. Colonel Shafer had insisted that his diplomatic immunity denied Detective Cross permission to enter the premises.

'I am therefore going to allow the prosecution to use the clothing Colonel

Shafer was wearing the night of the murder, as well as the blood on the carpet outside the apartment door, as evidence.

'The prosecution may also use any evidence found in the parking garage – both in Detective Hampton's car and Colonel Shafer's.' Judge Fescoe continued, and this was the key part of his ruling: 'I will *not allow* evidence found once Detective Cross entered the apartment against the stated wishes of both Colonel Shafer and Dr Cassady. Any and all evidence discovered during the initial or subsequent searches is suppressed and will not be allowed at the trial.'

The prosecution was also told not to make any reference, during the trial, to any other uncharged murders that Shafer was suspected of having committed in Washington. The jury was to understand that Shafer was under investigation only for the murder of Senior Detective Patricia Hampton. Both the prosecution and defense claimed victory at the end of the suppression hearing.

The stone steps outside the courthouse were swarming with a buzzing, unruly crowd on the morning of the first day. Shafer's supporters were wearing UK/OK buttons and waving crisp new Union Jacks. These wondrous fools made him smile as he clasped both hands high over his head in victory. He enjoyed being a hero immensely.

What a glorious time. Even if he was a little high and spacey on a few choice pharmaceuticals.

Both sides were still predicting 'slam dunk' victories. Lawyers were such fabulous bullshitters.

The press was touting the outrageous charade as the 'criminal trial of the decade.' The media hype, expected and ritualistic, thrilled him anyway. He internalized it as tribute and adulation. His due.

He purposely cut quite a dashing figure; he wanted to make an impression – on the world. He wore a soft-shouldered, tailored gray suit, a striped bespoke shirt from Budd, and black Oxfords from Lobb's of St James's. He was photographed a hundred times in the first few moments alone.

He walked inside the courthouse as if in a dream. The most delicious thing of all was that he might lose everything.

Courtroom 4 was on the third floor. It was the largest in the building. Closest to the double set of public doors was a gallery that held around a hundred and forty spectators. Then came the 'bar area,' where the attorneys' tables were situated. Then the judge's bench, which took up about a quarter of the room.

The trial began at ten in the morning, and it was all a rattle and hum to him. The lead prosecutor was Assistant US Attorney Catherine Marie Fitzgibbon. He already yearned to murder her, and wondered if he possibly could. He wanted Ms Fitzgibbon's scalp on his belt. She was just thirty-six, Irish-Catholic, single, sexy in her tight-assed way, dedicated to high-minded ideals, like so many others from her island of origin. She favored dark-blue or gray Ann Taylor wardrobes and wore a ubiquitous tiny gold cross on a gold chain. She was known in the DC legal community as the 'Drama Queen.' Her melodramatic telling of the gory details was meant to win the sympathy of the jury. A worthy opponent indeed. A worthy prey as well.

Shafer sat at the defendant's table and tried to concentrate. He listened, watched, felt as he hadn't in a long time. He knew they were all watching him. How could they not?

Shafer sat there observing, but his brain was on fire. His esteemed attorney, Jules Halpern, finally began to speak, and he heard his own name. That piqued his interest all right. He was the star here, wasn't he?

Jules Halpern was little more than five-four, but he cut quite a powerful figure in a court of law. His hair was dyed jet-black and slicked back tightly against his scalp. His suit was from a British tailor, just like Shafer's. Shafer thought, rather uncharitably he supposed: *Dress British, think Yiddish*. Seated beside Halpern was his daughter, Jane, who was the second chair. She was tall and slender, but with the father's black hair and beaked nose.

Jules Halpern certainly had a strong voice for such a slight and small fellow. 'My client, Geoffrey Shafer, is a loving husband. He is a very good father, who happened to be attending a birthday party for two of his children half an hour *before* the murder of Detective Patricia Hampton.

'Colonel Shafer, as you will hear, is a valued and decorated member of the British Intelligence community. He is a former soldier with a fine record.

'Colonel Shafer was clearly set up for this murder charge because the Washington police *needed* this terrible crime to be solved. This I will prove to you, and you will have no doubt of it. Mr Shafer was framed because a particular homicide detective was going through some bad personal times, and lost control of the situation.

'Finally, and this is the most essential thing for you to remember, Colonel Shafer wants to be here. He isn't here because he has to be. He has diplomatic immunity. Geoffrey Shafer is here to clear his good name.'

Shafer nearly stood up in the courtroom and cheered.

Chapter Eighty

I purposely, and probably wisely, skipped the first day, then the second, and the third day of the courtroom circus. I didn't want to face the world press, or the public anymore than I had to. I felt like I was on trial too.

A cold-blooded murderer was on trial, but the investigation continued more feverishly than ever for me. I still had the Jane Does to solve, and the disappearance of Christine, if I could open up any new leads. I wanted to make certain that Shafer would not walk away a free man, and most importantly, I desperately wanted finally to know the truth about Christine's disappearance. I had to know. My greatest frustration was that because of the diplomatic shenanigans, I had never gotten to question Shafer. I would have given anything for a few hours with him.

I turned the southern end of our attic into a war room. There was an excess of unused space up there anyway. I moved an old mahogany dining table out from the shadows. I rewired an ancient window fan and it made the attic space almost bearable most days.

Especially early in the morning and late in the evening, when I did my best work up there – in my hermitage.

I set up my laptop on the table, and I pinned different-colored index cards to the walls, to keep what I considered the most important pieces of the case before me at all times. Inside several bulky and misshapen cardboard boxes I had all the rest of it: every scrap of evidence on Christine's abduction; and everything I could find on the Jane Does.

The murder cases formed a maddening puzzle created over several years, that was not given to easy solutions. I was trying to play a complex game, against a skillful opponent, but I didn't know the rules of his game, or how it was played. That was Shafer's unfair advantage.

I had found some useful notes in Patsy Hampton's detective logs, and they led me to interview the teenage boy, Michael Ormson, who'd chatted online with Shafer about the Four Horsemen. I continued to work closely with Chuck Hufstedler of the FBI. Chuck felt guilty about giving Patsy Hampton the original lead, especially since I'd come to him first. I used his guilt.

Both the Bureau and Interpol were doing an active search of the game on the Internet. I'd visited countless chatrooms myself, but had encountered no one, other than young Ormson, who was aware of the mysterious game. It was only because Shafer had taken a chance and gone into the chatroom that he'd been discovered. I wondered what other chances he'd taken.

Following Shafer's arrest at the Farragut, we'd had a little time to search his Jaguar, and I also spent nearly an hour at his home – before his lawyers knew I was there. I spoke to his wife, Lucy, and his son, Robert, who confirmed that he played a game called the Four Horsemen. He had been playing for seven or eight years.

Neither the wife nor the son knew any of the other players, or anything about them. They didn't believe that Geoffrey Shafer had done anything wrong.

The son called his father 'the straight arrow of straight arrows.' Lucy Shafer called him 'a good man,' and seemed to believe it.

I found role-playing-game magazines as well as dozens of sets of game dice in Shafer's den, but no other physical evidence concerning his game. Shafer was careful. He covered his tracks well. He was in intelligence, after all. I couldn't imagine him throwing dice to select his victims, but maybe that helped to account for the irregular pattern of the Jane Does.

His attorney, Jules Halpern, complained loudly and vigorously about the invasion of Shafer's home, and had I uncovered any useful evidence, it would have been suppressed. Unfortunately, I didn't have enough time, and Shafer was too clever to keep anything incriminating at his home. He'd made one big mistake; he wasn't likely to make another. Was he?

Sometimes, very late at night as I worked in the attic, I would stop for a while and remember something about Christine. The memories were painful and sad, but also soothing to me. I began to look forward to these times when I could think about her without any interruption. Some nights, I would wander down to the piano in the sun porch and play songs that had been important to us – 'Unforgettable,' 'Moon-glow,' ''Swonderful.' I could still remember how she looked, especially when I visited at her place – faded jeans, bare feet, T-shirt, or maybe a favorite yellow crewneck sweater she liked, a tortoiseshell comb in her long hair that always smelled of shampoo.

I didn't want to feel sorry for myself, but I just couldn't help feeling miserably bad. I was caught in limbo, not knowing one way or the other what had really happened to Christine. I couldn't let her go.

It was paralyzing me, crippling me, making me feel so damn sad and empty. I knew I needed to move on with my life, but I couldn't do it. I needed answers, at least a few of them. *Is Christine part of the game?* I kept wondering. I was obsessed with the game.

Am I part of it?

I believed that I was. And in a way I hoped she was, too. It was my only hope that she might still be alive.

Chapter Eighty-One

And so I found myself a player in a truly bizarre game that was habit-forming for all the wrong reasons. I began to make up my own rules. I brought in new players. I was in the game to win.

Chuck Hufstedler from the FBI offices in DC continued to be helpful. The more I talked to him, the more I realized that he'd had a serious crush on Detective Hampton. His loss, and mine with Christine, had united us.

I climbed up to the attic late on Friday night after watching *The Mask of*

Zorro with Damon, Jannie, Nana, and Rosie the cat. I had a few more facts to check before going to bed.

I booted up the computer, logged on and heard the familiar – *you have mail.* Ever since that night in Bermuda, the message gave me a terrible fright, a chill that tightened my body from head to toe.

Sandy Greenberg from Interpol was returning one of my messages. She and I had worked together on the Mr Smith case and had become friends. I'd given her several things to check for me.

CALL ME ANY TIME TONIGHT, ALEX, AND I MEAN ANY
TIME. YOUR IRRITATING DOGGEDNESS MAY HAVE PAID OFF.
IT'S VITALLY IMPORTANT THAT YOU CALL. *SANDY.*

I called Sandy in Europe and she picked up after the second ring. 'Alex? I think we found one of them. It was your bloody idea that worked. Shafer was playing a game with at least one of his old cronies from MI6. You were spot on.'

'Are you sure it's one of the game-players?' I asked her.

'Pretty sure,' she shot back. 'I'm sitting here now staring at a copy of Dürer's *Four Horsemen*, on my Mac. As you know, the Horsemen are Conqueror, Famine, War and Death. What a creepy bunch. Anyway, I did what you asked. I talked to some contacts from MI6 who found out that Shafer and this one chap regularly keep in touch on the computer. I have all your notes, too, and they're very good. I can't believe how much you figured out from back there in the colonies. You're a very sick puppy too.'

'Thanks,' I said. I let Sandy ramble on for a few minutes. A while back I recognized that she was a lonely person, and, even though she sometimes put up a cantankerous front, craved company.

'The name he uses in the game is Conqueror. Conqueror lives in Dorking, in England,' Sandy told me. 'His name is Oliver Highsmith, and he's retired from MI6. Alex, he was running several agents in Asia at the same time Shafer was there. Shafer worked under him. It's eight in the morning over here. *Why don't you call the bastard?*' she suggested. 'Send him an e-mail. I have a number for him, Alex.'

I started to wonder about the other players in the Four Horsemen game. Were there four of them – or was that just the name of the game? Who were these players? How was the game actually played? Did all, or indeed any of them, act out their fantasies in real life?

My message to Conqueror was simple and straightforward, and not too threatening, I hoped. I didn't see how he could resist answering me.

DEAR MR HIGHSMITH,
I AM A HOMICIDE DETECTIVE IN WASHINGTON, DC,
LOOKING FOR INFORMATION ABOUT COLONEL GEOFFREY

SHAFER PERTAINING TO THE FOUR HORSEMEN. I UNDERSTAND
THAT SHAFER WORKED FOR YOU IN ASIA. TIME IS OF THE
ESSENCE. I NEED YOUR HELP. PLEASE CONTACT DETECTIVE
ALEX CROSS.

Chapter Eighty-Two

I was surprised when a message came right back. Oliver Highsmith, Conqueror,
must have been online when my e-mail went through.

DETECTIVE CROSS. I AM WELL AWARE OF YOU, SINCE THE
ONGOING MURDER TRIAL IS A RATHER BIG STORY IN ENGLAND,
AND IN THE REST OF EUROPE, FOR THAT MATTER. I HAVE
KNOWN G.S. FOR A DOZEN YEARS OR MORE. HE DID WORK
UNDER ME, BRIEFLY. HE IS MORE AN ACQUAINTANCE THAN A
CLOSE FRIEND, SO I HAVE NO EXPERTISE OR BIAS ABOUT HIS
GUILT OR INNOCENCE. I HOPE IT'S THE LATTER, OF COURSE.
  NOW, AS TO YOUR QUESTION ABOUT THE FOUR HORSEMEN.
THE GAME, AND IT *IS* A FANTASY GAME, DETECTIVE, IS HIGHLY
UNUSUAL IN THAT ALL OF THE PLAYERS ASSUME THE ROLE
OF GAMEMASTER. THAT IS TO SAY, EACH OF US CONTROLS
OUR OWN FATE, OUR OWN STORY. G.S.'s STORY IS EVEN MORE
DARING AND UNUSUAL. HIS CHARACTER, THE RIDER ON THE
PALE HORSE – DEATH – IS DEEPLY FLAWED. ONE MIGHT EVEN
SAY EVIL. THE CHARACTER IS SOMEWHAT LIKE THE PERSON
ON TRIAL IN WASHINGTON, OR SO IT SEEMS TO ME.
  HOWEVER, I MUST MAKE A FEW IMPORTANT POINTS. THE
APPEARANCE OF ANY MURDER FANTASIES IN OUR GAME
ALWAYS OCCURRED DAYS *AFTER* REPORTS OF MURDERS IN
THE NEWSPAPERS. BELIEVE ME, THIS WAS THOROUGHLY
CHECKED BY US ONCE G.S. WAS ACCUSED. IT WAS EVEN
BROUGHT TO THE ATTENTION OF INSPECTOR JONES AT THE
SECURITY SERVICE IN LONDON, SO I'M SURPRISED YOU
WEREN'T INFORMED BEFORE NOW. THE SERVICE HAS BEEN
TO SEE ME ABOUT G.S. AND THEY WERE COMPLETELY SATIS-
FIED I ASSUME, SINCE THEY HAVEN'T BEEN BACK.

ALSO, THE OTHER PLAYERS – WHO HAVE BEEN CHECKED OUT BY SECURITY – ARE ALL REPRESENTED BY POSITIVE CHARACTERS IN THE GAME. AND AS I'VE SAID, AS POWERFULLY INVOLVING AS HORSEMEN IS – IT IS ONLY A GAME. BY THE WAY, DID YOU KNOW THAT BY SOME SCHOLARLY ACCOUNTS THERE IS A FIFTH HORSEMAN? *MIGHT THAT BE YOU, DR CROSS?*

FYI – THE CONTACT AT THE SERVICE IS MR ANDREW JONES. I TRUST HE WILL VOUCH FOR THE VERACITY OF MY STATEMENTS. IF YOU WISH TO CONVERSE FURTHER, DO SO AT YOUR OWN RISK. I AM SIXTY-SEVEN YEARS OF AGE, RETIRED FROM INTELLIGENCE (AS I LIKE TO PUT IT), AND A RATHER FAMOUS WINDBAG. I WISH YOU MUCH LUCK IN YOUR SEARCH FOR TRUTH AND JUSTICE. I MISS THE CHASE MYSELF.

CONQUEROR

I read the message, then reread it. *Much luck in your search*? Was that as loaded a line as it sounded?

And was I a player – *the Fifth Horseman*?

Chapter Eighty-Three

I went to court every day of the following week, and like so many other people, I got hooked on the trial. Jules Halpern was the most impressive orator I had ever watched in a courtroom; but Catherine Fitzgibbon was effective as well. It would depend on who the jury believed more. It was all theater, a game. I remembered that as a kid I used to regularly watch a courtroom drama with Nana called *The Defenders*. Every show began with a deep-voiced narration saying something to the effect that 'the American Justice System is far from perfect – but it is still the very best justice system in the world.'

That might be true, but as I sat in the courtroom in Washington, I couldn't help thinking that the murder trial, the judge, the jury, the lawyers, and all the rules were just another elaborate game; and that Geoffrey Shafer was already planning his next foray, savoring every move that the prosecution made against him.

He was still in control of the game board. He was the gamemaster. He knew it, and so did I.

I watched Jules Halpern conduct smooth examinations that were designed to give the impression that his monstrous, psychopathic client was as innocent as a newborn baby. Actually, it was easy to drift off during the lengthy cross-examinations. I never really missed anything, though, since all the important points were repeated over and over *ad nauseam*.

'Alex Cross . . .'

I heard my name mentioned and refocused my attention on Jules Halpern. He produced a blown-up photograph that had appeared in the *Post* on the day after the murder. The photo had been taken by another tenant at the Farragut and sold to the newspaper.

Halpern leaned in close to the witness on the stand, a man named Carmine Lopes, a night doorman at the apartment building where Patsy Hampton was murdered.

'Mr Lopes, I show you Defendant's Exhibit "J," a photograph of my client and Detective Alex Cross. It was taken in the tenth-floor hallway soon after the discovery of Detective Hampton's body.'

The blow-up was large enough for me to see most of the detail from where I was sitting in the fourth row. The photo had always been a shocker to me.

Shafer looked as if he had just stepped out of the pages of *GQ*. In comparison my clothes were tattered and dirty. I had just come off my crazy marathon run from the zoo; I had been down in the garage where I found poor Patsy. My fists were clenched tightly and I seemed to be roaring out anger at Shafer. Pictures *do* lie. We know that. The photograph was highly inflammatory, and I felt it could cause prejudice in the minds of the jurors.

'Is this a fair representation of how the two men looked at ten thirty that evening?' Halpern asked the doorman.

'Yes, sir. It's very fair. That's how I remember it.'

Jules Halpern nodded as if he were receiving vital information for the first time. 'Would you now describe, *in your own words*, what Detective Cross looked like at that time?' he asked.

The doorman hesitated and seemed slightly confused by the question. I wasn't. I knew where Halpern was going now.

'Was he dirty?' Halpern jumped in and asked the simplest possible question.

'Er, dirty . . . sure. He was a mess.'

'And was he sweaty?' the defense lawyer asked.

'Sweaty . . . yeah. We all were. From being down in the garage, I guess. It was a real hot night.'

'Nose running?'

'Yes, sir.'

'Were Detective Cross's clothes ripped, Mr Lopes?'

'Yes, they were. Ripped and dirty.'

Jules Halpern looked at the jury first, then at his witness. 'Were Detective Cross's clothes bloodstained?'

'Yes . . . they sure were. That's what I noticed first, the blood.'

'Was the blood anywhere else, Mr Lopes?'

'On his hands. You couldn't miss it. I sure didn't.'

'And Mr Shafer, how did Mr Shafer look?'

'He was clean, not mussed at all. He seemed pretty calm and collected.'

'Did you see any blood on Mr Shafer?'

'No, sir. No blood.'

Halpern nodded, then he faced the jury. 'Mr Lopes, which of the two men looked more like someone who might have just committed a murder?'

'Detective Cross,' the doorman said, without hesitation.

'Objection!' the district attorney screamed, but not before the damage had been done.

Chapter Eighty-Four

That afternoon, the defense was scheduled to call Chief of Detectives George Pittman. The assistant district attorney, Catherine Fitzgibbon, knew that Pittman was on the docket and she asked me to meet with her for lunch. 'If you have an appetite before Pittman goes on,' she added.

Catherine was smart, and she was thorough. She had put away nearly as many bad guys as Jules Halpern had set free. We got together over sandwiches at a crowded deli near the courthouse. Neither of us was thrilled about Pittman's upcoming appearance. My reputation as a detective was being ruined by the defense, and it was a hard thing to watch and do nothing.

She bit down into a hefty Reuben sandwich that squirted mustard onto her forefinger and thumb. Catherine smiled. 'Sloppy, but worth it. You and Pittman are really at odds, right? More like you hate each other's guts?'

'It's serious dislike, and it's mutual,' I told her. 'He's tried to do me in a couple of times. He thinks I'm a threat to his career.'

Catherine was attacking her sandwich. '*Hmmm*, there's a thought. Would you be a better chief of detectives?'

'Wouldn't run, wouldn't serve if elected. I wouldn't be good cooped up in an office playing political ping-pong.'

Catherine laughed. She's one of those people who can find humor almost anywhere. 'This is just fricking great, Alex. The defense is calling the chief of detectives as one of *their* goddamn witnesses. They've listed him as hostile, but I don't think he is.'

Catherine and I finished off the rest of her sandwich. 'Well, let's find out what Mr Halpern has up his sleeve today.'

At the start of the afternoon session, Jules Halpern did a careful and thorough setup of Pittman's credentials, which sounded reasonably impressive in the abstract. Undergrad at George Washington, then law school at American; twenty-four years on the police force, with medals for bravery and citations from three different mayors.

'Chief Pittman, how would you describe Detective Cross's record in the department?' asked Halpern.

I cringed in my seat. Felt my brow wrinkle, my eyes narrow. Here we go, I thought.

'Detective Cross has been involved in some high-profile cases that the department has solved,' he said, and left it at that. Not exactly praise, but at least he hadn't gone on the attack.

Halpern nodded sagely. 'What, if anything, has changed his performance recently?'

Pittman looked my way, then answered. 'A woman he was seeing disappeared while they were on a trip together in Bermuda. Since that time, he's been distracted and distant, quick to anger, not himself.'

Suddenly I wanted to speak up in the courtroom. Pittman didn't know the first thing about Christine and me.

'Chief Pittman, was Detective Cross ever a suspect in the disappearance of his girlfriend, Ms Christine Johnson?'

Pittman nodded. 'That's standard police procedure. I'm sure he was questioned.'

'But his behavior on the job has changed since her disappearance?'

'Yes. His concentration isn't the same. He's missed days of work. It's all a matter of record.'

'Has Detective Cross been asked to seek professional help?'

'Yes.'

'Did you ask him to seek help yourself?'

'I did. He and I have worked together for a number of years. He was under stress.'

'He's under a *lot* of stress? Is that fair to say?'

'Yes. He hasn't closed a single case recently.'

Halpern nodded. 'A couple of weeks before the Hampton homicide, you suspended some detectives he was friendly with.'

Pittman's look was somber. 'Unfortunately, I did.'

'Why did you suspend the detectives?'

'The detectives were investigating cases outside the auspices of the department.'

'Is it fair to say they were making up their own rules, acting like vigilantes?'

Catherine Fitzgibbon rose to her feet and objected, but Judge Fescoe allowed the question.

Pittman answered. 'I don't know about that. Vigilantes is a strong word.

But they were working without proper supervision. The case is still under investigation.'

'Was Detective Cross part of the group that was making up its own rules to solve homicides?'

'I'm not certain. But he was spoken to about the matter. I didn't believe he could handle a suspension at that time. I warned him and let it slide. I shouldn't have,' said Pittman.

'No further questions.'

None needed, I thought.

Chapter Eighty-Five

That night after he left the courthouse, Shafer was flying high. He thought that he was winning the game. He was manic as hell, and it felt both good and bad. He was parked in the dark garage under Boo Cassady's building. Most manics aren't really aware that they're exhibiting signs of a manic episode, but Shafer knew. His 'spirals' didn't come out of nowhere, they built and built.

The irony, and the danger, of being back in her building wasn't lost on him. Scene of the crime and all that rot. He wanted to go to Southeast tonight, but that was too risky. He couldn't hunt – not now. He had something else in mind: The next few moves in his game.

It was unusual, though not unheard of, for the defendant in a first-degree homicide trial to be out roaming the streets, but that had been one of the prerequisites of dropping his immunity. What choice did the prosecution have? None at all. If they didn't agree, he had a free pass to keep him out of jail.

Shafer followed a tenant he'd seen several times into the lift from the garage and took it to Boo's apartment. He rang the doorbell. Waited. Heard her padding across the parquet floor. Yes, Act One of tonight's performance was about to begin.

He knew she was watching him through the door's peephole, just as he had watched Alex Cross there on the night Patsy Hampton got her just deserts. He had seen Boo a few times after his release, but then he cut her off.

When he stopped seeing her, she lost it. Boo called him at work, then at home – and constantly on his car phone until he changed the bloody number. At her worst, she reminded him of the nutcase Glenn Close had played in the movie *Fatal Attraction*.

He wondered if he could still push her buttons. She was a fairly bright woman

– and that was a large part of her problem. She thought far too much, double and triple think. Most men, especially dull-witted Americans, didn't like that, which made her even crazier.

He put his face against the door, felt its cool wood on his cheek. He started his act.

'I've been petrified to see you, Boo. You don't know what it's been like. One slipup, anything they can use against me, and I'm finished. And what makes it worse is that I'm innocent. You know that. I talked to you the whole time from my house to yours that night. You know I didn't kill that detective. Elizabeth? Boo? Please say something. At least swear at me. Let the anger out . . . Doctor?'

There was no answer. Actually, he rather liked that. It made him respect her more than he had. What the hell, she was more screwed up than he was.

'You know exactly what I'm going through. You're the only one who understands my episodes. I need you, Boo. You know I'm manic-depressive, bipolar, whatever the hell you shrinks want to call my condition. Boo?'

Then Shafer actually started to cry, which nearly made him laugh. He uttered loud, wrenching sobs. He crouched on his haunches and held his head. He knew he was a far better actor than so many of the high-priced fakers he saw in movies.

The door to the apartment slowly opened. 'Boo hoo,' she whispered. 'Is poor Geoff in pain? What a shame.'

What a bitch, he thought, but he had to see her. She was testifying soon. He needed her tonight, and he needed her help in the courtroom.

'Hello, Boo,' he whispered.

Chapter Eighty-Six

Act Two of the evening's performance.

She stared at him with huge dark-brown eyes that looked like amber beads, the kind she bought at her swanky shops. She'd lost weight, but that made her sexier to him, more desperate. She wore navy walking shorts and an elegant pink silk T-shirt – but she also wore her pain.

'You hurt me like no one ever has before,' she whispered.

He held himself under control, play-acting, a truly award-winning performance. 'I'm fighting for my life. I swear, all I think about is killing myself. Haven't you heard anything I've said? Besides, do you want your picture all over the tabloids again? Don't you see? That's why I've been staying away from you.'

She laughed, bitterly, haughtily. 'It's going to happen anyway, when I testify. The photographers will be everywhere I go.'

Shafer shut his eyes. 'Well, that will be your chance to hurt me back, darling.'

She shook her head and frowned. 'You know I wouldn't do that. Oh, Geoff, why didn't you at least call? You're such a bastard.'

Shafer hung his head, the repentant bad boy. 'You know how close I was to the edge before all this happened. Now it's worse. Do you expect me to act like a responsible adult?'

She gave a wry smile. He saw a book on the hallway table behind her, *Man and His Symbols*. Carl Jung. How fitting. 'No, I suppose not, Geoff. What do you want? Drugs?'

'I need you. I want to hold you, Boo. That's all.'

That night, she gave him what he wanted. They made love like animals on the gray velvet loveseat she used for her clients, then on the JFK style rocking chair, where she always sat for her sessions. He took her body, and her soul.

Then she gave him drugs – antidepressants, painkillers, most of her samples. Boo was still able to get the samples from her ex, a psychiatrist. Shafer didn't know what *their* relationship was, and frankly, he didn't care. He took some Librium and shot up Vicodin at her place.

Then he took Boo again, both of them naked and sweating and frenzied on the kitchen counter. *The butcher's block*, he thought.

He left her place around eleven. He realized he was feeling worse than before he'd gone there. But he knew what he was going to do. He'd known before he went to Boo's. It would explode their little minds. Everyone's. The press. The jury.

Now for Act Three.

Chapter Eighty-Seven

At a little past midnight, I got an emergency call that blew off the top of my head. Within minutes I had the old Porsche up close to ninety on Rock Creek Parkway, the siren screaming at the night, or maybe at Geoffrey Shafer.

I arrived in Kalorama at 12:25. EMS ambulances, squad cars, TV news trucks were parked all over the street.

Several neighbors of the Shafers were up and had come outside their large, expensive houses to observe the nightmare scene. They couldn't believe this was happening in their upscale enclave.

The chatter and buzz of several police radios filled the night air. A news helicopter was already hovering overhead. A truck marked CNN arrived and parked right behind me.

I met a detective named Malcolm Ainsley standing on the front lawn. We knew each other from other homicide scenes, even a few parties. Suddenly the front door of the Shafer house opened.

Two EMTs were carrying a stretcher outside. Dozens of cameras were flashing.

'It's Shafer,' Ainsley told me. 'Sonofabitch tried to kill himself, Alex. Slit his wrist and took a lot of drugs. There were open prescription packets everywhere. Must've had second thoughts, though. Called for help.'

I had enough information about Shafer from the discovery interviews preceding the trial and my own working profile on him to begin to make some very educated guesses about what might have happened. My first thought was that he suffered from some kind of bipolar disorder featuring both manic and depressive episodes. A second possibility was cyclohymia, in which case there can be numerous hypomanic episodes and also depressive symptoms. Associated symptoms could include inflated self-esteem, decreased need for sleep, excessive involvement in 'pleasurable' activities, increase in goal-directed activity – such as winning his game.

I moved forward as if I were floating in a very bad dream, the worst I could imagine. I recognized one of the EMS techies, Nina Disesa. I'd worked with her a few times before in Georgetown.

'We got to the bastard just in time,' Nina said and narrowed her dark eyes. 'Too bad, huh?'

'Serious attempt?' I asked her.

Nina shrugged. 'Hard to tell for sure. He hacked up his wrist pretty good. Just the left one, though. Then the drugs, *lots* of drugs, doctor's samples.'

I shook my head in utter disbelief. 'But he definitely called out for help?'

'According to the wife and son, they heard him call out from his den: "Daddy needs help. Daddy is dying. Daddy is sick."'

'Well, he got that part right. Daddy is incredibly sick. Daddy is a monumental sicko.'

I continued trudging forward toward the red-and-white ambulance. News cameras were still flashing all over the street. My mind was unhinged, reeling. *Everything is a game to him. The victims in Southeast, Patsy Hampton, Christine. Now this. He's even playing with his own life.*

'His pulse is still strong,' I heard as I got close to the ambulance. I could see one of the EMT workers checking the EKG inside the van. I could even hear beeps from the machine.

Then I saw Shafer's face. His hair was drenched in perspiration, and his face as pale as a sheet of white paper. He stared into my eyes, trying to focus. Then he recognized me.

'You did this to me,' he said, mustering strength, suddenly trying to sit up on the stretcher. 'You ruined my life for your career. You did this! You're responsible! Oh God, oh God. My poor family! Why is this happening to us?'

The TV cameras were rolling film, and they got his entire Academy Award-quality performance. Just as Geoffrey Shafer knew they would.

Chapter Eighty-Eight

The trial had to be recessed due to Shafer's suicide attempt. The courtroom shenanigans probably wouldn't resume until the following week.

Meanwhile, the media had another feeding frenzy, including banner headlines in the *Washington Post, New York Times*, *USA Today*. At least it gave me time to work on a few more angles. Shafer was good; God, he was good at this.

I had been talking with Sandy Greenberg nearly every night. She was helping me collect information on the other game players. She had even gone and talked with Conqueror. She said she doubted that Oliver Highsmith was a killer. He was late sixties, seriously overweight, and wheelchair-bound.

Sandy called the house at seven that night. She's a good friend. Obviously, she was burning the midnight oil for me. I took the call in the sanctuary of my attic office.

'Andrew Jones of the Security Service will see you,' she announced in her usual perky and aggressive manner. 'Isn't that great news? I'll tell you – *it is*. Actually, he's eager to meet with you, Alex. He didn't say it to me directly, but I don't think he's too keen on Colonel Shafer. Wouldn't say why. Even more fortuitous, he's in Washington. He's a top man. He matters in the intelligence arena. He's very good, Alex, a straight shooter.'

I thanked Sandy and then immediately called Jones at his hotel. He answered the call in his room. 'Yes. Hello. Andrew Jones speaking. Who is this, please?'

'It's Detective Alex Cross of the Washington police. I just got off the line with Sandy Greenberg. How are you?'

'Good, very good. Well, hell, not really. I've had better weeks, months. Actually I stayed here in my room hoping that you'd call. Would you like to meet, Alex? Is there somewhere we wouldn't stand out too much?'

I suggested a bar on M Street in half an hour, and I arrived there a minute or two early. I recognized Jones from his description on the phone: 'Broad, beefy, red-faced. Just your average ex-rugby type. Though I never bloody played, don't even watch the drivel. Oh yes, flaming red hair and matching mustache. That should help, shouldn't it?'

It did. We sat at a dark booth in back and got to know one another. For the next forty-five minutes, Jones filled me in on several important things, not the least of which was politics and decorum within the English intelligence and police communities; Lucy Shafer's father's good name and standing in the army, the concern for his reputation; and the desire of the government to avoid an even dicier scandal than the current mess.

'Alex, if it were true that one of our agents had committed cold-blooded murders while posted abroad, and that Intelligence knew nothing about it, the scandal would be a true horror and major embarrassment. But if MI6 *knew anything* about what Colonel Shafer is suspected of doing! Well, it's absolutely unthinkable.'

'Did they?' I asked him. 'Is this situation unthinkable?'

'I won't answer that, Alex, you know I can't; but I am prepared to help you if I possibly can.'

'Why?' I asked, then. 'Why now? We needed your help on this before the trial began.'

'Fair question, good question. We're prepared to help because you now have information that could cause us a hell of a lot of trouble. You're privy to the *unthinkable.*'

I said nothing. I thought I knew what he was alluding to, though.

'You've discovered a fantasy game called the Four Horsemen. There are four players, including Shafer. We know you've already contacted Oliver Highsmith. What you probably don't know yet, but will find out eventually, is that all the players are former or current agents. That is to say, Geoffrey Shafer might just be the beginning of our problems.'

'All four of them are murderers?' I asked.

Andrew Jones didn't answer; he didn't have to.

Chapter Eighty-Nine

'We think that the game originated in Bangkok, where three of the four players were posted in ninety-one. The fourth, Highsmith, was a mentor of George Bayer, who is Famine in the Four Horsemen. Highsmith has always worked out of London.'

'Tell me about Highsmith,' I said.

'As I said, he's always been in the main office, London. He was a high-level analyst, then he actually ran several agents. He's a very bright chap, well thought of.'

'He claimed that the Four Horsemen was just a harmless fantasy game.'

'It could be for him, Alex. He might be telling the truth. He's been in a wheelchair since eighty-five. Road accident. His wife had just left him and he cracked. He's an enormous fellow, about three hundred pounds. I doubt that he's going about murdering young women in the seedier areas of London. That's what you believe Shafer was doing here in Washington? The Jane Doe murders?'

Jones was right and I didn't deny it. 'We know he was involved in several murders, and I think we were close to catching him. He was picking up victims in a gypsy taxicab. We found the cab. Yes, we knew about him, Andrew.'

Jones tented his thick fingers, pursed his lips. 'You think Shafer knew how close you and Detective Hampton were getting?'

'He might have, but there was a lot of pressure on him. He made some mistakes that led us to an apartment he rented.'

Jones nodded. He seemed to know a great deal about Shafer, which told me he'd been watching him, too. Had he been watching me as well?

'How do you think the other game-players might react to Shafer's being so out of control?' I asked.

'I'm fairly sure they felt threatened. Who wouldn't? He was a risk to all of them. He still is.'

Jones continued. 'So, we have Shafer, who's probably been committing murders here in Washington, acting out his fantasies in real life. And Highsmith, who probably couldn't have, but could be a sort of controller. Then there's a man called James Whitehead, in Jamaica, but there have been no murders of the Jane Doe variety on the island, or any nearby island. We've checked thoroughly. And there's George Bayer in the Far East.'

'What about Bayer? I assume you've investigated him, too?'

'Of course. There's nothing specific on his record, but there was an incident, a possible connection to follow up on. Last year, in Bangkok, two girls who worked in a strip bar in Pot Pol disappeared. They just vanished into the noisy, *teeming* streets. The girls were sixteen and eighteen respectively, bar dancers and prostitutes. Alex, they were found nailed together in the missionary position, wearing only garters and stockings. Even in jolly old Bangkok that caused quite a stir. Sounds distressingly similar to the two girls who were killed in Eckington.'

I nodded. 'So we have at least two unsolved Jane Does in Bangkok. Has anyone actually questioned Bayer?'

'At this point, no, but he's being watched. Remember the politics, the fear of a scandal that I mentioned earlier? There's an ongoing investigation of Bayer and the others, but to some extent our hands are tied.'

'My hands aren't tied,' I said. 'That's what you wanted me to say, isn't it? What you expected? It's why you met with me tonight?'

Jones turned very serious. 'It's how the world works, I'm afraid. Let's do this together from here on. If you do . . . I promise to do what I can to find out what happened to Christine Johnson.'

Chapter Ninety

The trial resumed sooner than expected, the following Wednesday in fact. There was speculation in the press about how serious Shafer's self-inflicted wounds had been. None of the public's perverse interest in the case seemed to have been lost.

It seemed impossible to predict the outcome, a fact of life I tried not to let get me down too much. Both Shafer and I were present in the packed court-room that first morning. Shafer looked pale, weak, an object of sympathy perhaps. I certainly couldn't take my eyes off him.

Things got stranger and stranger. At least they did for me. Sergeant Walter Jamieson was called that morning. Jamieson had been at the Police Academy when I attended. He had taught me my craft, and he was still there, teaching others. I couldn't imagine why he was in court as a witness in Patsy Hampton's murder case.

Jules Halpern approached the witness with a heavy-looking hardback book open in his hands.

'I read to you from the textbook *Preserving the Crime Scene: A Detective's Primer*, which you wrote twenty years ago and which you still use in your classes: "It is *imperative* that the detective not disturb the crime scene until backup can be brought in to corroborate charges effected by the detective to unearth evidence, lest those charges be misconstrued to be those of the perpetration. Gloves *must* be worn at all times at a crime scene." Did you write that, Sergeant Jamieson?'

'Yes, I did. Most certainly. Twenty years ago, as you said.'

'Still stand by it?' Halpern asked.

'Yes, of course. A lot of things have changed, but not that.'

'And you heard earlier testimony that Detective Cross wore gloves both inside Detective Hampton's car and at the Cassady apartment.'

'Yes, I heard the testimony. I also read the grand jury transcripts.'

Halpern turned on the overhead projector in the courtroom. 'I direct your attention to prints number 176 and 211 provided by the DA's office. You see the ones denominated?'

'Number 176 and 211. I see them.'

'Now, the prints are denominated "Detective Hampton Belt Buckle: ID: Alex Cross/Right Thumb." And "Left Side Dashboard: ID: Alex Cross/Left Forefinger." What does that mean? Can you explain the markings to us?'

'It means that Alex Cross's prints were found on Detective Hampton's belt as well as on the dashboard of her car.'

Jules Halpern paused for a full ten seconds before he went on. 'And may we not therefore conclude, Sergeant Jamieson, that Detective Cross himself could be our murderer?'

'Objection!' Catherine Fitzgibbon stood up and shouted.

'Withdrawn,' said the defense attorney. 'I'm finished here.'

Chapter Ninety-One

Lawyers for both the prosecution and defense continued to regularly appear on Larry King and other TV shows and boast that their cases were 'slam dunks.' If you listened to the lawyers, neither side could lose.

In the courtroom, Jules Halpern had the fierce look and body language of someone brimming with confidence and determination. He was riding the case hard. He looked like a jockey whipping his thoroughbred to victory.

The bailiff stood and announced, 'The defense calls Mr William Payaz.'

I didn't recognize the name. Now what? Now *who*?

There was no immediate response in the courtroom.

No one came forward.

Heads craned around the room. Still no one responded. Who was the mystery witness?

The bailiff repeated a little louder, 'Mr Payaz, Mr William Payaz.'

The double doors in the back of the room suddenly opened, and a circus-style clown walked in. The gallery began to whisper loudly and a few people laughed. What a world we lived in; what a circus indeed.

The clown took the stand and both the prosecution and defense were immediately called forward for a sidebar by Judge Fescoe. A heated discussion ensued that none of the rest of us could hear. The clown issue was apparently resolved in favor of the defense. After being sworn in, the clown was asked his name for the record.

His white-gloved right hand raised, he said, 'Billy.'

The bailiff asked, 'Last name, please?'

The clown said, 'First name, Silly. Last name, Billy, Silly Billy. I had it legally changed,' he confided to the judge.

Jules Halpern took over, and he treated the clown with respect and seriousness. First, he asked him to state his credentials, which the clown did politely. Then Halpern asked, 'And what brings you here today?'

'I did a party for Mr Shafer out in Kalorama on the fateful and terrible night of the murder. It was his twins' fifth birthday. I did a party when they were four as well. I brought a video along. Want to see?' he said, speaking as if he were addressing a crowd of three year olds.

'Of course,' said Jules Halpern.

'Objection!' Catherine Fitzgibbon called out loudly.

The video was admitted over the prosecution's objections and yet another lengthy sidebar. The newspapers had claimed that Judge Fescoe was intimidated by Jules Halpern, which seemed the case.

The tape began with an arresting closeup of a painting of a clown's face. As the camera pulled back, everyone in the courtroom could see it was the sign on Silly Billy's van, which was parked in front of a handsome red-brick town house with a glass conservatory linked to the main building. The Shafer house.

The next scene showed Silly Billy ringing the front bell and apparently surprising the Shafer children at the door.

Once again the prosecution objected to the videotape. There was another sidebar. The lawyers returned to their seats and the tape resumed.

The other children at the birthday party ran to the door. The clown handed out toys from a sack over his shoulder – teddy bears, dolls, shiny red firetrucks.

Silly Billy then performed magic tricks and gags on the sunporch, which looked out onto the backyard. The yard was very pretty, with potted orange trees, white climbing roses, jasmine vine, lush green grass.

'Wait! I hear something outside!' He had turned and spoken to camera. Now he ran and disappeared from sight.

The kids all followed. The tension of surprise and imminent fun was in the children's eyes.

A pale white pony appeared, cantering slowly around the corner of the house. Silly Billy was riding on the horse.

But when the clown dismounted, the kids discovered that the clown was actually Geoffrey Shafer! The kids went wild, but especially the Shafer twins. They ran and hugged their daddy, who seemed the perfect father.

There were heartwarming, candid shots of the children eating frosted cake and playing party games. There were more shots of Shafer laughing and playing with several of the children. I suspected that Jules Halpern himself supervised the final editing of the tape. It was very convincing.

The adult guests, all dressed up and looking sophisticated, were a glowing testimonial that Geoffrey Shafer and his wife were outstanding parents. No longer in his clown costume but in a smart navy suit, Shafer modestly deflected the tributes. He had changed into the same clothes he had worn when he was apprehended at the Farragut.

The tape ended with the smiling and quite beautiful twins telling the camera that they loved their mommy and daddy for making their 'dream come true.' The lights came up. The judge granted a brief recess.

I felt incredibly angry that the video had been shown. It made Shafer seem such a wonderful father – and *victim*.

The jury was all smiles, and so was Jules Halpern. He had argued masterfully that the tape was crucial to establish Geoffrey Shafer's state of mind shortly before Patsy Hampton's murder. Halpern was so skillful an orator he'd actually made the outrageous request sound logical. At any rate, it was moot now.

Shafer himself was smiling broadly, as were his wife and son. It suddenly occurred to me that Shafer had been riding a pale horse at the party for his children. He was Death from the Four Horsemen.

It was all theater and games to him, his entire life.

Chapter Ninety-Two

Sometimes I wanted to shut my eyes tight and not have to watch another moment of the trial. I wanted things to be the way they were before the Weasel.

Catherine Fitzgibbon was doing a very good job with each witness, but the judge seemed to be favoring the defense whenever possible. It had begun at the crucial suppression-of-evidence hearing and it continued now.

Lucy Shafer took the witness stand early that afternoon. The warm, homespun videotaped images of the Shafer family were still fresh in the minds of the jury.

I had been trying to understand Lucy Shafer's odd and perplexing relationship with her husband since the first time I had met her, the night of Patsy Hampton's murder. What kind of woman could live with an unrepentant monster like Shafer and not know it? Could this woman be that much in denial? Or was there something else that motivated her, somehow held her captive to Shafer? I had seen all kinds of marital relationships in my therapy practice, but nothing like this.

Jane Halpern conducted the questioning and she looked every bit as confident and winning as her father. She was tall and slender, with wiry black hair tied in a bow with a dark crimson ribbon. She was twenty-eight, just four years out of Yale Law School, but seemed older and wiser.

'Mrs Shafer, how long have you and your husband known each other?'

Lucy Shafer spoke in a gentle but clear voice. 'I've known Geoffrey for most of my adult life, actually. My father was his commanding officer in the army. I believe I was just fourteen when I first met Geoff. He was nine years older. We married when I was nineteen, after my second year at Cambridge. Once when I was studying for exams, he showed up in full military dress: polished saber, medals, shiny black leather riding boots – right in the middle of the library. I was studying in a sweatshirt or some such awful getup, and I don't think I'd washed my hair for days. Geoff told me it didn't matter. He didn't care a bit about appearances. He said he loved me and always would. I must tell you, he's kept that promise.'

'Very nice,' Jane Halpern said, seemingly utterly charmed, as if she'd never heard the story before. 'And has he remained romantic?'

'Oh, yes, even more so. Scarcely a week goes by that Geoff doesn't bring me flowers, or perhaps a beautiful Hermès scarf, which I collect. And then there are our "ouch" excursions.'

Jane Halpern wrinkled her nose and her dark-brown eyes twinkled. 'What are "ouch" excursions?' she asked, with the exuberant curiosity of a morning TV show host.

'Geoff will take me to New York, or maybe Paris, or back to London, and I get to shop for clothes until he says "ouch." He's very generous, though.'

'A good husband, then?'

'The best you could imagine. Very hardworking, but not so much that he forgets about his family. The children adore him.'

'Yes, we could tell that from this morning's film, Mrs Shafer. Was the party an unusual occasion?'

'No. Geoffrey's always throwing parties. He's very joyful, full of life, full of fun and surprises. He's a sensitive, very creative man.'

I looked from Lucy Shafer to the jury box. She had them in a spell, and they couldn't take their eyes off her. She was also credible. Even I had the sense that she genuinely loved her husband, and more important, that she believed he loved her.

Jane Halpern milked the testimony for all it was worth. I couldn't blame her. Lucy Shafer was attractive and seemed nice, kind, and very much in love with her husband and children, but she didn't appear to be a fool. Just someone who had found exactly who she wanted and valued him deeply. That someone was Geoffrey Shafer.

It was the indelible image the jury took away with them at the end of the day.

And it was an amazing lie – spun by a master.

Chapter Ninety-Three

I talked things over with Andrew Jones when I got home after court that afternoon. I'd tried to contact Oliver Highsmith again, but so far hadn't gotten any response. Also, there was nothing new to link Shafer to the Jane Doe murders in Washington. Shafer didn't seem to have murdered anyone, at least locally, in the past several months.

After a dinner of chicken pot pie, salad, rhubarb pie, Nana gave the kids the night off from their chore of doing the dishes. She asked me to stay and help, to be her 'partner in grime,' as we used to call it.

'Just like the good old days, same as it ever was,' I said as I splashed soap and water onto silver and dishes in the porcelain sink that's as old as the house.

Nana dried the kitchenware as quickly as I got it to her. Her fingers were still as nimble as her mind. 'I like to think we're older *and* wiser,' she chirped.

'I don't know. I'm still the one getting dishwater hands.'

'I haven't told you something, and I should have,' Nana said, suddenly going serious on me.

'Okay,' I said, and stopped splashing water and soap bubbles around in the sink. 'Shoot.'

'What I wanted to say – is that I'm proud of the way you've been able to handle the terrible things that have happened. Your strength and your patience have given me inspiration. And I'm not easily inspired, especially by the likes of you. I know it has had the same effect on Damon and Jannie. They don't miss a thing.'

I leaned over the sink, suddenly feeling in a confessional mood. 'It's the worst stretch of my life, the hardest thing I've ever had to do. It's even worse than when Maria died, Nana, if that's possible. At least back then I knew for sure she was dead. I could let myself grieve. I could finally let her go and breathe again.'

Nana came around the sink and took me in her arms, which always surprised me with their strength.

She looked me squarely in the eyes, just like she always has since I was around nine years old. She said, 'Let yourself grieve for her, Alex. Let her go.'

Chapter Ninety-Four

G eoffrey Shafer had an attractive, loving wife, and that incongruous and monstrously unfair fact bothered me a lot. I couldn't understand it as a psychologist or as a detective.

The clever testimony of Lucy Shafer continued early the following morning, and lasted just over an hour. Jane Halpern wanted the jury to hear more about Lucy's wonderful husband.

Finally, it was Catherine Fitzgibbon's turn. In her own way, she was as tough, and maybe as formidable, as Jules Halpern.

'Mrs Shafer, we've all been listening to you intently, and it all sounds very charming and idyllic, but I'm troubled and confused by something. Here's what troubles me. Your husband tried to commit suicide eight days ago. Your husband tried to kill himself. So maybe he isn't quite what he seems to be. Maybe he isn't so well-balanced and sane. Maybe you're mistaken about who he really is.'

Lucy Shafer stared directly into the prosecuting attorney's eyes. 'In the past few months, my husband has seen his life, his career, and his good name falsely put in jeopardy. He couldn't believe that these horrible charges had been made against him. This whole Kafkaesque ordeal drove him, quite literally, to despair. You have no idea what it means to lose your good name.'

Catherine Fitzgibbon smiled, and quipped, 'Sure I do. Of course I do. Haven't you read the *National Enquirer* lately?' That got a laugh from the courtroom audience, even the jury members. I could tell that they liked Catherine. So did I.

She continued, 'Isn't it true that your husband has been treated for "despair" for many years? He's seeing a psychologist, Mrs Shafer. He suffers from manic-depression, or bipolar disorder, correct?'

Lucy shook her head. 'He's had a mid-life crisis. That's all it is. It's nothing unusual for men of his age.'

'I see. And were you able to help him with his crisis?'

'Of course I was. Although not with respect to his work. So much of what he does is classified and top secret. You must understand that.'

'I must,' the prosecutor said, then quickly went on, 'so your husband has a great many secrets he keeps from you?'

Lucy frowned, and her eyes shot darts at the wily prosecutor. 'In his *work*, yes.'

'You knew that he was seeing Dr Cassady? Boo Cassady?'

'Yes, of course I did. We often talked about it.'

'How often did he see her? Do you know? Did he tell you that? Or was it *top secret*?'

Jane Halpern shouted, 'Objection!'

'Sustained. Ms Fitzgibbon,' warned Judge Fescoe, with an arched brow.

'Sorry, your honor. Sorry, Lucy. All right, then. How often did your husband see Boo Cassady?'

'He saw her as much as necessary, I suppose. I believe her name is *Elizabeth*.'

'Once a week? Twice? Every day?' Fitzgibbon pressed on, without missing a beat.

'I think once a week. Usually it was once a week.'

'But the doormen at the Farragut testified they saw your husband much more than that. Three and four times a week on average.'

Lucy Shafer shook her head wearily and glared at Fitzgibbon. 'I trust Geoffrey completely. I don't keep him on a lead. I certainly wouldn't *count* his therapy sessions.'

'Did you mind that Dr Cassady, *Elizabeth*, is such an attractive woman?'

'No, don't be absurd.'

Fitzgibbon looked genuinely surprised. 'Why is that absurd? I don't think it is. I think I'd mind if my husband was seeing an attractive woman at her home office two, three, four times a week.'

Fitzgibbon moved swiftly. 'Didn't it bother you that Boo Cassady was a surrogate *sex* therapist for your husband?'

Lucy Shafer hesitated, seemed surprised, and glanced quickly at her husband. *She hadn't known.* It was impossible not to feel sorry for her.

Jane Halpern quickly rose from her seat. 'Objection! Your honor, there is no foundation that my client was seeing a sex surrogate.'

Lucy Shafer visibly pulled herself together on the witness stand. She was clearly stronger than she looked. Was she a game-player, too? Could she be one of the Horsemen? Or did she and her husband play a completely different kind of game?

She spoke. 'I'd like to answer the question. Madam Prosecutor. My husband, Geoffrey, has been such a good husband, such a good father, that even if he felt it necessary to see a sex therapist, and did *not* want to tell me about it because of the hurt or shame he felt, I would understand.'

'And if he committed *cold-blooded murder* – and did not want to tell you?' the prosecutor asked, then turned to the jury.

Chapter Ninety-Five

Elizabeth 'Boo' Cassady was in her late thirties, slender and very attractive, with lustrous brown hair that she had worn long since she was a young girl. She was a regular shopper at Neiman Marcus, Saks, Nordstrom, Bloomingdale's, and various chic specialty shops around Washington. It showed.

She had gotten the nickname 'Boo' as an infant because she always laughed and laughed whenever she heard the sound of somebody playing 'peek-a-boo' with her. She soon learned to make it herself, muttering '*boo, boo, boo, boo.*' In school, right through college, she kept the name, friends said, because she could be a little scary at times.

For her important day in court she'd chosen a single-breasted pantsuit, beautifully cut, very soft and flowy. Her outfit was an eye-pleasing mix of coffee and cashmere cream. She looked like a professional person, and a successful one.

Jules Halpern asked her to state her name and occupation for the record. He was amiable but businesslike, a little cooler than he had been with other witnesses.

'Dr Elizabeth Cassady. I'm a psychotherapist,' she replied evenly.

'Dr Cassady, how do you know Colonel Shafer?'

'He's a patient of mine and has been for over a year. He sees me at my office at 1208 Woodley Avenue once or twice a week. We increased the sessions recently since Mr Shafer's attempted suicide.'

Halpern nodded. 'What time are the sessions?'

'Usually early evenings. They can vary according to Mr Shafer's work schedule.'

'Dr Cassady, I direct your attention to the evening of the murder of Detective Hampton. Did Geoffrey Shafer have a therapy session with you that night?'

'Yes, he did. At nine p.m., nine until ten. I think he may have arrived a little earlier that night. But the session was scheduled for nine.'

'Could he have arrived as early as eight thirty?'

'No. That isn't possible. We were talking to each other on cell phones from the time he left his house in Kalorama until he arrived at my building. He was feeling a great deal of guilt about his latest dark mood coming too close to his daughters' birthday party.'

'I see. Was there any break in your conversation with Colonel Shafer?'

'Yes. But it was a very short one.'

Halpern kept the pace brisk. 'How much time passed between the time the two of you stopped talking on the cell phone and his arrival at your office?'

'Two or three minutes, five at the most. While he parked and came upstairs. No more than that.'

'When he arrived at your office, did Geoffrey Shafer seem unsettled in any way?'

'No, not at all. He appeared relatively cheerful, actually. He had just hosted a successful birthday party for the twins. He felt it had gone very well and he dotes on his children.'

'Was he out of breath, tense, or perspiring?' Halpern asked.

'No. As I said, he was calm and looked quite fine. I remember it very clearly. And after the intrusion by the police, I made careful *notes* to keep everything accurate and fresh,' she said, then glanced at the prosecutor's table.

'So, you made notes for the sake of accuracy?'

'Yes, I did.'

'Dr Cassady, did you notice any blood anywhere on Colonel Shafer's clothing?'

'No, I did not.'

'I see. You saw no blood on Shafer. And when Detective Cross arrived, did you see any blood on him?'

'Yes, I saw dark stains or streaks of blood on his shirt and suit coat. Also on his hands.'

Jules Halpern paused to let everything sink in with the jury. Then he asked a final question. 'Did Colonel Shafer look as if he had just murdered someone?'

'No, certainly not.'

'I have nothing further,' said the defense attorney.

Daniel Weston did the cross-exam for the prosecution. He was twenty-nine years old, bright, quick-witted, a rising star, and known to be a ruthless hatchet-man in the prosecutor's office.

Dan Weston was also good-looking, blond, and rugged. He got physically close to Boo Cassady. They made a fetching couple, which was the visual idea he wanted to communicate.

'Ms Cassady, you weren't Mr Shafer's *psychiatrist*, were you?'

She frowned slightly, but then managed a weak smile. 'No, a psychiatrist has to be a medical doctor. You know that, I'm sure.'

'And you are not a medical doctor?'

She shook her head. 'I am not. I have a doctorate in sociology. You know that, too.'

'Are you a *psychologist*?' Weston asked.

'A psychologist usually has a graduate degree in psychology, sometimes a PhD.'

'Do you have a graduate degree in psychology?'

'No. I'm a psychotherapist.'

'I see. Where was your training to be a psychotherapist?'

'American University. I graduated with a PhD in social work.'

Daniel Weston kept coming at Cassady. There was hardly a beat between question and answer. 'This "psychotherapy office" of yours at the Farragut. What sort of furnishings does it have?'

'A couch, desk, lamp. It's basically very spare. Lots of plants, though. My patients find the atmosphere functional but also relaxing.'

'No box of tissues by the couch? I thought that was a must,' Weston said with a thin smile.

The witness was clearly annoyed now, and maybe even shaken. 'I take my work very seriously, Mr Weston. So do my patients.'

'Was Geoffrey Shafer referred to you by someone?'

'Actually, we met in the National Gallery . . . at the Picasso Erotic Drawing Exhibit. That's been covered in depth by the press.'

Weston nodded, and a thin smile crossed his lips. 'Ah, I see. Are your sessions with Geoffrey Shafer erotic? Do you ever discuss sex?'

Jules Halpern rose quickly; a regular Jules-in-the-box. 'Objection! Doctor/patient privilege. It's confidential.'

The young prosecutor shrugged, flipped back his blond curls with his hand. 'I'll withdraw the question. No problem. Are you a sexual surrogate?'

'No, I am not. As I stated earlier, I am a psychotherapist.'

'On the evening of the murder of Detective Hampton, did you and Geoffrey Shafer discuss—'

Jules Halpern quickly rose again. 'Objection. If the prosecution is inquiring into the patient's privileged disclosures—'

Weston raised both arms in frustration. He smiled at the jury, hoping they felt the same way. 'All right, all right. Let me see. I'll take this out of the so-called doctor/patient realm and ask you, quite simply, if you, Ms Cassady, a woman, have had sexual relations with Geoffrey Shafer, a man?'

Elizabeth 'Boo' Cassady hung her head and stared down at her lap.

Daniel Weston smiled, even as Jules Halpern objected to the question and was upheld by Judge Fescoe. Weston felt that he had made his point.

Chapter Ninety-Six

'Call Detective Alex Cross.'

I took a deep breath, composed my mind, body, soul, then walked up the wide center aisle of the courtroom to testify. Everyone in the room was watching me, but the only person I really saw was Geoffrey Shafer. The Weasel. He was still playing the part of the wronged innocent man and I wanted to bring him down. I wanted to cross-examine him myself, to ask the real questions that needed to be asked, to tell the jury about all the suppressed evidence, to bring justice crashing down on him with all its force.

It was a hard thing to have worked honestly for so many years – and now be accused of being a rogue cop, someone who had tampered with evidence, and maybe worse. It was ironic, but now maybe I had the opportunity to set the record straight; to clear my name.

Jules Halpern smiled cordially at me as I sat down in the witness stand. He established eye contact, quickly looked over at the jury, then back at me. His dark eyes radiated intelligence and it seemed an incredible waste that he was working for Shafer.

'I want to start by saying that it is an honor to meet you, Detective Cross. For years I, like most of the jurors I'm sure, have read in the Washington papers about the murder cases you have helped solve. We admire your past record.'

I nodded and even managed a grudging smile of my own. 'Thank you. I hope you'll admire my present and future record as well,' I said.

'Let's hope so, Detective,' Halpern said. He moved on. We parried for half an hour or so, before he asked, 'You suffered a terrible personal tragedy a short time before the arrest of Colonel Shafer. Could you tell us about it?'

I fought the urge to reach out and grab the polite-sounding, insidious little man by the neck. I leaned closer to the mike, struggled for control.

'Someone dear to me was kidnapped while we were in Bermuda on vacation. She's still missing. I haven't given up hope that she'll be found. I pray every day that she's still alive.'

Halpern clucked sympathetically. He was good, much like his client. 'I really am sorry. Did the department give you adequate time off?'

'They were understanding and helpful,' I said, feeling my jaw stiffen with resentment. I hated that Halpern was using what happened to Christine to unsettle me.

'Detective, were you officially back on active duty at the time of Detective Hampton's murder?'

'Yes, I went back on full-time duty about a week before the murder.'

'Was it requested that you stay off active duty for a while longer?'

'It was left up to me. The chief of detectives did question my ability to resume my duties. But he made it my choice.'

Halpern nodded thoughtfully. 'He felt your head might be elsewhere? Who could blame you if it was?'

'I was upset, I still am, but I've been able to work. It's been good for me. The right thing to do.'

There were several questions about my state of mind, then Halpern asked, 'When you found out that Detective Hampton had been murdered, how upset were you?'

'I did my job. It was a bad homicide scene.' *Your client is a butcher. Do you really want to get him off? Do you realize what you're doing?*

'Your fingerprints were on Detective Hampton's belt and on the dashboard of her car. Her blood was on your clothes.'

I paused for several seconds before I spoke again. Then I tried to explain. 'There was a huge jagged tear in Detective Hampton's jugular vein. Blood was everywhere in the car, and even on the cement floor of the garage. I tried to help Detective Hampton – until I was certain she was dead. That's why there were fingerprints in the car and Detective Hampton's blood on my clothes.'

'You tracked blood upstairs?'

'No, I did not. I checked my shoes carefully before I left the garage. I checked *twice*. I checked because I *didn't* want to track any blood up into the building.'

'But you were upset, you admit that much. A police officer had been murdered. You forgot to put on gloves when you first searched the scene. There was blood on your clothes. How can you possibly be so sure?'

I stared directly into his eyes and tried to be as calm as he was. 'I know exactly what happened that night. I know who killed Patsy Hampton in cold blood.'

He raised his voice suddenly. 'No, you do not, sir. That's the point. *You do not*. In frisking Colonel Geoffrey Shafer, isn't it fair to say that you were in physical contact with him?'

'Yes.'

'And isn't it possible that blood from your clothes got onto his? Isn't it even likely?'

I wouldn't give him an inch. I couldn't. 'No, it isn't possible. There was blood on Geoffrey Shafer's trousers *before* I arrived.'

Halpern moved away from me. He wanted me to sweat. He walked over to the jury box, occasionally looking back at me. He asked several more questions about the crime scene, and then—

'But Dr Cassady didn't see any blood. The two other officers didn't see any blood – *not until after you came into contact with Colonel Shafer*. Colonel Shafer was on the phone until three to five minutes before he met his therapist. He came straight there from his children's birthday party. *You have no evidence, Detective Cross!* Except what you brought into Dr Cassady's apartment yourself. You have absolutely no evidence, Detective! You arrested the wrong man! You framed an innocent man!'

Jules Halpern threw up his hands in disgust. 'I have no further questions.'

Chapter Ninety-Seven

I took a back way out of the courthouse. I usually did, but on this day it was essential. I had to avoid the crowds and the press, and I needed to have a private moment to recover from my time on the witness stand.

I'd just had my ass pretty well kicked by an expert asskicker. Tomorrow, Cathy Fitzgibbon would try to undo some of the damage in cross-exam.

I was in no hurry as I walked down a back stairway that was used by maintenance and cleaning people in the building, and was also a fire escape.

It was becoming clear to me that there was a chance that Geoffrey Shafer would be acquitted. His lawyers were the best. We'd lost important evidence at the suppression hearing.

And, I *had* made a mistake at the homicide scene in my rush to help Patsy Hampton without putting on gloves.

It was an honest mistake, but it probably created doubt in the minds of the jurors. I'd had more blood on me than Shafer. That was true. Shafer might actually get away with murder, and I couldn't stand the thought. I felt like yelling as I descended the twisting flight of stairs.

And that's what I did, finally. I yelled at the top of my voice and it felt so damn good to get it out. Relief flowed through my body, however temporary it might be.

At the bottom of the concrete stairs was the basement of the courthouse. I headed down a long darkened hallway toward the rear lot where the Porsche was parked. I was still lost in my thoughts, but calmer after hollering my fool head off in the stairwell.

There was a sharp bend in the hallway near the exit to the parking lot. I came around the turn and saw him. I couldn't believe it. The Weasel was right there.

He was first to speak. 'What a surprise, Dr Cross. Sneaking away from the madding, or is it maddening crowd? Tail between your legs today? Don't fret, you did all right upstairs. Was that you yelling in the halls? Primal screams are the best, aren't they?'

'What the hell do you want, Shafer?' I asked him. 'We're not supposed to meet or talk like this.'

He shrugged his broad shoulders, wiped his blond hair away from his eyes. 'You think I care about rules? I don't give a shit about rules. *What do I want?*

My good name restored. I want my family not to have to go through any more of this. I want it all.'

'Then you shouldn't have killed all those people. Especially Patsy Hampton.'

Shafer finally smiled. 'You're very sure of yourself, aren't you? You don't back down. I admire that, to a degree. I played the game of being a hero once myself. In the army. It's interesting for a while.'

'But it's much more interesting to be a raving lunatic murderer,' I said.

'See? You just don't back down from your pig-headed opinions. I love it. You're wonderful.'

'It's not opinion, Shafer. You know it, and so do I.'

'Then prove it, Cross. Win your pitiful sodding case, will you? Beat me fair and square in a court of law. I even gave you home advantage.'

I started to walk toward him; I couldn't help myself. He stood his ground.

'This is all an insane game to you. I've met assholes like you before, Shafer. I've beaten better. I'll beat you.'

He laughed in my face. 'I sincerely doubt it.'

I walked right past him in the narrow tunnel.

He pushed me – hard, from behind. He was a big man, but even stronger than he looked.

I stumbled, almost went over onto the stone floor. I wasn't expecting the outburst of anger from him. He held it in so well in court, but it was close to the surface. The madness that *was* Geoffrey Shafer. The violence.

'Then go ahead, beat me. See if you can,' he yelled at the top of his voice. 'Beat me right here, right now. I don't think you can, Cross. I know you can't.'

Shafer took a quick step toward me. He was agile and athletic, not just strong. We were almost the same size, six foot two or three, two hundred pounds. I remembered that he'd been an army officer, then MI6. He still looked in excellent shape.

Shafer pushed me again with both hands. He made a loud grunting noise. 'If you've beaten better, then I should be a pushover. Isn't that so? I'm just a *pushover*.'

I almost threw a punch; I wanted to. I ached to take him down, to wipe the smug, superior look off his face.

Instead, I grabbed him hard. I slammed Shafer up against the stone tunnel wall and held him there.

'Not now. Not here,' I said, in a hoarse, raw whisper. 'I'm not going to hit you, Shafer. What? Have you run to the newspapers and TV? But I am going to bring you down. Soon.'

He came out with a crazy laugh. 'You are fucking hilarious, do you know that? You're a *scream*. I love it.'

I walked away from Shafer in the dark tunnel. It was the hardest thing I've ever had to do. I wanted to beat the answers out of him, get a confession. I wanted to know about Christine. I had so many questions, but I knew he wouldn't answer them. He was here to bait me, to *play*.

'You're losing . . . everything,' he said to my back.

I think I could have killed Geoffrey Shafer on the spot.

I almost turned, but I didn't. I opened the creaking door and went outside instead. Sunlight streamed into my eyes, half-blinding me for a dizzying moment. Shading my face with an arm, I climbed stone stairs to the parking area, where I got another unwanted surprise.

A dozen grim-faced members of the press, including some important reporters, were gathered in the back parking lot. Someone had alerted them; someone had tipped them off that I was coming out this way.

I looked back at the gray metal door, but Geoffrey Shafer didn't come out behind me. He had retreated and disappeared back into the basement.

'Detective Cross.' I heard a reporter call my name. 'You're losing this case. You know that, don't you?'

Yes, I knew. I was losing everything. I just didn't know what I could do to stop it.

Chapter Ninety-Eight

The following day was taken up with my cross-examination by Catherine Fitzgibbon. Catherine did a good job of redressing some of the harm done by Jules Halpern, but not all of it. Halpern consistently broke up her rhythm with his objections. Like so many recent high-profile trials, this one was maddening. It should have been easy to convict and put away Geoffrey Shafer, but that wasn't the case.

Two days later, we got our best chance to win, and Shafer himself gave it to us, almost as if he was daring us. Now we realized that he was even crazier than we'd thought. The game was his life; nothing else seemed to matter.

Shafer agreed to take the stand. I think that I was the only one in the court-room who wasn't completely surprised that he was testifying, that he was playing the game right in front of us.

Catherine Fitzgibbon was almost certain that Jules Halpern had lectured, pleaded and advised him against it; but there Shafer was anyway, striding toward the witness stand, looking as if he had been called up there to be ceremoni-ously knighted by the Queen.

He couldn't resist the stage, could he? He looked every bit as confident and in control as he had the night I arrested him for Patsy Hampton's murder. He was dressed in a navy-blue double-breasted suit, white shirt, and gold tie. Not a single blond hair was out of place, nor was there any hint of the anger boiling just under the surface of his meticulously groomed exterior.

Jules Halpern addressed him in conversational tones, but I was certain that he was uneasy about this unnecessary gamble.

'Colonel Shafer, first I want to thank you for coming to the witness stand. This is completely voluntary on your part. From the beginning, you've stated that you wanted to come here to clear your name.'

Shafer smiled politely, and then cut off his lawyer with a raised hand. The lawyers on both sides of the bar exchanged looks. What was happening? What was he going to do?

I leaned way forward in my seat. It struck me that Jules Halpern might actually *know* that his client was guilty. If he did, he wouldn't have been able to cross-examine him. Legally, he couldn't ask questions that disguised the real facts as he knew them.

This was the only way that Shafer could have his moment in the sun: A soliloquy. Once called to the stand, Shafer could give a speech. It was unusual, but absolutely legal – and, if Halpern knew his client was guilty, it was the only way that Shafer could take the stand and not be incriminated by his own attorney.

Shafer had the floor. 'If you will please excuse me, Mr Halpern, I believe I can talk to these good people myself. I really can manage. You see, I don't need a lot of expert help telling the simple truth.'

Jules Halpern stepped back, nodded sagely, and tried to keep his poise. What else could he do under the circumstances? If he hadn't known his client was an egomaniac or insane, he surely knew it now.

Shafer looked toward the jury. 'It has been stated here in court that I am with British Intelligence, that I was MI6, a spy. I'm afraid that I am actually a rather unglamorous agent, Double-O-Nothing if you will.'

The light, well-aimed jab at himself drew laughter in the courtroom.

'I am a simple bureaucrat, like so many others who toil away their days and nights in Washington. I follow well-established procedures at the embassy. I get approvals for virtually everything I do. My home life is simple and orderly as well. My wife and I have been married nearly sixteen years. We love each other dearly. We're devoted to our three children.

'So I want to apologize to my wife and children. I am so frightfully sorry for this hellish ordeal they've had to go through. To my son, Rob, and the twins, Tricia and Erica, I'm so sorry. If I had any idea what a circus this would become, I would have insisted on diplomatic immunity, rather than clear my name, our name, *their* name.

'While I'm making heartfelt apologies, I'll make one to all of you for being a bit of a bore right now. It's just that – when you're accused of murder, something so heinous, so unthinkable, you want desperately to get it off your chest. You want to tell the truth more than anything else in the world. So that's what I'm doing today.

'You've heard the evidence – and there simply isn't any. You've heard character witnesses. And now you've heard from me. I did not kill Detective Patsy Hampton. I think you all know that, but I wanted to say it to you myself. Thank you for listening,' he said, and bowed slightly in his seat.

Shafer was brief, but he was poised and articulate, and, unfortunately, very believable. He always held eye contact with the jury members. His words weren't nearly as important as the way he delivered them.

Catherine Fitzgibbon came forward to do the cross-examination, and she was careful with Shafer at first. She knew that he had the jury on his side for the moment.

She waited until near the end of her cross-exam to go after Shafer where he might be most vulnerable.

'That was very nice, Mr Shafer. Now as you sit before this jury you claim that your relationship with Dr Cassady was strictly professional, that you did not have a sexual relationship with her? Remember you are under oath.'

'Yes, absolutely. She was, and hopefully will continue to be, my therapist.'

'Notwithstanding the fact that she admits to having a sexual relationship with you?'

Shafer held his hand toward Jules Halpern, signaling for him not to object. 'I believe that the court record will show that she did not admit to such.'

Fitzgibbon frowned. 'I don't follow? Why do *you* think she didn't answer counsel?'

Shafer shot back. 'That's obvious. Because she didn't care to *dignify* such a question.'

'And when she hung her head, sir, and looked down at her lap? She was nodding assent?'

Shafer now looked at the jury, and shook his head in amazement. 'You misread her completely. You missed the point again, Counselor. Allow me to illustrate, if I may. As Charles I said before being beheaded, "Give me my cloak lest they think I tremble from fear." Dr Elizabeth Cassady was deeply embarrassed by your associate's crude suggestion, so was my family, and so am I.'

Geoffrey Shafer looked at the prosecutor with steely eyes. He then acknowledged the jury again. 'And so am I.'

Chapter Ninety-Nine

The trial was almost over, and now came the really hard part: Waiting for a verdict. That Tuesday, the jurors retired to the jury room to commence their deliberations in the murder trial of Geoffrey Shafer. For the first time, I allowed myself to actually think the unthinkable: That Shafer might be set free.

Sampson and I sat in the rear row of the courtroom and watched the twelve members depart: eight men and four women. John had come to court several times, calling it the 'best and sleaziest show this side of the Oval Office,' but I knew he was there to give me support.

'The sonofabitch is guilty, he's mad as little Davey Berkowitz,' Sampson said as he watched Shafer. 'But he has a lot of good actors on his side: doting wife, doting mistress, well-paid lawyers, Silly Billy. He could get away with it.'

'It happens,' I agreed. 'Juries are hard to read. And getting harder.'

I watched as Shafer courteously shook hands with the members of his defense team. Both Jules and Jane Halpern had forced smiles on their faces. *They knew*, didn't they? *Their client was the Weasel, a mass murderer*.

'Geoffrey Shafer has the ability to make people believe in him when he needs to. He's the best actor I've seen.'

I said goodbye to John, then I snuck out the back way again. This time neither Shafer nor the press was lying in wait downstairs or in the rear parking lot.

In the lot, I heard a woman's voice and I stopped moving. *I thought it was Christine*. A dozen or so people were walking to their cars, seemingly unaware of me. I felt fevered and hot as I checked them all. None of them was her. Where had the voice come from?

I took a ride in the old Porsche and listened to George Benson on the CD player. I remembered the police report about Shafer's thrill-seeking ride ending near Dupont Circle. It seemed a strangely appealing prospect. I took my own advice not to try and guess how the jury would decide the case. It could go either way.

I finally let myself think about Christine, and I choked up. It was too much. Tears began to stream down my cheeks. I had to pull over.

I took a deep breath, then another. The pain in my chest was still as fresh as it had been the day she had disappeared in Bermuda. She had tried to stay away from me, but I wouldn't let her. I was responsible for what had happened to her.

I drove around Washington, riding in gently aimless circles. I finally reached home more than two and a half hours after I left the courthouse.

Nana came running out of the house. She must have seen me pull into the driveway. She'd obviously been waiting for me.

I leaned out of the driver's side window. The DJ was still talking congenially on Public Radio.

'What is it, old woman? What's the matter now?' I asked Nana.

'Ms Fitzgibbon called you, Alex. The jury is coming back. They have a verdict.'

Chapter One Hundred

I was apprehensive as I could be. But I was also curious beyond anything I could remember.

I backed out of the driveway and sped downtown. I got back to the courthouse in less than fifteen minutes, and the crowd on E Street was larger and more unruly than I had seen it at the height of the trial. At least a half-dozen Union Jacks waved in the wind; contrasting that were American flags, including some painted across bare chests and faces.

I had to push and literally inch my way through the crush of people up close to the courthouse steps. I ignored every question from the press. I tried to avoid anyone with a camera in hand, or the hungry look of a reporter.

I entered the packed courtroom just before the jury filed back inside. *You almost missed it*, I said to myself.

Judge Fescoe spoke to the crowd as soon as everyone was seated. 'There will be no demonstrations when this verdict is read. If any demonstrations occur, marshals will clear this room immediately,' he instructed in a soft but clear voice.

I stood a few rows behind the prosecution team and tried to find a regular breathing pattern. It was inconceivable that Geoffrey Shafer could be set free; there was no doubt in my mind that he'd murdered several times, not just Patsy Hampton, but at least some of the Jane Does. He was a wanton pattern killer, one of the worst, and had been getting away with it for years. I realized now that Shafer might be the most outrageous and daring of the killers I'd faced. He played his game with the pedal pressed to the floor. He absolutely refused to lose.

'Mr Foreperson, do you have a verdict for us?' Judge Fescoe asked in somber tones.

Raymond Horton, the foreperson, spoke to Judge Fescoe. 'Your honor, we have a verdict.'

I glanced at Shafer and he appeared confident. As he had been for every day of the trial, he was dressed in a tailored suit, white shirt and tie. He had no conscience whatsoever; he had no fear of anything that might happen. Maybe that was a partial explanation for why he'd run free for so long.

Judge Fescoe appeared unusually stern. 'Very well. Will the defendant please rise and face the jury,' he said.

Geoffrey Shafer stood at the defense table and his longish hair gleamed under the bright overhead lighting. He towered over Jules Halpern and his daughter, Jane. Shafer held his hands behind him, as if he were cuffed. I wondered if he might have a pair of twenty-sided dice clasped in them, the kind I had seen in his study.

Judge Fescoe addressed Mr Horton again. 'As to count one of the indictment, Aggravated, Premeditated Murder in the First Degree, how do you find?'

Mr Horton answered, '*Not guilty*, your honor.'

I felt as if my head had suddenly spun off. The audience packed into the small room went completely wild. The press rushed to the bar. The judge had promised to clear the room, but he was already retreating to his chambers.

I saw Shafer walk toward the press, but then he quickly passed them by. What was he doing now? He noticed a man in the crowd, and nodded stiffly in his direction. Who was that?

Then Shafer continued toward where I was, in the fourth row. I wanted to vault over the chairs after him. I wanted him so bad, and I knew I had just lost my chance to do it the right way.

'Detective Cross,' he said in his usual supercilious manner. 'Detective Cross, there's something I want to say. I've been holding it in for months.'

The press closed in; the scene becoming smothering and claustrophobic. Cameras flashed on all sides. Now that the trial was ended, there was nothing to prevent picture-taking inside the courtroom. Shafer was aware of the rare photo-opportunity. Of course he was. He spoke again, so that everyone gathered around us could hear. Suddenly it was quiet where we stood, a pocket of silence, foreboding expectation.

'You killed her,' he said, and stared deeply into my eyes, almost to the back of my skull. '*You killed her.*'

I went numb. My legs were suddenly weak. I knew he didn't mean Patsy Hampton.

He meant Christine.

She was dead.

Geoffrey Shafer had killed her. He had taken everything from me, just as he warned me he would.

He had won.

Chapter One Hundred and One

S hafer was a free man, and he was enjoying the bloody hell out of it. He had gambled, and he had won big time. *Big time!* He had never felt anything quite like this exhilarating moment following his verdict. He'd wagered his life.

He accompanied Lucy and the children to a by-invitation-only press conference held in the pompous, high-ceilinged Grand Jury room. He posed for countless photos with his family. They hugged him again and again, and Lucy couldn't stop crying like the brain-dead, hopelessly spoiled and crazy child that she was. If some people thought *he* was a drug abuser, they'd be shocked by Lucy's intake. Christ, that was how he'd first learned about the amazing world of pharmaceuticals.

He finally punched his fist into the air and held it there as a mocking sign of victory. Cameras flashed everywhere. They couldn't get enough of him. There were nearly a hundred reporters wedged into the room. The women reporters loved him most of all. He was a legitimate media star now, wasn't he? He was a hero again.

A few gate-crashing agents of fame and fortune pressed their cards at him, promising obscene amounts of money for his story. He didn't need any of their tawdry business cards. Months before, he had picked out a powerful New York and Hollywood agent.

Christ, he was free as a bird! He was absolutely flying now. After the press conference, claiming concern for their safety, he sent his family ahead without him.

He stayed behind in the court law library and firmed up book deal details with Jules Halpern and the Bertelsmann Group, now the most powerful book publishing conglomerate around the world. He had promised them his story – but of course they weren't going to get anything close to the truth. Wasn't that the way with the so-called 'tell-all, bare-all' nonfiction published these days? Bertelsmann knew this, and still they'd paid him a fortune.

After the meeting, he took the slow-riding lift down to the court's indoor car park. He was still feeling incredibly high, which could be dangerous. A set of twenty-sided dice was burning a hole in the pocket of his suit trousers.

He desperately wanted to play the game. Now! The Four Horsemen. Better yet, Solipsis. *His* version of the game. He wouldn't give in to that urge, not yet. It was too dangerous, even for him.

Since the beginning of the trial, he had been parking the Jaguar in the same spot. He *did* have his patterns after all. He never bothered to put coins in the meter, not once. Every day there was a pile of five-dollar tickets under the windshield wiper.

Today was no exception.

He grabbed the absurd parking tickets off the windshield and crumpled them into a ball in his fist. Then he dropped the wad of paper onto the oil-stained concrete floor.

'I have diplomatic immunity,' he smiled as he climbed into his Jag.

Book Five

Endgame

Chapter One Hundred and Two

S hafer couldn't believe it. He had made a very serious and perhaps irre-
versible mistake. The result wasn't what he had expected, and now his
whole world seemed to be falling apart. At times he thought that it couldn't
have been worse if he had gone to prison for the cold-blooded murder of Patsy
Hampton.

Shafer knew that he wasn't just being paranoid or mad. Several of the pathetic
wankers inside the embassy were watching him every bloody time he stepped from
his office. They seemed to resent him and openly despise him, especially the
women. Who had turned them against him? Somebody surely was responsible.

He was the white, English O.J. Simpson. A weird off-color joke to them.
Guilty though proven innocent.

So Shafer mostly stayed inside his office with the door closed, sometimes
locked. He performed his few remaining duties with a growing sense of irritation and frustration, and a sense of the absurd. It was driving him mad to be
trapped like this, to be a pathetic spectacle for the embassy staff.

He idly played with his computer and waited for the game of the Four
Horsemen to resume, but the other players had cut him off. They insisted that
it was too dangerous to play, even to communicate, and *not one of them* understood that that was exactly why this was the perfect time to play.

Shafer stared out onto Massachusetts Avenue for interminably long stretches
during the day. He listened to call-in talk shows on the radio. He was getting
angrier and angrier. He needed to play.

Someone was knocking on the door of his office. He turned his head sharply,
and felt a spike of pain in the back of his neck. The phone had begun to ring.
He picked up and heard the voice of the temp he'd been given. Ms Wynne
Hamerman was on the intercom.

'Mr Andrew Jones is here to see you,' she said.

Andrew Jones? Shafer was shocked. Jones was a director from the Security
Service in London. Shafer hadn't known he was in Washington. What the hell
was this visit about? Andrew Jones was a high-level, very tough bastard who
wouldn't just drop by for tea and biscuits. *Mustn't keep him waiting too long.*

Jones was standing there, and he looked impatient, almost angry. What was
this about? His steely-blue eyes were cold and hard; his face as rigid as that

of an English soldier in Belfast. In contrast, his brilliant red hair and mustache made him look benign, almost jolly. He was called 'Andrew the Red' back in London.

'Let's go inside your office, shall we? Shut the door behind you,' Jones said, in a low but commanding tone.

Shafer was just getting over his initial surprise, but he was also starting to become angry. Who was this pompous asshole to come barging into his office like this? By what right was he here? How dare he? The toad! The glorified lackey from London.

'You can sit down, Shafer,' Jones said. Another imperious command. 'I'll be brief and to the point.'

'Of course,' Shafer answered. He remained standing. 'Please do be brief. I'm sure we're both busy.'

Jones lit up a cigarette, took a long drag, then let the smoke out slowly.

'That's illegal here in Washington,' Shafer goaded him.

'You'll receive orders to return to England in thirty days' time,' said Jones, who continued to puff furiously on the cigarette. 'You're an embarrassment here in Washington, as you will be in London. Of course, over there the tabloids have recreated you as a martyr of the brutal and inefficient American police and judicial system. They like to think of this as *DC Confidential*, more evidence of wholesale corruption and naiveté in the States. Which we both know, in this case, is complete crap.'

Shafer smiled contemptuously. 'How dare you come in here and talk to me like this, Jones. I was framed for a heinous crime I didn't commit. I was acquitted by an American jury. Have you forgotten that?'

Jones frowned, and continued to stare him down. 'Only because crucial evidence wasn't allowed in the trial. The blood on your trousers? That poor woman's blood in the bathroom drain at your mistress's?' He blew smoke out of the side of his mouth. 'We know everything, you pathetic fool. We know you're a stone-cold killing freak. So you'll *go* back to London – until we catch you at something. Which we will, Shafer. We'll make something up if we have to.

'I feel sick being in the same room with you. Legally, you've escaped punishment this time, but we're watching you very closely now. We will get you, somewhere, some day soon.'

Shafer looked amused. He couldn't hold back a smile. He knew he shouldn't, but he couldn't resist the play. 'You can try, you insufferable, sanctimonious shit. You can certainly try. But join the queue. And now, if you please, I have work to do.'

Andrew Jones shook his head. 'Well actually, you don't have any work to do, Shafer. But I am happy to leave. The stench in here is absolutely overpowering. When was the last time you had a bath?' He laughed contemptuously. 'Christ, you've completely lost it.'

Chapter One Hundred and Three

That afternoon I met with Jones and three of his agents at the Willard Hotel, near the White House. I had called the meeting. Sampson was there, too. He'd been reinstated in the department, but that didn't stop him from doing what had originally gotten him into trouble.

'I believe he's crazy,' Jones said of Shafer. 'He smells like a lavatory at boot camp. He's definitely going down for the count. What're your thoughts on his mental state?'

I knew Geoffrey Shafer inside and out by now. I'd read about his family: his brother, a long-suffering mother, the domineering father. Their travels from military base to base until he was twelve. 'Here's what I think. It started with a serious bipolar disorder, what used to be called manic-depression. He had it when he was a kid. Now he's strung out on pharmaceutical drugs: Xanax, Benadryl, Haldol, Ativan, Valium, Librium, several others. It's quite a cocktail. Available from local doctors for the right price. I'm surprised he can function at all. But he survives. He doesn't go down. He always wins.'

'I told Geoff he has to leave Washington. How do you think he'll take it?' Jones asked. 'I swear his office smelled as if a dead body had been festering there for a couple of days.'

'Actually his disorder can involve an accompanying odor, but it's usually steely – like metal, very pungent, sticks to your nostrils. He probably isn't bathing. But his instincts for playing the game, for winning and surviving, are amazing,' I said. 'He won't stop.'

'What's happening with the other players?' Sampson inquired. 'The so-called Horsemen?'

'They claim that the game is over, and that it was only a fantasy game for them. Oliver Highsmith stays in touch, to keep tabs on us, I'm sure. He's actually a scary bastard in his own right. Says he's saddened by the murder of Detective Hampton. He's still not a hundred percent sure that Shafer is the killer. Urges me to keep my mind open on that one.'

'Is your mind open on it?' I asked, looking around the room at the others.

Jones didn't hesitate. 'I have no doubt that Geoffrey Shafer is a multiple murderer. We've seen enough, and heard enough from you. He is quite possibly a homicidal maniac beyond anything we've ever seen. And I also have no doubt that eventually he's going down.'

I nodded my head. 'I agree,' I said, 'about everything you just said. But especially the homicidal maniac part.'

Chapter One Hundred and Four

S hafer was talking to himself again that night. He couldn't help it, and the more he tried to stop, the worse it became; the more he fretted, the more he talked to himself.

They can all bugger off. Jones, Cross, Lucy and the kids, Boo Cassady, the other spineless players. Screw them all. There was a reason behind the Four Horsemen, he knew. *It wasn't just a game. There was more to it than simple horseplay.*

The house at Kalorama was empty, much too quiet at night. It was huge and ridiculous, as only an American house can be. The 'original' architectural detail, the double living room, six fireplaces, long-ago-dead flowers, unread books in gold and brown leather binding, Lucy's Marmite. It was driving him up the twelve-foot-high walls.

He spent the next hour or so trying to convince himself that he wasn't crazy; specifically that he wasn't an addict. Recently, he'd added another doctor in Maryland to his sources for the drugs. Unfortunately, the illegal prescriptions cost him a fortune. He couldn't keep it up forever. The Lithium and Haldol were to control his mood swings – which were very real. Thorazine was for acute anxiety, which was fucking bloody real as well. Narcan had also been prescribed for his mood swings. The multiple injections of Loradol were for something else, some pain from he couldn't remember when. He knew there were good reasons for the Xanax, Compazine, Benadryl.

Lucy had already fled home to London, and she'd taken the traitorous children with her. They'd left exactly one week after the trial ended. Her father was the real cause. He'd come to Washington, spoken to Lucy for less than an hour, and she'd packed up and left, like the Goody Two-Shoes she'd always been. Before she departed, Lucy had the nerve to tell Shafer she'd stood by him for the sake of the children and her father, but now her duty was over. She didn't believe he was a murderer, as her father did; but he was an adulterer, and that she couldn't take for one moment longer.

God, how he despised his little wifey. Before Lucy left, *he* made it clear to *her* that the real reason she'd performed her 'duty' was so he wouldn't reveal her unsavory drug habits to the press, which he *would* have, and might do anyway.

At eleven o'clock he had to go out for a drive, his nightly constitutional. He was feeling unbearably jittery and claustrophobic. He wondered if he could control himself for another night, another minute. His skin was crawling, and he had dozens of irritating little tics. He couldn't stop tapping his goddamn foot!

The dice were burning a bloody hole in his trouser pocket. His mind was racing in a dozen haphazard directions, all of them very bad. He wanted to, needed to, kill somebody. It had been this way with him for a long time, and that had been his dirty little secret. The other Horsemen knew the story; they even knew how it had begun. Shafer had been a decent soldier, but ultimately too ambitious to remain in the army. He had transferred into MI6 with the help of Lucy's father. He thought there was more room for advancement in MI6.

His first posting had been Bangkok, which was where he met James Whitehead, George Bayer, and eventually Oliver Highsmith. Whitehead and Bayer spent several weeks working on him, recruiting Shafer for a specialized job: He would be an assassin, their own personal hit man for the worst sort of wet work. Over the next two years he did three sanctions in Asia, and found that he truly loved the feeling of power that killing gave him. Oliver Highsmith, who ran both Bayer and Whitehead from London, once told him to depersonalize the act, to think of it as a game, and that was what he did. He had never stopped being an assassin.

Shafer turned on the CD in the Jag. *Loud*, to drown out the multiple voices raging in his head. The old-age-home rockers Jimmy Page and Robert Plant began a duet inside the cockpit of his car.

He backed out of the drive and headed down Tracy Place. He gunned the car and had it up close to sixty in the block between his house and Twenty-Fourth Street. Time for another suicidal drive? he wondered.

Red lights flashed on the side of Twenty-Fourth Street. Shafer cursed as a DC police patrol car eased down the street toward him. *God damn it!*

He pulled the Jag over to the curb and waited. His brain was screaming. 'Assholes. Bloody impertinent assholes! And you're an asshole, too!' he told himself in a loud whisper. 'Show some self-control, Geoff. Get yourself under control. Shape up. Right now!'

The Metro patrol car pulled up behind him, almost door to door. He could see two cops lurking inside.

One of them got out slowly and walked over to the Jag's driver-side window. The cop swaggered like a hot-shit all-American cinema hero. Shafer wanted to blow him away. Knew he could do it. He had a hot semiautomatic under the seat. He touched the grip, and God, it felt good.

'License and registration, sir,' the cop said, looking unbearably smug. A distorted voice inside Shafer's head screeched, *Shoot him now. It will blow everybody's mind if you kill another policeman.*

He handed over the requested identification, though, and managed a wanker's sheepish grin. 'We're out of Pampers at home. Trip to the 7-Eleven was in order. I know I was going too fast, and I'm sorry, Officer. Blame it on baby brain. You have any kids?'

The patrolman didn't say a word; not an ounce of civility in the bastard. He wrote out a speeding ticket. Took his sweet time about it.

'There you go, Mr Shafer.' The patrol officer handed him the speeding ticket. 'Oh, and by the way, we're watching you, shithead. We're all over you, man. You didn't get away with murdering Patsy Hampton. You just think you did.'

A set of car lights blinked on and off, on and off, on the side street where the patrol car had been sitting a few moments earlier.

Shafer stared, squinted back into the darkness. He recognized the car, a black Porsche.

Cross was there, watching. Alex Cross wouldn't go away.

Chapter One Hundred and Five

Andrew Jones sat in the quiet, semidarkened front seat of the Porsche with me. We'd been working closely together for almost two weeks. Jones and the Security Service were intent on stopping Shafer before he committed another murder. They were also tracking War, Famine, and Conqueror.

We watched silently as Geoffrey Shafer slowly turned the Jaguar around and drove back toward his house.

'He saw us. He knows my car,' I said. 'Good.'

I couldn't see his face in the darkness, but I could almost feel the heat rising from the top of his head. I knew he was crazed. The phrase 'homicidal maniac' kept drifting through my mind. Jones and I were looking at one, and he was still running free. He'd already gotten away with murder, several of them.

'Alex, aren't you concerned about possibly putting him into a rage state?' Jones asked, as the Jaguar eased to a stop in front of the Georgian-style house. There were no lights on in the driveway area, so we couldn't see Geoffrey Shafer for the next few seconds. We couldn't tell if he'd gone inside.

'He's already in a rage state. He's lost his job, his wife, his children, the game he lives for. Worst of all, his freedom to come and go has been curtailed. Shafer doesn't like limitations put on him, hates to be boxed in. He can't stand to lose.'

'So you think he'll do something rash.'

'Not rash, he's too clever. But he'll make a move. It's how the game is played.'

'And then we'll mess with his head yet again?'

'Yes, we will. Absolutely.'

Late that night, as I was driving home, I decided to stop at St Anthony's. The church is unusual in this day and age; it's open at night. Monsignor John Kelliher believes that's the way it should be, and he's willing to live with the vandalism and petty theft. Mostly, though, the people in the neighborhood watch over St Anthony's.

A couple of worshipers were inside the candlelit church around midnight, when I arrived. There usually are a few 'parishioners' inside. Homeless people aren't allowed to sleep there, but they wander in and out all through the night.

I sat watching the familiar red-and-gold votive lamps flicker and blink. I sucked in the thick smell of incense from Benediction. I stared up at the large gold-plated crucifix and the beautiful stained-glass windows that I've loved since I was a boy.

I lit a candle for Christine, and I hoped that somehow, some way, she might still be alive. It didn't seem likely. My memory of her was fading a little bit, and I hated that. A column of pain went from my stomach to my chest, making it hard for me to breathe. It had been this way since the night she disappeared, almost a year ago.

And then, for the first time, I admitted to myself that she was gone. I would never see her again. The thought caught like a shard of glass in my throat. Tears welled in my eyes. 'I love you,' I whispered to no one. 'I love you so much and I miss you terribly.'

I said a few more prayers, then I finally rose from the long wooden pew and silently made my way toward the doors of the vestibule. I didn't see the woman crouching in a side row. She startled me with a sudden movement.

I recognized her from the soup kitchen. Her name was Magnolia. That was all I knew about her, just an odd first name, maybe a made-up one. She called out to me in a loud voice. 'Hey, Peanut Butter Man, now you know what it's like.'

Chapter One Hundred and Six

Jones and Sandy Greenberg, from Interpol, had helped get the other three Horsemen under surveillance. The net being cast was large, as the catch could be, if we succeeded.

The huge potential scandal in England was being carefully watched and monitored by the Security Service. If four English agents were murderers involved in a bizarre game, the fallout would be widespread and devastating for the intelligence community.

Shafer dutifully went to the embassy to work on Wednesday and Thursday. He arrived just before nine and left promptly at five. Once inside, he stayed out of sight in his small office, not even venturing out for lunch. He spent hours on America Online, which we monitored.

Both days, he wore the same gray slacks and a double-breasted blue blazer. His clothes were uncharacteristically wrinkled and unkempt. His thick blond hair was combed back, looked dirty and greasy, and it resisted the high winds flowing through Washington. He looked pale, seemed nervous and fidgety.

Was he going to crash?

After dinner on Friday night, Nana and I sat out in back of the house on Fifth Street. We were talking, and spending more time together than we had in years. I knew she was concerned about me, and I let her help as much as she wanted. For both our sakes.

Jannie and Damon were washing the dishes inside and they managed not to squabble too much. Damon washed while Jannie dried. Damon's tape deck played the beautiful score from the movie *Beloved*.

'Most families have a disher and dryer these days,' Nana said, after she'd taken a sip of her tea. 'Slavery has ended in America, Alex. Did you happen to hear about that?'

'We have a dishwasher and dryer, too. Sounds like they're in good working order. Low maintenance, low cost. Hard to beat.'

Nana clucked. 'See how long it lasts.'

'If you want a dishwasher we can buy it, or are you just practicing the fine art of being argumentative before you launch into something more deserving of your talents? As I remember, you are a fan of Demosthenes and Cicero.'

She nudged me with her elbow. 'Wiseapple,' she said. 'Think you're so smart.'

I shook my head. 'Not really, Nana. That's never been one of my big problems.'

'No, I suppose not. You're right, you don't have a big head about yourself.' Nana stared into my eyes. I could almost feel her peering into my soul. She has an ability to look very deeply into things that really matter. 'You ever going to stop blaming yourself?' she finally asked. 'You look just terrible.'

'Thank you. Are you ever going to stop nagging me?' I asked, and finally smiled at her. Nana could always bring me out of the doldrums, in her own special way.

She nodded her small head. 'Of course I will. I'll stop one day. Nobody lives forever, grannyson.'

I laughed. 'You probably will, though. Live longer than me or the kids.'

Nana showed lots of teeth – her own, too. 'I *do* feel pretty good, considering everything,' she said. 'You're still chasing him, aren't you? That's what you're doing nights. You and John Sampson, that Englishman, Andrew Jones.'

I sighed. 'Yeah, I am. And we're going to get him. There may be four men involved in a series of murders. Here, in Asia, Jamaica, London.'

She beckoned to me with a bent, crabbed forefinger. 'Come closer now.'

I grinned at her. She's such a soft touch really, such a sweetie, but such a hardass, too. 'You want me to sit down on your lap, old woman? You sure about that?'

'Good Lord, no. Don't sit on me, Alex. Just bend over and show some respect for my age and wisdom. Give me a big hug, while you're at it.'

I did as I was told, and I noticed there wasn't any fuss or clatter coming from the kitchen anymore.

I glanced at the screen door, and saw my two little busybodies were watching, their faces pressed against the mesh wire. I waved them away from the door, and their faces disappeared.

'I want you to be so very, very careful,' Nana whispered as I held her gently. 'But I want you to get him somehow, some way. That man is the worst of all of them. Geoffrey Shafer is the worst, Alex, the most evil.'

Chapter One Hundred and Seven

The game had never really ended – but it had changed tremendously since the trial in Washington.

It was five thirty in the evening in London and Conqueror was waiting at his computer. He was both anxious and feverishly excited about what was happening: The Four Horsemen was starting up again.

It was twelve thirty a.m. in Manila in the Philippines. Famine was ready for a message, and a new beginning to the game he loved.

And War awaited news of the Four Horsemen at his large house on the island of Jamaica. He too was obsessed with how it would end, and whether he would be the winner.

It was twelve thirty in Washington. Geoffrey Shafer was driving fast to the White Flint Mall, from the embassy. He had a lot to accomplish that afternoon. He was revved and manic.

He sped up Massachusetts Avenue, past the British Embassy and the vice-president's house. He wondered if he was being followed and assumed it was possible. Alex Cross and the other police were out there, just waiting to get him. He hadn't spotted them yet, which only meant that they were getting serious now.

He made a quick right, hit a traffic circle, and shot onto Nebraska Avenue headed toward American University. He snaked around back roads near the university, then got on Wisconsin, and sped toward the mall.

He entered Bloomingdale's, found the department store sparsely crowded, a little depressing actually. Good, he despised the American shopping scene anyway. It reminded him of Lucy and her brood. He walked at a leisurely pace through the men's clothing section. He picked up a few overpriced Ralph Lauren Polo sport shirts, and then two pairs of dark trousers.

He draped a black Giorgio Armani suit over his arm and took the bundle into the changing rooms. At a security desk inside he handed the clothes to an attendant on duty, to curtail shoplifters, no doubt.

'Changed my mind,' he said.

'That's not a problem, sir.'

Shafer then jogged down a narrow corridor that led to a rear exit. He sprinted toward the glass doors, then burst into a parking lot in back. He saw signs for Bruno Cipriani and Lord & Taylor, and knew he was heading in the right direction.

A Ford Taurus was parked there near the F pole. Shafer jumped inside, started it up, and drove up the Rockville Pike to Montrose Crossing, a little over a mile away.

He didn't think anyone was following now. He passed Montrose, and headed north to the Federal Plaza shopping center. Once he was there, he entered Cyber Exchange, which sold new and used software and lots of computers.

His eyes darted left and right, until he saw exactly what he needed.

'I'd like to try out the new iMac,' he told the salesperson who approached him.

'Be my guest. You need any assistance, holler,' the salesperson said. 'It's easy.'

'Yes, I think I'm fine. I'll call if I get stuck. I'm pretty sure I'm going to buy the iMac, though.'

'Excellent choice.'

'Yes. Excellent, excellent.'

The lazy clerk left him alone and Shafer immediately booted on. The display model was connected online. He felt a rush of manic excitement, but also a tinge of sadness as he typed in his message to the other players. He'd thought this through and knew what had to be said, what had to be done.

GREETINGS AND SALUTATIONS. THIS GLORIOUS AND UNPRECE-DENTED ADVENTURE OF SEVEN YEARS, THE FOUR HORSEMEN, IS NEARLY AT AN END NOW. YOU HAVE STATED YOUR CASE VERY LOGICALLY, AND I ACCEPT THE REGRETTABLE CONCLU-SION YOU'VE REACHED. THE GAME HAS BECOME TOO DANGEROUS. SO I PROPOSE THAT WE CREATE AN UNFORGET-TABLE ENDING. I BELIEVE THAT A FACE-TO-FACE MEETING IS A FITTING END. IT'S THE ONLY CONCLUSION THAT I CAN ACCEPT.

THIS WAS INEVITABLE, I SUPPOSE, AND WE HAVE DISCUSSED IT MANY TIMES BEFORE. YOU KNOW WHERE THE GAME ENDS. I PROPOSE THAT WE START PLAY ON THURSDAY. TRUST ME, I WILL BE THERE FOR THE GRAND FINALE. IF NECESSARY, I CAN BEGIN THE GAME WITHOUT YOU. DON'T MAKE ME DO THAT . . . *DEATH*.

Chapter One Hundred and Eight

At nine o'clock on Monday morning, Shafer joined the monotonous, stomach-turning line of workaday morons stuck in traffic headed in the direction of Embassy Row. He had the intoxicating thought that he would never be going to work again after today. Everything in his life was about to change. He couldn't go back.

His heart was pounding as he stopped and waited at the green light on Massachusetts Avenue near the embassy. Car horns beeped behind him, and he was reminded of his suicide run a year ago. Those were the days, damn it. Then he blasted through on the red. He ran. He had rehearsed his escape. This was for keeps.

He saw two blocks of clear roadway ahead and he floored the gas. The Jaguar leaped forward, raw phallic power, as it were. The sports car rocketed toward the puzzle of side streets around American University.

Ten minutes later he was turning into the White Flint Mall at fifty, gunning the Jag up to fifty-five, sixty, sixty-five as he sped across the mostly empty lot. He was sure no one had followed him.

He drove toward a large Borders Books & Music store, turned right, then zoomed up a narrow side lane between the buildings.

There were five exits out of the mall that he knew of. He accelerated again, tires squealing.

The surrounding neighborhood was a warren of narrow streets. Still no one was behind him, not a single car.

He knew of a little-used one-way entrance onto the Rockville Pike. He got on the road, heading out against the barrage of traffic streaming to work in the city. He hadn't spotted any cars speeding behind him inside the mall, or on the side streets, or on the Pike.

They probably had only one, or at most two cars on him in the morning.

That made the most sense to Shafer. Neither the Washington Metro police nor the Security Service would approve a large surveillance detail to follow him. He didn't think so anyway.

He'd probably lost them. He whooped loudly and started blaring the Jag's horn at all the pathetic suckers and fools stuck in the oncoming lanes, headed toward work. He'd been waiting nearly seven years for this.

It was finally here.

Endgame.

Chapter One Hundred and Nine

'We've still got him?' I asked Jones, nervously looking around at the half-dozen agents working in the crisis room inside the British Embassy. The room was filled with state-of-the-art electrical equipment including half-a-dozen video monitors.

'Still got him. He won't get away that easily, Alex. Besides, we think we know where he and the others are going now.'

We had a tiny, sophisticated homing device on the Jaguar, but there was a reasonable chance Shafer would discover it. So far, he hadn't. And now he was running in the Jag, running with the bait, at least that was what we thought was happening.

The Horsemen were all on the move. Oliver Highsmith had been followed from his home in Surrey to Gatwick Airport, outside London. Agents at the airport made sure that Conqueror got on the British Airways flight to New York, then called Washington to report he was en route.

A couple of hours later, an agent called from the Philippines. George Bayer was at Ninoy Aquino Airport in Manila. Famine had purchased a ticket to Jamaica, with a stopover in New York.

We already knew that James Whitehead had retired to Jamaica, and he was on the island at this time. War was waiting for the others to arrive.

'I'm trying to get a fixed pattern for the Four Horsemen game, but there are several points of view at work. That's what they like about the game, what makes it so addictive,' I said to Jones as we waited for more information to come in.

'We know that at least three of them have been playing the game since they were stationed in Thailand in ninety-one. Around that time, bar girls and prostitutes began to disappear in Bangkok. The local police didn't spend much time on the investigation. Girls in Pot Pol had disappeared before. The police have somewhat the same attitude here in Washington with respect to the Jane Doe killings. These girls didn't mean much. They were written off. Murders and disappearances in Southeast certainly aren't investigated like the ones in Georgetown or on Capitol Hill. It's one of Washington's dirty little secrets.'

Jones lit a new cigarette with the butt of his last one. He puffed, then said, 'It might just be Shafer who's involved in the actual murders, Alex. That, or the others are much more careful than he is.'

I shrugged my shoulders. I didn't think so, but I didn't have enough concrete evidence to argue my case effectively with Jones, who was no slouch as a detective.

'The end of the Four Horsemen is coming, right? Can they really end their little fantasy game?' Sampson asked.

'It sure looks like they're getting together,' I said. 'Four former British agents, four grown men who love to play diabolical games. In my opinion, four murderers.'

'Possibly.' Andrew Jones finally admitted that the unthinkable could be true. 'Alex, I'm afraid that you could be right.'

Chapter One Hundred and Ten

Jamaica must have been chosen because it was relatively private, and because James Whitehead owned a large beach house there. But perhaps there were other angles attached to the game of the Four Horsemen. I hoped that we would know soon enough.

Oliver Highsmith and George Bayer arrived on the island within minutes of each other. They met at baggage inside Donald Sangster Airport, then drove for about an hour to the posh Jamaica Inn in Ocho Rios.

We were on the move, too. Sampson and I had gotten there on an early-morning flight from DC. The weather was glorious. Blue skies, warm breezes. We heard strains of English and Jamaican Creole at the airport, reggae and ska. The rustle of banana trees, as the sea breeze rushed through them, was like a soft chorus.

The hotel in Ocho Rios was very private and old-fashioned, just forty-five rooms overlooking the sea. We arrived there simultaneously with four English teams. There were also two teams of detectives from Kingston.

The English High Commission office in Kingston had been alerted about our presence and our purpose here. Full cooperation had been promised. Everyone was committed to bringing down all four game-players, whatever the consequences, and I was very impressed with the English group, and also the local detectives.

We waited for Geoffrey Shafer. Sampson and I were strategically positioned to watch the narrow, shaded road that led to the hotel. We were on a lush hillside between the hotel and the sparkling blue Caribbean sea. Andrew Jones and another agent were in a second car hidden near the hotel's rear entrance. Six of his agents were posing as porters and maintenance workers at the hotel. Jamaican detectives were also on the grounds.

We'd had no news about Shafer. He had finally lost us. But we believed he would join the rest of the Horsemen. Jones complained that there weren't enough of us to stop Shafer if he was coming after the others. I agreed. If Shafer was playing kamikaze, there would be no adequate defense.

So we waited and waited. Continual updates came in over the car's short-wave radio. The messages didn't stop all afternoon. They were a kind of electronic heartbeat for our surveillance detail.

Oliver Highsmith is still in his room. Doesn't want to be disturbed apparently . . .

Bayer is in his room as well. Subject was spotted on the terrace about ten minutes ago, checking out the beach with binoculars . . .

Bayer has left his room. He's taking a dip in the deep blue sea. Subject is in a red-striped swimming costume. Difficult to miss. Makes the job easier. Not on the eyes, though . . .

A black Mercedes arriving at the front gate. Driver's tall and blond. Could be Geoffrey Shafer. You see him, Alex?

I reported in immediately. 'The blond man isn't Shafer. Repeat, it isn't Shafer. Too young, probably American. Young wife and two children tagging along. False alarm. It isn't Shafer.'

The radio reports continued.

Highsmith has just ordered up from room service. Two English breakfasts in the middle of the day. One of our people will bring it up to him . . .

Bayer is back from his swim. He's well-tanned. Little guy, but muscular. Tried to hit on some ladies. Struck out.

Finally, at around six o'clock, I made another report. 'James Whitehead just drove up in a green Range Rover! He's coming inside the hotel. War is here.'

Only one more game-player to go.

We waited. Death had yet to arrive.

Chapter One Hundred and Eleven

S hafer was in no particular hurry to flash the checkered flag. He took his
sweet time thinking through each possible scenario. He had spotted the
coast of Jamaica on the horizon, several hours before. He had originally flown
to Puerto Rico, then sailed from there in a chartered boat. He wanted to be
able to leave, either by air or sea.

Now he calmly waited for nightfall, drifting in his boat with the cooling
trade winds. It was the famous 'blue hour' on the sea, just past sunset, extraordinarily serene and beautiful. Also magical and slightly unreal. He had finished
five hundred more pushups on the deck of the boat, and he wasn't even winded.
He could see half-a-dozen large cruise ships anchored near Ocho Rios. All
around him were scores of smaller boats like his own.

He remembered reading somewhere that the island of Jamaica had once been
the personal property of Christopher Columbus. He remembered because he
admired a time when a man could take whatever he wanted, and often did. His
body was tight and hard, and he was bronze from three days of sun during his
trip. His hair was bleached even blonder than usual. He'd had the drugs under
control for almost a week now. It had been an act of will, and he'd risen to the
challenge. He wanted to win.

Shafer felt like a god. No, he *was* a god. He controlled every move in his
own life and the lives of several others. There were surprises left, he thought
as he slowly sprayed his body with cooling streams of water. There were
surprises for everybody who still chose to be in the game.

His game.

His plan.

His ending.

Because this wasn't just a game, it never had been. The other players had
to know it by now. They understood what they had done, and why there had to
be revenge. It was what the Four Horsemen had been all about from the beginning: *the endgame was revenge, and revenge was his . . . Or theirs? Who knew
for sure?*

His father had taught him and his brothers to sail, probably the only useful
thing he'd ever done for Shafer. He actually could find peace on the sea. It was
probably the real reason he'd come to Jamaica by boat.

At eight o'clock he swam to shore, passing several of the smaller sailboats and a few motorboats. He found the physical exertion a neat antidote for anxiety and nerves. He was a strong swimmer and diver, good at most sports.

The night air was peaceful and calm and fragrant. The sea was flat. Not a ripple disturbed the surface. Well, there would be plenty of ripples soon.

A car was waiting for him just off the coast road, a black Ford Mustang, glossy and shiny in the moonlight.

He smiled when he saw it. The game was progressing beautifully.

Famine was there to meet him.

No, Famine was there for another reason, wasn't he?

George Bayer was waiting on shore to kill him.

Chapter One Hundred and Twelve

George Bayer isn't in his room. He's not with Oliver Highsmith or James Whitehead either. Damn it to hell! He's loose.

The alarming message went out over the two-way radio. Sampson and I had been watching the south side of the hotel for close to eight hours, and we were sure George Bayer hadn't come our way.

We heard Andrew Jones's concerned voice on the radio. 'Remember that all of the Four Horsemen are agents like ourselves. They're capable and deadly. Let's find Bayer right away, and be extra alert for Geoffrey Shafer. Shafer is the most dangerous player. At least we *think* he is.'

Sampson and I hurried out of the rented sedan. We had our guns out, but they seemed inappropriate at the beautiful and serene resort. I remembered feeling the same way – nearly a year ago in Bermuda.

'Bayer didn't come this way,' Sampson said. I knew he was concerned that Jones's people had lost Famine. We wouldn't have, but we were seen as backup, not the primary team.

The two of us quickly walked up a nearby hill that gave us a perspective on the manicured lawns rolling down toward the hotel's private beach. It was getting dark, but the grounds near the hotel were relatively well-lit. A couple in bathing suits and robes slowly walked toward us. They were holding hands, oblivious to the danger. No George Bayer, though. And no Shafer.

'How do they end this thing?' Sampson asked. 'How do you think the game ends?'

'I don't think any of them know for sure. They probably have game plans, but anything can happen now. It all depends on Shafer, if he follows the rules. I think he's beyond that, and the other players know it.'

We hurried along, running close to the hotel buildings. We were getting nervous and concerned looks from hotel guests we passed on the narrow, winding sidewalk.

'They're all killers. Even Jones finally admits that. They killed as agents and then they didn't want to stop. They liked it. Now – maybe they plan to kill one another. Winner takes all.'

'And Geoffrey Shafer hates to lose,' said Sampson.

'Shafer doesn't ever lose. We've seen that already. *That's* his pattern, John. It's what we missed from the start.'

'He doesn't get away this time, sugar. No matter what, Shafer doesn't walk.'

I didn't answer.

Chapter One Hundred and Thirteen

Shafer wasn't even breathing hard as he made it to the white-sand shoreline. George Bayer stepped out of the black Ford Mustang and Shafer watched for a weapon to appear. He continued to walk forward, playing the game of games for the highest stakes of all – his life.

'You bloody *swam*?' Bayer asked, his voice jovial, yet taunting.

'Well, actually, it's a fantastic night for it,' Shafer said, and casually shook water off his body. He waited for Bayer to move on him. He observed the way he tensed and untensed his right hand. Watched the slight forward slant of his shoulders.

Shafer took off a waterproof backpack and pulled out fresh dry clothes and shoes. Now he had access to his weapons. 'Let me guess. Oliver suggested that you all gang up on me,' he said. 'Three against one.'

Bayer smiled slyly. 'Of course. That had to be considered as an option. We rejected it because it wasn't consistent with our characters in the game.'

Shafer shook his hair, let the water drip off. As he dressed, he turned halfway away from Bayer. He smiled to himself. God, he loved this – the game of life and death against another Horseman, a master player. He admired Bayer's calmness, and his ability to be so smooth.

'Oliver's playing is so bloody predictable. He was the same way as an agent and analyst. They sent you, George, because they thought I'd never suspect you'd try to take me out by yourself. You're the first play. It's so obvious, though. A terrible waste of a player.'

Bayer frowned slightly, but still didn't lose his cool, didn't let on what he felt. He obviously thought that was the safest attitude, but it was how Shafer knew his suspicion was true. Famine was here to kill him. He was sure of it. George Bayer's cool attitude had given him away.

'No, nothing like that,' Bayer said. 'We're going to play according to the rules tonight. The rules are important to us. It's to be a board game, a contest of strategy and wits. I'm just here to pick you up, according to plan. We'll meet face to face at the hotel.'

'And we'll abide by the throw of the dice?' Shafer asked.

'Yes, of course, Geoff.' Bayer held out his hand and showed him three twenty-sided dice.

Shafer couldn't hold back a sharp laugh. This was so good, so rich. 'So what did the dice say, George? How do I lose? How do I die? A knife? A pistol? A drug overdose makes a great deal of sense to me.'

Bayer couldn't help himself. He laughed. Shafer was such a cocky bastard, such a good killer, a wonderful psychopathic personality. 'Well, yes, it might have occurred to us, but we played it completely straight. As I said, they're waiting at the hotel for us. Let's go.'

Shafer turned his back on Bayer for an instant. Then he pushed hard off his right foot. He sprang at Bayer.

Bayer was more than ready for him. He threw a short, hard punch. It struck Shafer's cheek, rattled, maybe even loosened a few teeth. The right side of his head went completely numb.

'Good one, George. Good stuff!'

Then Shafer head-butted Bayer with all of his strength. He heard the crunch of bone against bone, saw an explosion of dizzying white before his eyes. That got his adrenaline flowing.

The dice went flying from Bayer's hand as he reached for a gun, or some other weapon. It was in the back of his waistband.

Shafer clutched Bayer's right arm, twisted with all of his strength, and broke it at the elbow. Bayer shrieked in pain.

'You can't beat me! Nobody has, nobody can!' Shafer screamed at the top of his voice.

He grabbed George Bayer's throat and squeezed with superhuman strength. Bayer gagged, and turned the brightest red, as if all the blood in his body had rushed to his head. George was stronger than he appeared to be, but Shafer was speeding on adrenaline and years of pure hatred. He outweighed Bayer by twenty pounds, all of it muscle.

'*Noooo*. Listen to me.' George Bayer wheezed and gasped. 'Not like this. Not here.'

'*Yes*, George. *Yes, yes.* The game is on. The game that you bastards started. Tally-ho, old chap. *You* did this to me. You made me what I am. Death.'

He heard a loud, crisp snap and George Bayer went limp against him. He let the body fall to the sand.

'One down,' said Shafer, and finally allowed himself a deep, satisfying breath. He snatched up the fallen dice, shook them once, then hurled them into the sea. 'I don't use the dice anymore,' he said.

Chapter One Hundred and Fourteen

He felt so damn good. So fine. God, how he had missed this. The mainline of adrenaline, the incomparable thrill. He knew it was likely that the Jamaica Inn was being watched by the police, so he parked the Mustang at the nearby Plantation Inn.

He walked at a quickening pace through the crowded Bougainvillea Terrace. Drinks were being served while the wretched song 'Yellowbird' played loudly. He had a nasty fantasy about shooting up the terrace, killing several dickhead tourists, so he got away from the crowded area immediately, for everybody's sake, but mostly his own.

He strolled the beach and it calmed him. It was quiet, restful, with strains of calypso music gently weaving through the night air. The stretch between the two hotels was eye-catching, plenty of spotlights, sand the color of champagne, thatched umbrellas at even intervals. A very nice playing field.

He knew where Oliver Highsmith was staying, the famous White Suite, where Winston Churchill and David Niven and Ian Fleming had all slept once upon a time. Highsmith loved his creature comforts almost as much as he loved the game itself. Shafer despised the other Horsemen, partly because he wasn't in their social class. Lucy's father had got him into MI6; the other players had been from the right backgrounds. Shafer's didn't quite match up. But there was another, more powerful reason for his hatred: They had dared to use him, to feel superior and throw it in his face.

He entered through a white picket-fence gate at the property line of the Jamaica Inn. He broke into a soft jog. He wanted to run, to sweat. He was feeling manic again. Playing the game had made him too excited.

Shafer held his head for a moment. He wanted to laugh and scream at the top of his lungs. He leaned against a wooden post leading up from the beach, and tried to catch his breath. He realized he was crashing and it couldn't have happened at a worse time.

'Everything all right, sir?' a hotel waiter stopped and asked him.

'Oh, couldn't be better,' Shafer said, waving the man away. 'I'm in heaven, can't you tell?'

He started walking toward the White Suite again. He realized that he was feeling the way he had the morning he'd nearly crashed his car in Washington. He was in serious trouble again. He could lose the game right now, lose everything. That required a change of strategy, didn't it? He had to be more daring, even more aggressive. He had to act, not think too much. The odds against him were still two to one.

At the far end of the courtyard, he spotted a man and a woman in evening clothes. They were loitering near a white stucco portico strewn with flowers. He decided they were Jones's people. They had staked out the hotel, after all. They were here for him and he was honored.

The male glanced his way, and Shafer abruptly lowered his head. There was nothing they could do to stop or detain him. He'd committed no crime they could prove. He wasn't wanted by the police. No, he was a free man.

So Shafer walked toward them at a leisurely pace, as if he hadn't seen them. He whistled 'Yellowbird.'

He looked up when he was a few yards away from the pair. 'I'm the one you're waiting for. I'm Geoffrey Shafer. Welcome to the game.'

He pulled a Smith & Wesson 9mm semiautomatic and fired twice.

The woman cried out and grabbed the left side of her chest. Bright-red blood was already staining her sea-green dress. Her eyes showed confusion, shock and then rolled back into her forehead.

The male agent had a dark hole where his left eye had been. Shafer knew the man was dead before his head struck the courtyard floor with a loud, satisfying smack.

He hadn't lost anything over the years. Shafer hurried toward the White Suite and Conqueror.

The gunshots certainly would have been heard. They wouldn't expect him to run straight into the trap they'd set. But here he was.

Two maids were pushing a squeaking cleanup cart out of the White Suite. Had they just turned down Conqueror's bed? Left the fat man a box of chocolate mints to nibble?

'Get the hell out of here!' he yelled, and raised his gun. 'Go on now! Run for your lives.' The Jamaican maids took off as if they had just seen the devil himself. They would tell their children that they had.

Shafer burst in the front door of the suite, and there was Oliver Highsmith freewheeling his chair across the freshly scrubbed floor.

'Oliver, it's you,' Shafer said. 'I do believe I've caught the dreaded Covent Garden killer. You did those killings, didn't you? Fancy that. Game's over, Oliver.'

At the same time, Shafer thought, *Watch him closely. Be careful with Conqueror.*

Oliver Highsmith stopped moving, then slowly, rather nimbly, turned his wheelchair to face Shafer. A face-to-face meeting. This was good. The best. Highsmith had controlled Bayer and Whitehead from London, when they were all agents. The original game, the Four Horsemen, had been his idea, a diversion as he eased into retirement. 'Our silly little fantasy game,' he always called it.

He studied Shafer, cold-eyed and measuring. He was bright; an egghead, but a genius, or so Bayer and Whitehead claimed.

'My dear fellow, we're your friends. The only ones you have now. We understand your problem. Let's talk things through, Geoffrey.'

Shafer laughed at the fat man's pathetic lies, his superior and condescending attitude, his nerve. 'That's not what George Bayer told me. Why, he said you were going to murder me. Hell of a way to treat a friend.'

Highsmith didn't blink, didn't falter. 'We're not alone here, Geoff. They're at the hotel. The Security Service team is in the grounds. They must have followed you.'

'And *you*, and *Bayer*, and *Whitehead*! I know all that, Oliver. I met a couple of crackerjack agents outside. Shot 'em dead. That's why I have to hurry up, can't tarry. The game's on a clock now. Lots of ways to lose.'

'We have to talk, Geoff.'

'Talk, talk, talk.' Shafer shook his head, frowned, then barked out a laugh. 'No, there's nothing for us to talk about. Talk is such an overrated bore. I learned to kill in the field, and I like it much more than talking. No, I actually love it to death.'

'You *are* mad,' Highsmith exclaimed, his grayish-blue eyes widening with fear. Finally he understood who Shafer was; he wasn't intellectualizing anymore. He felt it in his gut.

'No actually, I'm not insane. I know precisely what I'm doing, always have, always will. I know the difference between good and evil. Anyway, look who's talking, the Rider on the White Horse.'

Shafer moved quickly toward Highsmith. 'This isn't much of a fight – just the way I was taught to perform in Asia. You're going to die, Oliver. Isn't that a stunning thought? Still think this is a bloody fantasy game?'

Suddenly Highsmith jumped to his feet. Shafer wasn't surprised. He knew he couldn't have committed the murders in London from a wheelchair. Highsmith was close to six feet and obese, but surprisingly quick for his size. His arms and hands were massive.

Shafer was simply faster. He struck Highsmith with the butt of his gun and Conqueror went crashing down on one knee. Shafer bludgeoned him a second time, then a third, and Highsmith dropped flat on the floor. He groaned loudly, and slobbered blood and spit. Shafer kicked the small of his back, kicked a knee, kicked Highsmith's face.

Shafer bent and put the gun barrel against Highsmith's broad forehead. He could hear the distant sound of running footsteps slapping down the hall. Too bad, they were coming for him. *Hurry, hurry.*

'They're too late,' he said to Conqueror. 'No one can save you. Except me, Conqueror. What's the play? Counsel me. Should I save the whale?'

'Please, Geoff, no. You can't just kill me. We can still help each other.'

'I'd love to stretch this out, but I really have to dash. I'm throwing the dice. In *my mind.* Oh, bad news, Oliver. The game is up. You just lost.'

He inserted the barrel of his gun into Highsmith's pulpy right ear and fired. The gunshot blew Conqueror's gray matter all over the room, and Shafer's only regret was that he couldn't have tortured Oliver Highsmith much, much longer than he had.

Then Shafer was running away, and he realized something that actually surprised him. He had something to live for. This was a wonderful, wonderful game.

He wanted to live.

Chapter One Hundred and Fifteen

S ampson and I sprinted toward the secluded wing of the hotel where Oliver Highsmith had his suite. There had been gunshots, but we couldn't be everywhere at once. We'd heard the pistol reports all the way on the other side of the Jamaica Inn.

I wasn't prepared for the bloody massacre scene we found. Two English agents were down in the courtyard. I'd worked with them both, just as I'd worked side by side with Patsy Hampton.

Jones and another agent, in addition to a team of local detectives, were already crowded into Highsmith's suite. The room was abuzz. Everything had turned to chaos and carnage in a burst of homicidal madness.

'Shafer went through two of my people to get here,' Jones said in an angry voice strained with tension and sadness. He was already smoking a cigarette. 'He came in shooting, took down Laura and Gwynn. Highsmith is dead, too. We haven't found George Bayer.'

I knelt and quickly checked the damage to Oliver Highsmith's skull. It wasn't subtle. He'd been shot at point-blank range and the wound was massive. I knew from Jones that Shafer had resented the senior man's intelligence, and now he'd blown out his brains. 'I told you he liked to kill. He has to do this, Andrew. He can't stop.'

'Whitehead!' I said. 'The end of the game.'

Chapter One Hundred and Sixteen

We drove faster than the narrow, twisting road safely allowed, barreling toward James Whitehead's home. It wasn't far. We passed a road sign that read: MALLARD'S BEACH – SAN ANTONIO.

Sampson and I were quiet, lost in our own thoughts. I kept thinking of Christine, couldn't stop the images from coming. *We have her*. Was that still true?

I didn't know, and only Shafer, or possibly Whitehead, could give me the answer. I wanted to keep both of them alive if I could. Everything about the island, the exotic smells and sights, reminded me of Christine. I tried, but I couldn't imagine a good conclusion to any of this.

We headed toward the beach and soon we were skimming past private houses and a few very large estates. Some of the estates had long, winding driveways that stretched a hundred yards or more to the main house.

In the distance I could see the glow of passing house lights, and I figured that we had to be close to James Whitehead's. Was he still alive? Or had Shafer already come and gone?

Jones's voice came in spits on the radio. 'This is his place, Alex. Glass-and-stone house up ahead. I don't see anybody.'

We pulled in near the crushed-seashell driveway to the house. It was dark, pitch black and satiny. There were no lights anywhere on the property.

We jumped out of our cars. There were eight of us, including one team of detectives from Kingston. The detectives were Kenyon and Anthony, and both were acting nervous.

I didn't blame them. I felt exactly the same. The Weasel was on a rampage and we already knew that he was suicidal. Geoffrey Shafer was a homicidal-suicidal maniac.

Sampson and I ran through a small garden that led to a pool and cabana area on one side, an expanse of lawn and the sea on the other.

We could see Jones's people beginning to fan out in the grounds. *Shafer had come into the hotel with guns blazing. He didn't seem to care whether he survived. But I did. I needed to question him. I had to know what he knew. I needed all the answers.*

'What about this prick Whitehead?' Sampson asked as we hurried toward the house.

It was dark near the water, a good place from which Shafer could attack. Dark shadows stretched out from every tree and bush.

'I don't know, John. He was at the hotel briefly. He's a player, so he's after Shafer, too. This is it. Endgame. One of them wins the game now.'

'He's here,' I whispered. 'I know it.'

I could definitely sense Geoffrey Shafer's presence. I was sure about it, and the fact that I *knew* scared me almost as much as he did.

Shots came from the darkened house.

My heart sank and I had the most disturbing and contradictory thought: *Don't let Geoffrey Shafer be dead.*

Chapter One Hundred and Seventeen

One more target, one last opponent, and then it was over. Seven glorious years of play, seven years of revenge, seven years of hatred. He couldn't bear to lose the game. He'd shown Bayer and Highsmith a thing or two; now he'd demonstrate to James Whitehead who was truly 'superior.'

Shafer had noisily crashed through thick foliage, then waded waist deep into a foul-smelling swamp. The water was distressingly tepid and the oily green scum on the surface was an inch or two thick.

He tried not to think about the swamp, or the insects and snakes that might infest it. He'd waded into far worse waters during his days and nights in Asia. He kept his eyes set on James Whitehead's expensive beach house. One more to go, just one more Horseman.

He'd been to the villa before, knew it well. Beyond the swamp was another patch of thick foliage, and then a chain-link fence and Whitehead's manicured yard. He figured that Whitehead wouldn't expect him to come through the swamp. War was cleverer than the others though. He'd been committing murders in the Caribbean for years, and not even a blip had shown up to suggest a pattern to the police. War had also helped him in the matter of Christine Johnson, and that had gone perfectly. It was a mystery, inside a mystery, all inside a complex game.

Shafer lost track of everything real for a moment or two – where he was, who he was, what he had to do.

Now *that* was scary – a little mental breakdown at the worst possible time. Ironically, it had been Whitehead who had made him dependent on uppers and downers in Asia.

Shafer began to slosh across the fetid swamp, hoping the water wouldn't be over his head. It wasn't. He waded out and climbed over the chain-link fence on the far side. He started across the back lawn.

He had the most powerful obsession about destroying James Whitehead. He wanted to torture Whitehead – but where would he find the time? Whitehead had been his first handler in Thailand and then in the Philippines. More than anyone, Whitehead had made Shafer into a killer. Whitehead was the one he held responsible.

The house was still dark, but Shafer believed War was in there.

Suddenly a gun fired from the house. *War*, indeed.

Shafer began to zig and zag like an infantryman thoroughly trained in combat. His heart was thundering. Reality came in odd stop-and-go movements. He wondered if Whitehead had a nightscope on his gun. And how good a shot he was.

Whether he'd ever been in combat.

Was he frightened? Or was he excited by the action?

He guessed the doors to the house were locked and that War would be crouched low, hiding inside, waiting to take a shot without too much exposure. He had never done his own dirty work though. None of them had; not Whitehead, not Bayer, not Highsmith. They had used Death, and now he'd come for them. If they hadn't agreed to meet in Jamaica he would have come after them one at a time.

Shafer broke into a full sprint toward the house. Gunshots exploded from inside. Bullets whizzed past. He hadn't been hit. Because he was so good? Or because War wasn't?

Shafer suddenly threw both arms up in front of his face. This was it. He dived through the large picture window in the loggia.

Glass exploded everywhere as the window blew into a thousand small pieces. He was inside!

War was here, close. Where was his enemy? How good was James Whitehead? His mind was filled with important questions. A dog was barking somewhere in the house.

Shafer tumbled across the tile floor, hit the leg of a heavy table, but came up firing anyway. *Nothing.* No one was in the room.

Suddenly he heard voices outside – at the front. The police were here! Always trying to spoil his fun.

Then he saw War trying to run. Tall, gangly, longish black hair. War had blinked first. He was heading toward the front door, looking for help from the police, of all people.

'You can't make it, Whitehead. Stop! I won't let you get out! Stay in the game.'

Whitehead apparently realized he couldn't get out the front door. He turned toward a stairway and Shafer followed, only a few steps behind. War turned sharply, and fired again.

Shafer flicked his hand at a wall switch and the hall lights flashed on.

'Death has come for you! It's your time. Look at me! Look at Death!' he screamed.

Whitehead kept moving and Shafer calmly shot him in the buttocks. The wound was large, gaping, and Whitehead screamed like a stuck pig. He whirled and fell halfway down the stairs. His face slammed against the metal railing as he fell.

He finally lay writhing at the foot of the stairs, where Shafer shot him again. This time between the legs, and War screamed again, loudly. He moaned, then began to sob.

Shafer stood over Whitehead, triumphant, his heart bursting. 'You think sanctions are a game? Is this still a game to you?' he asked in the softest voice. 'I believe it's great fun, but do you?'

Whitehead was sobbing loudly as he tried to speak. 'No, Geoffrey. It's not a game. Please, stop. That's enough.'

Shafer began to smile. He showed his enormous teeth. 'Oh, you're so wrong. It's lovely! It is the most amazing mind game you could imagine. You should feel what I feel right now, the power over life and death.'

He had a thought – and it changed everything, changed the game for him and for Whitehead. This switch was so much better than what he'd originally planned.

'I've decided to let you live, not very well, but you'll live.'

He fired the semiautomatic again, this time into the base of Whitehead's spine.

'You will never forget me, and the game will continue for the rest of your life. Play well. I know that I shall.'

Chapter One Hundred and Eighteen

The moment we heard the gunshots we ran toward the main house. I raced ahead of the others. I had to get to Shafer before they did. I had to take him myself. I had to talk to him, to know the truth once and for all.

I saw Shafer slip out a side door of the house. Whitehead must be dead. Shafer had won the game.

He was running toward the sea, moving fast and purposefully. He disappeared behind a small sand dune shaped like a turtle. Where was he going? What was next for him?

Then I saw him again. He was kicking off his shoes and getting out of his trousers. What was he doing?

I heard Sampson come running up behind me. 'Don't kill him, John! Not unless we have to,' I yelled.

'I know! I know!' he called.

I plunged ahead.

Shafer turned and fired off a shot at me. The distance was too much for anyone to be accurate with a hand-gun. Still, he was a good shot and came close. He knew how to use a gun – and not just from a few feet away.

Sampson was kicking off his sneakers, pulling away his pants. I did the same with my sweats and T-shirt.

I pointed out to sea. 'He must have a boat out there. One of those.'

We saw Shafer striding into the low waves of the Caribbean, heading into a cone of light made by the moon.

He did a shallow dive and started to swim in a smooth-looking crawl stroke.

We were down to our underwear. Nothing very pretty. We both made shallow dives into the sea.

Shafer was a very strong swimmer and he was already pulling ahead of us. He swam with his face in the water, lifting it out sideways after several strokes to catch a breath.

His blond hair was slicked back and stood out in the moonlight. One of the boats bobbing out there had to be his. Which one?

I kept a single thought in my head, stretch and kick, stretch and kick. I felt as if I were gathering strength from somewhere inside. I had to catch Shafer – I had to know the truth about what he'd done to Christine.

Stretch and kick, stretch and kick.

Sampson was laboring behind me, and then he started to fall even farther back.

'Go,' I called to him. 'Go back for help. I'll be all right. Get somebody out there to check those boats.'

'He swims like a fish,' Sampson called.

'Go. I'll be fine. Hold my own.'

Up ahead I could still see Shafer's head and the tops of his shoulders glistening in the creamy white moonlight. He was stroking evenly, powerfully.

I kept going, never looking back to shore, not wanting to know how far I had come already. I refused to be tired, to give up, to lose.

I swam harder, trying to gain some sea on Shafer. The boats were still a good way away. He was still going strong, though. No sign of tiring.

I played a mind game of my own. I stopped looking to see where he was. I concentrated only on my stroke. There was nothing but the stroke; the stroke was the whole universe.

My body was feeling more in sync with the water and I was buoyed as it got deeper. My stroke was getting stronger and smoother.

I finally looked. He was starting to struggle. Or maybe it was just what I wanted to see. Anyway it gave me a second wind, added strength.

What if I actually caught him out here? Then what? We fought to the death?

I couldn't let him get to his boat before me. He'd have guns on board. I needed to beat him there. I had to win this time. Which boat was his?

I swam harder. I told myself that I was in good shape, too. I was. I'd been to the gym every day for almost a year – ever since Christine had disappeared.

I looked up again and I was shocked at what I saw.

Shafer was there! Only a few yards away. A few more strokes. Had he lost it? Or was he waiting for me, gathering strength?

The closest boat was no more than a hundred, a hundred fifty yards away.

'*Cramp!*' he called out. 'Bad one!' Then he went under.

Chapter One Hundred and Nineteen

I didn't know what to think, or exactly what to do next. The pain on Shafer's face looked real; he looked afraid. But he was also an actor.

I felt something underneath me! He grabbed hard between my legs. I yelled and managed to twist away, though he'd hurt me.

Then we were grabbing at each other, struggling like underwater wrestlers. Suddenly, he pulled me under with him. He was strong. His long arms were powerful vices, and he held me tightly.

We went down and I started to feel the coldest, most serious fear of my life. I didn't want to drown. Shafer was winning. He always found a way.

Shafer stared into my eyes. His blue eyes incredibly intense and manic and crazed. His mouth was closed, but it was twisted and evil-looking. He had me; he would win again.

I pushed forward with all of my strength. When I felt him straining against me, I reversed directions. I kicked out with my leg and caught Shafer under the jaw, maybe in the throat. I hit him as hard as I could and he began to sink.

His long blond hair floated up around his face. His arms and legs went limp.

He went down and I followed him. It was dark this far under the surface. I grabbed one of his arms.

I barely caught him. His weight was pulling me with him toward the bottom.

I couldn't let him go. I had to know the truth about Christine. I couldn't go on with my life unless I did.

I had no idea about the water's depth. Shafer's eyes had been wide open and so had his mouth. His lungs must be filling with water.

I wondered if I'd broken his neck with the kick. Was he dead, or just unconscious? There was some satisfaction in the idea that I'd broken the Weasel's neck.

Then it really didn't matter. Nothing did. I had no more breath. My chest felt as if it would collapse. There was a fire spreading wildly inside me. Then a severe ringing started in both ears. I was dizzy and I was starting to lose consciousness.

I let Shafer go, let him sink to the bottom. I didn't have a choice. I couldn't think about him anymore. I had to get to the surface. I couldn't hold my breath any longer.

I swam frantically up, pulled at the water, kicked with all of my might. I didn't think I could make it; it was too far to the surface.

I had no more breath.

I saw Sampson – his face was looming above. Close, very close. It gave me strength.

His head was framed against a few stars and the blue-black of the sky. 'Sugar,' he whispered.

He held me up for a while, let me get my breath, my precious breath. My head continued to swim. We both trod water.

I let my eyes explore the surface for some sign of Shafer. My vision was blurred, but I didn't see him. I was certain he'd drowned.

Then Sampson and I slowly paddled back to shore.

I hadn't gotten what I needed out there. I hadn't been able to learn the truth from Shafer before he drowned.

Once or twice I glanced behind to make sure that Shafer wasn't following us, that he was gone. There was no sign of him. There was only the sound of our own, exhausted strokes cutting into the tide.

Chapter One Hundred and Twenty

It took two more exhausting days and nights to finish with the local police investigation, but it was good to keep focused and busy. I no longer had any hope of finding Christine, or discovering what had happened to her.

I knew it was remotely possible that Shafer hadn't taken Christine; that it was some other madman from my past, but I didn't give that possibility more than a passing thought. I couldn't go there. It was too crazy an idea, even for me.

I'd been unable to grieve from the start, but now the monstrous finality of Christine's fate struck me with all of its brutal force. I felt as if my insides had been hollowed out. The constant, dull ache I had known for so long had become a sharp stab of pain that pierced my heart every waking moment. I couldn't stop, yet I felt as if I were never fully awake.

Sampson knew what was happening to me. There was nothing he could say, but he made comforting small talk.

Nana called me at the hotel, and I knew it was Sampson's doing, though both of them denied it. Jannie and Damon got on the phone, and they were both sweet and kind and full of life and hopefulness. They even put Rosie the cat on for a friendly long distance meow. They didn't mention Christine, but I knew she was always in their thoughts.

On our final night on the island, Sampson and I had dinner with Jones. We had become friendly, and he finally told me some facts he had withheld for security reasons. He wanted me to have some closure; he felt I deserved that.

Back in 1989, after Shafer arrived in MI6, he was recruited by James Whitehead. He had reported in to Oliver Highsmith, and George Bayer had worked for him. Shafer had performed at least four sanctions in Asia during the next three years. It was suspected, but never proved, that he, Whitehead, and Bayer had murdered prostitutes in Manila and Bangkok. These murders were obviously the precursors to the Jane Does, and the game. All in all, it had been one of the worst scandals in the history of the Secret Service. And it had effectively been covered up. That was how Jones wanted to keep it, and I had no worthwhile objection. There were already more than enough unfortunate stories to keep people cynical about their governments.

Our dinner broke up at around eleven and Jones and I promised to keep in touch. There was one bit of disturbing news, though no one wanted to overstate the significance of it: Geoffrey Shafer's body still hadn't been found. Somehow that seemed a fitting end.

Sampson and I were due to catch the first flight to Washington on Tuesday morning. It was scheduled to leave at ten past nine.

That morning, the skies were swirling with black clouds. Heavy rain teemed on our cab's roof all the way from the hotel to the Donald Sangster Airport. Schoolkids ran along the side of the road, shielding themselves from the rain with flopping banana-tree leaves.

The downpour caught us good as we tried to dash out from under the cover of the tin overhang outside the rent-a-car depot.

The rain was cool, though, and it felt good on my face and head and on the shirt plastered to my back.

'It'll be real good to be home,' Sampson said as we finally made it under the cover of a metal roof painted a bright yellow.

'I'm ready to go,' I agreed. 'I miss Damon and Jannie, Nana. I miss being home.'

'They'll find the body,' Sampson said. 'Shafer's.'

'I knew who you meant.'

The rain hammered the airport's roof without mercy, and I was thinking how much I hated to fly on days like this, but it would be good to be home, to be able to end this nightmare. It had invaded my soul, taken over my life. In a way, I suppose it was as much a game as any that Shafer had played. The murder case had obsessed me for over a year, and that was enough.

Christine had asked me to give it up, Nana had asked, too, and I hadn't listened. Maybe I hadn't been able to see my life and actions as clearly as I did now. I was the Dragonslayer, and all that it meant, the good and the bad. In the end, I held myself responsible for Christine's kidnapping and murder.

Sampson and I tramped past the colorful concession stands without any real interest, barely a passing nod. Street hawkers, called higglers, were selling wooden jewelry and other carvings, but also Jamaican coffee and cocoa.

Each of us carried a black duffel bag. We didn't exactly look like vacationers, I was thinking. We still looked like policemen.

I heard a voice calling loudly from behind, and I turned back to look at the commotion coming up from the rear.

It was the Jamaican detective, John Anthony, calling out my name in the noisy terminal, coming our way in a big hurry. He was walking rapidly, a few steps ahead of Andrew Jones, who looked powerfully dismayed.

Jones and Anthony at the airport? What in God's name was happening now? What could possibly have gone wrong?

'The *Weasel*?' I said, and it came out like a curse.

Sampson and I stopped, and they finally caught up with us. I almost didn't want to hear what they had to tell us.

'You have to go back with us, Alex. Come with me,' Jones said, slightly out of breath. 'It's about Christine Johnson. Something's turned up. Come.'

'What is it? What's happened?' I asked Jones, then Detective Anthony, when the Englishman was slow in answering.

Anthony hesitated, but then he said, 'We don't know for sure. It could be nothing at all. Someone claims to have seen her, though. She may be here in Jamaica, after all. Come with us.'

I couldn't believe what he had just told me. I felt Sampson's arm wrap tightly around me, but everything else seemed unreal, as in a dream.

It wasn't over yet.

Chapter One Hundred and Twenty-One

O n the road out of the airport, Andrew Jones and Detective Anthony filled us in on what they knew. I could tell that they were trying not to build up my hopes too much. I'd been in the same untenable situation many times, but not as a victim of a crime.

'Last night we caught a small-time local thief breaking into a house in Ocho Rios,' Anthony said as he drove, the four of us packed tightly in his Toyota. 'He said he had information to trade. We told him we would hear what he had to say, and then we would decide. He then revealed that an American woman had been kept in the hills east of Ocho Rios, near the town of Euarton. There's an outlaw group lives up there sometimes.

'I learned about it only this morning. I called Andrew and we hurried to the airport. The man says she was called Beatitude. No other name was used. I contacted your hotel, but you had already left for the airport. So we came out here to get you.'

'Thank you,' I finally said, realizing I had probably been told as much as they knew.

Sampson spoke up. 'So why does this helpful thief appear now, after all this time?'

'He said there was a shooting a few nights ago that changed everything. Once the white men died, the woman wasn't important anymore. Those were his words.'

'You know these men?' I asked Detective Anthony.

'Men, women, children. Yes, I've dealt with them before. They smoke a lot of ganja. Practice their hybrid religion, worship the Emperor Haile Selassie, y'know. A few of them are small-time thieves. Mostly, we let them be.'

Everyone in the car grew quiet as we hurried along the coast road toward Runaway Bay and Ocho Rios. The storm had passed quickly, and suddenly the island's hellified sun was blazing again. Sugarcane workers with machetes on their hips were tramping back into the fields.

Past the village of Runaway Bay, Detective Anthony turned off the main road and headed up into the hills on Route A1. The trees and bushes here were a thick jungle. The road eventually became a tunnel boring through vines and branches. Anthony had to turn on the headlights.

I felt as if I were drifting through a mist, watching everything as if in a dream. I understood that I was trying to protect myself, but also that it wasn't working.

Who was Beatitude? I couldn't make myself believe that Christine was alive, but at least there was a chance, and I clung to that. I had given up weeks before. Now I allowed myself to remember how much I loved her, how I missed her. Suddenly, I choked hard, and I turned my face toward the window. I went deep inside myself.

Bright light shone in my eyes. The car exited the brush after two or three miles that had seemed much longer on the twisting road. We were entering lush hills that looked something like the American South back in the fifties and sixties – maybe like Georgia or Alabama. Children in dated clothes played in front of small run-down houses. Their elders sat on uneven, slanted porches and watched the occasional car drive past.

Everything looked and felt so incredibly unreal to me. I couldn't focus.

We turned onto a skinny dirt road with a thick, high corridor of grass running between deep tire ruts. This had to be the place. My heart was pumping loudly, and it sounded like a tin drum being pounded in a tunnel. I felt every bump in the road like a hard punch.

Beatitude? Who was the woman they were holding? Could it possibly be Christine?

Sampson checked the load in his Glock. I heard the mechanism slide and *click*, and I glanced his way.

'They won't be happy to see us, but you won't need the gun,' Anthony said, turning to us. 'They probably know we're coming. They watch the local roads. Christine Johnson might not be here now, if she was even here at all. I knew you would want to check for yourself.'

I didn't say anything. I couldn't. My mouth felt incredibly dry and my mind was a blank. We were still involved with the Four Horsemen, weren't we? Was this Shafer's play? Had he known we'd eventually find this place in the hills? Had he set a final trap for us?

We arrived at an old green house with tattered white cloth over the windows and a burlap bag for a front door. Four men immediately came outside, all of them sporting dreadlocks.

They walked toward us, their mouths set hard, their eyes blazing with distrust. Sampson and I were used to the look from the streets of Washington.

Two of the men carried heavy field machetes. The other two wore floppy shirts, and I knew they were armed beneath the loose-fitting clothes.

'Just turn around, go back, mon,' one of them shouted loudly at us. 'Get out of here while you can.'

Chapter One Hundred and Twenty-Two

'No!' Detective Anthony got out of the car with both hands held high. So did Sampson, Jones and I.

There was the beat of traditional drums coming from the woods directly behind the main house. A pair of lounging dogs raised their lazy heads to look at us, and barked a few times. My heart was thundering faster now.

I didn't like the way this was going.

Another one of the men called to us, 'I and I would like you to leave.'

I recognized the phrase of speech. The double pronoun represented the speaker and God, who live together in each person.

'Patrick Moss is in jail. I'm Detective Anthony from Kingston. This is Detective Sampson and Detective Cross. You have a woman here. You call her Beatitude.'

Beatitude? Could it be Christine?

One of the men with a machete hanging from one hand glared and spoke to Anthony. 'Galang 'bout yuh business. Lef me nuh. Nah woman here. Nah woman.'

'This *is* my business and we won't leave you alone,' I said, surprising the man that I understood his dialect. But I know Rastaman from DC.

'Nah woman here. Nah American,' the man repeated angrily, looking directly at me.

Andrew Jones spoke up. 'We want the American woman, then we'll leave. Your friend Patrick Moss will be home by tonight. You can deal with him in your own way.'

'Nah American woman here.' The original speaker spat defiantly on the ground. 'Turn around, go back.'

'You know James Whitehead? You know Shafer?' Jones said.

They didn't deny it. I doubted we'd get anymore from them than that.

'I love her,' I told them. 'I can't leave. Her name is Christine.'

My mouth was still dry and I couldn't breathe very well. 'She was kidnapped a year ago. We know she was brought here.'

Sampson took out his Glock and held it loosely at his side. He stared at the four men, who continued to glare back at us. I touched the handle of my gun, still in its holster. I didn't want a gunfight.

'We can cause you a whole lot of trouble,' Sampson said, in a low, rumbling voice. 'You won't believe how much trouble is coming your way.'

Finally, I just walked forward on a worn path through the tall grass. I passed by the men, lightly brushing against one of them.

No one tried to stop me. I could smell ganja and sweat on their work clothes. Tension was building up inside me.

Sampson followed me, no more than a step or two behind. 'I'm watching them,' he said. 'Nobody's doing anything yet.'

'Doesn't matter,' I said. 'I have to see if she's here.'

Chapter One Hundred and Twenty-Three

An older woman with long and wildly frazzled gray-and-white hair stepped out of the front door as I reached the scarred, unpainted steps. Her eyes were ringed with redness.

'Come with me,' she sighed. 'Come along. You nah need no weapon.'

For the first time in many months I allowed myself to feel the tiniest flash of hope. I didn't have any reason to, just the rumor that a woman had been kept here against her will.

Beatitude? Something to do with blessedness and happiness? Could it be Christine?

The old woman walked unsteadily around the house and through light bushes, trees, and ferns out back. About sixty or seventy yards into thickening woods she came to half-a-dozen small shacks, and she stopped. The shacks were made of wood, bamboo, and corrugated metal.

She walked forward again and stopped at the next-to-last shack in the group.

She took out a key attached to a leather strap around her waist. She then inserted the key and jiggled it.

She pushed the door forward and it creaked loudly on a rusty hinge.

I looked inside and saw a plain, neat, and clean room. Someone had written *The Lord Is My Shepherd* in black paint on the wall.

No one was there.

No Beatitude.

No Christine.

I let my eyes fall shut. Desperation enveloped me.

My eyes slowly opened. I didn't understand why I had been led to this empty room, this old shack in the woods. My heart was ripped in two again. Was it some kind of trap?

The Weasel? Shafer? Was he here?

Someone stepped out from behind a small folding screen in one corner of the room. I felt as if I were in free fall, and a small gasp came out of my mouth.

I didn't know what I had been expecting, but not this. Sampson put out his hand to steady me. I was barely aware of his touch.

Christine gently stepped into the shafts of sunlight coming from the single window in the shack. I had never expected to see her again.

She was much thinner and her hair was braided and longer than I'd ever seen it. But she had the same wise, beautiful brown eyes. Neither of us was able to speak at first. It was the strangest moment of my life.

I had gone cold all over and everything was moving in slow motion. It seemed supernaturally quiet in the small room.

Christine was holding a light yellow blanket, and I could see a baby's head just peeking above the crown of the covers. I walked forward even though my legs were trembling and threatening to buckle. I could hear the baby softly cooing in the nest of blankets.

'Oh, Christine, Christine,' I finally managed.

Tears welled in her eyes, and then in mine. We both stepped forward, and then I was awkwardly holding her. The little baby peacefully gazed up into both our faces.

'This is our baby, and he probably saved my life. He takes after you,' Christine said. Then we kissed gently, and it was so sweet and tender. We held on for dear, dear life. We melted into each other. Neither of us could believe this was actually happening.

'I call him Alex. You were always right here,' Christine told me. 'You were always with me.'

London Bridges, Falling

Chapter One Hundred and Twenty-Four

His name was Frederick Neuman, and he liked to think of himself as a citizen of the European Community rather than any single country, but if anyone asked he claimed to be German. His head was shaved close and it made him look severe, but also more impressive, he thought, which was an amazing accomplishment.

He would be remembered as 'quite tall, thin and bald,' or as 'an interesting artist type,' and several people *did* see him that week in the Chelsea area of London. *He wanted to be remembered. That was important.*

He shopped, or at least window-shopped, on the King's Road and Sloane Street.

He went to the cinema on Kensington High Street.

And Waterstone's bookshop.

Nights, he would have a pint or two at the King's Head. He mostly kept to himself at the pub.

He had a master plan. Another game was beginning.

He saw Lucy and the twins at Safeway one afternoon. He watched them from a safe distance across rows of baked beans and aisles of shoppers. No harm, no foul, no problem for anybody.

He couldn't resist the challenge though. The dice started to play in his head. They rattled the number he wanted to hear.

He kept walking closer and closer to the family, careful to keep his face slightly averted, just in case, but still watching Lucy out of the corner of his eye, watching the twins, who were perhaps more dangerous.

Lucy was examining some wild Scottish salmon. She finally noticed him, he was sure, but she didn't recognize who he was – obviously. Neither did the twins. Dumb, silly little girls – mirrors of their mother.

The game was on again – so delicious. He'd been away from it for a while. He had book money, his advance, which he kept in Switzerland. He had bummed around the Caribbean after his escape by boat from Jamaica. He'd gone to San Juan and been tempted to act up there. He'd finally traveled to Europe, to Rome, Milan, Paris, Frankfurt, Dublin – and at last home to London. He'd only strayed a couple of times on the whole trip. He was such a careful boy now.

It felt just like old times as he got oh so close to Lucy in the shopping aisle.

Jesus, his physical tics were back. He was tapping his foot nervously and shaking out his hands.

He'd have thought she might have noticed that, but she was such a vacuous blonde cow, such a cipher, a waste of time; even now, as he got closer and closer, only a foot or two away.

'Oh Loo-cy . . . it's Ricky,' he said, and grinned and grinned. 'It's me, *darling.*'

Swish. Swish. He swiped at her twice, back and forth, as they passed like strangers in the aisle at Safeway. The blows barely crisscrossed Lucy's throat, but they cut her inches deep.

She dropped to her bony knees, both hands clutching her neck as if she were strangling herself. And then she saw who it was, and her blue eyes filled with complete shock and pain and what seemed to be terrible disappointment.

'Geoffrey,' she managed in a gurgling voice, as blood bubbled from her open mouth.

Her last word on earth. His name.

Beautiful for Shafer to hear, recognition that he craved, revenge against all of them. He turned away, forced himself to, before he did the twins as well.

He was never seen again in Chelsea, but everyone would remember him for as long as they lived.

God, would they remember.

That tall, bald monster.

The one in all-black clothes, the inhuman freak.

The heartless killer who had committed so many awful murders that even he had lost count.

Geoffrey Shafer.

Death.